ACCLAIM FOR

TONI CADE BAMBARA's

Those Bones Are Not My Child

"Astonishing . . . [a] triumph of realism. . . . Bambara dazzles with a prose that rarely flags and has the precision of a scalpel, the grace of a poetic angel, and the horse sense of a coven of grandmothers. She amazes with her wisdom, with the breadth of her knowledge, with the depth and acuity of her characterization . . . with an insight so piercing it takes the breath away. Rare. Amazing."   —*Chicago Tribune*

"A powerfully told story, likely to become for the Atlanta child murders what Kurt Vonnegut's *Slaughterhouse-Five* became for the firebombing of Dresden. . . . A brave achievement."   —*Time Out*

"An impassioned rallying cry . . . an extraordinary achievement; at turns as poetic as it is vitriolic, as personal as it is political, and always thoroughly heartbreaking. . . . Empowering and frighteningly real."   —*Emerge*

"Bambara's posthumous docu-novel conveys the period's fear and conflict with a powerful blend of fact, fiction and indignation."   —*Time*

"Splendid . . . a broadloom weave of lost children and child sacrifice. . . . [A] masterful mix of multitude, solitude, trajectory and vertigo . . . grand and grueling, exhaustive and exalted."   —*Newsday*

TONI CADE BAMBARA

Those Bones Are Not My Child

Toni Cade Bambara is the author of two short story collections, *Gorilla, My Love* and *The Sea Birds Are Still Alive;* a novel, *The Salt Eaters;* and a collection of fiction, essays, and conversations, *Deep Sightings and Rescue Missions.* Her writings continue to appear in literature anthologies around the world. A noted documentary filmmaker and screenwriter, Bambara's film work includes the documentaries *The Bombing of Osage Avenue* and *W. E. B. Du Bois: A Biography in Four Voices.* She died in 1995.

Those Bones
Are Not
My Child

TONI CADE BAMBARA

VINTAGE BOOKS

A Division of Random House, Inc.

New York

FIRST VINTAGE BOOKS EDITION, OCTOBER 2000

The Library of Congress has cataloged the Pantheon edition
as follows:
Bambara, Toni Cade.
Those bones are not my child / Toni Cade Bambara.
p. cm.
ISBN 0-679-44261-8
1. Afro-Americans—Georgia—Atlanta—Fiction. I. Title.
PS3552.A473t47 1999
813'.54—dc20   99-21534
CIP

Vintage ISBN: 978-0-679-77408-2

Author photograph © Joyce Middler
Book design by Fritz Metsch
Map design by Jeff Ward

www.vintagebooks.com

Printed in the United States of America

*We are the light
we are robbed of
each time one of us
is lost*

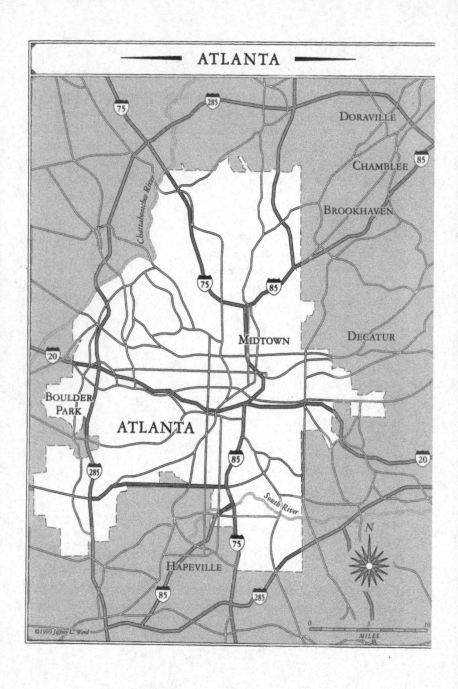

THE KILLER'S ROUTE

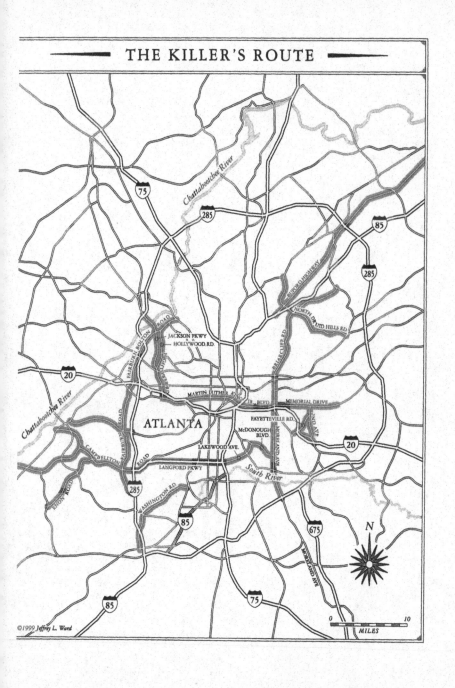

©1999 Jeffrey L. Ward

Contents

Those Bones Are Not My Child

PROLOGUE

Monday, November 16, 1981

You're on the porch with the broom sweeping the same spot, getting the same sound—dry straw against dry leaf caught in the loose-dirt crevice of the cement tiles. No phone, no footfalls, no welcome variation. It's 3:15. Your ears strain, stretching down the block, searching through schoolchild chatter for that one voice that will give you ease. Your eyes sting with the effort to see over bushes, look through buildings, cut through everything that separates you from your child's starting point—the junior high school.

The little kids you keep telling not to cut through your yard are cutting through your yard. Not boisterous-bold and loose-limbed as they used to be in the first and second grades. But not huddled and spooked as they were last year. You had to saw off the dogwood limbs. They'd creak and sway, throwing shadows of alarm on the walkway, sending the children shrieking down the driveway. You couldn't store mulch in lawnleaf bags then, either. They'd look, even to you, coming upon those humps in your flowerbed, like bagged bodies.

A few months ago, everyone went about wary, tense, their shoulders hiked to their ears in order to fend off grisly news of slaughter. But now, adults walk as loose-limbed and carefree as the children who are scudding down the driveway, scuffing their shoes, then huddling on the sidewalk below.

The terror is over, the authorities say. The horror is past, they repeat every day. There've been no new cases of kidnap and murder since the arrest back in June. You've good reason to know that the official line is a lie. But you sweep the walk briskly all the way to the hedge, as though in clearing the leaves you can clear from your mind all that you know. You'd truly like to know less. You want to believe. It's 3:23 on your Mother's Day watch. And your child is nowhere in sight.

You lean the broom against the hedges and stretch up on tiptoe. Big boys, junior high age, are on the other side of the avenue, wrassling each other into complicated choke holds. You holler over, trying not to sound batty. Maybe they know something. A bus chuffs by, drowning you out and masking the boys in smeary gray smoke. When it clears, they've moved on. The hedge holds you up while you play magic with traffic, making bargains with God: if one of the next four cars passing by sports the old bumper sticker HELP KEEP OUR CHILDREN SAFE, then you will know all is well, you'll calm down, pile up the leaves, make a burnt sacrifice, then get dinner on. Two cars go by, a mail truck, an out-of-state camper, then a diesel semi rumbles along. You can feel it thrumming up through your feet. Your porch windows rattle, so do your teeth. An exterminator truck pulls up and double-parks by the cleaner's. The familiar sticker is plastered on the side of the door, the word "children" under the word "pest." Your scalp prickles, ice cold. A stab of panic drives you onto the porch and straight through your door.

You dial the school. The woman who answers tells you there's no one in the building. You want to scream, point out the illogic of that, and slam down the phone. But you wheedle, you plead, you beg her to please check, it's an emergency. You can tell by the way she sucks her teeth and sets the receiver down that you're known in that office. You've been up there often about incidents they called "discipline" and you called "battering." Things weren't tense enough in Atlanta, teachers were sending "acting-out problems" to the coach to be paddled. In cut-off sweats, he took a wide-legged stance and, arms crossed against his bulging chest, asked, since it wasn't your child sent to him for punishment, what is your problem?

Exactly what the principal had wanted to know when the parents broke up the PTA meeting, demanding security measures in the school. Never enough textbooks to go around; students would linger after school to borrow each other's, then, having missed the bus, would arrive home to an hysterical household. The men voted to form safety patrols. The principal went off: "There will be no vigilantes in my school!"

City under siege. Armed helicopters overhead. Bullhorns bellowing to stay indoors. The curfew pushed back into the p.m. hours. Gun stores extending sales into the a.m. hours. Hardware stores scrambling to meet the demand for burglar bars, deadbolt locks, alarms, lead pipes, and under-the-counter cans of mace and boxes of pellets.

Atlanta a magnet for every bounty hunter, kook, amateur sleuth, sooth-sayer, do-gooder, right-wing provocateur, left-wing adventurer, porno filmmaker, crack-shot supercop, crackpot analyst, paramilitary thug, hustler, and free-lance fool. But there should be no patrols on the prin-cipal's turf. "Unladylike," you heard the gym teacher say when you led the PTA walkout. But how do you conduct a polite discussion about murder?

The woman is back on the line and says again that no one is in the school building. You repeat your name, say again why you called; you mention the time, remark that you're calling from home, and you add that your neighbor across the way is wearing a candy-striped dress and is packing away summer cottons. Then you hang up and interrogate yourself—establishing an alibi in case something is wrong? It's 3:28 and if grilled, you would plead guilty to something. It's 3:29 and you've got to get a grip on yourself.

From the start, the prime suspects in the Atlanta Missing and Mur-dered Children's Case were the parents. Presumed guilty because, as po-lice logic went in the summer of '79, seven or eight deaths did not constitute "an epidemic of murder," as the parents, organizers of the Committee to Stop Children's Murders, were maintaining; because, as the authorities continued to argue after STOP's media sit-in a year later, eight or nine cases was usual in a city the size of Atlanta; and because, as officialdom repeatedly pointed out, even as the body count rose from one to twelve, the usual suspects in the deaths of minors were the parents.

Monstrous parents, street-hustling young hoodlums, and the gen-tle killer became the police/media version of things. In the newspapers, STOP's campaign—to mount an independent investigation, to launch a national children's rights movement, to establish a Black commission of inquiry into hate crimes—would be reported, invariably, on the same page as stories about parental neglect, gang warfare, and drug-related crimes committed by minors, most often drawn from the files of cities outside of Atlanta. And frequently, photos of Atlanta's grief-stricken mothers would appear above news stories that featured "the gentle killer"—a man or woman who'd washed some of the victims, laid them out in clean clothes, and once slipped a rock under a murdered boy's head "like a pillow," a reporter said. Like a pillow.

Another pattern you've noticed, having kept a journal for nearly two years and your hallway jammed with cartons of news clippings, bulletins, leaflets, rally flyers, and memorial programs: Whenever STOP members were invited to lecture around the country, the authorities would call the parents in for another polygraph. Then a well-timed leak to the press: "The parents are not above suspicion." A name dropped: one of the parents most critical of the investigation, most outspoken about the lack of trained personnel on the Task Force. In '81, as thousands were scheduled to board the buses for STOP's May 25 rally in Washington, D.C., an FBI agent told a civic group down in Macon, Georgia, that several of the cases were already solved, that the parents had killed their children because "they were such little nuisances."

The father of Yusuf Bell had been treated as a suspect for more than a year; his wife, Camille Bell, the murdered boy's mother, co-founder and prime mover of STOP, was one of the more vocal critics of the authorities' response to the killings. A friend of the family of murdered girl LaTonya Wilson had also been considered a prime suspect; it was LaTonya's body that the civilian search team had found on its first outing, embarrassing the professionals, who'd maintained that they were not dragging their feet, were committed to an exhaustive search, were "leaving no stone unturned" in their efforts to find the missing children. The mother of Anthony Bernard Carter was arrested, released, tailed, questioned, dogged for months, and visited at all hours of the night until she was forced to move. The media kept harping on the fact that she was a poor, young Black woman who had only one child, "only one," as though that were sufficient grounds for suspicion, if not prosecution.

The sun is streaming in your hallway window. It's hot on your face. Your house smells like cooked cardboard. A flap on one of the cartons has come loose and is imprinting a corrugated design on your leg. You can't go on standing there by the phone, watching the second hand sweep around the dial. You need to get moving. You are trying. Trying not to think about the anti-defamation suit that the STOP committee, regrettably, dropped against the police, the Bureau, and the media. Trying not to think about the rally STOP held in D.C.—all the speeches, pep talks, booths, posters, buttons, green ribbons, T-shirts, caps, profiling, and blown opportunities to organize a National Black Commission to call a halt to random, calculated, and systemic assaults on Black people all over the country. Trying not to remember how swiftly the arrest came, the authorities collaring a man just as those back from the rally began clamoring for answers. What about the law-enforcement memo describing castrations? What about the mortician's assistant who reported, back in the fall of '80, the presence of hypodermic needle marks in the genitalia of several victims? And the phone tipster whose message, loaded with racial slurs, accurately predicted where the next body would be dumped? As the grapevine sizzled with charges of hate-motivated murder and official cover-up, the authorities made their arrest of a man who in no way resembled any of the descriptions in the Task Force reports, any of the sketched faces pinned to the corkboard in command headquarters. In no way resembled the descriptions in the reports of STOP's independent investigators, or in the reports of community workers investigating well out of the limelight. A man who bore no resemblance to men fingered by witnesses to homicides kept off the Task Force's list despite linkages of race, class, acquaintanceship, kinship, and last-seen sightings along the killer route. One man, charged with the murders of two male adults. The case against the arrested hanging by threads—carpet fibers and dog hairs, persistent enough to survive wind, rain, and rivers. Strong enough to hitch to the arrested man's coattails as many cases as the law would allow and the public would tolerate. A seven-, eight-, some said nine-million dollar investigation brought to a close.

You're most especially trying to keep your mind off the murders committed since the arrest in June, cases that match the six patterns devised by community investigators: Klan-type slaughter, cult-type ritual murder, child-porn thrill killing, drug-related vengeance, commando/mercenary training, and overlapping combinations. Your hallway table is tumbled down with reports you have to double-check before composing the next newsletter. You can't afford to think about any of the chores posted on your calendar under the pile. You need all your energy to figure out who to call, what to do. Where the hell is your child?

I sent him to the store, God forgive me. I should've moved right away, but you know, kids lolligag. The officers kept saying, "His trail is cold." What kind of thing is that to say about a child?

You dump your handbag on the floor, grab your key ring and purse, and lace up your tennis shoes.

I never should've grounded her, maybe she wouldn't've run away. Not that

I believe what they say down at Missing Persons. That girl did not run away. She was snatched.

You inspect your purse for cabfare, but reject the idea. A cab can't jump the gully back of the fish joint and can't take the shortcut through the Laundromat lot.

The main thing I got out of those sessions with the Task Force investigators, and none of them were from Homicide or anything like that at the time, was to keep my mouth shut. Said all this talking to the press made their work harder. Made them look bad is what they meant. And those sister detectives down at Missing Persons caught the same flack, except then it was "hysterical women." The officers and the parents, including my husband, we were all hysterical women. Crazy is what they meant.

You take off down the driveway, gathering speed.

The Task Force people wouldn't talk to me because my boy wasn't on the list, so I kept asking how to get him on the list. He's from Atlanta, he was missing, then they found him under the trestle with his neck broken. So why can't he be on the list? Maybe someone after the reward can do something. They had me so bulldozed, I'd actually apologize for taking them away from the "real" case to listen to me. Can you imagine?

You are running down the streets of southwest Atlanta like a crazy woman.

It's over because they've locked up one man? Only thing over and done with is that list they were keeping. Over—what's that supposed to mean?—go home and forget about it? They can forget about it. The whole city can forget about it. But I'm the boy's father, so how in hell am I supposed to forget about it?

Maybe you *are* a crazy woman, but you'd rather embrace madness than amnesia.

Less than five months ago, you would not have been running alone. Before Wayne Williams drove down the Jackson Parkway Bridge and became a suspect, your whole neighborhood would have mobilized the second you hit the sidewalk. But Williams did drive across the bridge. And a stakeout officer thought he heard a splash in the Chattahoochee, he would say days later, a splash he assumed was a dead body being dumped in the river. Though trained in lifesaving techniques, the officer did not dive in and attempt a rescue. Though equipped with a walkie-talkie, he did not request equipment to dredge the river. The police did nothing more that early morning than to stop Williams's car and ask a few questions. Days later, after a local fisherman did spot a body in the river, the authorities visited the Williams family's home, ransacked it, and hauled young Williams off for questioning. Before the media began calling Williams "weird" and "cocky," the whole of Simpson Road would have responded to your distress.

The tailor, hearing the pound of your feet on the pavement, would have picked up the phone for the block-to-block relay. Mother Enid, Reader & Advisor, would have taken one peek at you from under her neon and dropped her cards to flag down a car. The on-the-corner hardheads, heroes for a time when they formed convoys to get the children to and from school, would have sprung into action the minute you rounded the corner. Brother Chad, who turned his karate studio over to the self-defense squads, would have turned the bar next door out the moment you raced past his window. Everyone would have dropped everything to find a missing child, for when mumps have been replaced by murder, alarm is no longer a private affair.

But it's November, not spring. The Emergency Hot Line posters are gone from the phone booth at the corner of Ashby, removed too from city buses, school buses, MARTA (Metro Atlanta Rapid Transit Authority) stations, and schools. The Williams trial has not yet begun, but the reward signs have been taken down, extra police detail withdrawn from the neighborhoods, state patrol personnel returned to highway duty, the Task Force staff reduced from a hundred and seventy to six, out-of-town reporters told to go home. There is no sign of the Community Watch network along the avenue. Decals have been scraped off the windows. "Let the Community Mend Again," says the sign under the glass in the churchyard where you turn.

It's 3:40 by the clock in the taxi shed. You wave your arms as you run past the first window. An old-timer brushes the brim of his hat and keeps talking. His cronies, lounging in chairs of busted green vinyl and aluminum tubing, salute you with their bottles of C'Cola. You keep moving, hoping they'll figure it out and come on. But they're cabbies, and cabbies have good reason to turn a glass eye on any gestures that seem to spell "crisis." Cab drivers, who like so many others under the veil, now support the official drive toward closure.

Last spring, through Roy Innis, a witness had offered self-incriminating testimony that featured a cab-driving boyfriend. A member of a cult engaged in drug-induced sex and ritual murder, he'd boasted to the woman about his role in the child murder case. The witness, Shirley McGill, had been involved in the drug-traffic end of the cult's operations; she'd witnessed the torture of youths and adults, bound-and-gagged couriers who had tried to defect or had tried to shortchange. When a co-worker was killed, she'd fled to Florida. Her former boyfriend, the hack, had phoned her in the winter of '80–'81, bragged that the kidnap-murder ring would be changing its procedures in the spring. When the Task Force in spring began placing adults on the list of Missing and Murdered Children and reported that the pattern of killings was changing, she'd read that as confirmation of the cabbie's boast and sought the protection of Roy Innis's group. Cabbies joined the roster of suspicious characters—Vietnam vets, karate experts, dog owners, owners of vans with carpeting, anyone capable of lulling a child into carelessness or ordering a child into obedience—and remained there, even after the Task Force issued an all-clear bulletin: witness not credible, information unrelated to the case, cabbie not a suspect.

A number of community investigators, struck by McGill's drug-sex-murder-cult descriptions, and by the self-incriminating nature of her story, were not so quick to dismiss her as a showboating hysteric. She was willing, she said, to be questioned under hypnosis. She claimed that she could locate sites used by the cult responsible for a number of abductions and murders of both children and adults, some of whom made the Task Force list, others who were only on the victim list assembled by independents. Further discussions with McGill had produced another reason to credit her story. Her account of threats and tortures shed light on the mysterious entries in various coroners' reports: "death by asphyxiation, precise method unknown." The method, disclosed in McGill's version, was a plastic bag shoved down the victim's throat, then withdrawn after.

Caravans of independents had begun scouring the outlying environs of the city. The writer James Baldwin, a frequent visitor to Atlanta who'd been conducting his own inquiry, joined the searchers, as did Emory professor Sondra O'Neale, a cult specialist who'd been examining the case from that perspective. In September of '81, a group had discovered ceremonial grounds littered with animal carcasses and marked by a pile of bloodstained stones heaped in the shape of an altar. A twelve-foot charred cross was found nearby. By that time, though, only one out-of-town magazine expressed interest in the cult story. Atlanta authorities had already declared the theory groundless in general, the McGill version in particular.

You're only one block from the school, you tell yourself to spur you on through the brambled lot. You're on the only halfway-clear path, but can feel the nettles and briars scratch through your clothes. Up ahead a rawbony mutt is nuzzling a pile of trash. The dog looks up, bares its teeth. Hackles stiff, it shivers itself sideways and blocks your way. Skin that bags below its ribs puffs out a few times, but you don't hear the bark, you're breathing that hard. The dog plants a paw on a baby doll facedown in the trash. The doll's *ma-ma* box tears through its gauze-cotton skin. You growl at the dog, you're feeling that crazed. It moves its rump aside to let you pass. The doll lets out a croaked *ma-ma* that catches you in the back of your knees. You plow through a tangle of weeds and renegade vines looping up from clumps of kudzu and scrub grass. Now that you've passed, the dog is woofing at you. Your ears are cocked for attack. But the mutt resumes its raid on the trash and you concentrate on the booby traps the kudzu has set for your feet.

It's the first time you've been in a wooded lot since the wintry weekends with the civilian search teams. Muffler, boots, thick denim, flashlight, and always a stout poking stick for turning things over and moving sharp things aside. You'd rendezvous at dawn with total strangers because that was preferable to sitting slumped over a coffee mug staring at the TV. Someone always brought along an extra thermos or two. Several Chinese restaurants donated lunch. Hundreds of other people were drawn to the task—ministers, students, secretaries, upholsterers, masons, carpenters, lawyers—everyone turned out, got involved, tried to respond to the call, the crisis. By January, the civilian search teams had swelled to the thousands. There was, too, a group of white volunteers on those weekend searches, men in flak jackets whom the community investigators had been monitoring. They toted rifles, carried satchels of jangling equipment, resisted the command of the search-team marshals, and signaled each other through walkie-talkies. The other searchers learned to ignore them, fanning out as directed, letting the tracking dogs take the lead. Shivery people moving over brush-whipped unfamiliar terrain. Glazed ground crackling underfoot. Trees shagged with ice. Every shadowy thing in a hollow a dread possibility.

You stub your toe on brown glass. With the rubbery tip of your ten-

nis shoe you pry loose a crusty beer bottle. Caked mud and leaves that
cradled it break apart when you roll it over. Worms burrow down into
the muck. You gauge how long the bottle's been lying there. The
ground covering's autumnal; beneath the bottle is a rain-blurred Popsicle wrapper. *Late summer,* you figure, moving on, stooped over, eyes scanning the ground. You're no longer watching out for sharp-edged cans,
you discover. When you snap to, you still can't get your bearings.

"Remains," they called the discoveries, yellow tape ringing the
perimeter of the scene. "Remains" might mean a pouch burial, em-
balming powder sprinkled into a plastic liner, or it might mean a corpse
in a rose satin box. It always meant, first, families gathered around a
stainless-steel table. A woman clutching her purse, knuckles bleeding.
A man examining surgical instruments in a rectangular basin. White
men in white coats, buttonholes sealed closed with starch, standing
apart from the families, manila folders tucked under their arms. Relatives outside the coroner's workroom glued to portholes of the room's
double doors. One of the summoned stepping forward to slip a hand
under the rubber sheet. A pierced ear, missing molar, lumpy cartilage
in the left knee—the searching hand the only thing moving in the
room. A murmur from the white coats. All but one family is dismissed.
A tag is affixed to the toe that extends from the sheet. A mother backs
away. *Those bones are not my child.* But the tag bears the name heard soaring over rooftops on summer nights of kickball.

Your daughter has a mole on the right shoulder blade, you're thinking. You have a mole on the bottom of your left foot. There's a host of
scars crosshatching the back of your hands now. You rip through the
cobwebs spun between the trees. The wooded lot is just behind the
school, but no matter where you look, you can't spot the aerial on
the school roof.

The mother, back at the house, still insists there's been a mistake.
She holds out her arm to tell her pastor about a scar. The media invades
her home, setting up cameras, plugging in cables. A light meter is
shoved in her face. She's asked what she'll wear to the funeral. A city
representative shoulders his way through the crush of neighbors to say
that the city will pay for the burial. The mother is showing her arm.
Her child had a bad burn from an iron. The body downtown did not.
Her pastor pats her. Relatives shush her. Neighbors set down covered
dishes and envelopes of money on the table. Everyone who's kept the

faith through the whole ordeal wants to pay respect and leave. It's some-body's child downtown on a slab, so claim the bones, mother. Set the fu-neral date, mother. Don't make a fuss, mother. You're not yourself, mother. Let's close the lid, mother. Let the community sleep again.

You hear it first as a funeral drum, young schoolmates in new suits and white gloves hefting a coffin down the steps of a church. Then you hear it as band practice and follow the sound to the sidewalk. You can see up ahead to the left the shadow thrown by the school's flagpole. You lean against the railing of the community center to flick pebbles and dirt from your shoes. You're winded, out of condition. For a year your child would not go out for a walk even with you armed with a knife, mace, and a slapjack. Voices are coming from around the corner. You push on, hobbled by a rising blister and bits of twigs you couldn't reach.

A squad car parked on the school lawn has all its doors open, like wings. A trail of blood by the flagpole leads to a book bag sprawled on the curb. In the street by the manhole a group of eighth-graders are gathered around someone down on one knee. It's your daughter. She's clutching her chest and she's bloody. You bump the children aside and are ready to scream.

"Ma!"

She's hugging a cat. It squirms to get loose. A splint's on its leg. It bites at the tape.

"You forgot?" Your daughter stands up, passes the cat to a boy in blue sweats, and cocks her chin at you like you've done something stupid.

You're trying to hear her, roaming your eyes over her person for open wounds. But everyone's talking at once. Behind her two Bloods are slamming a middle-aged man over the hood of a car. The police pull one of them off, but the other keeps saying, "Man, this ain't the Indy 500." Hit-and-run driver, your daughter explains. Drunk, the boy with the cat offers. The two men, the cop is telling you, forced the driver to re-turn to the scene. The victim's the cat, one of the girls says. An elderly woman in a floral bib apron saunters over and sizes you up. A pair of scissors and a roll of tape pull her apron pocket out of shape.

"Mother." Your daughter, using her too-grown voice, grips your shoulders for a good talking-to. "This is the only free day at the pool. You were supposed to meet me 'cause you've got to sign. Forget?"

The woman in the bib apron brushes your shoulder with hers. "Some mother," she says out of the side of her mouth. "Leaving your girl to wait on the corner." She sucks her teeth. "This is Atlanta, honey, where is your mind?"

Your daughter drags you away and grabs up her book bag. You follow her through the double doors of the community center. She's talking a blue streak, using her neck. You lean across the table and sign parental permission. The chlorine fumes draw you across the tiles to the pool area. Your girl is still working her neck and cracking on you. You've got twigs in your hair, your clothes are a mess, and what's with them cornball, old-timey sneaks? She comes to a stop by the door to the lockers and dabs at your scratches with a square of gauze. At seven, she would have disowned you, but at twelve, she's your mama. Then she rears back, takes you in, and lets loose with more cracks. You let her. You help her. You perform a Raggedy Ann softshoe. She holds her sides and goes through the door. You can hear her throaty laughter ricocheting off metal and tiles long after you drag yourself past the pool to the bleachers.

You're beat, but she's laughing. She's twelve, she's entitled. For longer than you care to tally, it's been hard to laugh freely. Though at your house there've been no horrible nightmares, no bedwetting, asthmatic emergencies, anxiety attacks, depression, withdrawal, fits of raging or weeping, plummeting grades, or any of the other symptoms mental hygienists described over and over on radio, TV, in newspapers, in safety-ed comics distributed at school, and on panels after the child-safety films shown at community centers, films featuring Black male actors as bogeymen, there's been, nonetheless, a definite decrease in the kind of clowning around that used to rock your household, leaving you all sprawled, breathless, helpless, in a heap on the floor, dabbing at wet eyes, and talking in preposterous falsettos.

So you laugh a little too, brush the leaves from your clothes, and nod hello to the grown-ups on the benches above. Leaning forward, wrists loose between their knees, they're watching youngsters splashing in the shallows and preteens doing laps on the deeper side of the pool divided by a rope of blue-and-white buoys.

You settle down and rummage around in your daughter's book bag for an apple or a stray carrot stick. You find one of your journals. Once again, she's mistaken it for her math notebook, same color. When she enters the pool area, stuffing her hair under her cap, you hold it up and smirk. She rolls her eyes and prepares for a dive where the stenciling says six feet. You're not sure you want to watch that. You flip open the wine-colored spiral wondering how she fared in fifth-period math with your Missing and Murdered notes.

You began that first journal in September of 1979 with nothing particular in mind, journal keeping a habit. But you recorded the fact that your mailman had rapped on your screen back in summer to ask if you'd heard about the kidnappings reported in the McDaniel-Glenn area. Didn't you use to work at Model Cities over there? A few weeks later, Mother Enid, Reader & Advisor, had stopped you at the newspaper box to tell you about a psychic, a white woman in Waco, Texas, who'd been "seeing" a Vietnam vet in Atlanta relive the blasts of hand grenades lobbed by Vietnamese children, a white vet who was now on the rampage killing colored youngsters and depositing them near bodies of water. And did you see in the papers the case of two dead Black boys found out on Niskey Lake Road?

You recorded a third event that occurred in late August. The aunt of one of your students mailed you a copy of an in-house memo that had come across her desk down at Missing Persons, Youth Division. The memo referred to a rash of disappearances, attempted abductions, accidents where foul play was suspected, and several definite homicides in a twenty-block radius in the Black community. The memo writer, a female officer, had suggested to her superior that the cases not be regarded as normal runaways, that they seemed related. The response to the memo, if there'd been one, was not attached. But a yellow stick-on note called your attention to a magazine article enclosed celebrating 1979 as the United Nations Year of the Child. "Some celebration," the note ended.

Overheards and ruminations about men, women, and children mysteriously vanishing from the community are sprinkled throughout the first half of the notebook in between entries about books, movies, jobs, meetings, and your dreams. But sometime in the spring of 1980, entries on the case take over. Mothers of several murdered children happened to meet that spring at a community gathering and they compared notes. Weeks later, a group of them staged a sit-in. Organized as the Committee to Stop Children's Murders, they camped out in media and law-enforcement offices, demanding a special investigation of "the epidemic of child murders." During their press conference, they charged that the authorities were dragging their feet because of race; because of class; because the city, the country's third-busiest convention center, was trying to protect its image and was trying to mask a crisis that might threaten Atlanta's convention trade dollars.

"Know what they told me?" one mother asked, taking the floor at a community meeting. "They said it was my civic duty to cooperate because all hell might break loose with this news. In other words, to shut up." In July 1980, city hall responded to STOP's direct action tactics by forming the Metropolitan Atlanta Emergency Task Force to Investigate Missing and Murdered Children. Their staff was made up of not homicide detectives, but community relations personnel.

The second half of your journal begins with minutes of neighborhood meetings and comments on the skimpy items that appeared in the back pages of the dailies. Increasingly, the disappeared begin to crowd out everything else you normally log in your journals. Even your dreams revolve around the women found dead out on pistol ranges, men found facedown in culverts, children stuffed under floorboards of abandoned buildings.

Marked-up photocopies of bulletins the Task Force published on demand about the case are stapled to left-hand pages, factual errors circled, discrepancies in the children's names, ages, and dates of disappearances noted. In the margin you remark, "Doesn't someone proofread the copy before sending it out?" On the right-hand side, you've stapled fact sheets that were circulated by community workers who had examined police depositions, were in attendance at the STOP office, and who were dogging the steps of STOP's three volunteer detectives. The three white former APD homicide detectives had served under the notorious police chief dispatched when Maynard Jackson became mayor and ushered in, as folks were prone to say, the Second Reconstruction. One of the volunteer PIs, Chet Dettlinger, would make the first real breakthrough in the case by plotting the killer's or killers' route and charting the connections between a dozen or more victims. He was hardly rewarded for his efforts, however. The Atlanta police would eventually pull him in for questioning. The community workers remained to the end no less suspicious of his interest in the case.

The last few pages of the journal, written in October of 1980, are hurried but lengthy. An international convention of white supremacists had been hosted in nearby Cobb County by self-proclaimed racist and convicted bomber J. B. Stoner. Not fourteen hours after the convention adjourned, the Gate City–Bowen Homes Day Care Center blew up; four toddlers and a teacher died. That explosion, on Monday, October 13, 1980, brought the case of the Missing and Murdered Children—the tip of an iceberg that involved scores of men, women, and other children—to citywide, nationwide, and finally worldwide attention. While the Task Force called in forensic specialists to produce a victim profile, everybody else, most especially independent investigators, focused on the killers. There was widespread speculation about their identity and their motives:

White cops taking license in Black neighborhoods again?

The Klan and other Nazi thugs on the rampage again?

Diabolical scientists experimenting on Third World people again?

Demonic cultists engaging in human sacrifices?

A 'Nam vet unable to make the transition?

UFO aliens conducting exploratory surgery?

Whites avenging Dewey Baugus, a white youth beaten to death in spring '79, allegedly by Black youths?

Parents of a raped child running amok with "justice"?

Porno filmmakers doing snuff flicks for entertainment?

A band of child molesters covering their tracks?

New drug forces killing the young (unwitting?) couriers of the old in a bid for turf?

Unreconstructed peckerwoods trying to topple the Black administration?

Plantation kidnappers of slave labor issuing the ultimate pink slip?

White mercenaries using Black targets to train death squadrons for overseas jobs and for domestic wars to come?

Splashes of green reflecting from the pool bob across the pages in your lap. Seasick, you close your eyes. In a minute, your stomach's less swarmy. But your mind won't let go. It battens down on the heavy three-ring looseleaf in one of the cartons at home. That binder contains the other journals, separated by manila envelopes that bulge with scraps of letters, tear sheets from magazines and social science journals, news clippings, safety-ed comics, LEAA (Law Enforcement Assistance Ad-

ministration) circulations, *The Caped Crusader* and other Klan periodicals, and the various flyers and bulletins issued in fall '80 and winter
'80–'81 which signaled, as early as Christmas of '80, that you would
need cartons to hold the material that came pouring in from all over the
world.

Reporters everywhere were trying to make sense of what was hap-
pening in Atlanta. *Gone With the Wind* Atlanta. New International City
Atlanta. Atlanta, Black Mecca of the South. Second Reconstruction
City. Home of a bulk of Fortune 500 companies. Scheduled host of the
World's Fair in the year 2000. Proposed site of the World University.
Slated to make the Top Ten of the world's great financial centers. Local,
out-of-town, and overseas media all relied first and foremost, however,
on information supplied by the Metropolitan Atlanta Emergency Task
Force. For a long time, media was unaware—or rather, made uninter-
ested in the fact—that there were numerous other bodies of investigators conducting inquiries and coming up with findings more plausible
than the explanations offered by the Task Force, which hobbled itself
early on by insisting that there was nothing that linked the cases.

For all the authorities—city hall, the APD, the Task Force, the
GBI, the FBI—agreed that the important thing was that the idea of
a serial murder case not take root. A serial murder panics the public.
Embarrasses law enforcement. Makes professionals look outsmarted.
Serial murders are bad for tourism. Handling serial murders requires
a coordinated effort, a spirit of cooperation on the part of the various
epartments, bureaus, and agencies that careerists prefer to run as private fiefdoms, rewarding true-blue border guards, not liaison officers.
Worse, tracing a race-hate-motivated conspiracy would demand a no-
squabbling truce between the various branches of the law-enforcement
industry. Well aware of the pecking order, locals resist "serial" lest the
feds become in charge of the yard.

On complaints of civilian search team members, APD officials had
approached federal agents about the blustering, arrogant behavior of
the white commando types who attached themselves to the search
teams and tried to bogard their way into meetings on the south and
northwest sides of Atlanta. "Counterterrorist units," muttered one fed,
then exited quickly, perhaps because he had breached security. In any
case, the situation was not negotiable. The APD officials backed off.

And until a Black man was collared, it was unacceptable to speak of hate.

The Task Force itself was under the command of Commissioner of Public Safety Lee Brown, a Ph.D., formerly of Seattle, Washington, a well-respected administrator and family man. Mayor Maynard Jackson had created the Public Safety post early in his first term, originally to bring Police Chief Inman under control. Later, the Public Safety Office operated mainly as a liaison between city hall and the police department. Shrewd maneuver on Maynard's part, for as was/is an open secret in most cities, there are two police departments: a Black police force, comparatively new, having evolved as a result of the civil rights movement; and a white force, not new, and to a great extent pledged to the old order. Many a newly elected Black mayor has found him/herself embattled from day one by the reluctance, frequently bitter, ofttimes fierce, of the old-boy network to honor the voters' choice.

No one foresaw that Atlanta's Office of Public Safety would require a big budget, a large staff, a PR director, and a comprehensive body of policies and procedures. Its work had been, under Brown and under his predecessor, Reginald Eaves, of a community relations nature. Until the killers struck.

Eventually, the media began to ask pointed questions about the "conflicts" in the unfolding drama: bad-mouthing between the police and the community; between official investigators and community sleuths and out-of-town visitors armed with hunches; between STOP and organizations self-appointed to raise funds in the parents' names; between the parents and city officials; between local, state, and federal authorities, who each complained that the other agencies were conducting investigations in secret and obstructing their own investigations.

Many in the targeted neighborhoods were willing to be cast as passive spectators to the tug-of-war scenarios written by reporters. But others, not distracted by theatrics, cast themselves as undercover workers who sorted out the growing roster of characters into major and minor players. From the day the case became national news, the cast of characters kept growing—psychics, suspects, tipsters, bat squads, witnesses, hypnotists, journalists, forensic experts, cult specialists, computer consultants, fund raisers, dog trainers, filmmakers, visiting celebrities. Hundreds of people with theories, alliances, agenda clotted the arena, which began to take on the look of a fiendish perception test, challenging the most discerning eye to lift out of the dense design those players that could lead them to purposeful action. Those community workers who were not stymied by the cluttered ground design began to chart a particular part of the schemata—the crisscrossing paths of the feds.

Community sleuths clocked federal agents in and out of Atlanta as early as summer 1980. There were feds investigating alleged kidnappings even as the official word to the public and the parents was "runaways." But other feds, using the Missing and Murdered cases as a cover, were engaged in COINTELPRO-like operations, particularly against the Revolutionary Communist Party and the Central American Support Committee. President Carter, who made no secret of his suspicions and alarm over the dangerously clandestine nature of the intelligence operations, was the one hope clung to by citizens subjected to FBI break-ins routinely blamed on burglars. The election of President Reagan, though, changed the picture. Both the intelligence community and right-wing insurgents stepped up their covert activities, overseas and on home ground. And community-based detectives moved further away from the media spotlight in order to keep an eye on the feds.

Agents from the Treasury Department, from the Internal Revenue Service, and from the Securities and Exchange Commission were unusually active in and around Atlanta. Their subject of surveillance was a ring of counterfeiters, credit-card defrauders, junk-bond hucksters, bank robbers, and states' rights tax protesters that was bankrolling the ultra-right network through criminal activity. Agents from Alcohol, Tobacco, and Firearms crossed their path. The ATF was on the trail of ultra-right gangs that were knocking over armories in the Southeast and stockpiling weapons in and around Atlanta in preparation for race war. ATF agents, in turn, were covering the same ground as narcs, staking out private airports in the area. Both the ATF and narcs crossed the paths of INS agents. Immigration and Customs came into the picture in the fall of 1980. Violations of the Arms Export Control Act had been reported in Florida, Georgia, and Texas. Those in Atlanta were keeping watch on the comings and goings of international right-wing terrorists who'd been issued visas by the State Department to attend Stoner's convention the weekend before the Black day-care center exploded.

"Faulty boiler," city hall said. Black vets, other community workers, as well as a number of tenants who'd spotted white men on the roof of the day care, said otherwise. "Not related," said the six o'clock news, quoting the mayor and Commissioner Brown. But enough people felt a connection between the observation "white men on the roof" and the old question "Who would kill Black children?" to give the media a lead.

"Clean bill of health," came the announcement from the governor's mansion in spring after a three-week look at Georgia Klans. "Hothead," said the reporters, quoting no one in particular, in response to Julian Bond's outrage over the "whitewash" report. "War," screamed the *Thunderbolt* and other fascist rags of the region when the National Anti-Klan Network was formed in Atlanta. "No connection," said FBI director William Webster later that spring as Black citizen groups all over the country were documenting incidents of bigoted violence. "No evidence of conspiracy," as various fight-back groups demanded that the Justice Department check into and stop the escalation of attacks throughout the country based on race, class, gender/sex, religion, nationality, and sexual orientation.

"Opportunists," say the media when STOP persists in its efforts to ally with children's rights lobbyists around the country. "Mercenary motives" and "limelight greedy," the media says of the Atlanta parents. No one seems to remember anymore that prior to the arrest, a member of the Atlanta City Council, not totally persuaded by the Task Force version of the case(s), requested Lee Brown to submit by June 30 a list of all unsolved homicides in Atlanta. Suspect Wayne Williams was formally charged on June 22, making the report moot, as they say—that is, forgettable. Meanwhile, the slaughter continues.

Your daughter calls you from the pool. You close the notebook, rise, and look. Arms spread, legs wide, she's facedown in the water, in a dead man's float. Can you applaud?

A woman hands you the notebook you've dropped and you sit back down on the bench. Your daughter jackknifes under the water and kicks off. She swims under the rope like an arrow, surfaces, and turns to grin at you. Your joints settle back into position and you grimace a smile. Will you find your voice before she climbs out of the pool?

{ I }

FIRST LIGHT AND THE

SHAPE OF THINGS

Sunday, July 20, 1980

Marzala Rawls Spencer prowled the living room. With each step, the shag carpet bristled. The upholstery crackled when she brushed against the furniture. Each time she rounded the room, the pinned choir robe slung over the chair reached out, electric, clinging to the shivering hairs on her arm. At the door, she thought she might go out again to look up and down Thurmond Street. A smear of Brasso on the knob warned her hand away from the metal. The shock came when she turned and faced herself in the full-length mirror propped against the sewing machine.

She leaned in, close to the mirror furry with grime. She had worried the fuzz escaping from her braids into corkscrews. Smudged mascara from the day before ringed her eyes like a raccoon's. She looked feverish, her lips cracked and peeling, salt streaked across her breastbone. She looked about to boil over. He would stroll in, take one look, and know she had no good side to get on.

She set the mirror behind the sewing table in case he burst in. The sweat-crusty piping of her tank top chafed her underarms. She stepped back, the mirror out of danger. Her wraparound skirt hung uneven, limp. She had walked all the starch out of it and felt clammy. But she was not going to shower and change. Let him see she'd been up all night waiting, up all night and still wearing her shoes. Her arches ached and her soles burned, but she was keeping the sandals on for the height of the heels. Any minute now it would be eyeball to eyeball. And he was not going to get over on her, not this time.

A whir and a whine made her turn toward the archway that opened onto the kitchen. But even as she looked at the fridge, she was thinking the sound might be herself, an overwound spring. She felt like brittle clockworks trembling near the shattering pitch. It was a car coming. The seams of her skirt pockets strained with the thrust of her fists.

A car had turned into the street from Ashby. She backed up over the rug, grazing her hip on the table. The TV shimmied against the button box, the sour yellow of the sewing-machine bulb blinked. She planted herself in the middle of the room, her legs straddling the bald spot in the carpet. "Pushover," she'd heard him tell his scatter-tooth friends. Let him try. He was not going to get by her this time.

It was a car and not the van from the Metropolitan Boys' Club. Its headlights strobed the panes in the door. The lights hit the hedges, the jade, the window-glass spaces in the macramé drapes before they shut off. When last she'd been out, marching up and down Thurmond Street, the jade had been shaggy inkiness behind blocky hedges of black. Now she could see three different shades of green in the yard, a network of browns, and a halo of mauve outlining the bush.

It was morning. "Morning": The sound of it fueled her fire. Twelve years old and out all night long. She pitched forward, her toes sliding out of the sandals and clutching at shag. She mouthed all the things she would say to him, all the things she'd been lashing together to flay him with since the day before when Kofi had shrugged and said "Went." Sonny had actually gone to the Boys' Club cookout when she'd told him flat out no, he couldn't go. He was asking for it, and he would get it this time.

The car pulled alongside her Bug out front, then swung wide. It cruised up the driveway across the street. She could hear Mean Dog yank on his chain. She shoved the drapes aside and dust sprinkled down on her arm. She added that to the boy's crime sheet; he hadn't vacuumed. The car went all the way up to the carport. No doubt Sonny was directing the driver far away to avoid a scene.

It was not the camp counselor that got out, but Chaz Robinson. She couldn't figure out how Sonny had hitched a ride home with their neighbor. Robinson closed the door softly and waved the thick Sunday papers at Mean Dog. He got a frisky welcome, the dog nipping his own backside, nearly twisting in half. Robinson held his finger up to his lips and the dog wagged his head, backed into the butterfly bush, then sprang forward, forepaws scratching at air. The yelping was muffled low in the throat. She could hear Robinson's husky chuckle as he opened the side door and went in. Ears forward, Mean Dog waited, then dropped flat on the lawn. His tail beat the ground and petals spattered the walk.

No one else was getting out of that car, she could see that. Mean Dog nosed his dish toward the walk as far as his chain would allow. The back of her throat thickened, but she waited. The dog dropped his head on his forepaws and slept. Maybe Sonny had been dropped off at the corner and was coming around the back way. She moved too quickly, barking her shins on the sewing chair. The choir robe fell to the floor in segments.

"You stompin' again and waking us up, Mama."

Zala swung her head in the direction of the backroom. Her hemp-like braids swatted her cheeks.

"Never mind what I'm doing, you two. Go back to sleep."

She heard the wheeze of the cot, Kenti turning over. Kofi muttered; then his bedsprings squeaked. She went into the kitchen, skirting the drawer of the cupboard. She'd left it just as Sonny had left it, pulled all the way out on its runners. The food stamps were gone and a good fork was missing.

She leaned over the ironing board. The clothes she had sprinkled and balled up for church were now bone dry. The backyard was deserted. But once before, when she'd grounded him for running off with his singing friends who swore they were the Commodores, he'd pitched a tent under the dogwood near the other half of the duplex. She hurried into the bathroom. That was the window he'd used that time to lure Kofi and Kenti out to join him under her one good bedspread for a feast of raw hot dogs.

The nails were secure in the bathroom window. And nothing was moving in the yard. It made no sense. The counselor should have brought him home in time for dinner, then taken the others onto the campsite. How could they take Sonny without her permission? She'd always made a point of phoning the Boys' Club director to make sure the signed slip was on hand. Sonny lost things, like keys, like report cards. She always called too, to get the exact location of the outing and to find out the exact time of return. She made it a point to be among the early arrivals, leaving work early sometimes in order to do it. No one was going to say she was a single parent who couldn't cut it.

Wandering out of the bathroom, she added forgery to Sonny's

crimes. And though she knew he was too proud to use the back way, she'd take a look from the children's room just in case.

"Ain't you sleepy?"

Kenti spoke the moment she entered the room. On each eyelid, Zala saw now, were daubs of blue eyeshadow. Kenti's lips were red on top of Popsicle orange. Zala hadn't noticed that before. Tiptoeing in the dark and cupping the girl's chin to close her mouth, she'd been aware only of the perfume, the reek of it sickening, the fact that it had been a present from Dave, annoying. She had almost shaken her daughter awake to fuss. But she hadn't, didn't trust herself, hot with rage couldn't risk it.

"Sonny's gonna git it, hunh?" Kenti leaned up on her elbow.

Zala turned away from the scrape of skin against canvas, the girl's bottom sheet half on the floor. She went to the window with only a glance toward the top bunk. The cash-register bank was nested in a pile of dirty socks in Sonny's bed. The fork, bent from jimmying the bank's payoff lid, was missing a tine.

The yard on the Griers' side of the house was as quiet as her side.

"Is it the next day?"

"I'll get you up in time, don't worry."

Her seven-year-old fussed with her sheets, and Zala made a mental note to get cocoa butter for the girl's elbows . . . until she could see her way clear to get her a proper bed . . . to get them all better housing. Kofi grumbled and rolled away from the wall. He looked at her upside down, and she almost reached out to shake him by his hair. But he didn't like that, and this was no time to talk about haircuts.

She lost herself for a moment. One minute she was looking at the gray rings the fishbowl had left on their study desk, the next she was sinking into the blistered paint on the windowsill. She was falling asleep on her feet again. She tried stretching her arms up, but she couldn't sustain it long enough to work the crick out of her neck. Her arms flopped and she folded them on top of her head and tried to work out the knots in her back.

"It don't go like that, Mama. You suppose to stretch up on tippy-toe. That's how we do in the morning before the Pledge Allegiance. And Miss Chambers say, 'Reach me down a piece of sky, children.' She so silly."

"You better tell her something, Ma." Kofi's gruff-grumpy voice came up from under the covers.

"Beg pardon?"

Kofi kicked the covers off and drew his knees up. He walked the soles of his feet across the bottom of the mattress that sagged from above. "Ma." The fork clinked against the bank. "You call Dad?"

"Yes. I called your father."

"Dag, I was just asking." He dropped his legs down hard and the bunk ladder creaked. "Can't say nothing around here."

"I've been calling him all night," Zala said. "He's probably on the road. . . ." Her voice thinned, for try as she might she couldn't remember whether Spence was still driving for Mercer, showing houses for his sister and her husband, or peddling insurance again. "I spoke to Bestor Brooks, though, and he was supposed to meet Sonny and Cousin Bobby at the Boys' Club." She drifted over to the bunks.

"I know, you told us. Two times you told us. 'Bestor's under punishment,' " Kofi mimicked, making a face, "so he couldn't go."

"Sonny was under punishment, wasn't he, Mama? And he went, hunh?"

"Yeah, but he all the time do like he want." Kofi punched his pillow and flounced down in the hollow. And when Zala leaned in to draw the covers up over his shoulders, he shrugged her hand off. "He always do what he wants. And you let him. You don't never say nothing to him. You jump on me all the time, though."

Zala sighed and moved toward the door, but Kenti grabbed a fistful of her skirt and tugged her back.

"Don't forget," Kenti said, while Kofi mumbled a list of complaints that threatened to drown her out. "Pancakes and bacon 'cause it's Sunday."

"Keep creeping in here waking us up, asking me the same things all over again, like I know. He don't tell me nothing. He just go on and do like he wanna onnaconna you ain't gonna do nuttin' about it."

"Enough, Kofi." She could hear that he was reaching for dems, dats, and doses just to annoy her. "Enough."

"Enuf. You doan tell Sonny enuf when he say sump'n. Just get on my case alla time."

"Enough. I mean it now."

Kofi rolled to the wall and socked it. Kenti yanked on Zala's skirt and whispered the Sunday menu again.

"He could be in trouble, ya know." Kofi bolted upright in the bed, talking loud. "Maybe the cops got'm. Betcha they beating him up. And you just walking around and everything while he in trouble."

"So what should I do, Kofi?"

" 'What should I do, Kofi?' "

"You taking Mama to the bridge," Kenti warned, releasing Zala's skirt.

"Well, Sonny is in trouble all right. He's in deep trouble. With me." She thumped her chest, but the feebleness of the gesture made her flush, and she couldn't meet her almost nine-year-old's eyes. He saw that, and now she had to go because he was calling up the same pictures that had driven her up and down Thurmond last night, too keyed up to stay home, too embarrassed to knock on doors, her gas tank empty from shuffling back and forth to the Boys' Club, no one in sight, not even directions to the campgrounds posted on the door.

"Would you quit it!" Kenti was tumbling things out of the bookcase, looking for something to throw at her brother.

"He could be already dead, ya know, out in the woods. Could be a bear got'm, or a moose. Or the Klu Klux Klan!" Kofi shouted, falling forward on his knees to make sure she heard it before she closed the door.

Sonny hit by a truck. Sonny hitching a ride with a lunatic. Sonny ducking in an abandoned building to pee, crazy junkies jumping him. Sonny missing the van and striking out on his own, a branch felling him in the woods. The woods booby-trapped, people said, by 'Nam vets who lived wild on patrol. Zala felt the stitching in her pockets give. She was grinding her teeth. He played her. He depended on her fear being stronger than anger. So he could come home when he got good and ready, saunter in, the crooked grin, that chipped tooth in front a prize he would flash. And she, relieved, would let him outtalk her. But she was not going for it, not anymore.

"Well, this is a new day, so don't even try." She shredded the words through clenched teeth. She filled the Coke bottle with tap water and shoved in the sprinkler attachment. She hated ironing and so she ironed, determined to hang on to her rage.

"Come home now," she muttered. But each time the iron thudded against Kofi's shirt, she heard her younger son's taunts and couldn't fend off the horrors. Sonny stumbling down a ravine. Sonny trapped in an abandoned house. Sonny pole-axed by a maniac.

Zala flung open the doors of the cupboard and didn't bother getting a glass. She swigged a mouthful of Southern Comfort and the woods began to fade. The body facedown in the gully blurred. Blood seeping between the stones dissolved.

Now that she was on the toilet, she didn't have to go. The fishbowl was in the tub. She didn't feel like changing the water. It was too early yet and Roger the fish was still sleeping.

Kenti made herself get up. When she sat a long time, she'd start sticking to the seat and it would hurt to get up. She could hear the telephone wire slapping against the side of the house. Some pigeons were making noise up in the roofing somewhere. Everything else was quiet. No bacon sizzling. No choirs singing on the radio. Mama was on the couch, half in and half out of her nappy bathrobe. She had her legs over the arm of the couch so Sonny couldn't get in the door without waking her up. He was going to get it, 'cause she wasn't fooling this time. On top of the arts and crafts box was that long whip of leather.

Kenti leaned against the arch post, one foot on top of the other. She could feel grit when she wiggled her toes. Sonny wouldn't mop the floor or nothing. Even when she stuffed the pillowcase and dragged it to the hall, he wouldn't get the cart and take it to the laundry. Said, "Ain't my work, it's her work, wasn't me that kept having babies." Like he wasn't one of the babies she had. And like she didn't work a lot at the barbershop and the art center too. Sonny's work sheet was under the kitchen table. It wasn't crumpled up, so maybe he hadn't thrown it there. Probably it had slipped from under the banana magnet on the refrigerator door and blew there. Nothing he was supposed to do was checked off.

Kenti sniffed to see if maybe the refrigerator was open. Sometimes the wooden spoon stuck in the bowl of batter wouldn't let the door close. But all she smelled was gas, 'cause there probably was no bowl of pancake batter to begin with. She was sure the smell was gas, because the stove was broke. Sonny was supposed to go get the landlord about it. But she didn't think he did, 'cause she sure smelled something. And it wasn't just the bottle pushed down in the trash. Mama call herself hiding it under a bread wrapper. If Daddy came by he would get on her about that. But Daddy wasn't coming by so much no more.

Kofi's shirt was hanging on the ironing board, but her dress was balled up on the table. One of the table legs was sticking out funny. That was where Sonny and Uncle Dave had a fight. Uncle Dave was all the time saying something. So Sonny would say something right back at him. And it wasn't any use telling Sonny he better watch it 'cause Uncle Dave was big and a man and used to working with them rough boys down at the juvenile, 'cause that to Sonny wasn't nothing but a dare. So next thing you know they were shouting the house down.

Uncle Dave was okay sometimes. When he remembered to get peaches and whipped cream in a can. And he told good stories about the time he and Mama and a lot of cousins were little children growing up in Buttermilk Bottom. They played dodgeball and running bases. The movie was a quarter in the old days. And for a nickel they'd get two Tootsie Pops and change besides at Wellington Market. There was a pickle barrel there and a case with store cheese and baloney and another case with candy dots on paper and root-beer barrels and stuff, only it cost two cents 'stead of five. Uncle Dave was a good talker when it came to movies. They'd go to the Ashby movie house and have Milk Dud fights and Goober wars since stuff was cheaper then. Sonny would be listening and laughing up in his nose somewhere because it was funny, Mama being a girl with Jujubes stuck in her teeth.

But then Uncle Dave would get to the part when Grandmama Lovey married Widow Man and everybody moved to the Dixie Hill Apartments, only before the move, Widow Man's twins ran off to join the movement and Mama got sent to live with Great-Aunt Myrtle in New York. And that's the part Mama didn't want to hear about so much, 'cause she'd stop sorting groceries and say over her shoulder "All right now, Dave." But he'd keep on going, talking about people in New York thinking they so hot but not as hot as they think specially if they didn't even come from New York but came from some nowhere place south of Atlanta and meaning Daddy. And Mama would be shaking too many bread crumbs into the canned salmon, saying, "I'm warning you, Dave, you better cool it."

But Dave never did when he was doing that story. Then he'd get to the part where Mama was making up things to tell Great-Aunt Myrtle and Mama would slam down the bread-crumb can or whatever she had in her hand. Then he'd laugh and puff out his cheeks and round out a big belly with his hands even though his own stomach was pretty big anyway. And Mama wouldn't be saying nothing, her hands lost in the bowl with the salmon and stuff, and not moving, because this was always the part where Sonny would jump bad, and never mind that who he was jumping at was a grown man and was bigger than Daddy.

And Friday was the worst fight, and by the time she got to the kitchen, Dave was up out of his chair looking like Daddy do with his card friends and he fixing to slam down a good card and run a Boston. And Sonny was out of his chair with his neck swole up and they calling each other jive turkeys and Uncle Dave telling Sonny he's going to wind up in the juvenile and Sonny saying where he get off hanging around our mama and they so close leaning across the table they got to be spitting on each other. And Uncle Dave said, "Little nigger, I've loved your mother longer than you've been alive." That did it. And the table couldn't take it.

Mama don't allow the N word in her house and she don't allow nobody to pick on her children neither, so she's trying to put Uncle Dave out, only he's so big she couldn't get a grip nowhere on his body so she started shoving with her hip, but he didn't budge at all. And Kofi calling himself the karate champ start doing the iron fist of death and there was just time for her to climb the step stool and dive on Uncle Dave's back while Kofi chopped and Sonny was trying to get past Mama and haul off.

That was just how she'd tell it when Daddy came by. She'd show how she got on Uncle Dave's back and rode him all the way to the door, Mama yelling, Dave laughing, but how hard it was to pull her fingers off from round his throat. She wondered if her daddy would laugh, or if he'd go all quiet with rocks in his jaw.

Kenti moved up close to get a good look at her mama. From the kitchen archway, she'd looked like a little child sleeping all crooked on the couch, one arm in the bathrobe.

"I smell gas, you?"

Not even the eyelids moved. Sometimes she slept with her mouth loose and Kenti could wake her by touching her bottom lip. But her mouth was like the mail slot in the door.

"You get sick, you know, sleeping in gas."

Kenti opened the door a crack. "I can't move your feet, Mama." She opened it some more, until it touched her mother's shoes. Then she hooked the screen in case of burglars. Mailman didn't come on Sundays, no way.

Kenti looked across the street to the only house on Thurmond that was three floors high. Aunty Paulette's house. She made waffles Sunday mornings. But her car wasn't parked out front. Not home from the hospital yet. Sometimes she took them to church in her uniform and looked just like the ushers carrying the collection plates down the aisle, one white-gloved hand tucked behind their back like they were letting everybody know they were honest.

"Mama?" Kenti brushed against the shoes, but the eyelashes didn't flutter. "You going to church this morning?" She bumped her hip against the sofa arm, then trailed her finger along her mama's leg. "I can call Aunty Paulette later. She'll take us. Should I?"

Kenti leaned in close to make sure the gas hadn't killed her mother. She blew on her face, and the lips loosened. Kenti drew back from the smell. Straightening up, she could see the Robinson yard through the curtains they had knotted together at the art center. Mean Dog was digging up the lawn over there with his nose. Chunks of grassy dirt went over his head and fell right on his back, then broke up.

"Dopey dog." But on her way back to her cot she was thinking that maybe Mean Dog needed company. It was too bad Buster was a cat and Roger was a fish. She wondered if Daddy would maybe get them a dog. She could walk the dog over to play with Mean Dog. Daddy would have to buy a leash in case Mean Dog played too rough she could yank her dog away. She tried to wake Kofi to see what he thought about it. But even when she pinched him, he wouldn't wake up and talk. She climbed into the cot with one of her old dolls for company.

Birds in the woods were a whole lot noisier than pigeons on the roof. In the woods they really let loose, a buncha them. So they'd get them all up all right. Cousin Bobby would unzip himself out of his sleeping bag. Sonny probably slept wrapped in the counselor's extra blanket. And probably slept in his drawers 'cause he didn't do the laundry. The sight of them stumbling around groggy made Kofi smile in the hollow of his pillow.

There'd be a creek nearby for washing. A good camper always found a spot to bed down next to a creek or something. That way you just get up and jump in. But sometimes the big guys wouldn't wash up. They wouldn't say they were scared of the beetles and snakes and things. They'd say the water had germs. A good camper was supposed to have iodine crystals in his pack. They killed germs. Then you were supposed to let water boil a long time in the kettle before you added the pow-dered milk or the cocoa or eggs out of the box or whatever you were planning for breakfast. You made the counselor's coffee in a spotted pot. Whoever was supposed to get up first and do breakfast was supposed to have crystals.

He had some foil sacks of iodine crystals, but Sonny wouldn't talk up for him to go. Bestor Brooks always spoke up and looked out for his younger brothers, but Sonny only sometimes. And Kofi was a better camper than any a them. "Only the big guys, Kofi, just the big guys this time." Sonny wasn't all that big and still had to lie and say thirteen 'cause his birthday was coming up which the counselor was too lazy to look up in the book and catch him out.

Kofi propped his eyelid open on the corner of his pillow. Spider-Man was crouching between the mattress and the bedpost ready to spring. The Hulk had been hanging on the ladder, but he'd fallen down a long time ago, one of them times when she woke him up and made him go over everything again like it was his fault Sonny didn't mind. And like it was his fault he didn't know how to look Sonny's friends up in the phone book. How should he know what Flyboy's name was, he didn't hang out with them. "When you're older, kid, and develop a voice and some style, you can hang." Sonny was a better singer, but he was a better camper.

Kenti was awake. She had her petticoat smoothed out at the foot of the cot. She'd found some clean socks, but she was going to wear her bathing-suit bottom for panties. He had to laugh. She looked over and thought he was laughing at her doll. She was squeezing its rubber head to make it do ugly faces.

"Mama drinking again, Kofi."

Kofi roamed his eyes over the bookcase in back of her cot. The paint sets looked crusty. Sometimes they'd go off to the woods to paint, like when Sonny went on a cookout or a bus trip and Kenti would nag that everything was boring and quiet. She would mean McDonald's or

Stuckey's with her greedy self. But Ma would make like the best place to go was to the woods with paint things. Sometimes it was just the three of them. But if Big Dave went, they'd drive in his station wagon as far as the approach trail to Appalachia.

"Hear what I said, Kofi?"

He closed his eyes. There were lots of good things to see in the woods, but he didn't like her pointing things out all the time like she was teaching class over at the Neighborhood Art Center. He had eyes, he could see for himself. Sometimes she'd make a big fuss about how smart he was because he didn't need paints, he'd squash berries or smear bug juice on the watercolor paper. He didn't need a brush, he'd break off a bunch of ferns and dip them into puddles looking greenish gold down by the creek. He could almost feel her hand warm on his shoulder. She'd be bragging on him and he'd do a good painting. But sometimes Big Dave would start in, saying she bragged too much on her children and wasn't firm enough. Then he'd wish Sonny was there 'cause Sonny got Dave straight.

"You wake. I see you smiling."

"Quit it."

Kofi sank down deep in the mattress and returned to the woods. One time when they were bottling rinse water for the brushes, there was a scuffling over past the reeds where the frogs had flattened them down. Then he heard this weird witchy laughing, but before he could go see, she threw out her arm like she did driving and coming to a stop. It was a loon. They got to see it but they had to follow her walking squat like they do in the army.

It was a big bird with a tiny head and bright colors. It had a goose neck and a white stomach and it was rearing up and flapping its wide, big feather wings. It was cackling like a crazy person. And all that cackling made it clumsy. It wasn't the wings but the feet that got the bird going. Once it got itself together it skied off across the water then lifted, its neck stuck straight out. It was calling and calling, only now it was a pitiful sound. "Lonesome" was his sister's two cents.

On the drive back it was one of those lectures like they were her students and she was teaching about nature. The only interesting part was that flying loons sometimes took a shiny wet highway for a lake and tried to land. And one time, when Dad came by to get them because he was driving to Chattanooga to see one of his Omega brothers, there was a dead bird spread out on 95 so he said it was probably a loon looking for water. Dad was cracking his gum and nodding while Kofi told all he knew about loons. Dad didn't interrupt and when he had finished, Dad talked about how he liked water. Said the ocean was one of his favorite things to be on. Then Sonny leaned over from the backseat and said how come Dad was living in Atlanta if he liked the ocean so much. Then Dad said he didn't think he'd be living in Atlanta much longer. And the whole car got quiet and Kenti didn't even yell out when they passed a Stuckey's.

"Girl, would you be careful!"

"We told."

Kenti stepped in front of Paulette, who had turned to yell over to Mean Dog to shut the hell up. Kofi was shoving the door back with his chin. His key was in the lock. The lanyard he'd made in day camp was around his neck, choking him.

"You sew in your sleep now?" Lanky Paulette approached, stooped over, snapping her fingers under Zala's nose. "If you're dying for stitches, come down to Emergency on Saturday night like everybody else."

"We told."

"Everybody heard you." Kofi took the long way around to the kitchen.

Zala felt herself lifted up, a cool hand on her forehead.

"Raise up, girl, 'fore you sew your face to the table." Paulette clicked off the bulb and twisted the skin around on Zala's arm. "Hmph," she said, then pulled Zala's left arm away from the needle.

"We told Aunty Lette," Kenti said, trying to scratch her head through her Easter hat.

Paulette hiked her thumb toward her house. "Should I get my first-aid kit?" She cupped her mouth and called out toward the backroom. "'Cause somebody around here sure is asking to get his behind tore up."

"Save your breath," Zala sighed, the room swimming together. "He's not back yet. He and Bobby are expected at five o'clock."

"Is that five o'clock Sonny time or five o'clock standard time? Take my advice, girl, call the cops."

Zala looked at the welt on her arm. "I don't call the police on my children, Paulette." The welt was beginning to blister.

"Not 'on,' *for.* He's out there and some maniac's running around—" Paulette interrupted herself. "Hey, how about getting your poor old aunty something to drink?"

Zala reached out to help Kenti off with her hat. The elastic was biting into her neck. But Paulette pulled the girl into the folds of her dress and eased off the bonnet, tickling Kenti under the chin.

"Don't you bring me none of that diet soda they got you drinking over here. And no, I don' want skim milk either." Paulette made a face and Kenti giggled and squirmed but kept clinging. "I'll have whatever your mama's drinking." Paulette mugged a peek into Zala's glass.

"Tea." The glass had sweated against the pincushion.

"Tea. Right." Paulette shooed Kenti away but she kept coming back, butting the tall woman and burying her head in the yards of beige silk.

"Plain old tea, Paulette. It's just tea."

"Take it easy. I was just kidding with you."

Paulette walked Kenti backward toward the kitchen, her tickling hands locked under Kenti's elbows. "Whatcha got in there for poor ole Aunty Lette?"

"You not old," Kenti said, flirty. "Want some iced tea?"

"None of that cloudy stuff you guys brew up around here. Give me something I can see through."

Zala released the clamp and dragged the sleeve into her lap. The seam was zigzag and puckered, the tension too tight. Already a day late with the robes. She wondered if the choir had sung at morning service in their street clothes. It was the first Sunday she'd ever missed church. "Pressure," she murmured, as though her pastor was demanding an explanation. She searched among her sewing things for the seam ripper while her across-the-way neighbor horsed around in the kitchen with the children. It was noon. She'd promised her sister-in-law she'd return the machine by dusk. But who would take it over there? The kids had been looking forward to riding the new MARTA train with Sonny.

"The elastic's not supposed to go under your chin," Paulette was saying between sips of ice water. "You'll cut your own neck off."

"Then how I keep it on?" Kenti was using her baby voice. It was getting on Zala's nerves.

"Try combing your hair," Kofi said, sounding like Sonny.

"Mama," Kenti called out as Zala grabbed up the scissors. "We gonna do our hair now?"

"Sure could use it," Paulette cracked, coming up behind Zala's chair. She picked at her braids. Zala stabbed at the seam with the point of the scissors.

"Look here," Paulette said, coming around the chair. Smoothing yards of creamy silk under her, she bent down by Zala.

"What is the matter with you? You look like hell. No wonder, I guess. I'd be scared to death too, what with these kidnappings and killings. Want to take my car?" She patted herself down and found the keys. "I'll hang here with Stuff 'n' Such while you go get His Nibs."

"What killings?" Kofi and Kenti came in.

"Somebody killing somebody, Mama?"

"Go change your clothes," Zala snapped. "I don't work like a dog for you two to play in good clothes." They retreated and Paulette reached for Zala's hand.

"Now look, if you're tuning up to sing the working dog miseries, kindly do me the favor of putting your feet together, Marzala. I've only got one nail left."

"Very funny," Zala said, pulling away. She could hear Kenti giggling in the hallway. Kofi yelled "Kee-yagh!" and kicked the bedroom door open.

"Don't you think we should go look for him? All kidding aside, girl, there's a lunatic out there grabbing children. Where'd they go anyway, the camp group?"

Zala ripped open the seam and tried to focus on what Paulette was saying. "I don't even know where they are. Spence's sister couldn't find the slip."

"Couldn't find, my behind." Paulette stood up and flounced out her dress. "Too busy entertaining to go look, you mean."

"Yeah, well."

"Or looking for more real-estate suckers." Paulette poked her. "Call her back. I'll talk to her. This could be serious."

"Paulette, I've got a pile of work to do here."

"To hell with these robes. What's the matter with you?"

"Four mouths to feed is the matter with me! Rent overdue, two incompletes, and I may be fooling myself about this whole college thing I let you talk me into. I'm worn out and you're giving me a headache. That's what's the matter with me. How are things with you?"

"I don't believe this. Marzala, you were sitting right there on that broke-ass couch same as me when the women came on TV."

Paulette tugged on her arm as though she intended to drag her to the sofa to make her remember.

"They were talking about the child killings, remember? Kids disappearing in broad daylight and turning up dead. Don't give me that glazed-over look, girl, you ain't that drunk. Roll your eyes all you want, it don't faze me, 'cause this ain't about you. I'm talking about Sonny, 'cause I know you heard them. You must've seen it in the papers. And I know damn well they had to be talking it up in the barbershop. The child murders. Would you wake up?"

"Would you stop pulling on me, please?"

"There's nothing clean to put on," Kenti said, slouching into the room. "Everything's dirty."

"Well, don't whine about it." Zala threw the scissors down.

"No problem," Paulette cut in. "Gather up the laundry and we'll stick it in my washer. Now look—" she was tugging again—"I'll hunt up the newspapers. Maybe that'll—would you put that sewing down and listen to me? I know how you hate people getting in your business, but you better get the police over here. I'll drive over to Campbellton Road and see if I can find Spencer."

"Oh, you know where Spence hangs out."

"Would you stop. Sonny's been out all night and you're sitting here calmly sewing with a child murderer on the loose? I don't get this. I really don't. Explain it to me. Tell me something. I'm a quick study." Jangling the car keys, Paulette crossed to the couch and sat down on the edge of the cushion. "I'm listening."

Zala rubbed her eyes. They felt like sandpaper. She knew Paulette wouldn't remain seated too long. And since the Ted Bundy case was her notion of light summer reading, she was bound to start slinging gore on the walls with the latest from the *National Inquirer*.

"So school me, madame. Tell me how come Maynard ordered a special police force to look into these kidnappings. And I want to hear how the *Journal* and the *Constitution* are being silly for printing stories about it if I'm talking off the wall." She was up again, tapping her foot. The shoes were new, Zala noticed.

"But while you're at it," Paulette went on, once again at Zala's chair, "don't give me that downtown crap about gang wars. Some of those kids that disappeared were seven and eight years old. And spare me the wild-marijuana-party angle too. Seven-year-old kids at wild parties? A joint won't stab a kid or strangle him or shoot him. Am I reaching you yet? Do you want me to hunt up the newspaper so you can read it yourself?"

Zala was no longer listening. She was trying to piece together what she'd heard at Simmons's barbershop. She usually tuned out the checker players' arguments, the bootblack's state-of-the-race speeches, the customers' gossip. But she did remember talk of kidnappings. And she did remember a boy being found dead in an abandoned school building.

"I thought that was in . . . I dunno, Alabama?"

"No, girlfriend, wasn't in Mississippi or Arkansas either. Right here," Paulette said, tapping the machine with a tuck comb fallen loose from her hair. "Don't be the complete fool, you idiot, call the police."

"And you're going to stand over me calling me names till I do?"

Paulette drew herself up from the waist. Zala felt two holes being bored through the top of her skull.

"You know, this ain't about your silly ass, Marzala. This really and truly is not. But let me tell you this one thing, see. It's like I tell the patients down at Grady. You can bite my head off if you want to, but getting upset with me won't change the X-rays. Hear? You can hide the pills under your tongue, spit them out in the toilet, whatever you want to do, hey, you grown, and I don't give a good goddam, 'cause it ain't me. Okay?"

"No, it ain't you."

"You are one stupid bitch, Marzala Spencer, you know that? One sorry-ass, silly bitch."

When the door slammed, Kenti dropped the pillowcase on Kofi's foot and tiptoed into the living room. She bumped against Zala's chair. "What's Aunty Paulette so mad about?"

"Her?" Zala thumped her chest till her skin hurt. "What about me?"

The air was heavy with barbecue smoke. Porch gliders squeaked to the *twit-twit* of lawn sprinklers. Two doors up toward Ashby Street, an elderly couple stepped out and looked at the trio talking by the patrol car. The man diagonally across from the Robinsons' hauled a bucket out to wash his car. The two officers looked his way and stopped talking. Then they passed Sonny's snapshot back and forth until Zala handed over a second one. She turned from one to the other, answering their questions. Her head wrap began to slip down around her ears.

An ant carrying a speck of pollen crawled over the red ridge in the brick step near Kofi's foot, then disappeared down a hole in the grout.

"All of a sudden everybody got something to do outside," Kenti said. She rubbed her head through a towel, holding her elbows in so as not to drop the funnies. She sat down on the top step and shook out the paper. "I wish they'd get going and find Sonny."

"Waiting on Bobby." Kofi watched her for a minute to see if she was trying to make an airplane. But she was only pleating the paper into a fan. He saw lather on the back of her neck, but he didn't say anything. Paulette had made him rinse Kenti's hair twice.

"All they do is talk, talk," Kenti said, looking up at him standing on the hump of the stoop.

"Well, don't blame me."

The white cop was leaning back against the car like a board, his heels caught on the edge of the gutter. He said something to Zala and smacked a flashlight in the palm of his hand. "Well, ma'am, what about the boy's father? Do they all have the same father?" Kofi could see how she looked. When she looked like that, the answer was going to be real chilly or real hot.

The Black cop was standing on the strip of grass where Kofi had rolled the Herby Curby for garbage pickup. "And you've contacted both sets of grandparents, Mrs. Spencer?" He nodded at whatever she answered and mashed his lips together while she said some more. Then he hitched up his pants leg and put his foot on the water meter. Kenti looked up when the metal plate clinked.

"The streetlights'll be on in a minute," she said.

"So what?"

Kenti stopped fanning. "Then she'll make us go to bed, stupid."

"You got soap on your neck. There's some in your hair too. You're going to have dandruff."

Kenti cut Kofi off. "Everybody's looking at us."

"I got eyes."

He had spotted Aunt Paulette's boarder watching through binoculars from his room on the third floor. The window was empty now, but the shade pull was swinging. A big moth was plastered up against the boarder's screen. There were moths and dark bugs flitting around the streetlight too, and it wasn't even on yet. He saw a dragonfly nosedive into the bed of crispy brown petals on the Robinson walk. Mean Dog was looking across the street at everybody, panting with his tongue hanging out to one side.

"You don't think he might have gone for a swim, Mrs. Spencer, when he couldn't locate the campgrounds?" The Black cop took the flashlight away from his partner and shoved it into one of the loops in his belt. Then he leaned down on the leg resting on the water meter. Kofi looked at the bulge in the holster. And when the cop turned, hopping a little on one foot to do it, Kofi could see the handcuffs. The sight of them made his mouth taste funny, like drinking milk from a tin cup.

The cops hadn't come in the house to search up in the eaves or down in the basement, like they had. "Before I start making phone calls, let's look," she had said, when what she really meant was, "Before you go across the street and have a good time, let's work." The police didn't knock next door to question the Griers. They just took her word that Sonny was not on the premises and not with a neighbor or friend.

Kofi took a good look at the handcuffs. He slipped his wrist in the lock of two fingers. Those handcuffs couldn't hold a boy or a small woman or even a man if he was skinny.

The Black cop made the water meter clank again. The brass in Kofi's mouth was worse. He could've told them a few things. Like how Sonny took Mama's stitch ripper on his way out, like he was going off to have a fight with somebody. Kofi wasn't trying to hide it. He wasn't saving it to tell at a special time, either. He just forgot. And if he told now, he'd get yelled at. She'd been yelling so hard in the basement, Mr. Grier had to come down the cellar steps to see. The basement was spooky, like a mine that people had quit digging at once they found gold. She kept saying she'd dreamt about the basement. So she made them look around.

Kenti yanked on Kofi's pants leg. But he didn't see why until the car rolled over second base and the manhole cover rattled. The car was coming slowly down the middle of Thurmond Street. A big dark-green Buick. It looked like one of the cars their Uncle Bryant loaned Dad sometimes to show people houses. The driver slid the windows down and stuck his elbow out, then his head.

"Not Daddy," Kenti said.

She sat back down. That close to the house, Daddy would whistle. A woman leaned across the man to get a good look when the car slowed up. She was holding flowers done up in plastic like they do for running down the aisle at a concert.

"So nosy. And that funny-looking baby too."

In the backseat, a baby sat in what looked like a high chair to Kofi, feeding herself. She banged on the tray. She tipped over her bowl. She smeared food all over her clothes and clapped her hands. Then she tried very hard to pick up something to eat from the tray. Her fingers were fat. The spaghetti sauce slippery. It wore Kofi out to watch her keep trying.

"Stupid child," Kenti said.

"She's just a baby, Kenti."

"A fat ole nosy baby."

"Who's talking?"

Kenti tossed her head and swung the towel like hair. Then she crossed her leg high and fanned herself. When the car picked up speed and the baby bucked and let out a wail, Kofi thought she was going to call the parents some names, but she went on fanning. He roamed around the house in his mind, wondering where Sonny had stashed his cigar box. It was a better box than the one Kofi had.

Mama once threatened to throw his out, calling his stuff junk. He kept his baby teeth in it, some seashells, and a few magic things, along with the foil packs of Aqua Pura that Mr. Lewis at the Boys' Club had given him. Dad stepped in and made a big speech about privacy. On account of he once had a cigar box for his things. The box he gave Sonny was a Primo. Kenti spoiled hers the same day, trying to make it papier-mâché the newspaper strips sopping wet, more water than flour. The skinny doll she stuck in it anyway was mushy and blurred.

"Where you think Sonny at?" She was talking behind her fan and interrupted his thoughts of the crawl space. He'd been so sure Sonny's box was buried up there in the loose-fill insulation.

"You keep scratching, you going to get sores," Kenti said. "Mama told you to put on long sleeves and smear Vaseline on your face before you climbed up there. You a hard head, Mr. Kofi."

"Would you shut up?"

"A hard head will get you a soft behind every time," she said.

"I wish you'd be quiet. It's too hot to talk."

Zala went over it all again to fill in the time. "He left to come pick up the machine before I had a chance to talk to him. But he'll be here any minute. At least he'll know how to get to the camping area." She turned toward Ashby and felt the whole street turn with her. Mowers idled. Hedge clippers paused. Hoses splattered the driveways. A woman near the corner got up from her porch glider and leaned against her screen door, bowing it out. Two stoops up from the Griers', the elderly husband, seated, held his wife by the elbow while she stood up craning her neck. Then she sat down, leaning against him.

"So long as we don't get a call, ma'am, we can wait," the white cop, Officer Eaton, said.

Zala settled back on her heels and examined the curtains in the Griers' living-room window. They hadn't moved. But Mr. Grier had come down the basement steps while Kofi had been playing at being a coal miner down there, then a switchman, swinging the lantern behind the stony dirt mound back of the furnace. Mr. Grier seemed annoyed to be asked again if he'd seen Sonny.

"Mighty hot," said Officer Eaton.

"A scorcher," said Officer Hall.

"Think your boy might have gone to the pool? That's where I'd be. It's some hot," repeated Eaton.

"Can I get you two some ice water?"

"No thanks, Mrs. Spencer. Let's just see what your nephew comes up with."

Zala looked at the knob on the Griers' door. She hoped Mrs. Grier would let bygones be bygones and come out. She needed support. It was uncomfortable having to deal with police. Especially out in the street.

It was too hot indoors. And too, they'd torn the place up going through Sonny's things looking for phone numbers.

"Must be some kind of record, this heat wave."

"Hmm."

Looking down toward Taliaferro, Zala wondered if everyone was keeping a distance because of the police or because they weren't sympathetic. By nightfall, she thought, a sour taste in her teeth, some made-up story would be circulating. A version of it would eventually reach her in the barbershop a mile and a half away.

"Well—" pushing himself up onto the curb—"I guess we could check along the strip," said Eaton, talking across her to his partner. "But let's see what the nephew comes up with. Now, how recent are these snapshots?" He walked toward his partner, who was still standing with his foot cocked on the meter.

"She said they were taken in June."

"Sonny's sixth-grade graduation," Zala said. "I have a packetful." She stepped between them. "What strip is that you mentioned?"

"Over there along Stewart Avenue. The electronic game palace, the nudie joints, adult bookstores." Eaton licked his fingers and thumbed through his notes.

"My son is a twelve-year-old boy," Zala said icily, and the cop looked up from his little book.

"You'd be surprised, ma'am. And not just Black kids, either," said Eaton.

She turned on her heels and followed Hall, who shone the flashlight over the roof. Though it was still broad daylight, he flashed it along the gutters and around the lumpy tar edges of the dormers.

Kenti bumped down two steps and twisted around to follow the beam. "You think my brother's hiding on the roof?"

"Does he do that sometimes, hide from you?" asked Hall.

Kenti looked at him, turned to Kofi, then looked over the man's shoulder at her mother. Kenti tucked in her lip. When the policeman came into the yard, she pulled in her feet. She looked from the gun on his hip to the Robinson yard. She could see Mean Dog between the back of their yellow Bug and the police car's front lights. Mean Dog hadn't barked but one time, like he knew cops had pistols with bullets.

"I thought I heard something up there," the Black cop said, turning around to look straight at Kofi.

"Squirrels," Kofi said.

There'd been nights, though, when he'd heard something up there heavier than squirrels. He was thinking about saying so, but he saw his mother looking at him, so he didn't say anything. The Black cop went around the side of the house just as Eaton came up to the hedge and pointed.

"You need to get your landlord to replace those gutters. Rusted clean through in places. You renting or buying?" Eaton asked her.

Kenti watched how her mother came to a full stop by the jade tree and took a long time to turn her head to look over the hedges at the white man.

"I think my boy is lost in the woods," she said. Then, "My nephew will show you. He'll be along soon." That stopped him. But just for good measure, Kenti stretched her legs out. The cop looked at her bare feet, then went back to the car, his head turned toward the corner of Ashby.

"Mrs. Robinson's looking," Kenti said, watching out of the side of her eye. "She pretending to hold Mean Dog back by the collar when he ain't even barking."

"I can see and I can hear," Kofi said. The fiberglass was making him itchy all over. He prepared for a jump from the stoop. He wanted to see what the Black cop was looking at around the side of the house.

"She said to stay put."

"I didn't hear her say nothing."

"Said it with her eyes. You got eyes, doncha?" Kenti crossed her legs high again and fanned.

"Forget you." Kofi sucked his teeth but stayed put.

Staying to the narrow walk, Zala followed Officer Hall around to the back of the house, where he suddenly dropped down in a squat. He shaded his eyes and peered in through the basement window.

"You got a cat, Mrs. Spencer?"

"The neighbors'. We share the basement."

"Laundry room?"

She shrugged. "The washer and dryer broke down one month after we got here."

He swiveled around, the soles of his shoes gritty on the brick walk. It didn't seem dark at all until he swept the light under the dogwood, then directed the beam along the back fencing, then back again to the tree. He did it quickly, as though to catch something sly and elusive. The pool of yellow-green pollen below the dogwood bleached out to pale yellow. The clothesline Sonny had used to pitch a tent suddenly looked bright, almost clean. It was knotted in places. A web a spider had spun, using a knot for an anchor, had ensnared a victim. The husk of a beetle dangled in silvery threads.

"You get on with your next-door neighbors?" Officer Hall straightened up and pulled his uniform free at each armpit.

"We're fine," she said, suppressing the scenes that usually started over her gunning the machine late at night.

The flashlight swept across the tub-and-wringer a yard down. An old woman, resting her cheek on her knuckles, her elbow on the edge of the enamel table, was dozing on the back porch. Her stockings were rolled to her shins. She wore men's slippers. Wet wash hung over her head from a wooden rack. The door that led to her kitchen stood open. A shotgun house; every room was exposed by the APD flashlight.

"Look at that." Officer Hall shook his head, sending the light down to the house where the blue wading pool lay wrinkled and flat in the yard. The door there was ajar. She could make out the handlebars of a child's trike on the back porch. Then he focused the light on the house immediately behind Zala's. The ladder had been left up at full stretch against the side of the house. The screens in the windows were the slot-in kind.

"Lot of break-ins in this neighborhood recently. Getting worse every day. We got a call on the way over here. That's what took us so long."

"You get many calls like this? Children missing?" The spit in her mouth was pasty.

"Runaways? A fair amount."

"No, I mean . . . The papers say somebody's kidnapping children and killing them." She got the same response they'd given her at the curb: nothing.

He seemed determined to wake up the old woman, shining the light right in her face. He stepped a few times to the side, and now Zala too could see straight through the old woman's house all the way to the plants lined up on her front porch rail. They were sturdy, colorful plants in buckets, pails, and large cans.

Juice cans, Zala was thinking. Grapefruit juice, the lining of her mouth acid. At the Boys' Club they served the waiting parents grapefruit juice poured from large tin cans into plastic cups that were collapsible.

"I fault the new airport," Hall was saying. "Building an international airport as huge as Hartsfield is like putting the welcome mat down for organized crime. It's a whole new ballgame now." He strolled over to her back steps. "When you get major drug trafficking, you get an increase in petty crimes too." With the side of his shoe, he gathered scattered cherry pits into a heap.

"You think these murdered children were involved in drugs?"

"I'm saying that drug traffickers've got no compunction whatsoever about recruiting youngsters. We can't arrest a minor for possession, and the courts can't prosecute. Dealers depend on that."

"But the children . . ." Zala couldn't keep her mind steady. Hall kept looking from the cherry pits littering the back steps to the rope wrapped around the dogwood. A girl, she remembered reading, had been found strangled in a wooded lot not far from Spence's apartment complex. She'd been tied to a tree with an electrical cord. "Is that what they say about the child murders? That they were working for a drug ring?" It seemed far-fetched. Wasn't it easier to pay an adult to be quiet than to kill a child?

"My partner looked into the case and he feels it's a reporter using a sensational story to try to make the grade. There's actually nothing to make a case. Different MO each time."

She waited for him to ask about the cherry pits. She would keep her answer short. She would say only that they'd sat on the back steps two nights ago, she and Sonny, sharing a bowl of Bing cherries. It had been a peace offering, but she wouldn't say that. Sulking, he wouldn't come in to dinner. She'd burnt the salmon croquettes. But at least she'd gotten Dave to leave.

She dragged herself behind Officer Hall. He'd taken an interest in her garden plot. She was mostly interested in going to sleep, but Paulette's newspapers were scattered all over the sofa.

"The papers say the police chief's got a special unit to investigate. So there must be something to it," she pressed him, and followed him over to her garden.

"The commissioner formed a special investigation team, yes," he said, "because—just between you and me—a group of parents were pressuring city hall."

His remarks seemed to tire him out, and Zala could think of nothing else to ask. But then he was the professional, he should have been questioning *her*, pressing her to think of some thing, some person, some place she'd overlooked. Maybe there was nothing to be alarmed about. He was a cop; he should know. If there was something to the murder stories, wouldn't Maynard be on the news, mobilizing the city? Leave it to Paulette to come up with something scary. Zala glanced over at Paulette's empty driveway. She wished she'd come back and lend some support. Paulette would know how to take charge of the situation.

"You could use some yard lights around back, Mrs. Spencer. Just you and the kids here by yourselves?"

She nodded. And when he shoved his hat back to run his arm across his forehead, she knew he wouldn't leave it at that. He asked, "No man in the house?" just the way the Griers had, not butting in, but genuinely concerned. "Then who tells you what to do?": Mr. Grier had sounded sincerely worried about her welfare.

"A dog wouldn't be bad," Hall said, scuffing up dirt from her garden. "We've got a German shepherd, but a Doberman would be best. Keep a gun for protection?" He spoke quietly and seemed to know she wouldn't answer, not that it was a big thing. Most people kept guns in their cars, one in their houses, and it wasn't unusual to feel guns on a person out dancing.

"People have to take precautions," he went on. "A .33 or a .38, I think." He turned and looked at her. "Maybe a .32—you're small-framed."

He continued sizing her up. And Zala wondered if he'd now indicate what particular sort of man went with the preferred dog, the recommended gun, and her small frame. But he turned his attention back to the plot, tamping the top layer down as though testing how packed the dirt was. He shifted his weight onto his back leg suddenly, keeping his body well away from the tamping foot. He had her believing the earth would split open any minute and yank him down into its mud-caked maw.

"Must be difficult raising three kids on your own. Particularly two boys. And one's a teenager too." He puffed up his cheeks and blew out. "Adolescents can be rough." He shone the light on the shovel.

"He's a good kid," she said, feebly. "He's just twelve, not a teenager yet. He doesn't give me a rough time. Not at all."

"Problem is, you can't monitor them every second. They can be running with a bad crowd and you wouldn't know." He pulled a tomato stake free from the pile stacked and ready to mark rows for the vegetables.

"I screen his friends," she said, watching him slide his thumb over one end of the stick, testing its point. "He belongs to a singing group. Nice bunch of boys," she said, repeating what she'd already told them.

"That's good, because like I said, these narcotics dealers get young kids to do their dirty work. And drugs are big business. They'd kill a kid in a minute to keep the others in line." He hefted the stick, measuring its weight. "I assume you have a curfew for the boy. Who punishes him when he violates his curfew?"

"Well, I ground him."

"Uh-hunh." He sounded doubtful about something. With the stick, he moved her tools around in the toolbox. "Is your husband strict with the children? Does he whip them?"

"No, no." She felt uneasy, him bent over studying each tool and her not knowing what was going on in his mind. The ball of twine tumbled out of the box. Even to her, it looked suspicious: too thick for the width of the stakes, just right for tying someone up.

"Yeah," he said tiredly, dragging the word out. "Don't think these drug pushers don't use their own children, either."

"Are you saying that's what happened? To the missing children, I mean?"

She felt a little easier when he made a shrug with his mouth. But at the same time he kept turning over one of her gardening tools in his hand, the one she'd used to rake the dirt into an even grade so she could plant.

"The Iron Claw," he said, suddenly up and playful, except that she could see he was serious, lunging around with the tool, fencing with the shadow the loose telephone wire made against the side of the house. He was so completely unself-conscious it floored her. She wondered if a .32 Smith and Wesson strapped to her thigh would give her that kind of confidence. And she was wondering why she felt embarrassed and he didn't.

The phone ringing brought the swordplay to a halt. He leaned over on one leg and put back the claw, a golfer on the green. She heard the children shoving each other aside in a race to the phone.

Hall's partner walked up to the hedges. "Anything back there?"

"Nothing of interest. Any sign of the nephew?"

"Not yet." Officer Eaton looked off toward Ashby.

Kofi was swinging back and forth on the door with his knees when Zala reached the front steps.

"That was Nana Cora looking for Dad. He was supposed to be down there at two o'clock. He didn't show."

"And she's mad," Kenti said, coming to the door.

"Onnaconna she was waiting for him to pick her up at the Eastern Star 'cause Grandaddy Wesley took the car to go to the lodge."

"She still on the line?" From the doorway, Zala could see the phone had been hung up, but the heat of the house messed with her timing. "Kofi, please go to the bathroom if you need to. And cut off all these lights. It's like a furnace in here."

"We told her," Kenti said, taking Zala's hand to feel her hair. It was dry, which meant it would be a battle to comb through and braid up. Zala patted her head and went down the steps.

"We told her about Sonny. And she said Sonny was a caution. What that mean?"

"See if you can call her back, Kenti."

"She's not home, I told you that."

"Beg pardon?"

Kenti tucked in her lips and backed into the house.

She had to step between the two officers and the patrol car. They seemed to be ready to leave.

"It looks like the boy's with his father, wouldn't you say, Mrs. Spencer?"

"Took in an air-conditioned movie is my guess, ma'am. I know that's where I'd be," Eaton chuckled.

"Like you said, your husband comes by to visit the children on Sundays. I'd say the two of them hooked up on their own. What do you think?"

"Well, he doesn't come by every single Sunday," she began, but Hall and Eaton both seemed so sure. These men weren't rookies. They should know how things went. They'd told her already it wasn't an unusual situation. And before Old Man Murray talked Sonny out of his bike, Sonny often rode over to Campbellton to see Spence. She concentrated on the certainty in Hall's voice.

"So, missing the campers," he was saying, "feeling left behind, so to speak, he went to see his father. It's Sunday. And your husband, to make up for the outing, took him to a show, or maybe for pizza. Can you think of some regular place they would go? Six Flags, is that a possibility?"

"Makes sense, ma'am." Officer Eaton was encouraging her with his eyebrows. "Took a drive out to Six Flags. Some Sunday crowd, phew. Or just a drive, the kid and his old man. Air-conditioned car, I bet." He invited her to smile with him.

"The time got away from them and your husband neglected to notify you of the boy's whereabouts."

"Having such a good time, they got a late start heading down to the old folks. In the country, is it? They got a farm somewhere?"

"Columbus," she said.

"Don't discount the possibility of road trouble, either."

"Now, I'd say that was pretty likely in this heat. And God help him if he left antifreeze in the engine. Boy, that can get sticky." Officer Eaton was suddenly an old family friend ready to wire money to a buddy stuck on a "country" road down in Columbus, Georgia.

"They're together, wouldn't you say so? I think so." It was the first time Officer Hall had smiled a full smile. He looked radiant, turning from her to his partner, then to her again. He shoved his bottom lip out and bobbed his head the way Spence did after unloading a TLC house on a handyman.

"It'll occur to them to call."

"Sure. They were having a good time."

They agreed. They looked ready to throw light punches at one another's shoulders, so pleased with themselves. Mystery solved, case closed.

She felt lighter somehow. The knot toward the top of her spine—just under the one clenched for the overdue rent—loosened. She could

see it, the two of them in one of a half-dozen cars Bryant leased out, taking a drive, the radio blaring, a jumbo pack of gum divided between
them on the dashboard, singing and chewing and talking loud, without
a thought for Kenti, for Kofi, or for her. She could even smile about
their thoughtlessness. And she did, until the officers tried to hand her
back Sonny's pictures.

"I dunno," she muttered, wrapping her arms around her midriff.
"I'd feel better if we took a look around the campsite."

"We can do that, ma'am, sure."

"We can radio a unit in the area," Officer Hall corrected, "as soon as
we get a fix on the exact location."

"There go Bobby!" Kofi yelled. He jumped from the stoop and
took off.

"Is that the boy's cousin?"

"That's him," Zala said. The thud of Kofi's landing shivered in her
uterus. She told herself—and was sure of it, as she began moving up
Thurmond—that if Sonny were in any real danger, she'd feel it. She signaled Kenti to stay by the door and picked up her pace. She couldn't recall her womb having taken any elevator rides in the past twenty-four
hours. She'd experienced no sudden updrafts. He would be home before
nightfall. She felt free for the first time since Saturday afternoon, when,
coming in from the barbershop to change clothes to go teach her craft
classes, she'd been derailed by "He went."

"Damn if that don't look like somebody with him." Eaton came up
on her right, Hall flanked her on the left.

Zala had to laugh. Tucked under Bobby's arm was a buckram-
bodied woman with one long, glossy leg. Far from demanding the machine back, her sister-in-law was apparently asking her to sew.

The streetlights came on. Moths and large bugs circled the globes.
Moths were still trying to get at the old man's hat up the street. The old
lady slapped them away, but they kept coming back. The old man took
it off when Zala and the two officers went by. The old lady stood up and
looked at the sweaty backs of the police. Both had dark V's in their uniform shirts. Then the old lady ducked inside the house.

Kenti waited to see if she would come out again with a spray can and aim it at the old man. He had a bald head almost, just fringe around the back where the moths were playing around.

She watched her brother and her cousin come down the street carrying Aunt Delia's shape between them. The big-belly lady poking the screen of her door out swung it open to say something friendly to them. Cousin Bobby had a dip to his walk, now that he was the center of attention. Then all five joined up in the middle of the street and came down Thurmond like a parade. Bobby shook his head a lot when they asked him something. He would stop walking to say what he had to say. And Kofi would have to slow up, go back, and keep in step. Kofi was carrying the tricky end, the leg stand. And when they all bunched together to ask Cousin Bobby something special, Kofi got left out at the far end of Aunt Delia's dress form.

The old man slapped his hat back on just so he could tip it when the parade went by. It looked like the old lady wasn't coming back out. She was going to miss the best part, all the stopping and talking and then picking up the rhythm again.

Kenti was waiting to see who was going to pile into the car and go get Sonny and who was going to get left behind. She counted everybody coming and placed each one in the cop car. They all fit, with three laps left over for her to sit on. If Aunt Paulette hurried up, they would have two cars to go in. Then no one could say, "Draw a map, Bobby, and stay with Kofi and Kenti while I go, 'cause someone has to stay by the phone."

"Everything all right?" It was Mrs. Grier cracking her door open. She said it so sweet, Kenti's eyes filled up. She tried to smile and nod to Mrs. Grier without blinking. If she didn't blink, she wouldn't spill.

"All right, then." Mrs. Grier closed the door right on her own housecoat. It was a long time before she tugged it and the shiny orange disappeared.

Kenti tipped her head back like she had a nosebleed. The two cops looked like they were hurrying up to jump into the car by themselves. She looked up and down Thurmond for the familiar bronze car with the black top. At the Ashby end Old Man Murray was walking his bike, Sonny's bike, the one the old man paid Sonny ten dollars for when Mama had paid Goodwill twenty-five dollars, the one Daddy wouldn't go get cause he felt sorry because Mr. Murray's mother had died and he lost his job going South to bury her. And now Murray had Sonny's paper route too. So Kenti didn't want to look at him.

"Old fart," she said, the way Aunt Paulette had said it. "Look like the change of life."

A boy was coming up the Taliaferro end of the street. He had on black-and-white sneakers. The rest of him was in the shadowy part between the streetlights where the trees hung over the sidewalk. She hoped it wasn't him. She wanted Sonny out in the woods lost. She wanted to be the first one to see him from the police car. She would lean over from somebody's lap and tap the driver on the shoulder. She'd say, "Pull over please, there go my big brother Sonny."

Kofi drew his legs up at the foot of the sofa bed and folded the newspaper. "Listen to this. You listening?" Kenti squashed the pillows against her ears. Kofi sucked his teeth. Wasn't his fault only Bobby got to go. He slid the phone closer. And just to make sure it didn't slip out of place, he propped it against the schoolbook Sonny hadn't turned in yet.

"There was this little girl and she was your age. She was going to be eight the next day. But somebody stole her right out of her bed. And they can't find her. You listening?" He looked toward the kitchen. His mother was slamming things around on the back porch, so she wouldn't hear him.

"There was this boy around my age. He just disappeared. Then one day somebody found him under a trestle thing and said he musta fell from the trestle 'cause he was holding leaves in his hands when he died. You know, like he'd tried to grab hold on the tree while he was coming down. But one of the cops said he suspected foul play because the leaves couldn't come off those trees. So he said foul play. That means not an accident. Someone offed him."

"I know, dummy."

"Okay. So when the parents got together and started talking to the news people, the police changed their story from accident to murdered."

"I already knew that part. That was the boy named Andrew, like your friend Andrew, right?"

Kofi ran his finger down the newspaper looking for something

Paulette hadn't told them already. She mostly went dah-de-dah-blah over the scary parts and only read little bits just so she could tell them to watch out, be careful, behave, and don't take rides with strangers.

"I don't want to hear any more," Kenti said. "I'm mad with you. You coulda said something. You were scared, that's what."

Kofi put the paper aside. He couldn't understand why such a big story as somebody knocking off little kids was crammed between a lot of furniture ads. He opened Sonny's school book. At the bottoms of pages 93 and 94 a bunch of olden-time people in one-shoulder robes were running for their lives with their mouths in an O. And flames drawn like tongues were licking down the side of page 93, chasing them. Some of the people ran right off page 94. But on 95, the lava got them and all their houses and cows and carts and lumps of cheese too.

"Want to hear this? It's about some Romans who kept living in a place where there was this volcano." When Kenti played like she was snoring, he closed the book and slid it under the phone so it wouldn't tip over. He searched the clock face behind the dress form. Somebody should've called—if not the police, then Bobby. But Bobby was like that. He was going to summer school and had to get home to study for a test. Even so . . . Kofi reached for the paper again. He didn't want to read about people too stupid to build houses where no volcanoes were around.

It was quiet in the kitchen. To see her, he had to lean all the way down to the floor. Balancing up on the tips of his fingers, he could see the fluorescent ring in the kitchen ceiling. And when he leaned sideways, bracing his hip against Kenti, he could see what she was doing. She wasn't reaching around in the cupboard behind the dishes. She was bent over with both arms wrapped around the silverware drawer. At first he thought she was taking it out to put it on the table, like maybe she'd hid something back behind the drawer. But she was only lifting it. And when she shoved it in, the drawer went in strong and everything in the kitchen rattled. It rattled him too. He almost toppled over on his head.

"You scared to go to sleep, hunh?" Kenti bopped him with a pillow and moved to the window side of the mattress and curled up.

Kofi stretched out along the foot of the bed. He looked at the living-room wall, waiting to see what Mrs. Grier would do. Sometimes when they made noise at night, she started running the vacuum cleaner and rode it right into the baseboards to let them know. Maybe she didn't hear the drawer. Or maybe she felt sorry for them. He sure did. He had a feeling Kenti was sucking her thumb under the sheet. He rolled over and sucked his.

Zala locked up the back, checked the windows, cleaned the fish-bowl, tapped it to make sure Roger was still alive, and set it on the kitchen table. She checked the nails in the bathroom and backroom windows. She left the light on in the hall, then walked through to the front. She locked the door, pulled her bathrobe sash tighter, securing everything that could be secured.

They'd promised to call back. She couldn't remember all that they'd said about filing a report, but she wouldn't let them go until they'd assured her: "We'll get back to you." She set the phone on the floor and made sure it was plugged in at both ends. Holding Sonny's sixth-grade reader by the cover, she shook it. Nothing fell out. She pushed her finger through the tunnel of the spine. No "illegal substances," as Officer Hall had put it, Bobby stopping, pulling himself up tall, his chin digging into his chest, thoroughly offended by the question.

"A Doberman." Zala shook her head, staring at the dress form.

"What?" Kofi rolled over, knuckling his eyes.

"A damn Doberman," she told him. "Just what we need," she laughed. "Probably eat more than all four of us put together."

Kofi sat up trying to make sense out of what she was saying. Standing there staring, shaking her head, her fists on her hips, the head scarf gone and her hair all over her head, she looked like somebody else's mother. Bestor Brooks's mother looked weird like that sometimes on Saturday mornings, except she always had a cigarette in the side of her mouth. He was thinking how much he wished he was at Bestor's house when the phone rang.

It looked like she was just going to stand there staring at it with her eyes wide open. "Pick it up, Ma."

Cupping it with both hands, Zala breathed into the mouthpiece. "Sonny, is that you?"

Kofi could tell by the way her voice changed when she started walking back and forth talking that it was Dad. He climbed out of bed.

"Well, of course they told her. We were worried, Spence. They thought he might be down there, or that she might— Is he with you?"

For a second, Kofi thought she was handing the phone over to him. She did that sometimes after making faces at the ceiling then slamming her eyes shut. But was only dropping her arm for a minute 'cause what Dad was saying was driving her crazy.

"Lemme talk to him."

Zala held Kofi back, her hand hard against his chest. The line crackled as though water had seeped into the cable.

"Where the hell are you?" But he kept on talking and wouldn't let her get a word in. "Dammit, Spence, I am not playing around, this is serious. We had the police over here. They've been looking all night. Two nights now he—"

"Let me tell it." Kofi could see they'd only argue and get everything mixed up.

"He's gone, Spence. He's gone. Some lunatic's running around killing children and you ask me if this is a bit? What kind of bit? I'm out of my mind—the police, everything, you nowhere all day, neighbors gawking, and all you can say is your mother. To hell with your mother, your son is missing."

Kofi put his hand over the buttons just in case she tried to hang up. And that's when he noticed Kenti was on the other side of her trying to reach over to do the same thing. But neither of them could stop her.

Zala shoved their hands aside and slammed the phone down. " 'A joke'!" she shouted. "A *joke*. Did you hear that? Your stupid father thinks I'm making up stories just to upset his mother. A heart condition my foot. Since when has that woman had a weak anything?"

Kofi made himself small against the sewing machine to give her room. And she took it, walking back and forth raising dust from the carpet.

"Don't talk so loud," Kenti said, hunching her shoulders up and looking at the wall.

"What? You talking to me, miss? Where you get off talking to me like that, little girl?"

Kenti squeezed in by the mirror and poked the dress form in front of her.

"And he's upset. *He's* upset. And not once did he offer to do something. His own son. You see what kind of . . . dumbass . . ." She was hissing like a snake and she was reaching for words with both hands strangling Dad and Kofi tried to come up with something to make her stop it.

"Maybe . . . maybe we should call Mr. Gittens?"

"The landlord? Call the *landlord*, Kofi? What do you suggest, his PO box number or that little hole-in-the-wall office back of the beauty parlor where he never is anyway? The landlord." She was reaching again, like Mr. Gittens was hiding in the overhead light and she would tear him down from there with her bare hands.

"It would take Missing Persons to find that bastard."

When her eyes fell on him, Kofi nodded and moved away from the phone so she could call Missing Persons. But she went into the stare thing again. The phone book was on Kenti's side, but she wasn't even moving to get it.

"Call 911, Ma."

"911. Right. 911."

Her grip on the phone should have melted it. Kofi looked over at Kenti and she darted out from the corner and jumped into the sofa bed. Kofi stood by, hoping his sister wouldn't start crying. He listened hard by the phone, but couldn't tell what the 911 lady was saying back to her. But he could tell by the way his mother drew her mouth away from her teeth that she might explode any minute. Her hand was moving over the things on the table. He found the pencil and handed it to her. He watched her scribble a number on the back of Aunt Delia's dress pattern, then hang up.

" 'Not an emergency,' Kofi. Your brother is not an emergency. You got that? And you too, miss. Just remember that. You two better remember that."

She gave him such a hard look he felt his chest caving in. He felt like he was about to get yelled at for wanting to run away when he wasn't even thinking it. He moved out from under her stare and sat on the arm of the sofa bed. Kenti was looking out the window between a space in the knotted-up curtains. Fireflies were sparking in Aunt Paulette's yard. If he'd had the energy to lift his head, Kofi was sure he'd catch the boarder on the third floor spying on them through binoculars.

Zala sat down and strung some words together before calling Missing Persons. She rehearsed it quickly as she dialed, reminding herself of the officers' names. She was fully prepared on the third ring. But what she got was a recording. It said Missing Persons was closed for the weekend and to call Homicide. She held on, frozen, and the message was repeated. Call Homicide. She could not even move to write down the number; her thermometer stuck at zero.

Monday, July 21, 1980

The Youth Division of Missing Persons was an oblong room split down the middle by a counter. The room resembled the attendance office at the children's elementary school—wooden benches where people waited, a wall case with pigeonholes for mail, scarred desks and dented file cabinets, ringing telephones and clackety typewriters. At school, though, there was a sense of subdued order, and the workers, mostly women, were cordial. At MPYD, the bustle was noisy, and the workers, mostly men, wore uniforms and badges. There was no semblance of order anywhere, not even in the arrangement of furniture and fans. Aisles were interrupted by cardboard files and stacks of phone directories. And at the far end, near the closed-in office, tall army-green file cabinets were set in a U shape. Those typing at that end worked in shadows.

The squad room was dingy, and there was a graininess in the air, giving it the look and feel of newsprint. The form that a big-boned redheaded sister had slapped down on the counter for her to fill out was almost too faint to read.

Zala bore down with the chewed-up ballpoint, using the margins to report efforts made to locate the missing subject, Sundiata Spencer, a.k.a. Sonny Spencer. She'd started phoning at 7:30 a.m., and her efforts looked impressive on paper.

Mr. Lewis of the Boys' Club was out searching the woods. Presumably, the two officers had filed a report on whatever search had been conducted the night before. She'd tracked down Sonny's former band teacher, and he was making calls on her behalf. Simmons was going to have his regulars ask around. Dave was checking the juvenile shelters. Paulette was using a special hot line to conduct a hospital search for any young John Doe victim answering Sonny's description. Delia promised to track Spence down and tell him to meet her. Mercer, the man Spence drove for sometimes, vowed he'd deliver Spence to the Decatur Street Police Station by ten o'clock sharp. The clock over the window said 10:25.

The window, tilted open at the top, let in traffic noise from the street and student hubbub from Georgia State University. What sunlight came in was murky, filtered through panes green with soil mold. On either side of the window were children's photos, some glossies, some photocopied flyers. Sunday clothes, school-picture smiles: they were pinned to dirt-streaked corkboards gouged out by pushpins. Some pictures were cracked and dusty. Where pushpins were missing from corners, photos had curled up, covering the faces of the missing.

"You think this is bad, you ought to see Homicide on the third floor." A young sister with a short-cropped 'fro was speaking to a male rookie who was balancing a jar of pens on a stack of folders. "Four to a desk and only three telephone lines. They've got to sit on their collars to get their paperwork done," she laughed, tugging at her uniform. The blue material strained at the hips. Creases were deep at her thigh joints.

"How about support staff?" The rookie, a nervous-looking blond in a crisp new uniform, glanced over at Zala, who was trying to get the attention of the sister, whose nameplate said SGT. B. J. GREAVES.

"Say what? Support? Don't make me laugh."

"Excuse me." Zala leaned over the counter, but Greaves waved at her to be patient, after slinging a large paper clip across the counter.

Zala put one five-by-seven and two wallet-size pictures of Sonny together with his medical record and the map Mr. Lewis had drawn on Metropolitan Boys' Club stationery. She attached the papers to the form and waited, the edge of the counter hot and hard against her breasts.

"You could spend your life in here and they couldn't even find you to start with." An old man behind her on the bench kept rubbing his knees. At the other end of the bench, a young Asian couple sat staring. He drummed his fingers on a cloth-covered box crammed with documents. Her eyes were downcast; she seemed to be studying her wedding band.

A woman clutching a wad of tissues scraped her feet to get Zala's attention. "Polite will get you exactly nowhere," she said in a voice that sounded more steely than tearful.

Zala tapped on the counter. Heads turned, expressions fleetingly polite, just like at Sonny's school, except no one got up and came over. Zala flushed, arguing with herself to speak up.

Make a stink, Mama Lovey used to tell her when she came back empty-handed. "You go back to that store and you make them wait on you." The twins would try to pump up her heart, rehearsing her for the oral reports she dreaded. Shoulders down, back straight, she was to speak out, chin high. "Raise hell," Gerry would tell her, for some wiseass classmate was bound to make fun. "Give 'em this," Maxwell would say, bringing his fist close to his nose, and stiffening all over to show her how to look fierce. Mr. Lewis had told her that she might be badgered, bullied even, asked embarrassing questions of a personal nature down at the station. She'd been through "personal" with Spence's VA group, so she felt prepared for that. But she'd thought they would rush her into a patrol car and interrogate her on the way to the woods. This was not how it was supposed to go. This was like waiting on line at the phone company, or taking a number in the deli section of the A&P.

"I need to talk to somebody." Zala pumped alarm into her voice. "My son is missing."

A male officer turned, winding himself in the phone cord; he looked annoyed. A female officer bent over one of the cardboard files sighed in exasperation and looked around the squad room.

"Officer Judson will be with you in a minute. Please have a seat."

Zala turned toward the benches. Families that had been in the hall arranging papers and getting their stories together hovered in the doorway. A few straggled in and took seats. Others hunkered down in front of them, talking things over.

"I'm telling you," the woman with the tissues said straight at Zala, her voice full of warning and push. The old white man rubbing his knees bobbed his head to second the motion.

Her face went hot. She leaned against the counter. She was afraid that if Officer Judson didn't come soon, she might do something abnormal to show how urgent the situation was. Scarier still, she realized, standing there clutching the sisal straps of her shoulder bag, that she was longing to do something strange, something totally self-effacing, just to get it over with, so nothing anyone could say or do could embarrass her any further.

The fibers of her bag straps dug deep into her finger joints. Barely able to straighten her hand, she wondered if it was possible to sever a finger by sawing the strap across her hand. They'd move fast if a stump started spurting blood all over the squad room.

The hands of the clock were grinding into position. It was 11:00. Phones were ringing, fans whirring, the keyboards clacking away, file drawers gliding open, desk drawers being slammed shut. But no one was responding to her. There were hinges in the counter. She thought about lifting the panel and walking through. There were plants on some desks; on others, mugs with curdled coffee. There were, in fact, throwable objects everywhere. She was picturing herself hurling a staple gun through the window when the redhead lumbered up out of nowhere.

"Done?" She whisked up the forms, her red-lacquered nails scraping the counter. She brushed muffin crumbs from her shirt and leaned over, beckoning Zala closer so they could talk over the noise. Zala inhaled the spinachy smell of fresh henna.

"Has he run away before?" Officer Judson crimped her mouth, perusing the form.

"He hasn't run away," Zala said. "He went to find his friends on a camping trip and lost his way. At least that's what we think happened. We hope it's nothing worse than that, not . . . anything worse than that."

" 'We'?" The officer looked around at the invisible others, then detached the papers and spread them out on the counter, a gesture that set Zala to boil. She had not strolled into the gas company about a discrepancy in the bill. She wanted to be seated somewhere—in that office at the far end of the room, for instance—not serviced at the counter, where the people behind her could hear her better than Judson, who stood shifting her weight back and forth.

"Good . . . excellent." Judson slapped at the marginal notes with the back of her hand. "This is what we like to see," she said, like a teacher examining homework.

"Is there some place we could talk?"

"I'm afraid not." She invited Zala to look and made a face: you see how things are.

"Then could we get going, maybe talk on the way?"

"One sec," the big-boned sister said, turning the form over.

The woman with the tissues scraped her feet. Zala felt the prodding, knew she wasn't handling things well, and was tempted to pick up the pen and goad Judson with it. She was taking a long time to read.

"Has he been in trouble before? Truant from school, shoplifting, vandalism—things that might have brought him to our attention before this?"

"He's never been in any kind of trouble. That's why we're so worried. And why we're so anxious to get going." Zala motioned toward the door, but Judson only flipped the form over.

"No history of wandering off? Staying out late without permission? Visiting friends, relatives, neighbors without your knowledge? Spending the night with a friend? . . . No? Sounds like a model child," Judson said, not unkindly, but Zala fine-tuned her ears while the woman looked at the map and crimped her lips.

"So." She looked up. "No history of any kind with juvenile authorities, is that right?"

"Yes, none. I always know where he is. That's why we think something happened."

" 'Happened.' " The woman was studying her. It struck Zala that this was the moment to work in something about the STOP committee, as Mr. Lewis had advised. But Judson cut her off. "You listed three work numbers. You have three jobs and can keep track of three children? We need you down here conducting workshops, Mrs. Spencer."

It might have been a crack; several heads turned. Someone slamming a file drawer seemed to be doing it to say "Score."

"I was wondering, Officer Judson, if the special Task Force will conduct the investigation, or does it begin here?" Zala slipped with the "I." A woman with no "we" didn't even get served by waiters. But she'd been loud enough. Someone typing by a buzzing phone stopped, reached around, picked the receiver up, and dropped it back in the cradle.

"The officers who came to my house yesterday suggested I take the case to the Task Force. The mothers at STOP suggested that too." The double lie got a response from Sergeant B. J. Greaves, who looked over. Zala thought she saw her exchange a look with Judson before she stuck her nose back in the folder she was reading, perched half-buns on a desk.

"Can we begin now and talk on the way? The officer last night stressed how important it was to get on it now, before the trail gets

cold." She hoped there was nothing in the Hall-Eaton report to contra-
dict the statements she'd attributed to them.

"Did the officers explain to you, Mrs. Spencer, that Youth Division
cannot conduct a search for a runaway until the court issues a warrant?"

"He's not a runaway. He's not a wayward child. He's not a delinquent. He's a missing boy." Zala pressed her shoulders down to get
ready; Judson seemed to be about to address her as "dear."

"Technically, Mrs. Spencer, any minor who spends a night away
from his or her legal domicile without express permission from his or
her legal guardian is a delinquent, a runaway. Unless"—she arched an
eyebrow—"you have reason to believe he was kidnapped. Who has legal
custody?" she asked suddenly, running a fingernail down the form.

"I do. His father wouldn't take him without telling me. He didn't
kidnap him, I mean."

"Your husband, is he a vet?" And when Zala nodded, Judson leaned
closer. "Did a tour overseas?" Zala held up two fingers and raced around
in her mind for something to say to get things moving. No one was
going to lure her into a discussion on Vietnam vets. She had learned
how to skirt that, by keeping her mouth shut.

"He had permission to go," Zala said quickly, "so he's not a delinquent." Did they only look for well-behaved children from two-parent,
nonvet homes?

Judson set her elbows on the counter and laced her fingers under her
chin. "You say that you expected him home on Sunday for dinner. All
right. He had your permission to take the overnight trip on Saturday,
but not to stay out on Sunday night. But when the other boys returned
Sunday evening, no one had seen . . . Sundiata, is it? No one had seen
him, is that right?"

"That's correct. So something must have happened to him on Saturday, because he didn't show up at the outing at all."

Judson took a long time studying Sonny's photo, and Zala wondered if something had happened to make the boy familiar to her. There
was no fancy equipment in the squad room, nothing to suggest his face
might have come "over the wire." Unidentified boy in traffic accident.
Boy found in woods, amnesia victim. Male youth rescued from drowning. Zala was riveted to the flaky lipstick, the crimped mouth like
forked pie crust.

"Can you think of any reason why your son might have chosen not to go with the group?" She reached under the counter with one hand and picked up the pen with the other, prepared to make notes on a clean sheet of paper. "Please think back, Mrs. Spencer. Did he have a fight with any of the boys, or a disagreement with one of the staff?"

"Mr. Lewis and I discussed that. There'd been no problems."

"And at home, Mrs. Spencer. A row with a neighbor, or with your other children? Are they all natural siblings?"

"Natural?"

"They all have the same father? And mother. . . . All right. How about a row with a boyfriend? One of your personal friends? Nothing to be embarrassed about. You're an attractive young woman and legally separated, why shouldn't you enjoy male companionship? It happens like that." Judson gave a coy shrug. "Separations upset children sometimes. And when Mom takes up with a man friend, young boys have a way of getting in the middle. You know, to get in between. It happens." She shrugged at the ordinariness of it, arms out, palms up. "It happens," she repeated, inviting intimate disclosures.

"He gets along fine with all friends of the family," Zala said carefully, but Judson was holding her pose, adding an encouraging half-smile to lead Zala over the leaves into the pit. "And that's why so many of us are busy trying to find him."

Judson nodded and folded her arms on the counter. "Was it a legal separation or an informal agreement to separate?"

"Informal. And cordial. The courts weren't involved."

"And Mr. Spencer's a vet? Any problems there?"

"He contributes what he can, and he visits." Zala was hoping the footsteps behind her were Spence. But it was the Asian couple getting up. They wandered out into the hall.

"No trouble there, between the boy and his father? Broken dates, forgotten birthdays? Two tours overseas, you say?"

Zala emptied her face and nodded.

"You believe in spanking, Mrs. Spencer?"

"No, we do not, and we make sure their teachers don't whip them, either."

"There've been . . . situations at school?"

Can of worms. She had to tread carefully. There'd been a hearing at the district superintendent's office once. Teachers were too quick with their hands to suit Zala. She couldn't remember who they'd made the complaint about. A substitute throwing an eraser at Kofi, or the vice-principal striking Sonny with a ruler, telling her Sonny had threatened the teacher with the window pole. A cafeteria worker had once swatted Sonny on the behind with a metal tray and Spence had gone up there and let it be known that the Spencers didn't play that shit and didn't care what kind of punishment the law allowed.

"He has no reason to leave home, or to be afraid to come home," Zala said, sidestepping the question. "That's why I hope we can get the court warrant, though I don't know why it is needed. I mean, it's not like he's done anything criminal, so I don't see what a warrant's got to do with this."

"Have you got a family worker, someone who can help you?"

"A family worker?" Zala took a quick inventory. Had she come across as incompetent somehow? Had she forgotten to button her clothes or comb her hair? "You mean a social worker? What would I need with a social worker? I take care of my kids."

"Mrs. Spencer, you list three work numbers, and you're the only adult in the home."

"One of those numbers is my home. I do a lot of work at home."

"But the other two jobs keep you out of the home. You've lost a child, Mrs. Spencer."

Officer Judson's face was too close, a moon crowding her, blocking out the light. Pride. Zala wrapped her fingers around the sisal straps and squeezed. Pride. So busy showing she was not lazy, unresourceful, or destitute, she'd put down too much and fallen right into the pit.

"Please." The straps dug into her shoulder. "I am not a neglectful mother."

"I'm not saying you are." Judson leaned closer, lowering her voice. "I'd simply like to refer you to a family service worker. She's been very effective in cases like this."

" 'Cases like this'?"

Judson leaned back. "I'm trying to be of help here."

"Then come help me." Zala tried to lift her arm to indicate the patrol cars parked outside, but her hands were clamped to the straps. The moon face was kindly, but the hands meanwhile were folding the papers in half and running the crease between the hard, lacquered fingernails.

"This woman," Judson was saying, one hand reaching under the counter, "can get the ball rolling faster than we can." She slipped the folded papers into an envelope, flattened it out with the heel of her hand, and began writing on it.

It felt like a brush-off, one of those referrals that turned into a wild goose chase. She should threaten to go directly to the Task Force, or to the newspapers, or to the mayor.

"Let her speak to Captain Sparks." The voice came from behind Zala. The woman with the tissues. For a moment, she seemed to be walking over to give Zala some backup. But then she threw the wad on the floor and walked out into the hall, muttering.

"Yes, I'd like to see this Sparks person," Zala said.

"I'm sorry. He's not in at the moment." And then Judson raised the hinged panel. But she didn't come out, as Zala had hoped, or invite her through. She was in fact motioning for Zala to step aside, a gesture as mysterious as a teacher's asking her to pass out the *Junior Scholastics* just as she, having gotten the courage to raise her hand, was in mid-sentence.

A beefy officer brushed by her from behind, holding the top and bottom of a soaking bag. He edged past Judson and, broken-field-running, rushed toward the end office. Colleagues swiveled around to cheer him on. The bag left a milky trail, which no one moved to wipe up.

"I'll try and get things started," Judson said, lowering the hatch. "I'll have to make a few phone calls. Please have a seat."

"A seat!" Zala leaned over the counter, calling at the officer's back, and was not at all surprised to see Judson duck into the U-shaped arrangement of army-green file cabinets. Where a half-eaten muffin was waiting, Zala suspected.

She moved down along the counter, striking the floor hard to get the attention of Sergeant Greaves, who was strolling along parallel, pausing by the window where someone had set a revolving fan. A few officers looked Zala's way, but not long enough to engage her eyes so she could draw them over to the counter. She was wishing she'd put taps on her shoes.

"Would somebody help me please?"

"Officer Judson will be with you in a minute." It was Sergeant Greaves, who then turned her back and punched four buttons on the phone. An in-house call. Zala was hopeful; maybe she'd gotten a response. She strained to listen, but she caught no mention of herself. No wonder there'd been a sit-in. No wonder there'd been eight or more murdered children. These people were not doing their job.

The long hand grated and dropped down. 11:30, and Spence still didn't show. This was not something she should have to shoulder by herself. She was striking like flint and cursing Spence under her breath when she turned her ankle. A hot current shot up her leg. Her eyes felt scalded.

"Watch it." The man with the troublesome knees shuffled up from the bench as Zala let herself double over with the pain. Her shoulder banged against the side of the counter, the jolt knocking the breath out of her. She heard chairs being scraped back on the other side of the counter, a phone knocked over, people off the benches now; and even when the pain eased up and the throbbing in her temples subsided, she watched herself, curious, detached, to see if she would throw herself onto the filthy floor to writhe and moan and, without any pride or fight left, be utterly pitiful.

And the knowledge that she was thinking of doing it filled her with such disgust she had trouble straightening up, so she didn't try; she could see the bottom of her shoe and the tumbled contents of her bag; people brought ice, a glass of water, cologne dabbed on a hankie, a cushion, a chair; hold her head up, get her seated, take her pulse, press her head between her knees, get her a paper bag. If she really let go, she could sleep the first sound sleep in a week. Lying out cold on the floor, she could infect them enough with her desperation to get them mobilized. And maybe God, seeing how things were, pierced through as she was with hot spikes of self-disgust, would take pity and send Sonny home unharmed.

Sun flooded the barbershop through the wide-slat bamboo blinds, its heat quickly dispersed by the standing fan blowing from behind the manicure table, its bleaching brightness subdued by the backs of the chairs the checker players had shoved to that side of the shop. The radio droned low on V103; the TV's sound had been off for weeks. Those who lounged in the chrome-and-vinyl chairs flipped through *Ebony, Jet,* and some beauty-supply magazines, drifting in and out of the checker players' conversation and remarking from time to time on the heavy topics of the past few weeks—the sniping of Vernon Jordan and the hospitalization of Richie Pryor. The gentleman waiting for Zala to attend his nails sat in the high chair inspecting his shoes, lifting them one at a time from the metal footprints of the bootblack stand, turning his ankle, frowning, then fitting his feet back on the wrought-iron treads. Barber Simmons's customer was preening in the mirror, timing his leisurely flicks with the whisk broom to the *shoosh-shoosh* of Zala's emery board.

"That sound use to set my teeth on edge," Zala's customer said, breaking into her musings. She was at the point of deciding that what she'd taken for laxity in the squad room was nothing more than laid-back professionalism, that what she'd perceived as malevolence on the part of the first woman officer was probably more a reflection of her own panic. She'd been wound tight, on the brink of hysteria. She never wanted to be like that again.

"Are you psychic?" The woman's knees bumped hers. "I would imagine you are." Zala pushed her chair back a bit from the manicure table, more fully in the draft of the fan. "I can tell by your eyes." The woman lifted her left hand from the soak dish to point. Zala pushed it back down into the sudsy water and continued filing and shaping the woman's right hand. "Very deep-set eyes, piercing. Scorpio?"

"Libra, I think." She hadn't meant to encourage conversation just when it felt peaceful in the shop at last. Ten minutes ago, there'd been a wreck at the Cascade-Gordon intersection, but things had quieted down and she wanted to drift. Her mind hovered in the vicinity of her front walk. If Spence dropped Sonny off at the house, would they realize that her car was parked there because it needed a can of oil; or would Sonny, ringing the bell because he had no keys, think she was mad at him and not letting him in?

"Ah, a Libra," the woman said, scooching around in her chair. "That's interesting. Libras are misunderstood in such a particular way. For example, people think that they're highly susceptible to suggestion because they don't generate their own self-image or have an agenda of their own. They seem not to. Do you find that true?" She shifted again, throwing her legs to the side and crossing them. The loungers looked up from their magazines to examine the woman's legs, shapely and slender, though she was otherwise rather squat.

"Not really." Zala worked cuticle gel around the woman's nails and restrained the impulse to stab deeply with the orangewood stick. Out of the side of her eye she caught Preener grinning at her in the mirror as he slapped on aftershave, slapping sympathetically, she thought, so she smiled. She removed the woman's soaked hand and laid it down on the towel with exaggerated gentleness.

If Spence took off, she was thinking, leaving Sonny at the door to fend for himself, would the boy figure out where she was and take the bus? Did he have his bus pass on him? She reviewed the awful night before, going through his pockets, listening to his rehearsal tapes for the names of his friends, upending his gym bag, looking for clues. She rubbed the woman's nails dry, then massaged her hand briskly with a sassafras oil she had concocted years ago for Spence when he would awake chilled and tangled in the sheets. She would be too glad to see Sonny, she smiled to herself, to scold him right away. She'd fall all over him, muss up his hair, embarrass him in front of the men. He would try to fend her off, would slouch away to the counter to find a comb to re-pair his do. She could hear him as she came up behind him, unable to keep her hands off: "Aw, Ma, quit."

"In any case," the mouthy woman was saying, "I'm grateful for this meeting. Paulette Foreman's been promising for the longest time to introduce us. Besides those macramé curtains of yours that I've been coveting, I wanted to ask if you'd be interested in a dream workshop or an astrology group I'll be conducting in a few weeks."

"Would you look at this!" Barber Simmons mashed the pushbroom down on the floor and pointed in disgust to the TV. All heads except Zala's swung toward the screen. "Bad enough that Ramey fool put the sign up there like that for the whole world to see, but that don't mean the TV gotta keep playing it up. Dammit to hell. 'Scuse me, ladies. But just look at that." He banged the pushbroom a few times and the neat pile of hair clumps, butts, and elastic-tissue collars scattered.

Zala's customer grunted, then fished from her bag a packet of yel-low business cards that she passed around while the barber fussed and fumed. The lounger nearest the manicure table stood up, took off his golf cap, wiped the sweatband with a handkerchief, adjusted the cap at an angle, and asked the Reverend Mattie Shaw, Reader & Advisor, if she could tell her which numbers to box? The heavyset man in the high chair cracked his knuckles and read aloud the sign on the TV screen, as if there were anyone in the shop, anyone in the whole city, who didn't know the notorious downtown billboard by heart: WARNING! YOU ARE IN ATLANTA!! WHERE THE POLICE ARE UNDERPAID UNDERMANNED UNDEREQUIPPED—USE EXTREME CAUTION WHILE HERE. On the bottom line, grouped together under the rubric ATLANTA FACTS, were everchanging figures indicating MURDERS, RAPES, and BURGLARIES.

"They just won't quit," one of the checker players said, slamming his king around the board and collecting the fallen. "Anything to make the Black administration look bad."

"When in point of fact," Simmons said, warming to his favorite topic bar none, "the crime rate's gone down since Maynard took over as mayor and outfoxed Chief Inman." Golf Cap broke into "I Shot the Sheriff," bouncing at the knees. Simmons chuckled. "Yeah, outfoxed him and slid Reggie my main man Eaves over that sucker's head.

"But too bad my man Reggie didn't cover his ass," Simmons went on. "Scuse me, ladies. He should of known they'd be laying for him."

Zala swung the lazy Susan around slowly for Reverend Mattie to select a polish. The topic on the floor was good for at least a half hour of horseplay, a side bet or two about some disputed fact, and maybe even an argument or a throwdown—nothing heavy, the battlers could depend on being separated before a punch was thrown. She slathered on Carnival Red while the men told each other what they already knew: namely, that damn near every Black mayor elected in the South had to go through an OK Corral duel. The high sheriff wouldn't surrender up the keys or the roster or the requested letter of resignation, and/or he'd threaten to arrest, tar and feather, or lynch the duly elected Blood if he or she showed up to take the oath of office or insisted on appointing a new police chief. Zala's next customer climbed down from the high chair to re-enact a high sheriff calling in SWAT, or the Klan, or the National Guard to lay siege on the burrhead in City Hall.

"Don't forget how they trot out some handkerchief head too," the loser at checkers called to him.

"So now it's a draw, but in our favor, I'd say." The heavyset man climbed back up the bootstand as he summarized. "We have virtually two police forces: the Fraternal Order, or whatever it is—what's it called, Otis?" addressing a magazine reader who hadn't yet spoken. "Whatever it's called," the heavyset man continued without waiting for an answer, "and the Afro-American Patrolmen's League. Now, some people might regard that as unfortunate." He looked Barber Simmons dead in the eye. "But that's history. That's history's weight, or rather its wedge." He planted his feet once again on the metal treads and leaned back.

The two checker players picked up the thread, telling Otis the Silent what would have happened in '73 if the likes of them had put up a billboard downtown listing Blacks gunned down under Chief Inman's reign of terror. Golf Cap strained into falsetto. "Every time I plant my seed," he sang, "he say, 'Kill'm 'fore they grow.' "

"That would've been something," the losing checker player said, watching his men disappear off the board. "A memorial billboard." His voice was flat, dispirited. "Maybe we should've done it."

"I know that's right," Preener said from the mirror. He cocked his head as if listening for the TV over the whir of the fan, the clunk of the wooden checkers on the board, the liquidy slap of the nail-polish brush against nail, then strolled over to the manicure table and bowed slightly when Zala looked up. "Next time you and your old man have a gumbo party, put my name in the pot if you please." He swiveled on the balls of his shoes, bowed to the rest of the people, and was out the door.

How long had it been since she and Spence had done gumbo together? Sweaty afternoons playing hooky from work, doo-wah nights with the sheets thrown back, trading recipes as the sun rose. The pot washed and ready. A quick trip to Municipal Market for shrimp, clams, and crab. Friends over, card games, dancing in the yard, nobody minding that the food tasted of citronella. Zala reached for the seal coat and sighed. Those were the days, before Spence had been bitten by the Atlanta bug and started running around in business suits big-deal bragging, bar hopping, back slapping, power lunching with potential policyholders or real-estate investors at pretentious restaurants that featured seafood menus as bogus as the fishnet drapery and the cork-buoy centerpieces in landlocked Atlanta. As fraudulent as all the hail-fellow-well-met foolishness among men who in the sixties had called each other "brother" not "doctor" or "chief" or "admiral." Black men acting like white men, corny white men. It scared her.

Zala smiled wanly at whatever Reverend Mattie was saying to recruit her in an argument with Barber Simmons. She watched Preener through the slatted window as he paused just outside the door, raking his mustache with his fingers the way Spence did, looking across the three-lane traffic to the sidewalk opposite that dipped down into the

Cascade-Gordon shopping mall. She watched him hug his pelvis with balled fists, as most men did coming out of the shop, to announce their presence on the block, then stride off down the street. Preener was walking that walk that said, "Ain't going for the okeydoke."

Simmons knocked the broom handle against the manicure table to rouse Zala's support in his argument with Reverend Mattie about how the city should be run. Go ask Kofi, she wanted to tell them both. That was his class's term project, "The Running of the City," and she was totally drugged with the topic. Preener had crossed the street and disappeared into the shopping mall. How, she wondered as she applied a coat of sealer to Reverend Mattie's nails, did some people manage to be immune to the bug while others were so susceptible?

"Bite me," Spence had said to the Atlanta bug. At least that was what she'd thought and what she'd called it: the talking jags, the anxious pacing, punching the hand-held calculator with the eraser head, the sweating, the feverish race to plug in with the old guard or the new. But then the nightmares had begun again. In '75, when the fall of Saigon appeared on TV, his army buddy Teo had come so unglued, Spence had pulled himself together to help. Then, in November of 1978, when he saw the footage of all those bodies in the jungle clearing at Jonestown, something had snapped, and Spence came unraveled in her arms.

The official version of the situation didn't acknowledge the realities of shell shock or battle fatigue. At best back then it was "acute situation reaction," warranting a hit of Thorazine and back on the line. Later it was "posttraumatic stress disorder," justifying some stingy funds for readjustment counseling.

So in the spring of '79, Spence, Teo, and forty-three other Vietnam vets from Atlanta's Black, white, and Hispanic communities were rounded up by George McClintock, a counselor at the EOA Center who'd managed to secure some Operation Outreach monies for an encounter group. "Trip-wire syndrome," he told the wives—what few hadn't already thrown in the towel, what few could be cajoled into coming by Celia Hernandez, a combat nurse who'd done two tours in Da Nang and worked out her readjustment talking to wives at the EOA Center in the Southwest and organizing get-togethers for Latino vets through *Mundo Hispanico,* the Spanish-language newspaper.

McClintock had explained his role and the wives' role too by playing parts of the taped sessions he'd had with the men. He had to get three groups into one, and race and ethnic considerations were nothing compared to other differences, he maintained. First there were the vets who'd been shipped back with no breathing space in between the free-fire zone and home sweet home. These men and women went about in battle fatigues, bivouacked on the curb in front of the army-navy surplus stores on Pryor Street, eating C-rations with penknives, creating disturbances wherever they went, most especially in movie houses where *Taxi Driver, Coming Home,* or *The Deer Hunter* played. In and out of jail, in and out of drug-abuse centers whether drugs were the problem or not; two of the women committed by their husbands, one of the men sent to the state asylum at Milledgeville by his folks. Fourteen wound up in Mac's office, their recorded voices halting and breathless.

The second group had come home mute, sullen, bottled up, then took to the hills. Reported missing by their families, these vets were tracked down not by Missing Persons but by other vets who knew what to look for, knew how to trail civilians who thought they were still on patrol—the bark dishes, discarded buckskin clothing, makeshift shelters, half-dug bunkers, booby traps, cooking fires. Of the fifteen brought back, ten said they were interested in being with other vets in an encounter group. But except for a flurry of monosyllabic mutterings when someone brought in a case of Carling Black Label beer, the only voice on those tapes was Mac's.

The group Spence and Teo were in talked nonstop. They hated Carling, hated the woods, would not wear any shade of green. Guns shot off on the Fourth of July and New Year's Eve were rough on their nerves. And yes, they slept with their necks covered by their arms; and sure, anybody attempting to wake them up took their life in their hands. But they'd been doing all right on the job, in school, in their marriages. They knew of other vets suffering from addiction, depression, impotence, headaches, loss of hair, low sperm count, birth defects among their children—none of which, of course, was service-related, they'd all laughed raucously on the tapes. They'd heard the official response, for example, to the Agent Orange Vets, no different from the official response to the Atomic Vets: "Agent Orange effects? Well, maybe a little acne, but nothing to get hysterical about." But they were okay, or rather had been doing all right, until . . . until summer '75, or until the Travis Bickle character in the Scorsese movie, or until a daughter was born with a cleft palate and half a brain, or until the Jonestown massacre, divorce, someone trying to sell them a Vietcong skull souvenir, a death in the family. They couldn't stop talking—napalm, fragging, race riots, AWOL, desertions, defections, a loaf of jane laced with opium for ten dollars, the shelling. Couldn't stop talking. Couldn't stop shivering. Couldn't stop crying.

The wives trying to sidetrack Mac from his be-a-helpmate talk long enough to discuss what they'd been burning to discuss: that the behaviors they were living with had to do with dioxins that no one, certainly none of the government agencies, wanted to talk about. Agent Orange and other chemicals had deranged the minds and deranged the genes and had caused, two of the women argued before quitting the group, multiple miscarriages, deformed births, or no pregnancies at all.

Zala clicked off the lamp and held Reverend Mattie's wrists down on the towel so her nails would dry. At least Mac and the VA, after six months of hit-and-miss, had found a medication that didn't have Spence drooling and tiptoeing on eggshells one minute, raging around incoherently the next, though he would look chronically haggard from troubled sleep for nearly a year.

Zala looked up and signaled the heavyset man that she was ready, but he was absorbed in the discussion between the reverend and the barber.

"While I don't agree with the provocative sign," Reverend Mattie was saying, waving her nails in Zala's face to enlist her support, "I do think the time is long past due for people to stop confusing Atlanta's PR with Atlanta."

"Oughta be a law. That sign's messing with city revenue, scaring the tourists. It's in restraint of trade." Pleased with the phrase, Simmons repeated it. "It's operating in restraint of trade."

". . . serious unemployment, cutthroat competition, mindless ambition, and the wholesale abandonment of the family dinner tradition in favor of fast food on the run," Reverend Mattie concluded.

"A regular rat race," the winning checker player said.

"Which reminds me of an experiment we set up once in the lab." Reverend Mattie had cut into Simmons's remarks, her voice full of story. She uncrossed her legs, then crossed them again while Simmons retreated to the counter. The woman had everyone's attention. "We wondered if humans behaved any better in a maze than rats do."

"You work with rats?" Simmons let it be known that he was still in the game.

"Tell it," both checker players said at once.

"Well. . . ." Reverend Mattie slapped one hand down for a second coat of sealer. "We positioned six human volunteers in a large-scale maze that was an exact replica of the one we use with laboratory rats. But instead of cheese—" she eyed the men in turn—"we placed, at intervals along the maze, dollar bills."

"I heard that."

"Don't forget about dee-greeze."

"And trophies and shit. You know how we folks in Atlanta go for awards and plaques."

"But this is a true story I'm relating, gentlemen. An actual scientific experiment."

"Sho nuff. Tell it."

"Well, as you might expect, the human volunteers scored higher. They were faster at the money than the rats were at the cheese. The humans made more judicious use of memory, induction, deduction, and hunch. They absolutely showed up those rats and then—." For two beats she watched Zala's quick, sure strokes. She blew on her nails.

Simmons couldn't help himself. "So then what happened?"

"Well, it was like this. When the cheese and the money were removed from the two mazes, the researchers observed an odd thing. The rats ignored the maze. They would not run if there were no cheese rewards. And they would not respond to electric goads or other kinds of punishments, either. Nor would they budge when cheese was reintroduced. Because, you see, gentlemen, during the interim they'd discovered better things to do with their time, such as reviving old courtship rituals, dinner dances, loving, raising families. You know, gentlemen—" she blew on her nails—"living."

Suspicious that the Reverend Mattie, Reader & Advisor, was actually cracking on men, Black men, men like himself who were trying to get ahead, Simmons shot Zala a hot look, as though she were responsible for her customer's derisive tale. He pushed the broom toward the chrome-and-vinyl chairs to marshal his cohorts. Their eyes were riveted on the woman's legs, waiting for the other shoe to drop. Only Golf Cap seemed to be holding his applause till the real butt of the joke was revealed.

"And the humans?" Golf Cap asked.

"Well, gentlemen, the human subjects continued running the maze. Though the money had been removed, they ran. They could not be threatened or cajoled out of it. We called in loved ones, old grammar-school teachers, even their mothers to plead with them. But still they ran. We called in psychiatrists, hypnotists, professional bounders. . . ." She waited for the men to vocalize encouragement. "They would break into the lab at night in Adidas and jogging suits and—" Even Golf Cap got caught up in the call and response. "We put on extra guards, brought in attack dogs, and electrified the fence. But—" She winked at Zala when she intercepted a scowl relayed from the barber to the manicurist. "Gentlemen, we finally had to resort to tear gas. But do you know, from that day till this those men are still running."

Barber Simmons coughed a low, gruff cough of disapproval. Zala refused to look up. She slid her tip cup toward Reverend Mattie and shook out the towel. The men were slapping five and naming names. Simmons looked sternly at each of the men in turn. Didn't they realize that the woman had squired off of them? If not on them per se, then on those fine men and women framed above the ledge of his mirror? People with get-up-and-go, pioneers who'd founded Atlanta Life, Paschal's, the Yates-Milton Pharmacy, construction companies, undertaking establishments, banks, credit unions, colleges, law offices, and all such as that, all of which had helped make Atlanta what it was, the Black Mecca of the South?

"I don't hold with tales that disrecognize achievement," he said. He let the men see his eyes roving over the split dowel that framed the mirror. For over the mirror, lined up from the wall adjacent to the telephone to the alcove leading to the mini-kitchen in back, were the photos, old and new, that spelled out the history. There among the scions of the old Atlanta aristocracy at the opera, hundreds come to see Roland Hayes himself at the Civic Center, were the Colored 400, filling up as many box seats as the whites. And there at the groundbreaking ceremonies of Clark Normal were the members of the Negro Women's League, the Knights of Pythias, educators, solid citizens, his great-grandfather among them. There was history marching across the aquamarine wall, clean, cultured, levelheaded pioneers and their offspring, heirs to good fortunes not built from slavery, convict labor, red-light districts, or legerdemain with the public coffers, but from hard work and clean living, give or take a peccadillo here and there.

"Black Mecca of the South," he said when his private musings threatened to trip him up. "And the thing we got to appreciate about our accomplishments here in Atlanta is that nobody else, nowhere else did it. Know why?" He beamed an angry eye on Reverend Mattie. "'Cause we ain't sitting around playing crabs-in-the-basket. We all pull together here, that's what. Our ministers, our businessmen, our politicians, our educators—" he waved a sweeping arc in the direction of the photos—"all pulling together. Where else you got the . . . ah . . . the er—how you say it, Otis?—the economic floorboards to support a leadership like we boast here in Atlanta?"

"But there are problems," Reverend Mattie said, her voice so cool, so mellifluous, Simmons wanted to strike her with the dirty part of the broom. "And we're always so busy patting ourselves on the back about our achievements, we totally ignore those who can't get ahead."

"Anybody can get ahead," Simmons interrupted. "Don't hand me no alibi stuff about race prejudice and all such as that, 'cause I'm a living witness to that lie."

"Can you guarantee full employment, Mr. Simmons? Do you know what 'full employment' means to the government? Millions and millions out of work but business well oiled and running smoothly. I don't see any photos up there of the garbage workers who were out on strike. And where's a photo of those thousands of unemployed people who mobbed City Hall when a couple of jobs were announced? Don't you have any photos of the homeless who live under the bridges in boxes, Mr. Simmons? . . ."

Her voice nettled and her "Mr. Simmons" stung. Simmons counted to thirty-five and listened courteously, lest he lose advantage with the men for riding roughshod on a lady.

"You may be right," he said, when she came to a period at last. "Perhaps all that depressing stuff you're talking about is telling it like it is. Sure, there's been too much PR-type frosting and not enough . . . er, uh . . . not enough solid cake, so to speak. But if you ask me, the main problem is this city is growing too big, too fast."

"Amen," Zala said, surprising him. But it wasn't the city she was thinking of. "Too big, too fast," she said, and for a minute Simmons bobbed his head up and down to encourage her further.

Zala was grateful that the phone rang. She pressed a finger to her outer ear. Delia's secretary relayed the message to Zala, which took all of three seconds to say: Nate Spencer was scheduled to be at J. C. Penney's out at Perimeter Mall at four. She held on, listening to the dial tone, and waited to see if she had any more customers. None. She could leave to pick up Sonny right away. Spence delivering him. The men were rocking back on their heels and examining their shoes while Simmons talked on, as though they'd only dropped in to see if Lincoln would return, Lincoln the Leather Illuminator, as his business card read, who'd walked off in high dudgeon, leaving his stand and supplies behind, when Simmons allowed his wife to interfere and redefine the barbershop's function. That function was not to give haircuts and shaves and provide loitering space for men to dog-ear magazines, but rather to provide the kind of forum Simmons's father had had in mind, gent that he was, a place where intelligent men could run nations with their mouths, discuss the state of the race, and analyze the mysterious ways of female folk—who understood not to cross the threshold unless accompanied by a boy for Saturday specials.

Barber Simmons beat the floor with the push broom while everyone filed out, including his manicurist, leaving him alone with the cigarette smoke, the nail-polish fumes, and a mountain of debris being blown around like tumbleweed.

It was an impressive skyline, Zala supposed—the glass towers, the skyscraper hotels, the banks, the revolving club lounges on the top floors of buildings. "Battlestar Galactica," Kofi always said when he gazed around at satellite discs and radio towers. Too literal, she decided—too literal a statement about its intention to be a major city. Hulking machinery and building equipment halted traffic in the outer lanes. There was enough cable lying about to wrap up the whole world. She shot up a side street, giving a cable spool a thoughtful look. It would make a good table. She wondered if Spence would deign to appreciate the worthy looks of that obscene machine and haul the spool back to her house.

Zala had always prided herself on her knowledge of the city; its back roads, parks, and campuses; its architecture and monuments, the various ways brickworks had of signing their buildings; the iron mongers who kept African motifs alive without knowing it; the county borders; the voting districts that kept shifting their lines since the day Primus King cast the first Black ballot down in Columbus, Georgia. Her first training had come from her dad, tickled to death with the dollbaby born to him and Mama Lovey late, in their middle-age years. He would ride her all over the city in the old Ford truck as he replaced downspouts, flushed dormers, cleaned gutters, talked history, and shared his professional secrets with her as though the five-year-old Zala would grow up to be a carpenter, a glazier, a handywoman, or all three.

"The way to match raw new shingles with the old," Dad would say, fastening the safety belt around her so she could sit in an attic vent and keep him company on the roof, "is, you mix marsh and sea water together." She got to shake up one of the many crocks they hauled back and forth from Jekyll Island, where they spent summers and holidays with his folks. "You brush it on just so with a boar-bristle brush." He would demonstrate and she would watch.

Driving through the city, Dad spoke of their roots, tracing the blood through Africans, through Seminoles, to way in the past, taking every opportunity to pass by the Blackstone Apartments on Peachtree and Fourth where his father had been a janitor and one of the first Black Atlantans to drive his own car. Traveling further out, he would point out the site of the drugstore long gone where his father's father had been on the scene in 1886 when Coca-Cola was first concocted as a headache remedy. Later, they'd open the lunch pail and unscrew the thermos in the old cemetery yard and he would point out family headstones. One uncle's epitaph read: DIED FOR HIS COUNTRY. She understood by her dad's gargling of the lemonade and the spit-out that this uncle had been a first-class dud. Another relative's tombstone read: LIVED FOR GOD AND AFRICA. Her dad would always linger there, pulling up weeds, making neat the plastic bouquet.

When the name changed from Marthasville to Terminus and then to Atlanta, her dad never tired of telling, as they'd cruise by Five Points on the way back home, her people had been there too, at the lamplighting ceremonies. Even now, swinging around a bumblebee-striped barrier to detour around Central City Park, Zala could still imagine the buggies, the train sheds, the loading platforms as they must have been. Somewhere in the wooden keg behind her front door at home, somewhere under the poster roll from SNCC's Freedom School, was one of the original city flags bearing the phoenix emblem and the motto "Resurgens," a flag her Dad had once soldered to the side mirror of the truck—not to be confused, he took great pains to make clear, with the Confederate flags waving from the sides of cars and trucks that tried to shove them off the road when they went as far as Roswell.

Putting his finger on the tip of her nose to rivet her attention, he made certain that she understood that the Atlanta they had a stake in was not the mythical one drummed up in the guidebooks, the billboards, the newspaper ads, the novels, the glossy brochures with tables of figures and graphs and maps showing gray areas slated for "demographic changes and redevelopment." Atlanta, the real one, was documented in the sketchbooks, the scrapbooks, the photo albums, the deeds, family Bibles, in the memories and mouths of the elders, those who had stayed and those long since moved to Brunswick, Georgia, when their summer stints on Jekyll Island, servicing the Goulds, the Astors, and other wealthy families that playgrounded there in white linen and panamas, georgette and Milan-straw sundowners, played out.

Swinging off Peachtree, where the old Indian burial mounds used to be, by the pitch tree that gave the area its name, where later Dad's mother, in keeping with the curfew codes for the colored, walked along sporting the lisle stockings, black dress with lace apron and cap, the passport costume needed after six p.m., her dad would quiz her, holding out a pack of Bit-O-Honey as reward. Then they'd bounce and rattle down the hill to Buttermilk Bottom, where they'd sit outside the house, their mouths stuffed with candy, while he guided her hand drawing maps of the terrain and she dutifully recited, prying her jaws apart with her sticky fingers, the history learned on that day's trip.

That early training had stood her in good stead during her time with Delia of the speak-up-make-contacts-get-with-it-girl program. Zala hadn't done any better, though, at the job her sister-in-law got her with Tour Atlanta, than with the telephone jobs soliciting for carpeting companies. But she'd at least been able to contribute to the Black tour company's information bank and wasn't a total bust when Delia and Bryant opened a sideline in real estate. She knew what was where. But for all the jobs Zala'd had over the years making use of Dad's training, her favorite had been driving an ice-cream truck in summers, mostly because it required so little talking at all.

Now, leaning hard across the steering wheel on the lookout for blinking detour signs, she realized that the downtown area she'd mastered at five, then remastered at ten under the tutelage of the Twins (who, like other activist youth in the sixties, demonstrated, picketed, and sat in with such adamancy that white business interests had built shopping malls along the Perimeter so Blacks could never flex that kind of muscle again) was a confusion of sawhorse barriers, open ditches, plank sidewalks, and sandy pathways for yellow Caterpillars carrying boulders in their maws.

She pulled up short when a cement mixer trundling along went suddenly in reverse, then scooted through a newly excavated lane; and ducked instinctively when a line slung across the narrow street slackened and a clamshell bucket dropped a dollop of cement on her roof. She peered past the windshield lest she miss the new entry onto 75/85 north that would take her to 285 and out to Perimeter Mall.

She spotted the limo right away, the chrome lady on the hood slowing her down. It was parked outside of J. C. Penney's double doors. She pulled into the lot and parked in view of the plate-glass window. A motorcycle cop pulled up behind the limo and strode back and forth, examining its length, width, and sheen, tapping on the windows, cupping his eyes to inspect the interior. As she walked up, he was checking the tags, the plates, the inspection sticker, one hand on the violation book flapping against his hip. She leaned against the mailbox and waited for him to remount, rev up, and move on, reluctant to ticket so impressive a car, so likely a VIP's. She had to smile.

Her smile broke into a chuckle when Spence pushed through the double doors in a Chinese-blue outfit and boots. Spence as Bruce Lee as Cato in the old *Green Hornet* series. She couldn't wait to huddle with Sonny so they could crack up together. Spence propped the door open and was immediately hidden by a portly man in a green brocade burnoose and turban, leading a procession out; two women cowled in shimmering cloth filed out toward the limo, their coverall garments flapping crisply between their ankles like laundry on a line. Six children, she counted them, filed past her in elaborately embroidered gowns, the girls with lots of jewelry, the boys in turbans. She wondered how the limo would hold them all. A sharp-nosed man, nervous and wiry—she decided he was the tutor—lugged small valises. The tutor hunched his shoulder against the door and Zala stepped around the mailbox in anticipation. But it wasn't Sonny yet; it was a parade of salesclerks carrying bundles and bags to the limo. She was holding her breath as the door wheezed to. Was holding it still when the tutor moved away and Spence stepped toward her, calling.

Zala didn't like the surprise in his voice, the working of his face. Didn't like the way the people were closing the limo doors, the sales clerks backing away, practically bowing, bills in their hands, dismissed.

"Where's Sonny?" It came out garbled.

The horn was beeped. Spence actually turned away from her to respond to strangers while her knees were buckling.

"Sonny, Sonny."

He was genuinely perplexed. "Sonny?"

"Don't play with me." She lunged. "Where's my baby? Baby, please."

He caught her under the arms before she knew she was falling. She thought she'd simply stumbled over something on the pavement in her effort to see into the limo. She felt weightless and giddy, a hot spraining sensation like an electric current traveling from her neck to her armpit and down one side. He was saying something into her hair, nearly breaking her arm as he slung it around his shoulder and lugged her toward her car. He was telling her to be calm, to stop shouting, to take a deep breath. He was giving her a hell of a lot of instructions, but not saying the one thing she was desperate to hear.

Sergeant B. J. Greaves pushed the door with her hip and ushered Zala into a room, a storage closet actually, dusty and cluttered. She motioned toward a step stool and an old kitchen chair.

"We can talk here, Mrs. Spencer. It'll be a while before we get any feedback from the hospitals and shelters. Have a seat. I'll have a team from the evening shift scout out the woods where you designated. Be right back."

Zala sat in the chair, old paint on the armrest lodging under her nails. It could have been a jail cell—tight, smelly, airless, a mop-wringer pail and a disconnected toilet banked against old telephone directories and stencils. Smears of grime funneled down the dark hole. She was feeling swarmy and regretted having taken Spence's advice that she call Delia to come get her from the mall.

What was it the sergeant had asked her? Did she know of houses in the neighborhood that hosted pot parties, drinking, and dirty movies? Could she identify adults that her son might know who were involved in drugs and wild parties? There were more than a dozen cases in all, the sergeant had said: children who'd vanished in broad daylight, children murdered, others dead from undetermined causes—mysterious cases that didn't fit the normal pattern, the normal pattern of murdered children. And something about a child who'd fallen fatally from a railroad trestle at Moreland and Constitution. Zala dug into the soggy paint with her nails. There was no train trestle in that area.

"Okay," Officer Greaves said, returning from the squad room. She sat on the step stool and Zala sensed she was being closely studied, the woman gauging how big a dosage of information could be safely administered. She had a manila folder clutched under her arm. Zala was afraid of it.

"The children," Zala said. "You were saying that several children have been killed at wild parties?"

"That's the theory at the moment. Though the lab tests don't confirm it, I understand. And as far as I know, there are no corroborating witnesses. May I call you Marzala?" She extended her hand. "I'm B. J., and I'm here to help you. I swear."

It should have assured her. But a current of ice sped through Zala's veins. She was afraid to put her hand in her lap. She clutched the armrests.

"Some of the deaths were originally labeled accidental, Marzala." She flipped through the folder. There were typed sheets, handwritten sheets, and interoffice memos stapled together. "Others have been on the books as 'undetermined' for months. And in a few cases, the patrolmen on the beat reported 'suspected foul play.' Many of the children were apparently murdered, just as a number of parents have said all along. You've read about the parents? Heard about the sit-in they staged?"

"No . . . I . . ."

"At any rate, a few days ago a special investigative Task Force was set up. They're reviewing, I believe, fifteen cases referred by MPYD and Homicide." She took a long drag on her cigarette and flicked ash onto a pile of forms. "You'll want to see the director of the Emergency Task Force. No doubt, you'll want to meet with the Committee to Stop Children's Murders. Am I going too fast? I'm sorry."

"No, I'm listening and I . . ." She almost apologized for keeping Greaves beyond her sign-out time. A student dropped in for term-paper research. Normal, murder. It was clear from what Greaves had just said that she didn't expect Sonny to be found in a hospital or in a shelter, didn't think there was much hope that the police would stumble upon him wandering around, dazed, in the woods, either. Rings of smoke curled against Zala's knee and broke up, like ghosts, while Greaves puffed and continued talking about what was typical in cases of slain children.

"Maybe two or three per month we can solve, so in a given year, perhaps four cases still pending. But since last year Detective O'Neal and Sergeant Sturgis have been writing memos to call the division's attention to the fact that the numbers of deaths are way out of proportion. For a year too, the parents have been escalating their protests. Some of them, at any rate." She paused to lodge the tip of her tongue in her upper gums, signaling that she found it odd that only some of the parents were vocal. She ran her fingers across the form Zala had filled out, noting the address. "Surely you've heard about it? Several of the youths are from your neighborhood."

Zala looked toward the half-closed doors for a shadow, a swatch of navy blue, some sign of rescue, some news. How could Sonny be in any way involved in a string of murders? How could anything like this be happening in the Black community and Mayor Jackson not be on the TV nightly mobilizing the city?

"That's exactly what Mrs. Mathis has been saying." Greaves paused when Zala looked up startled, unaware that she'd been thinking aloud. " 'It's a hurting thing,' indeed, when you consider that not only is the mayor Black, and the commissioner, and the police chief, and half the city council and its president . . ." She massaged her gums again and took a long drag on her cigarette. "Which is not to say that . . ." She wrestled with whatever she'd been prepared to say, then shrugged. "Do you know Mrs. Willa Mae Mathis? Her boy Jefferey's been missing since—" Greaves consulted a sheet from the folder. "He left the house in the afternoon of March 11, 1980, to run up the block to get her some cigarettes. Up on East Ontario and Gordon. Isn't that near where you work? Do you know the family? The boy's your son's age. Maybe they went to camp together, or know each other from the park, a basketball team, something? Think now." She leaned forward, and the edge of the manila folder cut into Zala's knees. "So far we've got no links between the children. And no suspects, either. Or murder weapons. Or any witnesses. Or even a known scene of the crime. No hunch regarding motive. No leads. No clues. Which makes it all so unlike the routine cases." She held out papers stapled together. "Do you know any of these children?"

Zala allowed the woman to drop the papers into her lap, but she made no effort to read them. She was stalling, waiting for a tap on the door, verification that Sonny was no part of this "epidemic," this trouble, that these pages needn't concern her. Somehow Greaves had pulled her off the track she'd come in on and plunged her into a murky world of disconnected information. Parties, victims, memos, sit-ins, foul play, Task Force.

"Please," the sergeant *almost* whispered, the cigarette clenched in her front teeth. "I'm trying to help you find your son. Are any of the names there familiar to you?"

She planted a finger against her lips while Zala rustled the papers. Greaves flicked a shred of tobacco away and continued talking, keeping her voice low and leaning closer. "For my money, the families aren't saying all that they could about their children, their habits, their associates and hangouts. But then I'm not altogether sure my colleagues are probing as they should. And those Task Force donkeys can't seem to get off their duffs and hit the streets to . . ." Smoke streamed from her nostrils. She'd smoked the cigarette down to the lipstick. She stubbed it out on the side of the step stool and looked sideways at Zala. "Please talk freely, Marzala. This is a serious situation, and we'll be of little use to you if you sit on the facts." She waited, then lit up another cigarette and set the lighter under her thigh.

"Well, at least take a look." She was clearly annoyed. "Do you know any of the victims?"

Zala scanned the pages, still waiting for approaching footsteps to save her. The names ran together, boys and girls of seven, nine, eleven, fourteen, sixteen. Addresses blurred. Bludgeonings, stab wounds, possible revenge, a fall from a trestle. Last seen on a bike, at a park, a pool, a movie house. Statements from mothers, fathers, foster parents, grandparents, neighbors. Suspicious cars seen in the neighborhood. Visits by groups of parents demanding attention, refuting "runaway" and "accident."

"Quite frankly," Greaves said, "when I noticed how several of the girls' ages clustered around fourteen, that age when they start striking out on their own, I thought of prostitution—you know, some pimp getting rough. And then the boys—at that age when they start standing up to Stepfather or tussling with Mama's boyfriend. Are you okay, Marzala?" She stepped away from the stool to catch the papers falling from Zala's lap.

Zala was thinking of Dave and Sonny. Of Spence and the blackouts he used to have before the VA hit on a pill that didn't have him sleepwalking, or flaring up in fits of rage.

"Oh, God!" Zala wailed. Stand by me, she prayed silently, stand by me, Lord.

"What is it?"

"My husband," Zala blurted.

"Your husband?" Greaves tapped ashes into her palm, then sprinkled them behind her. "Your husband?"

Zala was afraid now of what was seeping through her brain, leaking into her mouth. Dave. Spence. She could not even prevent the notion from forming that she herself might have dragged Sonny to the back-porch pantry Saturday morning and done him bodily harm. *Boy, I will knock you down. Boy, I will knock the breath clean out of you.*

"Your husband, Mrs. Spencer. Might he have taken the boy? Hurt him perhaps? . . . Is he a violent man? Was your husband in 'Nam? What kind of discharge did he receive?"

Zala shook her head. What was it about these lady cops, so eager to pin something on husbands and fathers—or was it just Black men in general under suspicion? She found she could not make the officer back off simply by staring her down. Zala dropped her eyes.

"Sexually speaking, Marzala . . . ahh . . . This is difficult, but necessary, believe me, okay? Your husband . . . any offbeat tastes or habits? You know what I mean."

"Please." She kept her eyes down.

An ember from Greaves's cigarette had fallen onto the stack of forms. Zala barely registered it. It was just a place to rest her eyes. "My husband in no way . . . my husband." He's perfect, she wanted to say, once in fact had said to Paulette getting into her personal business. "Then why aren't you together, you and your perfect man?" Paulette had asked. Zala blinked. A blistering brown was spreading on the papers.

"I meant only," Zala said carefully, watching the brown circle widen, "that I wish my husband would get here. He's not the kind of man who would hurt anybody. Certainly not his children. Or myself," she added, meaning it both ways. "Or anybody." The brown circle was now eating down into the pile.

"Of course." Greaves settled back on the step stool, rolling her buttocks left, then right. She looked over the contents of the folder again. "There's a pattern to children's slayings as a rule. A distraught mother at the end of her rope, and the baby won't stop crying. A burdened father pushed to the edge by the job, or no job, and he's the family's disciplinarian. A zealous guardian with a pipeline to Jesus—" She cut short a snuffled laugh. "You'd be amazed how many good Christian folk scourge the youth for Jesus. 'Suffer the little children' indeed." She stared at the butt-end glow for a moment, lost in some private thought. Remembering a sad case, Zala figured, wondering how to move the woman back to the more hopeful discussion begun in the squad room when she'd dispatched several officers.

"Sometimes it's Mama's boyfriend," said Greaves, "irked by what he considers unfair competition with the child for her attention. As a rule, it's the perpetrator himself—or herself," Greaves added pointedly— "who calls the ambulance or the police. So as I said, there are rarely more than three or four cases pending in a given year. But here lately . . ." She shook her head and held her cigarette close to her nose. "Out of hundreds of reports of missing children, certain ones touch a nerve." She squinted at the filterless cigarette, then drew on it. "A pattern—" she started to say, then, following Zala's gaze to the smoldering stack, jumped up and stomped out the fire just as a circle of tiny flames licked at the toe of her black brogans.

"Damn!" Greaves swung the door back and forth briskly, fanning the air. "Maybe we'd better sit out there," she motioned. "My desk seems to have been vacated at last."

The photos over Greaves's desk seemed to have collected another layer of dust since morning. Zala sat in the swivel chair, her back to the faces, and followed Greaves's movements about the squad room. Her feet jammed against the desk leg, Zala braced herself; her mind, though, reeled—lesions, contusions, autopsy reports: a far cry from the discussion they'd had before heading for the closet. Despite the empty-handed gestures the officers offered the sergeant, Zala clung to hope, for before Greaves had launched into patterns of deaths, she'd remarked on Zala's good fortune in finding her back from vacation and knowing enough to move fast. Usually it took three to four weeks before the police were satisfied that a missing child was not a temporary runaway. Then, armed with depositions from frantic parents or teachers who'd not been thinking clearly at the time of the original report, they'd pick up the trail, grown cold, colder still now that memories of witnesses were fuzzy. So, though two officers gave Greaves an empty-handed shrug, Zala counted herself lucky. A heavy-heeled male officer approached Greaves at the copy machine; they talked, mouth to ear, the man's knees slightly bent, the shorter Greaves scribbling notes, tapping the eraser head against her teeth, nodding, scribbling some more. Then, standing alone, she nodded, arriving at some conclusion, her fingertips pressed against her temple, the pencil point recklessly close to an eye. Impatiently, she began pushing buttons on the copier.

Hundreds of reported missing children. A few touched a nerve. Greaves hadn't called in Sturgis or O'Neal, so didn't that mean Sonny's case hadn't struck that nerve? Zala turned slightly in her chair and examined the children marked MISSING. There were a few empty squares on the bulletin board marked FOUND with names and dates on index cards. That was a good sign, hanging as it was over Greaves's desk. People were reluctant to admit that their children had run away from home. So the session in the hot box had been a goad, that manila folder a scare, all of it a move to impress upon her the need to hold back nothing. Greaves had dropped her form on the desk midway between a file marked PENDING and her purse, packed to go, slightly open; Zala could see the built-in depression where a compact automatic was stashed. Another good sign, somehow, for the form was nowhere near the scary folder of bludgeonings, undetermined death, and suspected foul play. She prayed.

"Marzala." She'd come up quietly, catching Zala unawares. "Quickly." She handed Zala two stapled sheets warm from the copier and motioned for her to secret them in her bag.

"I've got a few ideas," Greaves said, leaning close. She made an attempt to moisten her lips; they were dry, cracked, particles of tobacco blending with shreds of lipstick-stained skin. "The thing for you to do is get over to 350 Peachtree—that's the special emergency investigative Task Force, Marzala. And get very pushy. Very, very pushy."

She stood up and led Zala to the door. "And then get the best damn private detective money can buy."

Gusts of grit blew into the window with waves of heat. Cars honked behind her. She drove down Forsyth in a blur mumbling, "Sonny, oh, Sonny." Sweat dripped into her eyes—the eerie seductiveness of store-window mannequins lured her up onto the curb by Rich's Department Store, their mouths parted to give her the word, the secret sealed over, enameled. She begged; they offered glazed stares. Shouts from late shoppers backing up against Rich's window reminded her she was a driver and not a pedestrian stumbling along on the sidewalk. The car bumped down the curb and she turned widely on Martin Luther King Jr. Drive, veering over to the opposite side where construction was going on. She tried to assess what she'd accomplished at the low-slung building out past Peachtree Towers.

Her visit to the Task Force had been brief. 350 Peachtree looked like a car showroom, hastily converted into a squad room, but still a car showroom. She had asked to speak to someone on the special Emergency Task Force investigating the missing and murdered children. A man in blue sent her toward a partition marked SALES MANAGER. It was a while before she found her way back again to the sign EMERGENCY TASK FORCE, on the double doors with the transom overhead that led back to the sales manager's office. One after another referred her to Missing Persons, to Juvenile Court, to her neighborhood service center, to family counseling. One officer explained that they were reviewing only old cases at the moment, not taking information on new ones not yet referred by Homicide. She was a customer come too soon to the new store, stock not yet in, sales personnel being interviewed, Sonny an item not unpacked yet, the price sticker not licked and stuck on.

Then she had yelled, "I want to see someone in charge!"—the words echoing deep within the showroom, richocheting off the walls, the hoarseness deep within her chest, grating, friction threatening to send up sparks. Greaves had said to get pushy. For nearly a year mothers had been put off and trivialized in in-house memos as female hysterics. The

parents, organized and adamant with the newspapers, TV and radio stations, had collared city council members, who'd put a bug in the
mayor's ear. They were a group. She needed to be in a group. "Come
back tomorrow."

At 6:25, alone, Zala had gone back and knocked again on the double doors of the locked showroom, hearing footsteps go past. She
banged her knuckles bloody. Then on the street she had smeared blood
on the pay phone calling Delia, who said she couldn't come down to
help because her daughter Gloria had taken her car to pick up Zala's
children, but if Zala could make it down to Spring Street, Delia would
drive her home, then bring the kids over later. Delia had hung up
abruptly. It was late. She had work on her desk. She wasn't paid over-
time.

"Bitch—you bitch!" Zala had screamed, kicking the glass doors.
"Bitch."

A driller was sinking his bit deep into the shoulder of the humped
street of Martin Luther King Jr. Drive. *I should have gotten on the case the
minute Kofi said "Went."* She damned herself. She'd gotten the cue and
not done as she should. Her son's trail was growing cold.

Shocks gone, nerves shot, she bounced over the resounding metal
plates covering the pits in the torn-up street and sped up the ramp toward Spring, scraping a fender against the base of *Resurgens*, the dingy
gray statue dividing the drive. She swung wildly in the direction of the
Russell Building, oncoming cars honking and veering. She hit the
brakes the minute she spied Delia moving rapidly down the wide, flat
stone steps.

Zala got out and negotiated to the passenger side of the car, holding fast to the dusty fender, its sap-smeary dents a series of hand-holds.
The streetlights came suddenly on, and something loud and urgent was
blowing against her back. Delia's voice.

"Gloria called. Said Nathaniel picked up the kids and tore out of the
place like a madman. He's got a pistol, Zala. What's he going to do with
a pistol?"

A pistol? A pistol seemed fine. She slumped against the car door,
yanking at the handle, not sure how to get the mechanism to work, but
sure that she had to get back in and strapped down tight lest she come
apart.

"Oh, my God." Delia jumped her from behind. "Please let me help you."

Zala spun around, her head falling back against the metal. Then Delia had her about the shoulders, tugging her, trying to get her to do something, she wasn't sure what. Delia's face was so close Zala could see the pores under the foundation, could lean away and take in the family trademark, that particular arrangement of features: the prominent jaw, the eyes that leapt forward from under the brows, the bold nose. Not at all like her own looks—soft, receding, the eyes deep-set and secretive, the features in retreat. She should have been able to say to anyone, "My boy looks just like this," and thrust her face forward. But he'd rejected her looks, accepted only her ginger-brown complexion; everything else was his father.

"I resent it," she said, and wondered if that hadn't always been true.

"Don't fight me, Zala. Please. I'm trying to help."

There seemed to be no way to twist free of the arms, those arms that weren't powerful enough to really hold her together, only thick enough to annoy, interfere. She had to get into the car, through the window if necessary. But strong arms held her about the middle, constricting. It felt like the elastic band she'd worn to school that time when she'd begun to bulge with Sonny.

"Oh, Zala. I'm so sorry. I didn't realize."

Bitch, she wanted to say. The last thing she saw were the street globes, their haloes blending with the sheen of the pale blue sky.

[II]

CONNECTIONS:
CONVENTION BUCKS,
INVESTIGATION FLACKS

Tuesday, August 5, 1980

For a split second the whole of the Cascade-Gordon intersection lit up like night baseball; eerily silent white flares were followed by a salvo of firecracker rockets. She waited in the barbershop doorway as he approached from the curb, moving as though each step would detonate a claymore mine.

"Leftover fireworks from the fourth?" Spence turned in the direction of the shopping plaza, his mouth bone dry.

She waited, one arm twisted up behind her at an odd angle. When he turned around again, she swept his face for news that would restore her life.

A few bars of an old sixties tune blared up from the lot across the street. "Dancing in the Street," Martha and the Vandellas. Burnt sugar was in the air. Noisy laughter accompanied the clangy hammering of the ragtag outfit setting up a carnival in the mall's parking lot. She could make out the tops of raw lumber stalls and booths; Kewpie dolls in pink feathers swung from crossbeams. Abruptly the tune, banned from the airwaves during the street rebellions of her childhood, stopped.

"Well?" She pulled the door shut behind her. Her arm ached. "You went down there? You saw him? There's a plan?" He seemed afraid to move, so she walked toward him.

"Dave been around? I want to see him."

"Is that what ya'll talked about down at Task Force headquarters? That detective, he suspects Dave?"

"I asked you a question." He backed up toward the limo motioning for her to follow. "He wanted to know if we'd be willing to take a lie-detector test."

"What!" she exploded just as he bumped against the limo fender.

"That's what they want? That's what the detective you met that time on Campbellton told you?" She moved closer to his face. The muscles were lax except around the eyes. He didn't look like himself.

"Take it easy," he said.

The music roared up again on the loudspeaker and then cut off. The wheeze and crank of rusty ratchets and unyielding sockets traveled up from the lot and over the traffic along Cascade Road. It could well have been her heartworks, or his, she was thinking. She leaned against the limo and watched cars cruise by, slowing down while passengers craned their necks to see the kiddie rides and food stands.

"Has Dave been around since Sonny disappeared?" He ran a finger across his distorted reflection on the fender. Then he sprawled across the hood. Slowly the heat seared through his jacket and shirt. But he didn't move.

"Dave's been by the shop once or twice," she said. "He calls, keeps in touch. Been talking with the kids down at detention, trying to help out. Came by the Neighborhood Art Center yesterday to bring me lunch. But no news." She looked at him sideways, but he was standing now, looking over her head in the direction of Burger King. Kids were racing from the food joint across Cascade to the mall. It seemed impossible that there could be so many children about and not one of them be Sonny.

"Don't you think it's odd, Zala, his not coming by the house since Sonny took off?"

"Took off," she said. They looked at each other. Neither would confirm or deny. "Wasn't like Dave was all the time over my house, Spence." She waited for him to explain. He was probing the tire with the toe of his shoe. "They plan to question Dave? That's what you were doing down there at the Task Force, throwing suspicion on our friends?" She waited to hear if he'd amend "our friends."

"Mostly we talked about Sonny," he said. "Height, weight, build. They made much of the fact that Sonny's not slight as the others were." He jumped his shoulders up and down to remind her of that, then flexed one arm slightly, just enough to crease his sleeve and disturb the symmetry of his jacket balanced on both sides by the even distribution of billfold, Sonny's medical and dental charts, and the pistol he'd been moving from the glove compartment to his nightstand to a pocket in his clothes. "Most of the boys were slight," he mumbled. She knew that.

He wanted to say that they were tiny, spindly, wanted to increase the difference and thereby increase the distance, putting their son at a safe remove. He couldn't summon the energy. Besides, she would hear the subterfuge.

"Most," she said. Their eyes met for a moment, then she looked away. What did "most" mean? At the Wheat Street Baptist Church meeting, there'd been two lists circulating. The one drawn up by the STOP committee had five names in common with the list compiled by the Task Force, but each list had additional names that didn't match. And neither was as lengthy as the one B. J. Greaves, with the help of colleagues at MPYD, MP, and Homicide, had assembled. Perhaps B. J.'s request for assignment to the Task Force had gone through at last and she'd been able to get the lists combined and to note a pattern— slight of build in young male victims.

"They're going to send over a squad car to help us search," he said. He jutted his chin in the direction of the barbershop. "When do you get off?" He was no clearer now about her work schedule than he'd been in the past. He wanted to know who was minding Kenti and Kofi, but was sure that would start an argument.

"I can leave now," she said, shrugging her smock off. "Where are we going to be searching? Do they have some ideas?"

"Your place. My place." He shrugged. Youngsters were moving into the mall from the three bordering streets. Some of the bigger boys helped the carnival workers to drag cables; others waited their turn to bark orders and horse around with the bullhorn. He watched a work gang of five raise a newly painted Ferris wheel, the strain of their heaving visible in the shirtless backs and sweaty arms.

"I see," she said after a while. "Then Dave's place, I suppose. Paulette's. Right?"

He cleared his throat and said nothing more. It had seemed a good move when the Task Force detective first suggested it. Many members of STOP, as well as supporters who dropped by the Campbellton office, seemed convinced that someone close was the culprit, someone right in their midst watching them perform treadmill hysterics. Committee members had been photographing those attending the funerals and had asked the Task Force to review the photographs taken by professionals as well. But now, hearing Zala's voice dripping with sarcasm, the suggestion sounded less than scientific.

"Me and Kofi been all up in the fiberglass stuffing under the roof," she said, touching her face as though it still stung with tiny cuts. "We've been down on all fours in the basement, lighting matches behind the boiler, shining the flashlight all over the unexcavated places in case we missed seeing an opening, a hole, where . . ." He heard the catch in her throat.

"What did you tell him you were looking for?" He regretted it the minute she beamed her hot eyes his way.

"A dead body, stupid. Naturally I told my eight-year-old son that we were on a treasure hunt for bones and skulls."

"I only meant . . ." He tried to touch her shoulder but she pulled away.

"I told him we were looking for clues. Sonny's keys . . ." She'd been looking in particular for a cigar box or the metal cash box his grandaddy Wesley had given him years before, a private stash of some sort that might contain an address book or a diary. She bundled the smock up and jammed it between her stomach and the hot fender.

Instinctively, he reached for her face with both hands when she closed her eyes and hunched her shoulders. Like his, her left ear was swollen from incessant phoning. She didn't pull away when he turned her face from side to side. He wanted to lean down and kiss her ears, but she felt so feverish and jumpy. He took his hands away slowly.

"Lots of places to search," they both said at the same time. Another luminous flare burst over their heads. He fought the impulse to duck.

"The woods again, I guess," he said.

And your mama's, she did not say. Her own mama, Lovey, had been shocked by the suspicion. But she'd worked around to asking Spence if they should visit both sets of parents, leave no stone unturned. Maybe Sonny had made up a horror story and been given asylum. Spence had given her a withering look: did she actually believe their families capable of tormenting them?

"So," she said, bumping against the balled-up smock, "we're the prime suspects, is that it? A lie-detector test and a search of our premises. Wonderful."

"Take it easy," he said. He kicked the tire and wondered which one of them would say it. It kept coming up. At the TF, at STOP, at MYPD, at the Travelers Aid Society, the shelters, the hospitals, the crisis centers, the agencies recommended by the National Youth Services. Grandparents. He ghosted a smile remembering a session he'd had with the kids over Sonny's homework one night years ago: theme. Kofi had done well with "Jack and the Beanstalk," saying "I guess the theme of the story is that sometimes beans are more important than money." Sonny had tackled some of the Sunday School parables for examples of them. Then Kenti piped up with the "theme" of "Little Red Riding Hood"—"Don't never trust your grandmother." Spence could feel wetness at the corner of his eyes and wrenched himself back to what they'd been told by the professionals. An infant disappears—first search the maternity-ward records for the mother of a recent stillborn, then visit both sets of grandparents. A child missing from school—examine custody battles in the parents' history, then visit the grandparents on the noncustody side, usually paternal. An older child missing—if the child's not well off, then write him off as a runaway. Like Mrs. Camille Bell of STOP had emphasized, "It's a class thing." No search party was mobilized to find a poor kid. A poor kid's supposed to run. Bon voyage. Case closed.

"Shut up," he said, and kicked the tire when he tuned in to what she was saying, that he'd been an ass to let the detective suggest a lie-detector test to his face, that he wasn't tough enough with the police, that he hadn't been tough enough or attentive enough with his son. He didn't know how she'd gotten onto that track so suddenly. They'd promised not to. He'd have to listen more closely and head her off the minute her voice rose. McClintock, the VA counselor, had asked if she shouldn't be sedated.

Cherry bombs blasted somewhere near the Ferris wheel. Fireworks shot out from the far end of the mall and burst yellow, then red, then orange over the roof of Popeye's Chicken, fountaining down on the sidewalk near the bus kiosk. A comet of blue came sizzling across the lanes of cars along Cascade, then fanned out like a peacock two feet from the limo. They both leaned away, though the sparkles vanished in a puff before reaching them.

"You think, then, that he's a runaway." She ducked under his arm and stood close.

"That's what they keep saying. But they don't say who's chasing him." He wrapped his arms around her and pressed against the fender.

Runaway. How heroic it had sounded in her daddy's mouth, in Spence's bedtime stories. The folks of old fleeing captivity and setting up bases in the woods, the swamps, the hills, and in the camps of the Seminoles. Runaway. The word figured too in Mama Lovey's family tales, in Grandaddy Wesley's chronicles of the Spencers. Uncle Thad, M'Dear Selestine, and the stalwart patriarch Spence had been named after, running off from slavery, from migrant camps, tramping along on foot with the North Star by night and the moss growing on the north side of the trees by day. Hopping boxcars, running north to make a way for those who would come later, who'd leave stoop labor and cramped quarters and the bow-bent life spent under the weight of billy clubs, whips, and guns. Runaways who made a place to stand up straight in. How soured "runaway" had become of late in the mouths of strangers who would not budge from swivel chairs and air-conditioned offices. But in the face of the heart-stopping anguish of parents whose children had been murdered, how it glowed again with hope. Runaway. Not snatched, not choked, not dumped, but run away. Run away, Sonny. Rail line, hot line, steal away home.

"Baby, don't cry." He rocked her. Music was on again, not the sassy sisters of the sixties, but the corny grind of a calliope, an old-timey tune he couldn't batten down, not with the front of his chest dampening and her back shuddering against his palms. A tune that would go round and round in his head demanding to be named when he was stark staring awake in the middle of night. Two youths were winding cable around their upper arms and shoulders, walking along the edge of the mall across the street. He'd heard that youth workers often got jobs for delinquents with outfits like these. Perhaps, traveling around neighborhoods, they'd picked up information.

"I'd like to talk with Dave," Spence said. He felt her stiffen. He loosened his arms.

"Then go see him. But if you want to be suspicious about someone, why don't you tail that creepy friend of yours up at the EOA Center." She slid away and left him standing awkwardly off-balance.

"Mac?" He laughed. "McClintock's about as capable of doing harm as . . ." As I am, he did not say. Despite all the blabbering he had done in the encounter group, he had never talked about it, and she'd never asked. He had killed. He had killed children. Others hadn't asked, either, they simply said it: "Killed babies, hunh?" One My Lai per serviceman. His arms hanging at his sides, mouth dry, no muscle energy to resist it, Spence drifted closer to the memory.

The thudding of mortar rounds that night had given him ample cover to zigzag noisily across the open terrain lobbing grenades at anything that moved. Then his foot struck a sandbag and he pitched himself sideways into the bunker, his helmet crashing down around his ears so he couldn't hear what he was hearing and denying, that the screams weren't those of grown men. And when morning came, the bodies hanging on the wire weren't full-grown, but he didn't draw that detail, so he hadn't had to inspect more closely. Even from squinting distance, his eyes level with the top of a sandbag, his boots sinking into the mud, he'd summoned his defenses, marshaled together all the firsthand and secondhand stories of preadolescents asking for gum, then rolling grenades into the PX or into the barracks.

"Why don't you take off your jacket?"

Sweat trickled down the backs of his legs. He felt woozy. Had he survived the mayhem of war thousands of miles from home only to return to Atlanta to be punished? He let her help him out of his jacket and took it from her the minute she began lifting it up and down, frowning at its weight.

"I only meant," she said, "and I'm serious, that Mac's right up there on Verbena Street not five minutes away from the Wilson home, where the little girl was kidnapped. Don't tell me you haven't thought of it, Spence. Don't tell me you haven't looked at the list and wondered how many vets are in those families, how many of those fathers and uncles and so forth might know Mac."

"I've thought of it," he said slowly. LaTonya Wilson had been removed from her bed on the eve of her seventh birthday. He didn't have information as to whether the children sleeping in the same room, in the same bed, recognized the child thief stepping in the window. But a neighbor of the Wilsons reported seeing two men standing near the apartment in the early morning hours on June 23, and one was carrying the sleeping child. Could one of them have been Mac?

"And?"

He pictured Mac at his desk tamping down tobacco in the bowl of his pipe, the children seated in a semicircle around the desk, bound and gagged in their chairs, as Mac, sucking and puffing, said, "As POWs in this undeclared war of age against youth . . ." He could get no further.

"Zala, that's off the wall. What about that weird witchy woman? Revun Whatsherface? She lives over there by Anderson Park, not ten minutes away from the Wilson home. Comes out of nowhere, attaches herself to you, invites you over for a séance or whatever it is they do. You don't find her a little peculiar, offering to hypnotize you?"

"She's just trying to help. Under hypnosis a person can remember things. Beats taking a lie-detector test." She felt her shoulders sag. "This is stupid," she said. Her heart wasn't in arguing, defending. The truth of the matter was, Mattie *was* weird. But then everybody and anybody was, if scrutinized closely. She'd learned that at least. "If having the house searched will help, and if taking a lie-detector test will get them on the case, what the hell."

"Not just taking it, Zala, but *passing* it."

"What's that supposed to mean?" She almost keeled over. It had never occurred to her that he might suspect her. How the hell could she defend herself against that? He caught her, but not before she'd banged her wrist against the limo.

"Let's not jump in each other's face every time we . . ." He exhaled loudly and opened the limo door. He threw his jacket across the back of the seat, then closed the door slowly, wondering what to do next.

"You'd let that detective say anything to you," she snapped. "Just because he didn't run you in that time."

His laugh almost choked him. He remembered the race up and down Campbellton Road, searching for two vets in particular he was certain were behind the kidnapping of his firstborn, Kofi and Kenti sliding across the back of the seat at each turn. He'd gotten out waving his pistol, collaring people, till someone directed him to a lot where a child had been found the spring before. He'd found Detective Dowell there, pushing bushes aside with a stick. He looked up as if he knew straightaway what, if not who, Spence was, and very calmly informed him that he was still checking into the murder of Angel Lenair, the twelve-year-old who'd been found tied to a tree with an electric cord, her panties stuffed in her mouth.

Spence had insisted Detective Dowell test him the minute the issue was raised down at headquarters. Had slung his arm across the desk, eager to have that out of the way so they could put their minds on what common sense and history taught them, where to look for the culprit in cases like this. But Dowell had told him that polygraphs weren't administered there. "I can make an appointment for you, though, with the state police," he'd said. "Appointment," Spence had mumbled. It had seemed sensible at the time, insulting but perhaps a necessary evil to show good faith, to clear the decks before proceeding to the next logical step. It frightened him now to discover how much he'd submit to in order to barter cooperation.

Zala looked through the windshield at the stack of handbills on the front seat. Sonny's face looked back up at her: MISSING HAVE YOU SEEN THIS BOY? She urged her tongue, plastered to the roof of her mouth, to work.

"So what do you think, Spence?"

"I think I've never missed anybody so much in my whole damn life, Zala. I can't breathe."

Spence lifted his elbows so Zala could wrap her arms around his waist. Very slowly she rested her head against his chest. He wondered whether an ice pack would help their inflamed ears. His back to the mall, her vision cut off, they had nothing to go on but the sounds of fiesta. But they could picture it: shelves of glassware, ceramic piggy banks, plush teddy bears. A parking lot of pitch-and-toss, pick a card, three for a dollar. The tick-tick of the wheel of fortune spinning against tenpenny-nail sprockets. The ding-ding of circling spaceships. The flirty bell of an ice-cream wagon.

"I'm probably holding Simmons up," she mumbled, but made no move toward the shop to retrieve her bag or drop her smock in the bathroom hamper. She held on to Spence's waist even as he turned to look at the fireworks.

Tracer fire. Used to mark locations. A red trajectory sizzling through the night. Spence shook his head free of ghosts and squeezed her. He wondered if anyone checked the personnel files of these fly-by-night carnival groups against police records—kidnappings, child molestation, murder, drugs, pornography, Klan affiliation. She wondered if anyone came around to examine permits, to give the bolts an extra turn, to inspect the gunk on the gears, the tape on the cables. A vendor in a moth-eaten clown suit and high-top sneakers came up from the lot with a tray of cotton-candy cones and caramel apples. Several passengers getting off the bus followed him along the sidewalk, then down into the lot.

"Well, we've got a new batch of flyers anyway," he said. She nodded against his chest but stopped abruptly. Her ears began to throb.

They'd gone through packets and packets of pictures looking for a suitable one, a photo in which Sonny wasn't squinting, making a face, or looking sloppy and uncared for. Zala hadn't noticed before that on most, he'd been walking away from them like a boy with something to hide. Spence had never noticed before how few there were of Sonny by himself—mostly they were group shots, the happy family crammed together, posed, no air between them. But how little usable information he'd been able to scratch together for the private detectives.

There'd been one photo that he'd removed from the pile. In it, Sonny, naked from the waist up, was staring into the camera with an expression he couldn't name, but it made him uneasy. Not defiant, not surly, but challenging in some way, sexual. There'd been a photo she'd never seen before, a Polaroid stuck in his geography book. She'd shoved it into her pocket and not mentioned it to Spence, gotten up in the middle of the night and burned it in a coffee can she'd kept her paintbrushes in. The photo had been a three-quarter back shot taken recently. He was looking over his shoulder, angry and furtive, furtive first, his hands somewhere below the picture frame, in the area of his crotch, then angry at having been caught by the lens. The room was tiled, but it didn't seem to be a bathroom, more like the stairwell near the boy's gym. She'd asked Dave, not Spence, to track down the school janitor and question him. In the photo Spence selected for the flyer, Sonny's graduation picture from elementary school, there was something of that same expression, crooked, up to something. But it came through the copying process as nothing more than a lopsided grin, an innocent preteen boy trying to hide a chipped tooth in the front of his mouth. The whole household needed to get to the dentist, she was thinking. Maybe her earaches were a symptom of an abscessed tooth.

"I'd better make an appointment," she muttered. She felt his chin sink into her hair, his breath hot against her scalp.

"Appointment?" He jerked his head up when "Dancing in the Street" thundered over the loudspeaker, this time played at the wrong speed, the jumped-up arrangement sounding tinny and garbled.

"Yeah," she said. The Board of Ed was now asking for dental slips during the first week of school.

"I was going to ask for an appointment," he said cautiously, "when I thought Dowell was on assignment from Missing Persons. He's from Homicide and not even officially with the Task Force yet. . . . Zala? Did you hear what I said? Homicide."

Her moan ripped through his chest like an electric drill. He rocked her, rocked himself.

Friday, August 8, 1980

A soup plate for a giant, the kids might have said, taxing their imaginations further to explain why, set on its rim, it didn't roll across the green. Smooth, white, cool in the shade, the satellite dish measured perhaps six foot three, Spence caught himself thinking, his foot slipping off the rung of the bar stool. It was the concavity of the dish that attracted him initially. It was nestled on the front lawn of a company that hid its identity behind a wall of bougainvillea. The upper story of the building, its Palladian windows outspoken above the bold Doric capitols, announced that the mansion had been built to impress, overwhelm.

"What's so fascinating about that estate?" Delia pushed her glass toward the bartender and studied her brother's face. "It isn't on the market, is it?"

He shook his head no. He was grasping at straws, thinking of what Judge Webber had said about the use of global telecommunications systems by securities exchange commissions, interlocking transnational conglomerates, and law-enforcement agencies. None of which applied, however, in cases of missing children unless industrial espionage was suspected.

"I'm sorry," she said, sliding down from her stool, "that noblesse oblige is such a smirky term, Nathaniel." He heard "Nay-thhhan-yule," the way Sonny would say it, mocking his grandparents. "Because personally, I think it's the obligation of the well-connected to assist the less fortunate. And the wonderful thing about the Black middle class and the rich here in Atlanta is that they do." She straightened her skirt and headed for the ladies' room.

She'd been speaking in a public way. Whether for the benefit of the serviceman who sat at the bar hunched over a newspaper sipping a beer, or for the young white woman nursing a Tom Collins and slipping her shoe off and on, chafing her stockings, Spence couldn't say. Certainly not for the bartender. He'd danced down toward the door when a majestic Black woman in African brass jewelry strode in, rubbed circles in the counter all the way up toward the cash register following behind her till she took a seat at the far end of the bar and ordered a Cuba Libre, stressing Appleton rum.

"Honey dripper," the bartender drawled, winking at Spence.

Spence was twisting his wedding band around on his finger and looking at the silhouette figure on the ladies' room door. He'd been sure that the purpose of Delia's summoning him to the real-estate office was to give big-sisterly advice about Carole, the crack saleswoman Bryant and Delia were grooming for partnership. But she'd said nothing to hint she knew of their relationship, had simply ushered him into Bryant's office and introduced him to an old friend of hers, a judge, then backed out of the room. It took Spence a while to adjust to the context, the unexpected offer of help; if not help exactly—for stocks, bonds, international banking security systems, and keyboard bandits seemed to be Judge Webber's special interest—then an ear. When Spence laid out what had been done and not done in connection with his missing son, stressing his dissatisfaction with the seeming inaction on the authorities' part, the white-haired man with the receding hairline had swiveled his watery eyes from Spence to the Venetian blinds and squinted till Spence played with the cord. In his overstuffed chair—a pope, a king, an Old Testament judge—Webber had proved as ill prepared for the meeting as Spence. He did ask, though, if Spence suspected chicanery in high places, involvement at the level of elected officials or government appointees. Spence had had to take a seat behind that. It was possible, he answered cautiously, to head off a lecture about libel laws. Perhaps, the judge went on to say, Spence suspected collusion between a band of child killers and some section of the government because that seemed to answer the question of why it had taken such effort on the parts of parents and lower-echelon professionals to galvanize the officials to act. That too was possible, Spence conceded, though it was no secret that Klan members and sympathizers were on the force. And that, coupled with the fact that mass murders were bad for business, might encourage a true believer at the level of file clerk to throw a monkey wrench into the case. The judge then gave a rhetoric lesson, insisting that "serial," not "mass," was more apropos, assuming the number of murdered children translated as something more than "natural attrition."

"Are we talking about human beings or rocks?" Spence had challenged. The two of them had sat in silence, the freckles on the judge's pate darkening, the muscles in Spence's face tightening. And in the silence, Spence heard Carole in the outer office asking for him. He hadn't seen her since the desperate ride of the day before. He made a move to get up, thank the man cordially, and split. But the judge relaxed at that point and held forth on a number of subjects, in particular the noncomprehensive body of legislation and the whimsical procedures governing the distressful situation of lost, kidnapped, and runaway children. It was no news to Spence that the way things were set up, the authorities were better equipped at locating a stolen truck than finding a stolen child. The old man had promised to have his office send Spence a national directory of organizations that had a better rate of success with recovering lost children than the authorities.

Spence sipped irritably at his bourbon-and-water. The bartender and the serviceman were looking at him slantways and seemed to be sharing a joke at his expense. He scowled. The bartender moved off to ask the Cuba Libre sister if she was a designer of jewelry. The serviceman spread the newspaper wide, then backed it to a story he'd been reading.

"It was your getup that caught my eye," he said, glancing apologetically at Spence's uniform. The China-blue jacket hung oddly opened, the weight of the five brass buttons and the pistol in the pocket pulling the shoulder seam down well past Spence's collarbone. He'd flipped the patent-leather visor up and pushed the cap far back on his head. Tapered pants and boots too: he supposed he did look ridiculous, especially with the raw band of skin over his top lip.

"There's this guy out of Oxford, Mississippi," the serviceman explained, tapping the newsprint. "Got dressed up like a chauffeur and picked up his two boys from private school and disappeared with them. One of them divorce cases where the guy pays through the nose and can't see his own kids." He looked at the two women at the bar for their views on the matter. The young white woman kicked off her shoes and wrapped her stocking feet around her stool's lower rung. The Black woman jangled a bracelet, then fished the wedge of lime from her drink.

"Last week the owner of a trailer park outside of Lawrence, Kansas, she spots the three of them and drops a dime." He paused to find his place in the article. "Seems the wife sicced the bloodhounds on the guy for taking off with his own kids. Probably had a price on his head or something and the trailer lady saw the Wanted poster. Doesn't say."

"More likely a missing-child bulletin was circulated with photos," Spence said.

"Makes sense. So the posse arrives and corners the guy in the trailer. . . ." The serviceman wet a finger and thumbed through the paper for the rest of the story.

"Smut," Delia said, climbing back on her stool. "Smut," she told the bartender, jerking her chin toward the ladies' room.

"Aw, hell," the serviceman said, slapping his forehead.

"What happened?" Cuba Libre sucked on the lime.

"Aw, hell," he said again.

The bartender moved back toward the serviceman with a fresh beer. "I bet the kids thought he was decked out for a costume ball when he got to the prep school, hunh?" He laughed good-naturedly at Spence's uniform, then cut it short when Cuba Libre leaned over the bar and rapped with her knuckles for the serviceman's attention.

"So what happened?"

"Three blasts from a shotgun. Man-oh-man." He folded the paper over and gulped his beer.

"Have you noticed," the white woman asked no one in particular, "when a woman commits suicide, she just kills herself. Why is it a man always tries to do away with his whole family? It's so macho."

"A good thing the wife wasn't there. Were there other children?" Cuba Libre set the lime rind on her napkin and shook her head. "You're right. He'd've wiped them all out if he could've."

Delia tried to steer away the conversation. "Well, Nathaniel, what are you going to do? Where do we go from here?" But it was clear that Spence was somewhere else.

He was on the road between Chattanooga and Nashville. The sign: LANE FOR RUNAWAY TRUCKS. That outer lane widening as the grade steepened, swerving in the middle of the bluff away from the rest of traffic on 75 north; the lane ending in an embankment of sand. He'd noticed the sign at the top of the hill and had smiled, recalling *Thieves' Highway*, an old black-and-white he'd stayed up one night to watch when Sonny came by on his bike just late enough to be invited to sleep over, but on the alibi side of dusk so as not to be fussed at for riding in heavy traffic, at night, at his age. Slick. One of those hardboiled stories, the hero and his sidekick as thuggish as the villain; the girl, a heart-of-gold streetwalker with a foreign accent, pretty much talked out of the side of her mouth too. Hollywood's version of the working class, he'd pointed out to Sonny. During commercial breaks, they crowded each other in front of the refrigerator talking like hoods: "Put a nab on that last apple, Pops, and I'll climb into your hair."

Apples: the drama hinged on getting a shipment of golden delish to market on time, otherwise the bad guy would take over the union and corruption would reign. The hero and his sidekick loaded the crates onto two broken-down trucks, then really pushed it, no pit stops, no sleep, barreling down the highway to market. They get to a hill, side-kick's truck begins to come apart. The gear stick's stuck, the brake pedal's juicy, the wheels won't catch, the speedometer needle careens, ropes snapping, crates sliding, apples bouncing all over the highway, close-up of sidekick's terror-struck face, the hero wrenches his wheel to head off the runaway truck—too late, it's crashing through the rails, plummeting down a mountain end over end, crashing in a ravine—explosion. They'd loved it.

So he took it.

He shot over into the runaway lane doing eighty-five, ninety-five, picking up speed, streaking down the hill, the thick white lines signaling when to ease into the turn away from the rest of the traffic. He plowed the hood of the limo into a hill of sand that stopped him. He'd been sitting there a long time, sand covering the windshield, motor purring, adrenaline draining away from the muscles it had flooded. Then she spoke. Hands folded over her briefcase, the bulge of her cosmetic bag outlined in the leather, the tube of lipstick like a vial of nitro from some other crazy-ride movie, her lipstick always the same shade of dark plum no matter the trademark or scent—Carole quietly asked, "Is something wrong with the car, Spencer?"

"He wants to know if you'll have another." Delia was elbowing him.

He threw down a twenty. "I want to be there when Zala picks up the kids."

"I should think so."

He turned to take a good look at his sister, realizing as he did that it had been a long time since he'd done it. She'd developed an uphol-stered look over the years. She'd never been anything but chunky, lay-ers of corseting garments underneath the stiff tailored suits; but now her face, her expression seemed built, stuffed, and covered with some-thing unyielding. He frowned.

"You've never liked Zala, have you?" Rather late in the game, Zala would have said, for nearly ten years ago Delia had summed her up— "The girl just doesn't have it, Nathaniel."

"You can ask me that? You can say that to me? To *me?*" Her voice snagged on all she had done for them both in the name of family and just because help was what people were supposed to do for each other.

He should have apologized, should have moved closer to his big sis-ter and said, "Hey, Dee, I'm hurtin'. I hurt bad." But instead he left the change on the bar, knowing that would get her goat. Overtipping was vulgar; pointing it out, worse; snatching up the excess and cramming it into Spence's pocket, unthinkable. So he chuckled on the way out, the cardboard disc hanging from the light fixture inviting him back to gusto, the clock over the till saying Happy Hour would begin in earnest in an hour or so, then the bar would become predominantly Black for two hours more and he might meet an old friend before the day gave way to the expense-account crowd, predominantly white. He paused in the doorway, one shoulder in the cool, dark interior, the other in the eye-stinging sunshine. He was feeling stupid, his mind mush, and feel-ing rude keeping his sister waiting on the hot pavement. And he was hurting all over.

"You'd better watch yourself, Nathaniel," she said as they headed for the limo. "Please drop me off at the Russell Building. And by all means, see about your children."

Spence parked at the corner he was sure Zala would be passing in a matter of minutes. The stream from the AC vents fluttered a list he'd begun after his session with the judge. He pulled it from under the ba-nana magnet Kenti had stuck on the ashtray to hold her drawings. Friends, associates, buddies, colleagues, people to contact, groups to pe-tition—it took up less than a third of the paper. Over a million and a half Black people in the city, two and a half million Black vets active and organized in the Southeast region, twenty-five of his thirty-one years on earth spent in Atlanta, and he could think of no one to drop in on and say, "Hey, man, I'm hurtin'."

In his haste to catch up with those who'd scaled the ladder while he'd been crouched down in the mud and the leaders at the Paris peace talks were debating the shape of the conference table, he'd let crucial ties slip. Couldn't even remember the last Thursday Night Forum he'd attended, the last African Liberation Day ceremony he'd helped organize, the last prison support committee he'd joined. If his life depended on it, he couldn't say if the Institute of the Black World was still there on Chestnut Street, or if Atlanta U's poli-sci department was still a progressive enclave. The last thing he'd heard, when Zala had insisted on having lunch in Leilia's Diner rather than at the Abbey, which he thought better for contacts, there'd been a lunch-counter philosopher telling an anecdote about the poli-sci chairman throwing two equal-opportunity officers from the CIA out on their ear only to receive a call later from the college president reprimanding him for interfering with the career prospects of AU students.

Ten years ago, Spence had still been serious about becoming a community organizer. General Giap, Malcolm, Che Guevara, Amilcar Cabral, C. L. R. James's *Black Jacobins,* Sam Yette's *The Choice,* Sam Greenlee's *The Spook Who Sat by the Door*—he wracked his brain for the books he'd read, the passion he'd had, the plans he'd devised before swerving away to another persona, another agenda, when one by one the firebrand combatants he'd come home expecting to hook up with left the city or left the path in some other way. He'd defected and hadn't even noticed. And now he was hurting, the skin under the gold band raw from twisting, the band of skin over his lip sore from touching.

He'd been a thorough asshole right from the start, running off to New York instead of standing up to Delia when she took over the house, all but turning their parents out. Asshole for trying to repair the damage to his warrior image by throwing himself body and soul into the campus thing, for not being a "pragmatist," as his roommate put it, for political activism was right on but not if your grades suffered and not if you risked losing draft-deferment status. "I hate to pull a fade, bro," his roommate told him just days before Zala broke her news, "but the heat's too heavy." Eugene moved out and transferred to another campus, where he immediately signed up for ROTC. No fool, Eugene had read the handwriting on the wall. They were talking troop withdrawal, but they were stepping up recruitment in the Black neighborhoods using War on Poverty programs as their cover, using the Moynihan Report for their slogan: Join the army, escape from Black matriarchs who're fucking up your male minds. Eugene planned to go in, not as cannon fodder, but as an officer. And in the meantime, his mother could use the monthly stipend he got from ROTC.

Asshole, his buddies at CCNY had told him—marry the girl and claim hardship status. But Spence had gone in the army, fled in fact, still using the Black Power salute to repair the damage, wearing his "No Vietcong Ever Called Me a Nigger" pin, hanging "militant" posters over his bed, playing Gil Scott-Heron records loud on his box, draping the black, red, and green over his foot locker. Dogged, brave, noble, right on. "Asshole," said the play-it-safers who cut off their 'fros and kept *Look Out, Whitey! Black Power's Gon' Get Your Mama* carefully tucked away. "Asshole," said the truly political brothers he'd been trying to impress.

He'd blown an opportunity to become a radio operator when he laughed at his squadron leader's suggestion that he stop listening to Hanoi Hannah. It might land him in the box; worse, might earn him bad paper and reduce his benefits later to zero. In Nam, when court-martial actions were streamlined to "administrative memo," a mere zing of the pen for behavior considered an offense by an officer, Spence got a haircut, straightened up, and buttoned up. But he refused to join the opportunists who brown-nosed their way to desk jobs in the rear, where they could stock up on souvenirs to make their fortune with back in the States, or wangled jobs in the PX that assured them a role in the local black market.

He hadn't thought he'd see combat at all, or if so, not for long. Asshole that he'd been, he'd underestimated three things: the government's gene-deep commitment to the national image as invincible cowboy; the utter demoralization of combat troops that had to be replaced by fresh blood, and fresh Blood and Latinos it proved to be; and the serious vested interest in the war by officers, journalists, and freelance profiteers. For all of Dave's johnny-one-note harping on drugs as the crucial piece in all things wrong, Spence had to admit that Dave was mostly right. The drive to establish the U.S.–Southeast Asia connection to challenge the France-Turkey drug trade in that part of the world was the only momentum Spence had observed in the otherwise winding-down war machine.

Spence stared at the half-moons in his thumbs and thought about

Zala's childhood friend. He'd been to see him once and they'd set up another meeting to compare leads. Hardly someone he could drop in on
for a can of beer and say, "Hey, Dave, I'm hurtin', brother man."

Going to STOP hurt all the more. So he didn't go there. And he
didn't know the other drivers of the fleet well enough to call by their
first names, much less argue with when they said, "They must've been
up to something dumb, those kids." His mind was mush from so many
years of thinking he was thinking when he was not thinking. Those
kids. Like prisoners. Wouldn't be there if they hadn't done something
wrong. Like the homeless who slept under the viaducts along the highways. Must like it, the bums—hell, they could always rake leaves or
something. And women. Looking for trouble, they got what they deserved. So he avoided the office, tallied his receipts in the car, visited on
radio waves only. Hardly men he could drop in on for a beer.

Then who? He'd traded gumbo and whist for pepper pot and
cricket when he'd thought the West Indian Association ripe for group
plan insurance. Traded pepper pot for backyard grills and leather bars
in finished basements when up-and-coming wheeler-dealers took him
in on the inside real-estate track. The last get-together he remembered
all too well. It had been a Mother's Day feast in '78, the men cooking
outside by the pool, the women on the sun porch drinking and talking,
the teenagers batting balls on the tennis court, the children in the basement den throwing darts. A gallon of Chivas Regal and a gallon of Jack
Daniel's had been killed waiting on a couple Spence was eager to show
a house to. The wife came in a cab, ducked in with a black eye and a
cracked wrist, and locked herself in one of the upstairs bathrooms. The
women rushed up to attend her. The men gathered at the bottom of the
stairs split into two camps—those who argued that domestic matters
were private matters, and those who felt nothing but disdain for men
who had to resort to violence to control their women. So he'd gone alone
to see Charlie, ice cubes clinking in his brain, a schematic forming on a
blackboard in a dim corridor far back in his head: the diagram shifting,
erasing, re-forming, turning at angles to show hierarchy one minute,
the grid the next. He'd driven to Charlie's trying to fit domestic violence into the scheme of things. Not that he'd planned to draw the
diagram on Charlie's wall and take up a curtain rod as pointer. Not that
he'd planned to lecture about personal violence as a sociopolitical im-

perative in a society based on dominance, militaristic solutions to conflict, et cetera and so forth. He knew only that the brother would be hurting and would be needing somebody to wrestle him to the mat and drag him off for professional help. Knew only that what the men swigging their drinks at the bottom of the stairs had said was wrong, though he couldn't nail it, couldn't pin it to the grid and argue. Knew only that he would want somebody to come rescue him, drag him back from the edge. They'd seen each other since the barbecue. Took in a movie, *The Great Santini,* which Charlie ran out on when Robert Duvall bopped Blythe Danner around the kitchen and the kids jumped him.

He'd waited in the bar across the street for Spence to come out. They'd laughed uneasily together about therapy, each of them in an encounter group. Not much to talk about.

Spence rubbed his eyes hard with the heels of his hands, then scanned the limo's complicated dashboard of dials and gauges trying to find out the time in Atlanta, Georgia, in the U.S. of A. He could circle the block and intercept Zala. Except he wasn't sure what he would do—beep the horn and pick her up like a sensible person? Cruise along behind, surreptitiously following? Follow her. Follow his wife. He would have to watch himself. There were granules of sand on the wiper blades the car washers had missed. He would definitely have to watch himself. Two and a half million vets. He would have to look into that. Child Find, Inc. He would have to see about that too. He cranked up, then shot up the wrong way of a one-way street, bumped over the curb and into the schoolyard a good distance away from the driveway designated for picking up children.

When they saw him, Kenti and Kofi came out of the doors holding hands. The other children pranced around hitting last tag. Kenti had a large sheet of drawing paper that was giving her trouble. They ran down the steps, the paper slapping against her legs, threatening to trip her up. Kofi wouldn't release her hand so she could roll up the drawing, so she put it on her head. Spence slid across the seat. He wanted to open the door manually. He wanted to be right there for a hug and a kiss when they climbed in, knees first, full of "guess what" and "that ole teacher" and "my friend" and then and then and "you know what, Daddy." He pushed the door open with his fingertips and sat there leaning, tangled, contorted, but safely away from the steering wheel. So if he planned to actually pick them up and take off, not waiting for their mother, he wanted to see himself deliberately turning the key, so he'd know it was not a mistake, not an oversight, not a move of habit.

"Ole naked-face Daddy, look at you." Kenti was pointing and laughing before she reached the door. By the time she climbed in and grabbed him, the chant had become a song.

"You need a suntan, Dad," Kofi said, pushing his sister in. "Look like you been drinking Clorox."

"Where's Mama?" Kenti had one knee on the seat and was reaching for his neck but hesitated. Hesitation and suspicion, he detected both. He grabbed her in a bear hug and growled in her hair, dragging them both toward the wheel to make room for Kofi.

She thrust the drawing between them and broke his grip. "Mama comin'?" She sniffed at his face and frowned, then settled down, kicking the ashtray, while he inspected the picture. A stick-figure mother with bushy hair. A stick-figure father with hat and pipe. A yard full of pencillike tulips. A boxy house with a red triangle roof. A radial-tire sun. And by a lollipop tree three children—two boys and a girl. Behind the tree a smeary purple thing, something stormy and scary.

"Hey, Dad, for real, what's up?" Kofi leaned across his sister to hug Spence, doing his best to mash Kenti's head under his armpit. She pummeled his ribs, then bit him, and he leaned back against the door. "No kidding, you look weird."

"I feel weird."

"Then don't be drinking," Kenti said, pouty, folding her arms over her chest. She kicked the ashtray harder till he patted her legs. "You smell," she said.

"Yeah, Dad. Don't drink so much, hear?"

"I'll watch it," he said, laughing.

"You laugh raggedy," she said, moving her legs away.

Friday, August 15, 1980

She didn't know where she was or which who it was dreaming, her day self in a half-doze or her night self sleeping. Nor was she sure if she was the dreamer or the being dreamt. And where was her body? Earlier, she'd thought she'd heard a scraping noise.

She was asleep, she was sure of that only. Asleep and uneasy. Too much effort at trying to be lucid was waking her. She sank down into dreaming as Mattie recommended, teaching her how to set up a movie screen while dozing off ("Since both you and your husband seem to be movie-oriented"), her unconscious mind registering in dreams what her day self had failed to make note of.

She tried to get up. There was an awful smell in the room. She might have put the tie-dyes away before they'd sufficiently dried. Someone might have left a damp mop about that had gone sour. But the funk wasn't fabric. It was something more organic, more noxious, more shaped than mildew. Maybe a skunk had gone in. She heard more thumping, then a rush of water, then scampering sounds not unlike the earlier scraping, which she'd attributed to the clock. Part of her wanted to wake up, another followed Mattie's advice. Part of her jumped up and skidded across the slippery Sunday-mag section of the *Journal-Constitution*. She threw up her hands to keep from falling. She fell anyway and bumped down on the mattress.

Zala's gaze poured into a black so pitch, so opaque, she was sure her blindness meant that the walls had finally closed in. Surely that had been the grating noise earlier, the walls moving in on her. She leaned up on one elbow and concentrated on piercing the dark. A pinpoint of light on the edge of peripheral vision turned a corner, then disappeared from sight. Was she in a tunnel? There'd been a poem that Ebon, one of the founders of the art center, had written—"Take heart, sometimes the light at the end is caught in the bend of the tunnel." She sat up.

"Mama gonna get after you," she heard from the backroom. She was home, then, the dreamer awakened, not the dreamt adrift in the limbo between episodes. She heard the click of the flashlight and a shush, then the rickety wheeze of the bunk bed's joints. She needed to attend to that while she still knew where the carpenter glue was. And while she was at it, she'd find the mug of brandy she'd thought she'd placed on the window ledge back of the bolster before rolling over, punching a hollow in the pillow to sink down into, away from their snickers. Kenti and Kofi had been entertaining each other all night with a version of "The Gingerbread Boy." She knew she should have stayed awake and monitored the story for clues, or for—what had McClintock said?—acting out, indications of coping strategems. She'd been too tired, too tired even to sleep soundly. Twice she'd shot up straight in the bed and reached behind the bolster and come up empty-handed. Then she'd stared at the walls, listening, stared in the dark till her eyes teared.

Of course Spence had noticed it. He'd come over again to pace back and forth, going over the details of that distant weekend, his footfalls bringing it closer and closer, and the walls moving in. Back and forth, slamming his fist into his palm, pounding each *maybe,* each *what if,* each *should have,* blaming her, blaming himself, faulting the police, suspecting everyone, socking his fist, pulverizing each hunch, each overheard, grinding it all beneath his knuckles. And the walls moving in, but not together, one sliding soundlessly on greased ball bearings, another scraping over the bunched-up carpet, the room a rhomboid. He knew it. She could tell by the way he reached for the tape measure around her neck. The way he touched it, then stared at the pinking shears. He hadn't taken them, though. Shears were hardly strong enough to wedge under a wall and keep it from crushing them. When he finally tugged at the tape measure, she knew he knew. Of course the room was getting smaller. He paced from wall to wall popping the coated cotton as though it were elastic. But what good would it do to measure? A tape, a ruler, a yardstick, whatever they chose would be off too. Inches, feet, yards foreshortened. The conventional laws of perspective shot. Their son at the vanishing point.

"Ma?"

"Go to sleep."

She pulled the tape measure from around her neck and threw it to-ward the sewing table. She flung back the sheet she was tangled in and swept it to the floor. Then she swung her legs around and tried to stand up. That's when it seized her, all of her bones at once gripped in the vise. How could she have thought she'd slip past it? The dark made no dif-ference. Daily it grew more relentless, cutting her legs out from under her. She fell back on the bed. It did no good to go through a checklist, because no, she hadn't left her purse at the grocer's; no, she hadn't locked her keys in the car. What seized her could not be reasoned with—the jets were turned off, the doors were locked. It didn't matter. In the middle of a sentence, in the middle of the street, it attacked with-out warning, without mercy. She'd double over gasping for air until someone ran up behind her, lifting, knuckles pressed into her di-aphragm trying to help her dislodge the bone stuck in her life.

"Ma, we getting up now?"

The vise melted, leaving her with a dull aching throb. She could at least tell them to go to sleep and put force into her words this time. She got up and steadied herself against the cable-spool table before ventur-ing toward the kitchen. Glue. Brandy. And what had that scampering sound been moments ago? A dog digging in the yard. She listened out, cautioning her mind to stay where her eyes were and not race ahead to that smell, leaving her a paralyzed woman marooned in the kitchen to-tally mad. On the ironing board, where she'd eaten dinner, staring out into the yard, rivulets of sweat running down to her feet, was the greasy skillet and the soup spoon. The mug, though, had been placed in the sink with a juice glass Kofi had drunk out of. He'd run water in the mug, but it was still faintly sweet. But that was not it, not the smell that had seeped into her dream. Something more pungent, more clot-ted and dangerous, and too familiar to blame on soil mold or on the fridge that needed defrosting. She couldn't pretend that she didn't know what it was.

She opened the porch door and sprang back from a snowstorm of feathers. Someone had left the yard door cracked. There was no sign, though, of the Griers' tomcat or of the dead bird's skull. And the scratchy, scampering noise had sounded more like a dog anyway, a dog digging in the yard, where the smell was overpowering. She stepped down into the dirt. What had the dog unearthed? What had it run off with?

Nostrils flared, sinuses burning with the effort to search it out, she moved through the yard, measuring the shape and weight of the smell and making bargains with God. Heavier than a sparrow, ranker than a chipmunk, it was the smell of something large decomposing, reaching out from the briars back of the dogwood. She picked her way carefully past a circle of pigeons in the yard, on the ground, heads on backwards, beaks nestled between their shoulderblades, sea gulls without legs. Bastards, she thought when she realized they were not the source of and therefore not the cure of her agony. Simply asleep. Mattie could make something of it. Didn't pigeons signify messages—and in the yard rather than up in the dormers, with a full-grown hunter cat on the grounds? She scuffed up dirt with her bare feet and sent two waddling away, ruffling their wings before squatting down in ruts made by the garbage wagon. She sniffed. The smell was not from the wagon. Thicker.

She eased around the dogwood, bark coming off in her hands. Her foot struck a rock. She stopped. That was a good sign. That was a saying, a slogan of the South African women who'd protested the pass—When You Strike a Woman, You've Struck a Rock! She waited for insight, for release, something, certain it was a good omen. It should at least put starch in her back, as Mama Lovey would say. She squatted down in the brambles and parted the weeds, sniffing. Nothing but Popsicle wrappers and a bald baby doll, its face disfigured by rain.

The odor seemed to be coming now from the shadows under the hedges out front. A sickening smell, fleshy, grim. Not the heavy oil-and-spearmint stink of a skunk's fear, but something dead. Maybe Mean Dog from across the way or one of Old Man Murray's pack of hounds had buried a meaty bone under a bush. Maybe the tomcat had made a raid on a family of squirrels and half-buried what he'd been too full to eat. She headed toward the light the street lamp threw on the front walk, hoping her eyesight would arrive before her feet did.

There were no signs under the hedges of bushy tails, bones, or shallow graves. And the stench seemed to have spread, she noticed, all over Thurmond Street and beyond, everything for miles and miles driven to some terrible putrefaction.

"Getting more like Savannah every day," a man passing said with a husky laugh. He moved his finger from the side of his nose to the brim of his hat in greeting, not once looking in Zala's direction with eyebrows that said, What the hell are you doing parading around in your nightie? She hadn't seen or heard him approach. But as he went past the house, leaving a trail of gentle perfume, she heard a door click, then the porch light went off three yards down.

Zala looked over toward Paulette's house, drawn by the glint of binoculars in an upper-story window. Peeper at his post, the brass knob of his bed a third eye. By tomorrow, a tale of romantic intrigue would have traveled the block, and the report that Zala'd been traipsing about in a diaphanous shortie would circle round to her ears by supper. She riveted her eye now on the open window, the shade pull swinging back and forth. Of all the people she knew, half-knew, Peeper was the most likely suspect. Sexual spying. Supposedly bedridden, perfect alibi. She'd turned over his name to B. J. Greaves. They'd asked Zala down at the Task Force office if she harbored negative feelings about the disabled, except they'd said "the physically challenged," and she'd bungled her answer trying to decode their question. No one had been over there to Paulette's to question anyone, she was sure of that. But it could be that Peeper was studying her face with high-powered lenses and now knew. But who said the glint was binoculars? She eased backward away from the light, sure that she was caught in the crosshairs of a rifle sight.

"Stop it," she told herself, just for the sound of her voice. It didn't sound like a crazy person's, but maybe that was a sure sign that she was. A chain rattling made her push through the hedges to look. Two boys were standing by the telephone pole half the block down. One boy waved goodbye and ran into a house near the corner; the other, a jaunty boy in cutoff shorts, methodically unfastened a ten-speed bike from the pole, stashing the chain in a bag that hung from the back of the seat. He was doing a drill-team step, throwing his legs around as he wheeled the bike into the street, ran with it, then jumped on and pedaled toward her. A high-school senior or college freshman, she judged, looking him over as he raced by. Did he know he was endangered? Or was the Task Force to be believed, that only younger children, boys of slight build, were qualified for slaughter? She stepped to the curb and watched him approach the lights and sounds of Ashby Street. From out of nowhere, a scrawny brown-and-white mutt took off after the bike, leaping at the boy's foot, nipping at the reflectors in back, then turning around in the street to bite its fleas.

Good thing we don't have a dog. That had been Kofi's two cents, going over the advice the cop had given: a man, a gun, a dog. "Good thing," he told Kenti, "'cause Ma's dog wouldn't know where to lie down." And they had laughed. That was a saying: The washerwoman's dog belongs to neither the house nor the river. Something Cora might say about a gallivanting woman. Something Mama Lovey might say about an itinerant worker. Zala applied it to herself, confused more and more each day as to what was her schedule—TF, Board of Ed, barbershop, art center, newspaper offices, B. J.'s, various stakeouts. Any dog of hers would run itself ragged trying to figure out where to lie down. That was the trouble with learning all these sayings, she sighed, pulling her hair at the roots. What to hold, what to discard?

The mutt had trotted back into a yard. The boy on the ten-speed was almost swallowed up in the neon haze of the one block still jumping after 10 p.m. She pictured herself a whippet, a greyhound, one of them bony fast dogs she'd seen at the races when her father-in-law tired of the zoo. A greyhound racing alongside the bike, then braking short at the intersection of Ashby and Simpson to howl and bring the nightlife to a stop. For nothing had stopped. That was the bewildering thing. Children had been bludgeoned, shot, stabbed, and strangled, and nothing had stopped. Conventions came to town. Save the Fox Theatre luncheons were served at fifty dollars a plate. Newspaper and magazine articles put asterisks alongside the Fortune 500 branches in Atlanta. Suits were pressed, briefcases polished. And nothing stopped. Students dragged trunks along the walk to their dorms, registered early for courses, purchased sweatshirts, made friends, and rode their bikes with no thought that they might never come back. Milton Harvey hadn't. Eric Middlebrooks hadn't. Children were sent on errands with no thought that a child could fall through a door in the air. Some said Jefferey Mathis had vanished in a puff of smoke before he reached the Star service station. Others, though, remembered a blue car cruising the neighborhood. But people saw blue cars, sent children to the store, or put them to bed with no thought that they'd be gone in the morning. LaTonya Wilson was gone. But nothing had stopped.

Along Campbellton Road where Spence drove up and down, jazz buffs crowded into 200 South, folks got down at New Orleans Seafood, and all up and down the strip from the Touch of Class to Cisco's to Greenbriar Parkway, people partied with no idea that a boy had disappeared on that route. Went downtown to the movies with no information of those two last seen on their way to the Baronet. And in parks and pools where she'd asked around, the lifeguards checked between the toes for sores but not the locker room for kidnappers, though she'd passed on the information that one of Mattie's psychic friends had offered, that Earl Lee Terrell had never left the pool at South Bend Park alive. A sex-for-hire ring had been busted by the team searching that area for the boy, but nothing had stopped. B. J.'s list kept growing. And the media was mostly silent, burying the story in the back pages under liquor ads. So parents disciplining their children gave no thought to the possibility that the last gruff word uttered would be the last word heard.

Zala spun around, a light full in her face.

"Ma?" Kofi and Kenti were huddled in the doorway in the crisp green-and-purple pj's their granny Cora had sent.

"Kofi, turn that thing off and go to bed."

He played the light around her feet for a second, then shone it on himself. Sea grapes and kelp. "Mama, you better get in here. You almost naked." Kenti ducked behind her brother before Zala could ask who she thought she was talking to with her fast self.

"We gonna clean up now? I tried to wake you, Ma."

"Did you hear what I said, you two?"

"You said we'd clean up on Friday so we could go to the movies on Saturday. Well, we ain't cleaned up yet."

"Don't play with me, mister. You heard what I just said. And lock up."

They stepped inside, grumbling. Kofi made a grand effort to slam the door, but the carpet was thick near the threshold. He made the most of putting the chain on, though, trying to wake up the neighbors who might have managed to sleep through the Spencer Family Sidewalk Theater. Zala heard a thud, one of them tripping over the sheet, Kofi most likely, deliberately not using the camp light so he could be hurt and let her know it. She heard more stumbling and thumping. Her home was a terrible mess. But only a terrible mess: It was her life that was uninhabitable.

Saturday, August 23, 1980

He pulled in between a Ford tow and a wheelless station wagon, a lousy taste in his mouth, as though he'd lit up a stale cigarette. He was about to get out when his scrotum tightened, the taste a warning, the diesel fumes and hammering registering at last. He'd actually been scanning the grease-gray terrain for sandbags and concertina wire, quickening the ghosts. *Watchit.* He steadied himself and tucked the folded flyer into his breast pocket. Getting out, he worked up the spit to whistle the ghosts away. Damn if he ever wanted to have the shape of his world determined again by vials from the VA dispensary. But the tune he was whistling, trying to armor over protectively, was Marvin Gaye's—"Don't punish me with brutality/Talk to me, . . . Oh, what's going on." Self-ambush. Spence slammed the door, hardened his stomach, and picked his way through a scatter of scrap-iron parts and hulks of vulcanized rubber.

It was a deep, open shed set squat on the ground, its front wall a corrugated door rolled up with padlocks hanging from loops. In the junked-up yards on either side, mounds of blasted parts poked through the weeds and bow-bent rust that might have once been fenders sunk under the assault of kudzu. The chaos inside the shed was lit here and there by sour blobs of yellow; heavy-duty trouble lights, oblong and caged, were hooked on a pegboard where fan belts gathered dust, and hooked on a slanted shelf that had spilled boxes of screws on the floor. Spence wondered about the man he'd come to question. Was the wreckage inside a sign of dotage or outright contempt for customers? Spence braced himself against the entranceway wall, trying to outline a path past spout cans furry with filth, boxes once damp that had dried, buckled, grayed, and become something other than cardboard. The more he could make out, the more worried he got for his boots, his slacks; his hand was already a lost cause. There was no space in the burl pattern of grease to wipe his hands clean. That's when he noticed the signs. LOOK OUT BAD DOG. He hadn't heard any barking as he'd approached, only the wheeze and hiss of a hydraulic jack being pumped, only loud banging that had stopped abruptly when he'd slammed the car door. WE HAMMER DENTS. He could believe that. Inside, leaning against a pegboard under a series of baldpeens, was a John Henry sledgehammer. The sign he was leaning against was a favorite from childhood: BEAR ALIGNMENT with the puzzling logo of the laughing bear, or, as Kenti maintained, a little boy in a bear suit holding out his hand to show that M&M's did so melt in your paw. What a bear had to do with front-end axles, welding arcs, and the din of iron knocking on iron—sounds he'd associated with machine shops ever since his Uncle Rayfield's—not even his uncle, who knew everything, had been able to explain.

Spence told himself that he was standing there smearing his greasy hand on the doorjamb and indulging in nostalgia because he was waiting for the man to appear and guide him through the chaos. An Oldsmobile was up in the air on orange runners, but no one was anywhere near the jack. Beyond the Olds, over a table where a pencil dangled on a string and the phone book looked like someone had been practicing origami with the pages, a pane of dusty glass showed an office beyond. No one was there, either. He expected to see on the walls the signs of old—VULCAN PLOW, HARNESS HITCH FIXED, FARM MACHINERY LOANED. There were two calendars, the obligatory pinup, the equally obligatory insurance-company version of a harp-strumming angel gazing down through the clouds.

He thought he caught a movement. The siphon hose attached to the Olds's underbelly swayed a bit. But when he cleared his throat and scraped his shoe against the pavement, no one stirred. A far door, near a series of small windows green with mold, was open, suggesting that whoever had been hammering was not now taking a crap. Spence waited. The more he looked, the more he was convinced that the chaos had been deliberately arranged. A battered tire rim leaned against three metal drums that had been punched with a serrated tool that had pulled the jagged ends out. A dangerous thing to go past, he noted. A waist-high, hospital-oxygen-looking tank had had its black lettering dimmed by a coat of navy deck gray, but the skull and crossbones had been revived or invented with thick gluey white now a light shade of gray. Not contempt, not dotage, he decided when he spied the wire running from the tire rim to a complicated construction of hubcaps and spare parts near a soda crate. Fear. The place was booby-trapped. The wire was so visible now he wondered how he could have missed it. Ankle-high, it snaked between the jagged drums and the Jolly Roger tank and coiled around one of the hubcaps, then disappeared behind the soda crate. And what might be behind the crate, he wondered, massaging his chin with his clean hand—a crossbow straining in tension, which would discharge a quiver of arrows after the hubcaps crashed in warning and broke the final connection?

Trip wire. "Den diz muz be de playze," he mouthed to himself, the way his uncle Rayfield used to, a punchline from some grown-up routine that had gone over his head as a child. There was another movement, a shadowy movement in the pit. A man? A bear? His heart quickened. The siphon hose was definitely swaying, then suddenly taut. Spence tried to call out. But it was too late. Too late for protective spit, for ghost-routing tunes, for muscle or shell or magical chants or even "Oh, shit." He'd been summoning the haints from childhood all along, unaware, wanting to be anyplace and anyone other than where and who he was and in such deep trouble. He'd only meant to flirt with the past a little, dance near it, circle, call upon someone from those days when he could curl up in bed with his thumb in his mouth and a grown-up someone would take care of troubles. Someone like his uncle Rayfield had been before he knocked his favorite nephew flat on his ass in the dirt and unnamed him.

They'd been going to get him overalls, at least that's what Rayfield told Wesley, overalls for Nathaniel to fish in—the first *he'd* heard of it, deciding "fishing" was a code word, for on the first day of the visit his uncle had called him away from Dee and the other big kids to ask if he'd ever seen a still. At eleven, Spence didn't know what a still was, but his uncle had flashed a mouthful of gold, so he'd grinned too. The family's return to Atlanta put off for the day, his father walked the two of them to the truck looking worried, stood in the road looking worried a long time after the truck rambled off. When they went past the main store, the only store, the store–post office–gun shop store, Spence pulled his head back into the truck and got worried too. When they took a side road past the lumber mill, he got scared. His mama had strict notions about fooling around with "them people" who stayed "out back there." Them people drank raw whiskey till they went crazy blind out back there. Lotta cussin' and cuttin' out back there. No house numbers even out back there. Don't go to church out back there. Just soon bed down with a hound as their daughters. This heard, though, through the swinging door of the dining room. He was excited to get there but Mama-scared too. They bumped past lean-to's, rattled past burnt stumps and blazed spaces between log piles. For all the cussin' and cut-tin', Spence was thinking, his head bouncing against the roof of the truck, the trees were still closely thick and coming right at them, try-ing to crowd into the truck.

"Diz muz be de playze." His uncle drawled his jokey line at a sud-den clearing no larger than the yard in front of the machine shop. There was a gas pump that surprised Spence, though he doubted it had worked since 1902, his mama's favorite year. The whole of it—yard, pump, house, laundry bush, side sitting bench—could've fit in the car-port back home in Atlanta. The house was a box with a chiseled-out window; its door had no steps, had to hoist up to climb in; a metal chimney stuck up with smoke coming out; and all over the front of the house were signs—Griffin All-White Maybry Feed & Seed, Watkin's Linament, A.J. Coasts & Threads, Duke Pomade. Spence didn't think for a moment that the house was a store carrying any of these items or overalls, but that's how they decorated out back there.

"Who dem?" he asked, not joking, and almost ducked from habit. His mama didn't play about English and "resorting to savage," as she would say.

"People. Folks. Can't you see that, Nathaniel?"

On the side of the house, on a crudely made bench, three old folks balanced, a jar of pig parts by the woman's left heel. Everything looked dark brown, the dirt, the people, the corn husks and cabbage leaves that littered the ground, the wet wash on the bush. Not even late afternoon, but the light brown too. The old woman had veins cording out of her ashy legs, her feet looked horny, her breasts were in her lap, and the dress not a dress was just some cloth stretched in front and held with a safety pin. The two men looked clouded over, so Spence figured they'd been drinking raw since 1902. A woman came to the doorway in a butcher apron, looked at the truck, and spit a glob of brown juice into the dirt, hitting the only part of the ground not covered with garbage. Then she turned back into the dark, the apron not covering much in the rear.

Uncle Rayfield wrenched open the door, seeming to want to make a big racket of it. The old folks didn't break their trance. He held his hand up to Spence like you do a dog: Stay. Spence was nobody's dog, he was a Spencer, but he stayed, 'cause he'd seen the children by now and they didn't look right. A little bandy-legged baby in only an undershirt was leaning against three teenage boys, who between them, Spence thought, had gone twenty-five years all told without a comb. They looked at him, then looked at Rayfield. Spence's uncle was walking funny, his arms hanging well away from his pockets, gunfighter-style, his elbows bent, his hands palms up in front, no weapons, no aces. He stopped by the door and said something to the old folks—something gentle, it looked like, by the way he dipped his head to bend around the corner. The old woman roused herself, rubbed her legs a little, and answered, dipping her head too. Then a light went on in the house, a weak light, so feeble why bother? Spence thought. Uncle Rayfield turned and waved him out of the truck.

Spence tried to walk the way his uncle had, slow, gunfighter style, nothing-up-my-sleeves Mississippi gambler. He tried hard not to stumble over the corn husks or let the stink rising up from turds make him lose his place as the favorite nephew, the cool one with smarts, merit badges, big future, bragged on when taken round back of Mr. Norton's rib joint and presented to the men: bestest kin to come down the pike, my nephew himself, Nathaniel Lee Spencer. But the cabbage leaves, brown as the dirt but slippery, proved worse than the turds, which he could at least look out for. It was just like his mama said, he thought, slipping and sliding, them people living out there with not a clue as to how you do it. He'd heard her say in the dining room that them people were just like them po' white trash still picking lice on themselves in the wildman caves.

Uncle Rayfield grabbed hold of the side joists and hauled himself up into the house. But Spence couldn't get past the baby tugging at him with a strength that was scary. He let himself be dragged around the side past the bench toward a ditch where the three boys were jiggling. Spence wondered if the still was in the ditch. He could see a shadowy movement. Hearing the clang of a cooking spoon against a kettle gave him the courage to lift his hand in preparation for saying hi. Maybe they'd understand "Hi" and let him look at the still. But he never got the word out, because a monster rose up from the ditch and scattered everything in his head.

He remembered running from the shaggy beast, remembered the boys cackling and slapping each other on the back when he peed on himself, remembered the baby hollering and clapping her hands. Remembered the matted hair and the yellowed teeth. But didn't remember being grabbed by the woman in the apron, though in nightmares he did recall her face peering into his, a sad face, wet, her features jumping out toward him. Didn't remember shoving her into the old folks or the bench collapsing, or his uncle shouting and wheeling him around. Did remember the thud against the side of his head and the woman saying, "Don't, Ray." And the second thud that went all through him when he hit the ground.

"I thought you'd know how to act, boy, and would thank me," his uncle said in the truck. "Don't you know who they are?"

Animals, he wanted to say, but his uncle was driving with one free hand, so he said, "Sharecroppers?" It was a while before Uncle Rayfield's mutterings became words again, but Spence wasn't listening. Part of him was flashing ahead, wondering if his mama would call down thunder when she saw the welt on his face, wondering if his daddy would punch Rayfield out. That part of him knowing already that he'd be found at fault somehow and would get a whipping, so that part teamed up with the other part, 'cause a whipping was nothing compared to being disowned, called "boy," having "favorite" taken away and maybe the bragging too and the visits behind the rib joint. So all of him gathered together to remember himself behind the rib joint in the circle of men. All of his young self pulled together to recollect the men the way he had his baby tooth from his mama's jewelry box, the three vertebrae bones from the garbage where his sister threw them, the bright blue-and-yellow feather from under the well bucket where he'd first put it for safekeeping, the seashell from Savannah he'd traded for an aviator decal, then won back in a mumblety-peg game, and the suede drawstring bag of marbles his father had played with as a boy. On dismal days, little Nathaniel Spencer would pull his special box of magic stuff from under his bed to look at. At thumb-sucking times he'd line up the bones and shells and feathers and other sacred things on his pillow to ward off evils, like loneliness and being teased.

"I thought you knew something. I thought you was ready to know something further. Guess not," his uncle said.

No smarts, merit badges a fraud, no future after all, Uncle Rayfield would now try to take the men from him. So Spence sent all the smells, sights, and sounds he could summon into his special box. The sting of the barbecue sauce, the smoke from the wet mesquite tossed on the charcoal for extra tastiness. The men's voices as they 'lowed as how Norton would never marry 'cause it might get good to him one night and he'd blurt out the secret recipe. The men's laughter. The men's singing. Always hearing a cue in the talk, two or three men would start singing the same snatch of the same tune at the same time like magic. The music. One of them blow-spitting across his fist to get a bottleneck sound, another strumming his belly for the guitar, another sticking his face way out and thumping his Adam's apple up and down for the bass. The men talking of other men. Blues men with crazy names—Tub, Stubbs, Pinetop, Furry, Cleanhead, Gatemouth, Iron Jaw, Howlin', Lightnin', Muddy. Then the hat. The feel of the warm, damp hat. Uncle Rayfield would clap his very own hat on his favorite nephew's head. One of the men would fit it, snapping down the brim and rearing back to admire. Another saying he'd drive the women wild. Then all the men talking at once and somehow hearing each other, pointing fingers to show who they were answering, and Spence dizzy trying to follow. Women they'd loved, fights they'd fought, ports they'd visited, promises they'd kept to those passed on. Eyes hot-pepper wet, they'd haul out huge handkerchiefs that snapped like ship sails. Men pinching his shoulders or poking his belly to call his attention to the places he had to visit for good times, good women, good brew, good music: Memphis, Greensboro, Chicago, New Orleans. Then more names—Tampa Red, Mississippi John, Sunland Slim. And it way past his bedtime and the hat slipping down over his brows and him feeling real small as the talk turned to Big Walter, Big Maybelle, Queen Ida, King B.B. But always someone would notice and sling an arm around his shoulder and turn the talk to the Sonny Boys, the Pee Wees, the Tinys and Juniors, and make him feel at home, late as it was, dark as it was, small as he was.

By the time they went past the main store that was locked up tight, overalls, fishing poles, and all, he had the men safely tucked away in his magic box. Uncle Rayfield could keep his hat and keep his bragging in his mouth.

"You nobody's Spencer, that's for true. I never knowed you to act like that, boy. You listening? Do you know what demoralized means?"

He could afford to listen now, and knew who his uncle was talking about, so he said, "Means they don't have no money?"

"Worse. Don't have much hope. Near 'bout give up. Know why?"

"Why?"

"'Cause they don't remember how it can be in the good days ahead."

Which sounded like his uncle had been tippling a jar of raw in that house. 'Cause how could you remember ahead? And remembering behind wasn't so good. His mama said wasn't nothing back there but slavery and the jungle, so he stopped listening again. And instead he thought about his own memories.

There was a picture feeling the boy had often strained after; it was the earliest memory of himself, maybe. He was standing in a dry, shuttered room with dust cloths on the furniture. People were whisperpraying around him, and a woman was in a chair with a lapful of folded money. She would take up a bill and smooth it flat across her kneecap while he looked at the shiny floor, outlining the shadow of the shutters with his big toe. Then he stopped, because of a hum outside, the sound of a kite string singing; he held his hand out, because he wanted to feel the string wrapped round his hand thrumming against his palm. The woman looked up and frowned at his hand till he let it fall. When he asked his mama about it, she called it a dream and cut him a piece of pie she'd just got through saying he couldn't have so close to supper. And his daddy would listen letting the rinse water slip through his hands, then would say to forget about it and reach for the soap again. All Dee would say was that he was one stupid boy and get out of her room. So when Uncle Rayfield parked the truck at the house and said to listen up good, that Negroes with no memory were up for grabs and pretty nigh hopeless, Spence leaned his ear against the past one more time and it swung away from him worse than the dining-room door the night he got caught when he thought the grown-ups were discussing his memory dream.

"Kennahepya?"

Greenish-yellow spots swam away from in front of Spence's eyes. He was staring at a caged light hooked onto the Olds's grill. The man in the pit, his elbows on the ground, was slapping a funnel back and forth between his hands and regarding Spence with an expression devoid of anything in particular and yet not blank. A heavy crescent wrench was dragging down the breast pocket of his baggy blue-gray uniform.

Spence swallowed and moved cautiously forward. "You Tyrone Gaston?"

"Need a tow?" He set the wrench down by the funnel and looked past Spence's legs toward the sledgehammer. He beckoned Spence forward with his chin. "Hope not. Winch broke." His eyes guided Spence through the danger course.

"I want to talk to you if you've got a minute."

"'Bout all I got," the voice empty of irritation and haste and sounding decades older than he looked.

Spence hiked his pants up and hunkered down but could not get eye-level with the man. His eyes were hooded under a cotton cap that had been washed to a raggedy shapelessness. He seemed no more than twenty-five or so, but he talked and moved like an old-timer.

"I wanted to talk to you about the Dewey Baugus case. You remember? Young white boy over on Primrose Circle who was beaten to death back in April. They said Black youths did it." Something in the dark, greasy face rearranged itself. Spence cautioned himself not to crowd the man. You don't crowd a man in a pit with an Olds on his head and a wrench in his grip. He should have started with the Missing handbill, his calling card, the object of his quest, the subject of his sentence. Spence reached into his chest pocket, conscious that the man was wary now.

"You remember the case?"

"Got somebody doing time."

"Yeah, I know."

The man's hand was resting on the wrench, not reaching for the flyer. A bill, a summons, some other troublesome piece of paper; his hand continued to rest. His nails were thick and split with black injury spots like half-moons. A scar ran from the middle-finger knuckle to his wrist, disappearing up under his dingy cuff.

"Then whatcha want, man? I got these cars to get after." He picked up the funnel and leaned back toward the siphon hose.

"My boy's been missing since July. Maybe you've heard about all these children getting kidnapped. Some of them have been murdered."

"So whatchu want with me?" He picked up the wrench, then crooked his neck a little to look at the flyer.

"Some people say a white vigilante group's been taking revenge for the Baugus boy. A friend of mine thinks you might know something."

The man reached up and loosened a bolt in the Olds's underside, then bent down out of sight with the funnel. The hose danced to the left, then the right, then was straight. Spence slid the missing handbill to the edge of the pit just as the man was setting a nut down on that spot. They looked at each other. Spence wondered what the other saw—a father in trouble, a brother needing help, or a boy who threw rocks at niggers who didn't own spoon nor fork nor comb?

"They picked you up for questioning, didn't they, Mr. Gaston?"

"Didn't pick me up—bust me up." He bent down again and tin knocked against hard leather.

"Who? Was it the cops that took you in for questioning, or was it some neighborhood thugs that beat you up?" While Spence waited for Gaston to reappear, he reviewed the multiple choice and congratulated himself on its simplicity. Gaston yanked the hose free and wrapped it around his knuckles and set it down by the flyer.

"This ain't the boy they got locked up."

"No, that's my son. Somebody's got him. I'm thinking that maybe the same guys that roughed you up might have taken him." Spence watched Gaston's eyes carefully, and when they looked past him toward Memorial Drive, Spence swiveled around and looked too.

"Jumped me right out there. Three of them. Split my lip. Broke two teeth out. Had my legs cross that curb tromping it like kindling."

"Who?" Spence swung around. Gaston was ironing the handbill out with his fist. Grease bled through. "When was that, Mr. Gaston?"

"Told me a beating was too good for my Black ass. Gonna torch my place one night they catch me in here. And it ain't even my place," he laughed, looking up at the windows and walls.

"Three men? You can identify them? How'd they pick you out to beat up on?"

"How come?" Gaston lifted himself up, scraping his hard work boots against the wall of the pit. He swung one baggy leg onto the ground and climbed out. Spence followed him to the hydraulic lift and waited while Gaston pumped the car down two feet. Spence felt the sound as congestion in his chest.

"'Cause one of the boys they tried to make say done it is my uncle. He thirteen, I'm thirty-one." Gaston laughed again. His broken teeth looked filed, as though he had weaponed himself after the attack. Spence followed him to the table, where he rummaged around for a tool, then took up a shoebox with rags and lengths of pipe in it.

"Can you help me find them? If you've got the license-plate number or a name or something, we can burn 'em, man. Get those bastards." He followed the loping, slow-moving man back toward the Olds. "Put their asses in jail for what they did to you. Burn 'em good."

"Fullashit," Gaston said. He sat down and dangled his legs in the pit and worked on the car.

"What?"

"Say you fullashit."

"I ain't fullashit, Gaston. I'm hurtin', man. I'm hurtin' cause somebody's got my boy, so maybe I'm a little crazy and ain't comin' on like I should, but please, look, I'm not tryin' to cause you no grief, but you're the only lead I got. So please. The cops don't know shit. Would you help me?"

"I don't talk to no po-lice," Gaston said, wrenching free a rusted piece of pipe near the gas line.

"I'm not a cop. I'm a father. Aw, hell." Spence paced back and forth, conscious that Gaston was eyeing him sideways. Spence unhooked the light from the Olds's grill and shone it on the area where Gaston was scrubbing with a scrap of sandpaper. "I don't know what else to say to you." He felt helpless. "My boy. Someone's got my boy, man."

"Your friend? The one that sent you here? How I know y'all don't carry bones?"

"Who am I gonna carry bones to? Look, nobody's got to know I've even been here." Spence squatted down and gave Gaston more light. He watched while a shiny new piece of piping was expertly inserted.

"Then you gonna want me to go to court."

"No, man. I swear. Just tell me how to find those guys and I'll forget I've ever been here. Who'll know?"

Gaston leaned away from the pit and rubbed his hands on a piece of terry cloth. He was looking toward the street again, this time at that part of Spence's limo that was visible behind the tow truck.

"What work you do?" He looked at Spence's smooth, soft hands, then back toward the limo.

"I drive them wheels and do a little real estate. Look, I can pay you."

"What work your friend do?"

Spence jumped over Webber and came up with Dave, though Dave hadn't thought much of the revenge theory. "He's a youth worker. Works with kids."

Gaston looked at him for a moment, then set the terry-cloth rag down by the shoebox. "Like them social workers. Carrying bones is they business." He returned to his work.

Spence lowered his head and massaged his chin, missing the reassurance he used to find raking his fingers through his mustache. He looked down into the pit. There was a vinyl-covered cushion from a porch glider that had once been floral yellow, an open cooler with cans of juice suspended in icewater, a half-eaten sandwich curled on top of an empty apple juice can, and a Bible. When he surveyed the pit again, he noticed one of the corners of the cushion was hiked up. Pistol, Spence thought. His eyes slid back to the Bible.

"As God is my witness, Mr. Gaston, I won't involve you with no police, no social workers, and no courts. I swear on my children's heads and my mama's soul."

Gaston laughed again. It was the tee-hee falsetto that dropped down and trailed off in a sigh sort of laugh Spence had always called "country" when he didn't say "swamp." Gaston looked at the flyer by his side then rubbed his hands up and down his legs.

"You gonna need plenty backup, Spencer. That your name?"

"Yeah. Sorry." Spence extended his hand. "Glad to know you, man. You don't know how glad," he added, hanging onto the rough, crusty hand.

"Think you know how to jack this crate up, then down again when I give the signal?"

"Sure thing." Spence moved quickly to the hydraulic, remembering at the last minute to step over the trip wire. He heard Gaston chuckle again behind him.

"You's in 'Nam, Spencer?"

"Da Nang, 1970. You?"

"Was a powder monkey."

"That right? Keep dynamite on the place?"

"Whatchu think?" He was sporting his filed teeth again when Spence faced him, one foot on the pump, one hand on the bar.

"I think you probably got a big surprise for them clowns if they come again." Spence pumped the car up on Gaston's signal, taking in the wheeze, the hiss, the dusty air, and the grunt as Gaston slid down into the pit. The prospect of standing there gripping cold steel in the midst of chaos for hours waiting on the next signal didn't make him uncomfortable. He felt hopeful.

"Da Nang?" There was knocking of iron on iron against the car's underbelly. "Guess that make us brothers," Gaston said. Then he signaled, his rough hand waving, like a man used to handling weight on his head.

En route to the airport to pick up the buyers that morning, Spence had avoided rush-hour traffic by going the back way along Sylvan Road. Just past the trucks on Murphy, seeing the day laborers, men of twenty-five, thirty-five, fifty, standing around waiting to be called over to the loading platforms if the foreman found himself shorthanded, he'd taken up the pencil, turned Kenti's drawing over on the clipboard, and written himself a memo to locate the other spot, somewhere along Hightower Road near Baker, where domestic workers gathered should someone require a cook, laundress, or yard man for the day. At the rate things were going he might have to hire a few helpers; or as Dave put it, relating how a phone call from the high command had canceled out eyewitness accounts to the Jones boy's murder, he'd have to raise an army and navy.

After delivering the three women to the Ritz-Carlton for the bridal show and opera collection, he'd driven from Buckhead to Hollywood Road, where the Jones boy was found on Thursday. Not that he doubted Zala's word, but he wanted to see for himself. Now, having dropped them off at Lenox Square for the Geoffrey Beene trunk show, Spence was heading for Moreland and Constitution, where the Wyche boy had been found back in June. He no longer knew what he expected to find at any of the sites—maybe Dave walking around with co-workers from Youth

Authority questioning witnesses rumored to have fingered the murderer, or the bastard already manacled and the key to the kidnap shack in the arresting officer's hand; Sonny was evidently too much to hope for—but he kept on pushing, the pencil grafted to his hand since morning, a spare index finger that pointed out the urgency of the list, the box of flyers, his worksheet, and other items on the front seat.

He went over his work and personal schedules. There was a lot to cram in. He had only an hour before the pickup at Lenox and the buyers' reception at the downtown Hyatt Regency; then two hours after, he could escort the women to their rooms in the Peachtree Plaza. Luckily, Carole had packed him a lunch in a thermal container. So all he had to do was resist distractions, stay focused on the front-seat memos, and keep on pushing. Slipped between the pages of his Atlanta street guide was Gaston's name and address. Judge Webber had relayed the lead in a roundabout way, the old geezer a master at laundering info. The drawing-memo was slid under boxes of flyers, and a copy of Sergeant Greaves's list was tucked under the rubber band around the jumbo map rolling across the width of the seat.

When he'd gone to his regular newsstand for his early-a.m. coffee and the biggest map on hand, the man had paused over the cash drawer—should he take out for the morning edition? Three days in a row, though Spence still ordered his coffee, he'd felt no impulse to pick up a paper. What that old habit since high school had been about anyway was a total mystery to him now. What news had he been looking for all those years, what word so important he braved blizzards till the delivery? What had he thought news was then? Disasters, celebrity divorces, the demented drivel of war-monger industrialists. When word came, it wouldn't come through the press two beats behind the police, the police ten paces behind STOP's volunteer investigators, the VIs miles behind the murdering, and the general populace sleepwalking on a blind road.

He'd almost let the women become a distraction. The sleek one in very high heels and severe ballet hair referred to him as "the, ahh, driver" and seemed hell-bent on picking a fight about his being out of uniform—he was "theirs" nonetheless for the day, she'd emphasized, so synchronize the watches. The nubby one in a raw-silk coat dress, who tried valiantly to countervalance her companion's flintiness by being down home, would lean forward to mention her childhood in Waycross, Georgia, and all the wonderful things she'd heard about Spence's city. The third one, born in Atlanta but now a London–Paris–Hong Kong–New Yorker, spent most of her time in the car adjusting a summer silk dress cut by Vidal Sassoon apparently, sprinkling talcum on her feet and patting her stockings, sending clouds of dust in his rearview, and snapping her head around to pronounce various billboards X-rated, evidence of how dangerously sleazy the States had become. He'd been stung with resentment at first, so haute couture, Mont Blanc pens and leather appointment books in their laps, exuding perfume and a passion for the high-tensile-strengthened threads of Bangkok tailors. Not much older than Zala, but so confident, unentangled. Then he'd found himself relishing the sting, listening assiduously for more to envy as they chattered on about wine cellars, the swing and drape of French crepe, their favorite runway models, the utter baroque of nouvelle cuisine, flirty princes and yacht weekends, predictions of Hong Kong hegemony in fashion, and the shit they put up with as Black women. Anecdotes on the last item sliding them into a brooding silence, one staring out of the window, another scribbling in her book, the third bent over powdering her toes, his foot going to sleep on the pedal. And in the lengthening quiet he'd felt a sharp hunger for corns, burning blisters, an all-out knockout fight about his abridged uniform—anything but the dreariness that threatened to envelop him whenever he slowed down.

Approaching the light along Moreland, Spence's eyes fell on the untanned ass of a curly-headed infant, half the Coppertone ad hidden by a building, the dog pulling the baby girl's panties down out of view. He tried to imagine what the crimped-hair woman would say about that. It had been a thigh-to-navel briefs ad that had originally set her off. Then, near an elementary school, a blonde sprawled across the roof of a Buick with her legs cocked in the direction of the schoolyard provoked a tirade about the sex-charged environment of infantilized America. Climbing out of the limo at Lenox, she'd vowed to get off a hot letter to Calvin Klein about his jeans ads as she scowled up into the crotch of Brooke Shields. Ahead, at the far end of the five-lane highway at Constitution, Spence saw the heavy-browed model/actress again smiling down from a billboard for *Blue Lagoon*—boy and girl cousins marooned on a South Seas island grow to puberty teasing the audience panting for the approaching hot moment. Disney porn. Spence recalled an earlier film of hers and the reviews Sonny quoted as part of his argument that Spence was a drag—"tasteful." *Pretty Baby*—a preadolescent prostitute in a New Orleans whorehouse becomes the obsession of an adult scopophiliac. Sonny. "I'm old enough." "No way." The memory of another child whore in the disturbing movie about the crazed Viet vet, *Taxi Driver,* still a little too vivid for comfort. A child actress, Jodie Foster, playing a twelve-year-old whore. Where the hell were people's heads at?

Spence drove slowly over the expanse referred to as a "railroad trestle" in the police report. Lanes of traffic, sloping abutments on either side, one could believe in a whole continent as concrete, but "railroad trestle" was what the report said. He hooked a turn and drove by the underpass, got out to examine the bushes and trees for two-month-old signs. Under which tree had the Wyche boy been found clutching leaves? Had the crime-lab techs confirmed that the leaves matched those in the vicinity? He stepped back and looked up at the overpass that had felt like nothing more, driving along it, than a widened extension of the smooth-graded boulevard. The cylindrical railings above the chest-high embankments of concrete seemed hardly inducive to acrobatics, most especially not for a small boy frightened of heights. Horseplay, they figured. No way, his family had said. Running from a maniac, the boy might have risked the climb, Spence thought, shading his eyes and trying to conjure the scene. Most likely thrown. But the case wasn't on the Task Force's list. "Probable accident," though the patrolmen originally had penned in "suspected foul play." Spence tried not to think about going down to the station and arguing his citizen's right to see the files.

By six o'clock he realized that each time he'd returned from a site to pick up the women, he cherished the reunions in an excessively sentimental way. They worked so hard, looked so good, moved so well among the crystal and ermine, smiling their smiles, making their deals, working their show with those Mont Blancs, tapping a bony shoulder for a swivel turn to see how the cape flared. So good that Spence forgot himself and the forgetfulness felt good, and he began to make up things about the four of them: cousins at a family reunion. Through glass, through openings in drapes, from behind lucite easels holding featured designs, he watched them, cherishing them, faces in the family album, characters in a yearbook. He let himself be talked into rushing them from the reception midway through the first setup of champagne to take in a bit of the trunk show at the Promenade way out on Cobb Parkway, miles from the Memorial Avenue address he'd planned to follow up on in that time slot, then doubling back to the Hyatt before the swan centerpiece melted and the crudités underwent transmogrification.

Earlier, before he pushed cordiality toward the familiar—the three women seemingly as glad to see him, as a rescuer who whisked them away from ascots, crisp linen jackets, and all that sucking in, to collapse in the backseat freshly vacuumed each time and the upholstery plumped, ashtrays gleaming, covers removed from the drop-leaf tables so they didn't have to interrupt their postgame analysis to hunt for the release catch—he would have found a way to discourage their going so far from the metro area. But the flinty one had mugged in his direction when a bronze-gelled man she'd been talking to turned away for a moment to cough into his handkerchief, transforming the peach-colored square into an iodine rag, and that fleeting drop of the mask revealing a cutup from elementary school chastened him; he was, after all, out of uniform, which could be misinterpreted as disrespect, an unwillingness to do the whole chauffeur number for sisters. Then Edie had slipped in the middle of an anecdote about some woman with a chocolate jones who'd been astonished that Edie too could afford Godiva, and called him "girrrrrl," but didn't backstitch to alter it, trusting him to translate it as "friend." So he suggested a mini-tour of Auburn later, feeling very generous about his time. Then, too, Deidre had squashed herself in the corner of the elevator, digging her elbows into the carpeted walls trying to hike herself up out of her shoes, and he'd wanted to bend down and gently remove them but instead made his body available to lean on, neither coming on nor making more of the moment than it was, her turning suddenly and asking if he was as nice as he seemed because she couldn't tell, her face so wide open. He answered quietly that yes he was a nice man, certain that careless others had stepped into the opening without removing their shoes. He would have agreed to go anywhere she had her heart set on going.

So by the time the four of them were walking through the corridors of the Hyatt, refreshed for a moment by the stone-cool of the lobby but obviously bushed, Edie and Deidre swaying on either side of him, Geneva ahead but no longer prancing on her lizardy stilts and no longer bothering to quickly recover her poise when her ankle twisted and she reached for the wall, he wasn't looking forward to depositing them at the Plaza, the Auburn tour having been declined. He was disappointed, worried, already feeling abandoned, rebuffed, so he hiked his elbows out for them to hook onto as he escorted them to the gift shop as they'd requested. He was reluctant to part company with the women even for the seconds it took to bring the limo around. Then reluctance turned to panic as they approached with their parcels, talking together and not looking at him. Maybe he could invite them to his place for a drink. Helping them in, he was about to ask if he could use their shower. Climbing behind the wheel, he was afraid he'd suggest something gross, unforgivable, sitting there scratching his balls.

"Maybe we can get it together after a shower and nap, hunh, girls?" Neither of the other women was giving the Auburn tour second thought, so Edie leaned back. When he heard the upholstery sigh he feared he would completely deflate. He snatched the slip of paper from his street guide and folded a missing handbill against the wheel. He needed something to hold on to beside the pencil to undistract himself, sensing that in the days ahead, if the fog didn't lift and the sun burn through, a car would whoosh by him and he'd be assailed by this same perfume and be reduced to sobs and a twelve-day binge on expensive chocolates.

"Sweet, sweet Auburn, they used to say. Girrrrrl, I wish I'd been there in the old days. Mary Lou Williams, Eddie Heywood, the Peacock Lounge . . ."

Spence fighting the wheel and searching for the equation his uncle Rayfield had presented to him as a child: memory equals hope. It had never worked before, or rather, it had never made much sense; he'd been unclear how to apply it. But he needed something to anchor him, flying through traffic and pain. There was no hope in memory of recent events, that was for sure.

". . . dances at the Odd Fellows Hall." Edie was giving the leather cushions a fit.

Zala and he in a red leather booth, on a date, in New York, the restaurant about to close. Their talk of themselves, movies, school, things in common besides both being late-arriving babies to very mature parents, finally converged on Auburn Avenue back home in Atlanta. Spence imitating his mother appraising the business enterprises, the pastors, the other solid citizens of Auburn who were a credit to the race as compared with the riffraff of Decatur Street. Then Zala imitating her mother in a black slip, a Lucky Strike dangling, one eye closed against the smoke, dancing from the closet to the bed to upend a hat-box of mementos. Zala moving around in the booth, unself-conscious for the first time, showing how the shoulder strap drooped and the ash collected, and how the wilted brown corsages looked against her mother's shoulder, how the dance programs had yellowed, how the group pictures of elegant folks at the roof dances at the Odd Fellows Hall had curled.

"Course we went to Friendship Baptist by the university," Deidre was saying, powdering her shoes. "But we'd visit the churches on Auburn. Wheat Street Baptist—Auburn used to be named Old Wheat Street, you know—Ebenezer, Big Bethel . . . Ahh, driver, you just went through another red light."

Wednesday, August 27, 1980

The boy stopped to fold down the neck of the bag he carried, balancing it on one raised knee while he juggled the radio on his opposite shoulder. Zala crossed the newly paved blacktop and almost stepped out of her sandals. She felt the strap on her left shoe give a little. She took cover under a spread of huge sunflowers and tightened the strap. Limp-headed and droopy, the sunflowers didn't offer much shade, or in fact sufficient cover if the boy turned around. But he didn't. She gave him a third-of-a-block lead before she resumed tracking. She could hear herself breathing.

In a vacant lot back of the MARTA station, children, stooped as if working a snatch-row, collected aluminum cans, dumping them into a plastic bag big enough to hold all four of them in a sack race. There was no play to their actions, though—no hook shots, no dunks, and no peekaboo either from the two younger ones dragging the bag through the mustard-colored brush. They worked as though the family budget depended on their seriousness. She was thinking of the Jones boy, who'd been visiting from Cleveland. He'd disappeared while gathering cans with his Atlanta cousins, the papers said. But Dave had said, and she'd heard it corroborated at the Task Force headquarters, that there were several people who, separately and independently, had seen the boy hours after his cousins reported him missing: one who'd witnessed the boy being molested, one who'd witnessed the boy being strangled, two who'd seen the murderer the next day carrying a body wrapped in plastic, and two who'd seen the murderer step into a phone booth to tip the police off as to its whereabouts. According to B. J. Greaves, after a brief interrogation the man had been released, whether in the hope he'd lead the police to the rest of the murder ring, B. J. couldn't say.

Zala slapped at the army of gnats swarming around her ankles. She moved past the lot where the children were scuffing up clouds of red dust and kept her eyes on the boy. She was seeing him through waves of heat thrown up from the ground like a curtain of Lurex fringe. He was moving quickly now. For the first time since leaving the store and running down Forsyth to catch the train, the boy was walking as if time meant something.

Originally downtown to intercept Delia's daughter Gloria, Zala had switched tracks the minute she recognized the boy going into the clothing store. She'd almost approached him, so glad to see him. But something told her to follow instead.

She wouldn't give two cents for the private detectives Spence had selected from the yellow pages, detectives who wouldn't budge from their air-conditioned offices, wasting Spence's time telling him what was possible, difficult, just too damn expensive in a city the size of Atlanta. She tried to calculate the worth of the Task Force personnel, grown now from five to thirteen. "You're not qualified to judge," Delia had told her. To hell with Delia.

The boy had paused by an ice-cream truck, the kind she'd once earned a living with in summers. A wooden bar with six bells, operated by a string on the inside, overhung the windshield, exactly like in the one she'd once driven. She knew by the slapdash arrangement of decals showing Fudgsicles, Creamsicles, rainbow pops, and assorted sundaes that they hid splotches in the white that needed epoxy. The freezer was set in on the side of the truck. She saw herself in white T-shirt and slacks reaching into the box, reaching into the hot-ice vapors up to her shoulder, up to her ear, her cheek flat against the freezer door while the boy changed his order. Three times was the general rule. She used to amuse herself conducting surveys like that. That seemed three lives ago, in another city.

She snapped to. The boy was moving. She followed, congratulating herself. She'd been right—he was heading for the Ollie Street Y. To hell with private detectives.

For all of Spence's misgivings about the ex-APD cops volunteering their services to STOP—and he had a point; they were part of the old Chief Inman crowd, so who knew what their motives were?—they at least knew the lay of the land compared to miscellaneous sleuths in the phone book, or at least the three did who'd entered the case when Mrs. Willa Mae Mathis accepted their help. Perry, who'd left the force in '79 for an unsuccessful bid for the Rockland County sheriff post, had been with Homicide when the first two children were found laid out within 150 feet of each other, both mysteriously dressed in black. Edwards, who'd been working in Criminal Investigations when O'Neal and Sturgis were writing the early warning memos down at MPYD, said he'd quit the force after nineteen years out of disgust; manpower was limited enough without squandering resources on community-relations nonsense. The Task Force's insistence that there was no discernible pattern to the missing and murdered children's cases, plus the fact that the TF refused to make use of Edwards's private agency, were proof positive of that unit's piss-poor approach. Barber Simmons had reminded her days ago that Edwards had been part of the clique that had blown the whistle on Reginald Eaves. She didn't know if that was true of Perry, and if it was true of the third VI, Dettlinger, she didn't much care. Dettlinger had said all along that instead of flapping their gums about the murderers' motives they ought to concentrate on finding the link between the children. A few days ago he'd found it. So simple, so reasonable; it had been right in front of their eyes. But the Task Force hadn't hit on it. She was reluctant to say that the TF wasn't hitting on much, for there was something to what Delia had said, she just didn't know enough about police procedures. But Dettlinger, plotting two or three points for each of the children—where they'd lived, where they'd last been seen, where those murdered had been found—had zoomed in on a geographical link that, charted on a map, outlined the killers' route. Bingo. Down at the low-slung car showroom they were not impressed. Nor were they impressed by eyewitness accounts. They were still calling the death of Angela Bacon three days ago a hit-and-run accident, so not for their list, despite the on-the-spot testimony of the girl's companion, who called it deliberate, intentional, cold-blooded murder.

Daily, Zala felt increasingly confused, despondent, and not up to the task of trying to second-guess professionals. Were they lying, were they stupid, or were they just playing things close to the chest? Every day the thing grew more snarled by misquotes, blank faces, charges of race, saving face, and recklessness. Had the children been killed because they were Black, or should she say because the murderers were white? Had the authorities marginalized Dettlinger because he was white, because the high command was Black? Had the memo writers' warnings been trivialized because they were females, their supervisors male? And was B. J. correct, that female victims would be continually overlooked because girls did not count to male personnel down at the showroom? It was generally said, by those who said anything at all, that had the families of Angel Lanier and LaTonya Wilson not been members of STOP at the time of the sit-ins and the meeting at Wheat Street Baptist, there'd be no girls on the list at all. It was beyond her. What did it take, if not the security of children, for every damn body to sit down and pool information?

Tied up in knots, she'd sought out her pastor. He'd listened gravely, then given her a selection of readings to study. She knew without looking which psalms he had cited, which figures, like God-wants-something-special-of-you Jonah and model-of-steadfast-faith Job, he'd recommended. She'd not anticipated, though, the stories of sacrifice—Abraham and Isaac, Hagar and Ishmael, Jephthah, and Lot. She'd always been befuddled by the sermons that hinged on these stories that to her were nothing more than atrocity tales of child abuse. Get out of Dodge, kid, your father's a psychopath. And what was the Abraham-Sarah-Hagar-Ishmael story but plantation melodrama, with Sarah as the evil Miss Ann?

She had worked herself up into a heat with the biblical tales and the squad-room tales while Mac, who couldn't even be counted on for food stamps, told her and Spence, sucking his pipe, that perhaps (puff puff) they preferred (puff puff) being up to their necks in convoluted theories (puff puff) because they lacked the courage (puff puff) to face the ordinary fact (puff puff) that their child had simply run out on them. "Don't vary routine," he'd said in his phony fatherly way, ushering them out of the door. "He'll turn up." Like a last piece of a jigsaw puzzle found in the dustpan next time she swept, or like something a dog unearthed in the yard.

The boy was crossing the street, turning up the volume on the radio. She recognized the song from the Peabo Bryson album *Crosswinds*, a song she and Spence had danced to over and over in their try-again days. "I'm so into you / Don't know what I'm gonna do-ooo-oo-ooo." Singing along with the blaring radio, a woman stepped around a bed of dahlias to shape up the front of her hedges. Zala nodded a brisk hello and moved toward the corner, walking parallel with the boy on the sidewalk opposite. He paused at the side door of the Y, then moved toward the front of the building. She waited in the shade of the hedges, bending down to remove pebbles, mud, and bits of glass from her sandals. Where does a boy that age, she wondered, get money for expensive equipment like that? Now she was thinking like the police, like the reporters, like Mac: Was your son involved in a gang? If not a peer-run group of hoodlums, then perhaps a ring run by an adult? Has he ever brought home items such as radios, jewelry, cash—things he couldn't account for? So casually they spoke of break-ins, car thefts, the boosting of clothes, the snatching of purses, the peddling of hot goods, drugs, defective merchandise, as though everybody in the community was in on it.

An old man and a panting bulldog crossed over from Washington Park and almost collided with the boy, who played it off like a star recognized in public by a fan too awestruck to ask for an autograph. Out of danger, the old man and the bulldog drooped their heads again and went down the street. The boy was dancing, moving with the assurance that the ground underfoot would always be reliable. Zala watched the old man for a moment, how he studied the street; a sudden trip-up could mean the end of a porous bone too played-out to mend. She pictured herself of late treading the ground with the suspicion that any minute it might crack open and suck her under.

A blue car swinging way to the left to make a right turn in front of the Y interrupted her musings. Using it as cover, she ducked across the street toward the side door. She inched up toward the corner like a sneak thief to take a peek at the boy. He had one leg cocked on the third step and was swaying his hips to the music. The blue car cruised by and beeped a short beep. Then, apparently realizing he'd made a mistake, the driver took off.

Zala leaned against the side of the Ollie Street Y. The DJ had switched from his rapping voice to his news-bulletin voice. Zala strained to hear, but the boy changed the station. She slumped back against the wall, her breath hot on her top lip. Earlier, while the newscasts continued the daily countdown on the American hostages in Iran, Zala had logged in her notebook the errors made and opportunities blown to rescue the child hostages in Atlanta. Five weeks of deprivation and desolation bordering on insanity, and she was told (her civic conscience being appealed to), "But we can't let this reach the front pages—all hell would break loose!" As if that wasn't exactly what she wanted, if only she knew how to do it. The authorities had told Mrs. Camille Bell that her husband had done their boy in but they just couldn't prove it. Mrs. Bell went right on raising the alarm. "Check it out," one of the parents at STOP had tried to school Zala, "the figures speak for themselves, so of course they'll say anything to keep you quiet. In 1969 one-half million convention delegates poured sixty million dollars into the local economy. You ready to hear the figures for last year? Hold on to your hat now." And each time Zala had said, "Well, I don't know," stalling, looking for something particular in them that could not be found in herself. Maybe it was true what the police told Mrs. Bell, so she studied her most especially, but she could not come up with anything better than that Mrs. Bell wore glasses and she didn't. Stupid. So the parents talked to her like the stupid person she was. "Don't you remember the trouble downtown last summer, Mrs. Spencer? A white woman, onetime secretary to a former governor, got killed, remember? And one hundred state troopers were on the scene just like that." Snapping fingers one inch from her nose, while one of the mothers kept saying, "You know it's true." And still she didn't know, because that was too impossible to think about, not about the mayor and the commissioner.

But she did write on tissue-thin airmail, "Convention dollars speak so much louder than an invisible community silenced by their very wealth of pigment and their very lack of dollars." But wrote it without rancor, wrote it to two not-quite relatives on the other side of the ocean, so it didn't count, didn't mean she was anything like the grief-struck, outraged parents. And true, she'd been watching the news for years, and there was no getting around the fact that the authorities were dragging their feet. On TV the Red Cross, the fire department's emergency medical team, unions, civic organizations, governments, citizens of neighboring towns or countries always rushed into a flood area, an earthquake region, a plane-crash catastrophe to restore order, rescue and treat, declare a state of emergency. In the movies, army generals, university professors, health workers, and ordinary people mobilized quickly, pooled resources, and brought things under control. The robot has run amok—quick, call in the welders, make room for the lab techs. Someone's broken into the lab and stolen the petri dish with the virulent virus—quick, inoculate the citizenry, all vacation leaves canceled by order of the superintendent and the mayor. We've got the alien creature trapped in the old silver mine—quick, bring in the torch throwers and dynamite setters, clear the highways for the tanks, evacuate the town.

Like a fool, she'd photocopied Sonny's medical records, packed a Moon Pie wrapper he'd stuffed in a corner of his gym bag, took along a pencil he'd chewed on, and the pick comb with his hair wound round the tines. With Kofi's help she'd lifted prints from the cassettes onto cellophane tape and took the bag down to the TF. She'd read some-where—and not in the comic strips, either, with crisp-angled arrows pointing out the crime stopper's two-way-radio wristwatch, she had to tell the ironic officer—that fingerprints could be taken from inside a rubber glove; that the sex, age, and blood type could be identified from a single strand of hair; that trained dogs could track a given scent through a crowded city; in short, that crime labs were being run by thinkers, so yes, of course, damn straight she expected results over-night. But when she'd gone back to follow through the next day, no one could locate Sonny's folder and she'd lost her momentum of the previ-ous day and decided to play on sympathies instead. From one day to the next she flopped back and forth between outrage, disbelief, and faith that a little wretchedness and courtesy could win the day, still mur-mured "I don't know," not wanting to link herself to those who did seem to know, parents whose children were dead.

The blue car went past again, turned tightly, and bumped its two right wheels up on the curb, barely grazing the boy's behind with a fender. The boy leapt up the steps and glared at the driver, who gunned his motor, then took off up the hill. Zala dug out a pencil and took notes in her checkbook. Blue Ford Galaxy. Fulton County plates. Male, Black, thirtyish, air-force-type sunglasses, arm slung over the backseat, driver and passenger side windows rolled halfway down, man roasting in a storebought safari suit. In her notebook at the barbershop and on the bulletin board at home was a category called "Cars"—blue, blue Ford Galaxy, blue-and-white sedan, green station wagon, yellow like a cab. Mattie's clairvoyant friend had said a blue Ford Galaxy figured in at least one of the abductions. And B. J., in touch with several families of missing children whose files had come back from the TF office with no comment, had mentioned a blue car at least once. "Blue car" was scrib-bled in the margin on the page of the dead who were not on the TF list. Was it the Tammy Reid case, the girl who'd been found stabbed to death behind a warehouse the same day Angel Lenair was found strapped to a tree? Zala wracked her brain. Beverly Harvey—killed the same week as Reid and Lenair, same week Jefferey Lamar Mathis vanished—was the blue car on the line next to that name? The Mathis boy's sister had been accosted on the same corner from which her brother had disappeared, by a man driving a blue car. Was it a Ford Galaxy? Zala's mind spun. One of Dave's boys had told a story of a nine-year-old kid who'd been taken from a store in the Stewart-Lakewood area by two men who put him out later near Pickfair when he refused to go down on them for a dollar. Or was that the green-station-wagon story?

Zala ran to the side door of the Y. Where the hell were the counselors while creeps menaced youth out front? A voice in the back of her head told her it was up to her: *You the one.* She tugged on the knob, knocked. What was she supposed to do—run the car down, smash his glasses with her key ring, gouge his eyes out with her pencil? *You the one.* She wasn't the one. There were people trained and paid for this work. Mama Lovey had told her to stick close to home and let the police do their job, Widow Man grumbling in the background about the phone bill. Sit tight, act normal, maintain routine. But "normal" had always been a threadbare throw rug Mama Lovey slung over the snakepit and called wall-to-wall deluxe as she swept up broken dishes and shattered light bulbs, then gathered her brood around her to pose for family portraits.

Zala raced toward the back in search of an entrance. Maybe she wasn't the one, but then, "Whatever the Task Force is doing is the best-kept secret in the world," Camille Bell had said. So she had become a one, 'cause the TF was ignoring half the victims, yet talking about a "composite profile." Like shopping for a wide-patterned plaid with a one-inch-square swatch of fabric for matching. She tried doubling back through the grassy yard, no other door in sight. Maybe she was the one, because in real life there was no bumbling Columbo dropping cigar ash on his rumpled trenchcoat as he pestered people and put the case together. There was only the STOP committee sifting through clues and keeping the fire lit under the TF's behinds. In real life Dave, not the Mod Squad, questioned kids in the shelters and detention centers. Dave driving up and down Dimmock Street showing Sonny's picture to the young dealers in case he'd been grabbed in a case of mistaken identity. Spence and his army buddy Teodescu, not Billy Jack or Sheriff Walking Tall, keeping tabs on the Stone Mountain yahoos. And there was no Lois Lane to emblazon headlines across the front page so all hell could break loose.

The side door was flung back and hit the brick wall as she approached. Boys crowded out pushing and shoving, twisting wet towels and snapping each other, taking over the sidewalk. Several boys bunched together separated and streamed past her on either side. Others grabbed their buddies in choke holds and drag-ran them across Ollie to the park. She tried to get around to the front of the building, but two boys were roughhousing on the corner and she could not get past.

"Hey, Jeeter," she heard, then shoved the boys out of her way. A rowdy kid about thirteen was pushing up against the boy on the bottom step, trying to wrestle the radio away. "Awww, c'mon, lemme hold it a minute."

"Forget you, Scoop."

So this was Scoop, the singer Kofi had tagged UFO, Unidentified Fat Object. Not so much fat as waddly, he walked on the back of his heels with his torso thrust forward, in imitation, perhaps, of a potbellied father. Another boy, whom Kofi had ID'd on the tapes as Flyboy, the neato dresser, was coming down the steps eating Chee•tos, lifting an elbow, twisting at the waist, fending off the boys pushing at his back and reaching around him trying to make a grab for the Chee•tos bag. His 'fro was freshly trimmed, a part on the side razored in. His towel was neatly folded around his neck like a pilot's scarf. His denim shorts were hot-starched and pressed hard, his shirt, striped a cool blue and white.

Several bigger boys sauntered out of the door tucking their shirts in. They took the stairs slow and easy, one of them breaking open a pack of cigarettes, another frisking himself for matches. Then Bestor Brooks came out, a taller version of the sandy-haired, square-jawed boy she'd followed from downtown. She held her breath waiting for the circle to be completed, the four boys already moving on. And in the doorway was a man, not a boy, a musclebound man in a white terry-cloth shirt, wrinkled beige pants, and white tennis shoes who was closing the door.

"Pig out!" Scoop was racing up to the rise of the hill, a stream of Chee•tos littering the street behind him.

"Your ass is grass!" Flyboy hollered, and the three boys took off after Scoop. Zala, following, was remembering that she didn't like Scoop. On the tapes he'd interrupted rehearsal to punch Sonny in the arm for not breaking off a line crisply enough to suit him. She'd been playing the tapes over and over, listening for a name, a place, a tone, a clue. But all she knew was that Scoop was older than Sonny and Jeeter and missed no opportunity to lord it over the two.

The blue Ford Galaxy was waiting at the very top of the hill, no moving traffic in sight. She stepped behind a bush when she saw Bestor Brooks, leaning in to speak to the driver, glance her way as if giving directions. The other boys had moved to the park side of the street and were bent down gathering up trash. Whatever Bestor Brooks told the driver did the trick. The car spun around in a juicy U-turn and sped her way, the boys leaping to the middle of the street bombarding the Galaxy with rocks, soda bottles, and beer cans. Veering from one side of the street to the other, the car sped past her, the driver doing a mean lean, head cocked, the tinted glasses covering half his face, the heel of his hand maneuvering the wheel. Hollywood. She took down the license-plate number and resumed her pursuit following the boys' voices, on the down side of the hill, laughing and congratulating each other.

Would they now lead her to Sonny? "Probably holing up with a friend," Dave had said. "Kids will do that," Mac had said. "When families break up, the child often feels it's his fault, and feels torn by conflicting loyalties. Often they run to resolve the tension." Zala had sat patiently listening to that crap while Mac talked and scribbled in his notebook as if she hadn't learned to read upside down all these years— "lower socioeconomic . . ." "a surfeit of problems . . ." "no perceptual set for . . ." "limited ability to . . ." "Poor orientation to civilian life," he'd written once, as if that took profound insight. He wouldn't join in filing suit against the army, but he sure could scribble. Medication, yes; litigation, no. "Passive aggressive," he'd written about her. "Carry on as usual," he'd had the nerve to tell them. You're lousy parents and your son has split, but carry on as before, what the hell.

She trudged up the hill on the lookout for the blue car. She was learning. There was no Kojak to grab a creep out of a car and slam him around while sucking on a Tootsie Pop, just the boys and their rocks and her pencil. There'd be no Virgil Tibbs arriving on the scene all scientific and articulate, bringing the culprits to justice and leading her boy safely home. *You the one* nagged at her and sent her scurrying down the hill, her feet sliding out of the front of her sandals. Real life; she had to stick to real life. Only in stories was there a detective to reach under the counter where the dead body slumped on its stool, coming up with a wad of chewed gum that a retired orthodontist hermit up in the hills could trace to the culprit minutes before the final commercial. In real life, all cops could do, they told her, was listen, keep an eye peeled, and wait, the squad rooms looking more and more every day like a fast-food annex, greasy white bags on the desks, bulgy Styrofoam cups on the file cabinets. In the movies they fine-tooth-combed an area and sent bags of clues to the crime lab. In her basement they'd overlooked the area behind the stairs and the area behind the furnace and had been so gruffly rude and clumsy questioning Mr. Grier when he came down his cellar steps to see what was going on, that her neighbors hadn't spoken to her since. Just that morning when Zala had run to set her garbage out, she heard the Griers' Herby Curby wheels stop short in their driveway. They'd rather live with garbage for a week than say good morning to her.

She followed the boys onto Mayson Turner. They'd found a dented lard can perfect for soccer. She'd thought the police would talk to these boys, would assign a detail to watch the comings and goings of neighbors and friends, would stake out the Boys' Club and the campsite they'd used, interrogate the counselors, grill Sonny's former teachers. She was learning. Maybe she was the one. But so far every time she'd listened to that voice she'd wound up a stranger to herself, a crazed woman with snakes in her hair and film on her teeth, spying on neighborhood children, squatting down in neighbors' driveways peering into basement windows with bloodshot eyes, intercepting boys her son knew on the way from the pool and following them home ready to tear the walls down or crowbar the floors up, but only breaking her nails on windowsills a little too high. One Sunday she'd seen the Brooks family walking from church and, telling herself she would overtake them in the next thirty feet and offer a lift, knowing good and well she wouldn't, the Bug couldn't hold half of the group, followed them home, parked around the corner, and crept close to the house, looking in every window for who might emerge from a closet or crawl from under a bed. The you-the-one self had been urging her lately to set aside the artsy-craftsy farting around and run up a navy-blue shirt and skirt that could get her past the inner-sanctum doors at headquarters and city hall. But would she find out anything from those quarters worth knowing?

What mild complaints she'd voiced about the lead-footed leadership had struck Delia as heresy and the twins, answering her letter, as naiveté. "The job of the police," wrote Gerry, a Peace Corps deputy in

Lesotho, "is to protect the interests of the ruling class and keep the animals domesticated." And Maxwell, a health worker there, had written on the same blue airmail, "The *comprador* class maintains its privileges by doing the dirty work for the real rulers." Zala had dropped on the sofa with two dictionaries, studying the letter for counterfeit, for the twins had been the ones who'd taught her that the Black leadership in Atlanta was a true leadership, not an appendage of, not operating at the whim of, an outside group, but accredited by its own community which had built the economic base to launch them. She had no gift for politics. All she wanted was for everybody to get out of her head and to have her son back.

She was glad that the game was a rousing one and that the boys had established a penalty for kicks that sent the lard can anywhere but up ahead. The street offered so little in the way of trees and bushes, the sun bright, starkly flat and unshadowed. She was glad to get past the railroad-track area back of Troy Street. How grim a vacant lot could be even in daylight. A few months ago, though, she would have paused to see if the pecan tree was bearing. Now all she could think of was getting away from that desolate spot. What if Blue Car returned, pulled up in a van with some helpers, grabbed the boys before they reached the back of Church's Chicken? What could she do? Who would hear her if she screamed? Scream? she asked herself from the back of her head, where she sat on a stool with her arms crossed over her knees, smoking a cigarette, you've barely learned to talk good, sister.

When the boys shoved each other into Church's Chicken, Flyboy pounding on Scoop's back and demanding he pay up for the Chee•tos with an order of corn on the cob, Zala posted herself by the Dumpster eyeing the parking lot, Troy Street, and Simpson Road, wondering where she could place herself to scream to best advantage. How exciting the simple heroics had looked on the screen in the Ashby movie house:

Doris Day and Jimmy Stewart running into the Albert Hall, the assassination scheduled to take place during a particular passage in the music. Doris rushes down the aisle scanning the audience for the assassin. The faces are calm, comfortable, attentive to the concert. Jimmy races up the carpeted stairs to find the dignitary's box and warn him that he's been targeted for murder. The security guards stop Jimmy. The music races on. The shot will be fired when the cymbals clash, he explains to the guards. He races along, yanking open doors to the box seats. Along the row the dignitary enjoys the music, out of it. Below, the audience enjoys the music, out of it. The musicians on stage turn a page of sheet music, into it. Only Doris and Jimmy to save the day. A gun appears through a curtain. The percussionist is about to clap thunder. Doris sees the gun and screams. The gun tilts. The shot is fired off its mark. A scream. A scream can save a life. And if she screamed? Someone would come along on the trot and offer to take her to church or to Grady's eighth floor.

"Miz Spencer, did you want to see me about something?" Bestor Brooks was peering around the corner, hanging on to Church's door, balancing on the loose step.

"Sonny." It was all she knew to say, caught out that way, her eyes seeping into the boy's pores. "Sonny." Surely that was enough. She watched him studying her, her hair uncombed, forehead furrowed, eyes bloodshot, the mouth hard drawn. She'd never felt uglier. A friend's-mother-who-followed-you-through-the-streets-and-skulked-around-a-garbage-Dumpster-waiting-to-pounce-on-your-bones kind of ugly. "Sonny," she said through her teeth when pity washed over Bestor Brooks's face.

"Say, Miz Spencer." He stepped down and shrugged. The door closing was stopped abruptly.

"Friendship and loyalty is one thing," she said, a grown-up. "I can understand that. But Sunday's his birthday. It's time he came home."

The other boys came out, looking embarrassed for her. They stood together in a tight clump hugging their square-shaped bundles.

"Sonny," she said to them. She fixed again on Bestor Brooks, the eldest, the one who broke up the squabbles, the oldest child in his family too. He would not play with her. "Sonny, Bestor—Sonny."

"We haven't seen Sonny since Fourth of July, Miz Spencer, I swear." He turned to the others to confirm it. They nodded. "That time we came by to see if he was going to the cookout."

"But he was on punishment," Scoop said.

"Except for that other time," Flyboy corrected, "the time I came by to walk him to rehearsal." They all nodded. "But then you called, right?" He rubbed his shoulder against Jeeter, who rearranged his radio on top of his bag and bobbed his head up and down. "Jeeter called to say we'd been locked out of the basement again, so we called rehearsal off."

"Yeah," they all mumbled, looking down at their shoes. Then one of them said something about being made late now and getting locked out again. She singled Scoop out, certain it was he trying to rush things.

"That's where we're going now," he said, looking straight in her teeth.

"To rehearsal? That's where you're going? You're still a quintet, the five of you?"

Jeeter was counting each of them with his chin, not sure what she was driving at.

"We got somebody else," Scoop said, knowing. He rocked back on his heels.

"Somebody else. You got somebody else." She looked at each of the boys and they all hugged their bags more closely, except Flyboy, who held his away from his clothes.

"Yeah," Scoop said, like he was picking a fight, "we got somebody else."

"But he's not as good as Sonny, though," Jeeter said quickly. "He don't even play a little bit of guitar."

"Yeah," they all said, shifting their weight from one foot to the other.

"He sings good, though," Scoop said. "Real good." Nobody echoed this.

She fixed on Scoop. What kind of name was that anyway? Did it mean he was an ass grabber? He liked to punch, but they didn't call him KO, they called him Scoop. And before that he was called something else, Kofi had told her. A kid with aliases. She moved in on him, thinking over what B. J. had said in the Busy Bee Cafe. She'd tossed down a packet of photos on the counter and asked Zala point blank, "Sonny a faggot?" Then asked if he knew the punks who hung around the Greyhound terminal or the bars she referred to as "S&M meat markets." Scoop was backing away.

"We ain't seen'm since then." Scoop's voice was suddenly whiny. "We told Mr. Spencer that the time he came looking with his pistol."

"What do they call you at home?" she hissed, and Scoop jumped back, hitting against a parked car in the lot. "How many names have you got?"

"Say, Miz Spencer," Bestor said. "We don't know anything, I swear. We'd tell you if we did. We just don't know where Sonny went to."

She turned around and looked at him. "Sunday, I told you."

"Ma'am?" He leaned his face forward but kept his feet planted where they were.

"Sunday's his birthday."

"Yeah?" Jeeter was interested.

"You think he'll be home by then?" Flyboy asked.

"Hope so. What do you think?"

They looked at each other, then looked at the ground. Flyboy did a quarter-turn and watched traffic along Simpson Road.

"If you ask me," Scoop said, "you oughta go see that newspaper joker."

"Mr. Murray?"

Flyboy arched an eyebrow and stared hard at Scoop. "Man, that's really outside," he said, leaning hard on the words, then jerking his shoulder against Scoop, nearly knocking him into Zala.

"Mr. Murray's all right," Jeeter said, stepping between them again. "He's just old and kinda crankety."

"Murray," she said.

"Say, Miz Spencer. We're looking too. We're asking around. He was our friend."

"Don't say that. Don't say 'was' to me."

Bestor stepped back and mumbled something, then pointed his bag toward a telephone pole on Simpson. "I only meant we're really looking." She followed his gaze, then nodded when she recognized the handbill tacked on the pole. Bestor tucked his package under his arm and reached for her. She almost came apart with relief till she realized he was simply pulling her out of the way of a taxi that had driven around the restaurant in search of a drive-up window.

"You all right, Miz Spencer?" Jeeter Brooks looked concerned.

Was she all right, a boy was asking, a boy menaced by creeps who cruised young boys, by drug dealers who used them dangerously, by numbers dealers who exploited their mobility and quick memory, by larceny-minded adults who had them climbing in windows or thieving from coat racks, going in men's rooms to roll homosexuals, menaced by Saturday-night juiceheads, by dogs, rats, reckless drivers, and don't-give-a-shit landlords, by leaky gas pipes and space heaters that fell over and sent curtains up, sleeping on roofs in summer with no retainer walls, crummy jobs or no jobs at all to prepare for, join the army and see the world from a body bag, student loans that kept you in debt past thirty, weirdo mothers of lost friends who stalked them, and maniacs on the loose grabbing and killing, and was she all right?

"Mrs. Spencer." Flyboy was offering his towel, but Bestor had already stuffed a napkin into her hand.

"Want us to take you home?" Jeeter piled his radio and package on top of Flyboy's and reached for her arm.

"You want us to walk you home," Flyboy asked, "or you gonna take the bus?"

The boys were patting themselves down for bus passes or change but already limbering up for a walk.

"Wait. Please."

But Bestor Brooks shook his head. Eldest boy of eight children, his gesture was the soul of economy. No, discussion over, nothing more to be done today, go home and go to bed, lady. Zala followed him out of the parking lot and the others fell in step behind her, quiet as no boys she'd ever known to be.

"Does the number 14 go downtown to Central City Park?" Her voice so light, so casual, it seemed to be coming from another time zone. She rummaged in her purse, then rummaged some more just for the there-and-now sound of it to ground her. "You all go on," she said listening to herself. "I've got to get downtown and meet the kids." She was already flashing forward to Margaret Mitchell Square, Kenti prancing along with her new library card, Kofi's nose stuck in a book about quasars, and Gloria leading them to the park, where boys her age hung out after their part-time summer jobs.

"There's no more 14 Dixie Hill bus, Mrs. Spencer. It's the 51 Simpson bus now." Flyboy had his towel draped over his arm in case she might need it.

"Does it go to Central City Park?" Such an ordinary question to be asking in the third-degree brightness of the afternoon. She heard the sentence echo as a caption, under an illustration in her Spanish text, *Preguntas y Respuestas.* What wouldn't she give to curl up inside the type and live that life: Is the book on the table? *Sí,* the book is on the table.

"It goes there after a while." Jeeter smiled when he saw her smile. He drew circles and loops in the air with his chin. "Quickest way to get there if you ain't in a hurry," he said, then laughed when she laughed.

Flyboy flagged the bus down and was the first to take her elbow. Bestor and Jeeter bumped into each other to take her other arm and help her aboard. Scoop hung back. And long after she'd chatted with the bus driver in translated Spanish text sentences, remarking how a fifty-cent fare was a sign of the city growing too big too fast, then seated herself by the window and waved adios to the boys still standing by the bus post, Scoop was standing way back where the sidewalk met the dirt, his back up against a wall of green leaves.

The young woman across the aisle had a handmade loom propped against the seat in front of her. She had reinforced a nine-by-eleven picture frame, then set nails in on four sides and strung her warp. Zala found it soothing to watch her send the smooth boat of a bobbin through the twine, drawing aquamarine yarn across the frame. Several small balls of colored yarn were in the woman's lap, together with a fork for tamping and delicate, filigree scissors for clipping. From time to time she worked in an inch or two of a contrasting color, plucking the threads with her fingertips. Slowly, Zala relaxed into the rhythm of the woman's weaving, her own fingers working in her lap in concord. When the bus braked suddenly for a cyclist, the woman looked over at Zala and they smiled. The ancient smile that weaving women secretively exchange in a country, Zala imagined, that once burned spinsters as witches. Burned at the stake. Zala leaned her head against the window. Burnt on the altar. She closed her eyes and begged for mercy. But there they were, the children, burnt offerings.

Abraham piling the kindling on Ike, whom he's promised to God. The good fairy arriving to save the day slips Abe a ram. Abe agrees. To save face in front of all that goodness, no doubt, same fairy from the drama of Hagar and Ish, the baby killed off by hunger, thirst, and over-exposure revived. Abe, in a sleight-of-hand, substitutes the ram for his son. Does he think his God is myopic? . . . Dusk, the sun going down on a field of carnage. With God's help Colonel Jephthah has smote a mighty army of enemies and so has promised to burn up in thank-you the first thing he lays his eyes on back at the ranch. At home, the household's excited with the news of victory. The lovely daughter dons her high holiday threads, puts flowers in her hair, a trimbal in her hand, and dances down the road to meet Daddy. Jeb lays his eyes on his daughter's loveliness and rends his clothes. "Alas, my daughter—what you have done to me!" Blood in his eye, he can't read the fine-print escape clause the way Abe did. Besides, she's asking for it.

The barrier was down at the railroad tracks, the bell clanging, the light a twitching red eye. As a schoolgirl Zala had tried to wade through the Old Testament without offending her teachers with her real thoughts; eager to be a good girl, she usually came up with the official version. But there were current voices now in her head: Mattie talking about the children's bodies laid out just so and expounding her cult theory, Paulette talking surgical sutures, and laboratory diabolics reminding anyone in earshot that the Atlanta-based Center for Disease Control had monitored the Tuskegee Experiment, using Black male subjects from the thirties to the seventies, Spence pounding his fist in his palm and talking Klan. Zala, gazing out of the window, could believe the whole city was made up of covens and klaverns and demons with scalpels. Burnt offerings were everywhere she looked. A trash heap on fire was a funeral pyre. Even a moldering blanket in the weeds past the cinder patch looked like it would burst into flames if she stared hard enough.

Clang-a-lang, clang-a-lang. Send them out that we might know them. Bam-a-lam. Give us the strangers that we all might know them. Bam-a-lam, bam-a-lam. Send the men out that we might know them. The mob in Sodom demanding that Lot turn over his male guests to be fucked.

Her minister fed her gore when she needed solace. No balm in Gilead for you, sister. What was she being punished for?

The hiss of the back door opening pulled her straight up in her seat. Passengers who'd glimpsed the length of the train passing preferred to get out and walk. Zala stared into the weeded lot and forced the dead bodies back into the shape of trash heaps. If worse came to worse, would she ever be able to see things as they were? Did she have the capacity to go on slogging through the days up to her hips in ice the way the others did, telling their story over and over, never quit of it, opening their veins to police, reporters, the caller from the obit section, the curious, the sympathetic, over and over, bleeding into each other's wounds, nursing mothers hearing it, turning away fearful of panic in their milk, over and over, throats rasped with the telling and hope that someone hearing would avenge the bones or at least bring the thing to a halt? And what kept her on her feet? The dark root of a scream coiled in her pit, draining her dry till she thought she would split open.

"Here, take it." The couple in the seat ahead were waving a tissue. They whispered quietly so as not to embarrass her further, all alone on the seat weeping, head at an odd angle.

The train picked up speed and rumbled past: flatcars, boxcars, double deckers carrying jeeps, yellow cars marked GRAIN, aluminum canisters marked PROPANE, sweaty refrigerator cars dripping in the cinder bed along the ties. The bus shook, the bell clanged, the light was a mad red eye. Several cars pulled out from behind the bus and U-turned for another route. More passengers got up, covering their exit with small talk. They jumped down into the gravel and cut through the ragweed. She searched the faces going by for someone who once knew Sonny. Children were playing in the high grass, decapitating puffballs with dry branches that withered in their hands.

Where would Sonny run to, running away? She pictured him hitching a ride to Epps, Alabama, and hiding out in Mama Lovey's bee colony. Stowing away in the restroom of a Trailways bound for Brunswick, Georgia, where the crazy Rawls relatives whooped it up but always held even the elders' rockers quiet if Sonny was in the mood to enact the tale behind his name. She saw him on the airfield running close to the ground on the runway, then, while the loaders' backs were turned, secreting himself in the baggage compartment of a jumbo jet on its way to New York. He and Aunt Myrtle would take to each other right away, her aunt the first relative to lay eyes on the newborn. They'd hang out together while Uncle Paul was on the road with the band. Uncle Paul would take to him too, encourage him to master the guitar instead of beating on it. But they would call. So would Mama Lovey and the Rawlses. Besides, Sonny was not adventurous stupid. She dabbed at her face with the shredded tissue and sank back down in her seat.

She had never thought much of Central City Park, a five-acre plot in the lap of the banking district. A few sweetgums, myrtle, and lindens, planted in two-inch-deep soil spread over the rubble of old buildings, looked temporary, makeshift. No benches, no band shell, no play-ground for children, it seemed designed for strolling through at lunchtime, for looking at while waiting for the bus, for glancing down on from a ten-story window while placing a file in a drawer and taking a daydreamy break. But she was glad that she'd come. The park was flooded with sunshine, and it was unusually crowded. There'd been a noontime jazz concert. Musicians were rolling big drum cases to vans at the curb. A white girl with headphones around her neck skated past and Zala caught a bit of Olivia Newton-John: "You have to believe we are magic / Don't let your aim ever stray." Zala smiled to herself and looked around for Gloria and the kids as the crowd thinned out.

Brothers in cufies and sisters in geles, merchants of jewelry, books, incense, fruit, bean pies, trying to create an African bazaar at MARTA's Five Points, had been dispersed by the police, she heard them saying as they lugged their wares past the park. A white couple with sheaves of newspapers slung over their arms stopped several merchants and sold a few papers, then attempted to engage people at the bus stops in con-versation about the headlines. As usual, Zala noted, people were cour-teous, attentive even when clearly not interested. Pretty sisters in back-out dresses sat on the low brick wall that bordered the park laugh-ing and talking. An intense middle-aged man with a receding hairline strode up and down thumping his Bible and haranguing the people on the wall; he and the radical newsdealers crossing each other's path nodded politely. Behind the pretty sisters, two brothers and an Asian companion admired the back-out dresses while doing slow-motion martial-arts moves on the green. Near them a circle of white youths strummed guitars and combed their hair, one girl in a prairie dress flinging a Frisbee for a dog to fetch. It was clear that Gloria and the kids were not there yet, so Zala was hunting instead for the Bureau of Cul-tural Affairs chief when she noticed several workers winding cable were wearing T-shirts she'd designed for the bureau last year. Maybe there was time to submit designs for the up coming Third World Film Festi-val. The curly-haired woman she'd thought was Shirley Franklin turned out to bear no resemblance at all close-up—heavier, darker, an older woman with big, round electric-blue glasses. They smiled and went past each other as a few pigeons, flustered by the unusual number of people milling about, flew up over their heads to perch on the ledge of the First Georgia Bank.

Zala drifted over by the waterfall fountain. Two boys on the top steps were daring each other to walk the water. Below, musicians snapped horn cases shut and slid cymbals into chamois cloth bags. She looked around again for her T-shirts, remembering that she was on the screening committee but hadn't been notified yet by the film festival coordinator. She saw again the woman in the blue owl glasses smiling slyly at her about a group of businessmen standing between them. The sister in her African print dress and sandals, carrying a straw tote bag, had the kind of style that would prompt Mama Lovey on visits to say, "Is she a friend of yours, baby?" then admire the hair and sniff at Zala's big bush, muttering, "Who ya gonna eat today, Wamba?" The businessmen were a self-consciously integrated group, they talked overloud and worked hard at laughing; each carried his jacket hooked on one finger and slung over the shoulder exactly like the models on the glossy Atlanta brochures: City Too Busy to Hate.

The summer before, she and Spence used to meet in the park for brown-bag lunches between her classes at Georgia State. They'd reminisce about picnics at real parks—Mozley and Adams on the south side, Piedmont in the northeast, especially during arts festival time, lounging on blankets, listening to jazz while the kids darted back and forth from the African Village the Neighborhood Art Center set up every year, reporting how many of Zala's halters, macramé hangings, tapestries, and weavings had been sold. Then, later, Kenti worn out and asleep in her lap, Kofi leaning against Spence the way old folks do claiming they're resting their eyes, Sonny would ask for Spence's whittle knife to turn a tree branch into a royal staff. Then he'd entertain them and other families on blankets nearby with the story of Sundiata the Bowman, pulling on the staff now a great bow and cueing Kofi when to keel over clutching his chest.

"Wake up, Africans!"

Zala spun around, knocked out of her reverie by the thunderous voice of a dark-skinned, bumpy-faced brother in blue seersucker overalls and knitted cap. He was standing on the low perimeter wall jamming the black-red-and-green into the dirt behind him. Several people got off the wall and boarded the number 23 Oglethorpe. The sister in the owl glasses sat down and pulled a tape recorder from her straw tote.

"People, what are we pretending not to know today?" He smiled a glorious smile and a group of college students from the number 3

Auburn moved into the park and sat down on the walk by the owl-glasses sister's feet.

"I say, what are we pretending not to know today, African people? The U.S. government is up to no good in Grenada. They're sending in-filtrators into Jamaica to bust up the trade union movement. They're down there in Miami training death squadrons for South American fas-cists. Can you hear me?" He straightened his cap. The martial-arts trio, moving like taffy, came closer and the radical newsdealers came in from the sidewalk. The Bible man wheeled around and scowled at the speaker. Two old-timers remarked that Jesus was one thing, but bring-ing politics into the park, hmmph. They shoved over for Zala to sit down between them.

"The Klan was barely beaten back in Dominica, good people. You know they're consolidating their international network. And every-where they forge a link with other pig-dogs, it's bloody murder for the people. They've got their eye on Guatamala now. So wake up!"

The old gent on her left nudged her. "Only one kinda killing 'poze to talk about in the financial district." His shoulders shook up and down as he chuckled.

"Are we sleepwalking Africans or what? People, the poultry work-ers in Laurel, Mississippi, need our support. The textile workers at J. P. Stevens could use a hand. Folks in Liberty City in Miami are calling us. And you know Central America's the next Southeast Asia. Don't let the state force-feed you knockout drops, Africans. *Aaaaafrrriicaa-aannzzzzz!*"

"What about Wrightsville?" one of the students said, smoothing down her Clark College sweatshirt while her friend slapped her shoul-der at her boldness.

"That's right. Wrightsville. Thank you, sister. People, the folks in Wrightsville shouldn't have to face the fight alone. And the chemical workers in—"

"Aw, shut up all that noise!" A flashily dressed dude was bopping through the park, shifting a toothpick from one side of his mouth to the other. He glanced over his shoulder at the speaker and tugged at the brim of his polished straw white as he disappeared.

"He's giving that toothpick a natural fit," the speaker said, hands on his hips, shaking his head at the man, dimples puckering. "But is his mind in gear?"

"Teach!" one of the Morris Brown students said.

"Shiiiit," came the dude's voice, carrying all the way from Park Place.

The pretty sisters on the wall got up, pulled their dresses from the back of their thighs, and stretched. "One monkey don't stop no show," someone yelled to discourage their leaving. The pretty sisters sauntered into the park, but others left the wall to wait for their buses at the curb. A couple and their two children, in four identical white caps with their names stitched on the brims, strolled into the park to see what was going on. The husband tugged his wife's arm, and she in turn pinched the children. They all stopped to listen.

"Hear me, Africans," the speaker was saying. "While the U.S. government is hogging the airwaves murder-mouthing Khomeini, big business has taken this country hostage again."

"Well, it's not my government," one of the students said petulantly.

"Oh yes it is," Speaker and Bible Man said in unison, then nodded to each other.

"Now, that's the truth," the old gent on Zala's right said. "America's my home and I'm proud of it." He leaned over to see if his buddy on her left wanted to argue.

"We got a stake in this place," Bible Man said loudly, cords rising where his hair receded. "Make no mistake. The white man tief it from the red man, den he tief us from the homeland, but all o' we got a stake in this place." He rapped the Good Book.

"We can't go to sleep and act like none of this is our business," Speaker said. "Things ain't shaping up so hot for the Tchula Seven or the Pickens County Two. What's that? you say—what's the Tchula Seven? An exact replay of the showdown that took place right here in Atlanta not so long ago. You were there," he said, pointing toward the old-timers around Zala. "Some of you were there," he said to the students sitting cross-legged below him. "When Maynard demoted Inman by creating a new post, what did the police chief do? Called in the SWAT team to hold *his* department and defy the mayor the *people* elected. History's repeating itself down there in Mississippi, good people. The ex-sheriff and his boys are trying to put Mayor Carthan and the whole City Hall staff under arrest, and to hell with the voters, to hell with the law."

"Whatchusay!" the old-timer on Zala's right growled.

"And the Pickens County Two?" one of the newsdealers shouted, holding up a copy of her paper that carried the story.

"Talking about the courageous women in Aliceville, Alabama, good people. Miz Maggie Bozeman and Miz Julia Wilder. Can I speak on it? Do I have your permission?"

"Tell it," Bible Man ordered. "Then hang down de phone."

"Talking about some serious voter-registration workers. Talking about little Miz Julia, who registered two hundred voters in Pickens County. How many, you say? Said two hundred voters, and in one day and on foot. And how old is Miz Julia? She's seventy. Hear me?"

"Whatchusay!" The old-timer slapped his leg a few times.

"But the good ole boys want to put Miz Julia and Miz Maggie in prison. Say they committed a crime registering all them voters. Say they committed voter fraud." Speaker paused for the groans and *tsk-tsks* to subside. "Five years of hard labor in Teitweiler Prison—that's what they want to give them righteous African women."

"We gonna put up widit?" Bible Man was challenging the gathering.

"No sir, nosiree," the old gent on Zala's right said.

"That's Alabama," the woman with her name stitched on her cap said. Her younger child fidgeted. The woman thumped the girl's shoulder and continued, "And this is Atlanta." It was apparent that she wanted to leave, having spoken.

"Now, that's an ignorant ole gal." The gent on Zala's left poked her. "Pure blind ignorant."

The man with his name on his cap seemed more disapproving of Bible Man's support of the speaker than the chuckler's remark about his wife. He scowled. His wife clung to his arm. He scowled some more. The son and daughter looked uncomfortable.

"Tell me we aren't a cosmopolitan people!" Speaker shouted. "Tell me we aren't one big family with kinfolks scattered all over the world. Mississippi, Grenada, Alabama, Soweto, Brooklyn, St. Ann's Parish, Brixton, Bahia, Salvador, Christiansted, Mobile, Chattanooga—" he was breathless. "Charleston, Frogmore, Mosquito Island, Kingston, Robbins Island, Parchman Farm Prison, the projects, ya mudder's kitchen, Catfish Row. Whatchu think?"

Bible Man beamed an angry eye around the crowd. "No fairyland place somewhere. Gotta fight the good fight." He stomped the ground and shook the Good Book.

"And people, good people, right here in Atlanta, in 'Lovely Atlanta,' someone is killing our most treasured resource, our most precious people, our future—our children."

The two gents grabbed Zala's hands when she slipped and scraped her legs on the brick wall. They patted her hands and urged her to sit back down. There was a lot of commotion in the park, but all she was aware of was the plane overhead streaking something illegibly in the blue. On the ledge of the Trust Company Bank she saw a woman with a wild look brandishing a crowbar. The woman threw back her head and shrieked rockets across the park.

"Did you hear what I said, Africans?" Speaker looked up and waited for the plane to roar past. "Thirteen or more children kidnapped, eight of them murdered. With our permission? With our consent?" He pivoted slowly, then crouched suddenly in a movement so swift, so percussive, several people close by recoiled. His hand shot out toward the sidewalk and people turned. Two white policemen were approaching the park with Burger King bags. They moved into the orbit of Speaker's churning finger.

"And what are the police doing about it? Or, better yet, what are they *not* doing?"

The two patrolmen exchanged a look, glanced around the park, then at their bags soaking through. The newsdealers moved in behind them. The martial-arts trio closed around Speaker. The students spread out on the walk, hemming in both the policemen and the businessmen, now hugging their jackets and loosening their collars. The family in stitched caps looked around at the gathering.

"That's not a rhetorical question," Speaker said, still crouched. "What haven't the police been up to?"

The shorter cop opened his mouth to say something but didn't. The taller shoved through the students and ordered the strummers in prairie clothes to get off the grass.

"Where I come from, we always know who kills young Bloods," Speaker said over the head of the short cop. "They shoot 'em in the back for fleeing the scene of the crime, though there's been no crime till that moment. But they shoot 'em in the back to, uh, arrest them. Or they shoot 'em in the chest because they swore they saw the flash of a knife, though there's been no knife except the one in a blue pocket for planting. But they shoot 'em in the chest in, uh, self-defense. Or the young Blood dies of, uh, complications on the way to the precinct. Or the Blood, uh, hangs himself in his cell out of, uh, despair."

The tall cop was coming around behind Speaker, trying to break through the martial-arts trio. They stood like pyramids, arms bulged across their chests, mouths in an O, breathing in and out, rippling muscles through their clingy polos. A cup of soda dropped through the bottom of one cop's bag. The dog bounded over and caught it, then raced over to his mistress. But nobody cheered. The old gent on Zala's right let go of her hand and stood up.

"Whoa time," he said, hitching up his pants with his elbows. "That kind of talk is for the old days." He turned to the businessmen who were trying to find an exit through the crowd.

"Old days?" Speaker whipped out a newspaper from his back pocket and snapped it open. "Latest issue of the *Thunderbolt,* good people." As he pivoted, showing the front page, Owl Woman handed him another paper, the *Torch.* "Note the photo at the top of *Thunderbolt.* African people superimposed on the bodies of apes. Note the bottom-half photo— our boys in blue palling around with the good ole boys in white sheets. And look here—note this 'survivalist' camp in the woods. Do you recognize faces on the targets?"

"Let's break it up," the tall cop ordered. The short cop had his hand on his holster. "Let's move it. Move it." A few people got up and discussed the Black leaders they recognized on the bull's-eyes. Others scrambled for buses. The businessmen squeezed behind the old-timer and hailed two cabs at the curb. Bible Man was urging Speaker to continue when the short cop told Speaker to get off the wall, he was defacing public property.

"Oh, wow," the boy with his name on his cap said. The cop turned red. The boy's father nudged the boy's mother and she thumped the son's shoulder.

"Where are his manners?" the reddened cop said, trying to appeal to the boy's mother and other females. "Wearing his hat in the presence of ladies."

Owl Woman smiled as Speaker slowly peeled the knit cap from his head. Heavy ropes of dreads sprang alive and tumbled down around his shoulders. Zala leaned forward, the old gent gripping her elbow.

"Whoa time," Old-Timer bellowed over the cheers. "You keep saying where you come from this and where you come from that, but you don't say where you come from, fella."

"The Black community, father—the Black community."

One of the martial-arts trio pulled up the liberation flag and held it high. There was more cheering. Only Owl Woman showed an interest in what Old-Timer was going to say next; she gave him the mike. Others had turned toward the street, where a patrol car was pulling up between two buses whose drivers were waiting to see how things would work out.

"No, sir," Old-Timer said, nonplussed to discover that the mike didn't throw his voice. "That's talk for the old days," nonplussed again to discover the businessmen he then turned to for support were gone. "Sure, sure, there are still gangs running the street getting themselves in trouble, but these kids you say were what?"

"Lynched." Speaker's lips were curled back, his gums showing. There was a hush. Then his teeth parted a little and his tongue looked swollen. "Noose South, father, Noose South."

The gent gripped Zala's hand in his for a moment, then got up and released it. He pressed through the people and tugged on his friend's belt and walked him away just as two new cops came into the park. Their arrival encouraged the other two cops to swagger, the short one with his hand on his holster, the other barking commands. The man with his name on a cap motioned his family toward the flowerbed gap in the wall, pushing his son along, who continued to watch over his shoulder. Taking their sweet time, the students got up and brushed off their clothes. Now what would happen? Zala got up. Would authority be challenged, the right to assembly recited, or would the police just burn them all? A god who beat up on his people and threw mega-tantrums at the first sign of disobedience gave bullies the right. She looked up at the ledge of the First Georgia Bank wondering how to call the wild woman down and smuggle her out of the park with the sheep.

Tuesday, September 9, 1980

"Before we go any further, Spencer, let me review." Mac planted his elbow on the desk pad and broke open a fresh box of paper clips. "I don't understand why the date of the attack on the mechanic is important. But I do see the significance of the station's location. I recall that on the map outlining the death route there were eight or nine points in the Memorial Drive area, and so—please," he said when Spence leaned forward as though to interrupt. "We've both been so distracted, I'm not sure we're listening to each other or even to ourselves."

Mac hooked several clips together and tried to resume his train of thought. "I think I've lost my third point. In any case, let me jump right to my main objection, if you don't mind my playing devil's advocate for a minute. You keep offering assumptions as though they were implications. But in terms of hard evidence, what have you got actually? As for the list . . . well . . ." He twirled the loop of clips around his finger.

"Look, I don't pretend to be an expert at detection, Mac. But I've read enough mystery novels to know that a paramount principle of investigation is, don't let your theorizing get too far ahead of the physical evidence. The Task Force are deliberately ignoring evidence in favor of theorizing without it. They've put together a composite profile of the victims while at the same time they're (a) dismissing eyewitnesses; (b) letting suspects go; (c) refusing to look at two-thirds of the cases; (d) not listening to the parents' versions of what they think is going on; (e) rejecting the links that both the STOP investigators and the STOP members have noted. Also . . ." Spence held on to his pinky finger, straining after more points to argue with. He found himself staring blankly at the calluses on his hand.

"Why not apply that principle to yourself, Spencer. You've reached conclusions based on what?—hearsay, hunch, anecdotal data. Question: Did the mechanic identify his attackers as policemen, or is that one of your 'contributions'? Now, you've arrived at the following conclusions, if I've heard you correctly: one, the three white men are police officers; two, these same officers have managed to divert crucial files to offices other than the special investigative team's; three, they have otherwise interfered with the investigation because, four, they seek to cover up their involvement in kidnap and murder. Is that right?" Mac pleaded for patience with one hand and mumbled an apology. With the other hand, he picked up the ringing phone. "She'll be back in a sec," he said for the third time, meaning his secretary.

Spence picked at his calluses and mentally drew a frame around the phone, labeling it "The Telephone as an Instrument of Torture."

He'd gone to pick Zala up at the screening room yesterday. Arriving early, he'd sat in the back, his mind elsewhere, not immediately registering what he was seeing. He thought he was looking at ordinary, everyday objects—a telephone, a radio, a set of jumper cables on a tabletop. When a cattle prod and a water hose were introduced, they pricked his memory. He changed his seat, moving closer to the projector and the sound, gripping the armrests when the tortures began, horror made mundane by the innocuous ordinariness of shirtsleeves, tweezers, soda bottles, eyedroppers, file cabinets, time clocks, cigarette lighters, saws. South American montage growing out of a sandwich on waxed paper next to a salary check—boots, tires growling in driveway gravel, thousands rounded up and detained in a stadium. The junta, hit lists, government by torture. The bullet-ridden corpse of Che Guevara; the attacks on the Tupermaro in Uruguay; the overthrow of Allende; the forced sterilization of Andean laborers; the wholesale slaughter of the Quiche Indians in Guatemala; Argentine Jewry one percent of the population, twenty percent of the disappeared. Strikers in U.S. companies in Central and South America disappearing. The Women of the Disappeared petitioning the government, appealing to the populace. Amnesty International's statistics. Floggings, chemical zombification, arrests and executions without trial. The interrogated bound and gagged, suspended from poles, and beaten. Cables plugged into crank-up radios. Jumper-cable pinchers attached to nipples. Electric prods slid past the penis to the anus, then shoved. The utter silence in the

screening room when the leader went white, flickering in its sprockets. . . . Then the fuzzy color of shaky camera shots: the streets of
Greensboro, North Carolina, U.S. of A. An anti-Klan demonstration,
an interracial gathering. Gun-toting whites leaping from cars and
trucks, a freeze shot of the FBI informant in the lead. Dressed in hunter
plaid and heavy boots, the white men spring open the trunks of cars for
heavy-duty weapons, taking aim in the direction of the camera. "Com-
mie!" "Nigger!" "Kike!" A second camera telephotos the men firing.
Falling bodies and pandemonium. Clear, interior close-ups of the killers
and their attorneys talking calmly into the lens. Patriotic duty. Ridding
God's country of the dangerous and the inferior. A voice over the rolling
credits brings the audience up to date: defendants acquitted, plaintiffs
appealing to a higher court, FBI disavows the involvement of its agent.
Lungs starved in the screening room had gasped for air.

"Sorry," Mac said, taking up the paper clips again. "You were about
to tell me why the date of the attack on the mechanic is significant. One
second," he said before Spence could pull himself back to the present.
"I've got to get these gifts wrapped so I can stop thinking about them
and give you my undivided attention." Mac swiveled his chair around
to face the bookcases, then got up and flung the lower cabinet doors
open. "In late July, you say?" He slid out a tray of scissors, tape, and
twine. "You were saying?"

Spence massaged his temples. "Late July," he mumbled. "Months
after the Dewey Baugus case was closed and pretty much forgotten."

"So?" Mac pulled on the tape without much success. He sank down
in his chair and looked attentive.

"July, Mac. Just after the families staged the sit-in and forced the
authorities to set up the Task Force."

"Meaning?"

"Why beat Gaston up then? Not for vengeance, not so many
months after the Baugus trial. Hell, that makes no sense at that late
date."

"You're operating on the premise that acts of that nature are sensible? Tell me about it," Mac said, rocking in his chair the way he always
did when he'd mouthed a phrase he thought currently hip.

"The beating was to silence Gaston in the future, not to punish him
for the past. It was a warning, a threat."

"He knows something, in other words? Tell me, are you any good at wrapping? I'm all thumbs."

"He may not realize how much he knows. But as the children's case breaks . . ." Spence studied the counselor's face. Usually it was placid, encouraging, the middle-aged lines counterbalanced by the boyish features; now his brows looked like tormented caterpillars, his mouth a gash in his face. "So I'm sticking close to the mechanic," Spence said.

Mac nodded, then ran his hand over his face. The phone rang again and he sighed, "Sorry," though he looked relieved. As he answered he swiveled his chair toward the window.

Spence concentrated on his calluses, but out of the corner of his eye he could still see the carton on the floor by Mac's desk. Only an edge of pale tissue paper was in his field of vision, but it bothered him anyway. Earlier, the first time the phone had interrupted their conversation, he'd had the urge to spring from his chair and tear into the box, for he'd spotted, beneath the throbbing reds and greens of a grasshopper kite and the bright orange shellac of a bamboo umbrella, a mask face down in the bottom of the box. It took all he had to keep himself in the chair, trying to break down the impulse to spring into an orderly succession of questions: What is that churning at the pit of your stomach about? And what makes you think the box has a false bottom? Why is the mask disturbing? What the hell is the matter with you? Now, pale as the tiny corner of tissue paper was, it was splitting his head open with the same incessant throbbing he'd left the screening room with, gotten up from bed with, only a fragment of the troubling dream lingering: walking across a prison yard under the eye of the tower guards who might shoot out of boredom. Back toward the lockup, the strip search, the guards instructing him to bend over and spread his cheeks, then massage his hair to show he carried no weapons in his bush, but mostly to spread the funk in his hair, the guards laughing as he moved into the corridor, the gates slam-locked behind him.

"This will only take a minute," Mac assured him, swiveling around, one hand over the receiver. Spence stopped picking his calluses when he realized Mac was watching him. When he looked up, Mac self-consciously looped the necklace of clips around the base of a Lucite cube of photographs. Mac's children looked out at Spence, their smiles frozen in the block.

Speechless, he and Zala had gone from the screening room to pick up Kenti and Kofi. A boy's face seemed to fill the frame of the windshield. A husband had broken while watching his wife being questioned. A mother had passed out when her children were ushered into the room by the interrogators. A ten-year-old boy was forced to watch his mother being hoisted up to the ceiling on a pole, forced to watch, forced to smile, prodded whenever his face muscles sagged or he attempted to look away or drop his eyes.

When they reached the schoolyard, Zala had jumped out while the car was still moving, grabbed the children, embraced them stiffly, her hands balled and turned out at the wrists. When they thought themselves released from her grip and headed for the limo, she'd grabbed them again. He'd had to step in, afraid to touch her. . . . At the house, he brushed up against her and both of them winced. She moved around the living room touching things but not him. She reached for pinking shears, the sewing box, and a fold of navy-blue cloth. And he'd thought, pulling himself together to deal with the present, that that was how best to deal with chaos—turn your back and get to work. He knew he couldn't stay, shouldn't be there, could best get himself together by leaving her alone and getting on with his own work, whatever that could be. Except he couldn't leave. And when the phone rang, she'd dropped the tracing chalk. They'd both backed away, staring at it on the floor until Kenti, filling her fishbowl in the kitchen, had called out, wanting to know if they'd gone deaf.

"I concede," Mac said, replacing the phone in its cradle, "that it's premature for the investigators to establish a profile of the victims. As you say, it violates a scientific principle known even to readers of pulp. It does set limits. Dangerous, I suppose, most especially if, as you say, there are people on the scene in a position to gum up the works. But I'm not convinced that your procedure is a whit more sound, though of course I understand why you're forcing the issue." He lowered his eyes and looked uncomfortable for having voiced his doubts. He knuckled his lower lip and coughed.

"It's not a matter of early or late, Mac. It's not a matter of 'premature' or 'unscientific.' Don't *you* think it's suspicious? Can't you see the possibility of what I'm proposing, or is it beyond you to imagine that police could be involved in kidnapping and murder?"

Mac leaned over and gathered up the tissue paper and gifts. "I can understand why you insist on viewing things that way," he said over the cover of the carton. "Too garish?" he laughed when he saw Spence frown at the articles. "My wife's on a Fulbright. This papier-mâché mobile is from Bhutan, I think. Gifts for our girls. My wife hates to wrap worse than I do." When Spence didn't answer, he returned to the main topic. "Have you talked all this over with the detectives working with the parents' organization?" He fastened the grasshopper to the lampshade rim, its wire talons puncturing the cellophaned silk.

"I thought it was a kite," Spence said.

"Kite?" Mac examined the grasshopper. "From Indonesia, I think." He opened and closed the umbrella a few times, then took out the mask and set it face-up by the lamp. "And this is from Japan, if I'm not mistaken."

"I thought sure it was a kite," Spence said again, then looked at the mask, the empty eyes, the expressionless face.

Mac settled back in his chair. "It reminds you of something?" He waited. "An army helicopter, perhaps?" He placed two fingers on the edge of the desk pad as if marking off the lengths of tape to be cut for the packaging. "What is it?" Mac listened, thinking Spence was hearing footsteps in the outer office, the secretary returned. He stared at the grasshopper that wasn't a kite, hoping to see whatever it was that had arrested Spence's attention. "Ghosts?" Mac looked from his top drawer, where he kept aspirin, to the Lucite cube, which Spence was now turning around on his desk.

"My wife, Charlotte," Mac said, wondering what Spence was seeing.

Spence was seeing the Women of the Disappeared. Widows in veils, mothers in drab dresses, sisters and aunts and cousins chalking ghosts on government buildings, block-printing the names and dates of loved ones dragged from schools, from jobs, spirited away in the dead of night. Silent processions in the Greensboro public square. Chile, Colombia, Argentina, Brazil, Uruguay. The still-unaccounted-for in Soweto township. The four films of yesterday afternoon merging into one.

"Spencer? You're not equipped to maintain round-the-clock surveillance of either the mechanic or his attackers, to say nothing of keeping track of every police officer on the force. What are you going to do? And how can I help?" Mac reached in the drawer for the bottle of aspirin and set it down by the mask Spence was staring at. "I gather Teodescu's involved in this now and intends to infiltrate an ultra-right group. Do

you think that's wise?" He searched in the drawer, waiting for a response. "I gather you're convinced that there's a connection between the
attack and your son. I don't suppose I can talk you out of that." His eyebrows made it a question.

"You don't think there's a connection?"

"What I think isn't important, is it?"

"I'd like to hear it. But please don't—" Spence added when Mac
plopped a pad on the desk—"please don't ask me if I'm sleeping well or
if I want to see someone about having my subscription renewed."

"I think you mean 'prescription refilled.' "

"You think I'm the villain in the piece, or my wife is."

"That's not the term I would've used. I'd like to see your wife, by
the way. How's she holding up?"

Spence was seeing his wife: picking up the chalk, the phone still
ringing, walking to the door without her bag, her keys, or her eyes focused. Where had she been going with the chalk, looking like a zom-
bie, a duppy, a jumby? He'd knocked over the sewing box to break the
spell. The phone had stopped ringing. She'd returned to the table and
cut something wide. Wing sleeves for the minister, he'd thought, but
navy blue? And she hadn't been to church, choir rehearsals, or fellowship in weeks.

"Of course," Mac was saying into the phone, two lights on the panel
blinking. "Put him through. Thank God she's back," he muttered to
Spence, meaning his secretary. "Please wait, Spencer." He moved the
bottle of aspirin within Spence's reach, but Spence had already turned,
heading for the door.

"Call you later, Max."

"Mac." He replaced the bottle in the drawer and took the call.

Thursday, September 18, 1980

A fluorescent light over the nurses' station was sputtering and buzzing, getting on the nerves of the nurse Paulette had handed a record to. Both irritated, they spoke curtly to each other. Then Paulette turned on Zala.

"Routine, my ass! Go sit down somewhere and get out of my face."

But when Zala headed for the elevator, Paulette came up behind her. "I've got to answer this page, Zala, but I'll be right back. We'll have coffee and you can run it by me again."

Zala hung on to a vacant gurney someone had wheeled off the elevator. How could she concentrate and convince herself all over again that the test had been routine?

She listened to the disembodied voice paging staff. Any minute she would hear, "Young amnesia victim identified. Will Mrs. Spencer please report to pediatrics." A boy can't stay lost forever. She'd said just that over breakfast a few days ago, aimlessly turning pages of a fly-specked newspaper, trying to rev up her motor. She'd blown two CETA job interviews and fall registration at Georgia State, and Simmons was making no secret of the fact that he thought her unreliable.

"Like Peter Pan, Mama?" Kenti had reached for the syrup. "Peter and the Lost Boys?"

Zala had forked another piece of French toast onto Kofi's plate and listened as Kenti chattered. Clap if you believe in Tinker Bell. Sonny a faggot? The psychological consultant to the Task Force had said, "We may be looking for a former child prodigy." Peter the adventurer who didn't want to grow up. "From a singular childhood to an unspec-tacular adulthood. Become ordinary, he seeks to recapture childhood through kidnapping and then cancel it out." She had no contribution to make to the killer profile the detective and the psychologist were discussing, only her list and the killers' route that volunteer investigator Dettlinger had worked out.

"Peter the Pansy," Kofi had snickered. Zala had had to participate in the breakfast conversation long enough to tell Kenti that her brother hadn't meant flowers and to tell Kofi he had a backward attitude. Peter the Venus Flytrap. "Any adults in the neighborhood, Mrs. Spencer, who throw wild parties, use drugs, show dirty movies?" Peter the Pied Piper. Dave was on the trail of a man, maybe a minister, who frequented playgrounds around public housing apartments, telling kids that his church was setting up camps in the summer for the musically promising. The kids tagged him the Pied Piper.

The children off to school, Zala had set her second cup of coffee down on a book review she had no intention of reading. But the black type arranged itself around the edge of her mug. A book about the father of gynecology, a man who'd used captive African women as guinea pigs, conducting surgical experiments without anesthesia, one slave woman the subject of seventeen different operations. Zala had gotten up to rinse her cup, to rinse her mouth, when the doorbell rang. And with the plausibility of dreams she greeted Paulette before she'd even opened the door. Paulette surprised but she wasn't. Though she was disappointed with the latest bulletin—that the one unidentified young John Doe patient traced through hospital services turned out to be Vietnamese. Sitting down while Zala put the kettle on again, Paulette began to read a pre-pub review of a book about the Tuskegee Study in Atlanta. "Aha," Paulette had said, ripping it out. Zala was not surprised about its being there. Daytime was being overrun by nighttime logic. All she had to do was pay attention and read the signs. Something was about to connect, she was sure.

Between customers at the shop, she had flipped through old *Jet* magazines and heard Preener say that Otis the Silent had gone into the hospital on the twenty-fifth of July. Aha. Same day as the Richard Pryor Burn TV Telethon, and same day Reverend Carroll, one of STOP's founders, had mentioned trying to do a telethon like Jerry Lewis's annual muscular dystrophy fund-raiser to raise money for an independent STOP investigation. The twenty-fifth was also midway between the disappearance of Sonny and the disappearance of Earl Lee Terrell. She wrote it down, convinced that the puzzle was coming together.

The same day B. J. had reported that an investigative unit from St.

Louis specializing in cases of sexually exploited children was assisting the Task Force, Zala had found under her soak dish an article someone had left there for her, she'd never asked who. It was about the John Wayne Gacy case in Illinois, a fuzzy photo of Gacy's yard where he'd buried his young victims in quicklime pits. And in the bathroom a customer had left a newspaper folded to an update on Vernon Jordan, gunned down in Fort Wayne, Indiana, by a sniper in May. "Special Agent Wayne G. Davis denies probe stall," the paper said. She paid attention to numbers. The day Jordan announced he'd be back on the job as National Urban League head was September 14, the day Darron Glass disappeared. All she had to do was pay attention to those connections. A force was directing her, she was sure.

"Irrational," was Delia's diagnosis. "Paranoia," said the media to Blacks pointing out connections. "No connection," the FBI said in response to Black organizations all over the country dissatisfied with lackluster probes of the Jordan sniping, other snipings, slashings, cross burnings, and attacks on Black people by assailants unknown or known to be white; an avowed racist, member of an organization calling itself Defenders of the White Seed, was wanted in several states in connection with attacks and in connection with the Jordan case too. Might he be a kidnapper and killer of children as well? Zala's notebook was bulging.

"There's no such thing as nonsense. Pay attention to these promptings," Mattie had urged, cracking a coconut open on Zala's kitchen counter and catching the milk in a saucepan, then ordering Zala to drink the milk. "It'll come clear," she'd said, soaking the remainder up on a washcloth and laying it across Zala's brow as she explained the clarifying properties of coconut. "It will come clear, if you just come clean," handing her four pieces to chew, as if "come clean" wasn't plenty to chew on.

So in place of "coincidence," she learned to say "synch occurrence" when, in the space of two hours, three and a half things echoed each other. 12:30—the Busy Bee, B. J. slapped down on the counter still another collection from the chicken porn file: glassy-eyed youths languorous against pillows, clothes open, lipstick-painted aureolas round their nipples and the head of their penises, one naked boy with one hand tugging the end of a silken scarf knotted around his neck, the other arm under his balls, a finger, perhaps, stuck up his ass. If someone could do that to children, then she could look, she had to know what Sonny

might be coming home from. 1:15—the sculptor back from a conference on the coast stopped her to show her a brochure that had been in
everyone's conference kit, a two-page booklet from the San Francisco
Visitors' Bureau containing safety precautions for out-of-towners attracted to the S&M communities in the city; a yellow marker emphasized passages concerning the lengths one could go in strangling a sex
mate for the ultimate get-off without the ultimate bump-off. 2:20—
batik class over, students scraping wax from the floor, Zala bunching
newspapers from the table, an item about a sodomy trial, youngsters
taking the stand to say the defendant had been otherwise kind, stunned
parents had thought the defendant a praiseworthy scout leader, had had
no idea of the bondage games and the sex. 2:30—Teo running in to say
that he'd missed meeting Spence because a customer at Daily's had
choked on a fishbone, and did she know where he might be, and why
was she laughing so hard, and did she want to smoke a joint, shouldn't
she try to calm down?

Convinced that there was a force steering her, placing people on her
path, setting items in her line of vision, knocking down the barrier between night dreams and daytime consciousness, Zala had pressed the
cruise control button in Dave's car that she'd borrowed and dared the
force to present itself and take over. The force took over. She removed
her foot from the pedal, at times her hands from the wheel, and glided
along will-less in the car enjoying the lascivious pleasure of surrender.
And without quite deciding to, though she'd bargained with the TF detective, she had found herself heading for the state police office.

"You're out on your feet and don't even know it, girl." Paulette
seemed to come out of nowhere, her firm hand steering Zala through
the crowded corridor of Grady. She pushed her toward a chair and went
to a bank of vending machines.

She would have to get a grip on herself. No telling what Sonny
would be like. She was scared. But then he had scared her before. He'd
grabbed Kenti once in the yard and was swinging her around by an
arm and a leg when Zala got to the window, afraid to yell *put her down*
'cause he might have; mad about something, surly, unpredictable, he'd
reached that stage she'd thought only other people's sons went through.
And a time after that when he and Kofi had pooled their allowances to
order an anatomy chart from a karate supply house. She'd been at a delicate phase in a stained-glass project and they were identifying death

spots on each other's bodies. She'd dropped her soldering iron when Sonny told Kofi that one deft slam with the heel of his hand between his nipples and it would be all over. She had shattered the glass.

"Here, it's beef bouillon. Good and hot." Paulette put the Styrofoam cup in Zala's hand. "You'd better see a lawyer, Zala." She tossed a package of peanut-butter crackers in her lap. "Routine! What did you think you were doing?"

"I thought it might help."

The TF detective and the consultant had both said it might help, so she'd agreed. She would cooperate with them if they would do likewise; if they would review all the cases and take the map seriously. But when they ushered her into the room and walked her around the industrial shelving, she knew they'd made a mistake. The detective had made a mistake. She'd made a mistake. There was a definite misunderstanding somewhere. She'd come to be hypnotized, not electrified, she'd tried to explain.

They led her to a chair, a scarred-up old library chair with wide armrests and a curved ladder-rung back. Not the brother she'd expected to see, the operator at the machine was a wispy-haired white man with skin like sidewalk. They drew down the shades and strapped her in, a band across her chest, taped buttons at her pulse points. Then they left her alone with the wispy-haired man, who would not look up from the machine, from the needles, the dials, or the praying mantis that moved across the grid paper.

"Relax, please. Do not change position in any way and simply answer the questions. Your name is Marzala Rawls Spencer?"

"Yes."

"You live with your children at 109 Thurmond Street, Southwest, Atlanta?"

"Yes."

"Your oldest child is named Sonny Spencer?"

". . . Yes." She could feel throbbing just below her left ear. The operator glanced at her wrists on the armrests, the wires curling out from the back of her hands, then straightening at the attach points on the machine.

"His name is Sundiata Spencer. We call him Sonny."

"You last saw Sonny on Saturday the nineteenth of July at approximately 10:30 a.m.?"

"Yes, that's right."

"Do you know where he is now?"

"No."

"Do you masturbate?"

"What?" He was deadpan at the controls, the metal mantis scooting across the grid. She held her breath. He would ask it again and she'd be ready.

"How old are you, Mrs. Spencer?"

"Twenty-seven."

"Do you have any idea where Sonny Spencer is?"

"No, I do not."

"Has he run away before?"

"He's never run away from home. From anything." Her throat felt swollen and raw. The back of her left hand was inflamed.

"Do you resent it if your husband has an orgasm and you do not?"

"None of your business. . . . No. . . . I don't remember."

"Please don't gnash your teeth. Relax. Do you know where your son was going when he left the home on July nineteenth?"

"I thought at the time that he'd gone to the Boys' Club four blocks away. I thought later that he might have gone to the campground. I also thought that he might have gone to his father's place on Campbellton Road." Her mouth went dry. "But I don't know for sure where he was headed." Went. "He disappeared." She looked down at the band across her chest, expecting her heart's pounding to snap it in two. "No."

"Do you suspect anyone of having kidnapped your son?"

"No. No one in particular . . . no one I can think of." She wondered if the machine could pick up her nightmares, could reach below her daytime thoughts and pull names and faces up through her pores. Everyone she knew, at one time or other, had skulked about in her nightlife with hooded eyes and dread schemes, featured as the number-one suspect.

"Does your husband whip or spank or otherwise administer corporal punishment to your children?"

". . . Last time Sonny got spanked, he was nine years old. I did the spanking. Once or twice after that, his father shook him by the arm or yelled at him a little." She could fix on nothing. Sonny was vanishing from her mind's eye. She clamped her jaws tight and fought down a hiccup.

"Relax, please, and answer the questions as simply as possible. Have you ever stolen anything, Mrs. Spencer?"

"Yes."

His eyebrows went up.

"I was pregnant with Sonny," she said, catching the operator looking at her fingers. She spread them flat on the rests. "I went into a drugstore on St. Nicholas Avenue in New York City and slipped a pack of Bit-O-Honey into my sweater."

He was studying the paper rolling across the machine. He seemed to want more.

"And light bulbs. I once stole some light bulbs. About two years ago. I had an argument with my husband and walked out to get cigarettes. I smoked then sometimes. I paid for the cigarettes but forgot I had the package of bulbs in my hand. I walked out. Nobody stopped me." She remembered standing on the corner crashing the bulbs to the ground one at a time, then grinding them into the pavement with the heel of her boot. "That's all."

"Did you have a fight with your husband this past summer?"

"No."

"Your son?"

She scrambled his earlier question around to make sense of the new one, frantic that she was taking so long. "No. We don't 'fight' with our children."

"Did your son and your boyfriend get along?"

"Who?" She felt wet under her right armpit. The pulse button seemed to be slipped down. "Sonny and my childhood buddy got along all right. They've had some disagreements sometimes. Naturally." Again he seemed to be waiting for more. Maybe he too was listening to the whir, wondering if it was the machine, the traffic outside, or her blood beating against the tape and the wires. How did he know things about her?

"Did your son and boyfriend get along?"

"Yes."

"Has your son Sonny ever stolen anything?"

"No. Well, not that I know of. . . . Yes, he once borrowed a guitar thing from the band closet. A clamp you put on the neck of the guitar to hold the strings down. He took it back the next day. His band teacher told me he put it back."

"Does Sonny use drugs?"

"Definitely not."

"Does anyone in the household or in the family use drugs?"

"No. . . . My husband was taking medication last year under VA supervision."

"And you once stole an item of candy and years later a carton of light bulbs?"

"Yes."

"Has anyone in the household or in the family ever been arrested?"

"My stepbrother was in jail once. With Martin Luther King," she added proudly.

"Did you kill your son, Mrs. Spencer?"

And there it was. Routine question in cases like this, the police said. Did you kill your child? She'd heard the parents at STOP comparing notes. Did you kill your very own child? She'd been dreading it since the moment they led her past the industrial shelves. Pull the shades. Give her the chair. Turn on the juice. Come clean, woman.

Isn't it true you were in a rage when your son challenged your authority? Isn't it a fact that you are particularly sensitive about your inability to make people take you seriously, having never been able to strike an imposing figure, having always been diminutive in stature? Isn't it true that you deliberately left the camping-trip flyer in the napkin holder where it would provoke the boy? You wanted a showdown. You'd been humiliated two nights before by your son in front of your boyfriend.

You hid across the street behind the hedges in the Robinson yard waiting for Sonny to come out. Of course he did. You knew he would. You followed him in your car to the Boys' Club. The van had gone. You then followed the boy to the bus stop. You got out of the car and confronted him. He sassed you, challenged you, made you feel ridiculous there in the street with your hands on your hips trying to make the boy mind you, the boy three inches taller, twenty pounds heavier, a mind of his own, an agenda of his own. He defied you, criticized you for two-timing his father. You lashed out and struck him. He stumbled, he fell, he hit his head on the curbstone. It was an accident, to be sure. We realize that, Mrs. Spencer. You hadn't meant for things to go that far. It's hard to raise children without a man in the house. We understand that. An accident. It happens. But you covered it up, and that is a crime.

"Zala, give me the cup."

You realized he was not breathing. You dragged his body to the car and dumped him into the backseat. You know this city well, Mrs. Spencer, and you know how to handle tools. You're an arts-and-crafts worker, you're the daughter of a handyman. You're handy, you're crafty. You knew just where to take him, knew just how to dispose of him. Come clean. You killed your child.

"Take it easy, girl."

It's not necessary to keep denying it. We know. Would you like a tissue? Would you like a blindfold, one last cigarette? Perhaps a drink of water—you seem to have a severe case of hiccups. Guilt? Guilty as charged.

Paulette was scrubbing her dress with a wad of paper towels. Zala felt two men standing over her, their lab coats so heavily starched the buttonholes were glued shut. One of them leaned down to whisper something to Paulette. She waved him away.

"Dammit, Zala, let go of the cup."

[III]

THE KEY IS IN

THE BOOT

Tuesday, October 7, 1980

S he wouldn't look. He had something to ask, but he couldn't get
her to look at him no matter where he stood. He felt lonesome.
Kenti was falling asleep between Zala's knees, and no one was talking.
And he couldn't hear the TV. He could make it louder, but then she
might fuss. And if she was angry, then he couldn't ask what he wanted
to ask.

"Ma?"

"Hmmh?"

Zala parked the comb in Kenti's hair, then dipped her head toward
the bunk lamp. He was standing right there, but she wasn't looking,
just at the lamp. He clicked it on, figuring that's what she wanted.

"It did it again, Ma." Kofi hooked his arm in the bunk ladder and
swung right in front of her. "The phone." His arm hurt. Least she could
do was look. "Ma?"

"Hmmh?"

"The phone. Just now when I put out the garbage, it rang twice,
but nobody was there." He stopped swinging when he heard the ladder
creak.

"Hmm."

Kofi dropped to the floor in a cross-legged position and drew his
shirt up over his head. He flung it down near Kenti's feet, but she was
drowsing and didn't look up. Zala was leaning way over from the bottom bed, braiding and braiding, her lap full of beads.

"Ma, do you think it's Sonny trying to call us?" He held his breath.
She was holding hers too. Then her fingers started braiding again. He
heard her tell somebody one night that she was through, that Sonny was
in charge of his own skin from now on. Who was she talking to? There
was no phone in the bathroom. Who was she yelling, at, waking him

up, loud through the wall, saying she didn't want to look at any more pictures?

"My neck hurts." Kenti's chin was in her chest now, her knees on the slide. Kofi watched how his mama's legs hugged tighter around his sister's middle. "Whatchu think? Was it Sonny like Kofi said?"

He whipped his belt out of his pants and slung it toward the closet.

"Probably a wrong number," Zala said, cutting her eye at his belt on the floor. "Gonna run your bath?" Talking to him but looking at Kenti's hair.

Kofi rolled over onto his stomach and picked at the rug. He let his feet kick against the chair by the desk, but nobody looked.

"Kofi, turn off that TV. Nobody's watching."

"Am too watching, Mama."

Kofi rolled over toward the TV and punched the belly of Kenti's cot. "You ain't watchin'. You sleepin'."

"Am not."

"I said to turn it off. I don't want you all watching that show."

"I like Gary Coleman." Kenti was whining, and it wasn't even Gary Coleman, just a scene from what was coming later on that week.

"All that program is doing is telling little boys to run away from home," Zala said. "See how they do it?" She was pointing the comb at a Mop 'n Glo commercial and not at *Diff'rent Strokes* like she thought. "Nice rich white man and nice big house with a housekeeper and such nice furniture, even got a nice little white girl to be your sister. Sooo much nicer than being in Harlem with your own people who use drugs and steal and kill and look dirty. So run away. Some nice rich white man will take you in and be your daddy. See?"

Kofi didn't say nothing. When she started talking like that it was best to be quiet. Kenti was quiet too, thinking it over. She didn't have no better sense, though, than to answer.

"You a mean mommy, Mama," Kenti said after while.

"If you don't hold still, missy, I'll show you mean. And you too, mister. And turn that TV off."

Kofi snapped off the TV. She'd been like that all week. At the meeting she stood up and told the people they had to attend the rally coming up and had to form safety squads in the neighborhood too. Like she was the boss and they'd better listen. And they did. That was the funny part.

"You all need to clean up in here," Zala said, sounding tired. "Time to put summer stuff away and get out whatever the moths left us." She was trying to smile. Kenti could feel it and turned around.

She pushed Kenti back down, then looped the thread around the end of a braid and slid three beads on. Kofi watched. He'd been watching a lot lately, and he knew how to fix a tuna casserole and how to fold the fitted sheets without the round corners bunching out. He straightened the games in the milk crate, thinking over what all it took to be on his own, taking care of himself.

"Ma? Why can't we get this cot outta here and make room? Then it wouldn't be so junky." He looked at the top bunk. It was stripped. Fresh sheets and cases were stacked at the foot. Kenti didn't catch on, so he threw a Parcheesi man at her foot and looked toward the top bunk again. He pulled bent cards through the bars of the milk crate and made a neat deck, waiting for Kenti to say what he'd told her to say. But she didn't.

"Hey, Ma?"

"Dammit, Kofi, what is it?"

"Never mind." He made a neat pile of the games, then shoved all the books upright and propped them with the cash-register bank. He picked up his comics from under the desk and piled them on top where he'd finished his homework. "Want me to feed Roger?" The fishbowl was already freckled with food Kenti had shook from the shaker. He asked just to be saying something, just to get his mother to look up. And then she did.

"Must be awful." She was looking at him like she used to. His face got hot. He tried to smile. "Poor Roger," she said, like he should do something. "Must be terrible living in a bowl like that. No place to hide."

"Maybe we could buy him one of those bridges they make for fish, or some bushes."

"A castle," Kenti said. "Roger needs a castle."

"Hmm," Zala said, then she got lost again in Kenti's hair.

"Ma, is Sonny a delinquent?"

"What! Where did you hear that? Who said your brother was a delinquent, Kofi?"

"Mama, you pulling my hair."

"Mrs. McGovern, I bet. Mrs. McGovern say that? Damn that bitch."

"Ooo!"

"Nobody said it. Mrs. McGovern wasn't even there. We had a substitute."

"Then who said it?"

"We were just talking. Me and my friend Andrew, we were just talking." Kofi picked at his laces. "I was telling him about Sonny a little bit." He tugged on his shoe.

"Who Andrew? What were you telling?"

Kofi tugged harder and heard the rip up the back seam of his tennis shoe.

"It helps, Kofi, if you untie the laces first. I don't work like a dog so you can bust up good shoes."

He let his foot fall down on the rug. Dust rose. "Good shoes," he muttered, looking at the way his little toe was coming out of a hole in one shoe and now the back of the other was wide open. Zala burst out laughing. So Kofi leaned back on his hands and modeled his shoes, one at a time. But she didn't laugh long, 'cause Kenti started modeling her bare feet, saying she needed new shoes too and did they have some money.

"This Andrew person—what were you telling him?"

"Well, I wasn't exactly telling. More like I was asking if maybe he kind of knew something, 'cause . . . Andrew, he like knows things."

"Knows things?"

"Yeah."

"Pardon?"

"Yes. He's . . . my friend."

"Your friend." Then she was braiding again, yanking Kenti's head every time she tried to look over at the window. Buster was on the ledge outside, brushing against the screen like he felt itchy. Kofi couldn't wait for him to turn around and spot the goldfish. And wait till Roger spotted him. Kofi chuckled.

"Am I almost done?"

"Get your hands out of the way, please."

Kofi pulled the laces nearly out of both shoes before he pulled them off and let them drop. Now he would ask. He put the shoes right where she could see them. Now he would ask for real. But she went on braiding and braiding and beading and braiding, lost in the hair. He hit the rug and some dust came up.

"Ma, would you listen?" He glanced toward the closet and swallowed.

"I'm listening, Kofi. And watch how you talk to me. Now, tell me, what did your friend Andrew who knows things say? I'm really listening."

"Nothing. That's not what I . . . I got a question."

"He said your brother was a delinquent."

"No, he didn't."

"Well, where did you hear that? Who said it? This Andrew, what did he say?"

"Mama, quit pulling my hair."

"Who you talking to, missy?" She popped her fingers against Kenti's shoulder. "I'm waiting, Kofi."

"Nothing, Ma. It was nothing."

"Don't tell me 'nothing' when I'm talking to you."

"It wasn't anything. Dag."

"Beg pardon?"

"Maaaa." He slouched over toward the closet door and pulled his socks off one at a time. She was bearing down on Kenti's head with the fine end of the comb, scratching up dandruff that wasn't even there. Kenti was scrunching up her shoulders but she didn't say a word.

"Now. You were at school talking with this Andrew person. And then what?"

"He said maybe Sonny got put in that . . . you know . . . hall."

"Juvenile hall? He said that?"

"Yeah."

"Which?"

"Yes."

"Then what? Did you break his nose for saying that?"

"Nawww, Ma."

"Pardon?"

"No, ma'am."

"So what happened?"

"You don't get on Sonny when he says yeah and naw and worse stuff. You don't make him talk right all the time."

Zala stopped braiding. She stopped breathing. Then she was braiding again with her face tight. "Sonny's not here, Kofi. Your brother's not here."

The tom raked the screen with his paw. Roger dove to the bottom of the bowl where Kofi couldn't see him.

Zala sat up. She put her hands against her back and pushed like the big girls did in assembly, showing off their boobs.

"Jesus," she muttered. "Now they've got the children calling the children delinquents and my son right up in the middle of it." She looked at Kofi.

"Nobody called nobody nothin', Ma. You always making something out of something." He moved toward the closet and acted like he didn't see how she was looking at him. "Since Sonny ain't here," he went on boldly, "can I sleep on top and Kenti can take my bed? Then we can get that cot out of here. It stinks." He waited for Kenti to say what she was supposed to say. But she didn't say a thing. Then he heard his mother mutter something about beating Andrew up for what he said.

"I'm telling you, Ma, didn't nobody say nothing. And I ain't beating up on my friend just 'cause you say so, 'cause you wasn't even there and Andrew's my friend. I know what I'm supposed to do when somebody cracks on my family. You wasn't there and Sonny's my brother, not yours."

Kofi yanked the closet door open and went on in and got the cowboy boots like he'd been wanting to all along. If she got mad about it, then she'd just have to be mad, that's all.

"Can I have these boots? I mean, can I wear them till I get new shoes?"

She wasn't looking at the boots. She was looking at him, her hands rubbing her knees and her head bobbing, just missing the bump where the top mattress sagged.

"Sonny gonna get you for botherin' his things," Kenti said.

"Well, Sonny ain't here," he said. "He ain't here."

"You two be careful," Zala said. "And don't be slinging them nasty socks all over, Kofi. If we got nothing else, Mister Kofi Spencer, we got a hamper for dirty clothes."

"I know we got a hamper." He set the boots down and gathered up his socks and shirt.

"Told you before dinner to run your bath, now do it. And pick that lint out of your hair. Hear what I said?"

"Yeahhh."

"Pardon?"

"Yes. Mother."

Kofi stomped toward the door. His arm bumped the bunk lamp. It shone right in her face. He didn't do it on purpose, the clamp was loose. But she didn't accuse him, so he didn't explain. She leaned over and slapped the shade down like she wanted to slap him. But he was already in the hallway.

"Tell me something." She was yelling through the wall, so he banged the hamper lid and turned on the tap for his bath. "This Andrew friend of yours, he ever been in juvenile hall? Does he know Dave? Think Dave might know him?"

Kofi slammed up the toilet seat and unzipped his pants and drowned her out. She kept on talking, coming right through the medicine cabinet when he went for his pick. So he ran the cold water and flushed the toilet again. She was asking about the boots. He picked his hair out a little. Then, since the water was on, he wet his washcloth and ran it across his face. She was still going on about the cowboy boots, the boots he had taken from Sonny's bag without asking first so he couldn't tell her 'cause that was way before they'd started looking for keys and clues and he shouldn't have done it. He looked in the mirror. He had to admit he looked a lot better, but he wished she would shut up.

"Would you leave it," he said. He thought he heard her grumble, so he took his time coming out.

She was yawning when he walked into the bedroom.

"You sleepy, Mama. You oughta go to bed."

Zala held the comb out so Kenti could study it. "So, Kofi," she said, looking up, "was 'delinquent' one of your spelling words?"

He brightened. "Yeah."

Zala parked the comb again and sat back. "Listen, you two." Kofi dropped down onto his knees. "The police and the newspapers don't know what the hell is going on, so they feel stupid, because they're supposed to know, they're trained to know, they're paid to know. It's their job. Understand? But it's hard for grown-ups to admit they're stupid, especially if they're professionals like police and reporters. So they blame the children. Or they ignore them and fill up the papers with the hostages in Iran. Understand? And now . . . Jesus . . . they've got people calling those kids juvenile delinquents."

"Don't cry." Kenti tried to lean into her lap and got pushed away.

"They don't know a damn thing and they act like they don't want to know. So they blame the kids 'cause they can't speak up for themselves. They say the kids had no business being outdoors, getting themselves in trouble."

"You let us go outdoors."

"Of course I do, baby. We go lots of places, 'cause a lot of people fought hard for our right to go any damn where we please. But when the children go out like they've a right to and some maniac grabs them, then it's the children's fault or the parents who should've been watching every minute, like we don't have to work like dogs just to put food on the table."

Kofi walked on his knees toward the bed, but he didn't lean on her like he wanted 'cause she might push him away. So he just put his hand on the mattress next to hers.

"Those bastards are calling the children hustlers 'cause they had jobs." Zala wiped her arm across her face and Kofi patted her leg; then he scooted closer and patted her back. And she looked at him. "Oh, Kofi. Just because they had little jobs. Those bastards."

"Who's a . . . can I say it, Mama? Who's a bastard?"

"The damn police and them stupid reporters who don't know how to get out on the street and talk to people instead of taking down whatever the police say."

"Is a hustler like . . . ?" Kenti scrambled up and started dancing.

"Not that hustle, Short Legs."

"A hustle is a sort of bad word for a job."

"Like Sonny and his paper route," Kofi explained.

"What's bad about that?" Kenti wanted to know, looking at both of them, then sitting back down.

"Nothing, baby. That's what I'm trying to tell you if you would listen." Zala pulled Kenti back between her knees but didn't start braiding. She was biting her lips. "It's people's prejudice is what it is, and using language in a hateful way. For example, if you look a certain way and live in a certain part of town and you're a kid who rakes leaves and carries groceries, then people say, 'Isn't that nice. What a fine, industrious child to be helping out.' Understand? But if you live in another part of town and are doing the same thing—"

"And you're Black."

"Okay, Kofi, and you're Black, with not much money—then people say, 'Why don't their parents look after those kids running around ne-glected? They're little hoodlums, street kids, hustlers.' Understand?"

"They so mean," Kenti said, punching the mattress.

"Now, for example, if I lived in a certain part of town, people would call me a working mother. 'There goes Mrs. Spencer. She works so hard raising her children. Bless her heart. She's taking courses at college and working three jobs. And such lovely children. So smart, so cute, so well-mannered.' " She tweaked Kenti's nose but she couldn't hold on to her smile and next thing she looked angry. "But don't let me be who I am, then people say, 'There goes a terrible mother. Always going off here and there, leaving her kids all alone. How awful.' "

"Mama, you don't leave us alone. Do she, Kofi?"

"She sure don't." He sat back on his heels knocking the boots over.

"You a good mother, Mama." Kenti fitted herself between Zala's knees and wrapped her mother's legs back around her middle.

"Understand? About using words for this and that?" Zala held out her hands, smiling at one and frowning at the other.

"Like when Ma's in a good mood," Kofi said, leaning toward Kenti. "Then we're her sugar dumplins and her punkin pies. But when she's in a bad mood," he bared his teeth and growled in Kenti's ear, "Then I'm *Mis*-ter Kofi and you're *Missss*-y Kenti."

" 'March yourself to bed, missy, with yo' fast self.' *You* do it, Mama." Kenti tugged at Zala's legs. "Do how you do when *you* mad."

"Oh, lamby pie, I simply couldn't," Zala cooed like a pigeon. "Mother dear is so weary, so please don't elbow me, dahlins, or I will surely collapse—then who will fix you wonderful children dessert and put you beddy-bye?"

"Dessert? What's for dessert?"

"First we must finish your hair, my sweet. And you, my precious scruffy one, quick like a rabbit before the water overflows. Or mother will be mad and gobble you up like the gingerbread boy."

"Ooowee, Mama. You losing your beads!"

Kenti dove under the bed after bouncing beads. Kofi scrambled after those sinking into the rug. Zala leaned over, picking up some but mostly tickling the kids. Kofi hated to leave. He dashed as fast as he could and turned off the bathwater and skidded back, sliding to home plate in time to get tickled. Leaning over, she was playful and silly. But when she sat back and the top sagging bunk touched her head she froze, then kind of caved in.

They poured the beads into her lap, waiting while she poked the needle a couple of times before hitting the hole. Then they watched for a while as the beads slid down the thread, clicking into place. Then Kofi sat back on his heels.

Kenti felt her head, then sat back down and hugged her knees.

Kofi picked up the boots and ran his hand over the toes. They were a little scuffed, but he could fix that with red polish. The saddle stitching was gray, but he could scrub it with an old toothbrush. They were a little too big, but they'd fit if he wore two pairs of socks.

"Ma, can I have 'em? I mean, can I wear 'em?"

"Hand them here." She looked them over carefully, then shook each one like they were supposed to rattle. "Hot as it is?"

"Least let me see if they fit." He was reaching for them when Kenti laughed.

"You already had your ole stink feet in 'em. And I'ma tell Sonny too."

"How'd they get in there, Kofi? We went all through that closet. Where'd they come from?"

"How I'm supposed to know? They Sonny's."

"Don't raise your voice to me, please."

"Dag. I just wanna wear 'em. I didn't do nothing."

"Nobody said you did anything, Kofi. I'm just asking who brought them into the house. I've never seen them before." She rolled the tops of the boots down, looking for something. "Get Cousin Bobby on the phone. Maybe he knows."

"But can I try them on?"

"Hear what I tell you?"

"Better march yourself to that phone, Mister Kofi," Kenti yelled at his back through cupped hands.

What a drag, Kofi thought, bumping his shoulder along the hallway wall. Kenti could be fresh, but he better not try it. Sonny could talk like he felt like, but he'd get punished. A bunch of birthday presents in the closet and Sonny wasn't even home. And here he was nearly nine but nobody said boo about what he wanted for his birthday. And all he'd asked for was some boots. Now she'd probably give 'em to the police and he'd have to go to school barefoot. At Andrew's house they had dessert right after dinner. But no, he had to take a bath first. Well, next time the phone rang like that, he was going to be ready. He didn't have to stay around where nobody combed his hair or smiled at him.

"I want to speak to him, Kofi."

"Yeahhh," he said, making a face in the direction of the backroom.

Saturday, October 11, 1980

I t was a new neighborhood with no definite look of its own yet, with no tales and gossip to be spun into lore in the local barbershop. No shops had opened yet. And on either side of the one-story complex of spaces to lease, two rows of townhouses with fresh cedar shingles stared, curtainless, tenantless, at the partly bulldozed woods across the street, the Cat sunk up to its hocks in mud, the driver lounging against the smeared yellow machine, smoking and gazing off into the distance where the soft, gray haze scrubbed out the building lines of DeKalb County. In the block they drove through, though, things were sharply etched—a moving van, a landscaper's truck, a convertible sports car dripped on by the leaves of trees bitten into the landscape. Zala felt the neighborhood with her teeth. It was a community-to-be for self-invented people unsaddled by nightmares and conflicting dogmas, people who could toss mamasay and preachersay over their shoulders with a pinch of coke and, applying one of Atlanta's upbeat sobriquets to their lifestyles ("City too busy to hate"), required nothing further to move ahead. Zala looked out at the trees, newly planted, held in place by clean stakes and near-invisible guy lines. She wondered what it would take to live there, how much she would have to cut, tuck, and gore to fit herself to such living.

"I feel I'm aging by the second," Spence muttered, cruising slowly past the rental office.

"Mmm," she said, her cheek against the window.

On the corner was a vacant house from a former time of mills and farms and company stores. Rainwater tinted red by leaves and clay puddled in the well of the bottom step. She imagined boarders pausing there to chat with the mailman. Weeds and twigs and vines had closed in on the porch altogether. Wasphives and cobwebs clumped in the corners of the windows of a large room, the dining room no doubt. She pictured mill hands rising from sturdy chairs to spear potatoes from plain, chipped bowls. The food platters set in the middle of a long, wide table covered not by a tablecloth but by shiny oilcloth stretched tightly and held firmly underneath by thumbtacks, so it could be wiped down in a flash with a dishrag while the cutlery soaked.

"Baby, we've got to start," Spence said. "Where do you want to go? We've got another hour before Teo knocks off at Daily's."

Zala shrugged, and Spence lingered at the intersection, watching pigeons on the ledge of a building slated for demolition.

Less than thirty minutes after Paulette had chased them away to spend the day together, they'd found themselves in the East Point section of town, not far from the airport, cruising along Redwine Road, where a body had been found the year before. They tried to keep up a conversation about the library books she'd checked out from the Uncle Remus branch, ten minutes from the house, midpoint between four marks on the map rolling across the backseat. Driving through the southwest district, they'd chatted relentlessly about Kofi's birthday party, carefully avoiding calling the names of friends to be invited, as though Paulette were breathing down their necks from the backseat. Discussing the birthday present for Kofi, repeating themselves, not listening to each other, they'd moved onto Cascade from Gordon and headed toward Fairburn, still keeping up the pretense as they reached Niskey Lake Road, where the first two bodies had been found. They were not patrolling, merely driving, talking, reminding each other that they'd meant to drop in to Paschal's for iced tea and pie when they'd left the library. So they'd headed back to MLK Drive and forgotten they had a destination until the drive led them to Hightower Road, a rock's throw from the Verbena Street–Anderson Park area where the Wilson girl had vanished, Mac and Mattie carefully expunged from their conversation as stale suspicions rose afresh in their minds. Then, hesitating where Hightower split into Jackson Parkway and Hollywood Road, they'd grown nervously silent, taken the fork along Hollywood, where another victim had lived, and when Spence could stand it no longer, pulled over for gas though the needle read three-quarters full. Then, in spite of themselves, they were drawn back to East Point, speeding north of Washington Road to Forrest Avenue to Norman Berry Drive, doing five mph over the new site neither had yet charted on the map.

Spence had taken eagerly to her suggestion that they get back to the Southwest, go by the Neighborhood Art Center and see the new exhibit hung in the center's Romare Bearden Gallery. But somehow they'd turned off Georgia Avenue and wound up in the McDaniel area, where Camille Bell lived, not letting each other know that they were scrutinizing each passing car and rehearsing what they would say to each other if they spotted any STOP members going over the route and signaling for the limo to join them. Forgetting the exhibit altogether, they'd picked up Memorial Drive and headed east toward DeKalb County, Spence wrenching the car off the route the minute he recognized the houses, the lots. Frantic to bypass the sites and give the day a chance to develop into something casual, he lost all sense of direction. But each side street, each turn only showed how a schoolyard or alleyway shortened the distance between the victims on the list, linking more closely neighbors, schoolmates, youths who'd ridden the same bus routes, frequented the same fast-food joints, knew people in common from old neighborhoods. This boy's sister was that boy's brother's girlfriend, B. J. had told her. This child's backyard was that one's shortcut to church, one of the parents had told her. The playground bordering the house where she'd been killed contained the basketball court where two others had played ball. His neighbor, her uncle. His hangout, her workplace. The store where one boy ran errands next door to where another bagged groceries, the store's parking lot a third had ridden through on his bike passing the Laundromat where a fourth had been seen being strangled, on his way to visit an aunt in a housing project where a fifth had disappeared.

"It's not a light, Spence. It's just a stop sign."

"I know," he said, but didn't move other than tapping his foot on the pedal and jogging them in their seats. She wanted to get going. She didn't care where.

"I can't seem to shake off this . . . It's as though we're being compelled . . . or surrounded." He pumped the gas pedal. The limo rocked at the intersection. He didn't know where they were, and that was good. But he didn't trust any direction, not left, not right, not straight ahead. "Where to?" he demanded.

Lost, they were safe for the moment. Zala squinted at the overcast sky for signs of a seam, for an entry into the other Atlanta where they'd been safe from moment to moment. "Anywhere," she said, afraid she might blurt out what she was thinking, longing for. She leaned again against the window as a jet roared overhead.

Adjacent to the abandoned house she'd people with mill hands was a small gabled building from that same old time, the street dead-ending into an excavation plot courtesy of MARTA. The building housed a Laundromat and a grocery store below, a dentist's office above, and pigeons in the dormers. A woman in a coarse hair net and stockings rolled below her dress hem was stiff-joint walking around large paper bags lined up on the sidewalk. The laundry or groceries or jawbones-and-teeth didn't fill the bags but left sagging pockets of dark space in the sides of the heavy brown paper. Perhaps she was a sculptor, or arche-ologist, or astronomer, or a bone-casting diviner. It seemed inconceiv-able that she could be merely a stranded woman trying to figure out how to get herself and her belongings home before the downpour. When the woman suddenly reversed herself, circling the bags counter-clockwise, then turned to watch the limo finally go through the inter-section, Zala busied herself with the books in her lap, rocking forward, trying to hurry the car and get out of there.

"*American Drama in the Thirties,*" she said loudly. "*Eugene O'Neill and the House of Atreus, The Plays of Jean-Paul Sartre, Aeschylus and Attic Drama, Gluck's Opera Libretti.*"

"Un-hunh," Spence muttered, trying to get interested.

She went through the books again, stacking and restacking—*Iphi-genia,* the *Oresteia, The Flies, Mourning Becomes Electra, Freud and Greek Myth on Broadway*—keeping her eyes downcast, averted. Because if the woman caught her eye, she'd rip off that hair net and there'd be nothing stiff-jointed about her once she shed her disguise and called Zala out.

"What's the matter?" But he didn't want to know. He only wanted to know how they were going to work themselves out of the sandtrap. "Baby, we've got to," he said again, wagging his head, his tongue a wasp in his mouth.

Make a clean start, she quickly phrased in her mind. Act like it never happened. Of course it never happened. It was just as Spence had said that day on Aunt Myrtle's stoop. Never could count straight. Made it all up. The girls at school had quizzed, examined, and said she couldn't be pregnant. She wouldn't have dared, not after Mama Lovey had worked so hard putting things in her head, like Do Not. There'd been no son, because with a son, her aunt had told her, you spent your life praying in the window and cursing the streets.

"Whaddawedo?"

Begin again. Fresh start. Square one. It never happened. Couldn't have. Bad dream gone nightmare. She hadn't been down on all fours in the basement. Hadn't searched the yard for his body. Hadn't been trying to dig up the woods with her nails. Hadn't seen the dogs blunt down in the meat of her son. No son. *Una buena madre empleada cuida su trabajo.* A good mother does her work. Then goes to bed and sleeps tight if the sherry holds out, so in the morning Paulette can tromp in with a friend and a cleaning brigade of neighbors, whip off the covers so the whole block will know by supper that Marzala Spencer sleeps in her panties and bra on filthy sheets. No such boy. The body found on Norman Berry Drive did not concern her directly. So she could fix coffee and ask Paulette's friend all about Miami and promise to visit. No Sonny. Another family had claimed the body from the morgue. So she could let Paulette fix her up with a blind date who turned out to be—small world—the boyfriend who'd kissed her in the vestibule of her aunt's apartment house, mailboxes imprinting on her back. A date, a drive, fresh start. This time she'd be more careful, not allow "orphaned at both ends" to drive her engine. So she dressed and put on makeup and skipped down the steps. Because it never was. So of course the boys had acted strangly, how else should boys act when a nut in mother-detective disguise follows them through the streets? Not her. Some wild woman dreamt up after too much wine.

"What's funny?"

"My mother. How she didn't know that 'Marsala' is wine. Thought she was naming me after a flower, using a z to make it more Southern, more cullid," she laughed.

"It can't be that funny." He was annoyed that her laughter didn't include him, didn't infect him. He ghosted a smile, then dropped the attempt. "I don't understand why your mother doesn't get here."

"She's got a dying man on her hands, don't forget. And what about yours?"

"After you told her not to come? Hey, look, let's take it easy." He leaned over the wheel. "I wish it would go ahead and rain. The clouds just hang there."

"Wake up," she snapped. The windshield was dotted, then dappled, then streaming. She flicked on the wipers, then moved to the far end of the seat where the leather was cool and dry. "What do you want to do?" She forced herself to sound pleasant, casual.

He wanted to see the boy but not the body. That made no sense, so he didn't say it. They might have made a mistake in identification. He didn't dare say that. He didn't want to say anything or see anything, and hoped it would be dark and stormy by the time they picked Teo up from work to hear what he'd found out. He wasn't sure he wanted to hear what that might be, but he was certain he didn't want to go to headquarters or to the coroner's. And never again to the woods, even if the others were game. He'd chunked rocks at the dogs right up to the very second he realized it was only a half-burnt mattress and not a body the dogs had been nuzzling. If she reached around and got the map, he'd insist that the flashlight was weak and that the dark would catch them down a dangerous ravine. On the first time out, when three vets and two of B. J.'s colleagues had joined their caravan, zigzagging around Primrose Circle to the "trestle," then north along Moreland to Memorial Drive, moving in and out and around the points, night had overtaken them before they could rendezvous back of Gaston's station. And no one had thought to bring a torch; no one had thought it would take so long to cover the ground.

"I can't truthfully say you ever penned me up," she said, turning to him matter-of-factly, as though they'd been discussing just this point for the past few minutes. "And yet," she continued, oblivious to his efforts to follow her, "somehow my life was bordered by the house, the yard, the classroom, and work. Now why was that, do you think?"

"What brought this on?" He looked at the books in her lap for a clue. Maybe Delia and his mother were right; but then he talked off the wall on occasion too, or so Carole had been saying. "Baby, what are we talking about?"

"Adam and his pumpkin shell. And don't use that tone with me. That's how Paulette talks to her patients, the ones she's trying to sweet-talk into bed so she can jam an enema up their ass."

"I thought it was Peter and the pumpkin shell."

"It's Peter and the Lost Boys. Peter and the cave."

He looked at her sideways. "Is this a conversation about something?"

"God, I hope it rains," she said.

He dropped the lever to its slowest beat so she could watch the rain hit the glass.

"And what did you call me?"

"Call you?"

"I'm a grown woman with three children," she said.

"Noted," he said, willing to humor her, but only up to a point. He'd stop her cold, though, if she hinted that they should go downtown to inquire about the body. If, on the other hand, she suggested going to City Hall to chalk four-letter words on the walls, he'd have to give that serious consideration.

"What I mean is, please don't call me 'baby,' Spence."

"Right. Check." He swung the car around a partially cleared woods and pleaded with his hands to relax on the wheel. Taut, they looked like his mother's hands. He settled back, remembering how he'd had to explain to Zala that his mother didn't wear gloves out of affectation. Piecework, production step-up, tendonitis, no compensation, no medical coverage either—for years after she was laid off she wore white cotton gloves that smelled of wintergreen. He'd tried to remember to always take his key. He hated the sound of her fumbling with the lock, while he stood, feeling guilty, listening, and smelling wintergreen through the door.

"What's the matter?" she said. His face looked twisted.

"The smell of spruce and pine seems awfully strong for this time of year," he said, the rumbling of the Cat drowning out the tumbling of the lock. "Echolocation," he said. "Remember? The bats?" He took his hands from the wheel and shook them. "Smells can tell time and sounds can see space."

"What?"

"Echolocation. At the zoo," he said. "How bats locate themselves because they can't see. They send out a high-frequency pitch, then listen to sounds reverberating from their surroundings. Remember?"

"Bats?" She examined the trees and rooftops. She saw only pigeons, sparrows, and starlings. "You can turn off the wipers," she said. "It's stopped again."

"Don't you remember? How could you not remember? It's called echolocation. We were all at the zoo."

"I wasn't with you," she said. "Don't get me confused with your other women."

"All of us," he was saying, frantic to have this bit of history confirmed. "My parents had driven up and we all . . . What women are you talking about?"

"We're going in circles, Spence." She reached for the wheel when she spotted seven large grocery bags by the curb. "Don't turn down there. MARTA's digging. We'll never be able to turn this boat around."

"Take it easy, Zala. Let go." He swerved to the left when an elderly woman stepped into the street and flagged him. He swung into a side street he hadn't seen the first time round.

"Jesus," she said, peering over her shoulder.

"I wasn't going to hit her. I had the car under control, dammit. Don't do that again," he warned, tapping the steering wheel. He thought she would argue, would point out some reckless act on his part that he hadn't noticed. Perhaps a cat had darted across without his being aware. But she said nothing, merely flung herself back against the upholstery and pulled at her hair.

"There's a comb in the glove compartment," he offered.

"Whose?"

"Aw, shit, woman. I need this shit? Look, I don't need this shit. I really don't."

"We're riding around in circles, Spence."

"I can see that. You don't think I can see that? Well, I can see that. I know where I am." He took a deep breath and blew out. Then, trying to get his body to remember his usual driving position, he eased his arm on the sill, but the window was rolled up. His elbow thudded against the glass.

They were moving through that part of the neighborhood yet to be transformed, part of it hanging on, the other already reduced to rubble. Three buildings scheduled for demolition bore large white X's on the doors and windows. One was an old-fashioned pharmacy, its front window crisscrossed with tape. Boxes of diapers were stacked in a pyramid. Would Mattie call that a sign?

"We're doing it again," Spence said, his voice tight. "We're back on the route. I can't seem to get away."

They'd each heard it separately on the radio more than a month ago, the DJ sandwiching in the news of the route between community bulletins of upcoming Labor Day weekend events. She'd been in the Morris Brown Post Office near the campus flipping through FBI Wanted

posters on the lookout for a name, a face, or a record that included kidnap and murder. A student buying stamps had set his radio down on the
Xerox machine near where she was learning again, in law-enforcement
language, that militancy was synonymous with crime: wanted for questioning in connection with armed robbery, the suspect is a member of a
revolutionary organization and should be considered armed and dangerous. Spence had been pacing back and forth in his one-room efficiency pursued by the dinnertime demons: eat out, eat in, pick up, call
for delivery, invite himself over to Carole's, or invite her out? Each possibility raising a fresh set of questions: what to do with leftovers, eat and
run or spend the night? The DJ's announcement that a former APD officer had discovered a clue in the case halted him in his tracks. The route
was used, the DJ speculated, by the killer or killers regularly, by day
traveling from home to work, by night from work to a girlfriend's. "Or
to a Klan meeting," Spence amended, the demons routed for the moment and the roller-coaster car his stomach rode in clicking up the
tracks.

"We can't live like this," he said. She seemed so far away on the
other end of the seat. He made a sharp left so she'd come sliding toward
him. Only the books did. "We've got a problem, Zala."

"Yes," she said. She was watching the sideview mirror and listening
to the map roll across the backseat. Any minute Jesus would loom up in
the tinted glass and announce that the ordeal was over, that they'd come
through the test. If Never Happened had happened, there was still This
Too Shall Pass.

"We've got to come to some decision about what we're going to do,
Zala."

"I vote we get Kofi a proper karate outfit."

"Zala."

"You can turn off the wipers. It's not raining now."

Spence hit the brakes when a dog wandered into the street. From
habit, he threw his arm out across her chest. She fell against it, then
slammed back against the cushion.

*Hockey stop. Sonny at the Omni rink skating fast and low, pulling up short,
scooting ice on Spence's good pants. Laughing.*

"I wish you'd buckle up," he said. He'd meant to say, "Sorry, reflex,"
from driving the kids around. But she tugged up the belt with no comment. It seemed that no matter how he maneuvered the wheel, the map

rolled across the backseat, slapping up against the near door, then the far.

Bales of chicken wire hitting against the sides of the panel truck. Sonny on his lap steering Widow Man's truck around the edges of the farm, dipping down into ruts, bouncing up over mounds, lurching from mud slick to pothole when they reached the cement of the main road.

"What's the matter?" She plucked at his sleeve when he pulled the car over. She asked it again when he rubbed his eyes with the heels of his hands. She answered herself: Yes, we've got a problem. They used to tell her in Sunday school that five verses a day would help solve problems. Told her in junior high that algebra sharpened that ability too. Was told at home that the community that named her, claimed her, sustained her, held the answers, she had only to listen. She moved across the seat and embraced his shoulder. She didn't remember his being so broad. One minute hating him for making it happen, the next wanting to wrap her legs around his hips. What would it mean to unbutton their clothes and tumble into bed? That they were desperate to replace a life. That it had happened and happened and they'd given him up for dead.

"I'm okay," he said when she took her arms away and bent down to stack the books on the floor.

"Good," she said. "Why were you afraid to break into Murray's place?"

"Are we back to that?" He pulled off without looking, then swerved when a camper nearly sideswiped them.

"Want me to drive?" She was holding the buckle and waiting.

He grunted and drove.

Once again they cut across Interstate 20, designed, it would seem, for the purpose of splitting up clusters of Black neighborhoods. Rather than ease up on the gas when a couple huddled under a newspaper were crossing, he hit the horn and made them run.

"You're being stupid," she said, then heard her mother: "Quit picking, baby. It may be a long haul up the rough side of the mountain. And y'all can't pull each other up if you're both face down in the muck." She'd hung up and gone to get the toolbox.

"I'm stupid? I jimmy open a neighbor's basement? A neighbor known to raise vicious dogs? Yeah, right. I'm stupid, but you—"

Standing in the doorway, his voice like sandpaper but his eyes giving him away. We're trying to do our homework back here. We'd go to the library if it was open. Then turning away—I sure would like to go somewhere and get on out of here.

"Finish it. Can't you complete one damn sentence? Say it, I can't even keep track of my own child."

"He's mine too." He hadn't meant to start anything, so he put a plea in his words.

"I heard a question mark on the end of that sentence. What's that supposed to mean?"

"Shut up, Zala. Just shut the fuck up."

"Pull over."

"Let's knock it off," he said, and they rode in silence for half a mile.

They were driving through what he called mixed neighborhoods, meaning a mix of real-estate values. Big homes with wraparound porches and dentil moldings. Across the way, a golf course where retired men raced electric carts to the clubhouse for two fingers of Jack Daniel's on the rocks. And in the middle of the block were rental units with no landscaping. Children were sitting on the curb pulling crusts from mayonnaise-and-sugar sandwiches and dropping them in the stream to race to the sewer. And then a Spanish-tiled building with a shingle out front: Notary Public, Chiropractic Clinic, Norma Baines Charm School. Then an adults-only apartment bloc with swimming pool and clay courts. On the opposite corner, the Resurrection of Christ the Nazarene, a whitewashed weatherboard rectangle that rocked three nights a week and all day Sunday. And sharing the driveway, a huge house with mullioned windows and a widow's walk.

Mixed, he called these neighborhoods. Middle-class, the people called themselves, job-starved and poverty-pinched, doily-fine and blue-veined privileged alike. A family of five, four with two jobs apiece, but look out if one library book was overdue. Couples who'd pulled themselves up from day-old wares at Colonial Bakery and greens from the cemetery, fighting the mockingbirds for first licks on the purple-green leaves of the pokeberry bush. Called themselves middle-class so long as there were down-the-street neighbors still battling the birds and stopping the meat truck for fifty cents' worth of salt pork to cook up the poke salad with. Middle-class up-and-coming. Bachelors who lived in their two-toned Sevilles, performing their a.m. toilette in bus-depot restrooms, their evening ablutions in bars, continually changing "address" two steps ahead of the collection agency. Teenage mothers on stoops rifling through *True Confessions* while their babies drank formula stretched with Kool-Aid. And where was he, what did he call himself? His daddy used to say, "A working stiff with apologies to no damn body," rising proudly each morning to walk the high steel.

"You think they're sure, Spence? Suppose the family says he's not their boy?"

He didn't answer. Instead he looked at the freshly mown lawns and inhaled, though double-glazed tinted glass separated him from the green.

"We're on the route again," she said. "I believe the Middlebrookses live over there." When he didn't respond, she sat quietly looking at houses and stores she had stopped at while tacking up handbills and showing Sonny's picture around. Some eyed her with misgivings: "I suppose you're taking up a collection as well?" Others heard things she hadn't said and responded: "Why do you want to make trouble for Maynard Jackson? Don't you remember how things used to be before we got him elected?" And there were those who examined her closely the way she had done at STOP: happened to her, can't happen to me because I wear stockings and wouldn't dream of leaving my hair like that. Some made things up to offer assurance: "But those were hoodlums, I thought. Yours looks like such a fine boy." Mostly people were kind, wanted to help but didn't know how.

"Know a shortcut downtown? To Daily's," Spence added quickly so there'd be no misunderstanding as to where they were going. She leaned against his arm, pointing him into a turn. He had doubts about the narrow lane, but bumped through it, cinders beating against the underside of the limo like hailstones, tree branches scraping the side windows trying to get in.

"When we patrol again," he said, astounded to hear himself saying it, "let's pay attention to where army camps and police stations are on the route."

"Army?" she said, her voice trailing off.

A boy of twelve with squared-off shoulders seemed to come out of nowhere, and they couldn't take their eyes off him. He stepped off the curb and stopped traffic with his hand. He wore khaki shorts and a green polo knit, hiking boots laced mid-calf with green socks cuffed at the top. He toted an army-green backpack. There was as much equipment clipped to his hip as to B. J.'s—a battered canteen, a flashlight, a leather pouch pointy at one end, lumpy at another. He clanged across the street as if off to war.

"Is he by himself?" She scanned the sidewalk for a counselor, a troop.

"Looks like it." He leaned forward, expecting to see the boy take up position on the double lines and wave across younger children temporarily hidden by the hedges.

The boy walked without breaking his stride, stepped up on the curb, jounced the pack on his back a bit, and walked on, solid, there— defiantly so, thought the two in the car, who half-expected to see him swallowed up in the haze. They sat staring till traffic closed in on them, one hasty driver beeping, then passing, an infant standing in her lap playing with the driver's glasses as she drove.

"He was so . . ."

"Actually he wasn't, Zala."

"Maybe we should double-check downtown."

"Think so?"

"But then the Stephens family already . . . And I don't think I could bear it."

"Maybe there's something on the news," he said.

"Do we have to have that thing on?"

"Yes." After a few seconds of blasting music, he turned it off, but she turned it on again. "Make up your mind. What do we do?"

"Why do you keep asking me?" She snapped the radio off. "This is your outing."

"Mine! How did it get to be mine? You and Paulette cooked it up."

"She said that you said . . . I could've stayed in bed."

"Why didn't you? I could be working. Saturday's a fat day."

"Then work," she said, pulling the radio phone from its catch and handing it to him. "Don't turn off the beeper for me. Nothing I like better on rainy days than reading." She flipped open a book and angled it in her lap.

He set the radio phone back on its catch. "Tell me where to drop you off. I'm not going through these changes."

"Just tell me, dammit."

"Tell you what?"

She threw the book on the floor. "Your hunch. The army and the police. He's my son too."

"Boots, that's all. Them damn boots. Combat boots, mounted police boots, motorcycle copy boots. I can't get them damn boots out of my head."

"You don't have to yell. I can hear you."

"Well, I told you." He stroked his neck, pinching the skin where it felt clammy. He would have to grow his mustache again. He missed raking it. And in shaving, he would have to approach his lip with more caution.

"Please don't do that," she said, turning her face away. There was a page in her notebook called strangulations. They said the last two boys had had rope burns on their necks.

Sitting at the kitchen table knocking his knees together in fury, rage swelling his neck like a puff adder, except that she didn't have time to make comparisons because Dave was trying to be funny cracking on the boy's father and Sonny making his eyes small as he plucked at his neck while she beat the eggs chasing the bowl around the wet counter and the more they talked the more the kitchen heated up.

"Spence . . ."

Spence raced to the curb in front of Daily's, braked in a whiplash stop, then gunned the motor to discourage her from talking. He leaned on the horn till Teo came out, jerking his thumbs in the air and all tuned up to launch into a narrative of his workday. Teo jumped into the car, filling it at once with the pungent smells of the restaurant and the jangly electricity of the tales he was about to spin. Spence cut him off quickly and asked him to find the gum he was sure he'd tossed into the glove compartment the day he'd taken the Saudi children to Grant Park Zoo.

"This y'all's anniversary?" Teo wrestled off his bow tie, ripped his shirt collar open, and released the catch on the compartment. "Must be somp'n up, you in that purty dress and him with enough grease in his hair to fry a possum."

"Just find the gum, man, and cut the cracker comedy."

"Don't raise a blister, good buddy. I'm a-looking and a-cooking with Crisco."

Teo's face was mottled red except where he needed a shave. Zala wondered how he always managed to affect a red, white, and blue look when he played at the drawl. She felt pressure against her left thigh, Spence signaling her not to ask about Sue Ellen, their marriage rocky.

It struck her as funny that Spence should be so delicate about somebody else's marriage.

"Aha," Teo said, holding up a blue paisley scarf by a corner. "Who's been going to the girlie shows?" He dangled it so the fringe swayed.

"Gum, Teo."

Zala took the scarf and shoved it toward the back of the compartment. Amid a jumble of matchbooks and business cards was a cigar box. She drew back, staring at it; the hairs at the nape of her neck prickled. While Teo rummaged for the gum, Zala carefully slid the crumpled page of the telephone directory from under Spence's pistol. She ran her eyes over the eagles and enlarged eyes that dotted page 579 of the Atlanta Yellow Pages, but her mind was riveted on the box.

"Leave it," Spence said when he saw her smooth the wrinkled paper across her kneecap. He glanced down at the advertisements and tensed.

The big ads at the bottom of the page boasted of specially trained undercover agents operating throughout the world with the help of consultants in overseas branches. They boasted of the latest in photographic and surveillance equipment and a policy of efficiency and discretion. A cat burglar kneeling before the bottom drawer of a filing cabinet had a heavy flashlight for spying, and maybe for clubbing unconscious the night watchman. In another sketch, the artist had drawn a man who looked like a respectable banker and at the same time the neighborhood flasher; in a foreign-intrigue trenchcoat, he was reaching behind a drape doing something efficient discreetly—planting a bug, or signaling his cohorts to swing across the airshaft and kick in the window, or removing a gun planted in the valance. The largest graphic showed a grim-mouthed killer in dark turtleneck and beret straddling the globe; under one arm he hefted an M-1; under the other, mountain-climbing gear. The ink of his boots dripped down into the longitudinals and latitudinals of the world.

Spence grunted and hoped she'd tire of reading the page and put it out of sight. How little he'd been able to tell the private investigators he visited. One had clamped a chummy hand on Spence's shoulder and told him not to feel bad for being unable to come up with much about the habits and quirks of his son. "More than half the men who come here looking for runaway wives can't remember what color her eyes are."

"I didn't send you in there to do spring cleaning."

"Hell, buddy, it's a mess of stuff in here," Teo said. "So it's more'n a ramble. But I'm dead on the case of the missing gum."

Spence felt the muscles in the back of his neck tighten. He flexed his driving arm, his driving foot, and tried to get comfortable. Zala placed the yellow page back where she'd found it and was now staring into the compartment as though peering into the mouth of a cave. That was how she'd looked the day after the rally when the police called her in and she'd had to face them alone. He felt damp and salty thinking of it. He should have been with her. But he'd been leaning over the desk in the outer office placating Carole. But then Zala should not have gone down there, he argued to himself, to no avail. He should have been there, planting his fist in the cop's jaw or wherever the professional venom was distilled.

"Quite a collection." Teo was looking from the gun to Spencer to Zala, who sat motionless.

"Gum, not gun," Spence said, remembering the day he'd shoved his bullet clip in, torn the yellow page out, then raced from his sister's house sure that he knew where he was going and whom he was gunning for. Guys from his unit who'd approached him near the end of his tour had asked for his help in setting up conduits in Georgia for drugs, money, and the skull, ear, and pelvic-bone souvenirs of the war. There'd been twice as many threats as entreaties each time he put them off. That hunch turned out to be a bust, making less and less sense the more he learned about other missing children. As the days dragged at him, nothing was making sense except that somewhere in the middle of it—drugs, cult, porn, Klan, sex for hire, or whatever it was—were cops covering their tracks before they could be caught red-handed.

"Very fancy," Teo said, tapping the pack of gum against the edge of the cigar box. He passed two slices of gum across Zala as she took the box from him. "Expecting?"

There'd been a cigar box like the one in her lap on the shelf in the children's closet last winter. "50 Hand Made Valencias" from Brazil, she'd thought it had said. The one on her lap said "50 Hand Made Caballeros." A small box behind the Christmas bulbs, it had been just large enough to hold the fret clamp, a tortoiseshell guitar pick, and a prism the size of a pecan. She'd asked Sonny about it, and that's when the story of the clamp came up; "borrowed," he'd said. Zala ran her hands over the lid, staving off what it might mean if this was Sonny's box in Spence's possession.

"So what did you find out, man?"

Teo skinned down a stick of gum and folded it into his mouth. He thrumbled the foil into a ball and rolled it between his palms.

"Dammit, Teo, have you heard anything?"

"I hate to tell you, good buddy, but you're driving with your emergency on." Teo licked his thumb and riffled through several pages of his scratch pad, then folded them back, creasing the fold with the side of his thumb.

"Sometime this week?"

"You're as bad as Sue Ellen," Teo said, prying his damp shirt from his skin. "Welp, you know that guy I've been telling you about, the one in Sue Ellen's drama group? Been talking with him just about every day since last we talked. And it's just like the paper say. There's gonna be a big hoedown in Atlanta this weekend. Getting under way right now, as a matter of fact." He checked his watch and chewed. "Hosted by that great American, your friend and mine, J. B. Stoner."

Spence hissed and chomped down on his gum. "Indicted in the Birmingham bombings. He wasn't convicted and now he's running for office. Just what we need."

"Churches and synagogues too," Teo said, flipping pages. "Let's see . . . in 1958, and in 1963—"

"Let's not make heavy weather of this report. Just let me hear what you've got. So what about this guy?"

"Welp, I'm waiting for Sue Ellen to get through with her scene, so we gets to gabbing, me and this guy I'm telling you about. And we're talking about how the colored senator's trying to get Stoner's racialist ads off the TV and all and he says Stoner's a right guy and gonna chair this big convention of white-is-right groups from all over the world."

"Great," Spence muttered, worrying the gum. "A city full of Nazis." And with nothing in place, he was thinking. The Black community becoming a killing ground, fascists from all corners of the globe marching in, and nothing was in place. "When the hell are you guys going to take responsibility for civilizing your community?" Spence snapped. "How come you're sitting around with this bastard talking about Julian Bond instead of taking some action?"

"Jeez," Teo muttered. "I thought we were." He turned to Zala for support. She seemed a million miles away, clutching the cigar box in her lap.

Spence bumped his leg against hers. Didn't she have something to say? He slid the window down when he realized it was never going to be a good chew; parts of the gum stayed separate in grainy bits. He spit it out, then thwacked the wheel. Storm troopers gathering in the city and the community had forgotten how to defend itself. His attention had been so focused on the rally that STOP and SCLC organized, the right-wing convention had slipped his mind altogether. He'd heard nothing more on the news than that immigration had refused entry to a few of the more notorious extremists.

"What are you so riled about?"

"They don't like you, either, don't forget." Spence slid the window up. "Because you're a good guy," he added without irony, he thought, but he could hear Gaston saying "fullashit."

"So about this guy," Teo said. "He bears watching, so I'm on the case. First of all, all he talks about is disaster. You know what I mean? Floods, earthquakes, nuclear accidents, revolutions, riots—especially riots." Teo turned his head to study his audience. "Race riots, of course, being his favorite topic."

"Right," Spence muttered.

"Course . . ." Teo skinned down another slice of gum. "Sometimes when I go and visit my folks and see them crops rotting in the fields 'cause it don't pay to harvest no more if the government's gonna play footsie with the Russians, and I tell you the truth, I get to thinking 'bout guns and revolution myself." He stopped chewing and looked out the window.

Spence glanced across the seat, feeling suddenly alone in the car. "Has he talked about the case at all? Has he mentioned the children?"

"Guns and revolution," Teo said. "That's mostly what he's been talking about lately. I haven't worked the conversation round to the case as yet. Just dropping a few hints. Mostly he does the talking. And can he ever talk, this guy. He gotta grab you when he talks." Teo seized Zala's arm for a joke but let go when she jumped.

"Real beefy type," Teo continued, swelling his chest out and deepening his voice. "But solid. You can tell he lifts weights and works out. You know the type—always wants you to sock his stomach and break your damn hand. Always selling, that guy."

"What's he selling, Teo?" Zala asked.

"Yeah, what's his story? Give me something I can use."

"Survival's what he's selling. Always saying, 'Make your choice now, either you're a survivor or a victim.' The guy runs survival workshops in the woods somewhere—Alabama, I think. A hundred bucks per couple per weekend. Physical fitness, how to cure meat and freeze-dry veggies, how to build a fire without smoke, set booby traps, keep your weapons dry fording streams. Like that. Hundred bucks per couple." Teo whistled through his teeth. "I don't know what he charges for kids, but them's the rates for grown folks. Readying up for the big war. The *big* one," Teo emphasized when he got no reaction. "The race war, you guys. Hello?"

"War, right," Spence said. War was being declared again and nothing was in place. A bogus peace had been proclaimed and the community warriors had placed their shields on the public pile and buckled up their honor in *GQ* suits. Out of the side of his eye Spence caught Zala watching his face. He wondered if she was reading his mind and would sneer "I told you so," though she'd never really understood what he'd told her about warriors, she'd only been adamant—not scared, he corrected himself—when he'd outfitted himself for upward mobility, afraid of being left behind. He was sure he had that right, but her staring unnerved him, nonetheless.

"And his clothes," Teo was chuckling. "You oughta see this guy in some of his getups."

"You tailing him or getting engaged, T?"

"Funny guy, your husband." Teo shoved against the door to give himself dressing room. "Wears a flak jacket, air-force flight glasses, fatigues, hiking boots, and an assault vest, Spencer, with a hundred pockets. Carries everything in them but attack dogs—got bolo knives, hand claws, and these watchamacallits. Ever hear tell of 'Brute Vitality Energy Paks'?" Teo was scraping the plastic pen case in his breast pocket to show where Brute Paks were fitted on his subject. "Super energy food done up like K rations. The guys wacko, I'm telling you, well-educated and sharp as hell but wacko. And you gotta see the flight bag he lugs around with him all the time. Not just his scripts and costume gear, he's a walking library too. *The SWAT Team Manual, The Survivor's Almanac, American Defender, Strike Force, Gung Ho, Soldier of Fortune*—that type of stuff. Them magazines with the bodybuilding ads and Help Wanted mercenary columns and 'Clip This Coupon for a Course in Hypnotism to Have the Ladies Do Your Bidding.' That type of stuff." Teo ran a finger across his brow and shook it.

"You've looked over the material?"

"Hell, yes. That guy could sell anything. Got me taking out subscriptions to them field-and-stream and shoot-and-kill gazettes. You bet."

Spence turned it over in his mind: hypnotism, costumes, weapons. He turned to Zala to see what she made of it. She was sniffing at the cigar box, not the least bit listening to Teo.

"Sue Ellen says he's got an ammo crate at his place. Some of the actors get together, between rehearsals at the church, to go over their lines," he explained, slightly crimson in the crinkles as he smiled, or tried to. "And he's got one of them Remington ammunition crates—foot spikes, carbines, handguns, grenades, tools the likes of which—well, hell, I don't know what kind of tools they are. But the point is the guy's a walking arsenal. Wacko. Except he ain't altogether wacko, 'cause he makes a sort of sense, in a wiggy sort of way."

"Yeah?"

"I worry about the company you keep, Teo," Zala said suddenly. "I really do." She took another whiff of the box. But how did a piece of faceted glass smell, or a pick?

"Like I say, he's real persuasive. 'Don't get dinosaured out,' he's always saying. 'Get with the times.' Sounds like paranoid, I guess, hunh?" Neither Zala nor Spence answered. Teo braced his back against the door again and blew his chest out, walking his fingers across the front of his waiter's shirt until Zala looked up. "He's got this T-shirt that says 'Gun Control Is Hitting Your Target.' " Teo laughed, then cut it short when they didn't.

"Like you said, T, this guy bears watching."

"Welp, I'm on the case." Encouraged, Teo flipped through more pages. "His other job," he said, folding the pages back, "I got onto this one night when he had the director hemmed gainst the costume rack talking a blue streak about ballistic-proof armored vehicles. Bug-proof, too." He ran his hands over the dashboard. "Got a little device that jams any kind of transmitter. He's a security consultant for overseas corporations. Kidnappings his specialty. Guarding against them, I mean."

"Kidnappings!"

"Ahh, now you're both perking up." Teo danced around on the seat, jerking his thumbs around. "Why do you think I've been on his tail? From the first day I spotted the guy in Daily's taking lunch with one of the reporters, I sez to myself, Tune in on this one, and sure enough they were discussing kidnappings. So I sez to myself, Fucking right, get on it, Teodescu."

"The children?"

"Naw, not children. Terrorist stuff. And not here. You know, in them countries where they take an American businessman to trade for one of their own buddies locked up. That kind of thing. Hasn't mentioned the case yet, and doesn't pick up on my cues, so I wait. Talks a helluva lot, so he'll get to it if there's something to get to. But he sure knows all about the kidnapping racket."

"Like what?" Spence leaned away from the wheel to hear.

"Well, for instance, in 95 percent of all kidnap cases, an automobile is involved."

Spence looked at his army buddy thumbing through his notes. "That's it? That's the extent of four weeks of sucking up to the creep?"

"It's something," Zala said. She kept her hands securely folded on the box lid while Teo and Spence argued back and forth across her about what was worth spending time on. It was Spence who was making heavy weather of the report. Teo, Beemer, and one other white vet who'd stuck it out in McClintock's encounter group were keeping tabs on the Stone Mountain right-wingers and were renewing old associations with school chums, 'Nam vets, and cousins who could help them keep tabs on known Klan members and sympathizers on the police force. But what if it wasn't outsiders but someone right in their midst?

"How long have you had this box?" she asked just as Spence leaned across her to ask Teo what the wacko guy's name was.

"Calls himself Bedford. One minute it's not, next minute it's Pat. I don't set much store by what he says. He's got three initials stamped on his flight bag—NBF—but the first time I met him he told me to call him Pat. You figure it.

"NBF. Nathan Bedford Forrest," Spence said dryly.

"You know him? You know this cookie? Hot damn, Spencer, you know everybody. And here I was tailing the guy and calling myself Barnaby Jones. I'll be damned." He poked Zala. "Ain't he somp'n?"

Spence shook his head. "Hell, Teo, half the city streets are named after Forrest, come on. Civil War hero, Klan founder, great American patriot—which is probably where 'Pat' came from. He's messing with your mind, T." Spence laughed. "Soon as they figure how to work ole Nathan up there on Stone Mountain next to General Lee and Stoney, they'll chisel him in. That's the kind of shit they used to teach us in civics class—to write letters to have ole Nathan up there on the wall. One of the benefits of so-called integrated schools, T, you get to worship at the shrine."

"Now that's inneresting," Teo drawled, his jaws working. "You don't suppose NBF is like a class ring—say, like one of them pins Masons wear to court and flash from lawyer to judge to jury? A secret-society pin?" He chewed awhile, thinking it over. "You don't guess there's a bunch of these NBFers marching around the city with initials stamped on their briefcases?"

"Or on those black leather cases cops wear on their hips."

"Jeez, this is getting scary, and this sorryass gum don't help."

"Best way to conquer fear, ole buddy, is to have at it." Spence pressed the button to slide the window down on Teo's side so he could get rid of the gum. "What say you get yourself an invite to the party, T?"

Teo gagged, then spit out the gum. "Is this what ya call Black comedy? All joking aside, Sarge, ain't there somebody else to pull this duty?"

"C'mon, a haircut and you'd blend right in. I thought you guys were gung ho to make use of all these contacts you've been making?"

"Gung ho my ass. It'd be a haircut all right." Teo yanked up a shock of his hair and hung himself. "First thing I'm gonna do when I get home is study that insurance policy you wrote up."

"Got an address at least?"

"Address? Have you got my family covered is the question."

"The convention site, T. Where's Stoner hosting this hoedown?"

Teo tore out a page and plastered it down on the lid of the box in Zala's lap. "Hotel out in Cobb County," he said guardedly, then leaned back and let out a long, breathy, spearminty sigh. "Pardon me, folks, while I catch some shut-eye."

Spence tapped the horn at a brown dog lying curled and sleeping in the middle of the tunnel that a year ago marked the line of demarcation between the new International Boulevard and the old Magnolia Street. Lazily the dog roused itself and shook all over, then blinked at the grill of the limo. Spence beeped again. The dog trotted down toward the Magnolia end of the tunnel, veering around trenches and digging equipment, signs of convention center encroaching inch by inch on the old neighborhood. The takeover schemes of the seventies had been foiled, for the time being at least, first by the unexpected appearance of hundreds of young Black professional couples who bought up the re-gentrified homes, second by the Black Christian Nationalist Church, which bought up a whole block on Gordon for the Shrine of the Black Madonna Center. The West End secured, community workers no longer studied the master plan of the Atlanta 2000 Project, which targeted several districts for "demographic changes" in time for the Interna-tional University and the World's Fair, both slated for the turn of the century. Malik, one of the brothers who'd accompanied the caravan weeks ago, had said that if they were to study the plan, they might note a relationship between the series of fires set in the West End area, the proposed school closings there, the proposed reapportionment schemes, and the aggressive offers real-estate dealers were making to old-time residents of the neighborhood to get out.

Spence wondered if there might be a gathering of warriors at Malik's place. One of Dave's friends, Malik lived near West End Park, where a sect of Muslims owned homes and stores. He'd offered his home as a meeting place one night so they could divide up the route—Dave's group, starting out from where the Carter boy had lived, traveled north-west along Gordon Street till it became MLK Drive, then swung up into Hightower Road toward Jackson Parkway, covering some seven points on the map and ending up where the boy from Cleveland had been staying; B. J.'s group drove east to Memorial Drive and Conway, covering nine points on the map, and stopping where the Richardson boy had last been seen alive; the limo went south to the Lakewood and Campbellton area, where Detective Dowell promised to meet them off the clock. At the appointed hour, 8:30 p.m., each stopped to make notes, then headed toward site number 1 on Niskey Lake Road. Spence supposed there would not be a meeting at Malik's, for come to think of it, Saturday was their Sabbath. Where, then, might someone be raising an army to defend the community?

"Boots," Spence muttered. The ballot secured, reps in office, relying on the intricate etiquette of minuet steps meticulously choreographed, folks had lain down their weapons in the public square and sauntered off to read the papers, mad as hell if the ten-cent discount coupon for a mouthwash they never heard of was missing from their edition.

"What boots?" Teo opened one eye, then closed it when no one answered.

Spence drove past the lumberyard at Northside wondering where he should check in to say he was available for drafting. A sawyer covered in dust, paper-thin wood shavings in his hair, came out of the lumberyard beating a butter-yellow cap against his work pants till it returned to green. Was he a warrior? There'd been a time when Spence could gauge at a half-block distance the warriors, the amazons, the queens, the obeahs, the griots, the seers. Something had happened to his eyes in the past ten years. Zala had said as much one evening when they'd been cruising along Bankhead looking for the gun shop one of the STOP men had said offered target practice for youths. "Is it my eyes," he'd said, watching folks stream out of the mosque heading for their cars, "or have Muslims changed? They used to glow. They used to have such a light around them." She'd said that everyone and everything had changed a little, most especially his eyes, which had changed a whole lot.

Spence turned off Northside into a side street. A hasty row of new housing among the old had the air of a bivouac encampment. Were these the residents digging in, or the annexers slipping in to commandeer turf? By the construction foreman's padlocked shack, a watchman, an old man, sat cross-legged on a stack of bricks covered by cloudy plastic. He was taking off his vest to cover his head from drizzle. Spence turned on his lights. In the cone of yellow, rain fell like Zala's sewing pins. It was a city of elders and endangered children. If warriors were somewhere marshaling their forces against the goose-steppers afoot in the city, they hadn't thought Spence rated a call-up. His eyes burned. Disinfectant, puddled gray in the gutters, overpowered the smells of raw lumber and wet cement. He slid the windows all the way up when rain slanted in, pelting the sleeve of his jumpsuit.

It was a weird state of affairs, psychopaths coming to a city of psychopaths. What else could he call the up-and-comers who smiled how-I-got-over smiles on the screen and on magazine covers, the I-made-it photos never having to be airbrushed, for the whole city was touched up, everyone falling for the ad-agency slogans created to attract out-of-town dollars. The same programmed notions of invulnerability, progress, health, and superiority plagued the whole country, boasting of big bombs, good teeth, strong bones, a miracle science and an advanced technology—meanwhile spending half their income on pills, booze, doctors, psychiatrists, sex manuals, sleeping potions, and assorted witch doctors to help them un-mismanage their lives. He right along with them.

"Spence?" Her voice seemed to echo from within a cave. "I want to know about this box."

"Me, too. Pass me one. I didn't even know you two were back together." Teo flipped up the lid and drew a cigar under his nose in pantomime. He bit off an end of his air caballero and lit up, doubling over in a coughing fit. Zala didn't bother to smack his back. She knew a cover-up performance when she saw one. She'd watched Teo's throat redden as his own words played back on his ears. It struck her as funny, Spence pressing her thigh, Teo embarrassed for indelicately referring to their rocky marriage, and an empty box on her knees. She ran her hand around the inside. As in life, so with boxes, she thought—emptiness weighs.

"Where did you get it, Spence?"

"Quit clowning, T. Will you guys do it? At least poke around out there in Cobb and see what's what?"

"I dunno, Spencer. I'll talk to Beemer, see what he says."

"I asked you a question, Spence. Whose box is this?" Zala struck him lightly with it to get his attention, then tuned up her hearing. She'd developed a pitch-perfect ear. She waited, ribcage clenched, to hear a catch in Spence's breathing, a false note, a cover-up. "Whose box?" she repeated, trying to keep her voice light.

"Nobody's."

"Had me one of those once," Teo said, glad for a shift in the conversation. "Had me a Prince Albert can too. Kept my aggies in the can and my holding stones in the box. I don't guess a kid can grow up without one, hunh?" His voice trailed off in reverie.

"Nobody's," she said. She searched for the courage to goad him into translating "nobody," but she drew herself back, afraid, unprepared, her bomb bays empty.

"Think about it, T, and let me know," Spence said.

He veered to the right to glide by the Pool Checkers Tournament Association Building, near Griffin and MLK. The library books fell against Zala's ankles, and she was spooked again. A box, five books, several unknowns. There had to be signifying grammar that could help her factor. It was obvious that Spence had no intention of taking her question seriously. So she started with the books.

Of all the characters in the spring course, why had she chosen Clytemnestra? And why the delay in doing the paper? She'd never risked an incomplete before. She was lagging enough behind her life schedule as it was. Perhaps she hadn't been able to reconcile herself to the official line espoused by the Southern-belle instructor and the few old books she'd gotten around to. Adulteress, murderess, Clyt had spelled sin, crime, and disorder and little more. But would she, Zala, have sat still while General Agamemnon sacrificed their child for favorable winds to get the warships to Troy?

Sacrificial children. Little Lamb, they'd called their firstborn long before he was Sundiata, Sundi, Sunday, Sonny. Who didn't call their babies little lambs? In the beauty magazines that cluttered the barbershop, she'd read about rejuvenation clinics that performed lamb-gland transplants to revivify aging clients. Injections of lamb-placenta extract were routinely sought in movie-star and celebrity circles, she'd read. Were there explorers in Atlanta hunting for the fabled Fountain of Youth, spilling blood again in their expeditions? Hadn't the forensic psychologist down at the Task Force been speaking of metaphorical cloning of some sort?

Zala sat up straight and moved closer toward the arena of danger. "What do you mean, 'nobody's'?"

"What?" His voice was light, smiling. When she turned to confront him, he was waving to a group of elderly men crossing from the Pool Checkers building to Canopy Castle restaurant.

She opened her mouth, then closed it. There was a streak of lightning poised just above her right brow. She waited to be struck dead for what she was thinking. *Careful,* she cautioned herself, drawing back from the danger line.

"It's just a box, baby."

"What's with you guys?" Teo said. "You muttering about boots and her with this box."

"A damn cigar box," Spence said, driving the limo through a cloud of vapor spiraling up from the sewer in the middle of Martin Luther King Drive. "Relax. It's only a box."

"Are you sure?"

"About what?"

She reached for the dashboard and held on.

"I have to know where you got this cigar box. It looks like Sonny's box."

"Get off my bones, woman. It's not Sonny's. It's from Bryant's office, if you need its provenance. A grateful client. His property had been tied up in probate."

"Provenance?" Teo grinned. "Kiss me quick, somebody."

"Sonny had a box just like this."

"Don't put boxes in my head. I'm having enough trouble with them damn boots. Here, give it to me." He made a grab for it, but she was holding on. "Let's throw it out if it's going to haunt you."

What good was it? Spence had cajoled Bryant to smoke up and pass the cigars out so he could take it to Sonny. It had been on the seat beside him the Sunday he'd gone by the house for his family to join him on the trip to Columbus. Sentimental, or maybe superstitious, he'd been peopling it with the men who could call up Ironjaw and Gatemouth. Now, worse than useless, pointless, the box mocked him. He yanked it from her and tossed it to Teo.

"For your holding stones," he said.

"Some of those old geezers must be a hundred," Teo said, drumming on the box. "Are we stopping or what?"

"Retired merchant seamen, cooks, teachers, journalists, bricklayers." Spence followed the men with his eyes into Canopy Castle. "Old Garveyites, Southern Tenant Associates, race men." Walking encyclopedias and atlases. Mobile archives. Storytellers.

Spence used to rush from sixth-period English so he could catch the men during their coffee break at the restaurant. Taking up the booths, tables, and counter stools, they'd talk history across the room, telling how it had been when old Hunter Street had been a mud-and-plank cowpath. Telling how voluntary tithing in the old days had created a common pot to dip out of for community-benefit enterprises. Telling what Du Bois had been like during his days at Atlanta University. And how they'd pooled money to send a trainload of supporters to D.C. to protest Mussolini's invasion of Ethiopia. How important it had been to visit Garvey in the Atlanta Pen, going back again and again no matter how often they were turned away. He couldn't have gotten through English or history or economics without those men, who'd put on support hose and slipped foam-rubber cushions in their shoes to march in the sixties. "Mayhap too late for us, but we're marching for the generations."

"Is someone going to clue me in about the boots and the warriors?" Teo nudged Zala, but she gave no response. "Another movie company in town shooting in this area?" Teo examined the streets for a film crew.

On Teo's side of Hunter Street, renamed MLK Drive, a youngster was slogging through a pool draining from Mr. Cooper's Gulf station. On Spence's side, in the liquor-store lot, three boys on bikes had found a slick perfect for hydroplaning. Listlessly, Zala watched as spray whooshed out from the bike tires. The drinkers who usually sat on the wall at Jeptha shooting the breeze with customers in and out of the Busy Bee Cafe weren't there. The only adults who could be said to be keeping an eye out for the children were five men under the roofing of Paschal's, the community landmark, tapping their cigar ash onto the wet pavement and holding the big palaver. One ducked out from under the roofing and scooted along the buildings' edges past the Metro Pool Hall. Spence slowed down, anticipating a blind dash across the street to a Cadillac parked by an expired meter near Sellers Funeral Home.

"Traded breastplates and shields for houndstooth."

"Would you mind repeating that for the West Coast audience?"

Spence ignored Teo. Nowadays when Bloods moved up and down the block, streaming in and out of the real-estate offices, insurance companies, and Bronner Brothers stores, he saw no salute, no secret sign, only a two-finger touch to a hat brim in greeting, an acknowledgment of the blood, but not of the tribe. He rubbed his eyes.

"Is something the matter with your eyes?" Zala reached in her pocket for a tissue.

"Yes, yes, that's it." Spence gripped her hand suddenly. "It's got to be my eyes. Got to be. And that's only half of it."

"What's he so perky about? Did you goose him or somp'n?" Teo leaned against the dashboard, expectant; he'd missed the gag somewhere. "If you were planning to hook a right here at Ashby to drop me at MARTA, I'm in no rush. Nothing cheerful about walking into an empty house." Teo sighed and shook something down from his sleeve. "Course, if you two got something going for the evening, I'll cut out."

Spence wheeled around in the intersection being widened and made a U-turn back up Ashby. "What makes you think it's all right to smoke dope, man, just because you're in a Black neighborhood?"

"I thought you guys might want . . . Damn, you sure do change up, Sarge."

"Can it." He turned to Zala suddenly. "You all right?"

She nodded, but didn't take his hand in time, and now he was maneuvering the limo into a space in front of the pool hall. She promised herself a long, hot bath in the deep tub. If the water were hot enough and she slid down low enough, she'd be too slack to torture herself trying to decipher her thoughts and feelings. An obviously new cigar box that hadn't been scratched, dirtied, written on, a box that smelled mannish, not boyish, and it had sent her right over the line anyway, so eager to trade her allegiance and sense of what was for—what?—sensation, the sensation of having answered a riddle cleverly, having fitted in a troublesome-shaped piece of a puzzle no matter how terrible the cost? She hugged herself and smiled wanly when Spence turned down the air-conditioning and massaged her arms. She shook her head; she didn't mind the cold. It was a good, punishing cold cutting across her knees.

"Tell me that ain't the axe-murderer and I'll try to believe you," Teo whispered, meaning the man out front of the pool hall. "Friend of yours?"

"Not yet." Spence dragged his tires against the curb to get the brother's attention. He liked his looks. One leg bent up in back against the black plate glass, his thumbs hooked in his side pockets, elbows taking up lots of room so no one could sidle up on either side, the Blood looked as though he'd said no to all manner of seductions and had never turned in his weapons. He wore a red leather cap ace deuce which he now tugged down as he eyed the limo, eyed Spence, then Zala, then Teo, then Spence again. He folded his arms and pushed away from the glass, kicking the crease back into that gray linen leg. He held Spence's gaze for a second more before he strolled off toward the men in Paschal's doorway. Spence turned off his lights and tapped his horn. Several more men his age came out of the pool hall and stood in the doorway waiting for Spence to approach.

"What's up?" Teo had one hand on the handle but he didn't get out.

Zala shrugged. She had no explanation for the stop, and had expected none. She was grateful for the room to spread out in. They'd been too close too long, turning the air between them phobic. She sat there thinking about the other parents in the city quarantined in their misery, no way to be comfortable, at ease, even asleep. She tried to get comfortable and breathe deeply. But even with Teo close to the door sensing her need for room, she felt crowded. It was worse than the ninth month. She'd needed countless pillows to plump under elbows and knees, to prop against her back, to stuff under her neck. Six hadn't been sufficient. Their double bed shrinking each day. Spence had usually given up fighting for his share of the covers and padded into the kitchen to raid the fridge, eating out of bowls by the tiny light, settling down in the living room to read baby manuals. She'd find him in the morning balled up in a chair.

"Please don't," she said when Teo leaned across her to turn on the radio. On every station they seemed to be forever playing "Another One Bites the Dust," as if prearranged in a monstrous plot. She couldn't hear that, not when the twelve-year-old Stephens boy had been found on Norman Berry Drive strangled. And she didn't want to hear campaign speeches. What did they know, what could they promise? And no more about the hostages, when right here in the city was a house, a garage, a toolshed, attic, basement, closet, filling up right now with her longing seeping flammable under the door.

Zala peered into the blue-tinted rearview mirror. Didn't goodness count? Were the barbarians to inherit the earth after all?

"Sure you don't want a toke?" Teo was rolling a joint, leaning over to do it between his knees. He looked up at the windows of Paschal's Motor Lodge as if addressing someone looking down. "Cool you out a little."

"Teo," was all she said, because the rooms signaled too much to think about. It was easier to pray than search the hotel. She pushed up on her hands for a good look in the mirror. There was nothing but herself, so she looked beyond the windshield to the L-shaped building across from Paschal's. Part of it abandoned, an old beauty-supply shop below, an office above, the two-by-fours in the upper window eased away from the nails, months of trash in the doorway, the plywood on the downstairs window weathered, graffitied, and burned through in places by people bored waiting for the bus. The ground-floor hinges looked hungry for action. A good omen, she decided, and tried then to mold the dark beyond the upstairs window into knowable shapes. Why couldn't she coax Sonny out of the cave as she'd coaxed him down the birth canal? She could urge him down the stairwell and press him into view in the rain-soaked doorway if God helped.

"Want me to take a look over there?" Teo got out and stretched his legs, then jogged across the street to the L-shaped building.

It would make, she was thinking, an excellent hideout, right there on the main street in ten-minute striking distance of nine points on the map. In the corner of the L was a grocery for food and a beauty salon for news. A quick skip across Mayson Turner was a drugstore for sleeping pills to keep the captives quiet. Sonny liked Moon Pies, did they know that? Hated milk but loved him some Donald Duck orange juice, but only if it was Kofi's turn to shop: Tropicana if Sonny had to ask for it himself.

She waited as Teo kicked a path through the garbage to the entrance of the building. Waited as she did by the phone, aching; as she did in the low-slung showroom out past Peachtree Towers, hurting; in the new STOP headquarters, straining, by the radio, hunched over the papers, the map. Waited as the net was flung out, clenched in terror of what might be hauled up. And she would have to beg to look. Couldn't look. Had to look.

Anna and Kenneth Almond had had to look at the bullet hole in Edward Hope Smith's back. Venus Taylor had had to look at Angel Lanier's mutilated face. Eunice Jones had had to look at the wounds on Clifford's head and throat. The Stephens family were looking now at Charles, arranging his funeral. She'd have to ask for permission to look. Couldn't look. Couldn't go to the woods again looking, branches grabbing at her courage, snapdragons dry and jabbing, the leaves brown mottled lace on her clothes that stuck like burrs through two washings. Couldn't step into that old school building another time, the dark dank, the mildew and soil mold sour, the sweat of couples that fucked there, the winos who pissed there, the dogs who slept in that crypt and left half their hair there in mangy clumps. Couldn't walk those hallways, enter those classrooms where children had once recited their lessons, sung the school songs, saluted the school colors, worn the school emblems till a backstabbing law in their favor said sitting next to each other was a handicap compared to the good fortune of sitting next to children taught to despise them, and closed E. P. Johnson Elementary School down so years later the worst of blasphemers could carry a stolen, murdered child into that place and stash it beneath rotting floorboards, dropping a stone on top to keep it down.

"I've done all I know how," she pleaded. "Please." The image of Teo in the doorway kicking at the litter blurred. "Please. What else can I do?" she begged. Five verses a day, she'd done it. Nearly every day of her life she'd slid the red satin bookmark across the crinkly page and turned the gilt-edge sheets, slowly reading, absorbing, her eyes moving along the familiar black type to the red. Done it. Fallen asleep with the Bible flat on her face. Faith can defeat grief. Sung it. Trouble doan lass alwayzz, like her mama and her mama before her over the ironing. Done. This too shall pass, changed. Prayed nightly on her knees.

"But where, Lord, are you?" Not an accusation, she cautioned herself. God don't like ugly. But not too resigned, either. God don't favor the mealymouthed. She angled her chin in the mirror and shaded her eyes just so. But not too much. It wasn't a case of heysugarwhereyabeen? It had to be done right or it didn't count. She'd been well taught by hundreds who knew how to get along with God, the church, and ministers of the moment. So she'd get it right. Had to be right or it wouldn't work. And it had to work.

"Lord?" A humble summons from a humble servant. Course, Maker don't come 'cause ya call, and Maker don't come 'cause ya need. But when Maker come, come right on time. "Time, Lord."

She saw Teo and Spence in the street talking. No Sonny. No angels. The streets ink soup. The cars trumpeting them out of the middle of traffic to the sidewalk. Teo hung by the curb, rained-on. Spence and three other men took off in the direction of Griffin.

By the time God, Jesus, and the Holy Ghost arrived there'd be no time for whatkeptya? With great dignity she'd state the time and place of the funeral and let the Trinity feel the sting of her disapproval collectively and individually as she waltzed off in a rustling black dress. Yes: a turrible numbah she'd whip up on the machine. Hah. Singing the hell out of "Lord, don't move that mountain, just give me the strength to climb." How she'd sing it—head thrown back, hair wild, sarcasm dripping from her fanged teeth! Hahn. Wouldn't look back over her shoulder either. Hahn. And let one of them crook a mouth to mention Job. Hah. Have you considered my servant? Don't even try. Unmerited grief and suffering and blah blah blah. Shut up. Peradventure fifty righteous souls in Sodom. Blow it up. Salt my ass. Turned to stone when she saw what Lot had done, when she saw what the Great Father allowed, what the city fathers allowed.

"I've done my bit," Zala said. "Through," she said, dusting her hands off, through with God since God was through with her. There was nothing left in her repertoire, nothing undone on her list of to-dos. She'd come out of the garden and learned to speak up. Made many a scene. Tracked like a cat. Worn her knees out. Prayed herself hoarse. And where were the tribes to go up against the base city that put family after family on the altar rather than change their notions of order or edit a single line of their job descriptions?

"Forget you," she said, feeling wild and free and crazy fine. "Forget you altogether, God. No more," she said, enjoying the sweet, crooked pleasure of hearing her voice so strong and defiant. . . . She laughed and the streak of lightning turned milky. "Yeahhhh, I've been here, Lord. But where the hell were you?"

Sunday, October 12, 1980

The fishbowl was full of sky, and Roger was blue, then orange, then Casper the Ghost scooting through clouds on his rock castle. Kenti sat up and knuckled sleep from her eyes. And for the third time since Mr. Grier's drill had stopped and the oven door slammed, she got up and told her baby doll it must be time for Sunday school by now.

She heard Kofi saying something fresh in the kitchen just like Mama hadn't been warning him all morning about his mouth. He was hammering in the freezer when she got there, and a chip of ice skidded across the floor and hit her on her foot. The kitchen was only half a mess now, so Kenti waited, one foot on top of the other, wriggling her toes, for somebody to say something about getting to church.

"Mama, we gonna eat now or later on?"

"Not now," Zala said, grabbing the saucepan from the fire. Kenti drew her shoulders up. She would've used a pot holder. She would've kept on the pink rubber gloves. But Mama didn't even run the cold water over the eggs. She had her head to one side, not to duck the steam but to hear the radio. It was talking about the funeral of the new dead boy. And she told Kofi to shush when he was fixing to say something. Zala cracked the eggs against the sink with her bare hands, listening, peeled the eggs one by one without dropping them, slit them open with a knife and scooped the yellows out, mashed them up in a bowl, not even looking at what she was doing. It had to hurt. Them eggs were hot, Kenti figured.

"We going on a picnic?" But neither of them said boo, so she guessed the devil eggs were for ordinary lunch. She went to the cluttered table to find the puzzle key ring to play with. There were pans of dirty water with frosty ice swimming in it, bowls of green fuzzy stuff, cups of hard, dark things graying around the edges, and a potato with a spooky pink finger poking out. Kofi was on the floor trying to roll up the soggy newspaper Mama had put down early in the morning. It kept tearing and making him mad. There was blood on the floor where the chop meat had dripped. There were dead moths curled up with celery leaves in the melted ice puddles. Dirty footprints walked across the newspaper and the tile all the way to the counter where the rubber gloves were plopped. They looked like Miz Penner's pink gloves held against her big chest when she got up to sing with the choir.

"Ain't we going to church, Mama?"

"I don't see why I got to do this," Kofi said. "Paulette and them already cleaned up in here. And now the whole house stinks of oven-off."

"Just do it." She sounded far away, but she was right there, her neck bent, her head to the side, listening to the funeral. And when the drill began again, she wheeled around and spattered eggshells in Kofi's hair, which gave him something new to fuss about.

"Dammit." Zala looked toward the front of the house. Then she looked at Kenti like maybe it was her fault Mr. Grier was drilling holes. Kenti rummaged among the stuff on the table and found the key ring number puzzle next to the juice jug, syrupy orange and sticky on the numbers side. Kenti backed out of the kitchen out the door when she saw her mama staring at her hands, red shiny slashes across her palms going white and puffy.

Mr. Grier gave Kenti a look, then wound up the cord, picked up the stepladder, and called his wife to come see what he'd done. He'd put a light over their front door. Seemed like he could've put the light between the two houses to share it, but Kenti didn't say so, 'cause Mr. Grier hadn't said a word to her since summer. She thumbed the numbers around in the puzzle tray and almost had 1, 2, and 3 in order by the time Mrs. Grier poked her head out and twisted around to see the lamp.

"He won't reimburse us, ya know." Mrs. Grier sucked her teeth in that special way, so Kenti knew she was talking about the landlord. Kenti wanted to try sucking her teeth too, but she didn't want them to think she was mocking. Mr. Grier flicked the light off and on, and then the two of them looked at her like she should be shame still in her nightgown. Her face felt hot, her fingertips cool, though, on the plastic puzzle.

"You don't suppose we should have offered to buy a pair of coach lamps and go halves?" Mrs. Grier said, scratching her head scarf. She wore it pirate-style, and one of the tails was caught in her earring. "Neighborly," she added, looking at Kenti's feet and then her ashy legs. Kenti yanked her gown down, waiting for somebody to say good morning. "Silas?"

"I'm not keen," Mr. Grier said, sounding strict. "I'm not keen atall."

And then he backed Mrs. Grier into the house with the ladder, the two of them looking at her funny like there was some bad thing going on that had made her come out of her house. Kenti skipped back into the living room singing the Christopher Columbus song she'd learned in school. She added a few extra tra-la-las and piped up when she got to the good part about the *Nina,* the *Pinta,* and the *Santa Maria,* real loud, to show there was nothing bad going on in her house. She heard the couple's door click and the chain drawn across the lock, and her face felt hot again. She kicked back the edge of the carpet and slammed the door as hard as she could.

"Dag, Ma, I don't know nothing about it," Kofi was saying in the kitchen. Kenti heard her mama's slippers clopping across the floor fast, fast, so she hurried in to see if Kofi was going to get it. But Mama was only screwing the lid on the mayonnaise and shoving it in the refrigerator. Kofi was banging cereal bowls down on the table looking like Daddy dealing cards, leaning high over the table, his legs on either side of the chair, butt stuck out, popping them cards, slamming them down, and telling the players they were going to Boston. But Kofi wasn't playing, look like he was trying to bust up them bowls. And Mama wasn't playing at nothing, either. She threw herself down in the chair and started studying in her books. And nothing about the kitchen looked like Sunday.

Kenti's good dress wasn't hanging on the ironing board. The bowl of batter wasn't on the counter with the wooden spoon sticking up in it. The rubber gloves were flopped over the side of the sink like Miz Penner was drowning in the catch cup trying to climb out. The black griddle was hooked over the stove on the board next to the skillet, not heating up on the burner with bacon sizzling on the back jet. The funnies weren't on the table, the Bible neither. Books and notebook paper were on the table. And the killer map was on Sonny's chair but not

wound up. Mama had the rubber band on like a bracelet, so Kenti figured she'd been drawing on the map on account of the new boy that got
killed.

"Mama, Mr. Grier wouldn't speak to me." Kenti waited for a hug or
something, but her mama went right on reading, moving from one
book to another, and scribbling on three-hole paper. "Her neither,
Mama."

"Aww, so what," Kofi said, dropping the spoons on the table. They
went clang-a-lang, and one of them bounced real close to Mama's arm.
She looked up and Kofi tried to play it off, but Kenti felt hot in the face
again, her feet cold on the damp floor. She leaned against her mama's
chair waiting for her to say that if she hurried and washed up, pancakes
and bacon would be ready by the time she got back. She didn't want
cereal. It was Sunday. And Sunday was supposed to be bacon and pancakes.

"I don't know nothin' about no box anyway," Kofi said, dragging a
chair. It made a trail across the mopped floor. "So we might as well go
to church."

"First the box," Zala said, looking at the marks on the floor. "Just
like you found them cowboy boots, mister, you find that cigar box."

"What box?" Kenti looked at her mama and then at her brother.
But neither of them would look at her. They had spears in their eyes.

"Some ole cigar box," Kofi said after while. "Like I'm supposed to
keep up with Sonny's stuff. Ask *him,* why don't you."

"How we going to ask Sonny? You stupid." And then she was sorry
she said it, 'cause both of their eyes stabbed her before they looked away.

"How'm I pozed to know where his stuff at?" Kofi was talking that
lazy way, but Mama didn't get after him about it. "For all I know it
could be his locker or someplace."

"What locker?" Zala dropped her pen, and it rolled toward Sonny's
chair.

"How should I know?" Kofi's voice shot up into his nose. "Maybe at
school he got a locker, or the Boys' Club. Dag. How I'm pozed to know?
You the mother." He dragged on the chair some.

"See that window over there?"

Kenti moved away. Her mama didn't sound like her mama. But
Kofi wasn't paying no mind. He was standing hip-shot by the table and
sighing like it was a real boring thing to have to look at a window. He

took his time about it too, roaming his eyes over the laundry basket where their Sunday clothes were balled, then he walked his eyes up the wall to the window and drawled some more. "Yeahhhh, I see it."

"Pardon?"

He flounced around and put his fist on his hipbone like he wasn't supposed to, not to no grown-up. "Yes," he said, baring his teeth.

"You see that wide-mouthed Ball Amber Buffalo home-canning preserves jar next to the spray starch?" It made Kenti's hair shiver. She eased around to the far side of the table and sat down on the edge of the chair, rubbing her arms.

"Yeahhhhh," Kofi said, two hands on his hips, asking for it.

"Pardon?"

He bared his teeth again and slit his eyes. "Yes. I. See. It." His gums were fire red.

"Can you picture how your head would look crammed in that same jar?" Zala picked up her pen and jabbed it in one of the books. "Find the box. Period."

Kenti was hoping Mr. Grier would find something else to put up with that noisy drill, 'cause it was dead quiet and the bottoms of her feet were cold. Kofi grabbed the back of the chair like he was going to drag it on the floor again, but he didn't. He picked it up high over his head like he was fixing to throw it. Mama didn't even look up, but when he set it down hard against the table her pen tore through the page. Kofi climbed up and threw his leg over the top rung, being a cowboy maybe, or a mountain climber. Kenti didn't know what he called himself being, but when he dropped down in the chair, he bumped the table again and Mama turned one of the books facedown so hard, he jumped. Being a fool was what he was being. "Keep it up . . ." was all she said. Then Kofi started playing with the milk carton, trying to figure out how to pour it on his cereal so it would splash and wet up her papers.

"Sunday school ain't closed on account of Christopher Columbus, is it?"

"If you don't want to take us," Kofi interrupted, "call Daddy. Let him take us."

"I don't like calling your father for every little thing."

"You call him for that thing." Kofi pointed his spoon at the killer map, and wet cereal dropped on the table.

Zala pushed the napkin holder toward Kofi's side of the table. He bumped his knees trying to make the map slide off Sonny's chair, but she caught it in time and spread it out on top of her papers. Kenti could see that a new house, and an eye, and an X were on the map for the boy they found strangled in the woods. Mama was going over one of the lines with her fingernails.

"So where you think Sonny at this time?" Kenti hadn't meant for it to come out like that. She tried to think of what to say to make her get up and fix breakfast. All week Kenti had been waiting for Sunday. She wanted her ruffled petticoat pulled down over her head. She wanted to lean her back against Mama's chest and step into her good dress noisy with starch and warm from the iron. She wanted to stand up in big people's church and give the lesson from her Sunday-school group. But before that, she wanted to slouch down in her chair and kick her Mary Janes against Miz Butler's chair so she would look her way and ask how come candy-face Kenti had her mouf all poked out. Then she could tell how they kept doing like they were doing. Cleaning up but not putting her drawings back on the refrigerator. Daddy taking the banana magnet but using it to hang other stuff in his car. Doing stuff like that. And it wasn't right.

Every time they were supposed to go somewhere, Mama would pull the stop bell before they got there. And they'd have to get off the bus and trot after her while she tacked up Sonny's picture on a pole. And everybody'd be looking at them too and come over and pat her on her head and ask her did she miss her brother and was she saying her prayers, cupping their hands under her chin like one-potato-two-potato and Mama not saying nothing about them people's hands on her, except one time when she said real low that children deserved respect. But when Kofi said that, 'cause Mama had snatched one of the drawings off the refrigerator door to write all over the back of it with one of Kofi's markers, he got hit when Mama got off the phone.

Sometimes they'd start out for the zoo in Unca Dave's car but drive right on past the grizzly bears, and she'd say, "Hold your horses, this'll only take a minute, next time bring your coloring book." Then they'd drive to a train track or a trashy lot and the grown-ups would poke under bushes with sticks or dump dirt in a sifter and shake it for clues. And if they said anything it was "Hold your horses, next time bring your crayons." Then they'd ride some more to a school nobody went to 'cept to park for games at the stadium. And all the grown-ups would get out of the cars and talk to people about the little boy somebody stuffed under the floor. One time an old man with a gold tooth in front like Grandaddy Wesley leaned his head in the car to say to Daddy that maybe the crust of the matter was that white boy that got beat up bad and now white folks were killing back. And when they said they wanted to go see the seals, it was them horses they had to hold.

One time they almost got to the zoo, but first there was a house nearby where the papers said grown men and little boys were doing nasty and went to jail. Everybody sat and sat in the cars till Kenti's legs were stuck to the seat and it burned them to move. That's when one of the men with a dog on a chain gave her the number puzzle to play with. But by the time they all started beeping at one another and drove off, the zoo was closed, everybody gone home. And didn't nobody say they were sorry, either.

Then yesterday didn't Mama or Daddy remember to come get them. And when Aunty Paulette walked them home, nobody asked if they'd had a nice day. Well, it wasn't a nice day, it was a terrible day, 'cause Aunty Paulette and her friend wouldn't stop smoking cigarettes and crossing and uncrossing their legs drinking iced tea and talking about when they were girls at nursing school together, and kept saying all right, all right, and smoking some more instead of going right to the zoo like they promised. And when they finally got to the zoo, there was a lady in a long dress and bells in her hair who kept getting in their face with her bug-eyed glasses, looking just like the fly Sonny let her look at one time through his magnify glass. And the bug-eye lady kept inviting them to her house for lunch, saying she was a friend of their mother's when they hadn't even gotten to the zebras yet. And not only that, the bug-eye lady's daughter took the number puzzle without asking and did all the numbers zip-zip, showing off.

And when they got to their house they had to eat some funny-looking salad off a wooden plate, and the lemonade was so thick with honey Kenti couldn't drink it. And all the while the show-off was bringing out games and saying she guessed they were too little to understand the games and putting them back. That's when Kofi jumped in her chest and said, "Don't be calling my sister stupid." And Aunty Paulette got after Kofi for showing out but didn't say boo to the bossy show-off. Didn't say boo to the bug-eyed lady neither when she hauled out her tape recorder and started asking nosy questions about Sonny and the lost children. Kofi had to tell her to mind her own business. And all the way home Aunty Paulette said they'd torn their drawers. Right in front of the friend from nursing school when it wasn't even true. Then dark came but nobody came to get them. Lights were on in their house across the street, but nobody came. They had to get Aunty Paulette up out of bed to walk them home. And when Mama unfastened the chain and opened the door, she gave a squint and then said, "Oh," which was a terrible thing to say.

"I'm gonna call Daddy myself," Kofi said, pushing his bowl away so it sloshed. He sounded like he was going to get the police after Mama for not fixing breakfast two days in a row. But Daddy was just as bad, Kenti was thinking. If they said they wanted dessert or something, Daddy would go in the store and start talking to everybody about the lost children and then come out saying, "Hunh? . . . what? . . . Oh yeah, keep your shirt on." Then maybe they'd drive to another place and they'd see him through the glass pasting Sonny's picture in the store window. And he'd come out empty-handed with some more "Hunh, what, just hold your horses." It was the same thing with the planetarium. They kept not getting there. And that wasn't right, either, after all the fussing Mama had done to get Kofi a card with her hard-earned money. Kenti shook out some cereal and poured in milk. But she didn't want it.

"I'ma get him," Kofi said again, not moving. And Kenti tried to suck her teeth, but Mama was sucking hers and it was loud. It didn't thrill the way the Griers did, though. "Right now," Kofi said, kicking the table.

"Daddy," Kenti said, the cereal mushy in her mouth.

"You nasty," Kofi said, banging his spoon against her bowl. "I'm not gonna eat in this smelly kitchen with some crybaby wiping her nose on her nightgown."

Zala stood up fast. Kofi ducked and Kenti lifted her head so she didn't drip in her cereal. Zala pressed down on one of the books and the spine cracked and two pages slid out. She threw the pen down and stomped across the floor, leaving damp prints. Kenti and Kofi's mouths dropped when she flung the porch door open and it hit against the fridge. Stuff inside was rattling even after they heard her slippers scuff down the back steps, then get quiet. She was probably sitting on the bottom step with her head in her hands, looking at the rock garden Sonny built one weekend when he was under punishment. It was supposed to be a victory garden for Africa, but Daddy didn't bring the flags like he said he would. Then Bestor Brooks came by and they painted musical notes on the stones and called it a rock concert.

"What's a rock concert, Kofi?"

"I ain't talking to you. You nasty. You a nasty crybaby."

"And you a fraidy cat!" she yelled back. "You so big and bad, why don't you call Daddy?" She was sorry she'd dared him the minute he flew out and left her alone in the kitchen with them pink rubbery hands catching hold to the sink, and the eye looking up at her from the map, and the jam jar on the window sill waiting on a head.

"Tell Daddy to come right now," she called out. "It's my turn." She held her breath and listened hard, but bigmouth Kofi was talking low all of a sudden. It was her turn and she wanted to tell the people 'cause now she had it all straight in her head.

Last Sunday it was mixed up. Everybody kept saying they didn't see why the Prodigal Son got special barbecue and new clothes just 'cause he'd come home. What about the other children who hadn't run off and worried their parents? She kept getting the Prodigal Boy mixed up with the Gingerbread Boy until Jimmy Crow said there was no witch in the Sunday-school story. But then Sandy Johnson got her mixed up talking about Pinocchio. And by the time Miz Butler got around to asking Kenti what she thought, she was busy thinking how she never did like that ole Geppetto anyway, always getting on poor little Pinocchio to behave himself when all Pinocchio wanted to do was go on the road and see the world and become a real boy 'stead of a wood doll. And seem like if Geppetto wasn't going to be nice, then he shouldn't have made Pinocchio in the first place, if all he was going to do was be grumpy all the time. If he really cared, Kenti told the group, he would've packed a picnic box and gone on the road with Pinocchio and had a nice time.

But Kenti was sure she had it now. And it was her turn to stand up and give the lesson. It was only right that the Prodigal Boy have a new bathrobe, 'cause while he was away he'd probably missed his birthday or Christmas or maybe Easter. And if she'd been there at the party feast, she'd've let him have the pick of the turkey. And if Jimmy Crow and them started grabbing at the platter first, she'd kick them under the table and tell them to quit being so hoggish.

"I bet you in there digging in your nose."

"Am not!" she yelled. Then it looked like the rubber gloves moved. Kenti went into the bedroom and curled up under the covers with her Baby Crawler. Course Baby Crawler hadn't crawled in a long time, 'cause every time Mama went out to get batteries, she'd come back with newspapers instead.

"I'll wash up first," Kofi said, running in and parting the curtains. "Daddy be here in a minute, so don't go to sleep." He looked down into the fishbowl, then looked out the window in the backyard, drawing a corkscrew near his ear with his finger. Kenti huddled deeper under the covers and hugged her doll baby closer. She hoped Kofi meant Roger, 'cause there was a girl at school named Marva, and they said her mother went crazy and was down in Milledgeville. Marva's clothes were never clean after that. And whoever was taking care of her didn't know how to do hair 'cause her braids stuck straight out and underneath was knotty. Every day Kenti would sit next to her in the lunch room trying to be her friend. But Marva wouldn't talk. And she wouldn't eat. She'd pick up her milk, holding the container to her mouth a long time but not drinking. And when Kenti would take it from her and set it down, Marva would just sit there with a dry white mustache.

Kenti prayed she would get to church. She wanted Miz Butler to hug her. She wanted to hear Miz Penner sing out while the choir clapped and swayed. She wanted to see Revun Michaels hit the pulpit, rearing up on his toes and straining, his throat gravelly and his tongue fat, calling the Lord a shoving leopard and even the grown-ups giggling. And when he said, "Let's bow our heads," she'd pray for Sonny to come home and put on his birthday bathrobe and get everybody to act right. And though house praying wasn't as strong as church praying, Kenti clutched her hands on Baby Crawler's back and prayed and prayed, sinking down to the place where the seals poked their whiskered noses over the back of the pews. There were three husky zebras munching hay in the choir stall. And she could hear the rodeo ponies trotting down the aisles. Kofi was riding one of them and saying, "Daddy's coming, Daddy's coming." Well, Daddy could just come on and grab hold them ropes and hold them ponies, 'cause she was going to go up and feed her cornflakes to the zebras. And then she'd give the lesson. 'Cause it was her turn.

Holding the phone loosely, Zala looked over Kofi's shoulder and conceded that Paulette's cleaning brigade had certainly done a job on the table. She could no longer tell where the stereo had been, the whole tabletop a sheen. While Mattie expounded on the pros and cons of capital punishment, Zala nudged Kofi by way of telling him to go fix his plate, but he jerked his shoulder away and went on reading his comics and eating cookies. She carried the phone to the couch and let him smolder alone.

"Not in general, Mattie. But do you think Clytemnestra had a case for executing her husband? Although in some versions of the story, the goddess Diana whisked Iphigenia off to safety at the last minute."

"I get the feeling, dear friend," Mattie said after a pause, "that either you're trying to tell me something or you're setting me up."

Zala went over it again, trying to keep to the version of the drama closest to her feelings. "Even so," she said, "I mean, whether the girl was rescued through divine intervention or not, the point is, Agamemnon had murder in mind."

"But did they consider it murder? Was that the consensus?" Mattie jangled her bangles over the wire, or someone else did. Zala realized she hadn't asked first if Mattie was free for a lengthy chat.

"Are you alone?"

"Never."

"Never?"

"You'd be amazed. One day I'll explain," Mattie said; then a match was struck close to the phone. Zala heard it sizzle, then flare. Instinctively, she held the phone away from her ear, then replayed Mattie's response, hearing "a/maze" and "ex/plane," for Mattie had a way of leaning on key words making them sound other than conventional.

Now Mattie was talking about the ancient Greeks' borrowing of ethical systems from a culture more advanced than their own, a culture that they'd conquered but not mastered.

"Well," Zala sighed, "it's all Greek to me."

"It may be Greek to you, dear friend, but it's all Egyptian to me."

There was laughter in the background, at least three other voices. Then once again Mattie invited her to join a study group investigating the mysteries. Zala heard, though, 'come mass-store the miss stories.' " It was no simple thing talking with the likes of Reverend Mattie Shaw, Reader & Advisor.

"I've got to go, I've got makeup work to deal with," Zala said. "I refuse to fall behind anymore. I've been at this thing too long as it is."

Seven years, she calculated, setting the phone on the floor by the stacks of books and newspapers Speaker had loaned her. She opened to the introductory notes on Gluck's opera based on the drama and settled back in the corner of the couch where the light was good. She was determined to double up on courses in the spring and get her degree by winter '81–'82 no matter how pinched they'd be by the budget. All around her people were busily re-educating themselves—the poli-ed study group led by Leah over Hakim's Book Store, the various workshops Mattie led at her house, and B. J.'s project with her husband and her brother, designing new curriculum for police training—while she was still struggling to get to the stage where she could afford to look back on her education and call it bogus, as Speaker had, urging her to consider doing her graduate work at Atlanta U poli sci, though she kept explaining that she was an arts type.

Those thoughts made her read impatiently, wishing the musician of the family would return to the house and sight-read the overture to *Iphigénie* as an additional spur. But could Sonny pick up a piece of unfamiliar sheet music and sing out? That she didn't know disturbed her. She shoved her back against the bolster and reread from the top of the page, riveting her eyes to the type.

Kofi turned on the lamp so he wouldn't have to hear her mouth about ruining her eyes. He put the last of the Lorna Doones in his mouth and let it dissolve so he wouldn't have to chew. He was too tired, too fed up, and he had only two comic books left unread from the pile he'd traded Sonny's tapes for with his friends Andrew Pierce and Kwame Penn, a *Super Heroes Atari Force* comic and an *Incredible Hulk*. He discovered that he wasn't following Dr. Orion and Commander Champion's exploits closely, just looking at the pictures and turning pages. He was listening out. He even skipped over his favorites, the guy called Singh and the other one named Perez, 'cause he heard a car coming. He looked toward the door, careful not to look at her. He wasn't going to look at her, eat her food, or talk to her again. He hadn't decided yet about his father. He'd see first what he had to say for himself. The car went by. Kofi dropped his eyes. The boots were propped by the door so that company coming in would see them and maybe solve the mystery. He wanted to tell her that it'd been stupid to take the stereo to the pawnshop just to buy them new shoes. But he didn't say anything. He wasn't talking to her.

Kofi shoved the comic aside and could have caught the falling records, but he let the Stevie Wonder album hit the floor. He'd heard her talking to Aunty Delia earlier about the secret life of a boy. Did Cousin Bobby have a secret life? she'd asked. Like he was a plant. What a stupid question. If Aunty Dee knew, then how could it be secret?

Kofi wiped the smirk from his face when he heard a car door slam out front. Then he heard his father whistle the signal. He didn't move. Let her get the door.

Spence came in empty-handed. That made Kofi mad. But then his father looked pretty scuzzo too. Kofi didn't know how he felt about that—pleased, worried, curious? He folded his arms over *The Incredible Hulk* and watched his father, trying to decide. He was kissing her. Nothing heavy, third-grade stuff. Then when Kenti came running in, he swung her up with one arm and hugged all over her. Then, kind of late to be thinking about it since he was right there, he started shadow-box-dancing in Kofi's direction. Some hello. Kofi waited to see how the explanation would go, but first there had to be an apology. He was firm about that, because he'd promised to come get them hours ago. And when Kofi called again there were people there talking and his father said he'd come as soon as he could but it would be closer to supper than lunchtime. So Kofi had asked him to bring dinner along. Kofi had gone to a lot of trouble too, putting in his order—extra crispy for Kenti with salad and yams, and a double order of macaroni and cheese for himself. If his father remembered *her* on his own, that was his business. Kofi wasn't going to order for her.

"You forget?" Kofi timed it just as Spence was almost sitting all the way down on the couch with Kenti hanging on his neck.

"No, I didn't forget, little man. I'm broke, busted." Spence tried to turn his pocket inside out, but Kenti was sitting on it.

"That's pitiful," Kofi smirked, turning quickly to his comic book when Kenti drew in her breath sharply and looked up to see how her daddy heard it. The Hulk was kind of pitiful himself when Kofi got to thinking about it, but not as bad off as he was. At least the Hulk could go into any restaurant and eat up everything without paying.

Spence sent Kenti for the TV-page pullout and the map while he brought Zala up to date. There'd been a meeting at his house; Teo had brought the news that several of the Cobb County conventioneers were sticking around for the TV special on the Klan scheduled for Monday night. He asked her again if she was going to take up the minister's suggestion that she speak in church, or Speaker's suggestion that she address the audience at the film festival. She gave him a lukewarm response. He sensed something in the air. It wasn't like Kofi not to greet him, not to want to wrestle a little. He supposed the boy had reached that handshaking stage where kissing and hugging were out. Spence twisted around and turned on the radio. Maybe a little music would help.

"I've been wondering," Spence said, when Kenti climbed back into his lap and fingered his gold chains, "what some of these symbols mean, Kofi."

Kofi recognized the invitation to come over as a "ruse," as Dr. Singh would have called it. He turned the page and watched Banner go through his changes, puffing up, turning green, busting out of his shirt but never out of his pants. That would've been something, the Hulk streaking through the city. Kofi muffled a smile, then took his time getting up. He'd sure like to bust out. Bust out of the house. Bust out of his almost-nine-year-old life. He wondered where Sonny had run to when he busted out. He was sure it was Sonny calling on the phone like that, waiting for the coast to be clear before he spoke, before he told Kofi how to come where he was. Next time, Kofi decided, he'd say, "Coast clear, where do we meet?" As soon as his father left, he'd pack a bag and keep it ready.

"I think the circle with the dot represents the sun," Spence said, leaning forward and unhooking the necklace.

"Yeah." Kofi fingered the oblongs set at intervals in the chain. "And this one, the crescent, that's the moon. And the circle with the cross underneath is the mirror of Venus. So we know which planet that is. The arrow's for Mars. Course," Kofi looked up, "if I could get to the planetarium sometimes, I'd really know this stuff."

"And the zoo," Kenti chimed in. "And the liberry."

"I'm gonna get a bad mark if I don't turn in my report on my class project."

"Tuesday," Spence said. "I'll pick you both up from school and we'll hit the library, then McDonald's, then the planetarium."

"I'll pay you Tuesday for a hamburger today," Kofi and Kenti said in unison.

"Just like Wimpy, Daddy." Kenti played with his jewelry.

"Tuesday," Spence said. "I promise."

Zala sighed and nudged Spence with her foot. Would he never learn?

"You promise," Kofi said, dangling the chain over the map. He could tell that he was being given the chain. A bribe, to be friends, and with her too. And he could tell by the way she kicked his father, then drew her foot back under her, that she didn't want him to give Kofi the chain, which made Kofi want it, but not on bribe terms. This was what Commander Champion would call a "dilemma." Kofi let the chain coil on top of the map. Then he sat back on his heels.

"Where'd you get all these necklaces, Daddy?" Kenti was counting the ones around Spence's neck.

"Yeah. You sure got a lot of them." Kofi saw her draw her legs up even tighter, and his father looked uncomfortable.

"Gifts . . . from a friend." Spence patted Kenti's leg in time with the music.

"All of them? And from the same friend? Must be a good friend. They cost a lot, don't they? This one looks like the real deal." Kofi had seen Sonny dog her around the house, signifying, and her trying to get away, justifying. Kofi leaned forward for the kill. "Valentine Day's gifts?"

"Friendship gift," Spence said, picking up the chain from the cable-spool table and gesturing for Kofi to come closer so he could fasten it on. But just when he almost secured the clasp, Kofi pulled away.

"But is it okay to give away a present a real good friend gave you? Your friend wouldn't be mad?" He was careful not to use a pronoun. It made it more fun. While he looked at her foot, he fixed the clasp himself, then plastered the oblongs down on his chest bone. He unbuttoned the top of his shirt so the chain showed, so she would see. He was sure now that the pretty woman with the dark lipstick up at Aunt Dee's and Uncle Bry's office had given his father the jewelry. She was always falling all over herself getting him and Kenti sodas and comfortable chairs and trying to teach them how to typewrite.

"You're sure?" he said when his father nodded, then threw his hand around like he was catching flies. "You're not going to go back on your word, are you?" Then Kofi looked at her, straight in her face. She was mad all right, but trying to play it off like it didn't matter. He stared her down like his brother had taught him. *Always stare 'em down, Kofi, ain't nobody so damn tough they won't back up if you stare 'em down and work some telepathy on their mind.*

Once they were hopping the fence to take the shortcut through the Robinson yard and Mean Dog got loose, and a whole pack of his dog friends backed Kofi up against the hedge, barking and snarling, leaping forward trying to bite his pants legs and drag him down. Sonny had doubled-back to get him. "Stare him down, Kofi. The leader. Stare him down. Use your mind powers." And Kofi had stood his ground and stared the yellow-eyed beast down, sending him messages that he'd get a foot in his nose or a stick upside his head if he messed with Kofi Monroe Spencer. And the leader had blinked and backed away, backed up into the pack, nipped one of the smaller dogs on the ear for getting in his way, then slunk off, and the rest of them followed, barking at Kofi from the curb.

Kofi stared his mother down till she closed her eyes, little damp marks squeezing out at the edges. Tough nuggies, Kofi thought, until he noticed that his father was looking at him, his jaws bunched as he lifted Kenti off his lap and set her down on the cushion beside him. Kofi didn't know whether to crawl, run, or apologize. He ducked when his father rose and lifted his hand.

Slowly, in time with the music, Spence rolled up the frayed cuffs of his work shirt, one at a time, trying to think how he could change the climate in the room. Something was definitely wrong, and the way Zala had been nudging him with her foot he feared he was at fault. Spence looked at his son crouched on the floor watching him.

Rapt, Kofi watched the sleeve being rolled up like his father was getting ready to lead an orchestra, take his own pulse, throw a knife, or slap him across the living room. When Spence didn't lean over and hit him, Kofi felt like a fool for ducking. He watched his dad pivot in that cool way of his and put out his hand to her. She took it and he pulled her up from the corner of the couch. Kenti drew her legs in so they could squeeze past the spool table and the couch. Kofi did a parachute roll out of the way to give them room to dance.

Spence hummed the song in Zala's hair, compensating for her initial clumsiness by dipping her backward, then holding her tight in a half-spin. For a moment it felt like old times, the kids up late watching them dance around the living room, the two of them holding each other close no matter what the music said or the latest craze demanded. There'd be pots on the stove and bags of ice for drinks in the sink, friends in for cards and gumbo, laughter and flirting and loud-talking mock debates filling up the rooms, and always the two of them dancing. Then the music ended and Zala was pulling away, and Spence reminded himself that he'd yet to ask her to call Dave about getting a group to monitor that part of the route nearest Cobb County so Teo and the others could relay the clues from their snooping.

"Awww, y'all looked so nice," Kenti said, as another song began, blocking Zala's way back to her books and papers.

Zala bumped against Kenti's legs in time with the rocking tune till Kenti let her go through the turnstile. Zala bounced down on the sofa to get the girl to laugh. She was groggy, but in a good mood. Spence bounced down too, to keep Kenti laughing; then, counting on the fact that Kofi could never resist a cool move along with a little romance, stretched out his hand to get five. Kofi slapped his palm rather hard. Kenti looked up to see how her daddy was taking it. Spence smiled.

A band of light from the table lamp cut across the slats of light coming through the macramé curtains from the street. The map, curled and creased, lay latticed in shine and shadow on the cable-spool table. Spence set the jug of pencils and markers on one furled corner to hold it flat. Kofi and Kenti scooted forward and held down two corners with their elbows. Reluctantly, Zala surrendered up the opera libretto as a paperweight and joined the huddle. The four of them focused and close, shoulders touching, Al Jarreau soft on the radio, it was like that Christmas in Epps, Alabama, the logs wheezing and crackling in the fireplace Spence had helped Widow Man build, Mama Lovey shaking the long-handled cast-iron popper and singing along with Nat King Cole crooning about roasted chestnuts on an old 78 while they worked an impossible puzzle that Sonny had put three allowances by to get for the visit so he could sit back with the top of the box facedown in his lap while they tried to get the picture together of the Great Sphinx, the one whose nose Napoleon had blown off riding into the Nile Valley like John Wayne.

Zala, her arms crossed lightly over her chest as she leaned toward the map, pressed her arms against her breasts thinking of a tarot reading Mattie had done. She'd sat on Mattie's rattan couch watching the cards being spread: the figures were Nubian; the designs on the back of the cards showed dense vegetation with scarabs, birds, snakes, salamanders, and clusters of stars worked in the vines. Mattie was attempting to teach her about the ancient arcana, riddling her speech with hissing sounds—synodical, synchronic, celestial, Isis, Osiris, Horus, systemic, asp, uraeus. Zala looked for serpentine patterns on the map. There were none, only the right-angled intersections of streets and avenues, the curves where an old street turned into a new one and changed its name; the squares, circles, and X's she'd drawn.

Spence flicked the bent corner of the map and cleaned two fingernails before he spaced again. "My family," he had grinned that Christmas, one side of him radiant from the fireplace heat. "My family," confident that he was experiencing the core of it—heart, hearth, heartworks—though he'd only been skimming the outlines of the form of it, following the course of an airbrush. Zala, looking up from the hassock, had given him a look while she flipped the heavy pages of Mama Lovey's photo album.

Spence selected a purple marker and thickened the line outlining the killers' route. Family. Six out of ten nightly calls to the police were to report domestic violence. Twenty percent of all homicides were family related. One-third of all female deaths were at the hands of husbands or boyfriends. He hadn't run across figures of how many men were annually maimed or murdered by female relatives, though as a child he'd eavesdropped on plenty of stories of women throwing lye, pulling razors, burning up beds, or garnishing salads with diced onions and ground glass, Uncle Rayfield's second wife singing "Cut'm if he stands still, shoot'm if he runs" in between the bits of gossip. The tales the drivers of the fleet told each other about city life were fairly mild in comparison—wives tipping the collection agency as to where husbands had stashed their Mercedes on girlfriends' property, wives stuffing husbands' doctoral theses down the garbage disposal. Only lately had Spence perused data concerning children murdered by relatives, driven to research in order to weigh how serious Zala's performance on the polygraph was from the police point of view and from, he was finally admitting to himself, his own.

"There's a little frog in your throat, Daddy." Kenti placed her fingertips on Spence's neck when he cleared his throat. "You sick? Daddy feels hot," she informed them. Kofi reached up to feel his dad's forehead but Zala's hand got there before his.

"What is it?"

"Nothing, Zala. Just thinking."

"Them bats?" She chuckled.

"Naw." He was thinking about home, longing to be home, at home, longing for Atlanta the way he had in the jungle, in the swamps, at the bottom of mud-filled trenches, reading off dog tags and helping to swing the bodies up.

"Thinking about Sonny, aincha?" Kenti leaned her head against his chest and patted it.

"Sort of," realizing that he wanted Sonny to be there not so much to complete the family portrait as to give him the opportunity to alter it and his own relationship to it. "My family," he said aloud, to see what it felt like to say it now. He hugged his daughter's shoulder and with the tip of his fingers grazed his wife's back. He stretched his leg out on his son's side of the table so he could feel the warmth of Kofi's knees against his instep. "Family," he said again.

"What about it," Kofi wanted to know.

"I think the Chinese have the right idea," Spence said, "or at least the way my bunkmate explained it." With family, relations were fairly formal, particularly between postadolescents and their parents. Casual and informal relations were fine with nonrelations. He wondered if he'd gotten that right. One thing was for sure, familiarity bred twenty percent, one-third, and six out of ten. Chin had been delirious at the time, though, burning up in his bunk with marsh fever, the soles of his feet spongy with jungle rot. But, how could a man with a name like that be taken seriously, and in wartime too?

"Cliff Chin, can you believe that? Sounds like a cousin of Rock Hudson and Mark Trail." Spence fell against the sofa pillows laughing while the rest of them looked at him and mugged.

"Chin the Chinese dude that came by that time? I think I remember him."

"You were so little, Kofi, I can't see how," Zala said.

"That was a long time ago." Spence had pulled some of his unit together to try to get a buddy released from jail in their custody. So many vets had wound up in jail when what they needed were jobs, medical attention, detox programs, review of bad discharges that had resulted in loss of benefits, and maybe just some attention, a breaking of the silence which not even the uprisings of Vietnamese refugees at Fort Chaffee had been able to crack. Spence continued darkening the line around the target area, wishing he had the energy to break the hush that seemed to be settling again in the room. He stuck his tongue out and worked on the map like a kid at a coloring book. He felt them smiling at each other.

"Sounds like they saying 'I believe in mackral,' don't it?" Kenti poked Spence in the stomach and pointed to the radio. She tried her hand at the hillbilly twang. Kofi joined in and Spence tried, but only Kofi seemed to know the words of "I Believe in Miracles." Zala had half a mind to join in but held back. It seemed just another snare that would get her caught up and entangled all over again.

"You hungry, aincha, Daddy?" Kenti poked him again when his stomach grumbled. "Want me to fix you a baloney sammich?" She crawled under the table. "I know how to fix it. And there's devil eggs too."

"That'd be nice."

"There's tuna salad," Kofi said, "but she put apples in it." He rolled his eyes.

"Well, I like apples."

Kofi made a face but got up. Then, inspired, he chopped the air with the side of his hand. "I know how you like salad, with tomatoes in it, chunked up like lemons for iced tea, not sliced roundways like some people do."

"Sounds good to me." Spence smiled, smacking his lips. He feinted a jab to Kofi's shoulder and the boy dropped into a crouch and threw a left hook. Spence fell over on his left hip and threw Zala down against the books.

"Coming up," Kofi said, striding off to the kitchen.

"And you like mustard, doncha?" Kenti was talking loudly for Kofi's benefit. "Not on the bread, just on the baloney, right?" She leaned over the table and yanked on her daddy's pants leg but he was trying to hug Mama. "Right? 'Cause I seen you fix it like that." Hands on her hips, Kenti marched off saying "Seeeeee," lest her brother think for one silly minute that he was champ in the Know Dad contest.

When the news went off, Zala glanced up from the map. Spence was facing the kitchen, a faraway look in his eyes. She eased the marker out of his grip and finished outlining the danger zone. They'd tried to convince themselves that there were two Campbellton Roads, two Martin Luther King Jr. Drives, two Gordon Streets—one crowded with squares, circles, and crosses, the other clean and spacious, where Spence lived, where she lived, where the barbershop was, safe behind a veil that separated that city where they continued to live out their lives troubled by nothing heavier than bills and disagreements about lifestyle, and this city of torment.

"I don't know about you, Zala, but I can't continue like this." He took her hand and drew her closer. "We're entitled to live, you know, no matter what's happened." He felt her stiffen. "What the hell will we have to show for all this time and worry? To Sonny, I mean. Bills, tension, confusion worse than before. At the rate we're going . . . I don't know," he whispered, leaning against her shoulder.

"You feel feverish," she said. "You really do."

"I picture it sometimes," he said, sweeping his eyes around the room. "Sonny coming through the door with a satchel of dirty clothes and a sheepish grin. And what'll he see?"

"What?" she said, her eyes on him, her throat constricted.

Spence laughed. "I should have made this speech a few days ago." Despite the piles of ragged papers—*Burning Spear,* the *Public Eye, Klanwatch,* the *Revolutionary Worker,* items that had boiled his blood until he met Leah and learned who'd supplied them—the place looked good. He'd been a clumsy gumshoe trying to find out if the hat in Zala's car had come from the same source; but Leah, a step ahead of him, had smiled slyly, telling him if he had to live one day as a woman he'd understand the mad strategems one had to resort to for safety's sake. He'd felt stupid, exposed.

"He'll come in the door, you were saying."

"We should have something to show. We should be trying to build something—a community organization." A family, he did not say, for she was watching him curiously.

"You think he'll be walking in that door soon, Spence?" She put the marker down.

"I can see that you've gotten yourself back on track," he said, indicating the library books. "But I was talking about us, Zala."

"I see," she said, waiting for a confession. Soon, then, she could be done with it—the dread, the blame, the masquerading as a wounded animal collecting praise and hoarding sympathy. "Promise?"

"Don't be stupid. How can I promise?" He dropped his face in his hands.

Kenti had found a faded bib in the bottom of the kitchen cupboard and, climbing over the sofa bolster, she tied it around Spence's neck. Kofi, taking his cue, fed his father forkfuls of salad, conscious of his mother's eyes on him whenever tuna fell on the carpet.

"That's a good boy," Kenti encouraged over Spence's shoulder. "Daddy a big boy."

"You still say you like apples in your tuna fish?" Kofi had his doubts, for his dad was making a face, but maybe it was because Kenti, thinking she was patting him, was thumping him on his head.

With the kids in such a playful mood, Spence didn't mind the mustard plastered all over the sandwich, nor the two-inch column of sugar that stayed stuck at the bottom of the glass, nor the tomatoes that had gone soft and slightly sour. Zala's spirits too seemed to lift once Kofi took the napkin and wiped up the crumbs. And Spence didn't have to coax her when a good rocking tune came on. She even got fancy on him, swinging him around while she did a tricky cross-step, then challenged him to rock hip to hip, knee to knee, ankle to ankle, right on down to the floor, the kids beating on the table, Kofi grinning, Kenti swearing she heard bones creaking, Zala shaking her shoulders, and Spence congratulating himself for not wondering too much if Dave and/or the owner of the hat in Zala's car had taught her the new steps.

"It looks like a shoe, don't it?" Kenti was darkening the circles on the map with a red pen. "Don't it look like the Old Woman Who Lived in a Shoe's shoe?" She made crisscross markings with her finger back and forth between the eyelets along Memorial, Gordon, MLK, and Hightower, lacing up the shoe. "Really like a boot, don't it?"

Zala dropped down by the spool table. "Oh my God."

"It's too crumpled-up-looking to be a shoe," Kofi scoffed. "Where's the heel?"

Kenti took up the fork and prodded the East Point area where four X's lined up in a square. "See?"

"It does look like a boot, Spence."

Spence squatted down beside Zala, wishing it didn't.

"Them some weird toes," Kofi said, taking the fork from his sister and dragging the tines across the McDonough/Moreland area where a bridge was drawn. "It scoots up here like somebody's bent the foot up, then all of a sudden it gets fat. . . . Naww," he said when he saw how crazy his parents looked staring at the map. He rapped the fork in the upper-left-hand corner of the purple figure, where Bolton Road swung over into Jackson Parkway. "Plus, it's all closed up. How ya gonna get a foot in? You can't onnaconna it's closed. Whoever heard of a boot with no way to get the foot in?" He searched the figure for more wrong things to point out. He felt his dad burning up beside him. "Naww, naww," he said, wishing the radio would go loud and they'd get back to dancing.

"How'd we miss seeing it?" Spence's voice was trembly.

"Well, you could cut the top open and put your foot in." Kenti was reaching for the fork, but Kofi wouldn't let it go. She picked up the pen again and pointed. "You could cut it open with Sonny's camp knife right here. Couldn't you, Daddy?"

"You stupid!" Kofi wanted to stab her. He stabbed the map instead. "That's stupid. Tell her, Dad. Tell her."

But Spence had already run to the phone, drying his damp hands on his jeans and carefully choosing what he would say to the vets, to the Task Force, and to any parents who might be at the new STOP office on MLK Drive.

Kofi was at the window with his packed bag rehearsing his getaway when a crowd of boys came marching down the middle of Ashby Street, singing.

"Sardines, ugh, and pork 'n' beans, ugh." The marching team broke rank as a car drove by; then the boys filing on either side streamed together again, getting louder. "Sardines, ugh, and pork 'n' beans, ugh."

"There's a moose," they stomped. "On the loose." March, march. "And it jumped." Boom. "In my juice." March, march. "Sardines, that'sallIeat. And pork and beans, that'sallIeat. Ugghhh."

Standing on the chair, he could see over the Griers' bushes. He counted seven boys. Coming home from a game, Kofi thought enviously, maybe from the stadium or their high school. A long-leg boy with a high behind was in front calling the moves. The others marched in ranks with pretend instruments. Bringing up the rear was a big guy in glasses banging like he carried a huge drum. They were doing it like the Grambling Band, shuffling forward, bending and dipping, skipping backward, gliding sideways, then hiphaw marching ahead in precision drill steps.

"A parade?" Kenti was crowding him at the window, stepping all over the runaway bag. Kofi hoisted her up in the chair, then onto the desk. She propped the curtains back with the fishbowl.

"There's a snake," the lead yelled.

"On my plate," the group yelled.

"And it ate"—boom, boom.

"All my steak."

"Uuuugggghhh!" Kenti joined in.

Kofi had just enough time to kick Sonny's gym bag under the desk before Kenti turned around. "What they doing out so late?"

"Having a good time," he said. In searching the hall closet, he'd found everything but the cigar box. He'd wanted the box for the open-sesame to the hideout. But he'd have to settle for "Valencia cigars" as a password. He'd ask Ms. McGovern how to pronounce the word.

"There's a bear in my chair / And it ate my underwear."

"Awww, they're going, Kofi." Her face was pressed against the screen.

"We'd better close this window a little. Getting cold." Part of the curtain hem was wet from the fishbowl, but he didn't tell her. He wanted her to get to sleep in a hurry. "Roger'll be okay," he added when she started baby-talking the goldfish. Kofi climbed up to the top bunk as the cadence grew faint.

"Sardines on a Monday
That'sallIeat
Sardines on a Tuesday
That'sallIeat. Ugh."

"I don't like sardines. You?"

"Go to sleep, Short Legs."

"But I didn't finish my story from before," she said, poking his mattress from below.

"Go 'head."

"Well, for my second wish, I want a big o' sausage pizza and some beer."

"You don't even drink beer."

"Well, I wish I did. This is my wishing story, don't forget. I'm talking about me and Moon Fairy, ya know."

"Okay. It's just that it's stupid wasting a wish to wish you liked beer. Why can't you just double up on pizza and soda and that'd be one wish?"

"Soda make ya pee the bed."

"So does beer," Kofi said, punching his pillow. "You could wish soda didn't make you have to pee, or you could get up and go."

"Then I'd be wasting a wish wishing to wake up before I peed the bed."

Kofi rolled over and slapped his foot against the wall. "Well, I wish you'd finish."

"It's not your turn to wish." Kenti adjusted her covers. "You want to hear what the Moon Fairy grant me or not?"

"Go 'head."

"For my third wish, I wish myself to where Sonny at. And I tell him, 'Come on home, Mr. Sundiata Spencer. It's your turn to stuff the laundry in the bag.' And I'ma tell you took his tapes too, Kofi."

"Shh."

"Shh yourself. I saw you at school."

"Go to sleep."

"Go to sleep yourself, Frog Face."

"Betchu pee the bed. All that ice tea you drank."

"Won't."

"You oughta go pee now so you won't be stumbling around later waking me up with your crybaby self."

"Better quit talking mean. I'll tell Daddy and he'll come in here."

"No he won't." Kofi leaned over the edge of the bunk. "'Cause they don't have no clothes on."

"Oooh."

"Go to sleep." Kofi held himself still and waited. After a while he heard her mumble nighty-night. He counted to twenty-eight, then thirty-six, then nine, then seven, then three. When he couldn't think of any more of the magic numbers his mama's fat friend had been talking about, he answered nighty-night. Kenti had to be asleep, 'cause she always wanted to have the last word but she didn't say anything.

Kofi turned toward the moonlight, trying to stay awake and go over his plans, but the curtain was puffing up, then going flat, then puffing out again, making him sleepy. The house was quiet, not even the clock was ticking. He thought about tiptoeing into the front room to get the boots. If Dad woke up, he'd play like he wanted to ask if he could go to the Halloween party at Kwame's. He'd planned to go as a cowboy, but when he ran across his birthday present in the closet, he decided to go as the ghost of Bruce Lee instead. The house creaked like someone was coming in. But it was only the curtain getting sucked against the scratchy screen. He settled down and worked on his costume. He decided to make up a character—the Karate Cowboy. He almost woke himself up, smiling so hard.

A finger of gauzy white reached out toward the bedpost. The breeze grazed the side of the bed, then bounced off the door into the hall, streaming under the arch into the living room, flowing into the cross-current from the front window. The boots stood upright side by side near the door as though an invisible boy were standing in them listening to the still, waiting for the two figures to roll toward each other again. The under-door draft bellied the carpet, and one boot leaned against the other as though the boy were standing hip-shot now, hugging himself, chilled.

Monday, October 13, 1980

Five minutes after Spence drove off and Zala curled up again in the warmth they'd made, the phone rang. Kofi stumbled out of the bathroom, saw his mother hopping toward the table with the quilt wrapped around her, and continued on into the kitchen, where Kenti was trying to fit two heels of bread into the toaster.

"It don't work, Short Legs. And anyway, you got to plug it in."

"I know it." She went to the fridge to get the jelly. He went to the cupboard to get the matches.

Before Zala could get out the second hello, the three middle toes of her right foot cramped. She cursed the drafty house and threw her weight onto the ball of her foot, massaging it against the floor. Kofi was lighting the oven to knock the chill off, she noticed groggily. She snapped her fingers to get his attention. The oven was tricky; he should be careful.

"Cora?" Zala adjusted the quilt under her armpits and sighed—two grown women acting the fool, it was time to call a halt to the game. "That you, Cora?" She could picture her mother-in-law smiling, payback, though she barely sensed any breathing. Suddenly wide awake, Zala gripped the phone with both hands. "Sonny?" The quilt slid down as she heard the click.

Kofi pulled the broiler pan out and sniffed. "You sure you want toast? Oven stinks."

Kenti pointed her knife toward the living room. "Who she fussing at?"

Kofi listened. It was the bossy voice telling somebody what to do. "Landlord probly."

Kenti pried the lid off the jar and looked again toward the living room. Her mother was wrapped in the quilt, the curly cord wound round her. "She look like a mummy and calling somebody else."

"You pozed to toast it before you put all that junk on it, ya know."

"Then never mind." Kenti painted both pieces of bread red, clapped them together, and bit. "Mama look like a mummy."

"I heard you. Don't talk with your mouth full. It's nasty looking."

Kenti held the jelly bread in her cheek and sucked her teeth at her brother. He rolled his eyes and turned slowly around in front of the oven, soaking it in, storing it up.

"Wish me happy birthday," he said.

"It ain't yet."

"You might forget."

"Can't talk with my mouth full, ya know."

Kofi stood as close to the hot draft as he could get. It might be real cold where he was going.

Ten minutes after Paulette left to take the kids to school, Zala eased the receiver up and listened. The security officer at the telephone company hadn't called back, nor the police. If they didn't know the importance of a tracer, she did. They hadn't believed that Earl Lee Terrell's aunt had gotten a ransom call, so the FBI were not called in, but the newspapers ran the story, and that, the boy's family said, had scared the kidnappers off. Darron Glass's foster mother was certain a silent call she'd received was from the boy who'd vanished in September. Zala tried to remember if any of the parents had been able to get a tap on their phone. She couldn't calm down enough to figure out where her blue notebook might be. She'd begun a section under the yellow tab the day she'd learned that Venus Taylor hadn't had a phone when her daughter's classmate saw Angel crying on a corner near home. Zala secured the receiver in place. It was working. She hoped that the APD, the Task Force, and Southern Bell were too.

It wasn't a telephone van that drove up as she was stepping into her skirt. Nor was it Detective Dowell arriving in a police cruiser. It was Sergeant B. J. Greaves pulling up in a Charger.

"This will take some doing," B. J. warned, handing Zala forms to fill out. She declined coffee, saying she was in a hurry. But while Zala completed the tracer request forms, B. J. continued smoking and talking, running topics into each other without pause—red tape, new slant on the case, a rescheduled test, the sudden change in the weather. Zala gave up trying to follow the woman's train of thought and simply found her an ashtray, then sat down by the phone with a bundle of shoes, knee-highs, and a vest.

"Have you seen this?" B. J. shoved a stack of albums aside and laid a copy of *The Caped Crusader* down in front of Zala.

"For the kids? Thanks." She pulled one sock on and massaged her foot.

"You're not listening, Marzala. I was saying that this comic book is a convention souvenir from the United Klans of America."

"Oh." Zala straightened her sock and looked at the comic. She knew it should ring a bell, but with B. J. standing over her stubbing out a butt and rattling the ashtray, she couldn't concentrate. A test? Whose, hers or B. J.'s? Back in the summer, when a squad-room memo stated that the moratorium on promotional exams was still in effect, B. J. had taken the news of her continued suspended status badly. Chain-smoking and rambling. A new child's folder under her arm, she'd gone on and on about how hard it was to hide a dead body in summer, oblivious to the effect she was having on mothers of missing children. Bacteria activated by the heat, swelling, the odor—any corpse looked like a homicide when it burst. Lousy detail having to take charge of the gore, B. J. had told them, before she noticed that one of the mothers had rushed to the bathroom.

"No, I guess I'm not listening, B. J. Sorry."

"Understandable." B. J. stirred in the ashtray with a match stem. "But I wanted you to know, though I may be jumping the gun, that it looks like my assignment to the Task Force has finally come through."

"Really? Thank God. Maybe now we can get somewhere," Zala said, slipping on her shoes. "With you on the team, we can break this thing wide open."

"Not so fast. It's just a maybe, a good maybe, but . . ." B. J. broke up clumps of ash till the match stem bent. "There's something to be said for working quietly behind closed doors." Zala froze, one arm through a hole in the vest. "I mean working without interference, okay? Being able to do the job without the eyes of the world boring through your head. Once the press charges in, the pressure mounts."

"You always said that publicity and pressure was what this case needed." Zala buttoned her vest slowly, giving herself time for something to register. What was the woman talking about? Sensationalist reporters, undramatic police work, things out of control. Nerves? An impending interview, perhaps; B. J.'s leather and metal were highly polished, the three-inch-wide belt, her badge, her earrings. She'd done something with her hair too, either a hot comb or a relaxer; it fit like a cap.

"Publicity don't always work in our favor," she was saying, using a lighter this time. "Especially when it's out-of-town reporters poking around looking for something flashy but not taking the time to get the facts straight." She snorted; smoke streamed from her nostrils. "Police reporters at least have to. They can't afford to get on the bad side of their main source of info." Her mouth set, B. J. flicked, and ash broke over the rim of the ashtray.

"I suppose so." Zala wondered if B. J. was working up to say something about the lie-detector test. Had someone sent her to demand a retesting?

"We've got to have room to turn around in. That's what I tried to explain to that woman your husband sent to interview me. Which I didn't appreciate worth a damn, okay? I'm not interested in spotlights, Marzala. I leave that to the egomaniacs. I'm good at my job. I've had to be." She crushed out another butt.

Zala had heard it all before, of course—how female applicants were shunted off into typing pools or into juvenile services; how a woman officer, until recently, had to have a college degree and background in social work; what an uphill battle it had been to be issued uniforms, and equipment, to get training, and be assigned to details like the men.

"Yes, I know," Zala said.

"Once a case blows open, all the chuckleheads come out of the woodwork. It's hard enough trying to shake something loose from informants, but if they can't come and go on the q.t. . . . ." She took a slow drag. "You don't know. Wide open, everybody jumps in, and we've got to cover our ass 'cause city hall got to look good, the high command got to look good, and nobody gives a shit for those of us bustin' the bricks. We're the dirty dogs coming and going. If we're on the scene, we're harassing the innocent. If we ain't on the scene, the public's up in arms. And who backs us up? Hell, the high command's loyalties are to the administration and all them other politicos. So when they bear down, it's our backs that catch it. And who's gonna chance asking for help? You look like a fool if you do. And don't think colleagues eager to move up a rung won't stab you in the back if you've got the ball. Dammit, I could do this job if these flakes would stay out of my hair." She jabbed the ashtray for emphasis, and gray sifted out onto the table.

"I hear what you're saying, B. J., but I don't know why you're telling me all this." Zala leaned over and buffed the table with her sleeve, embarrassed when she caught herself doing it.

"That Eubanks woman—your husband's friend?—she said you were bringing in the TV networks to blow the case open. I thought we had an agreement to keep each other informed. This morning I find out through the grapevine that you parents got a medium stashed in a hotel here in town, some woman who's been making headlines up north with cases that supposedly have the authorities stumped. If you knew how much work has been done on this case—no, listen, don't interrupt me. Then I find out—and not from you—that some of you parents are planning to tour the country cracking on the investigation. That's not too smart. And you should have told me."

"Now wait a minute. You act like the case belongs to you. No, you let *me* finish. You've thrown a lot of things at me, B. J., and I listened." Zala tried to stand up, but B. J. wouldn't move to give her room. "I know about the psychic. I assumed you did." Zala didn't know much about Dorothy Alison. She'd only gotten a glimpse of the energetic Italian woman when one of the parents suggested Zala bring by some of Sonny's personal items for the woman to "scent." She had only a smattering of the woman's background—the Patty Hearst case, five honorary badges from police departments who'd benefited from her help, particularly on the Debbie Kline case in Waynesboro, Pennsylvania.

"One of the volunteer investigators brought her down from New Jersey," Zala said, shoving her chair back to make B. J. move. "But I haven't called anybody in." She scanned the room again for her notebook. At the tenants' meeting, Speaker had given her the name of a network newsman in D.C.

"Let me get this straight," B. J. snorted. "You're telling me that you don't plan to use this TV contact to get on the air?" Her lips curled. "I don't think I believe that. Your husband's friend was pretty damn sure about that point."

"Since when am I answerable to you? I haven't called anybody. But what if I had?" Zala stood up and backed the officer away from the table. "I don't know what's wrong with you. All this time you've been bugging me to speak up, get pushy, try to get the help of the media to open the case. Now what are you saying—sit down and be quiet? Why?" she demanded.

"I'm trying to put a flea in your ear, Marzala."

Something about the way the phrase was whispered made Zala soften her tone. "Is this about the lie-detector test I took?"

B. J. chewed on her lips. "I wouldn't worry too much about that." She seemed about to say something more but didn't.

"No?" Zala waited for an explanation, for exoneration. Maybe she had passed the test and they'd lied to her. Zala reached under her skirt and tugged her turtleneck down. "I don't know what you're telling me, B. J., I really don't."

"I'm telling you, among things, to be careful. And you can tell Mr. Spencer that if he wants to know something about me, to come ask me himself. I want that tape. And another thing," she added, cutting Zala off. But then she stopped and tipped the chair back and forth. "These outsiders come in," she said, heating up again, "and don't take time to get to the nitty-gritty, so to liven things up they turn the cruds into heroes and we're the bad guys."

"I know you're not telling me that the media hasn't had time to dig into the real story. You can't be telling me that—not you, not to me."

"I meant outsiders, okay? As for the press here, they'll get to it. I'll see to that. But your contact, for example—how much can he accomplish? He'll come into town, on the weekend naturally, when half the offices are closed, so what good can he do? Make up shit. And next thing you know he's got the public rooting for the criminals."

"Not this, B. J. A bank robbery maybe, or a stickup at a fancy jewelry store. But not this. Thugs that don't even soften up for Mother's Day cringe about this case. I know what I'm talking about, so don't sigh that sigh at me. I've tacked up handbills and talked to all sorts of people. And I know. Not this."

"You don't know how media works, Marzala. They're after a story. You think they give a good goddamn about the facts? We get a suspect, catch 'em dirty even, and what do they say in the paper? Social misfit, rotten childhood, temporarily nuts because of junk food—like that creep out in California who shot up the mayor's office. The criminal's a misunderstood victim and we're a bunch of shits for making the collar without a please and a may I."

"Maniacs that attack children? No way. They've got to ask for protection in jail from other prisoners. You're talking off the wall. I'll get you the tape from Leah Eubanks, if that's what all this is about." Zala brushed past B. J. and headed for the hall closet. "Heroes," she snapped. "You must think you're talking to a two-year-old. You may have more experience with media, but I'm not stupid. To hell with it anyway," she said, swinging hangers back and forth. "Should I go with you down to the telephone company?" She yanked a sweater from the closet.

"You know that this out-of-town contact of yours is not going to get any cooperation from us. And neither is that fortune-teller. And how do you think folks'll feel reading about you all blasting the administration? Don't be too quick to accept invitations to speak around the country. You don't know. All those reporters are interested in is whipping up a good story. They'll have things coming out of your mouth you don't even mean. Then how will you feel when you try to correct something and get mad and they spring your polygraph on page one?"

"I see." Zala elbowed her way past and got into her sweater.

"Why are you catching an attitude with me? I'm trying to tell you something. They can't get very far on what you know, so they'll make up the rest, and you'll take the fall. You can travel all you want, but you've got to come home sometime."

"I see."

"All I'm saying," B. J. pleaded, following Zala back to the phone, "is that there are a million things the police are privy to that the public never learns, can't. You've had fringe access to information at best. Mostly what I've been willing to give you."

"Fine," Zala said, raising her right hand. "I swear I won't mention your name or what you've spilled. And I'll get the tape. Satisfied?"

"There you go again."

"That's right, 'cause it's crazy, B. J. Now that you're finally in position to really help us, you tell me you can't afford to be associated with us. That is what you're saying, isn't it? Tell me that's not crazy. Agreement? You come in here and I hear three kinds of 'we' and 'us' and none of them include the people you're supposed to be helping. If I had the time, B. J., I'd laugh, I really would."

"You're not listening," B. J. said, shoving the ashtray aside with her hip and sliding onto the table. "Let me break it down for you."

"I wish you wouldn't. I don't know what's bothering you, but I've got problems of my own. And seesaws ain't my thing, never was. Always hated getting bumped down hard. I wish you'd get those papers working," she said, and unlocked the door. But B. J. had hiked one pants leg up and was talking again, explaining how things had to be done by the book sometimes to assure maximum control so the job could get done. Her words tumbled out with the smoke, lost on Zala, who was shoving the door back over the carpet. Sergeant B. J. Greaves was sitting on her furniture, turning her house into a squad room, and refusing to be shown out until she'd finished sermonizing and patronizing. Zala heaved the door back till the knob banged the wall. Nobody was going to pull rank in her home.

"Get the tracer put on my phone, please."

Sliding off the table, B. J. looked like she might pitch forward onto the floor. She pulled herself up straight, then patted the leather case on her hip. "You can count on it," she said, and moved through the door.

"And thanks," Zala called out. B.J. paused, as if there were something further she would say; then she unlocked her car door and patted her hip again in a gesture of reassurance. It would probably be, Zala thought, B. J.'s last act as B. J.—hooking her up before cutting her off.

By 9:30, the house was upside down, but the notebook and the slip of paper with the phone number were in Zala's hands. Perched on the arm of the sofa, she chewed on the paper, wishing the phone would ring and give her another chance, though she wasn't sure she was up to anything stark yet. Maybe a call from a storm-window salesman first asking to speak to the man of the house. She could hear her niece Gloria—"The man of the house? Ooooh, sir, he died this morning, my daddy did. Washing the upstairs windows, he fell off the ladder and broke his neck. And I dunnoknowhawegonnadooo." Or maybe a market researcher would call asking after Zala's brand of brassiere and how much snap it had left after twenty-three washings. Or better yet, the Board of Ed informing her once more that Sundiata Spencer was truant and that things would go hard for the Spencers if she didn't bring in a sworn affidavit verifying the story she'd offered last time. Then she could let loose for five blazing minutes, discharge all the feelings jamming her system; then, calm, she'd wash her face and fix a cup of tea sweetened with the home brew Mama Lovey had sent up by Greyhound to make the fruitcakes drunk. Maybe then she'd be up to a phone call that mattered.

She peered through the macramé curtain when she heard a tapping in the street. She half expected to see legs sticking out from under her car, the back of her Beetle thrown open, its innards exposed, and Spence down on the ground by the fender, handing tools underneath to the mechanic. Months in the shop, untouched till she could come up with a deposit, the car had been towed home by Spence's new friend, who promised to give her an estimate of an installment plan. The tapping went past. It wasn't someone Simmons had sent to bring her to work, but a taxi, one of the old gents who hauled shoppers back and forth to the A&P at West End, its tailpipe bouncing in a bent-hanger girdle and sparking against the ground. Once, while sitting here waiting, she'd been startled by Sonny hopping out of a cab. He'd come strolling in blasé blasé, leaving her on tenterhooks until Kenti nagged the story out of him: he'd sassed Aunt Delia, who sent him home in a cab. How he'd bragged about beating Delia out of cabfare—how he'd boasted about beating the driver out of a tip!

"Obnoxious chile," she heard herself say before she could censor it. "And I tried so hard." The counterfeit of the whimper shamed her all the more. She clamped down on the paper till her teeth hurt.

She went over the call of earlier that morning foraging for some morsel of information that could settle her stomach. Had there been background noise? No, no Ping-Pong, no traffic, no machine sounds or music. Cora? Sonny? An anonymous tipster encouraged by the handbill, then scared at the last minute to get involved? All that the handbills had yielded thus far were calls from people who prayed for her, or people who warned that God was putting her whippings on the shelf. The intelligent thing to do, she told herself, running her hand over the upholstery, was to call Cora. But she couldn't get her legs to move. Her hand snagged where the fabric had lost its texture, then tore. A knobby weave that used to give her a tactile pleasure on lonely nights, its threadbare state only reminded her now of her own. She noticed that a corner of the sheet had gotten caught on the mattress strap when she'd folded the sofa bed back in. She looked at it and stopped chewing, trying to gauge how she felt about the night's lovemaking. She plopped the notebook down covering the telltale sheet and turned her attention out the window again.

There was no one on the street and no other sound now but the yapping and straining of Mean Dog tethered and pacing in the Robinson yard. The Griers' cat on the walk was slowly moving its head, tracing the dog's path.

"Can't pay the phone bill anyway," Zala said, trying to rouse herself, "so why not call D.C.?" Before inertia set in. In another minute paralysis would take over, locking her joints. Her mind would thrash about, but she'd stay stuck in the nightmare with the it, the thing, the them gaining on her. She tried to think of nasty names to call B. J. to fuel herself, but lacked the reserves necessary to even begin.

Zala turned on the arm of the chair. The trees along Thurmond were just beginning to mottle. They promised bright vermilions soon, burnt orange, golden-tinged russets.

In another time, in another life, gazing out the window, swinging her foot against the sofa, she'd be planning a trip to the Tombigbee near Epps, or the shore in Brunswick where her daddy's folks lived; or to where autumn colors looked best, planning an outing to the approach trail of the Appalachian. Staring a pleasurable stare and not minding the prickly feeling in her foot, she'd consider which weight of watercolor paper she'd pack, which brushes, which tubes of pigment for when Kenti tired of painting pictures with grasses, flowers, berries. Then they'd up and go, on the seeming spur of the moment, giving the girl no time to get excited and run a fever. Mother and daughter off for the day, no boys allowed, nyah, nyah, nyah. Kenti leading the way over the switchbacks where lichen sparkled, leaving the path to point— "Foxfire, right, Mama?" Picking up twigs to burn for charcoal, finding rocks just right to sharpen the charcoal sticks against, a picnic on a carpet of needles—deviled eggs, sausage and biscuits, a thermos of hand-squeezed orange juice, and apples for munching as they made their way to a watering spot. Mama and Chile gathering bouquets of brights and delicates, predicting which would be stingy, which generous giving up their colors. Then, leaning over a finger inlet of the Tombigbee River, or crouched down by a creek in the north Georgia woods, bracing themselves against each other's legs, they'd jar water, not minding too much the bugs and sediment that went in, for sometimes happy surprises occurred when bits of things mixed with the pigments and were laid on the paper with brushes of ferns.

The throaty cooing of pigeons somewhere over the bathroom dormer called her out of the mood. She snapped to attention at the sudden flapping of wings, brisk, panicked, as though a shot had rung out in the woods and geese were breaking from cover. How she hated pigeons. But did they care? They came and went as they pleased, on her front steps, on her car windshield. How she hated that yapping dog, the wind, the emptiness that ached like a severed foot. Who cared? Whether the phone rang again, or a cab arrived, or she got up and found a tissue, the grass grew anyway.

From the moment the man got on the line it was clear that dialogue would consist of one mouth and two ears if she wasn't aggressive. Glib, flip, in love with his facility for lists and impersonations, the newsman didn't sound like a serious someone Speaker would recommend calling for help. She didn't know where to break in, how to get him back on the track. Yes, he agreed, there was a media whiteout on the Atlanta situation, on Blacks in general for that matter, then off he went cataloguing stories that came up over the wire each day, got clipped, and collected in the waste bin—cross burnings, firebombings, snipings, pejorative slogans smeared across Black workers' lockers at Bethlehem Steel, hate mail delivered to the Black Student Association at Harvard, mysterious drownings, beatings, burnings, truckloads of bigots with bats ambushing interracial couples in parks, gangs of white youths on the rampage at skating rinks, the police rioting in Black communities around the country.

"Then how come—"

"What can I tell you? Blacks just aren't news anymore, Mrs. Spencer. Take those women that were bludgeoned to death in Boston. A group called a press conference and no media showed. Let's face it, if it hadn't been for Mount St. Helens blowing her stack, the Miami story would've received no coverage at all."

"I'm not talking about Boston or Miami. I'm talking about Atlanta and the children who—"

"Lady, Black boys getting killed in the South just ain't news."

"And girls," she inserted. "And women and men."

"Oh?" He was rustling papers. She didn't know what to say next. "The information Earl Reid clipped to his letter seems to be about boys . . . two pages full of typos and contradictions under an official letterhead . . . hard to believe this bulletin is from Atlanta's Commission of Public Safety. They've listed one boy as missing, for instance, three days after his death. What kind of Amos 'n' Andy operation—"

"I've seen it. But I can forward better information if you'll give me your address."

"I know how you feel, but I don't make network policy. The news of the moment is Iran, when it's not the election or stories about international terrorism." And off he went again, while she reached for the newspaper, grasping at straws. He was ticking off headlines, mimicking newscasters, referring to Ted Koppel of *Nightline* as Alfred E. Neuman, a.k.a. Howdy Doody, impersonating Jimmy the C speaking on the hostages, but calling the President Tom Sawyer, then rustling the papers again that Speaker had sent and tagging him Earl the Curl, which threw her, but maybe before Speaker had dreaded, he'd jerried.

"But if you could—"

"The problem is—and I don't mean to sound insensitive to your situation—but the Atlanta story lacks scope, if you will, as opposed to, say, Iranian women putting the veil back on to become revolutionaries, or terrorists skyjacking jumbo jets."

"Please! There's terrorism right here in Atlanta. Atlanta, I'm talking about, the 'New International City.' We're not some mail-order postal address you see on late-night TV—smokeless ashtrays, bamboo steamers. Look, mister, children and not just children have been murdered here, and you've got to do something about it. Earl says you're a newsman. Well, this is a news story I'm talking about. Terrorism."

"Formations on the left are the sort of terrorists that—"

"Then you think it's a right-wing group here, is that it? A lot of people would agree with you. I can put you in touch with them. Listen, here's an angle. Let me read this item to you. 'Self-proclaimed white racist J. B. Stoner and his National States' Rights Party will host an international conference in Atlanta.' International," she underscored, moving her finger down the column. "Here, about the State Department and the Immigration people. 'Nazi leaders from Belgium scheduled to come to Atlanta for the Saturday, October 11 meeting had their visas revoked on Friday.' Quote—'Their presence in the country is not in accordance with the U.S. public interest'—unquote. So what about that? International enough for you?"

"As American as apple pie and H. Rap Brown," he laughed, icing the wire.

"He's here too," she sighed, tallying up what the clock now said about her phone bill.

"Is he?" The man sounded interested. "And he's involved with the community's handling of the case?"

She couldn't think of a lie fast enough, and he took off again, the second hand sweeping around the dial as he mused about his apprentice years covering firebrands and mastering the gimmick of news pegs.

"As in the Miami uprising," he said. "Nature supplied a savvy reporter with something to hang the story on—two kinds of eruptions, a volcano and a community. It worked. The networks snapped it up."

"You're a journalist," she jumped in. "You could find a peg. I can set up interviews, introduce you to the STOP committee, to the volunteer investigators, to someone on the Emergency Task Force. You could interview my family. Our boy's been gone since July, but I believe he called this morning. That's a beginning. I can help. I really can." Sweat soaked through the ribbed cuffs of her sweater.

"Today? He called you today? You didn't mention that." He was about to laugh that not-quite-laugh again.

"Please listen," she said, cupping her hand over her outer ear to tune out Mean Dog. His howling sounded like something more than a cat was tormenting him.

"Mrs. Spencer, I don't make policy. What can I tell you?"

"Tell me *something*."

"I know how you feel, but—"

"Do you? Do you really? Rot in hell!" she yelled, slamming the phone down. Chips of plastic hit the wall.

She stomped along toward the bus stop, heaping curses on the heads of the newsman, Speaker, B. J., Cora. And herself. "Rot in hell." So lame. First Amendment rights was what she should have launched into. That's what was in the news lately—adult-bookstore owners, porno-mag editors, fascist fundamentalists, the ACLU, radicals—even Kofi running off at the mouth about the rights of the governed. The right to speak, the right to know. So what was the media whiteout but a viola-tion of everybody's First Amendment rights? That's what she should have told the bastard up there in the nation's capital, so dry, so droll.

The dogs in the side street were baying like wolves. Furniture was piled on the sidewalk. First cold day and someone was being evicted. Ain't it the way, she muttered, grinding her heel in a patch of dande-lions between the paving stones. Crazy damn mad, man, as Mr. Grier said of the world, coming in from work every day, wiping his feet on the mat and wagging his head. A greasy skillet full of steaming beans had been set on top of a sateen slip, then dragged across towels to a better perch on top of a mattress, the sheets fallen away, showing a pattern of stains. No privacy for the poor, she wanted to tell somebody, the "any-body" who should be there to do something about it, to at least snatch the dirty underwear spiked on the plastic dish drainer and stuff it in the chest of drawers sitting upside down in a chair. Who gives a shit! she thought, but she didn't feel better, she felt fake and as ineffectual as she had when she'd broken her phone. She approached the high curb and spied discolored pots and pans with dents in them, a burnt muffin tin holding earrings and old tarnished keys. She shivered. Hobgoblins, un-leashed early, were driving the dogs up the scale into the tenor range.

"*Marzala!*" Hearing her name thundered, she wheeled around, frightened.

"Get in," the driver of the green minibus ordered. "Dammit, sister, get in!" The passenger door sprung open and Zala jumped in. The bus shot past the heaps of furniture, leaving her stomach behind.

"Quick, stash your bag under the seat and change the batteries. Load all your pockets with tapes, sister. This is it."

"What is? What's happened?"

At 10:12 a.m. a roar had gone up from the boiler room of the Gate City Day Nursery in the Bowen Homes project of the Black commu-nity's northwest district, hurtling hot metal helter-skelter into the sunny playrooms of preschool children. Falling walls wrecked toy chests, splintered cribs were upended; floorboards unmoored spun in an avalanche of plaster; tables, picture books, and wooden blocks tumbled against plastic clocks that ticked away on pastel blankets spongy with blood.

A locket and chain torn from the neck ripped the skin of a toddler running with a slashed femoral artery through hot debris. Bawling babies crawled over blistered pacifiers, dropping scorched dolls on dump trucks smashed flat by scrambling knees cut on the metal edges of robots leaking battery juice. Soaked socks, torn drum skins, hands clawing at the mesh of playpens while tinny xylophones plunked eerily pinching fingers. Spines rammed by table legs busting the strings of ukuleles curling into black lumps. Teddy-bear stuffing like popcorn in the gritty air where glass spattered into the wounds of toddlers. Flashcards fluttered high against Venetian blinds clattering down on brightly painted furniture collapsed on a baby boy's life.

The cook, preparing lunch when the blast blew the juice can from her hands and sent the metal trays flying, got trapped in the kitchen when the stove was thrown in the doorway and jammed from the hall by flooring hurled from the office where the director reeled in her swivel chair phoning for help. The social worker snatched up a child as the ceiling caved in on them both. A teacher, broken-field-running through heat and fear, a child tucked under each arm, made it to the lawn strewn with rubble slippery underfoot and collapsed for a moment into the arms, bosoms, blankets of neighbors come on the run who couldn't hold her for more than it took to deposit the two and turn back to the building, one teacher diving through the pebbly air to cover a little girl knocked down on the tiles when a face bowl broke away from the bathroom wall.

Residents poured out of Bowen's buildings to pull screaming children, shocked mute children, stark-eyed children from the arms of the women who wrenched themselves away again, slipping on the dew-red grass where chipmunks had given way like grapes underfoot. Squirrels, tumbled down from swings and jungle gyms fifty feet away from the blast when a door sailed through the playground and ricocheted off the cyclone fence on the Jackson Parkway side, were trampled by motorists who thudded down the slopes to help. Birds, perched on the voltage wires along the perimeter of the hill, were felled by a storm of bark and twigs when a desk blew two hundred feet from the nursery below into the brambled lot on the high street, tire treads of delivery trucks and a church excursion bus scored across their feathery backs. Flung over the two-story apartments next to the nursery, soaring three hundred yards along Yates, a metal door landed in a parking lot, cracking cement and blistering paint from the cars rocked by the explosion.

Across the way, children in the A. D. Williams Elementary School took cover when the orange-brick valley shook, teachers racing to the rattling windows to look up at the hill for signs of cannons or tanks attacking. No assault platoons, only cars stopped in the middle of the streets and drivers crowding down the slopes, the teachers hustled their classes out of the rooms to huddle under the stairs and wait for the principal's voice over the PA system.

Stiff-legged and shivery, dogs whined alarm, relaying the disaster to Bolton Road, to Hollywood Road, to Hightower, and down to Martin Luther King Jr. Drive as more neighbors sped across the open terrain of the low streets from Walden, Chivers, Yates, First Street, Grant Drive to arrive stupefied at the scene of destruction.

"Oh my God," Zala gasped, yanked along on the cord of the tape recorder as Leah Eubanks moved through the crowd angling her mike— "I thought it was MARTA blasting below," "I thought it was Judgment Day," "Wh-who'd do th-this?"—stunned, stammering, a man in a bathrobe gritting his teeth, a woman in a dress ripped from the waistband, a stutterer in a tattersall vest holding a boy limp in his arms.

A school crossing guard whose yellow harness was streaked with char ran up. "Get that damn thing out of my face!" she bellowed. "What kind of people are you?" She spat in the direction of Zala's foot and flung her arms about for the group to break up. "Get these people cracking. We need bandages!" She sprinted past them along Yates to Fields, then uphill to the firehouse.

Dave heard the dogs, the sirens, the car horns, and stepped out to the stoop of the Job Corps Center at Westlake and Ezra Church. A scooter cop was wheeling around in the street, dragging his feet, holding up traffic, trying to get his walkie-talkie to work. Dave stood on the steps and looked up and down Westlake, cocking his head to pinpoint the crisis. Traffic followed the motor scooter toward Hightower, though the dogs seemed loudest in the direction of Bankhead.

"What is it, Mr. Morris?" A youth in a wine-red ski jacket came out of the building as Dave jingled change in his pocket and tried to get straight the seven numbers scrambling around in his head.

"Whatever it is, it ain't far. Listen up, Jonesy—I'll be right back. Don't blow your appointment. Get back in there in the line."

"A line? A damn line? Hey, Morris, I can't relate to no line," the youth drawled, swaying on rubbery legs, his hands making duckbill passes in the direction of his youth worker's back. "Dig it. A line is a Western concept and I'm an Afrikan. Dig yourself, imposing a white man's concept on a Black man's mind. Wow. That's deep. That's cold, is what it is. Yeah, in line, keep in line. Wow, that's some cold shit, Morris."

Dave left the youth weaving and jabbing on the steps and ran down to the corner of Simpson. Cars were U-turning in the lot of the Smoky Pit, then speeding off in the direction of Bankhead.

"An explosion over at Bowen Homes!" he heard the druggist shout across to the peddlers who had paused in their stacking of jeans, tapes, and ceramic tigers on tables lined up in the Pit's lot. "The day-care center, he says."

Dave reached the phone as the druggist bent toward his informant, tuning the dials on a shortwave radio.

"Holy shit," the druggist's informant said. "Bomb threats are coming in over the wire so fast, the cops don't know where to go first. It's Code One all over the place. Wait now." He shushed the druggist, who in turn held his hand up in the direction of the peddlers to put them on alert for the next bulletin.

"The dispatcher just told them to go on silent band. I think they're going to scramble the rest of us." He pulled the aerial up as far as it would go.

Dave yanked the phone off the hook, remembering how they'd used scrambling devices to delay the news of King's assassination. But the word spread from Memphis to the place he'd called home in a matter of minutes anyway. He slammed coins into the phone, one ear cocked in the direction of the two men standing in front of the pharmacy glued to the radio. There was crackling static, then a sudden burst of messages of numbers. He turned aside and got his own numbers together, already cursing Teo and Beemer, the two gray boys Zala's ole man had such faith in, doubting beforehand whatever they'd say if they couldn't name names, license plates, and precise room numbers of the hotel out in Cobb County.

Speaker directed the student to let him out near the church and then to get back to his frat brother at the Radio Shack who'd first called in the news to the campus. He followed on foot the crowd that ran into the firehouse. Finding all lanes empty, the rig, pumper, and the rescue wagon gone, the crowd about-faced and ran down the slopes to Bowen. From the steps of a house back of the station, a woman in a shower cap beckoned to Speaker.

"Here now," she said, holding out a dishpan of ointment jars, Band-Aid cans, and wads of cotton batting. "Take this along," giving him the load, then turning to take up a quilt folded on her porch glider. "They'll need this too." She came down the steps sideways, piling it on top of the pan and backing Speaker out of the yard. Slow and easy but not weary or old, the woman was the essence of calm.

"Did they catch anybody?"

"Catch?" She crimped her mouth and moved around to the side of the house, where a rooster, cockade wilted, was dragging his tailfeathers in the dirt. A white hen was moving around the yard in circles, its pale yellow feet spattered with shit. "When you find that out, baby, you come tell me," she said, then turned away, calling out to someone round back to take the coffee off the burner.

"Then no one's been arrested?" Speaker stepped between a row of plants standing on end in tall tin cans to follow the woman.

"You know better than that," she said, sticking two fingers up under the cap's elastic to scratch her head. But before he could ask about that, she began talking again. "I was sewing on my quilts when I heard it. It sounded like someone was rending fabric. Except it went on too long. You know? No fabric in the world tears like that." She looked past him—the apartment complex, a terra-cotta bowl set down in a hollow of green, had had a fist thrust through the side of the clay and was crumbling. "Ain't satisfied killing them one by one—now they feel they gotta blow 'em all up at once. Want coffee?" she added, before he could ask about "they." "May be your last chance to get something hot in your system." She hugged her jacket around her and continued moving toward the rear of the house.

"I'd better get these things down there," Speaker said, conflicted. "What have you heard so far?"

"Heard? What's to hear?" The woman turned and looked at him, seeming to age suddenly. Her gaze was quiet as two hens waddled near her legs. "My father use to ask me, bless his soul . . ." She laughed huskily and the hens moved away. "Ever notice how chicken mess is gray and white? Whatchu think the white is?"

Speaker lifted his brows till they met the edge of his knit cap.

"The white is chicken shit too, baby. It's chicken shit too." she said, heading round toward the back and talking over her shoulder. And then she was gone, a screen door swinging open on squeaky hinges, then bamming shut.

Speaker stepped back through the row of tinned plants. He carried the load carefully down onto Yates, dizzy with the attempt to take it all in and not lose the quilt. Leah's van was parked on the grass by Chivers, men in army-green parkas were giving first aid, the rescue medics daubing with gauze pads on tongs, people bundling children, one child's arm wrapped in a towel with an apron sash as a tourniquet, staff racing back and forth doing a head count. Speaker spotted Lafayette's shaved head among those tending the children, and he headed for him, the vet who'd suggested that the caravan patrolling the killers' route stop by the state police to request the help of the K-9 search team. Lafayette was applying Mercurochrome to the face of a little boy. Speaker caught a glimpse of another vet, Mason, who always wore a hachi-maki headband and had nunchaku sticks stuck in his back pocket. Heading toward him, Speaker saw Leah and Zala recording and paused just as Mason ducked into the wrecked building.

"I heard the wind screaming and screaming," a woman cracking ice trays against her front steps was saying. "But I told myself it's not the season for tornadoes and hurricanes now, is it? But who'd've thought . . ." she began and could go no further. She handed ice cubes packed in dish towels out to neighbors who passed them down the line to those administering first aid.

"Taste it? You can still taste it," a man in a bathrobe was saying to those clustered around him. "A sour taste in the air. I first thought tear gas, then I thought Three Mile Island. Remember last spring on TV? A taste in the air, they said." He moved around the recording women when the school crossing guard ran up to disperse them again.

"What's the matter with you people? Help pass out these blankets and try to find more antiseptic. Can't you see this is an emergency?" She reserved her hardest look for Leah, who was wiping her glasses with the hem of her dress. "Put that damn thing down and pitch in!" she ordered before she sprinted off, yelling to people in doorways to get more ice and not to tie up the phones.

"Don't think for a minute, sister, that this isn't important." Leah fitted the electric-blue glasses back on. Zala nodded, looking around at the wreckage. "And don't get squeamish," Leah added, retrieving the mike from between her knees. She angled it toward a brother in sweats unwrapping a cartridge of film.

"Somebody's got a lot to answer to," he said, loading an Instamatic. "A helluva lot." He glanced at Speaker, muscles taut in his jaw, then headed in the direction of the playground to document.

Speaker shook out the quilt and draped it around the little boy Lafayette was attending, mostly clowning around now with his khaki cap on funny, trying to distract the boy from his pain. The welts that ran down the boy's face and neck crinkled when he decided that Lafayette was a sketch, bald head and all, and smiled a tentative smile.

"See about that guy," Lafayette said quietly to Speaker, motioning his chin in the direction of the man in the tattersall vest carrying a child in his outstretched arms. Part of the boy's head had been blown away. "Wh-where the fuck the police?" the man kept saying as one of the rescue medics tried to get a pulse, then tried to take the child from the man. He resisted, still stammering the question. Two medics worked on the child.

"Let me have him, brother," Speaker said gently.

"Wh-where the fuck the police?"

"We called them. Didn't I call?" A woman in a floral apron was talking into the mike. She shook the arm of the man standing beside her holding a crock pot rapidly being filled up with bloody gauze. "He saw me," she told Leah. "He can tell you. A neighbor lady up the way rang me up and told me to look out the window. Must have been five or so this morning. Still darkish, but it was plain as could be what she was talking about." She pointed toward a building near the day care. "Two white men on that roof just like she said. Sure as I'm standing here, two white men were on that roof. So I called the police. Didn't I call?" She tugged at the man's sleeve again. "Woke up my husband and told him, then went right to the phone, 'cause what white men doing around here except on Sundays, when you see a few up at the old church on Bankhead? But did the police come?" She elbowed her husband.

The paramedic dropped a gauze pad in the pot, and the woman's husband eased the quilt-draped boy toward a chair two young women had dragged to the walk from their apartment. "That's right," he said, tucking a blanket around the child. "That's exactly right," he said again when Leah held the mike toward his mouth, tugging the cord for Zala to follow.

Spence rode the bumper of an ambulance, then parked the limo at Hightower Place behind Dave's station wagon. The ambulance continued on, lurching down the slope and across the grass toward the cordon, attendants jumping from the vehicle even as it moved, gurneys clanging to the pavement. He could hear the police roping off the area to preserve the scene for evidence, and the fire department hosing down the dust, issue stern injunctions to staff, parents, tenants, and the vets not to cross the line. He'd heard nothing yet about the bombers since the fleet owner had come roaring over the limo radio, reception murky, for in the background the owner had his CB up high, encrypted police calls vying for Spence's attention. He made his way through the band of people ringing the hillside, then down into the area, his ears like radar. Had the bastards been caught? Had the ringleader talked? Did they now know where the missing children were?

He spotted Mason, the munitions expert in the karate headband, inside the cordon arguing with a tall man in a slicker who was apparently ordering Mason off. Mason took a long drag on his cigarette, then field-stripped it, holding the pinched-off coals in his hand, but refused to leave. That was the man who would know something, Spence thought, moving through the crowd, listening: Who would kill little children? Keep the faith, we don't want to give in to hate. But I heard that. Leave off rumor mongering. But . . . Things ain't bad enough? Who would kill, keep the faith, I heard, hang on now—the words chased around in his head, offering nothing. Spence pressed his way past two women in heavy sweaters recording people and tried to keep his

eyes on Mason, who was inching backward toward the building, ignoring the tall man in the slicker, who gestured but made no move to stop
the vet or to follow.

"I didn't understand what was happening," one of the staff was reporting when Zala turned around but got no look of recognition from
her husband. At the first concussion, the woman explained, she'd been
slammed against the extra cots stacked against the wall, a rain of plaster clouding her vision. "All I could think of was, where's the broom?
Where's the broom? Can you imagine that? That's what I was thinking
when I heard little Andre scream and saw Nell running toward me.
How are we ever going to clean this place up?" The woman clutched her
face and wheeled around. "Where's Nell Robinson? Did Nell get out?"
She stumbled toward the building and was stopped by chest-high ropes
and heavy hoses at her ankles.

"Wh-where the fuck the police?" An attendant took the child from
the man in tattersall and used his shoulder to prevent a woman from
climbing into the ambulance.

"His shoe," the woman whispered. "Where's his other shoe?" The
man in the bathrobe held her from behind.

"That's right," a man in a dark flannel lining from a topcoat said.
He cleared his throat and moved closer to the mike. "I called the police
twice in one day. I was out walking the dog along Jackson Parkway this
morning." He pointed toward the hole in the fence back of the nursery,
then slapped his leg with a rolled-up newspaper. "I saw two white men
skulking around by the fence there. Maybe five o'clock or five-thirty, I
didn't have my watch on at the time, but that's generally when Prince
gets me up. Now, you can ask any of the community workers around
this way and they'll verify that not two weeks ago we had to run off
some bigots come around here with their hate literature. Pretty brash,
wouldn't you say, handing out hate sheets to us? To *us!*" He smacked his
leg with the newspaper bat.

"And you called the police?" Leah asked.

"That is correct. I called them as soon as I got back to the house. As
a matter of fact, I cut the walk short to do that. Reported two prowlers
to the police and gave their descriptions. I called again when the dishes
started rattling in the cupboard not a half hour ago. I knew it wasn't nobody's earthquake. My wife kept saying it was an earthquake. But I
knew it was something just like it was. I'd been feeling uneasy ever

since I walked the dog and saw them. But do the police come when you need them? They come pretty damn quick when you're getting put out the clinic for having the nerve to think health is your right. Come mighty quick then," he concluded, swatting his leg, the anger he vented as much self-distraction from horror as commentary on the police.

"Would you repeat that description, please?" Leah was saying as Zala, moving in close, asked, "Did you see a car or a truck in the area? Did you notice Cobb County plates? Or out-of-town plates?"

The man smoothed down his pajama top through the opening of the lining and thought. Those around him were pooling information about the colors of various counties' plates, hoping to jog the man's memory.

"Walk me over there," he said. "Maybe being there by the fence will refresh my memory. But don't try to feed me information," he said, pointing his newspaper to Zala. "We want to get this right, now don't we? The rumor mill is already operating at full swing. I don't wish to be a part of any of that."

Zala nodded and held the mike's jack in place as she followed the man. When Leah tried coaxing a description of the two suspects, the man stopped short to chide her for trying to put "suspects" in his mouth.

"I'm using the word 'prowlers,' " he said, "just as I reported it to the police." He waited till he was satisfied that the two women had that straight before he proceeded up the hill.

Two more police cruisers were coming into the area from the east entrance and three TV vans were trundling in from the west. Spence moved the man in tattersall out of the path of a cameraman. His arms still outstretched, his eyeballs rolling up and revealing a lot of white, he looked delirious.

"Was that your boy?" Spence took out his handkerchief, but the man was unable to take it. He shook his head no, a glistening rope of snot and saliva dangling from his chin. Spence wiped the man's face and lowered his arms. "Take it easy, brother man. I know you hurting." He thumped the man on his back until he stopped gagging, trying to speak.

"Get a shot of where the door landed in the parking lot," Lafayette was saying to the brother in sweats jogging through the crowd taking pictures. Lafayette sidled up to Spence and tapped his arms locked around the sobbing man. "No boiler did this kind of damage. No way."

"Is that what they're saying, a faulty boiler?"

"No telling what they'll be saying. But Mason's inside with the fire inspector and Vernon's getting pictures. Ain't that your lady up there?" He pointed to the slope behind the day-care center. "Them sisters been taping like champs."

"Then no suspects have been taken in?"

"A couple of tenants spotted some jokers early this morning, but that's about it."

"Wh-who would k-kill li'l children?"

Lafayette wagged his head then reached up to pull his cap down, re-membering only when he touched his scalp that he'd given it to one of the little boys the ambulance had refused to take, saying only the most severe cases would be transported. "You thinking what I'm thinking?"

"Been thinking that all along," Spence answered.

Tattersall, wiping his clothes and looking from Spence to Lafayette, was trying to speak. "J-just like before," he managed to get out before he gagged again. "In '79. One of them m-meetings."

"Whattayamean?" Lafayette moved closer to the stammerer as Spence turned, his attention on someone behind the cordon. "What'd you say?" Lafayette propped his shoulder against the man lest he keel over with the effort to speak. Tattersall's eyes seemed to be staring at a new darkness opening up within. And when he caught his balance and moved off to follow Spence, everything he looked at was branded by what he suspected, knew.

"There was a gathering of one of them Klan groups in '79 when the killings started? Is that what you're saying?" Lafayette caught up with Tattersall, who was coughing into the handkerchief. "Is that what you mean?"

"If the fire inspector's inside," Spence said, looking at the tall man by the nursery entrance, "then who's Murder Incorporated, dressed to kill?" He shouldered his way through the crowd and vaulted over the barrier, the two men close behind.

While the fire brigade wore smeary rubber jackets and knee-high boots with dirty soles, the man they headed for wore a long, gunmetal-gray slicker with silver galosh closings and new Wellington boots, silver stripes around the tops. He had a Lucite clipboard tucked under one arm, his hands deep in the slash pockets. He surveyed the three men, then surveyed the scene, and took no notes.

"From the FBI field office maybe?" Lafayette ran his hand over his scalp. "I know they've changed since the Hoover days, but I didn't know they had Pierre Cardin designing for the bureau. What say I slip around back and see what Mason's found out while you keep an eye on Slick. I'll be damned if they're going to jerk us around with some bull-shit about a bum boiler."

Dave spun an officer around by the shoulder and found himself star-ing into the face of a rookie fresh from the academy.

"What's the story on the bomb threats?" He didn't expect an answer any different than the one he'd been getting.

"Bomb threats?"

"Duh," Dave mugged, feeling like one of the wiseasses from his caseload. "You've been getting bomb threats over the wire since this ex-plosion went off. That's why it took you guys so long to get here. So knock it off. What's the deal?"

"Please step back, sir, we're trying to form a second perimeter here."

"Yeah, great. But did a description come in on any 'tentative look-outs'?" He waited. And the rookie was obviously waiting too, for Dave to show his shield. When he didn't, the rookie piped up again about stepping back.

"Yeah, right, a second perimeter." Dave moved on, looking for the official in command. He grabbed the arm of one of the TV cameramen and asked him.

"I don't know who's in command," the man said, brushing hair out of his face. "And no, I haven't heard about any other bombings."

"Did you ask?"

"Hey, wait a minute," the man yelled, turning on his camera and trying to follow Dave through the crowd. "Can I ask you a few ques-tions?" Somebody was giving a physics lesson. Someone with metallur-gical smarts was inspecting fragments on the ground. Others leaned on history to add weight to their speculations. And one old man kept re-peating how he'd stepped from the shower to see his bath mat suddenly speckled with glass and grit. Dave bumped into a woman threading sheer curtains on a bent rod and trying to reach an apartment house up ahead. He stepped in front of her and ran interference, holding on to the gauzy hem.

The police were demonstrating their skills in crowd control, the fire department its usual efficiency in securing order around the site and dispensing coffee to its workers; the medics were swift, eight hands apiece it seemed, swabbing and bandaging and moving the injured out. Workers from the day care kept ramming into him, frantic, for not all of the eighty-two preschoolers and eight adult staff had been accounted for yet. Dave sidestepped his way toward a door propped open with a red plaster Buddha and let go of the woman's curtain and continued on, trying to spot an official. He took note of the scraps of information being passed around in the crowd, but it wasn't much—prowlers, the missing and murdered, would the feds step in now and investigate?

It could've been summer '64, Neshoba County: missing—three civil rights workers; question—when would Bobby Kennedy get the feds to move? All Dave could remember was the feeling of the crowd, the three names—Chaney, Schwerner, Goodman—and the amount the feds later paid an informant for other names: thirty thousand dollars. He looked toward the destroyed building. It could've been his freshman year, Orangeburg: the bullet-ridden dormitory, the police, the crowd, a Browning automatic aimed at his window.

"Excuse me." A reporter stopped him, poking Dave's arm with a blunt copy pencil. Dave sized up the brother; he too looked fresh from the classroom. "Many here today say that they've never seen the likes of this. May I get your views?"

"The sixties, man. Bethany, Mount Moriah, Bethel Baptist." Dave tried to keep the growl out of his voice. "And the Sixteenth Street Baptist Church in Birmingham, where the four little girls were killed." He tapped the notepad and ordered the young man to write.

"And would you say there's a similarity—"

"Take off your tie, brother, it's choking your brain." Dave patted the reporter's shoulder and moved on. There was a sock on the ground, green and orange like peas and carrots out of a can, and so small it took him a second to realize it wasn't a doll's. He felt his throat tighten and hurried on, not seeing very clearly where he was going, but needing to get out of the crush.

"I heard a buzzing like a thousand wasps," the woman in tattered clothing was saying into a camera. "Then I felt the sting of bricks and glass." She touched herself, astonished to be alive. Her dress dropped away from the waistband.

"An awful thing, awful. Them people will have this on their conscience for the rest of their unnatural lives."

"Who?" Dave grabbed the old man by the back of his collar and tried to ease him around. "Do you know who did this?"

"Their sins will find them out," the man said, turning. He stroked the back of a boy clinging to him.

The boy looked up at Dave, then drew the old man's jacket back around himself. Dave had seen teenage toughs roughed up in gang fights or worked over by the thugs on payroll who called themselves youth workers. He'd seen pyro kids who'd lit one fire too many and gotten caught in the fry. But he'd never seen that look on a little kid before. And when he examined the faces of people around him, he realized they all had that look. And now he was trapped in a circle of people listening to a dude in a camel's hair coat and a fifties beret ace deuce. He held a brown scarf between his hands, popping it, twisting it, as he spoke.

"I'd only just gotten back to the city last night. Jet lag sacked me out, bam. Next thing I know, I'm rocking and bobbing like there's air turbulence. I sat up and reached for the oxygen mask like they show you before I realized I was in my crib. What got me moving was the knowledge that there's no nuclear plant in this district. So what could this be? Never, never ever," he said, wrapping the scarf around both knuckles, "would I have imagined this." He reached suddenly for Dave and pulled him out of the way of a green minibus leading an ambulance to the high street. "You know, they're trying to give that brother over there some hooey about this being a corroded boiler." He turned and the group swung around with him to face the rubble.

Mason and the fire inspector were behind the ropes arguing about whether the jacket casing of the furnace had imploded or exploded on detonation. One scrap of metal was bellied out, another caved in, a lever jammed, the rest of the jacket casing missing. Then Dave saw Zala slipping under the ropes with a tape recorder and heading for her old man, who was lockstepping the clown slicked out in silver and Lucite. It wasn't a cop but the tie-choked reporter who loud-talked Zala, an amateur claim jumper, and made her leave. Hemmed in by reporters with bulky equipment, Dave couldn't get to her. Reporters were shoving mikes into the faces of children and attendants dressing wounds as the gurneys and the cameras rolled. "How many dead? . . . How many injured? . . . How many in shock, would you say?" One reporter, writing as he spoke, bent over a prostrate woman—"And you're the mother of which dead child?"

Dave picked him up and buried his fist in his stomach. Easing him down to the ground, he saw Eldrin Bell, the deputy police chief he often ran into out on the strip. Bell seemed not to have seen Dave drop the reporter, or if he had he was giving it a glass eye. Bell had just found Mrs. Nell Robinson lying over a child she'd died to protect. He was breaking the news to director Betty Smith. To the right of the ambulance, Dave heard police exchanging information: twelve bomb threats had come in between 10:10 and 10:45. He put that together with the report of prowlers on the roof, the story of ofays being eighty-sixed from the neighborhood, and the comings and goings of conventioneers Teo and Beemer had been shadowing.

"Is the school over there targeted?" Dave pulled out ID for the police and jerked his thumb in the direction of A. D. Williams Elementary. "I know people on the scene here who can assist in evacuating the school without a panic." He gave the cops two seconds to study his card and size him up. "Come on, we ain't got all damn day. Is it only Atlanta Housing Authority schools?" He tried to remember where Zala's kids went.

"We're taking care of this," an officer said. "Now suppose you step back. We're trying to form a second perimeter."

"Swell." Dave turned around and headed for Deputy Bell, never one of his favorite people to hook up with; Dave's memory of Atlanta's SNCC days were enough to make him wary. but Bell outranked anybody else on the scene, and hell, it was an emergency.

It wasn't reasonable, it made no sense, but she couldn't shake the feeling that somewhere in the middle of the phone conversation with the network man, she'd wished for something like this, like a stupid, self-dramatizing child: Just you wait and see, you'll be sorry, then see if

I care. Zala heaped ashes on her head listening to the tape play back. "I guess they'll yank that TV special on the Klan scheduled for tonight," a newsman handing down a tripod had told his colleague. A motorist who'd pulled over his VW with oversized tires had looked down from the parkway and shaken his head—"Like ducks in a shooting gallery." She backtracked to the description of the prowlers, the man interrupting himself to point out a cruiser speeding away with two motorcycle escorts—"I hope someone snapped a picture of whatever they're in a rush to remove from the scene. And no, I don't care to speculate about what it might be or if the public will be informed. I'm simply making an observation for the record."

A woman with a thermos was motioning Zala to put her machine down. "Coffee?" Her pockets bulged with jars and cups. "Cream and sugar?" The woman's gesture was a reminder that there was a world beyond this chaos. Zala accepted the cup.

Two women were dragging kitchen chairs along the pavement. The brother in sweats ran past them shouting, "Here comes Maynard," then crouched to snap a picture of the mayor and his retinue gliding onto the scene. "Thank God," the two young women said in unison, parking their chairs.

The woman with the thermos crimped her mouth, then turned. "Pull that chair thisaway," she instructed. There was a pregnant woman on the ground behind her, Zala saw, down on the ground blotting the grass with a fuzzy beige sweater.

"Please," the thermos woman said, going to her. "Get up, baby. Get on up off your knees."

Paulette trotted from Emergency to Pediatrics to the twelve-by-ten windowless room where people waited for news about the casualties. Leah, at her heels, having helped to bring in the wounded and the prostrate, had been using a miniaturized transistor recorder to pick up comments from the hospital staff, the police, the media, and parents outraged that so many children had been denied treatment at the site and ambulance rides to the hospitals. Paulette took a deep breath.

"They're still coming in. But so far, six are here with serious injuries, two in critical condition with third-degree burns and a skull fracture." That was all she would say in exchange for five minutes' peace to talk with two families alone.

Kofi, at the blackboard drawing the connected boxes of city government, was just turning to answer Bernie Parks, Mrs. McGovern nowhere in sight, when he saw his father in the doorway, holding his sister's hand and looking at him funny. Lots of parents were in the hall, crowded around the vice-principal and talking in hoarse whispers.

All morning the class had been so caught up in the excitement of fire engines clanging past, raising their voices with the police-car *wee-ahh* and the dogs, they hadn't noticed when the teacher stepped out, their attention on the window, the streets, the wild goings-on beyond the flagpole. And Kofi, the chalk in his hand, none of his boxes complete figures, for he too was impatient with the closed-in, left-out feeling, was already jumping out the window, running the streets after a hook-and-ladder, free to go anywhere, reckless and happy, though he knew sirens didn't mean circus or rodeo or tent revivals. Even though he knew sirens were nothing to be glad about, he was excited and wanted to be part of whatever it was. Till he saw his father in the doorway looking like that. His excitement fisted and turned on him, for whatever was wrong had come to get him and there was nowhere to go except up against the cold blackboard. A small boy, he'd meant no harm, he wanted to tell his father, already denying inside his clothes that he'd ever thought about running away, ever wished for anything more exciting than putting his part of the project on the board. He was caught. Found out. So when his father reached for him looking like he was looking, looking like he was looking through him, Kofi raised his arms to ward off the blow or whatever it was coming to him.

From the moment the two motorcycle cops had pulled on their gauntlet-style gloves and revved up, cutting a swath for the police cruiser to leave, rumors of what had been surreptitiously removed from the scene spread across the slopes like grassfire. A fuse, a detonator, fragments of plastique, an unexploded grenade, bomb, or stick of dynamite? Lafayette, a bullet-headed trajectory, outdistanced Speaker winging through the crowd last numbered at two hundred and found finally the man he was looking for. A drab, flat-faced man who'd been mistaken earlier for someone from the coroner's office, he'd been allowed through the cordon with the techs from the mobile crime lab unit. Barely whispering, his arms hanging straight down, his right encumbered in the telling by the black bag he carried, his left extended an additional eight inches by the magnifying glass he held, he told it simply—"A black metal box, so big, so high. It caused a lot of excitement. They flew out of there like a bat out of hell."

"Well, of course," the young reporter in the tie said. "They took it to the crime lab to dust it for prints."

"Maybe," Lafayette said. "But didn't you notice that a lab unit was already on the scene? Are you covering this story? How come you didn't follow the patrol car?" Lafayette rubbed his scalp until the reporter picked up his cue and hurried off, but only as far as the ropes to ask one of the police where the crime lab was that the metal box had been taken to. "Reid," Lafayette said to Speaker, blowing through his teeth, "do you believe this guy?"

Speaker pulled the reporter aside and learned that he'd gotten nowhere with his questions. Speaker offered to help him track the police cruiser, pulling him through the crowd, cheek by jowl, toward the house back of the fire station. Reluctant to leave now that Maynard Jackson was present, the young reporter resisted.

"What makes you think they'd try to bury evidence?"

"Come, African," was all Speaker would say, lining up the phone calls he would have to make to locate the cruiser.

Gaston's wasn't the only tow truck circling in the vicinity, simply one of the late arrivals and one of the few who knew from the giddyap that it wasn't a wreck he was heading toward for business because one of his part-time helpers had come crashing into the shop, triggering two of the three booby traps and barely escaping getting maimed, and told him. And Gaston, pulling clear of the pile-up of garbled words two things—"children" and "dynamite"—snapped the padlocks shut and hurried to the Ford wrecker, not stopping for his toolbox, only the pliers he needed to tune his sometimey CB, the helper still talking at him about fifty to a hundred pounds' worth of dynamite damage done to a school out at Bowen Homes.

Buses, delivery trucks, and cars double-parked, triple-parked in some of the side streets left Gaston no alternative but to pull up in someone's yard, knocking over a row of tin cans and upsetting the plants. He slipped his card between the cushions of the porch glider by way of saying he'd be responsible for the mishap and lumbered down into the crowd, not sure where he was going, but sure that he could help out in some way. Everywhere he moved he heard people damning somebody's worthless soul to hell, then saying in the next breath not to let this outrage provoke. He looked in vain for wide-shouldered Spencer and his wife with the deep-set eyes.

The corps of bodyguards was posted around the makeshift platform, and Mayor Maynard Jackson took up the bullhorn. But the crowd did not settle down immediately. It seemed too soon, a mere half hour on the scene commiserating with parents and staff, for speaking lines. Time out while blood-pressure medication vials were popped open. Time. The trees flayed to the pith, dust still spiraling from the rubble of bricks, a fine mist in the air as the fire brigade wrapped up the hoses, bits of twine being plucked from clothes that had been pressed by the swell up against the ropes. Time. The enormity of it all hadn't been parceled out yet to be shouldered by the many lest it land on too few. There were still those hum-talking about the evil of this world, girl, the evil of this world, to restore, hopefully, their equilibrium. And those who latched on to every event as a sign of the Final Days weren't finished arguing against those of the seize-the-time persuasion. And those well-trained to expect no inheritance other than more bitter bread were caught in between. Youths, glancing shyly at each other when their parents interrupted their weeping to issue dire threats, made plans for day-night vigils and clever diversions to protect their parents from jumping a meter reader or dusting a social worker doubling back to check on ADFC eligibility. For others, though, it was time to get it on.

"If he's the Maynard I know," a man shouted toward the front of the crowd, "he won't dillydally about this, 'cause he knows we're not prepared to swallow nonsense. And if he says 'Let the trenches be dug,' I'll be the first to pick up a shovel," drawing a scatter of applause here, harrumphs there, loose talk of picking up other things, and questions the mayor began trying to answer, saying that the evidence so far, so far, so far . . .

"Hold it down. What did he say?"

"What the hell you expect him to say? He's the mayor. What other recourse he got?" A shove in response to this outrage—raising a leg on the mayor. Others agitated by mothball fumes, stale coffee, bay rum, nicotine, sweaty Noxzema, bad breath, and thoughts of actions they were pretending might not be necessary in order to live with themselves with honor, shoved back.

"Tell the truth, Maynard!" a woman shouted. "'Cause we know the devil is never at just one door. Have bombs gone off anywhere else?"

Something visibly faltered in Jackson's face. And for a split second he waffled, first to the right as though to confer with a police official, then to the left as though to signal the corps to get him the hell out of there. But he was only trying to find his footing on the shaky platform, several members of the crowd assured each other as Jackson confidently raised the bullhorn again.

"Let him talk, for crying out loud!"

"I second the motion!"

For this, after all, was no bow-bent grin-the-vote-in politician, no shade-tree fixer, no jackleg hustler or despoiler. This was Himself, the Mayor, Big M, His Honuh Bruthu J, the Chief, the Silver-Tongued Emperor who knew just how to enliven dull newsprint, telling the good ole boys of big biznis to kiss his royal yellow behind while he ushered in the Second Reconstruction. And yeah, sure, people reminded each other, he'd messed up on occasion, the man's human and give me a break, like his handling of the garbage workers' strike, yeah, yeah, but chalk that up to that diet Dick Gregory put him on without adding the postscript that in case of emergency brainwork to grab a fish sammich, un-huh, that ain't gonna git it but okay. They became a collective ear. Some because they remembered Big M's father, most likable gent in memory; others because they had a vested interest, having put His Honuh in office and admired his regal ways, and had never had cause to think their trust in the Emperor misplaced; and some because they wanted this scenario over and done with. Silence, cameras rolling, a zoom-in on the mayor's black armband as the bullhorn was lifted once more.

"There is no evidence of foul play. I repeat. There is no evidence of anything other than an accident, a tragic accident."

Relieved, betrayed, nonplussed, hard of hearing, groans and curses mingled with amens and questions. Then jeers, boos, hoots, and hissing roared up higher than the media voice-overs—"Opinions are sharply divided here today. . . ." The mayor's eyes, fixed for a moment, overbright, on a spot midway between the front of the crowd and the first straight-ahead camera, wavered, then retreated into the gloom as Mason, hoisted on Lafayette's shoulders, challenged.

"That's not what the fire inspector said. Among other evidence of foul play there's the safety valve that was rigged not to work."

"That's not what the inspector said," the tall man in the slicker countered. "He said that the triggering mechanism that regulates the steam was defective. That is, the safety valve wasn't working properly."

The overwrought seized on triggering, while Tattersall, straining to inform the crowd that Slick hadn't exchanged more than two or three words with the inspector, gave up and lunged, his attack plan thwarted by the overwrought shoving to get closer to Slick to have him repeat. Mason slid down and tried to grab Slick's lapels, but the rubbery fabric repelled him.

"Man, don't play expedient politics at a time like this," Mason pleaded. "People have died here today." He searched the crowd for the tape-recording sister who might have caught some of the conversation he'd had with the inspector before he left; or failing that, if the recorder was at least present, perhaps Mason could finesse an admission from Slick.

"What about the jacket casing the police raced off with?" someone challenged.

Perhaps Lafayette was pushing people to form an aisle so witnesses could move down front and speak. Police reporters, huddling with the uniformed, muttered that even if it was only a corroded boiler, there was still the problem of "race paranoia."

"I caution you as your mayor," the familiar voice broke out over the heads of those who'd moved up to the platform—the vets, the brother in sweats, the man in the plaid flannel lining, the woman in the apron, the man with the black bag and glass, "do not engage in spreading rumors. If you know something factual, tell the police."

"Bullshit!" Dave jerked his thumbs in the direction of the high street, and several men and women began moving off.

Most people stayed to question, to argue, to demand to hear the testimony, to try and mend what seemed irrevocably shattered, urging those splintering off to come back, to not form factions. A few stepped away, bowed by a double bereavement; others to privately piece together what they would say and how they would say it at work, at home, to neighbors, to friends on the phone before some bland man with media sheen in his hair robbed the event of its valence. Stepping away from the noise, stepping over the stains on the ground sluiced by a basin of sudsy gray dishwater, they attempted to shape the story.

To be told right, lest it dishonor those who'd lived through it and those who hadn't, it had to have a particular beginning. A small, quiet, personal thing was called for—the evil iron that had scorched a collar that morning, exact change lost through a hole in the clothes. Insignificant in the scheme of things, it would be offered as a sign of the teller's humility, as confirmation that cataclysms do give warnings, for there's an order to the knowable universe, and too, to signal that the teller would not distance himself or herself from communal disaster. The freakishness of the event itself defied description. So, hearing at their backs the announcement of an evening meeting where testimony from the residents and the authorities would be compared, the storytellers jumped over the muddled middle to compose a possible ending. Given what they'd heard so far and sensed, they composed the capture scene. A citizen's arrest, one Blood was thinking, looking at those racing to follow the broad-backed man muscling his way to the streets, a man possessed, a Popeye Doyle pushing through trains, through airports, through traffic, fixated, no eye for danger, no ear for caution, hellbent, in hot pursuit of the death merchant.

Outside the Fulton County Morgue, Lieutenant John Cameron broke the news to the television audience. Nell Robinson, fifty-eight-year-old teacher of the Bowen Homes Day Care Center, was dead. Ronald Wilcoxin, three-year-old preschooler of Wilkes Circle, was dead.

Andrew Stanford, three, of Chivers Street, was dead. Terrence Bradley, three, of Wilkes Circle, was dead. Kevin Nelson, three, of Wilkes Circle, was dead.

John Feegal of the Fulton County Medical Examiner's Office was asked by a young reporter in a loosened tie if metal fragments indicative of a bomb blast had been noted in the wounds of the deceased. Feegal explained that he couldn't comment on that yet with certainty, but said he predicted that none would be found.

"I guess we all heard that," Lafayette said, as the others groaned, then dragged themselves toward the quilt Speaker and Gaston had spread in the middle of McClintock's office. Lafayette turned from the TV set to open the office door for his cohorts returned with the food.

"Well," Mac said, "are we all assembled at last?"

Since two o'clock, when Spence had asked for the use of Mac's office for a strategy session, people had been coming and going—out to Cobb County, down to the Task Force, over to STOP, then to North Druid Hills to pick up Teo and Beemer, then out to the secretary to have their depositions typed, then downstairs to the notary, then out again to the store to pick up batteries and tapes, then off to meet with members of the citywide Tenants' Association. Now that the food had arrived, there seemed to be little time left to make plans for the evening meeting. But perhaps, Mac thought, they didn't require a discussion leader and an organized list of goals and objectives. They seemed to think they were ready, so maybe he'd simply missed the beat of their style. He had a few comments to make about the dangerous mind-set of the gathering and of the city, but he kept them to himself; earlier, Mason had upbraided him: "You'll never change, Mac—always offering psychological solutions to political problems." So Mac accepted a plate of chicken wings and potatoes and sat down with the others, his desk taken over by children.

"You know those mugs ain't gonna confirm the phone calls made to the police this morning," Dave broke the silence. He hooked his arm around the tobacco jars on the counselor's shelves, not trusting himself to join the circle. If someone put up an argument or squirted ketchup on him, he'd boil over. "In fact, they ain't gonna do a damn thing but cool us out. A bunch of pussies."

"Is that your idea of a curse?" Leah snapped, handing the children their plates as they made bubble eyes at each other.

Dave muttered then busied himself reading the labeled cassettes on the lower shelves—Bud Powell, Roy Ayers, the Chicago Art Ensemble, Betty Bebop Carter—there was more to McClintock than met the eye, Dave was thinking, trying to think of anything other than what he was thinking, fingering the tightly laced shoe in his pocket, a little Buster Brown shoe he'd stumbled over in the yard of A. D. Williams Elementary. He was thinking of Jackson's reduction of the massacre to a five-word fraud: nothing but a tragic accident. The police-media insistence: no connection to the Missing and Murdered case. The cops in the school hallway—shoptalk: full-moon killings, payday brawls, holiday suicides—while he was demanding an evacuation. No need, they told him, calm down, negative report from the bomb squads, it's over. Over, all but the dying. Signing out at the office, he'd walked in on three co-workers. The shoebox on the table with the bills lying in it. The squares of paper with numbers printed on them. Caught, they copped a plea. Not satisfied with the office football pool, they'd turned the case into a goddamn lottery. More than the Boston Strangler? More than Son of Sam? Or the Zodiac Killer? Would the body count top the Gacy thirty-three, the Texas nineteen? Dave was now on suspension and facing assault charges too. He set the Buster Brown shoe down hard on the shelf and the tobacco jars shook.

Kenti scooted onto the quilt to watch Unca Dave from the sanctuary of her mama's lap. Spence and Zala exchanged a glance. All morning they'd hoped the same thing; then, no one handcuffed, had feared the same thing; that after the eighty-two children and eight workers were counted, someone would announce that other bodies had been found in the debris. Older than infants, younger than adults . . . Zala had been wondering where a set of Sonny's medical papers were when Leah left to help transport the wounded, leaving her with the task of recording. Spence had been keeping one eye on Slick, the other eye roaming the rubble for familiar clothing, when Dave jumped the barrier to tell him other schools had been targeted. Kofi set his plate down between Spence and Beemer. And his parents exchanged another look—would the police move before the culprits left the city or left the country? Dave had expressed his doubts. The Spencers watched him rifling the no longer neat rows of tapes.

Tormé, Mose Allison, Diana Ross, Dionne . . . but where was Nina, Nina the Nasty, the Black Sorceress? Dave grimaced a smile at the memory of the 1968 concert at the Atlanta Stadium—Nina, Miles, Cannonball. Thousands come to hear Nina give the word—Tear the sucker down. It would've been done. So after that, it was called the Kool so-called Jazz Festival. And tonight it would be more of the same. Cool out. Where was it? he questioned himself. A campus in Florida. He and Norma had driven down to hear Nina. She told the audience slyly that the bookers had begged her not to get "militant," not to sing inflammatory songs. Then she laughed and held up the check, striding across the stage waving it. The suckers had paid her already. Riiiight, the crowd roared. "Mississippi Goddamn!" "Pirate Jenny." She looked out from the keyboard toward the administration building, singing, "I don't expect to see it standing in the morning." Nina. Nina.

Dave unlaced the little shoe. Tonight there'd be filibustering windbags, go-slow knee-benders, agents, hymn singers. But no Nina. "Alabama, Georgia too, but Mississippi, goddamn!" Atlanta needs ya, Nina. "Asking me, kill them now or later . . ." Riiight. "I'm counting your heads as I'm making the beds." A Buster Brown shoe. He should find the parents, but what could he say? What if someone came knocking at his door with his son's shoe? What if Norma rang up from wherever she'd gone to, taking their son with her, leaving no clue first of why, and told him that all that was left of David Morris Jr. was a goddamn shoe?

"We should get there early," Spence said to no one in particular.

Leah tossed Speaker a clean tape and got up to get confirmation that reliable Black media would attend the meeting.

"What's the matter with your phone, brother?" She held it toward Mac; maybe he was familiar with the odd sound.

"We've got several electronic wizards in the neighborhood," Mac smiled, glad for a chance to smile about something. "One kid—course he's hardly a kid anymore—used to run a radio station around here. He had such powerful equipment, he'd come through the stereo, the radio, and the UHF channels. Sometimes, all I could get on the phone were the police calls he monitored."

Leah looked at the phone with interest while the others urged Mac to locate the operator in case he'd heard something that morning that wasn't public yet.

"Well, he doesn't broadcast anymore," Mac explained, but he

reached for his Rolodex anyway. "Wayne Williams, you know him?" he asked Speaker, who'd been preparing notes for the WCLK and WRFG community broadcasts. "I think you know his father," Mac said to Zala. "Homer Williams, the photographer."

Zala nodded. "He covered some of the children's funerals."

"Did he cover the rally a few weeks ago?" Mason asked. "It might be interesting to see who was there."

"And who wasn't," Leah added.

"Mayor wasn't. Lee Brown either."

"A green-light invitation to the killers," Lafayette said.

"I don't know that we fully appreciate the situation the administration is faced with," Mac quickly inserted before the group tuned up to rehash opinions. He glanced toward Mason, but he'd gotten up to show Kofi how to wield the nunchaku sticks. Teo gave Mac an encouraging look, and Mason turned around. So though Speaker excused himself to retire to a quiet corner, some people seemed predisposed to hear Mac out.

"What we should be asking is this." His back to the circle, Speaker spoke quietly into the mike. "Whenever a crisis strikes a foreign nation, be it ally or archenemy of the U.S., the State Department pulls a team of experts together to map out the U.S. response to that crisis. Where is Big Brother now, good people? Has Mayor Jackson asked the State Department to respond to the domestic crisis in Atlanta? Four preschool children and a teacher were killed today in an explosion. Scores of others were injured. In the context of what has been going on in this city since the summer of 1979, that explosion today at the Bowen Homes Day Care Center warrants a full investigation. In the past year and four months, at least fifteen other children have been kidnapped and many of them murdered. City Hall says there's no connection. We're being told that the explosion this morning should not be viewed in the context of what is happening nationally to Black people—physically, economically, and politically. That argument is a con text. Wake up, Africans. Check it out. War's been declared again.

"And we know it will get worse if Reagan's elected and the full force of the right wing is unleashed. You heard Ronnie down there in Mississippi talking states' rights. Wake up, people! The explosion today, so hastily labeled an accident, and the children who've been dying through no accident but through murder, tell us this—it is time we moved on Malcolm's recommendation of nearly twenty years ago, and go to the UN once again, this time ten times the number as last year. We've a crisis on our hands, African people!"

Speaker was about to punch the pause button to find his place in the notes, but the next idea came in a rush. "What's the Intelligence Division doing? The Atlanta special investigation unit set up in the sixties to keep an eye on you know who. The unit that provides security for visiting diplomats, the Pope, and international figures whose safety must be guaranteed. The special intelligence unit mandated to infiltrate any clandestine groups that threaten the security and well-being of America. What are they doing about these kidnappings, these murders, this explosion? When last we heard from this special intelligence unit, it was in 1979, when the infamous billboard went up opposite the Omni. Put up in plain view as an attack on the Black administration. The unit was asked to investigate the billboard's origins. The then head of SPS said it was "distasteful" to be investigating a noncriminal matter. "Distasteful." "Noncriminal." If security and well-being were taken seriously, any overt and covert act of racism would be a felony, an antisocial crime. Wake up, Africans!

"What else has the SPS been doing? In 1974 they broke the case of the kidnapping of Reg Murphy, then editor of the *Atlanta Constitution*. Fine. Why haven't they been called in by the special Emergency Task Force to Investigate Missing and Murdered Children? And called in to investigate the bombing this morning? We know why. Can we get justice in Babylon? Mobilize, people. Organize. It is time to take our case back to the UN, thirty million strong."

From the backseat, Kofi leaned over Spence's shoulder.

"What if the mayor and the chief and them know who's killing but can't arrest them 'cause they're cops?"

"You can lock up cops cancha, Daddy? Betchu the mayor can."

"We need to stop for more tapes," Zala said.

"And cookies."

"But what if it's the police doing the killing? Can cops lock up other cops?"

"Give it a rest, Kofi."

"Well, I gotta know, Ma. You always saying to ask if you wanna know something, so I'm asking. Say like a bunch of cops and them Kluxers are killing the kids, would the mayor be scared to say so? He's the head of the city, ain't he? He's the boss of all the police and the fire department and the water company, so what would he do?"

"What would you do?"

"I'd get on TV and tell everybody, that's what I'd do."

"Then they'd come and shoot you. And some cookies, Daddy."

"Kenti, you just ate."

"Not cookies, Mama. Didn't have no cookies or nothing."

"Well, then, I'd write down everything I know and make lots of copies to send to the newspapers. And I'd put a set of them papers in my safety-deposit box in case they get me."

"What safe-deposit box? You don't have no safe-deposit box. You hear him?"

"Would you shut up. That's what I'd do, Dad. Dad? Hey, Daddy, you think maybe the mayor and them know? They got to know, don't they? So maybe they waiting till everybody gets organized like you said, you know, to back 'em up and everything!"

"Could be, Kofi."

"Is that what you think? Dad?"

"I want me some cookies and some choc'late milk. Choc'late milk is good for you, right?"

"If I knew who it was, Dad, I'd write everything down while the people are getting organized. Then I'd send the information to the newspaper and the TV and the radio. But then ... what if ..." Kofi dug his fingers in Zala's shoulder. "But, Ma, you remember what happened in that picture *Three Days of the Condor?* What if it went down like that? 'Member in the end when the main guy is talking with the other guy, the one with the wig on his head like a rug, and he says he's going to take the information upstairs to the newspapers and the wig guy says, 'What makes you think they'll print it?'? It could go like that, hunh? Whatchu think? Can't you pay 'em to make 'em print the story? Does it cost a lot of money?"

"There's a store, Daddy."

"Kenti, we're trying to get to the meeting. We'll go for dessert after, all right?"

"Will somebody answer me! Dad? What if it was you? Would you hide out in one of them embassies and ask for protection? Then maybe they'd give you a bodyguard to get you on TV without getting shot. But maybe the TV people would be scared to give you a mike 'cause the killers sent them a threat note. But then maybe the mayor and them could call up the TV to let you talk. Wouldn't they have to do it if the mayor told 'em to?"

"If you had a gun, they would," Kenti said. "I'd take Baldy Bean with me if I was you, Baldy Bean and the Kung Fu Man, that's what. Daddy got a gun."

"Dad—"

"Actually, Kofi, the idea of asking an African nation for asylum is swift. It would attract media attention. So under protection, you could hold a press conference once the forces got themselves together. It's a good idea," Spence added, hoping that would cap it. But his son's breath was still hot on his neck.

"Is that what Speaker was talking about, going to the UN for protection?"

". . . Not exactly. Well, yes."

"Well, what if the killers took a shortcut and got to the UN first? And what if they told them a bunch of lies and then—"

"You sure got a lot of what-ifs. All I want is some cookies and some choc'late milk. Ainchu hongry?"

"Dad?"

"Kenti, we can have dessert later. Now, please."

"Dad?"

"We don't seem to be early after all," Zala said when they turned onto Hightower. Vehicles were parked bumper to bumper. Buses were making unscheduled stops in the middle of the street for passengers come for the meeting.

"I hope this amounts to something," Spence said grimly.

"Dad, would you listen. You think the mayor and them know something?"

"Might."

"Do you? Like, maybe you sort of know who's doing the killing?"

"I've got thirty-two years' worth of informed suspicions," Spence said, sitting up straight; Kofi was about to tear the back of the seat out from under him.

"What if they know you know? What if they come after you, after all of us?"

"Kofi, don't work yourself up."

"Tell him to be quiet. He's scaring me."

"I gotta know what ya gonna do onnaconna they might come after us. Answer me! Dag!" He flung himself hard against the seat. "Mize well be dead awreddy, cuz you ain' gonna do nuthin'."

"Daddy got a gun, stupid. Anybody bother us, he blow they head off, scaredy cat."

"Somebody better tell her to quit pulling on my clothes, 'cuz when I hit her y'all gonna say it's my fault."

"Kofi, would you leave it."

"See—see there! I knew it. Gettin' on me and don't even care if them killers come after us."

"Kofi." Zala turned around. "Try to calm down. That's the trouble with people, they get too scared to do their own thinking. Then anybody can tell them anything. You remember what your grandaddy use to say about the Ku Klux Klan, when they'd announce they were going to parade and everybody better get off the streets? They'd turn the power off in the Black community, remember? Just to show they could do it, just to have people shaking in the dark, afraid to defend themselves. And what did people do? Did they hide under the bed? Did they get paralyzed with fear? That's what the newspapers said. But what did Grandaddy tell you?"

"Said they pulled ropes across the roads if they were coming on horses. Said they dug up the roads and made ruts if they were coming in trucks. They put bottles in the trees and stakes in the ground and nails and tacks and stuff like that. Sent the dogs out to get 'em when they climbed out of the trucks. Got them some rakes and pickaxes if they tried to set things on fire. Said they drove 'em off."

"In other words, they didn't panic. They got together and made plans. Well, that's what this meeting is for," she concluded, watching folding chairs being unloaded from the back of a van and handed along a line and up the steps of the Greater Fairhill Baptist Church.

"But what if they throw a bomb in the house? Whatchu gonna do then?"

"They think you the mayor, Daddy." Several people had rushed forward to look into the limo as they cruised past.

"Dad, if you were the mayor, would you tell people to get their guns?"

"Why don't we wait and see what the real mayor has to say," Spence sighed. Far from early, they were late, Spence realized. Hosea Williams and other SCLC heads were talking with groups of people clustered around the church steps.

"But what if—"

"Enough. Period." Zala looked for somewhere to park. She spotted Mattie directing a Buick onto the sidewalk, its radio drowning out her instructions. Zala scanned the crowd scattered along the sidewalk, looking for STOP members. Near the corner she recognized several of the radical newsdealers from Central City Park. Kenti was leaning over her, staring at a priest heading for Fairhill, his rosary chain swinging against his robes.

"You just missed a space, Spence."

"I think I'd like to miss the whole thing," he said wearily.

"What are they doing here?" Kenti tapped her.

Zala leaned her head back against Kenti's hands.

"Are they light people or white people?"

"Whatchu got against white people all of a sudden? You was just with some white people, stupid."

"Was? Was I, Daddy?"

Kofi sucked his teeth and caught Spence's eye in the mirror. He was smiling.

Light bread or white bread, which your Uncle Rayfield eat, Nathaniel? Miss Sudie holding the fish on the spatula, waiting on an answer. Wrong answer. His uncle had ribbed him mercilessly all day about bringing some funny-looking Silvercup into the house.

"We getting out or what?" The car was parked and someone was rapping on the window, but nobody moved. "Ain't we going in, Dad?"

Mattie held Zala's hand as she got out, then pulled her toward her in a motherly embrace. "Looks like everybody's here," she said, pointing. "Undercover police, plainclothes nuns. Political ragamuffins on one side, telltales on the other. That's what you call working both sides of the street. They evidently suspect the worst," she added, walking Zala toward the church. "Puts me in mind of a story my research mentor use to tell—"

"Let's go in," Zala interrupted. She was in no mood for stories, especially shouted over the Buick radio the children were running past, their hands over their ears. Why would anyone play music that loud and in front of a church and on this day of all days? Zala pulled away from Mattie. She didn't want to be mothered either, not by someone whose arm trembled.

"I'd rather be a blind girl," Etta James sang out of the Buick window as Commissioner Brown was accompanied up the steps by back-slappers and by those anxious to have their questions answered immediately. "I'd rather be a blind girl than see you turn your back on me, babe."

Zala raced up the steps, breaking the grip of two men in the doorway shaking hands. This was no time for pressing flesh and asking after each other's grandmothers. Were people going to see to it that justice was done, that the bombers were caught, that people organized and brought the terror to a halt?—those were the questions. She moved swiftly down the carpeted aisle to a pew near the front, not noticing who was there, not seeing her children waving from the side section, or her husband motioning her toward two chairs set at the end of a row. She coughed up grit into a tissue and did not sit down. She wanted to be on her feet when the meeting began. And if they were slow to begin, every minister in the hall eager to individually lead them in prayer, she wanted to be ready to cut short any delay. She scrutinized the leaders as they took their places on the pulpit two feet above the congregation. She feared the worst but muttered "Keep the faith," keepthefaith, hanging on to the back of the pew in front of her, digging her nails into the wood.

[IV]

THE STATE OF
THE ART

Friday, December 19, 1980

The wall loaded now with glistening statements, the graffiti artists capped their markers, wiped clean the nozzles of their spray cans, then looked in the direction of Ashby and Thurmond, where the music was coming from. A piano rendition of "We'll Understand It Better By and By" had begun when they first surveyed the wall, asked access of the three men sitting on the chain in front of it drinking, then bit off their cold-stiff gloves to draft their urgent communiqués to the neighborhood. From the Mount Moriah Tabernacle came the old song, the left hand brooding, somber chords of resignation sounding the bass line while the right hand skittered up and down the keyboard improvising sly comments till the thick bass chords broke into a nervous olio of signature themes from other anthems, hymns, and spirituals.

"That's one crazy fool up there on the ivories," one of the wine drinkers said over his shoulder. The graffiti writers packed their tools inside their jackets, zipped up, and headed toward Thurmond. "Make more sense to put your backs to the wind," he called to them, then huddled under his scarf and hat as the wind whipped across Ashby, spinning garbage can lids into the middle of halting traffic.

Clusters of notes tumbled free-form, crossing the axis and turning the left hand loose to blues some, gospel, bop-doo-wop, as the writers trudged backward up the street. The left hand chased the right in a relentless effort to do it—to make the terrible bearable. Both hands stretched out in self-generating rhythms, the pedal pumped to the floor to state it, music rolling, rolling, rolling thro' an unfriendly world. And ain't we got a right to the tree of life? God, the inexhaustible possibilities. Lord, help us. Oh, must Jesus bear the cross alone and all the world go free. Take up the cross. Whomp. Take it up. Whomp. Even as we stumble through another Golgotha of bones. Whomp. Take up the cross.

Then both piano hands collected themselves below middle C to take refuge in a bit of "Go Down" and "Swing Low" and "Nobody Knows" before "We'll Understand It" thundered up again, shaking the rafters. The writers mounted the steps and saw the lock rattling in the tabernacle door. They opened it and were shoved in by the wind.

Bundled to the eyes, Zala turned the corner. The wind digging branches through chinks in chimneys was no less fierce than the testifying piano. It gusted litter up out of hiding places and hurled it against windshields, slowing traffic to a crawl. It swept under coats, blew away hats, stole the greetings out of the mouths of neighbors. Sent brittle leaves skidding down the gutters to dam up the sewers. Newspapers plastered thick against the back of Zala's legs. She turned, stomped, turned again, and papers glued themselves to the front of her legs tripping her up.

Their legs shivering, the three men held. They would not be unseated from the stout chain links that they sat on, swung on, their heels rooted in depressions in the sidewalk. They passed judgment on females who swept by and voiced warnings to the endangered on skateboards. Bloodshot but sharp, their eyes condemned cars that slowed too near children dawdling with schoolbooks. They kept steely watch on strangers walking too near the candy store. Taking turns on the bottle, they kept all four corners under surveillance while they sang songs worth braving the cold to sing.

" 'The way you mooooove, you know you coulda been a—' "

"Jailbait," one of the men sang out, getting raunchy with a young girl coming out of the cleaners, the wind ripping the plastic from the clothes slung over her back. His companions pulled him back down by his coat and leaned against him on either side to remind him what he was supposed to be doing.

Zala used her package to anchor her coat down and inched carefully across a patch of ice browned in spots by the contents of a bottle that lay smashed up ahead, the shards offering noisy traction. No way then to slip past the men singing and carousing beneath the wall that urged the people to unite their wrath and take control of the city before it was too late.

" 'The way you loooook, you know you coulda been a—' "

"Hey, sweetmeat, you married?"

The wino tried to peer in through Zala's coat collar and scarf, smiling blearily. His buddies yanked him back to his seat, apologizing to her through wool. The three men seemed to be well fortified against the cold.

Whatever they were drinking was more powerful than the half-jar of Mama Lovey's brew she'd downed when she could no longer take typing the tapes. Next door Mrs. Grier had been rinsing rice over and over, running the tap, shaking a colander, scraping it against the sink. There were more typos than Zala could handle with the thickened white-out. She had yanked out the used-up typewriter ribbon and gone to the sink. She ran her tap on, off, on. Distress signals ignored, she drank down the last of the wide-mouth jars and bundled up, the underarm seams of her coat straining over two sweaters. Despite petroleum jelly, hat, scarf, and collar, cold had needled her face before she'd reached the hedges. By the time she got to the corner where the wind battled the piano for attention, her face felt like cheap silk crepe.

"Ha, ha, ha!" the drinkers were laughing, their voices loud in her ears long after she was seated on the bus, loosening her wraps.

Near a lot slated to be a park in the spring, four boys threw down a piece of corrugated cardboard and got ready to practice, cold as it was. Passengers on the bus fussed with their holly and silver bell corsages, clucking about children allowed to roam about like that. Others rubbed circles in the glass to watch when a neighbor woman taking plants in from her sunporch called out to the boys to go home before they broke their necks or got them broken. The boys were respectful. More, they looked grateful. For if someone called you by name, or only "son," "junior," "boy," even if they were scolding, then you were alive, alive to that community that named you. They ma'amed the woman until she took in the last of the plants. Then they dragged their dance floor closer to the lot and threw it down again.

"They're not going to let cold nor fear keep them from the dance," the man next to Zala said. "You have to admire these kids."

Zala nodded, but several people across the aisle disagreed. That led to a general discussion about the curfew, the puzzle and pain of it. Camille Bell of STOP had pointed out on TV that most of the children had disappeared in broad daylight, so what was the 7:00 p.m. ban but another way of blurring the facts and dumping on parents?

"That's right." A woman on the long seat behind the driver added to the conversation going on toward the front of the bus. "It's another way of blaming the mothers and mothers in general."

Her companion began explaining to the passengers that "motherhood" and "woman's place" were being bandied about at work. "Getting ready to cut back women workers' hours. That's the point of it all."

The people behind Zala were talking about the effect of the curfew on family budgets. Teenagers were discouraged from seeking afterschool jobs, and employers were reluctant to hire them because of the ban.

"I'm telling you," the woman on the long seat spoke up, "if the community doesn't rally behind women workers, we're going to lose the whole city to foreigners."

Several people toward the front chided the two women in deference to the driver, a Filipina. The two women on the long seat paid no attention.

"It's a fact that the situation is serious," the one in the brown coat continued. Vietnamese were taking over the wig shops and small clothing stores in the West End. Didn't people realize that Cubans, Koreans, and anybody who was not a hometown colored person was grabbing up all the small-business loans and setting up along Peachtree where not even Black people had stores?

"Not Black Cubans," someone inserted. "They're up in Atlanta Federal Pen."

"Don't get us wrong," the other woman worker said. "We don't have hard feelings against foreigners. It's the government. They open the doors and open their hands to them refugees."

"While they backhand us," her co-worker added.

"Please turn that up," one of the passengers across from the driver requested.

The driver leaned over and turned her radio up. It hung from a loop on the fare box. When the bus reached the corner, she swung the lever to open the front door, then turned in her seat. She planted one foot down hard near the base of the coin box and looked at the two women behind her on the long seat. The two women nodded briefly, then looked away.

Two young men dressed for the labor pool escorted an old gent down the aisle and turned him over to the driver, who stood up to take his hand and ease him down the steps.

"They'll be lifting the bans soon," the old man said, poking the radio with his cane as he got off.

"What'd he say?"

"Says the roadblocks and the curfew will end soon," one of the labor-pool brothers reported, going back to his seat.

"All this talk about it's under control. Just like the recession. But you see how they keep talking patriotic talk about buying American goods to get the economy up."

"Yeah, they keep talking about competition," the other laborer said, "with foreign businesses. Now, I ask you, who's kidding who? Them so-called foreign companies ain't nobody but Americans who ran out on us to avoid taxes and decent salaries. Competition my ass. We're supposed to compete with each other," he told those sitting in aisle seats. "Me and you. But not them. They cooperate with each other to hold us all down. Then when some shit get in the game, it's time to go to war. Who's kidding who here?" He took a seat in the back of the bus with his buddy and slapped the pole with his work gloves, disgusted.

"That's what I was saying," the woman on the long seat called out. But people shushed her as the bus took off. They wanted to hear the news on the radio.

Quiet was the word. There'd been no abductions since Aaron Jackson disappeared over a month ago and was found on the south bank of the river. Everything was quiet, according to the authorities.

Zala sucked her teeth. Quiet, if they didn't count the others. Patrick Rogers, considered the linchpin in the case by one of the VIs because he knew so many of the victims both on the list and not on the list, had disappeared nine days after Jackson. Found in the river, Pat Man was still not on the list. Nor was the Armstrong girl. A neighbor of LaTonya Wilson's and found strangled the week after Jackson's body was found, the same week Pat Man vanished, the same week *The Call* added three women, two men, and three children to the community-kept list, the Armstrong girl had been all but ignored by the press and was unknown to the Task Force.

"Looks like they've got this thing just about solved," someone seated near the rear door commented. Several people leaned into the aisle to hear what someone up front said in response. A fusillade of coins hit the box as boarding passengers dropped in their change. People sat up and drew in their feet, continuing to talk as the bus took off.

Where the bus turned to leave the 'hood for the straight shot down-town, girls were jumping rope with a fury. The two turners were lash-ing the sidewalk. The jumper was burning up the soles of her shoes. Waiting her turn, another girl was getting her hair cornrowed by a friend whose hands worked quickly. Then the girl tore loose and was rocked back and forth by one of the turners, her mouth grimly set, her hands balled into fists, her chin beating out the rhythm of the rope. She jumped in and so did the braider. They jumped with an attitude, refus-ing to duck, forcing the turners to step in to accommodate them. They were practicing their art, defying the cold and the fear. They eyed pas-sengers as the bus sped by. The braider waved when the man seated next to Zala leaned over to give them the power salute. The other girls smiled. To be seen by members of the community, no matter how fault-finding some of them were, was encouraging, their smiles said.

"I guess I'd do the same thing if I were a child," a woman across the aisle conceded. "In any case, it'll soon be over."

"You believe that, you believe anything," one of the new passengers snorted, grabbing a strap. It was a mucousy snort, and he hawked and hacked for a minute. Those who sat below him frowned and leaned away.

The floodgates were open, seven or eight conversations going at once. Would someone be arrested? Was it the Klan after all? What was the mayor going to do about all the bounty hunters pouring into the city? Maynard Jackson was likened to the little Dutch boy with his fin-ger in the dike.

"Everything quiet and under control is something to put in your Christmas stocking," the snorter said, his voice struggling through lay-ers of phlegm.

"Quiet" was a can of green beans put in the holiday baskets for the poor, called "needy" two times a year, called bums, welfare chiselers, or nothing at all the rest of the time.

"Peace on earth and good will to men," the man said. "In other words, go downtown and shop in peace and put yourself in hock. Maybe you'll climb out in time for Easter shopping to throw you right back on in." He strode toward the rear.

People busied themselves with breath mints or loose threads in coat buttons. Others held their lapel bells quiet and tried to think of ways to resume conversations with those around them. But the snorter in the peely bomber jacket had managed to kill the mood on the bus.

Zala rang the buzzer and got off. She thought of her own children. Away from the fear and the bulletins, they would be practicing no arts with dedicated fury—no singing, no dancing, no jumping rope. Primly seated between Nana Cora on the couch, they'd be turning the pages of the family album, looking at the commemorated moments that fulfilled the Spencers' expectations of the good life. Perhaps that was a defiant art, Zala thought. Spence, a baseball cap slung over one ear, washing a dog in the carport. Delia under the trees holding hymnal and gloves, her feet close together, her knees greased. Zala couldn't recall having ever seen baby pictures of Spence and had commented on it more than once. "We weren't studyin' cameras in them days," Cora would say, quickly changing her statement into good English, which made it no less a lie, for there were lots of snapshots from those years, but none of Spence. But then Cora was a notorious liar anyway. "Gone visiting." "At the movies." "Down to see his uncle Rayfield." The only way Zala had been able to reach the children was to call late at night, when they habitually got up to use the bathroom. All Kofi had to say was to hold his place in the Christmas pageant. Kenti asked after Buster the cat, Roger the fish, and Aunty Paulette, still away in Miami.

Zala pushed through the revolving doors and scribbled something in the sign-in book that the guard didn't challenge. She went to the bank of elevators and scanned the directory.

The one time she'd tricked Spence into coming to the phone by disguising her voice, he'd held her off with a bunch of statistics. Last year more adolescents died from booze, dope, and suicide than from disease or accidents. More children under five were murdered by their parents than died from natural causes. One out of four females was raped before twenty-one. Over a million children were sexually abused per annum. Over five hundred thousand children were reported missing per annum. What did that have to do with bringing the children home? In autumn he'd told her that she was a jerk for letting B. J. convince her that it was a porn ring and not the Klan. But what were his statistics about? It was all so stupid. How could anyone carry on a conversation with a person who said "per annum"? He hadn't even given her the satisfaction of hanging up on him.

"I'll fix his ass." She punched the button for the twelfth floor on the elevator panel, and four people stepped to the rear of the car to give her plenty of grumbling room.

She leaned the bundle against the elevator wall. She fingered an index card with the day's errand in her left coat pocket. In her right was a wad of address labels to remind her to pick up typing supplies. Crumpled there too was the Child Find brochure she'd found so disturbing. A minute ago she'd felt ready. Now she couldn't free herself of the memories of that day. It had been depressing from start to finish.

In the morning she'd gone to see about Dave. They'd thrown him in the holding tank after he squared off on an officer of the court who kept saying, "I gave him a direct order, a direct order." Then she'd doubled back to the house: no sign of Spence and the children. The barbershop was crowded, but she'd left her kits at a Mary Kay demonstration. So she'd gone to the STOP office to help out with the mail. The smell of burning leaves behind her, she'd gone up the stairs through a wave of floral perfume left, no doubt, by one of the many self-appointed spokesladies who were forever volunteering their services for the poor unfortunate mothers who could not possibly be regarded as spokespersons of even their own tragedy. Tragedies, after all, happened in castles, not in low-income homes. Good speechifying was done by the gentry, not by common folks. Folks could hang around the palace courtyard commenting on the king's business, or they could narrate the adventures of the captain obsessed with the whale. But dramas of common folks were not good literature. So reporters came to ask loaded questions designed to get poor Black women in trouble to crack on uppity Black men in office. And the gentry came to suggest what to say and how to say it, most surprised when they were shown the door.

Near the top of the landing, Zala had been hit with a mixture of coffee, overflowing ashtrays, and the musk of hucksters bringing in logo designs for T-shirts and bumper stickers, outlining how to bankroll a regional investigation for only one thousand down. In the doorway air deodorant took over. But there was another odor too. It emanated from people come to tell the office workers what couldn't be safely told to the police. The office itself smelled of secrets, fear, exhaustion. The phones were ringing off the hooks with callers wanting lists, maps, charts, chronologies, and the personal bios of STOP's members. And the volunteers were patiently explaining that the office was not equipped with computers or a full-time staff.

Zala hated going to STOP, but hated not going. She didn't want to be disconnected from people who felt as she felt. But she also didn't want her presence mistaken for greed now that contributions were coming in. She never knew where to sit, with the mothers or with the volunteers. When people invited the volunteers to lunch and included her, she always felt like a moocher. She would nurse a HoJo cola while the others ate fried clam platters. The family men had allowed the media's emphasis on the mothers to rob them of their identity just as she had allowed the Task Force list to steal hers. Neither the men nor the families of children not on the list were official.

At the office, she would fix herself a cup of horrible instant coffee, dawdling; then, when no one called her, she would find a quiet corner and break open a pack of mail. The piles had already been started by those who'd driven from as far away as Tuscaloosa, Talladoga, and Tuskeegee to lend a hand. Real workers, they had clear-cut motives and moved about purposefully. Zala felt like a fake. Fear of her lonesome house drove her to STOP. Since Thanksgiving, she'd been on her own for the first time in her life. And it was spooky.

On the top of the pile that day had been still another copy of Kübler-Ross's *On Death and Dying.* From local hospice centers came offers to conduct workshops for the survivors. Church groups, sororities and fraternities, families, prisoners, schoolchildren and senior citizens sent condolences and contributions. A Golden Age group wrote about the methods used to "calm" elders concerned about the awful situation in Atlanta: In nursing homes, medication was increased; in centers, lunch portions were enlarged and the thermostats turned up. They urged the STOP committee to speak out on behalf of prisoners, who were no doubt being "calmed" more brutally.

"This pile is for letters that want an answer," Monika had told Zala that day. It was a hopeless task to even sort them, much less respond. Often people sent tips and clues requesting feedback. But their letters sounded like overtures from lonely people reaching out with the one thing they were sure would not be rebuffed.

Karen was handling the mail from angry parents everywhere who wanted STOP to help improve child-protection laws. These parents had lost children to drunk drivers, malpractice, experimenting pharmaceutical companies, to child molesters who'd plea-bargained for lesser charges and early parole, to patients released from the back wards because of overcrowded conditions in state asylums, to companies who dumped chemical and nuclear waste near schools, to ambitious developers and corrupt politicians who went ahead and built houses on contaminated sites.

Without comment, Sandra had passed Zala a leaflet calling for an all-out attack on men, from the porn shops to Capitol Hill.

"We need to recruit more volunteers," Monika said. "You look burnt out already. Take a break."

"Talking to me?" Sandra worked nights at a crisis center handling a hotline. She divided her days between classes at Clark, STOP, and the Ronald McDonald House for ailing children and their families. "I can make it to spring break before I collapse," she said matter-of-factly.

"You," Monika said, pulling Zala's chair out from under her. "Take a walk."

So Zala had fixed herself another cup of instant and walked around the office, trying to concentrate on the Child Find brochure she couldn't seem to put down. A movie was showing on the Sony someone had loaned for the day: *Ransom!* with Glenn Ford and Donna Reed. Ford looking steely with no top lip. Donna Reed rich, twitchy, and dogged. Ford, an industrialist, refused to pay the kidnappers. Zala went back to work.

There was a bunch of crank notes and hate mail that applauded the killers. Less explicit were letters clipped to pages torn from the *Torch* and the *Thunderbolt*, newspapers that had been whipping up a fury about unsolved homicides of whites. "What's ten or ten thousand nigger lives compared to the loss of one white life!" the hate rags slobbered.

There were outraged letters demanding STOP to get more vocal about the media's depiction of the child victims as passive and willing. There'd been an outcry when Aaron Jackson's laid-out body was described as "peaceful," the rock under his head "a pillow." The children were called street hustlers and the killer "gentle." "Like a kind slave master?" one writer posed.

"Is there a pile for drawings?" a new volunteer from Spelman asked.

"Drawings from psychics go to the left, drawings by children to the right," Sandra instructed.

Many letters in Zala's pile confused STOP with the UYAC-led search teams. They referred the searchers to Birmingham, where recently unearthed graves had disclosed the bodies of civil rights workers missing since the sixties. Assuming STOP was an adjunct of the Task Force, other writers directed attention to the situation in Trenton, New Jersey, where a pattern of missing and murdered children was being suppressed. Some assumed the Black vets group was the paramilitary arm of STOP and recommended an invasionary expedition to free captives on slave plantations in Florida and North Carolina.

"Here's another for the Jekyll-and-Hyde pile," Zala said, handing over a sheaf of papers. Lectures on the split personalities of the Boston Strangler and Son of Sam were mailed in by forensic psychiatrists who quoted their consultant fees. From Jonesboro, a woman named Detwyler forwarded a page from her "murder scrapbook" about the still-unsolved Wynton Stocking Strangler Case of Columbus, Georgia. "It could be related," the woman wrote.

"The cult pile is getting too big to handle."

"Who's going to read through this material?" the new volunteer asked and was immediately sent to find a box. No one wanted to hear that.

In a thick manila envelope was a grisly account of a cult that had operated in St. Jo, Florida. For years the cult had been kidnapping hitchhikers and using them as sacrifices in LSD-induced rituals. They dismembered the bodies. Six hours before a scheduled raid by the sheriff, the cult's church mysteriously burned to the ground, its congregation dispersed. The tipster urged that a white plainclothesman be sent to St. Jo to research the connection to the cult killings in Atlanta.

While the piles grew, Zala thought of Jan Douglass down at the Office of Community Relations in the City Hall Annex. Douglass was compiling a news-clipping file on random and systemic attacks on Black people. The first time Zala had visited the Annex, to accompany the vets who'd written a position paper responding to psychic Dorothy Alison's allegations that Black men were the killers, Douglass had been using three legal pads to log her clippings: violence by the police, by white groups, by persons unknown. When next Zala went there, accompanying a delegation led by Teo and Sue Ellen to counter an all-white group demanding to know what "responsible Negro leadership" was doing to defuse "militants," the three legal pads had given way to large cartons for major categories like "Campus Violence" and smaller boxes for subcategories like "Drownings," "Beatings," and "Arson."

"Here's the end of the blue cow serial, Marzala."

Zala recognized the blue stationery. For weeks, someone from Carson City had been sending newspaper and magazine articles about a case in the 1970s that had affected cattle ranchers in seventeen states from West Virginia to Utah. Cattle had disappeared from herds, then turned up dead days later with broken legs and shattered ribs. An unusual number of UFO sightings had occurred in fifteen of the seventeen states during a given period. But ranchers were convinced that the culprits were not from outer space or even from out of town. First they investigated the agricultural barons. Then they began watching the skies, not for spacecraft but for army helicopters. They went into court armed with photos of government choppers with heavy nets carrying massive brown cargo. The autopsy reports on the dead steers indicated surgical tampering and viral infection from intravenous injections. Broken bones were attributed to having been dropped from the choppers.

"Ask the government," said the writer on blue stationery. "It's the work of a well-organized occult group operating in collusion with government researchers." The second page of the letter compared the condition of the steers with the description of Angel Lenair's body— leatherlike skin, missing lower lip and left ear, so aged in appearance her mother had not recognized her.

The packet was handed around the office while Zala broke open a plain brown envelope with three dollars' worth of canceled stamps on it. Zala shook out calendars, a how-to manual, and promotional material for a group called NAMBLA, the North American Man-Boy Love Association, dedicated to "liberating" young boys from loveless situations. News clippings from Troy, Auburn, and other cities in upstate New York identified defendants in child molestation cases as NAMBLA members. The writer urged STOP to investigate before the network of doctors, teachers, lawyers, and other "respectable" types went underground. Zala tried to pass it around, but everyone was preoccupied with the cattle story.

"In this article, the marginal note says we should be monitoring biochemical warfare centers in this region. Here's a map. The Anniston Center in Alabama is circled."

"Sounds out to lunch," the new volunteer said. "The government?"

Monika and the office manager gathered up the checks, money orders, and international bank drafts and slipped them inside the ledger to be placed on the main desk.

"Have you heard Dick Gregory on the subject? He may be thin, but the man's heavy."

"The government? He thinks the government is involved? That's too crazy. . . . Isn't it?"

"Well, you know the Health Department with the backing of the Catholic Church sterilized over thirty percent of the women in Puerto Rico," Zala volunteered.

"Why go all the way to Puerto Rico? Right here they've been sterilizing Indian women and men for generations."

"Well, what about the sisters? In some places you still can't get on welfare unless you sign away your womb."

"That can't be right," the new volunteer resisted.

"Come on, girl, wake up. More than half the doctors where I come from won't deliver your baby unless you agree to have your tubes tied, snipped, or cauterized. Every time the census comes out, white folks start getting nervous. So they make Mexicans honorary white folks to beef up their numbers. Then they roll up their sleeves and reach for the surgical knives."

"Are you kidding?"

"Are *you* kidding?"

"I hope we're not going to spend the afternoon trotting out horror stories for her edification. Let her read the mail, she'll see."

"Well, who's heard Dick Gregory?—that's my question? Zala, you still have that tape? School this child."

"But he's not a . . . a learned person. Okay, okay, I'm listening."

"Basically, his lecture was about interferon. It's produced in collectible amounts by people who have sickle cell. So it's collected from African and Middle Eastern people mostly, wherever the malaria is rampant and people's immune system produces the substance to combat it."

"So?"

"So, it's important to cancer research and to longevity research. I typed up part of an interview a friend did at the Centers for Disease Control last week. The CDC workers have been studying the missing and murdered children's medical histories for background in sickle cell."

"Get to the good part. Sit down, sister, while Marzala tells you how much they sell this interferon—which, incidentally, is collected from the foreskin of Black males. Give her the bottom line."

"It's worth two billion dollars a pint."

"Now get to that. Folks are wondering how come the reward hasn't pulled in defectors from the killer gang. The reward is chump change compared to . . . hell, I don't even know how many zeroes there are in a billion."

"But the government?"

"Please go find me a small carton to put these bank drafts in," Monika interrupted, and the new volunteer walked away, grateful to be out of their midst. Monika sighed. "We've been watching *Mission: Impossible* all our lives, but some of us still don't get the message."

The credits were rolling. Zala scanned the faces of those nearest the TV. She'd missed the ending of *Ransom!* Had the industrialist father relented and paid the ransom? Had the child been returned? Had Donna Reed rallied from her sickbed? There was nothing in the expressions of the STOP workers to give her a clue. Zala turned back to the pile of brochures she'd set aside for her own mailing list. The volunteers, worn out from haggling with the true-believer college girl reluctant to return to the table with the carton no one really needed, were quiet. Zala unfolded the Child Find brochure and concentrated on the story she'd found so troublesome.

Through the efforts of the parent organization, a young boy had been returned to his family after a four-year absence. But he was so changed by his experience with the salesman who'd stolen him, who locked him in an old coal bin when he went on trips, that the boy's parents began to doubt he was their son. And who had the forethought to fingerprint their children in anticipation of monstrous events years later? Footprints on baby records, fine for avoiding mix ups in the hospital nursery, were too uncertain after ten years. The boy was a definite look-alike, gave credible enough impersonations, but one morning when his father woke him for school, the boy said, "These aren't my clothes. Whose house is this?" The therapist quoted in the brochure

said that formation of dissociated selves was a not uncommon conse-
quence of trauma, but most people managed to integrate their multiple
personalities without undue difficulty. Sometimes, however, trauma
caused a separation, a split, and barriers grew up between the parts of
the self. Memory lapses turned into long bouts of amnesia. Worse, those
barriers could harden and the former core self be banished to the wings,
leaving a minor player to hold center stage ever after, with only a portion of the life script.

The brochure did not say what had happened when the family took
the boy to visit their former house, the one he'd grown up in. Nor did
it say what had possessed the family to move from that home in the first
place. That was the part that kept sending Zala back to the beginning
of the story looking for a footnote. Why had they left the one place the
six-year-old boy knew as home? And why hadn't someone proofing the
brochure not thought to place a note of explanation somewhere? It was
supposed to be a success story.

The more she read, the more disturbed she'd felt. She'd begged off
sorting mail and taken the bus to the Omni to shop for Christmas gifts.

Stumbling off the escalator, banged in the back with boxes, as-
phyxiated by perfumes, and suffocated by fur coats, Zala had veered to
the right, away from the stream of shoppers. She'd stood in front of the
Rizzoli international bookstore a long time trying to catch her breath.
In the window was an old, brown-shellacked circus poster. Busy, a cast
of thousands, animal acts, a full palette of colors, the poster would have
caught the children's attention. She could hear Kenti and Kofi pleading
with her to take the escalator down to the ticket booth for the circus
that came to town every February. Alone, she stared at the center circle,
where a family of gymnasts in blue and white tights formed a preposterous pyramid.

Zala had stood at the window studying the poses, the lines and
curves of the bodies, the strain of the muscles, the pattern of weight and
counterweight. How could any move on anybody's part result in anything but broken bones, torn ligaments, and all seven facedown in the
sawdust? Who would do what to make a springboard turn the family
into an aerial act? But there was the parasol. And there was the wire.
And there were the seven faces shining with belief in their ability, in
their future.

Zala turned and elbowed her way through the shoppers to the railing, leaned way over, sucking in the blue-mint chill of the ice rink below, where her three children should have been skating.

Zala sniffed back the tears with such force, her scarf was sucked into her nostrils. She mashed her bundle against the panel and eyed the emergency button. She might not get what she came for from Austin. She was already dreading the trip back home through the darkening streets, past the garrisoned homes to the empty house.

On the twelfth floor, the elevator doors opened onto a meadow of lavender moss. Mushroom-colored modulars arranged in an L were propped against potted plants six feet tall. Beyond was a wall of glass sun-splashed by the skylight. Behind the glass, blond desks floated on a creamy carpet with magenta zigzags. Zala got a good grip on her package and on herself and followed the sounds of a typewriter toward what she hoped was the entrance to Attorney Austin's office.

"Glass," she said, easing around the sofa. "Glass, glass," in case she hadn't given up on the dream of finding a permeable membrane to pass through to the other Atlanta where newspapers spoke of earthquakes in Italy, uprisings in Poland, the murder of a diet doctor in Scarsdale; the only hometown count the final score in the last Hawks game. But there was no place to dream anymore. No matter how far she fanned out from the killing ground with her manicure kit and her makeup and hairdo case trying to fill in the gap left by CETA and the Board of Ed's nonrenewal of her contract, it was the same. People whispering "phantom" and "random" like little children running to the edge of the subway platform to scare themselves. Fathers nailing up hasty basketball hoops and grounding grumbling teenagers. Mothers racing door-to-door with a coffee can to take up collections. Babysitters arriving with an escort of friends and relatives. Paper boys slipping pay-due envelopes into the folds and slinging the bundles from the safety of the sidewalk. Bored and sullen children reciting the dos and don'ts for travel to and from school. Yard boys dismissed early, leaves still blowing across the walk. Red pepper and pigeon-feather charms in doorways, asafetida bags around necks, garlands of garlic set in tubs of oil on front steps. All over, the same talk. Street crime was down, liquor sales were up, ditto for locks, flashlights, and baseball bats. No place to dream and no way to live a rational life.

Do you know you're stolen? Is your father talking bad about me? Don't let him turn you two against me.

She was in an irrational state, her husband on the phone had told her, citing his statistics, refusing to put the children back on the phone. Afterward, on the radio a sleuth played with the dates of the victims in order to prove a periodicity pattern that pointed to a murderess with an irregular menses. On another station, a policeman was being interviewed: No, ransom was definitely not the motive in the M&M case, the kids were poor, keep in mind, so poor they'd do anything for a buck. Robbery? Why, no—poor, I'm telling you; we found nothing on them. That was rational thinking? And then: There's no substance to the rumor of bickering between the various bureaus, and we've good communication. Yet Cynthia Armstrong had been in a city shelter while her mother had been badgering MPYD, was in the city jail while the APD assured her they were searching high and low. And then the girl was murdered. But there was no dead cat on the line, as Mama Lovey would have put it. Zala had flipped the dial until she found the Wailers. Babylon, Babylon. But her per-annum husband had hung up on her.

If she had indeed been insane, insane enough to cling to the dream, the looks she got upon entering the attorney's office would have cured her. Fingers froze over the keyboard, one hand battened down on the phone. She was scrutinized, her scruffy package eyed. The typist stared, but the receptionist smiled, dimpling, and offered a patient, sisterly look. Zala relaxed and took in the office.

Newspapers were spread out on desks, the photos of the children peppery. Telltale slips of paper were tucked under the phones—junior at school, junior at neighbor's, hubby at work. On the corkboard were the SAFE flyers and the Task Force posters, six emergency numbers in the lower-right-hand corner. On a dropleaf table between two bookcases, a foil-covered cake tin for office donations. On a glass-top coffee table in front of the sofa, photos of Austin and his wife in hiking boots, quilted down jackets, and ski pants, shaking hands with the Reverend Arthur Langford, the city councilman who'd organized the civilian search teams. Sticking out of copies of *Southern Living, Ebony,* and *Variety* were slips from a notepad, someone free-associating with the reward in mind.

"May I help you?" The receptionist's voice was soothing and her smile earnest. Zala rested her package and handed over the old business card she'd found among mildewed supplies when Paulette came by to borrow the last of the suitcases for her trip to Miami.

"I'd like to see Mr. Austin," she said, flipping the business card over for the receptionist to see where Austin had written. More than two years ago he had approached Zala about doing tapestries for his office, but then she'd started work at the art center and had let it slide. Meeting his wife at a Mary Kay party had reminded her of this resource. She waited while the receptionist read in Austin's hand that Zala should drop by. "I think he'll see me," she said. "Marzala Spencer."

The typist looked up. "Marzala Spencer? Didn't I just read about you in *The Call?*" The receptionist stuck her pencil in her topknot, but the typist ignored the signal. "Well, what do you think?"

"Think?" Zala hoped that whatever the typist was searching for under her desk would give her a clue.

PEOPLE'S POWER was emblazoned across the front of *The Call.* The typist was looking for something particular in the center sheet to speak about. "A People United Will Prevail Over Terror." Lynchings, rapes, bombings, nations brandishing nuclear weapons. Don't give up your power in exchange for the false security of deadbolt locks. What little Zala had had to say was lost in the avalanche of fight-back proposals and slogans. Think? She was thinking of the children, popping, breaking, turning, jumping, refusing to let the power of terror drive them under.

"You wouldn't remember me," the typist said, ignoring the receptionist, who turned in her chair and dug once again into her topknot. "I was at the Greater Fairhill meeting that night. I took your picture."

"Picture. Fairhill," Zala echoed.

So many that night at Fairhill had reached back for childhood memories of their country schools. Modest efforts at education, barely open more than two seasons out of four. No floors, most of them, without roofs some of them, a few backless benches, waxed-paper windows, one lap chalkboard per ten students. But still it was too much, an affront, for they'd actually painted the walls when many poor whites in the county had houses without paint. So the county spent less, eight dollars per white child, seventy-six cents per Black, the salary differential more criminal than that. And still an affront to whites, felling trees to block the road, turning the children back, waylaying the teacher, threatening the minister, eventually storming in to send the few assembled to the fields. And still it was too much, for in the canebrakes the children taught each other counting; in the snatch rows they practiced spelling; the crops laid by, they pulled those lapboards out of root cellars and set up again. So the school buildings, such as they were, were targeted. Kerosene was sloshed against the clapboards even as students inside were bearing down with stubs of chalk. Torched, bombed, and the grounds salted over so not even a weed could rise again. "But this is a new day," some of the country elders had said at the Fairhill meeting, surely meaning that the old taboo against retaliation no longer applied.

"I had those photos in here for the longest time," the typist was saying as she searched through the drawers of her desk. "I must have put them in the album already." Then, pressing three fingers against her collarbone, she whispered, "I was so glad you said what you said." She had trouble swallowing. "It's so awful. And I'm so sorry." She patted her throat to get the words out.

Zala nodded and waited for the young woman to lean over the keyboard again.

"Please have a seat. Attorney Austin's on the phone."

"Of course," Zala said.

She gazed around the walls of the office. Among Austin's certificates, degrees, and plaques were numerous well-wishing glossies, from Keisha Brown, the Commodores, Jean Cairn, Curtis Mayfield, and Peabo Bryson. Zala took comfort in the familiar faces of several musicians, Ojeda Penn at the piano, Kofi's friend Kwame's daddy; Joe Jennings the percussionist, one of the drummers at the Neighborhood Art Festival booths in Piedmont Park, and his group the Life Force. And below a photo of Austin and his wife at a celebration was the son of the Gulf station owner on Taliaferro, Al Cooper, and his partner in comedy, the actor Bill Nunn.

All over Atlanta, men were on the phone. In blazers, in shirtsleeves, in sock feet jogging on electronic treadmills, upside down in strapped boots hanging from orthopedic contraptions to improve circulation and forestall baldness, men were on the phone, curly cord, cordless, red, round, cylindrical, or see-through, making the long-distance run on an exercise bike while making the long-distance deal on the phone. Men on the phone sparring with a tetherball or dropping a golf ball into a teacup, or seated at the console, activating the Dictaphone by slight pressure on the foot pedal, so that the administrative assistant will have the confirmation letter typed and ready for signature before the receiver is placed in the well of the panel that boasts a memory disc of one hundred numbers, gives the temperature and barometric reading for the day, the time in Honolulu, and plays the *Bridge on the River Kwai* theme song on Pause.

Loan officers, art directors, detectives, school superintendents, doctors, the limo fleet owner pulling out the bottom drawer for a footrest while they talked on the phone, rapped on the fish tank with school rings, leaned over and set silver balls swaying one, then two *click,* three *click,* four, head bobbing in time as they filed her resumé, turned down her loan application, warned her about sleeping pills, or told her to come back tomorrow when they'd once again be on the phone, wondering why she's brought in her son's medical papers again, or her marriage certificate, or her bills, and wait if you wish but I can't release your husband's salary to you.

Then through for the day, the phone too greasy to handle—*I'll see what we can do about your gas bill, about your children's truancy, about your insomnia, about your son's disappearance*—then out to the assistant—*did you call the garage about my car, did you pick up my suit while at lunch, did you confirm my first-class nonsmoking aisle seat*—and, unable to resist, pick up that phone for one last call of the working day before a drink at the bar and a quick call from that phone before going home to the pine-paneled den to fix a drink at that bar and make a call from that phone while some other woman waits till the state-of-the-art equipment is demonstrated, touted, and explained—call waiting, the new video-telex, "Lara's Theme" while someone is put on hold, as men talk on the phone, each boasting that his equipment is bigger than his.

"He'll see you now, Mrs. Spencer," the receptionist said, holding the door open for Zala.

"Thank you."

Zala passed under the woman's arm into the short corridor. Lester C. Austin rolled forward in his wheelchair, clasped her free hand in both of his and ushered her into a comfy office of rust suede and semigloss coral.

"Diligent" was the word she came up with, appraising him. Pen and pad in his lap, he was rubbing his hands together. The gesture if done by anyone else would have seemed oily and full of shit. Zala relaxed and listened carefully as Austin went over his rates, smiling at the tapestry she'd brought along. No problem there, art for counsel, fine.

She got up without the least self-consciousness when he indicated the silver tray of stemware on the sideboard. She poured two generous drinks from the decanter while Austin discussed his views on her mass mailing campaign.

"I wonder if you've considered what you're letting yourself in for, Marzala." He glanced briefly at his desk, then pressed a button. "Loretta, please hold my calls."

He rolled his chair closer to Zala and pulled up from one side a writing shelf that fit across the wheelchair's padded arms. "Maybe Anne told you the story. My aunt and uncle also thought it was a good idea to mail pictures of my niece all over the country. They hired private detectives, engaged lawyers, and dunned the FBI and the local authorities for years. In those days, there weren't as many child-find agencies as there are now, but they managed to connect with numerous groups. You have no idea how many tips a mass mailing will elicit. How many people, crackpots included, will swarm into your life with reports of having seen the missing child.

"Eight years after my niece eloped, a retired social worker located her in Englewood, New Jersey. She'd been working under the same social security number she'd used in high school. She'd used her Georgia learner's permit to file for a New Jersey driver's license. She used her birth certificate to get a passport for the honeymoon. Even on her renewed passport, she used her given name and maiden name in addition to her husband's name. In all those years, she'd done nothing spectacular to change her appearance either, nothing one couldn't have anticipated given the change in styles since the time she left high school as a sophomore and the time she was located again, a married, working mother with an M.A.—in her surname, I might add.

"What I am saying, Marzala, is this. Finding a missing child is a priority for no one but the child's parents. You could spend the rest of your life on one wild goose chase after another."

My Life As a Goose. Zala wondered how that essay would sound. Not long ago, Leah had called her a silly goose when she'd accused Leah of hiding two of the B. J. tapes. And not long ago, Paulette had called her a crazy loon for not accepting her invitation to visit Miami. It had a lonesome sound, "loon." "Wild goose" sounded not wild but pathetic. She had no use for the pathetic anymore, and the wild woman no longer shrieked in her dreams, daytime or night.

"Actually, I wanted to talk to you about a few other things," Zala said.

"Shoot." He was rubbing his hands again. "Then let me take you downstairs for a bite to eat. Or we could have something sent up. If you don't mind my saying, you look all in."

She didn't mind. Even if he refused to take her on, or rather to take on the authorities she wanted to sue for criminal negligence, and even if he tried to talk her out of slapping a kidnap charge on Spence, or didn't agree that Leah had invaded her privacy, at least she had his ear, had a chance to focus, talk, sort things out. She held her glass as he placed the order and took another call, picking over what she'd tell Austin and what she had no intention of telling anyone, ever.

That she'd been jealous. And, jealous, had stopped transcribing Dave's tape. No longer an interview, it had become a seduction, a game of double entendre between interviewer and interviewee. Paint fumes coming up from the bookstore below, the room she worked in unheated, Leah not back with the correction fluid, no one around to give her a hand, and getting dark too, Zala couldn't be expected to continue typing. She'd cleared away Leah's cup and the silver tea infuser she'd coveted. She pressed it open and released the aroma of sassafras. The Spencer men for Fourth of July used to take a whole day to marinate a fresh ham in sassafras beer, garlic, rosemary, thyme, and crushed peppercorns. She didn't want to think about that. She wanted to think about why she kept having the suspicion that Leah had doctored the tapes.

Zala remembered having asked some pretty good questions out at Bowen Homes in October, but only now and then could she hear her voice on those tapes. And the session that Leah had taped with Speaker and one of the study-group students and Zala, with Paulette cracking in the background, definitely had cuts in it. "You took my reasons off your tapes," Zala had complained. "I sound so stupid." Leah had leaned over her shoulder to read from the page, letting the word hang in the air much too long before she offered the observation that the presence of equipment did funny things to people; instead of giving one's true opinion, people often made "public" statements when confronted with a microphone or a camera. Zala's remarks about how haggard Maynard

Jackson and Lee Brown were looking lately sounded like an endorse-
ment. Her remarks about STOP, when Leah asked if it wasn't the most
natural magnet around which working-class Atlantans should be mobilized, sounded like petty gossip, like she thought the members were too
distracted—worse, too evil and jittery—to work along class lines. She
was sure she'd said more.

All afternoon Leah had kept assuring her that it was the nature of
interviews. Sometimes respondents opted for received wisdom rather
than their own good judgment. Microphones tripped people up.

Spence's tape, for example, Zala was to learn. Hearing his voice had
been shock enough. But hearing him speak of personal things had outraged her.

SPENCE: Two of Paulette's boarders set floodlights in our backyard.
Just came by one morning and did that. Some woman I've never
laid eyes on rang our bell and offered to lend us her TV, said
she'd noticed no blue light flickering from our living-room
window . . . only house on the block . . . seen our names in the
paper. The couple next door slipped an envelope of money under
the door. A little note saying how much all the newspapers they
see bundled at the curb must have cost us. Zala and them haven't
said good morning to each other since summer. They used to ring
our bell to complain about the kids making noise. Used to bang
on the wall when Zala ran the sewing machine at night. . . .
Envelope full of money . . .

Zala had used the last of the fluid whiting out his references to her.
Only now and then could Leah, the interviewer, get Spence off the kind-
ness theme to discuss his theory of the case.

SPENCE: I've had policemen walk right up to me in the squad room
and say it's Klan cops on the force. I tend to regard some of those
tips like marked money, if you know what I mean. But there's this
one patrolman, he was by the house the night Zala reported Sonny
missing, he dropped in to STOP a few days ago. Reverend Carroll
was suspicious. He's thinking about suing the police department
for harassment. I understand they patrol Carroll so closely, he's
stopped taking cabs. He just hops in the prowl car. . . . Anyway,

the brother dropped in to STOP to jaw, see if he could help out in some way. Good people. From Savannah. He thinks it's government research gotten out of hand. Remember "Operation Buzz" a few years ago? The Army Chemical Corps released contaminated mosquitoes in Carver Village down there in Savannah. That's where he's from. Good brother . . .

Toward the end of side A, Zala had stopped typing. Spence was telling Leah things he'd never told her.

LEAH: Spencer, do you think the roadblocks and armies of occupation in our neighborhoods are safety measures or terror tactics?

SPENCE: You know, I was stopped at a roadblock . . . on my way to Zayre's one night to pick up some socks. There was this guy standing by a table of underwear, rubbing a pair of boy's drawers against his cheek. Right away, my geiger counter starts ticking. I'm ready to nab him. Rubbing the drawers, inspecting the crotch. He sees me watching him and his eyes well up. He's got a nephew down at Grady's Trauma Center, a burn case. He wants me to help him pick out soft underwear for the boy. Got to be soft. No rough seams. I felt like a dog.

LEAH: I'm inclined to go with your first thought. Don't you think his behavior warrants investigation?

SPENCE: Leah, you had to be there.

At that point Zala had taken off the headphones. If Leah's answer came in that same purry tone of voice, she'd find them coming on to each other on side B. Maybe in the privacy of her home she could listen to more, but not in that cold room over the bookstore.

Zala had stood at the window, watching the streetlights go on along MLK Drive. She could hear caroling down the block, a junior choir rehearsing. She tried to justify going the short distance from the bookstore to home on the bus. She didn't relish walking through the streets, seeing grandmothers putting up doilies and sugared leaves in the windows, kids on sunporches stringing popcorn, fathers on the roofs setting reindeer in place. She thought of the Christmas she'd spent in New York. Aunt Myrtle at the stove reaching under her long-line bra to scratch as she stirred the pot of boiling cranberries.

Coming down the stairs to the bookstore with the load she had told herself she was removing for legitimate reasons, she was stopped in her tracks by a bull mastiff curled up by the back burglar door. It lifted its pushed-in snout from its haunches and peered. The satchel inside her coat was cutting into her shoulder; the typewriter weighed a ton. The dog stood up. His medallion clinking against his collar bought one of the painters out of the bathroom. He insisted on helping. She had to get rude refusing before he'd back off. Help? Where was he six weeks ago when she needed help? She'd found Kenti in the Reading Corner eating paste and staring at the smashed pumpkin that had spattered her socks and summoned up nightmare pumpkin-head monsters. She'd had to lug the half-sedated child the whole seven blocks home.

The dog came up behind her when she hefted her load toward the front of the bookstore. She could hear his claws scraping against the newly laid tile. The entry to the bookstore was blocked by a ladder and a can of adhesive. A short-barreled .38 was on the lid of the can. The men in the store were busy handing up shelves to the owner, who was setting up a new section for hardbacks. She backed up and into the storage room and set the things down on a box of books. She heard the dog go back to the rear door and sit down with a clink. His forelegs kept sliding, his claws trying for traction. She waited till he gave up and lay down again.

The box was full of dictionaries, the kind with tabs in the back for medical, legal, musical, and literary glossaries. She learned in one flip toward the front of the book that "chaos" for the ancient Chaldeans was "to be without books." Well, that would be her story if anyone asked. Why she'd removed the things from upstairs. She was taking them home to finish transcribing, for without records there'd be disorder. And hadn't Dave's major complaint in the interview been that people kept getting sidetracked reacting to media instead of doing the work they'd said they would do?

Mason and the other vets, instead of organizing self-defense squads, kept editing the position paper they'd drafted in response to Dorothy Alison's allegations, going over the wording so that the criticisms they leveled at the authorities would not play into the hands of the militant right that seized on every opportunity to trash the very notion of Black leadership. Mac was supposed to help Dave organize youth workers and undo what the police canvassing of the juvenile shelters had done—

namely, pry open mouths clamped shut, for kids called anyone who even stood still to hear the cops' questions snitches. But Mac, like other workers at the OEO Center on Verbena, was shitting in his pants ever since the Wilson girl's body was found in the area. Youth workers were as useless as Mac, according to Dave. They ran for cover each time links between the victims were reviewed and the Boys' Club was mentioned. Dave joked that Mac, Mattie, and anyone else who worked or lived in the area were running around getting character references. It looked bad for everybody, especially for Mac and Mattie. The media was still harping on the idea that the killer had "hypnotized" or "psyched out" the victims. As for Spence and Lafayette, instead of getting Mason back on track, they were helping one of the vets put a handbook together—how to upgrade bad discharges and challenge the 201 forms, how to get retroactive benefits, how to press the VA to come across with some of the dough earmarked for Operation Outreach. After some newspaper pundit theorized that the killer was a disgruntled vet done out of his benefits and trying to crack the official silence about the whole Vietnam War, vets forgot about securing rooms for karate lessons and started running around asking about benefits. "The kids are getting dusted, and we're standing around with our dicks in our hands reacting to shit!" Dave had bellowed.

Well, she at least was on the case. She was guarding against chaos. That would be her story if anyone stopped her to question the bulge in her coat.

The painters cleared the ladder away and she headed for the front of the bookstore.

She had trailed across MLK Drive behind one of the transvestite whores, telling herself that if the dictionary was not meant for her, it would have opened to "honesty." Miss Thaang had run interference for her along Mayson Turner, where men from the bar grabbed at his leopard skin boots, red hot pants, and short lamb fur jacket. Miss Thaang would not be put off. He swung Zala's satchel around one furry shoulder, grabbed up the typewriter case by the handle, and walked Zala to the bus stop. Despite his frequent side glances, Zala offered no explanation for her rectangular breasts.

Maybe it was best that Spence had taken the kids. But for how long? There'd been a mother who'd written from New Hampshire that it wasn't until her baby girl was returned three years later—plump, cheerful, her ABCs and a few numbers in her repertoire—that she acknowledged the disintegration around her. Her husband had become a drunk. Her older daughter was suffering from double vision and malnutrition. Her son was withdrawn, had failing grades and a juvenile record. The mother had collapsed.

An old Chevy hardtop and a red Mustang were parked out in front of the Griers' home. Zala could hear company stretching out the goodbyes just behind their door as she came up sideways, one step at a time. Leaning the machine against her door, her body about to give out, Zala had stolen a little of their warmth to drive the goblins to the back of the house.

"Pass the night safely," someone said to the Griers in such a lovely way.

"Give a kiss to the pikney," Mrs. Grier said. She sounded so cheerful, so warm. How Zala missed Mrs. Grier's long ago hugs, missed hugging in general.

Zala had tripped on the doorsill and bumped her chin on the typewriter case. Nothing seemed broken. More important, nothing had sprung from the dark to attack. The crash hasn't brought the people in from next door, either. She kicked her door to. They were still saying goodbye and giving regards to each other's kin in the Islands, in England, in Brooklyn. Door locked, Zala had raced toward the bathroom by the light from the front. The toilet was running. It needed a tap. Legs crossed at the knees, she'd felt for the switchplate. A loose screw ripped her finger on its grooves. She'd nearly peed on herself, trying to remember where the light bulb she kept moving from one socket to the other could be. Two weeks and she still hadn't gotten to the store.

She had set the stolen dictionary on the sink and gotten up shivering. She'd done it all wrong. The bulb was in the living-room lamp. She'd seen to it before going out so she could enter as she'd rehearsed, but she'd forgotten. And now the coach lamp had gone off, and she could feel the dark streaming at her from four different directions as she inched along the hall.

Those nights when she'd lingered too long at candlelight vigils or meetings, she'd come back to the house chanting a spiel to get her courage up. *Yes, evil things happen, but people must live through it all, so stop*

at the cleaners, buy a new broom, buy some light bulbs. But she'd be distracted, something on the ground. A wad of gauze. Had a child been
chloroformed and tossed in a car trunk? She'd have to start all over
again. *Yes, evil things happen, but life must go on, you must flush that dead
goldfish, been put off too long. Keep moving for the usualness of it. Act usual,
Zala, and it'll be usual, Zala.* And if swaggering through the house
didn't get it, touching her name in the phone book sometimes did.

Zala had marched herself to the front, not stopping when the
sewing box the goblins had hung shoulder-height in the air fell. She
recognized the rolling spool of number 6 mercerized cotton thread as it
pursued her. She stepped on the satchel and nearly slid when the canvas
smooshed out. She grabbed the table and turned on the lamp. The room
sprang at her. It looked awful in the dim light. She lifted the load in one
heft, remembering to bend her knees. She carried it into the kitchen
and set it down. She felt along the side wall for Kenti's Easy Sew pattern placed just so to lead her to the refrigerator handle. She opened the
fridge door for the additional light and took a slug of ice water while
she was at it.

In the hall, she'd pulled the light string in the closet and picked
up the fishbowl and gone to the backroom. The eight of clubs was
waiting for her in the switchplate. She'd turned on the light and doubled back to the bathroom. She'd scooped Roger out with the card and
flushed him, giving the handle a tap. Passing the sink she'd said olé
to the book that stared back in Spanish. She was doing okay, olé, oyeh
Zala.

She'd put the kettle on, a tense energy propelling her toward the
important task next. She'd set up the recorder, the tapes, paper, and the
typewriter. She was going to be all right; she could feel it in the urgency
of her fingers tearing open the cellophane, freeing a fresh ribbon from
its wrapper. She'd sat down and put on the headphones. The keys were
lined up and waiting. She'd turned on the recorder and was striking
rapidly, watching the letters scurry across the page, when the paper
started shuffling. *No problema, máquina*—she would insert the next page
properly. Suddenly she stopped. There was a third voice on the tape, a
prior voice, a conversation in fact under the interview Leah had conducted with an epidemiologist from the CDC. Maybe she should have
let Leah continue transcribing this tape herself. She turned up the volume and typed, the under voices increasingly familiar.

DOCTOR: On the contrary, the term "epidemic" is quite apt, Mrs. Eubanks. Whenever the rate of an occurrence exceeds the national norm, when statistics show an increase in incidence and a rate of increase in incidence that law enforcement is unable to prevent, contain, or even accurately record, and, moreover, a sense of hopelessness colors the situation—then that social situation can be likened to the outbreak of a virulent disease. Unlike approaches in the other sciences, the public health model—

VOICE: We don't know where he went. Why you keep asking us about that?

DOCTOR: —considers the victim, the disease, the agent, and the context, that is to say, the environment.

LEAH: And "environment" would include a climate of receptivity? If the public health model is applicable to the Atlanta situation, Doctor, then you're saying that the incidence of racism—that is, the pernicious disease of racism—could be measurably reduced?

VOICE: Well, how would you feel if you lost your little girl?

DOCTOR: I'd say that racism was a factor in the environment. So is the entertainment industry's promotion of violence; so are firearms. Not that the CDC addresses the issue of gun control, per se.

LEAH: I wouldn't imagine so. Government funds would not be forthcoming. Not if the National Rifle Association had a say. But of course there are funds to study Black-on-Black crime, Black suicide, or the serial murders of Black children—all that good stuff.

VOICE: 'Cause it's none of your business, that's what.

Zala hit the pause button. She thought back to what the children had said coming in from the zoo months ago, and how she'd barely listened. No wonder Leah had selected particular tapes for her to type. Zala continued. She wanted to have it all beautifully typed and waiting when Leah came calling. And she'd have to, for Zala decided she would not be returning to the room over the bookstore. She would make Leah come to her.

LEAH: In assembling the medical data on the missing and murdered children, what did you have in mind in terms of the "agent"? Are you specifically looking for the sickle cell trait or disease in their histories? I understand sickling interferes with the output of the substance that suppresses the body's manufacturing of interferon. In other words, those with a history of sickle cell produce interferon in above average amounts. Is that so?

DOCTOR: Ah, I've heard about Dick Gregory's lecture. Of course, he's not a medical man.

LEAH: What's the value of interferon?

DOCTOR: It functions in the immune system as a defense.

KENTI: I want to go home.

DOCTOR: In other words, it's valuable in cancer research? I understand there's a growing market for it in longevity research. An acquaintance recently informed me that a Swiss clinic, long known for use of lamb placenta, is now using interferon.

Four times Zala heard the children pleading with Paulette to take them home. What the hell had Paulette been doing that she didn't notice what was happening? Zala let the tape play on. The scientist and Leah got into it hot and heavy about racism, the scientist arguing that it wasn't factored in because he was examining the environment of the victims and the Ku Klux Klan did not reside in high-risk neighborhoods. Zala wasn't listening to that. She was thinking about the story one of the mothers had told at a STOP luncheon in October.

An out-of-town visitor had stood up in church when the minister asked visitors to rise. The mother had invited her home, as Zala had often done in her church. The visitor began to prolong her stay as though she intended to be a permanent houseguest. One day when the mother came in the back way, she saw the woman interviewing her children in the kitchen, the tape recorder hidden under the tablecloth's hem. The visitor finally admitted she was working on a magazine article and knew of no better way to get a good story. Could the woman have been Leah? Zala made a note to call Sirlena Cobb, mother of the still-missing boy Christopher Richardson.

Zala had looked through the satchel, wondering what other surprises it held in store. She'd turned off the kettle when the water boiled away and had listened to Spence, side B. Didn't he realize he was being taped? Or was this his chump way of telling her things? She'd typed it up in a dead heat to mail to him. Then she'd found another familiar voice in her ear. The tape's label bore a coded ID. She'd chuckled as she began typing, imagining Leah's surprise. Her laughter, though, was short-lived as the pages piled up.

MURRAY: Sure I knew the Spencer woman was prowling around my place. I keep a room with Miss Needles and she's the eyes and ears of the world. She told me Mrs. Spencer was fooling around up there with her flashlight. I'm glad I had the dogs tied up good. I don't wish the woman no harm. And I know in her heart she don't mean me no harm. You do crazy things when you got troubles. She'll be crazy till she shed of it. I told their boy, that Cuffy fella, anything I can do, call on me. What the colored people got in this world but one another?

LEAH: You knew the older boy, Sonny?

MURRAY: Sure I knew him. I know most youngsters round through here. Related to most of them one way or another. I hire them on to help me fold the papers here and load the truck. Course now, that gets me in trouble with the busybodies. They be buzzing thick putting out tales on me. But I pay those youngsters good wages for them chores. And I get after them about their schoolwork and proper rest. Treat 'em all the same, same as my own. . . . Now, don't you know Mr. Spencer come to the station here one early morning asking after a made-up address so I wouldn't be put wise. I didn't know him right off, thought he'd come to spy on me, you know. I wasn't hospitable right off. He had a pistol bulging in his waistband. I saw his and he sure saw mine. I ain't going to be caught out if the killer come along. Some of these GIs are crazy. War will do that to you. . . . My wife used to work up at the VA and the way she tell it, these boys still walking around with poison gas in their systems. Pitiful shame what happened to our men overseas. But one of them come around looking cross-eyed at any of these boys, I'll send him straight to his Maker.

LEAH: You think it's a disturbed veteran who's murdering the children?

MURRAY: I don't say I do and I don't say I don't. First wind I got, I

figured evil ole white folks. But the papers say a colored man did
it. Say he used a special choke hold. I didn't know choke holds
different from race to race.

LEAH: You think it's a vet?

MURRAY: Could be. Look like nobody has hard information.
Everybody tripping over the bottom lip to outthink the thinkers.
I say best let the police do the job. And they better shake a leg
too. Getting fractious.

LEAH: You've observed . . . tension and strange behavior?

MURRAY: Sure tension. Old man, a friend of mine, stay in the room-
ing house down there by the Am Vets Bar. Poor ole soul, he don't
know what's going on. He don't read the papers; he wears them.
Gets up in the morning to put on the boil, come up with a
played-out tea bag. So he stuffs some newspaper in there between
his long johns and his undervest and zips himself up and goes out
to get him some breakfast. Sees the youngsters going to school,
traveling in twos and threes like the bulletins say to do. Then
what happens was, he says hello . . . hmph.

LEAH: Then what happened, Mr. Murray?

MURRAY: People gone crazy, that's what's happening. Don't you
know I saw a policeman pull a gun on a dog the other day. On a
dog! What a dog know about some gun? Well, that dog did. The
police got his legs bucked, kind of squat down, arms out stiff.
That dog say lemme get on away from here. This a fool here. . . .
People high-strung. . . . See this? Lost that finger to a harvester
combine in '47. You wouldn't know it to look at me now, but I
was strapping in them days, a built-up chap. Had my own plot,
a Vulcan plow, two mules in harness. . . . But some people can't
stand to see the coloreds with something. Poisoned the stock.
Just like they did them Muslim people down in Alabama.
Poisoned the well . . . Lost a finger. Been using a scythe ever since.
Course I don't do no more than that piece of yard of Miss Needles.
Got my dealership now . . . Sent that scythe to my nephew in
College Park. Used to be that part of Atlanta was a little village
like you'd run across in Africa somewhere. But now some of it's
part of Hapeville, which people say Hateville cause that's the
Klan there, the Klan there. Sent that scythe to my nephew
special express.

LEAH: You've seen the flyers the Black vets put out? They're
    protesting the resurgence of right-wing extremists. They feel the
    Klan might be behind these murders.

MURRAY: Sure I seen the handbills. Nothing much gets by me.
    Didn't hold their meeting like they said they would. Seen that.
    Like I said, I sure did think so in the first, till the papers say the
    police say a colored fella behind it all. All in all, we in a world
    of trouble. That's what I say. I just look after these youngsters,
    so on that day I can say I done my best, now I'll take my
    rest . . . like the song say.

LEAH: You knew Sonny Spencer?

MURRAY: That boy had a fine mind. Speak right up. Wouldn't stand
    for no foolishness around him. Now if Sonny Boy had
    been out there that morning when Meachum was trying to find
    him some breakfast . . . Now see, you don't hear much about
    folks like Meachum. People say Atlanta, average person think
    big homes, big cars, pretty women looking like the cover of them
    magazines. Average person don't want to know about Meachum.
    Who he? Where he went to school? How much money he give
    his church? Nare cross their mind that we ain't got to go through
    all that who-struck-John. Just give the man a tea bag and a can
    of tuna fish and let him cut the grass so he can live. Folks like
    Meachum freeze to death every winter and you don't hear a thing
    about it. They tell you about the wrecks on the highway, but you
    don't hear a thing about folks freezing to death, now do you? This
    a good town. Can't find no better people nowhere better than
    Southwest Atlanta. But if you poor, it can be cold . . . same all
    over the world I expect.

LEAH: Mr. Murray, what happened that morning when Meachum said
    hello to the children?

MURRAY: What happened was this. The children commenced to
    running. Some woman at the bus stop started screaming and
    beating Meachum with her pocketbook. I'm laughing now but it
    wasn't funny then. Life'll drive you crazy if you can't grab you a
    laugh on the run. See, Meachum got nare tooth in his head. He
    don't put in a good appearance, his clothes and all. But what kind
    of way is that to treat a person? Bunch of men run up and wrench
    his arm up behind his back. . . . . What kind of way is that to do?

LEAH: And you feel if Sonny Spencer had been on the scene . . .

MURRAY: Maybe.

LEAH: You said, Mr. Murray, when I first asked if I could speak to you, that you could understand why Mr. and Mrs. Spencer suspect you.

MURRAY: Listen at it and it'll size up. The killer can get to the children. Could be a teacher or one of them parkees. Could be a person like me who hires on youngsters. Read in the paper where the children had jobs. Now, the killer knows the streets, be up and down and across that map that was in the papers. Cab driver maybe. Delivery man. I'm a delivery man . . . Okay now. Lots of them children disappeared around places where children be, like parks and movie shows. Let's figure the killer using a youngster to get the drop. I go around with my nephews all the time . . . Two last things now. Paper say nobody saw nothing forcible to recollect. So figure the killer the police or dressed like the police, or a minister, or an old man like me. . . . Course, the papers lie. I know for a fact that many of the youngsters in the families and some neighbors too saw the boys being taken off by force. But we'll pass over that . . . Last point now, the time gap. Big gap between the killings of '79 and the killings in '80 starting up again. Could be the killer was in jail or some mental home them four months. Could be the killer was called out of town. My mother passed in '79 and I was out of town for four months getting things squared away. . . . How that sound to you? I don't fault the Spencers. The woman friends with a mouthy gal up there on Thurmond. She probably put that bee in their bonnet.

LEAH: It does sound like a good case against you, Mr. Murray.

MURRAY: You know, for all I know they could have the police on me. One time I kept catching a little blue foreign job with one brown fender in my rearview. Two or three times it was back there. I said to myself, "Get reconciled, Murray. That Spencer woman dogging you all over the city." Then the little foreign job with the odd-lot fender turned off and went on about its business. I had to laugh at that myself. Couldn't laugh long, though, had three hundred pounds of newspapers waiting to be picked up, folded, and delivered over a thirty-five-mile route in less than two hours. May not seem like much to you. You got a good education and a good job with a newspaper. But it's punishing work, delivering. Punishing work.

LEAH: And Sonny Spencer worked for you for a time?

MURRAY: He did. Punishing . . . Got to get up early, in the dark most times, and get out there on them empty streets when other people warm in bed, and that thought don't help much at all when it's cold. There's a lot to my job. A lot. Got to know each customer's preference. Some take evening, some take morning, some both, some only Sunday. All kinds of combinations. Some want it stuck in the mailbox, some it's all right to sling it across the yard. One lady in a trailer park you got to reach under there and tuck the darn thing between the cinder blocks so the dog can't get at it, neighbor neither. Another customer wants it placed right in the middle of the welcome mat. Don't want it dropped, heaved, or set to the side. The middle of the welcome mat or you got trouble on your hands come collection day. And you know some people don't pay you. And that comes out your envelope.

LEAH: Mr. Murray, from what you've said, you sound like a prime suspect. Doesn't the reward make you a little nervous that someone will turn you in?

MURRAY: I'd say it to the police just like I say it to you. I'd like to drive you over my route. It'd ease your mind. You'd see what it takes to do what I do. Got no time to be murdering people. . . . Sure it bothered me, Mr. Spencer coming around like that. I was embarrassed for him. Grown men should act like grown men and not play the fool asking after a made-up address. But it hurt me. It hurts me to hear you say they think I interfered with their son. But if they think so, let them tell me to my face in front of the police. And front of my lawyer too. 'Cause I don't bother nobody and I sure ain't going to stand for nobody bothering me. You can tell them that.

LEAH: Thank you very much for talking with me, Mr. Murray. I appreciate your spending so much time explaining things.

MURRAY: You don't fool me, you know. I ain't fooled for a minute. I know you thinking about that reward yourself. Tell the truth?

Zala had listened a long time for the answer that never came. She'd switched off the machine and removed the headphones. Maybe all of

Leah's work had originally been about documenting the facts and spreading the word in a community newsletter. But what else was Leah Eubanks up to? She seemed to have the Spencer family surrounded. She'd interviewed everyone Zala knew except her pastor. And what had she done with B. J.'s tapes—blackmail?

Now Austin pressed a button on the intercom, and the receptionist walked in almost immediately to remove the restaurant trays. Austin had the tapestry on his lap, fingering the metallic threads that gave the rugged jute webbing a touch of elegance. She'd done some open-work knotting in the center section on the order of a Peruvian rug she'd seen at a High Museum exhibit. He held it up and watched the light reflect. She hadn't laundered and blocked it, but he didn't seem to mind.

"It's like a runaway production," he said, not meaning her work. "Like going onto the set of a much-touted multimillion-dollar picture directed by last year's Oscar winner and starring the top box-office names, and finding the whole thing totally out of control."

She murmured and poured herself another Drambuie. He draped the tapestry across the desk. The ochres, purples, and turquoise went well with his rust suede decor.

"I'd say your instincts were sound," Austin said, placing his hands on the rims of the wheels and pushing himself around in little semi-circles.

She'd been expecting an argument at every turn. But not once during her review of her four-month ordeal had he interrupted other than to have a point clarified. And now, "going electric," as he'd joked, dancing a little in his chair when they'd been discussing the TF foul-ups, he drove up behind his desk and parked, looking all business. He was doing something clunky with the metal footrests; then he locked the wheels and shut off the zizzing motor.

"Now," he said, moving a praying-hands ceramic to the side, "I will set things in motion." He rubbed the bronze plate soldered below the praying hands, a prayer inscribed in the metal. Zala sipped at her drink. Drambuie was new to her, and she liked it. Austin drew the phone toward him and lifted the receiver.

She did not bother to listen or take notes. He knew what he was doing. He would see to it that Sonny's folder was found and included in the special investigation. He was a Morehouse man, a Kappa, and a fifth-generation homeboy. Wasn't that what it was all about? So how could he miss? He had something particular in mind for getting Leah Eubanks checked out. And he had Spence's address and number in Columbus. It was all in his hands now. She would lay her hands on some quality raffia and sisal and weave again. The thought made her rub her fingers together pleasurably.

Attorney Austin seemed to take her seriously enough. He was certainly making a lot of phone calls. She would have to work some wizardry with her fingers to do justice to his walls. Her eyes drifted onto a shelf in his glass étagère. A brand-new doll stood upright in a see-through box, hemmed in by three walls of cardboard and one of cellophane. The doll's limbs were pinioned by white plastic rings that bound her ankles and wrists to the backboard. Her hair was stapled to the cardboard, a slice of white around her throat. And in the glass, Zala saw herself reflected and turned away.

Not long ago, Leah had guided her and Paulette through a number of glamour magazines, pointing out the increasing youthfulness of the models, the more recent issues featuring preadolescents made up to look like adults. The backlash response to the woman's movement, Leah had explained. Paulette and Leah had kidded her that she was the petite, new-womanly ideal, the backlash ideal. Paulette had joked that they should concoct a line of cosmetics with an S&M look and get over like fat-cat capitalists. Leah hadn't thought that very funny. To hell with Leah, Zala muttered to herself.

For a second, she feared she'd said it aloud, for Austin glanced her way. He was arguing with the security officer of the telephone company. She could've saved him the trouble. If she could produce a ransom note or proof of a threatening call, the police would ask Southern Bell to put the trap back on her phone. But not for a runaway. Runaways did not count.

Tuesday, February 10, 1981

E ach time Spence returned to Atlanta he experienced a rush at the city limits. The same feelings surged as in years before when he'd come home from the war, back to The World from the smoke, the smoldering sandbags, and the blood-soaked heaps of fatigues. Spotting the capitol dome, he would rock forward in his seat, his face as close to the windshield as the seat belt allowed. The sense of expectancy as intense as in his search-and-destroy days, he would race recklessly toward Atlanta, driving the feeling into his lungs till he became the excitement itself and was protected, momentarily, from the dread collecting just below eye level, where a mortar might discharge at any second.

Steering with the heel of one hand, he always had to double back, having overshot the downtown exit to Austin's by a good thirty miles. Then the feeling would begin to ebb. Fear would seep in. And the only thing keeping him buoyant was the sound of the radio. He'd touch whatever was on the seat beside him—the envelope of pages Zala kept mailing him, or the narrow green book of actuarial tables from Delia's real estate office, to assure himself that he hadn't gone under.

Now, tooling along Northside Drive, he grabbed a month-old issue of *Newsweek* to fend off the demons that had once lured him, years ago, into taking off his helmet to cook in.

With the Coca-Cola sign in his rearview, Spence turned up the radio. It droned on about MIRVs, MIGs, SALT, SAM, and *Pershing II,* everything but the case, everything but news of the two women MPYD officers who'd been busted in rank when the family of Lubie Geter caught the Task Force napping. He rolled up the copy of *Newsweek,* after glancing at the spread of pictures and stories from Charlie Company. The silence finally had been broken. The featured story on the 'Nam vets had revived the night sweats for a time, but it also loosened him up; something wooden and blocky came unstuck.

On the radio, in between reports on the Camp David Accords, Poland, Iran, Iraq, and Afghanistan, the announcer burbled about the parades, gifts, and job offers for the released hostages. There were still confetti storms all over the country for the fifty-three Americans come home after 444 days of captivity. But for the Vietnam vets there was only that January *Newsweek.* Testimony from brothers who'd been in Charlie Company hadn't been quite on the mark. Edited with a heavy hand, Spence supposed. He glanced down at the crinkled pages, at the chopper blades, tattooed arms, jeeps, battery radios, and tried to be calm. But it was the same eerie calm he'd experienced under heavy shelling, sensing a high-caliber finality sailing through the dark toward his heart.

He'd tried to explain to McClintock how the stories and pictures of C Company had been both sickening and protective, a shield against the very terrors *Newsweek* evoked. Mac hadn't understood. Later, when Spence read the interview Leah had conducted with Mac, he could see why. Spence's babbling to Mac on his first trip back to Atlanta to see Austin about custody had become grist for the counselor's mill. Estrangement, Mac had told Leah. Both husband and wife were estranged from their generation, she by early pregnancy, he by the draft, the polarization, and the silence. Lacking friends among peers, the Spencers sough professional confidants. Mac was hopeless.

So on his solitary rides into Atlanta, Spence invented someone who would understand what he meant. A bunker buddy, a front-line buddy, someone who continued to value and search for the intense camaraderie of war when a whole unit was but one life they all held in their hands. This someone was always about to pull up at the next light or at the next gas pump, ready to talk. Would take the stool beside Spence at the diner counter or, turning around in a booth, spot 'Nam laid out between Spence's coffee cup and his toast plate and initiate conversation. Then Spence would not have to explain anything. This someone would be able to see with Spence's eyes—'Nam, Bowen Homes, the look of the woods during those search weekends, the artificial busyness at the TF headquarters when Spence had been drawn back to Atlanta by the discovery of two bodies.

Now, maneuvering past the rubber cones and orange barrels where a section of Northside Drive was under construction, Spence tried to get his bearings, feeling that the invented friend was at that very moment traveling great distances to meet him, to read Spence the coordinates, for Spence had doubled back too far and was lost, vulnerable, about to do something stupid, like years ago when he was tempted to extend his tour just for the few days' leave in exchange. He'd ached that much for one hour of normality.

On his last trip to Atlanta, Spence had actually pulled over by a lean Johnny Reb in high-heeled boots who'd bent down to pick up a dime from the sidewalk. Spence had swung over to the curb because the reb looked vet age and had a magazine stuck in his back pocket. Spence had felt a kinship so strong, he'd cut the motor and slid down the window, certain that something crucial would be exchanged once the man, straightening, shoving his cap back with his thumb, revealing a stark white forehead above his windburned face and clearly more akin to the Deep South recruits who'd made 'Nam holy hell for Black men, finally turned in Spence's direction and seemed about to speak. But the reb had only been working his mouth up to spit on the sidewalk. Then he hitched up his jeans and clomped down the street in his cowboy boots, his shirt coming untucked as he walked. *Popular Mechanics*, not *Newsweek*, had been in his pocket.

And once, missing his turn so repeatedly he'd had to admit that he was fooling no one, that he had no intention of keeping the appointment with Zala and Austin, he'd wound up in a cul-de-sac thinking about Sonny, thinking about POW training—had he told his son that the best time to escape was in the first few hours of capture?—and thinking about this buddy, who'd say, "Yeah, sometimes I think I died over there too." Spence had sat in the limo surrounded by woods and wept over his dead self. Face wet, throat sore, he had wheeled the limo back to the main drag and blamed his blurry vision on the draggy wiper blades. Then, swearing he heard the motor cough, he had decided to go see Gaston. For something was wrong with the steering mechanism too.

Clear now of the construction near the Northside exit off I-85, Spence leaned over and changed the station. He wanted to hear an update on the suit the medical examiner had threatened to bring against the authorities for tampering with evidence and ruining a site before the coroner's office arrived. As he fiddled with the dial he felt a definite yank in the wheel. It was as pronounced as it had been weeks ago when he'd made up his mind to let Gaston look things over but had followed a Big Bethel AME van instead. Finding himself near Paschal's, he had then decided to drop in on the Institute of the Black World. What did they make of the coroner's suit? What would they make of Judge Webber's latest news? A suspect the DA's office had been interested in had turned out to be a stool pigeon living incognito in Atlanta under the Federal Witness Relocation Program. Webber couldn't say whether the man was mafioso, Klansman, or porn kingpin, only that the interrogation had been kept off the police blotter. But he'd keep digging. So many separate and secret investigations being conducted by the various bureaus, it took some digging. Spence had wanted to talk things over with the members of IBW.

But he had not been able to find the Institute. Chestnut Street kept eluding him. He found himself on Drummond Street, slowing up behind a sheriff's car angle-parked by a truck. There were Black men in the panel truck. Had Kofi been breathing down his neck, Spence might have been encouraged to step out and ask what was going on just to swagger a little. Alone, he had merely looked. Were the men a work gang from the pen being rounded back up? Where, then, were the tools they'd used to repair the streets? Maybe there'd been a roundup of winos from the wall near the liquor store on Jeptha and the sheriff had processed the vagrants on the spot and given the white truck driver, a crew boss, sole custody. In which case they'd be hauled off to a plantation to work. One of the men huddled on the bench in back under a tarpaulin had called out "Stretch!"—meaning the limo. An SOS or a hello, Spence didn't take time to find out. The sheriff had waved him around the truck and he'd driven on.

Whether day laborers, winos, vagrants, or convicts, they'd been Black men and he'd wheeled the Flagship around them, merely looking at them lined up on the benches of the panel truck, a grungy tarp thrown over their shoulders. In '69, the benches at the induction center had been lined with brothers. His platoon was three-quarters Black. The casualty list was four-fifths Black. Not one officer of color on the set. Always Bloods on points, Bloods on the front line. The double war, internal war, the total nuthouse reality took over with Bloods actually trying to make themselves equal to the mad-dog tasks before them, behind them, surrounded by hatred. In the end, they were all addicted to the adrenaline rush that kept them in a state of emergency even back in

The World, driving their families nuts with it, but propelled up the ladder by it, if, with luck, a job came their way that called for an all-time jittery high.

Spence had driven away from Drummond Street without finding out where those passengers were being taken in the middle of the afternoon. On promise of work, perhaps they'd voluntarily gotten into the truck, the sheriff's presence a mere coincidence. It didn't wash. The promise of clean cottages, running water, three squares a day, and good pay they had to know was a lie. Everyone knew, no matter how drunk, no matter how desperate for work or empty-handed in the face of a badge, the truth was flea-ridden pallets, mealy-bug grits and green slabs of baloney, no showers, no rest, one outhouse per fifty workers. And the day before payday the booze and the whores were brought in. The morning after, that cold day of reckoning, you learned you were in debt for that pallet, those meals, the whiskey at five dollars a pint, the women at twenty dollars a hump. And try leaving. Try making a call to the authorities. They'd turn out to be the plantation bosses, or their in-laws, their lodge brothers at least.

He'd driven away with the same half-minute's worth of camouflaging concern that people showed to the situation in the targeted neighborhoods. What a pity, what a shame. Meaning, if only those people out there would go away, we'd all look better, fare better, rest easier. He'd gone downtown beating himself up with those thoughts when the smell suddenly enveloped him. It had filled the limo on Peachtree Street and forced him to slide all the windows down and pull into a parking space across from the Fox Theatre. He'd been taking a round-about route to Gaston's, not quite letting himself in on his real plan, which was to get to the Task Force and see about the bodies. But he couldn't chance going there or to the coroner's, not with the smell of death in the car.

It had been a call from the authorities, not the boastful phone tip-ster who'd sent the police to the Stewart-Lakewood area, not the two bodies still not identified on the radio, but dynamite and boots that got Spence to the Task Force office. And for once, unlike the previous trip to Atlanta he hadn't had to ask for Detective Dowell to help find Sonny's records. For right there on the table in a scramble of photos was Sonny's, his file, opened; the files of Christopher Richardson and Earl

Lee Terrell propped against a can of pencils to one side. On the back of Sonny's dental record something had been scribbled.

"Oh, that," the officer had told Spence. "We thought we had him. But he's still at large."

The obscenity charged straight for his heart, but he remained absolutely still. The phrase richocheted off the plywood nailed over the transom and coursed its way through the maze of tables and partitions. Muscles hard, fingers gripping the wood of the officer's chair, he was totally still. He'd learned how to do it, how to stand so absolutely fucking still even he couldn't distinguish between his cams and the landscape. Let the other grunts race around chasing tail, running off at the mouth Abel Baker Condition Red, squirreling away Baby Ruths, grenades, Dexedrines, smokes, steaming up their uniforms and entangling their rifle straps in shrubs. He would be still. He'd learned how watching rigor mortis set in.

So he'd stood motionless, rain pelting the windows, phones ringing, red creeping up the side of the officer's face. A composite sketch fell away from its pin on the corkboard and drifted down to the baseboard, where it lay like a slumped-over corpse. He neither blinked, winced, nor heard the apology when the officer shot out of the chair, its wheels banging into Spence's ankle. Then he'd looked down at the chipped tooth, the crooked grin, and something gushed in him. He'd wanted to remain hard and still, but most of him had turned to mush. And the part that didn't was beating in his throat.

"Awww, man, get it together," Spence scolded himself over the hum of the heater.

Now he gunned the motor for the downhill run on Northside Drive. Cars below were stuck in the flood of the underpass where ice dripped and rain collected. He flicked the *Newsweek* cover closed and pushed the pedal to the floor. With the rush came a raging impatience as the limo took the upgrade. Cars, mailboxes, buildings, everything that stood between him and the TF office he wanted to demolish, wanted to sail in through the double doors and get back the file, the face, the strands of hair, the breath on the cellophane tape, the tooth prints, the X rays, wanted to undo the click that had ghosted the bones, that had captured the smile.

He wrenched the limo away from the median and back on course and followed a trailer rig around a curve. It was funny, all while he'd been absorbed in big-bucks making it, he'd been an heir and didn't know it. He'd become a man of property at last, thanks to a relative from out back there. He laughed, leaning toward the glove compartment, at the last minute remembering that he'd removed the papers Rayfield had brought him. His uncle had rushed in, his father trailing behind, unable to meet Spence's eyes. Spence had stored them in a strongbox he found in Cora's attic. Each time that kite rose, he stomped it down flat again. He'd come thudding down the steps from the attic to check on the children.

They'd abandoned the tight fetal positions of Atlanta to resume their old sleeping positions: Kofi facedown hugging the mattress, steering his spaceship to a newly chartered asteroid; Kenti on her back, one leg bent, her arms up over her head, fingers gently curved in toward each other on the pillow, her face to one side in a dreamland pirouette. Cora had come up behind him in her bathrobe to ask what he was looking at. He was looking at absolution. He felt exonerated. He'd been right to get them out of Atlanta. His eyes told him that.

Though for a long time he could never be sure what he was looking at from moment to moment. Seven years had passed and the sights and sounds had not been expunged from Spence's inner eye. Bodies hung on wire. Cracked earth strewn with fires. Orange and black napalm smoke. White phosphorous figures dropping pongi sticks and running down the road of Quang Ngai, flesh flapping like old wallpaper.

There'd been a lieutenant in his unit who had no sympathy for the spaced-out games men at war played to keep the horror at arm's distance. "Everything we see we are responsible for," he'd say, scorning drugs, tinted goggles, and self-induced madness. He reserved his most scathing rebukes for the white-collar boys in lab coats back in The World who kept inventing things that made life unlivable.

Spence sat up straight and flicked on the wipers. He exhaled and felt quiet again. But he didn't trust it. He remained on guard as the trailer rig pulled into a lot where a new fast-food restaurant was being erected.

He'd been living outside the wire too long and gotten careless. He let the wheel slip between his hands and suddenly heard metal buckling, glass crackling, hard-knocking things grinding against each other, and a hot spewing up under the hood. But there were no spongy gobs of lung on the dashboard, no gray spatter on his sleeves. He was still breathing. He was still there, his life not yet unspooling along Northside Drive.

Someone was making a racket, pounding on the door. A brother in a thick, woolly poncho was running around the limo, whacking the hood, hitting the fender, coming around to the passenger side and yanking on the door. The woolly poncho gave Spence heart. It wasn't the rubber kind used to wrap the dead in till a supply plane could drop body bags.

"Get out!" The brother stuck his head in the window. Picket teeth on parade and a tiny gold nose bead in his left nostril. "C'mon, jim, slide over."

The brother threw his weight against the door, then pulled. Papers flew out. Spence was pulled out to his feet. The brother was feeling him up and down, making him lift an arm, coaxing him to speak even as he continued to talk nonstop.

"My fault . . . my fault! I was trying to avoid the roadblock down there. Last time I got stopped, there was a computer foul-up that got me confused with some guy with unpaid tickets. You look bad, jim— don't pass out on me! What's your name? C'mon, you know your own name!"

"Spence . . . Nathaniel Spencer."

"Great. That's great. Where you live? C'mon, Nat man, you know where you live. Tell me where you live. And keep moving. . . . C'mon, talk, man—don't fall out on me! Where do you live?"

"On the route . . . not far from . . . but not anymore." Spence was reaching for his wallet, but the brother pushed him against the car and propped him up with the stick he'd pounded the car with. Spence could see now that it wasn't a stick but a rolled up magazine. Part of an address label said Mr. Claude Russell. Well, Spence thought, nothing wrong with my eyes.

Two cops were coming up on either side of the nose-bead brother just as Spence was making out the California address on the label. He looked up and squinted. He was pretty sure there were two cops, not double vision from a concussion.

"I'm all right," Spence said.

"Well, I'm not, jim. My license, my wallet, my rental papers—shit, everything I own is in my hotel room." Claude turned and looked past one of the cops to the crumpled Chevette at a tilt on the median.

"Awwww, shit," he said, dropping his arms. Claude's *Newsweek* plopped to the ground. Spence leaned down and picked it up.

"What do you want to do, sir? You sure you don't want a doctor to look you over?"

"I'm all right," Spence told the patrolman, though he was puzzled. How had he gotten to the service station? Had he been carried? He remembered staring down at the Claude's feet—the black Chinese slippers, the thick white socks. The next moment, the officer was leaning over him in the chair. A definite break in continuity. No big deal for a 'Nam vet, Spence thought, discovering as he stood up that he was now clutching two copies of *Newsweek*. Someone behind him reported that Mercer was sending the company tow for the limousine. Spence nodded and walked to the window. The treaded rubber carpet underfoot felt familiar.

"Sure now? We can run you over to Grady."

"I'm all right." Spence looked out of the window to get his bearings. The Chevette was being dragged to the service station on the end of a tow chain. The limo stood scarred but unperturbed near the intersection. Several yellow cones were around it to deflect traffic. Spence wondered how much time had elapsed between the spotting of Claude's shoes and his coming into focus against the ribbed runner on the garage floor.

"We can take him in," one of the cops said, less concerned than his partner with anyone's health.

"If you want to be a hardnose," the other added, touching his cap like a pitcher. "Based on the information he's given . . ." He waited, pencil poised for Spence to signal that he could close his notebook.

"You look a little shook up." Claude gave Spence a pleading grimace.

"It's all right," Spence said and, hearing himself, realized he'd been talking all along, had been holding up his end of the conversation. He had asked to see papers, instructed the officers to make note of the information. His own notes, together with his license, registration, and insurance card, were curled up in the magazines. He took a deep breath. A car pulling up toward the window swung around to the premium gas pump. MEET YOU IN THE RAPTURE, its bumper sticker said. Next to the license plate was a metal plaque that read, GOD IS MY CO-PILOT. The combination struck Spence as funny.

"I'll make good, believe me," Claude said, stepping between the two cops to touch Spence's shoulder. Spence nodded. The two officers translated his nod as agreement to let the insurance companies handle things and went out the door. Claude gave them a parting wave, then increased his grip on Spence's shoulder. "I'll see to everything. Trust me."

It was not until they were going up in the hotel's rear elevator that Spence thought to ask for one good reason why he should.

"Smokey," Claude said, picking at the stitching in the green quilted padding on the walls. "We prevent forests."

Spence studied the face, subtracted a few years, changed the clothes to various uniforms, but still could not find in the man pulling threads from the wall pads anyone who'd been with him on defoliation missions in 'Nam.

"What outfit? What year?"

"Talk civilian, jim. Memories ain't good for the health." But all the way down the corridor, he spoke of nothing else. He'd been an airman, 101st Division, Jimi Hendrix's old outfit. Spence would not be dissuaded. He had questions. Even while telephoning the lawyer, he bombarded the brother with questions.

"You worse than the law. But them cops were decent, jim. You don't know how lucky you are. Cops, man. Philadelphia? New York? Chicago? Detroit? L.A., man." He was shaking his head as he moved around the room picking up clothes, searching for papers to verify his story.

"I'm lucky?" Austin's voice came on the line.

"Only in a manner of speaking, Nat." Claude upended a flight bag on the bed, explaining that he'd expected more from Atlanta. "I thought there'd be skywriters announcing the latest news of the case. I don't know—some meetings, marches. Something," he said, going to the table to get matches. "Atlanta. Atlanta. Great place to be Ozzie Nelson."

While Spence fought off the overwhelming desire to drop down on the bed, Claude talked about the efforts he'd made to plug into community work in Atlanta. He listened as Austin went through his calendar trying to reschedule in Spence's left ear.

On the night table was a Ziploc bag of photographs. Spence shook them out. None were of Claude; not as an airman, anyway. They were mostly of women and children. He sat down on the bed and reached for the joint Claude passed. The brother hadn't come up with his papers, but he'd found something just as good in the bottom of the flight bag.

"Who are you?" It wasn't the question Spence intended to ask, but it was close enough. Spence took a toke and hoped he could take the brother at his word. He could feel himself falling over onto the pillow and hoped Claude Russell could be trusted to at least take the joint from his hand before they both went up in smoke.

Zala came down the stairs in the City Hall Annex. From inside, looking through the window set below street level, it seemed to be raining upward. Heavy drops hit the sidewalk and split in two, then sprang up. Gullies ran from a hump in the street pavement, threatening to flood the building of the community relations bureau. Someone was at the door. A good push and a couple fell in.

"It's like going through the car wash," the woman said breathlessly, not closing the door behind them. She whipped off her rain bonnet and shook it. The man, already on the stairs, unbuttoned the top of his trench coat and scratched the head of the fox terrier whimpering inside the coat.

Zala secured the door as the woman ran up the stairs calling endearments to the pooch inside her husband's coat. When the door to the office overhead was opened, conversation drifted down to Zala. A group of community workers were discussing the Angela Bacon case. The driver who'd run over the girl had been indicted on a hit-and-run murder charge back in the fall—on the same day Aaron Jackson was found, Zala found herself thinking, linking dates second-nature by now. Released on bond despite a lengthy record of criminal violence, the driver had been scheduled to return for trial in January.

"Giving him plenty of time to get to the witness," one of the community workers said, meaning the Bacon girl's friend who'd said all along the death had been no accident.

"Plenty of time to get to somebody," another man added.

She strained to hear the rest of the talk but was cut off abruptly when the door closed. Neighborhood workers whom Preener had talked with were convinced that keeping an eye on the Bacon suspect, on any of the suspects the police had released, would lead to the killers; the killers, the workers were convinced, also kept their eyes on the suspects, selecting their victims from children the pimps and other creeps drew into their circle to exploit, children in no position to blow the whistle on the killers. These conjectures, discussed in Simmons's barbershop and continued on the street, Preener returning to fill them all in, the neighborhood workers based on three facts. One, that there was so much testimony from witnesses linking Black men of unsavory reputation with white men unknown in the area. Two, that many of the descriptions were carefully kept from the media, the public. Three, that the suspects were always released and the witnesses discredited and dismissed—the Bacon suspect a prime example.

For in January, all charges had been dropped, the file and all evidence lost. Any other time, the media might have jumped on that. But the girl had not been on the list. So from the beginning it was a back-page story. And in January even the investigation took second place to the major story of the day, the release of the hostages in Iran. The driver's trial had gotten less than two inches in the local papers. Days ago in the *L.A. Times,* though, Atlanta-based correspondent Jeff Prugh had made much of the fact that Commissioner Lee Brown could only blink when asked why the Bacon girl had not been made part of the Missing and Murdered investigation, blink because Brown had never heard of her. Not a rookie but an investigator was then called away from command center to locate the Bacon file, found, strangely, in another county's possession.

The Call had included the girl on its list, which doubled the official tally, but Lafayette and Mason had shown no interest in the information Zala brought them about the case. The vets could envision no connection between the driver of the car, a Black man, and the prowlers spotted at Bowen Homes, white men. The vets did stake out the Stewart-Lakewood area, not because of Bacon's connection to the area but because the caller who'd tipped the authorities about the next dump had been described as "the redneck tipster," and the FBI had traced the call to the Stewart area.

The Stewart-Lakewood area, in particular the shopping mall and the Pickfair Way section, was requiring a tab of its own in Zala's notebook. Its connection to the case dated back to the summer, when attempted abductions were reported there and the first sexual kidnap hit the paper. The police had corrected Zala's terminology at the time, explaining that it wasn't a kidnap, wasn't a crime for an adult to offer a minor a ride so long as there was no coercion; nor was it a crime to make an indecent suggestion to a minor so long as no act ensued that could be said to corrupt the morals of said minor or otherwise contribute to the delinquency of the minor, and after all the boy had voluntarily gotten into the car for a ride; further, he'd not been harmed. Zala had backed out of the squad room that day appalled. Since then, through the STOP mail, she'd learned from the numerous child-advocacy groups that child protection laws left children vulnerable.

The Stewart-Lakewood area was further connected to the case in that many on the list, and many not on it, had lived there, like Angela Bacon, and/or disappeared from there. Or, like Lubie Geter, peddled wares in the shopping-mall parking lot, or bagged groceries, or, like Charles Stephens, hung out along the strip. Faye Yerby had been found there stabbed to death and tied to a tree. What had made the vets move, what got them out in a caravan to follow Dettlinger's car as he was showing reporters and TV news people how various victims were linked to the locale, was the connection between the "redneck" caller, the threat made to Lubie Geter by white men, the description two boys gave of would-be assaulters as white men, and the closeness of South Bend Park and the porn-ring leaders who'd been arrested, white men. It seemed that no one was sufficiently concerned about the girls and the women. Was it the fact of a white man, the fact of a boy, or was the man-boy combination the galvanizer?

Rain was seeping in around the frames of the annex window. Rain was drumming the building and it was cold. In the last few days, while logging the contents of Jan Douglass's cartons stacked far from the radiators, she'd had to keep on her gloves.

Upstairs was the delegation come to the community-relations bureau once again to demand that Black militants capitalizing on the crisis be censured before race relations thoroughly deteriorated. Already, they claimed, there'd been too much reckless talk about the anonymous phone caller and too much dangerous speculation about the authorities' refusal to play the phone recording on the air. Teo's wife had walked in with them and flashed Zala a signal. And Zala was still resenting having to close up the cartons and leave not knowing whether Sue Ellen had infiltrated the group or joined them.

When Zala had first arrived from Austin's, Spence having failed to show, there'd been a group in the office discussing a conference they were planning on poverty. An integrated group of civil-rights workers, progressives from the Highlander Center and the local Southern Regional Council, and clergy who identified with the *Catholic Worker* tradition, they gave her hope that maybe the whole world wasn't crazy damn mad. Zala had gotten to work on the news clippings, listening to their discussion and feeling at peace, though the material was anything but peaceful and the conversation about the impact of poverty on young people anything but restful. But there was hope. Just that morning the Burpee seed catalog had come in the mail, and setting out the garbage, she saw earthworms wriggling in the dirt along the brick walk. Morning had smelled loamy and warm for a while. Spring was coming. All day she'd tried to get hold of something Mama Lovey used to say to drown out the ugliness around her: the something something, but ohhhh, the faith of the gardener. The buoyant phrase waltzed in Zala's head, lightening the anger of another day's pay lost because Spence didn't show.

In January, caught in the crush of frantic relatives come to the Quonset hut that served as the pathologist's headquarters, she'd had nothing like "the faith of the gardener" to bear her up. Though the news had said two young Black males, white families were there too, and people looking for missing adult relatives. Lord knows, there'd been errors aplenty before, people kept telling each other. And the latest bad-mouthing to reach the papers—coroners, from behind their degrees, taking pot shots at medical examiners, the "unqualified" examiners calling their colleagues pompous quacks; both vowing but not in concert, to bring suit against the various investigative teams for creating chaos with physical evidence—did little to sustain any faith in white-coat expertise or blue. Those who'd arrived early enough, often enough, to get to know the janitor relayed the news that the team behind closed doors were using only those medical charts of persons on the Task Force list. When it was learned that the team felt confident to identify, by process of elimination, the bones the investigators had scrambled, all hell broke loose, and the relatives were quickly removed from the area.

Zala and two other determined parents had shouldered the terrible chore of trying to get the experts to consider their children while handling the bones on the steel tray. Others whose relatives were not on the list stayed put on the sidewalk trying to convince themselves that the janitor couldn't know, that they'd done all they could to make the medical charts of the missing available so when the news broke, they could go home and wait in anguish till the next said bodies were found. Zala had been pounding on the Task Force doors when the names of Earl Lee Terrell and Christopher Richardson were announced on TV, the news having bypassed the waiting families and official couriers too. No one had knocked on Sirlena Cobb's door beforehand. She heard about the death of her son, Christopher, on TV a split second before a mob of reporters invaded her house shoving microphones against her teeth and cameras in her face.

With no faith of any kind, Zala had stayed in bed for days till Simmons came by himself to coax her back to the shop. Then two other boys were reported missing. The following day Terry Pue was found where the redneck who'd boasted over the phone that he was the killer predicted a body would be. She did not get up again on her own steam till one of the STOP volunteers called to say Lee Gooch had been found alive.

Zala then had set about cleaning the house, making gingerbread, and putting the finishing touches on Austin's tapestries. Delia came by with new gadgets to try, leaving the sewing machine without Zala having to ask. The Gooch story had changed the climate in the shop, the STOP office, the whole neighborhood, people stopping in at the grocery for a single can of tomato sauce just to tell the story of how Dettlinger had walked into the Gooch home, spotted mail addressed to the missing boy from motor-vehicle bureaus in Florida, made a few calls, and bingo, located the boy in a Tallahassee jail for failing to respond to traffic violations.

Never mind that it hadn't happened as simply as that, that the actual story had a cast of characters, that grueling time had been collapsed to a narrative second, that the boy had been released whereabouts unknown, that when he was apprehended again on another joyride charge he explained why he'd fled Atlanta—he knew one of the kidnappers and his life was in danger. The bingo version was the preferred version. When local reporters attempting to follow up on the out-of-town coverage were told by Atlanta authorities that there was no substance to the Gooch story of knowledge and threat, the bingo version became the only version. Zala did nothing in the daytime to correct the story with the facts she knew; but at night, hunched over her notebook, she notated in scrupulous, meticulous detail every scrap of information she could get from B. J., Detective Dowell, the vets, Simmons's customers, and the brothers in the neighborhood who knew people on the APD. Kept faith with the record, because it mattered. Because she was no longer a good little schoolgirl raising her hand to recite the Plymouth Rock Covenant. Then on February 5, she'd lost all voice, all faith, and fled to bed once again.

She'd been standing on the landing at the STOP office with Monika, who was spraying rose scent on the stairwell, when the news came over the radio. Lubie Geter had been found strangled. Weeks before, while most of the mothers were on speaking tours, Sandra had taken down testimony from three separate witnesses who'd come to report an incident in which two boys had run their go-cart into a car full of white guys, one of whom had threatened the boys with "Klan justice." One of the boys had been Earl Lee Terrell, the other Lubie Geter. The STOP office was abuzz—had the witnesses gone to the Task Force? Had the information taken down been transferred? Had any media picked up on "Klan justice" since *The Call* ran the story? Was this carload of white men the same guys the vets and community workers were patrolling? That night, Zala was dictating copy to Speaker when the next news broke. Patrick Baltazaar was missing. Running from an attacker, he'd ducked into a phone booth and called the Task Force, but no one came. The radio commentator, paraphrasing someone from Commissioner Brown's office, said the boy had failed to call the right number—the third number on the poster, or was it the sixth?

Later, crawled up in a corner of the sofa bed, Zala had been going over those portions of the B. J. tapes she'd transcribed months earlier for Leah. A white woman had written to Missing Persons, among other divisions, to say that her father and his Klan buddies were killing the Atlanta children just as they'd killed numerous Black children in their hometown in North Carolina while she was growing up there. Other things going on in her household had made growing up horrendous and Zala's typing sloppy, a rattler lashing around in her stomach as she'd listened, the earphones clapped to her head. So when two office volunteers from STOP knocked on the door, she was too frightened to answer. It was not until the next day, when Speaker insisted she go down to the City Hall Annex and log material, that she learned that someone had walked into STOP to say he could identify the whites who'd threatened Geter and Terrell. Further, he could identify a professional informer who was palling around with them who might, might not, be passing information to the APD, the Task Force, the GBI, the FBI, one of the various county bureaus, or keeping the information to himself in order to cop the reward.

"Even if that information goes over the transom or is phoned into the hot line," Speaker had said, "there's no guarantee it won't be handled the same way the phone call was handled. Too hot to share with the people," he'd muttered, shaking his head. "Leadership that has no faith in the people is dangerous."

And so Zala had been at the annex every hour she could spare, determined to put in order material on two groups in particular: Coverts—Kluxers, survivalists, Birchers, Minutemen, the Posse Comitatus, La Rouchites, Defenders of the White Seed, states' righters, and other ultra-right extremists; and Overts—fundamentalists, right-to-lifers, evangelicals, born-agains, creationist leagues, and other right-wing pulpiteers. Material in the cartons showed that, emboldened by the Reagan administration's green light and the President's frequent references to Armageddon in our time, the overts and the coverts had begun to persuade farmers, unions, church and business groups to march to the right.

Zala turned, hearing footfalls on the stairs, and was glad it was not Leah Eubanks coming down and maybe reading her mind, for she would call her an historical idiot. Hadn't Christianity, slavery, and capitalism developed side by side, hand in hand? Zala could hear the condescension in Leah's voice, and was glad she'd cut ties with the woman. It wasn't Sue Ellen either; Zala could hear her in the upper hallway arguing with one of the community workers. It was one of the secretaries taking out the late-afternoon mail wrapped in a plastic picnic tablecloth. Time for Zala to leave too. The woman was looking up over her shoulder through the staircase balusters, not, Zala noticed, at the debaters near the radiator, but further down the hall. That locked brown door. Mason and Lafayette, and others too, were sure the FBI was using the room for surveillance of City Hall visitors.

"This has got to be the wettest ever," the secretary groaned as they both went out.

"Yeah, it's a mess," Zala said, catching the woman's eye and hoping for a more substantive tête-à-tête. But the woman paused in the doorway only long enough to pull up her collar and hug the mail tight before she hurried out into the rain.

On Pryor Street, police vans were unloading their cargo in front of the courthouse. Riders in a tour bus craned their necks to see the handcuffed men being prodded to jump from the vans. Shackled too, the men shuffled up the steps of the courthouse between the white lamp globes; some looked up at the scales of justice and spat before going in. The women climbed down from a smaller van. Unlike the men, they were predominantly white and were not cuffed. Self-consciously, a few reached under their coats, those who had coats, to tug sweaters down over jailhouse flab. A few ran pocket combs through brittle hair.

There were three Black women. One, with greasy, tight curls from a curling iron and not combed out, ran up the stairs quickly and was the first into the building. Zala wondered what these women had done, what they'd been charged with. At the barbershop sometimes, but most often listening through the wall at home, Zala had been hearing about mothers who wound up in jail after going to court about their curfew-defying children and ringing off the metal detector, having forgotten to remove from their purses the can of mace, the scissors, the knife, or the pistol. Few could pay the fine for the curfew violation, much less the fine slapped on for bringing weapons to court. Customers in the shop were definitely talking about Atlanta. But Zala realized, after eavesdropping on the Griers one night and hearing a roomful of people putting together money to get someone on a plane to London, that the Griers were talking about the situation in England since the revival of the "sus" laws. On mere "suspicion," Black Britons were being collared, especially the youth, most especially those who sported a reggae style, and taken to jail. After the firebombing of a West Indian teenage party in the New Cross district that left thirteen dead, twenty-seven seriously injured, the police got worse, for the community had organized to fight the authorities' attempt to blame the deaths and the fire on the revelers and not, as the New Cross Massacre Action Committee charged, on the fascist British National Front.

"Same all over," Zala muttered. She huddled inside her coat and walked around to the side entrance of City Hall.

The downstairs lobby smelled of wet wool and hair relaxer. The tile was sloppy, and the security guards had their hands full with tourists, workers, and customers come to pay bills at the Water Department slipping and sliding. A tour guide was pointing out the architectural features of the windows, the entranceways, the ceiling, the oak banisters and wrought-iron risers, its pattern repeated throughout the five-story walkup. And along the stair wall were numerous cracks where the stairwell had pulled away. But no one pointed that out, or the makeshift attempt to patch the splits with spackling compound.

Zala had been among those who'd heard the rumble of the staircase the day a handful of city jobs was announced and thousands of unemployed showed up. Straight out of a postwar Italian movie she'd seen once at Ashley Mall, the unemployed had stood five deep in the lobby, blocking the doors of the Water Department, and the entranceways, jamming the staircase. Shoeshine boys had fought their way in and up to the second-floor landing where Zala had been heading with her manicure kit to meet her customer.

One of the mayor's elite corps, he'd held his camel hair coat draped over his shoulders clutched closed with one hand like a matinee idol, as though brilliantine suavity were sufficient to handle the crowd. It had taken muscle—a scarifying lot of muscle, as she recalled—to disperse "the mob," as the media had termed them, and as Zala heard herself say once, focused only on the fact that they were interfering with her livelihood. Blue-collar, white-collar, men, women, young, old, Black, white, Latino, Asian, domestic, foreign—they'd begun to speak with one voice against the measures used to evict them from the building. Then the crack resounded, and someone screamed seeing the fissure run along the wall. Those above saw those below look up alarmed, plaster dust in their hair.

Though clammy and uncomfortable, now Zala couldn't help grinning as she moved up the stairs, looking at the patching along the wall. Painted over at least once since then, the wall seemed to be inhabited now by a family of lumpy snakes. But had Mayor Jackson learned a lesson? She stepped aside for three people coming down the stairs with overnight bags. They could have been the last wave of the rush from Ohio, come straight from the depot, luggage and resumés in hand. Not long ago, while speaking in Ohio, the mayor hadn't been able to resist boasting about Atlanta, only to have Ohioans pouring into the city to pluck the last nerve of overburdened CETA workers.

On the third floor, waiting on either side of tall doors with frosted panes, were a group of Japanese men and a group of Indian women. The men stood in a semicircle, their overcoats over their arms. Some of the women were squeezing rain from the saris showing below their coats. One woman with a cherry-red spot in the middle of her forehead was looking over the shoulder of a younger woman slowly turning the pages of her passport. They looked up at Zala, then up the staircase, then back at her, their faces creased with sorrow. The doors opened and someone beckoned the women in. Zala acknowledged the men's nods as she rounded the bend to mount the stairs to the fourth floor.

Back in the days when Delia was running her life, Zala had escorted a group of Japanese men to a business luncheon as part of her job with a tour company. The Southern gents had gotten a head start with Southern Comfort, and she'd barely had time to lead the Japanese businessmen to their seats before the foolishness started: "Hah so, Mr. Yammy Wobby, hear y'all are putting up them Benny Hanny chop shops with your own lumber and your own workers." The Japanese men got up and walked out, sending her back in with their cards so that in the future the hiy'alls could be followed by proper names. A nervous, high-pitched, red-faced man was taking two Georgia men to task: didn't they realize how much money them Japs were bringing into Atlanta?

A City Hall employee, steadying a stack of phone books with his chin, came down the stairs in a careful one-step. He smiled, all tuned up to talk, but when he glanced up the stairwell he continued down past Zala.

A quiver of excitement quickened her step. Before she came into earshot of the murmured conversations, she could feel a high-tension current spiraling down the stairs in her direction. Something—an announcement? was about to break. She could feel her own excitement spring out from her fingers and travel up the banister, registering with those above: newcomer coming. Voices lowered. Heads swung her way as she came into view of those on the stairs. In rain-spotted hats, water beading their scarves, people were leaning against the wall and the railing, others were seated on the steps hugging damp shopping bags. Midway, the staircase angled for a turning, and there on the wide step was a small man with a face like an old leather glove. She felt her breath catch. He motioned her up, instructing those around to make room.

She took a zigzag course up the stairs. She sensed that some were there because, if bad news was coming, they wanted an inkling beforehand, not to hear it as Sirlena Cobb had. Some were there because they had information they didn't trust sending over the transom, and were tired of waiting for the police to come. Others had come simply to lend support. It was as good a place to be as any, she thought, climbing. For a directive had been circulated: no one got in to see the Task Force anymore without first going through the commissioner's press secretary. There were gatekeepers in the squad rooms as well, though wily reporters circumvented the gag order by transporting officers to restaurants in outlying counties.

Commissioner Brown wasn't the only one cracking down. Employers said the case polarized workers, so collections were prohibited. Posters and clippings were taken down from bulletin boards. Memos went around to the effect that discussion interfered with productivity. Supermarket managers instructed their security guards to keep a close eye on customers wearing green ribbons, possibly troublemakers come into the store to provoke. Everybody was jumpy. Demonstrations kept being called. The gathering on the stairs looked like a sit-in. Zala stepped over a sodden brown bag of groceries. Many were angling their heads up to look at the rope barring entrance to the corridor where Aquarius was installed. But it wasn't a sit-in, she knew, working her way up to the old man who kept beckoning.

Ex-sergeant B. J. Greaves had been on the radio several times in recent weeks calling for a community show of support for Detective O'Neal and Sergeant Sturgis, demoted when officials had been caught with their pants down on the Lubie Geter case. "Why should those two women take the fall just so those men can pull their nuts out of the fire?" B. J. had put her job and her pension on the line by reading from her daybook particular entries that proved that her sister officers had moved quickly and efficiently and done were what they were supposed to do, but their supervisor hadn't, hadn't been at his desk all day. Served with disciplinary action for unprofessional behavior, B. J. went back on the air to report that the women officers were being scapegoated and had had to hire a lawyer to get a hearing that should have been pro forma. She read off the awards and commendations the Black women officers had received over the years.

As far as Zala knew, there'd been no community show of support for the two policewomen. Nor had the demonstrations called to pressure the authorities to play the "redneck" recording on the air materialized. "How ugly could it be?" Barber Simmons had asked when his customer quoted officialdom: "The phone caller's racial epithets were too inflammatory to air."

"What's he saying?" A woman with groceries yanked Zala's hem as she attempted to reach the turn in the landing.

Zala identified the aroma drifting down the stairs as Irish Mist pipe tobacco. But she couldn't pick out McClintock among all those crumpled coats and rain-darkened collars. She could hear part of his litany on the "information fallacy"—"We are informed about everything, it would seem, so we understand nothing in fact." He was sharply cut off by a City Hall employee leaning over the rope and scowling. Zala heard the knocking of a pipe against the wall, saw several people on the stairs step back quickly looking down, then heard another brusque remark from the woman leaning over the barrier rope. She wore her hair in a bouncy mushroom cut, had on a pinstripe suit with the City Hall badge on the lapel, a lacy jabot at the throat. Directly in front of her was Leah, holding her miniaturized recorder near the lace. Next to Leah was Mac.

A tall, rugged-looking brother in a pea jacket and seaman's cap had folded his arms across his chest and planted himself just so on the wide step. Zala accepted the invitation and leaned against him. On his other side the old man with the leathery face motioned that he wanted to speak to her at the first opportunity.

"She back to that again?" The woman with groceries, three steps below the turn in the landing, broke open a loaf of bread.

Zala did not bother straining to hear what the City Hall woman in the jabot was saying. She knew the tone, so knew the spiel: Aquarius, the supercomputer, on loan from TBS in Dallas, is comparable in CPUs to ten IBM 370s; Mr. Samit Ray, our computer director, reports that we can now extrapolate seventeen thousand bits of data per minute; thirteen thousand separate pieces of information have come in from psychics alone, and those can now be tabulated and cross-referenced with Aquarius in one-tenth or better the time it would take with more conventional equipment; fifteen hundred calls can now be placed by computer in a twelve-hour period; electronic searches of similar cases can be sorted, cross-indexed, filed, stored, retrieved for patterns that blah blah blah.

"Instead of just playing the damn phone call," the seaman said, picking at his razor bumps.

A familiar face in a peely bomber jacket braced himself against the banister, looked around at the seaman and nodded, then leaned past Zala to join the discussion the woman with groceries was having with a high-strung youth with wild hair—something about dead bodies in a hotel. Each time Zala moved to position herself to hear, the old man reached across the seaman to pluck her sleeve to stay put. The wild-haired youth moved further down the stairs to take issue with something someone below had said about the STOP committee.

"Sshhhhush." A pregnant woman on the fourth-floor landing pointed up through the railing in the direction of Leah's back. "She's been asking good questions."

Zala leaned forward to listen. There were certainly plenty of good questions to ask. And Leah asked them. Now that Medical Examiner Stivers had dropped his suit against the FBI, the GBI, and the APD for not protecting the site until his office got there, was someone going to investigate why the authorities had been in such a hurry they'd thrown the bones of two bodies in one bag and left eleven teeth and a sternum behind? Had the site been meticulously searched since then, if not for footprints and tire tracks, obliterated once the professionals tromped through the scene, then maybe for a button, or a watch spring, or a spent bullet that might have rolled away from the skeletons? And what was being done in response to the charge by the civilian search team that evidence they had unearthed and turned over to the police was not heard about since? What about the things, for example, the team had discovered in the abandoned building last month, drawn to the place by the overwhelming stench of decay? According to people in the neighborhood who continued to go out by the hundreds on searches, there'd been weapons in the building, boys' underwear, Polaroid debris, an altar, and a Bible nailed open to the wall with a knife.

Zala thumbed through her notebook. Had she gotten the contents of the "cult" building in January mixed up with the contents of the "porn" building in summer?

"Yes," she said aloud, for there it was on the page. Polaroid backings and boys' underwear were found in the building near Lakewood, the building across from the park where the Terrell boy had been sighted. The altar and Bible, then, were from the building the civilian search team had found. But hadn't there also been photographic evidence and clothing?

She felt a warm hand on her leg. The woman eating bread was asking her to move a little to the side.

"We can't hear down here," someone yelled up from the bottom of the steps.

Whatever Leah had asked and the woman with the ID badge was attempting to answer, Mac interrupted.

"It's natural," he said, "that is to say, human," turning to project his voice down to the fourth landing. "We derive a certain pleasure from making connections. And so we often force causal connections just for the pleasure of the pattern. Or we see parallels that make no sense beyond the superficial level." So we often mistake coincidence for meaning."

"What's the deal? What's the deal, man?" The youth with the curly mop straddled the banister and attempted to shimmy up it to resume his conversation with the woman eating bread.

"Patterns." The pear-shaped man in the bomber jacket coughed, then leaned over to answer the impatient youth. "They're talking about patterns."

"Well, I could talk about some patterns myself." The woman set the loaf aside and stopped chewing.

Everybody could relate to that. Had anyone noticed that when the papers write about the mothers cracking on the investigation, they always lay the story alongside one about parental neglect and abuse? Looks funny, don't it? Anybody from the community say "Klan" or "cult," they come back with "gentle killer" and "Black man." Even when the authorities themselves say "porn" they don't mean porn *ring*, notice that? They want it to be a lone killer, nobody with any group associations. If the community says "porn ring," then it's "Street kids are little whores." Well, how about when the papers cover the mothers traveling around the country? Next day the word is out that they've got to take the lie-detector test again.

"But where there's fire, there's smoke," someone said below, in response to what no one could be sure with so many conversations going. The youth slid down the banister to the person who'd said it, and those on the landing near Zala turned all the way around to listen.

"That's shit," the boy said.

Zala caught the phrase "for instance" before the youth cut the speaker off again.

"How you gonna say something like that about the mothers, man? What your mother ever done to you? It's about ass, man. I'm telling you. You want some white ass? Well, you get one helluva situation on your hand, like in Detroit. Remember Detroit? Well, you stupid anyway, you don't remember the Algiers Hotel in Detroit."

"Who the hell is he yelling at?" The man in the bomber jacket was leaning far over the banister, watching the mop of hair disappear down the stairs, people moving aside, not sure whether to read the boy's intensity as passion, madness, or danger.

Zala could hear him thudding his shoulders against the wall on the floor below where those who'd been sitting were now up stretching their legs, some arguing Klan, others arguing cult.

"Now what is the Klan but a cult," the seaman said quietly and scratched his neck.

Zala pressed her hand against the memory churning in her stomach and muttered, "Cult, porn, Klan."

"Now you got it," the seaman said, without taking his eyes off the City Hall woman in the jabot. From the way he was slitting his eyes and scratching, Zala was sure he was arriving at a definite conclusion about the woman.

"What's the sister talking about now?" the bread eater wanted to know.

The official behind the rope was talking about profiles in response to a question Leah had raised. The killer profile that the FBI Behavioral Science unit in Langley, Virginia, had produced; the killer and victim profiles that Dr. Lloyd Bacchus, the brother there in Atlanta, a forensic psychiatrist, had composed; the victim profiles the Fulton County Health Commission together with four epidemiologists from the CDC had fashioned. The information relayed down the stairs, her question answered, the woman closed her bread package with the plastic twist and gathered up her bags.

The old man leaned across the seaman. "What did she say?" he asked Zala.

The man in the bomber jacket cleared his throat. "She said the turning point came with the fibers."

Zala grabbed the banister and was trying to walk up along the railing to get close enough to ask a few questions of her own. Had the laundry attendant been arrested finally? She was helped up by those on the stairs. But she couldn't get the City Hall woman's attention.

". . . dog hairs from Siberian husky or an Alaskan malamute, and of course carpet fibers and clothing fibers . . ."

"And rope fibers," a woman in a fur coat said, hooking her arm around the banister knob. "And don't forget Caucasian hairs. 'Cause my nephew works in the lab. That's right. Hairs from some white person's head."

"What about the laundry attendant?" Zala went up another few steps to speak. "A suspect that was identified back in August worked in a laundry." She turned to people around her. "Fibers." They nodded. "There were eyewitnesses."

"When was that?"

"Last summer. In August."

"Was it in the paper?"

"Not much. But I was in the squad room every day back then."

"Squad room? How come?"

The old man motioned for Zala to say more. When she turned, Leah was looking at her, pushing her glasses flat against her face. She held up one finger in the air and grimaced. Zala had seen that gesture, that expression, knew the tone that went with it, "I'll handle this," and the labels—"novices," "political virgin."

"Ask her to discuss the Laundromat suspect in connection with the fiber evidence, Leah," Zala called out.

Leah turned to the woman in the jabot, who leaned forward. But when she resumed talking, it was the spiel again.

"In hard cash $100,000, an additional $46,000 in pledges, an anticipated, hmmm, who knows, from the Sammy Davis–Frank Sinatra benefit . . ."

"Speak up." The old man was gesturing for Zala to continue up the steps. He turned to those around him. "That's the gal who broke up all the chitchat at Greater Fairhill Baptist." He motioned several people on the steps below to encourage Zala.

Thinking she was being addressed, the City Hall woman began to speak more loudly. "Two thousand traffic citations have been issued since the road blocks were instituted. I don't have figures on the over-time hours that represents. Suffice it to say that the investigation is costly. But the city council is considering stiffer penalties for curfew vi-olations. A five hundred dollar fine or a year in jail for the parents."

She'd gone too far. The old man was still waving Zala on with one arm, and with the other he was trying to quiet the crowd. Zala stayed put. It was pointless. The City Hall woman was not there to take notes. In any case, only data tailored to fit the profiles, patterns, and theories the Task Force was already committed to were considered. Any printout from Aquarius would bear as much resemblance to the actual situation as freshman plot synopses did to Greek tragedies.

The seaman, no longer squinting at the woman behind the rope, grunted. "Think she gets a bonus for baby-sitting the crowds?" He lifted his chin toward the fifth-floor landing, where the woman was still spieling out figures.

A tourist attraction, Zala was thinking. Aquarius was a tourist at-traction for home folks. Groups of supplicants came daily to consult the oracle. And the old man from Greater Fairhill was still insisting that she take part in the spectacle.

Someone below was shouting up the stairwell that he wanted his tax dollars accounted for. Black supercops were flown in, mentioned briefly in the papers, then flown out again, citizens none the wiser about what they made of things than a flea in his dog's collar. Scotland Yard came and went. ABC, NBC, CBS, 20/20, 60 Minutes, the BBC, German tele-vision crews, mystery writers, psychics, detectives who'd made their reputations from the Onion Field Case, the Zodiac Murders, The L.A. Freeway Killings. "We get the tab but don't get the facts."

"Tell them what you know," the old man pleaded with Zala.

"You know something about them fibers she was talking about?" The fur-coated woman with the lab-technician nephew said it loudly, in challenge.

Attention turned to Zala. But what did they want? Why did people keep demanding to hear what they already thought, muttered about, suspected, knew, but kept resisting? She could begin by telling them how a single phone call inside the precinct house had sprung the Laundromat suspect fingered by five separate eyewitnesses. Or she might begin with the letter B. J. had read on the tape. Maybe the writer was just some crazy white woman who wanted her father locked up, but it did seem relevant.

A victim of father rape, she'd been handed over to the sheriff and other Klan friends of the family to fuck. At twelve, she'd become a regular in home-movie orgies. The minister's wife, the sheriff's wife—or was it the mother?—someone put her in a home for wayward girls and then an asylum because she wouldn't shut up about the death of her brother. He, too, had been raped by the father, then beaten to death, according to the letter writer, who called herself not a victim, but a survivor, though her childhood, fingered and mauled, was still being shown on the screen, her terror still entertainment for rent.

Zala heard herself speaking too loudly, rushing her words, though she did not hear what she was saying. She could feel a wall going up, not unlike her own in summer, when she'd been listening to the STOP mothers and trying to separate herself from their calamity. She tried to slow down. She went over the witnesses—the mortician's assistant, the Bowen Homes tenants, the father who'd seen the boiler door spirited away and was visited later and urged to be mute lest all hell break loose.

"Take your time, daughter," the old Fairhill Church man whispered.

She tried to choose her words carefully, to find polite, calm, tax-free words that wouldn't make them back off from the horror with "Oh, how awful, what's anybody doing about it?" What did they need said? They knew, and they knew they knew, that the official version was off the wall, shot through with so many contradictions even a fool could figure it out. And when the whole report was neatly done up like a roast, would they cluck, tsk-tsk, give her a hug and a pat and a pill, or would they storm the computer center and take over the investigation?

"My God," the woman in the lacy jabot said, holding her face in her hands.

"That poor woman," drifted up from below as Zala made her way down.

"It's not how little we know that hurts so," the old man was saying, "but that so much of what we know ain't so."

"I know one thing," the seaman said, "one way or the other, this city's gonna explode."

Zala stood by the cyclone fence where three police horses were tethered, waiting for Leah and Mac to come out. Maybe they'd already left by another exit. Everyone else who'd visited the oracle had come out, chewing over this riddle or that. There had been no move to take over the computer room. There would be no protest promenade around Central City Park, no storming of the doors at the car showroom. No action to bring the city to a halt. Resisting what they knew and what knowing obliged them to do, the people were willing to buy official lies a little while longer. Lest all hell break loose.

She continued to wait, the hem of her coat heavy with rain. She eyed a chrysalis slung in the crook of a branch like a bag of garbage, wondered vaguely what was inside the parchmentlike pouch—wasps? hornets? Maybe Austin had served papers on Leah and she was too embarrassed to face her. But maybe there'd been no action at all, Austin's reassurances a hoax like everything else. Zala thought for a moment that she detected a movement in the chrysalis and wished the larvae well, thinking of Widow Man, not as he was now, cranky and dying, but as he'd been in the very beginning when he took time to tell them things.

He'd called them down from the ladder one day when, washing the windows, they'd discovered a hornet's nest. Closing up the house with them all inside, he'd sent the twins to fetch the kerosene. He wrapped an old dish towel around the broom and began. Once-upon-a-time not his style, he went directly to the heart of the matter. There was the bee, who flat-out stung you, then went on about its business. Unlike a wasp, that chased you indoors with welts, then buzzed menacingly at the window. Then there was the hornet that would call out its whole army and navy to chase your ass to the ends of the earth, hellbent on your total destruction. Outside, decked out in long sleeves, heavy pants, a mesh helmet cut from an old window screen, and his flaming lance, Widow Man went up the ladder to do battle, leaving them indoors with great respect for those singleminded, non-negotiating, taking-no-prisoners winged maniacs that put their whole life agenda aside to kill you for disturbing their young.

The lights went out in the lobby of City Hall. The guard locked the front doors and went away. The fifth floor dimmed. Whatever else Aquarius had accomplished, its work as distraction was done for the day.

Leaning far forward in his chair, chest pressed against the edge of the table, Claude was rapping on the wood underneath. Ice cubes tinkled in the plastic tumblers.

"What?" Spence didn't know why he was whispering. The hotel restaurant was half-empty.

"The dark ages, jim." It was a secret message being tapped through a prison wall.

Spence began making room on the table. He moved the pepper mill, the red candle jar, then the tumblers to one side. Familiar now with his dinner companion's sudden breaks and startups, Spence figured Claude would be laying the photos out on the table again like cards. Seeing them lined up in rows seemed to help him think.

Claude was finger-spelling against the bread basket. Then he gathered crumbs in piles. His nose bead gleamed in the red candlelight.

"You're not eating." Claude dipped his fork in his wineglass and scratched lines between the crumbs. "Feeling all right?"

"I'm mellow," Spence smiled. Claude had complained that he'd come to Atlanta ready to do the do, only to find everyone laid-back and oh-so-mellow. Everyone, that is, but a cartoonist he'd met who was frantically searching for the agency producing the safety-ed comics. The only passionate discussion of the case he'd heard thus far was between the hotel chambermaids, fiercely defending the STOP mothers, and the head housekeeper, who'd called them mercenary so-and-sos for charging lecture fees. "As if Kissinger don't or Jimmy Carter don't," the maids had argued.

Spence watched Claude and waited.

Claude threw down his fork. "What about the feds?"

"I thought we'd exhausted that topic." Before they left the hotel room they'd agreed that the feds were good for finding a stolen dune buggy, a yacht taken from a marina, an AWOL perhaps, but not children.

The waiter cleared away the dishes and brushed the crumbs into the breadbasket. Claude emptied out the Ziploc bag and began lining up the photos.

"Why don't we hear more about that sex ring they caught in a dragnet a few months ago?"

Spence shrugged. While searching for the Terrell boy, the police had collared three men. And for a time the reigning theory on the block was S&M gotten out of hand. The official story was that Wilcoxin, St. Louis, and Hardy had exploited white boys only. The story had died down.

"The trial's set for spring," Spence said. "They made a point of saying that no Black children were involved."

"I noticed that. But how often do you see that in the papers— so-and-so, white, and so-and-so, white? Think they hit paydirt and are holding the media off with the ruse? Or are they afraid to say the three white men were roughing off young Bloods?"

"Could be."

"You don't think so?"

"I know only that they're lying. A friend of my wife works with JDs and the word is young Bloods were originally scheduled to give testimony. They'll probably do it in judge's chambers now. But . . ."

"I don't think so either, Nat. The sex angle may be a small part of the total scheme, but . . . In a word, what do you think?"

"Klan."

"Just as everybody thought the minute the story broke. Which brings us back to the feds." Claude leaned down again to think, his chin wobbly on the back of his hands.

Spence moved the candle jar closer to inspect the photos. One was crackled and had been cropped, evidently, to fit into a wallet case. Another bore signs of yellow tape at the corners. Apparently it had been in an album. In the three hours they'd been together Spence had learned few facts about his companion. On the hotel dresser there'd been an envelope with HOT SPOT: ELECTRONIC EQUIPMENT CO-OP printed in the return-address section. That, and the address label on the second *Newsweek,* was about it for print. For the rest, he had to take the brother at his word.

In the wallet-cropped photo were two women. The older, thirtyish, wore her hair swept up in back and brushed over her forehead in fifties bangs. She gripped the handle of a baby carriage, glancing over her shoulder to smile broadly at whoever took the picture. The younger, eighteen at most, wore her hair pulled back and brushed to the side, held with a tuck comb. A chiffon scarf was around her neck, tied to the side. A cardigan, pushed out in front by an ice-cream-cone bra he remembered Delia wearing in those days, was buttoned up the back. The skirt, long, straight, and tight, was the kind Cora used to call a "hobble skirt." "Fast" they called the girls who wore them; "slack," the mothers who permitted it.

When Spence reached for the color prints, Claude spun several of them across the rows like a card sharp. But he made no attempt to identify the subjects. In one print the woman and the girl, older, were joined by a middle-aged woman with a hearing aid. In another, taken on the steps of a church, foxes chased each other around her broad shoulders, dead teeth clamped on dead tails. Spence picked up a jumbo print of a family picnic. A boy who might be Claude was rassling with a teenager under the trees. Men lounged on a patchwork, laughing and lifting paper cups. The girl with the pointy tits held a cup under a thermos spigot. The two women sat back to back supporting each other. Their legs were tightly crossed at the knees, the fox-fur woman tugging her skirt down.

Once again, Claude spun a snapshot across the table. Taken in 'Nam, it showed barechested servicemen posing in front of a supply tent. Whoever took the picture was more interested in the tent than in the men. Heads were cut off, elbows out of the frame, but the tent was carefully centered. The angle had been selected for optimum light on the side of the tent where the flap had been tied back, exposing the weapons—M-60 machine guns, M-79 grenade launches, 155-millimeter guns, howitzers, Uzis. Was the brother from California trying to tell him something?

"A wiretap," Claude said, hitting his fist on the table.

"What wiretap?"

Claude opened his napkin and unfolded the blue airmail letter from the Ziploc on top of the napkin. He used the same meticulous gestures he'd shown in the hotel room rolling joints. Though his hands were calm, his legs weren't. He was swinging his knees back and forth, rocking the table.

"If not the feds, then who, Nat?"

"I don't follow."

Claude drummed on the table a while, then looked over the airmail letter. Everything about him was still now. Spence drew from one of the rows a photo that looked the most recent. The three women were in a densely thick, green landscape. On one side of the photo the sun seemed scalding hot. The woman who'd worn bangs now wore her hair braided in front. She was lowering a heavy skillet onto a sawhorse table. A bunkhouse behind her, though blurred, had a readable shingle over the doorway—JANE PITMAN PLACE. On the dark side of the photo, where the surrounding green was nearly black, the fox-fur woman in a bib apron bent over a cook pot. At first glance she seemed doubled over in laughter. But the smile was forced. The bend in the middle was real, though, and pained. Sweat spread on her back like Rorschach blots. She cocked her ear toward the camera in an "Eh?"

It was the girl who dominated the scene, though she stood at the far end of the table in shadows. No longer a girl, her breasts were a soft line across her T-shirt. She held a wooden shoveler, the kind used to remove pizzas from ovens. A peel, Spence thought, remembering the last time he and Zala had curled up with the Sunday papers and worked the cross-word together.

Claude was watching him closely for his reaction. Spence looked at the photo some more. The young woman had mastered the art of ap-pearing before the camera and commanding the eye. A manifesto was being stated in the lift of her chin, her grip on the peel. But what? He noticed then that the fox-fur woman was not wearing her hearing aid. Eh? Was there a message in the Rorschachs on her back? Eh . . . eh? On the flipside of the print was written, "Paradise at Last—Love, Alma, Theresa, and Pat."

"They ain't playing," Claude said, leaning back in his chair and sig-naling the waiter. "I don't know if you've been following their es-capades, but they're knocking over banks now, counterfeiting big bills, cleaning out armories, bombing public utilities. They've got their own wire service. They're computerizing their mailing lists. They've got more front organizations than *Klanwatch* can keep up with. David Duke, their talk-show pinup, may have split with jet-setting Bill Wilk-erson, but those two managed to cover a lot of ground, a whole lotta ground, jim. And now with the Carolina senator as ideological point man—"

"Jesse Helms," Spence inserted, now that he'd caught up.

"Damn straight. They're recruiting everybody that the center and the left overlook—parolees, mental patients, bag ladies. Figure it out. There you are on the streets, no driver's license, can't vote, don't nobody want to be bothered with your sorry ass, no place to live, no job, bad credit, bad risk all around—ripe, jim, ripe. The Christian Front is recruiting leftover flower children by the vanload on the West Coast. On the East Coast, the guardians against smut are aiming to make common cause with the antiporn feminists. Never mind what they used to say about the Pope, they're recruiting Catholics now, and not just in front organizations. They've got a Black klugle out in the Midwest. And they've begun soft-pedaling the Jewish thing, if you've noticed. They no longer say in the newest literature "Onward to the White Christian Republic." Now it's "Save Judeo-Christian Civilization." Now, how do you read that? But my question is," Claude said, leaning over and tapping the table in front of Spence's arms, "do they have the balls to wiretap the white boy?"

"Maynard and them, you mean?" Spence couldn't see how, not with the GBI breathing down their necks, the FBI at their heels, the media dogging them door to door, and the good ole boys waiting to pounce. He bit his lip and thought it over. "Police Chief Napper was relieved of duty on the Task Force. That might mean something. We thought it was because he moved too fast when one of the VIs brought in a psychic. The city got stuck with her bills. But maybe he was moved so that with less visibility . . . hmmm."

"More likely the feds. There's no love lost between the Bureau and the Klan. There are as many agents in the Klan as Knights in the Bureau. It'd be prettier, though, if the brothers were trump-tight. Maynard and Jackson and them, I'm talking about."

With a quick sniff at the coffee carafe, Claude waved the waiter away with the tray, then called him back and ordered a bottle of cognac and a fresh pot.

"You look worried, Nat. You think I'm going to stiff you for the bill?" He grinned, sporting two rows of picket teeth. "So what do you think?" he asked after a long pause.

Before Spence could brush his top lip where his mustache was coming in bushy, Claude began lining things up on the table. He positioned the candle jar to the rear of his wineglass. When the waiter put down the bottle and two balloon glasses, Claude made them part of the battle formation. The lecture part of his brandy demonstration, though, was not forthcoming.

Wiretap. His niece Gloria's boyfriend, a ham operator, boasted that he would bag the reward once he caught the killers on the wire. Tap. How much time would it take? Spence wondered.

More than ten years had passed between the bombing of the church in Alabama and the trials. Robert Chambliss was finally doing time for the murder of the four little girls. But he'd been loose to plot and scheme for fourteen years before going to jail. Stoner beat the rap and was running for office, despite the well-known secret that his roommate was the brother of James Earl Ray, still in Springfield prison for the murder of Martin Luther King Jr.

"File an FOA, Jim. That's the answer," Claude said. "That's it, Nat. The Freedom of Information Act." He reached across the table and grabbed Spence's arm, tipping his brandy glass.

Spence rescued the rolling snifter. Claude jumped up when the stream reached his side of the table and poured into his lap. He didn't use his napkin on his pants but moved quickly to grab the photographs from the spill.

"Shit," was all Claude said when he sat down again, holding the Paradise print and the airmail letter close to his chest. He seemed a million miles away. Spence sat down, uneasy. It didn't seem a good time to leave the table to phone Judge Webber. He scooted his chair closer to Claude's when the brother slumped and let the photo drop.

"What is it we don't know to say to the sisters, Nat?" Claude said, reaching for his cognac. His voice seemed to be coming up through loosely packed earth. "What do these self-styled messiahs know to say that we don't?" With the hand holding the snifter he gestured emphatically over the floor where the color print lay. Brandy dripped onto the carpet.

"Take it easy, Claude!"

"Our pastor refused to bury them. All up and down the coast, Jim, ministers refused to hold services. Suicide and holy ground, that shit. Some admitted they were scared of the People's Temple."

Spence placed a steadying hand on Claude's arm and brought the brandy glass safely down to the table. "Take it easy. I know you hurting, brother."

The waiter threw down a towel, pressed, snatched it up and flipped it over his shoulder and left.

Claude twirled his snifter and inhaled. "Would you believe it? I once worked for Jones. Did promotional films for the Temple when he had the place on Geary Boulevard. Used to fly up to San Francisco every week. Every week, jim. Worked my buns off. We all did. Huey Newton, Angela Davis—anybody who was anybody spoke up for him. Shit, he was doing good things then. My sister left a good job—social worker, Black adoption stuff. Went to work for Jones. That was in the days when he was getting awards from the Human Rights Commission for the orphanages, the old-age homes."

"This is your sister?" Spence picked up the Paradise print from the floor and laid it on the table.

"Yeah . . . I had some serious questions when they started getting the children. You know, placing Black children with white couples. I said heyyyyyy, wait a minute. But she talked me out of it that time." He drew the photo closer. "But Charles Garry—you know, the Panther lawyer—he stuck to the bitter end. The bitter end, jim." Claude poured two fingers of brandy into Spence's glass.

Spence waved the waiter away after he set down the coffee tray. Claude rubbed a finger over the rim of the carafe, satisfied that it was freshly brewed.

"When I realized what was up . . . man! We started hearing about the beatings and the rapes and the drugs." He shook his head and the table shook. "All them sisters. All them children. We wrote letters everywhere—FBI, State Department, CIA, the President, the U.S. embassy down there—all the finks you swear you'll never deal with, much less beg. I mean *beg,* Nat. And that Burham . . . Why do we have to rubber-stamp those bastards just because they're Black? Burham's a bastard all around, Nat."

"I hear you."

"We went to see the Panthers. We tracked down every senator and congressman we could. You know what got Leo Ryan to take it on? One of his students was a defector from the Temple and he got murdered. His family pleaded with Ryan to look into things. We were running around trying to put a fire under anybody's ass. But you know the coast, Nat. Everybody's spaced out and fucked up. Everybody sipping wine and stoned out on Acapulco Gold and quoting the yogis and burning incense and catching the view—the Palisades, the Bay, the bridge, the this, the that."

Spence moved things out of the way when Claude began gesturing. He moved closer and rubbed the brother's back till the shuddering subsided. When Claude began to smooth out the airmail letter, Spence expected to hear the stories. The infrequent long-distance calls that sounded monitored, rehearsed. The powerlessness one felt at the other end far away while defectors predicted serious trouble from the step-up of suicide drills in Jones's paradise in Guyana.

On public radio there'd been interviews with Atlantans whose friends and relatives numbered among the nine hundred and eleven massacred. The old letters were read over the air, monotone but a stray phrase took on sudden import—a coded SOS, a goodbye, a warning to watch your own back? Defectors came on the air and told of the floggings, the rapes, the venereal disease, the currency kept in mothballs, then transported periodically in hand luggage to Switzerland, Brazil, and the Soviet Union. Lawyers hired by relatives gave updates on the trials for a while, on the lawsuits brought against the two governments by the families, by Congressman Ryan's widow, by the colleagues of the newsmen murdered on the airfield in Georgetown. Then silence. Just as the town criers had warned and as the defectors had predicted if there was no mass voice raised in protest, silence set in. By the time the movie *The Guyana Tragedy* came to town, the suppression of news had taken effect. Amnesia reigned. Pulled after two days, the movie didn't even finish the week out.

"The Dark Ages, Nat. They're close at hand." Claude straightened up. "That's why you were speeding, Nat."

"*I* was speeding! You hit *me*, man."

"Ghosts—we're both trying to outrun the ghosts who want to make us ghosts. Well, here's to them," Claude said, raising his glass. "You're not drinking. You got something better to do?"

"A belligerent drunk. You total my limo and now you get nasty."

"It was my Chevette that got totaled. And it wasn't even mine. Here's to the Dark Ages coming at us."

"I'm not drinking to that," Spence said.

"What are you going to do? You've got a few choices."

"I know, you've told me. Apathy, misery . . . conformity, madness, and . . ."

"Just two. Either you do or you don't. Believe it. Trust me. I know what I'm saying."

"You're drunk, Claude."

"And getting drunker. I hope you got some money on you," he grinned, rubbing his nose bead.

Spence looked around for the phone. In the bar a TV was bolted to the wall above the till. They were running a review of the case—the searches, a boat in the water, the grappling hook, a covered gurney being heaved into the coroner's wagon, the mayor in a black armband, the commissioner looking weary, the mothers making a charge, an on-location reporter, classmate pallbearers gripping the handles with white gloves. Then the familiar school pictures crowded the screen.

"Close at hand all right," Spence said, standing up. "As close as the TV set."

"Closer than that, jim. Closer than that."

The horn blew a third time before Zala thought to look. Headlights were blinking through the macramé slits. She peered through the pane in the door. Two drunks were stumbling up her walk, one in a blanket, the other half in a coat, a sleeve empty and dangling. She opened the door. They reeled into the hedges, grabbing at each other's clothes. The cabbie got out to assist, waving X's in front of his chest; he wasn't in this mess, he wanted her to know. The coach lamp went on in her neighbor's doorway. Spence scrambled to his feet and looked up. His eyes were half-closed, the veins in his lids thick, his lower lip wet and droopy. She'd never seen him so smashed. The drunk in the blanket was waving his arms to speak. The cabbie caught him under the armpits and walked him from behind over to Spence. He clamped his hands on Spence's shoulders and pushed him toward the steps.

"Marazuuuul?"

"It's Nat," the man in the blanket said and stepped back.

They were waiting now for her to claim him, this man who'd told a stranger things he hadn't told her.

She took her time before she nodded.

"You all right now, jim. You home." The drunk in the blanket gave Spence a pat on the back and turned, bumping into the cabbie who pulled him again to his feet, then headed for the curb.

"Hold it!"

They stopped by the hedges and looked at her. The cabbie lifted his cap, rubbed his head, then fitted it back on. The man in the blanket adjusted the folds that threatened to trip him. They leaned over at the same time to encourage Spence, who'd missed the first step, to untangle his legs and try it again. He bent down. He intended to come up on his hands and knees.

"Can you take it from here?" The driver went to his cab, not waiting for an answer. He sat down on the front seat, turned on his TV set.

The blanket man was yanking at the cab door handle. The cabbie was making no attempt to help.

"Take him to Greyhound," Zala said.

"Say what?"

Zala pictured Spence waiting slumped over in one of those molded chairs, a coin-operated TV bolted to a reinforced arm the only thing holding him up from the coffee-spilt floor. Wrappers, butts, newspapers stuck in dried puddles of pop. Cops looking for someone to break up the boredom.

"Nat's your ole man, ain't he?"

Zala looked down at Spence, fallen over sideways on the third step. She looked at a spot in the top of his head. His hair needed picking, his clothes were a wreck. He belched and giggled up at her. Miss Purple Mouth might find this amusing.

"The depot," Zala said, then stepped back inside, closed the door, turned the lock, and drew the chain.

V

FOXGLOVE AND TANNIA

LEAVES

Sunday Afternoon, April 26, 1981

From the northern breezeway of Judge Webber's estate, the new housekeeper watched the guests in the carriage house. Parlor games among the leisure set. Who could they be that even before she could load the butcher-block cart with rolls, salad, cake, and chocolate cordials, as her employer had told her to, her nibs had tiptoed out there herself to serve them a tray?

"Those are no miscellaneous Negroes out there," she said aloud, setting a pitcher of iced tea down on the window ledge.

In the carriage house, a man in a white athletic suit was folding paper, then tearing it along the edge of a carton cleared of demitasse cups. "Number your responses one to ten," he could very well be saying. And the guests passed around the paper and the short, pointy pencils that Mrs. Webber's club used for bridge and Scrabble.

The housekeeper steadied the plate of sandwiches on the ledge with her hip and waved to the packers coming across the patio to come in and eat. But they stopped by the trellis to watch the men and women in the small building at the far end of the flagstone walk.

"Must be a prayer group," one of the packers said.

"Looks more like one of those singles groups."

The packers moved on when the boss, a rawboned man with a goatee, a leather cap cocked on his head, came up the patio steps from the moving van. He waited until they had all wiped their feet on the mat and gone in, then rubbed his knees and sighed. Unaware that he was being observed, he planted his hands on the small of his back and twisted to work a crick out of his massive body. Then he turned in the direction of the carriage house.

"Too old for the work," the housekeeper mused, watching the big man walk away. "And too hip for the room, as they say."

The big man set his heels down hard on the walk so the guests would know he was coming. No telling what they were doing in there with their charts and maps and movie equipment. An election of some sort? They seemed to be casting ballots. Not secret ballots; they openly conferred. A guessing game, he decided, when several screwed up their faces. The stakes were high. There was no mistaking their seriousness. When a woman in a batik dress looked his way, he lifted one of the doors out of the bed of bluebells and set it in place, disguising a grunt with a cough. He took a look at a list taped to a portable blackboard. Families . . . a list of families.

He shoved the second door in place and, shielding himself, spied through the crack between the jamb and the hinge. At the far end of the room was a lineup, women's favor. The men were in for it, if it was one of those man-woman speak-outs.

He leaned over and hammered in the linchpin with his fist. He would need the ladder again to put the top pins in the hinges. Not that anyone in the main house would mind if the doors hung aslant. No one inside the carriage house seemed to.

The grass was still moist from the morning shower, and the air held the fragrance of damp earth and blooming flowers. The raw-boned man chuckled to himself as he moved across the yard. No less than five people had expected him to use the side entrance to the main house. They would have to race to the front hall now if they planned to intercept him for a report. He moved toward the eastern end of the estate, drawn as much by the clonking of stones thrown against a tree as by curiosity to see what the main foyer looked like. Loose grass collected on his shoes and muffled his steps. When he came up behind three children, they didn't turn around.

A boy in a sky-blue parka was putting his feet together on the sharp shadow line of a security alarm sign stuck in the front lawn. He took aim at a dogwood flowering pink and white. A girl, smaller, was not interested in target practice. She was prancing through the hyacinth and the crocuses. An older girl, her hands shoved in the pouch pockets of her sweatshirt and her knees hugging a poster roll, kept her eye on the two youngsters. Her vigilance made the big man rethink the carriage-house group.

It had something to do with the child killings. He was sure of it. Five days in Atlanta, waiting to pick up a job that would take him back home, was enough to know that it took heart to even get together, what with everything jumping. He'd heard more about the police moving on community groups than he had about the investigation itself. He stepped into the marble foyer of the Webber home. Whatever the game plan of the people inside the carriage house, Ed Bingham of Trans-America Movers tipped his cap to them.

"I want to say one thing." Dave turned slowly around in his chair and waited for the others to look up. "Let's not be stupid when we get out there," he said, jerking his thumb toward the map on the wall. "We get stupid, somebody gets killed."

Mason leaned across the table with a cigarette in his mouth.

Lafayette flicked his lighter and lit it. "Too true," the vet said, running his hand over his scalp, glad that someone had broken the silence. "We can assume that many of the victims were dusted to cover the killers' tracks. Since so many knew each other, it's a reasonable guess. No telling who might be watching us. So like Dave said, let's not be too anxious to question people along the route. I'm sure I'm not the only one who has the feeling that the cops, the investigators, and reporters too have been careless about witnesses' safety."

"I second the motion." A brother in a white crocheted cufi stood up, and several people groaned. Dave was heard to mutter, "Here comes another 'prison letter.' " But the brother in the cufi would not yield the floor. " 'Cause it's been open season on the Black man all along. Ever since we were brought here from the motherland in chains, the Black man has been an endangered species. So while we're out there reconnoitering, we need to cool it, like the brothers said, because the Black man—"

"Write it," the schoolteacher snapped. "That's what the paper is for."

Several people seconded that motion. Earlier, when discussion had threatened to degenerate into slogans and lectures, the teacher had made the suggestion that people put their positions on paper, then let Mason do a summation.

"While we're at it," Lafayette said, "I'd like to volunteer as an advance scout."

"Good idea," several murmured, for Lafayette had more than once demonstrated his ability to move swiftly and to stay on the case.

Mason got up from the table and went to the blackboard. From the sash of his white kung-fu jammies he withdrew a piece of chalk. He wrote the vet's name alongside "Roy Innis and Company" under a listing of people to contact. The word was out that the CORE splinter group had moved from the Hyatt to the Americana and had then checked out to the Atlantan Hotel. It would take someone like Lafayette to track Innis down for the story on the witness in CORE's protective custody.

"Well, good people, since we're taking time out, maybe we should distribute the papers Brother Spencer had copied for us." Speaker waited until he got the nod from Zala before he passed out the contents of a manila envelope.

"Make sure you get both packets," Speaker instructed. "The top sheet of the first pile is National Security Council Memo number 46, dated March 17, 1978. You'll notice that it's addressed to the secretary of state, the secretary of defense, and the director of Central Intelligence. It talks about the whys and ways to keep African people of the Americas separated from African people on the Continent. The documents stapled to it are also top secret. Local version," he added. "They speak to our situation—namely, to the isolation and muzzling of the community voice." He paused long enough for the group to react to the "Confidential" stamped across the security memoranda before he handed out the next batch.

"The second pack are guidelines and forms for filing under the Freedom of Information Act. The top sheet is a copy of title 5 of U.S. Code 552, which explains procedure. Be sure to spread the word. Do not reveal your source for the security papers, but do spread the word. And quickly," Speaker added ominously, then sat down.

Zala slipped carbon between sheets of foolscap. It would probably have been better for Speaker to hold off until she'd completed the pledges for the members of the newly formed Community Committee of Inquiry to sign. But no one seemed uncomfortable about being in possession of security documents. Discussions were brief. Then everyone returned to the writing.

Renegades, Delia had called them—or so Gloria had reported. It wasn't half off the mark, Zala was thinking, looking around the carriage house. Preener, for example, had defected from his neighborhood patrol when the police ambushed the Techwood Homes Defense Squad. His squadron got cold feet after the arrests and rescinded an earlier decision to arm themselves. Preener was sitting between ex-officer B. J. Greaves and Detective Dowell, who'd asked to be transferred from the Task Force because information was neither coordinated nor shared. "I knew more when I worked in my old unit," he'd told the group.

Sitting between two fathers who'd complained loudly about the treatment families not on the list received from both the Task Force and STOP was a STOP office volunteer who could no longer stomach the squabbles between STOP and organizations raising funds in the name of the victims. The volunteer had walked out with Alice Moore, one of the mothers, who felt that STOP should charge city hall with theft and tampering with the mail. She carried in her handbag the sympathy cards she'd been called to City Hall to pick up. The envelopes, addressed to her, had been emptied of the "tokens of sympathy enclosed" that the notes on the cards referred to.

Next to the wood-burning stove set on a block covered with Mexican tile was a woman who'd worked in the SAFE office designing flyers. She'd thrown up her hands in defeat after being repeatedly discouraged from putting together fact sheets designed to inform residents right away of abductions in their neighborhoods rather than have them wait, ignorant and vulnerable, until the victim made the list or the media decided to grant coverage. "I thought safety education was the business of that office," she had told the group. "Tell me about it," the schoolteacher had said in response. He was on suspension for organizing a PTA safety patrol in defiance of his principal's order to "remain calm" in the face of daily reports of disappearances in early spring.

On the bench with Leah and Speaker were Paulette Foreman and two co-workers from Grady. Like Dave, who'd used up his sick time and annual leave to fly to La Crosse, Wisconsin, to visit his wife and son, Paulette was filing for reinstatement too, having overstayed her vacation in Miami doing refugee work with a girlfriend from nursing-school days. Dave and Paulette, disturbed by the erratic services set up for the stricken families, had organized a group of Grady workers with city youth workers to help lawyers, doctors, and psychologists volunteer their services to the families.

Zala wasn't sure if Mattie's new mode of dress represented defector status. Never a model of dress-for-success, the reverend, research lab aide, and metaphysical counselor was wearing dark-pink textured tights under a dropped-waist, scooped-neck, striped dress. The bangles she customarily wore on her arms she now wore in her ears—three on each lobe. Her makeup was close to garish and hot-pink peau-de-soie heels capped legs crossed purposefully in the direction of Bible Man. Next to her was a woman dressed completely in white, with a double strand of myrrh beads tucked inside her dress. Bible Man and the two women had been working on the pierced-through passage of the Bible found by the search team back in January. "I was nowhere near Damascus," Bible Man had told the group, "when I saw the light and went to look for this young man here," hugging Speaker around the shoulder.

Behind them, the projectionist straddled a chair between a brother wearing a Gay Rights button and a brother in an Atlanta Street Academy jacket. The projectionist had been a mass-com intern at CNN when two of the STOP volunteer investigators appeared on a talk show. The show's host had double-crossed Chet Dettlinger, who'd specifically requested that she not set him up to criticize the official investigators. The intern had wanted to work with the VIs, but instead hooked up with several community workers he met during the demonstration protesting the arrest of the Techwood Homes Defense Squad. For a while he'd filmed the activities of the Guardian Angels, the New York subway patrol that had been invited to Atlanta by a politico who preferred not to be interviewed. Then he'd met Preener on the march organized by Coretta King and SCLC. Zala had introduced him and Preener to Mason and Lafayette the day Spence brought the children home and cooked up a pot of gumbo.

Beside the Florida narc, lured from his own jurisdiction by Lee Gooch's testimony and the fat Atlanta reward, sat a young reporter in the loosely knotted tie who kept turning up mud. Children reported seeing two men smear "mud" on the face of a boy they grabbed and threw in a yellow cab that drove off; "mud" was the neighborhood kids' word for the substance in a can found in a corner of the house on Gray Street they had taken him to see for himself; it was "mud" that the boys reportedly sniffed to get high on before doing what they came to do, were paid to do, with the men in that infamous house that both his editor and the Task Force ignored, even after Dettlinger, pulled in for questioning, told them that several of the victims had frequently visited there.

"Anyone interested in hearing what we have?" The projectionist was going through the stacks of cases and canisters from Hot Spot.

"Not yet," Zala said, passing out the pledges.

She had to smile. Spence's drunken friend Claude Russell had turned out to be a fraud in one sense. Mercer's insurance company reported that Claude Russell was a plumber in Oakland who'd never been to Atlanta and could prove it. Whoever the brother from California was, though, he had sent a shipment of film to Spence at Zala's address. Spence had vowed to return the films in person to Hot Spot. She wondered where he planned to get the money to fly to the coast.

"I'd like to get you on film," the projectionist was saying to the Street Academy brother, as Zala headed for the side door to check on the children.

"I'm ready any time you two are," the young reporter said. He'd planned to say more, but the schoolteacher looked over his shoulder and frowned.

Zala walked through an area that had once been a stall and was now lined with sheet-music racks built into the corral walls. She stepped out into the sun and headed toward the front yard, composing.

How I Spent Our Anniversary. She wasn't sure whether it would be an entry in her notebook or a letter to the Twins. Gerry was down in Epps with Mama Lovey. There'd been no further word from Maxwell since his wire from Frankfurt, Germany, while on the first leg of the trip from Lesotho. *Under each tree is a green pool of pollen.* She paused on "pool," recalling how some members of the Committee of Inquiry reacted when Bible Man opened the meeting with a reading of Psalm 81. "Sheol" put them in mind of "Flat Shoals Road," one of the marks on the map for Eric Middlebrooks. Mattie still maintained that the murders were the work of a cult and that bodies of water held the key.

The Bible passage Mattie and the others had been working on was from Isaiah, the most motley compilation of all the Old Testament books. Zala had never much thought about how many different Bibles there were besides the hotel Gideon and the family King James, but Bible Man and the woman in white had brought along the Dartmouth Bible and six other versions in an effort to break the code. A complete

Isaiah text, Zala had learned, was contained in The Dead Sea Scrolls, discovered by several Bedouin boys in a cave in 1947. Mattie had been free-associating all morning: dead, boys, cave, sea; Pied Piper, Peter Pan, the Chattahoochee, Flat Shoals Road, Middlebrooks.

"Is it two o'clock yet?" Gloria was hobbling forward, a cardboard cylinder between her knees. The children ran through the flowerbed to hug Zala.

"My mom said to give this to you at two o'clock, when y'all married. But it's a nuisance."

"What is it?" Zala uncapped the cylinder.

"I hope you like it. It cost a fortune," Gloria said, stepping back when Kofi crowded her to help Zala unroll the poster.

"The circus, Mama! Can we go?"

"It's already gone," Kofi said. "While we were at Nana's."

"That's me." Kenti reached across Zala's hand to tap the cardboard. "I have an umbrella like that. It don't have all that stuff on it, but it's pink. Right?"

"That's the poster you were talking about, isn't it?" Gloria looked worried.

"Kiss your mother for me, Gloria."

"Can we go to the playground? It's just down the street."

"This neighborhood is the pits," Gloria said. "Round our way the creeps yell out nasty things. But around here they wave money at you."

"Wave money?"

Gloria pulled one hand free from her sweatshirt pouch and gestured. "They wave dollar bills as they drive by. So I give them my look." She leered, then chomp-chomped exposing her braces. Kofi and Kenti laughed.

"For a little while if you want," Zala said, and the two raced down the front lawn toward the street. Gloria pushed her face close to Zala's and showed off her braces again.

"Get on out of here, Gloria."

Zala watched the three jump from the grass to the sidewalk, then cross the street toward what looked like a sculpture park. Large wooden and fired-clay structures were set in a five-pointed-star pattern in a field of wood chips. She supposed the children would find a way to turn the art to their advantage. She slid the brown-shellacked circus poster back into the roll and started back to the carriage house.

The former instructor from the Atlanta Street Academy was leaning against one of the half-opened doors talking to the projectionist and the reporter. He'd already told the group how he'd hung in long after undercover infiltrators backed by the Justice Department had staged a coup at the Academy and had several community organizers fired. While his account tended to be self-serving, with numerous ellipses leaving his motives for staying on board open to question, his story of the infiltrators had been of interest, particularly to Speaker, who continually reminded the group of the necessity to close ranks and bring no one into Inquiry who couldn't be personally vouched for.

By the time the infiltrators hit the Street Academy, it was hurting for funds and suffering a split, one faction nervous about the Afrocentric philosophy another faction used to inform the Academy's curriculum. The infiltrators moved in and, according to the ASA defector, began keeping dossiers.

"I started a few dossiers of my own," the brother was saying. "Pretending concern about the children, they're pulling in staff one by one now to question them about community workers, neighborhood hangouts, and other staff members. The day we heard that the STOP mothers were going to have a rally in D.C.," the brother was saying as Zala came up, "they started asking about the mothers' connections."

"You can tell from the intelligence memos," the young reporter interrupted, "that there are a great many things going down behind the so-called investigation that are not being reported."

"That's a fact." Herman, the brother wearing the Gay Rights button, leaned out of the doorway and began cataloging the various abuses of civil rights suffered by the gay community as police raids on bars, antique shops, bathhouses, bookstores, coffeehouses, and cabarets stepped up in frequency and brutality. "All in the name of the investigation," he said. "And the thing is, the silence about it corrupts everybody. You know what I mean?"

This is how we spent the first part of our anniversary, Zala continued composing as she walked back into the carriage house. The Hot Spot film cases on the butcher block cart were stacked high. *P.S. Your cousin Gloria is wearing braces on her teeth these days.*

One minute's worth of eavesdropping on the moving-company boss and his employees confirmed what Mrs. Webber had ascertained for herself: namely, that the guests, whose presence the judge had declined to explain, were part of the very affair that was routing them from their home. Hardly an enclave, not with the front doors hanging ajar, it was nonetheless a private meeting, closed even to her, their hostess—their unprepared, hence initially reluctant, hostess, but their hostess all the same, who'd wanted nothing more than an opportunity to place at their disposal whatever it was they might need. She was not without resources. The judge wasn't the only Webber who could marshal human and material aid.

Merely irritated at first by their lack of civility, her gestures of hospitality and concern all but rebuffed, she'd been above all disappointed that they'd failed to recognize in her a person of good sense and good humor; moreover, of discretion. They apparently preferred, some of them at least, to view her as a paragon of aristocratic uselessness—such a deplorable cliché—and then to act accordingly. Persons of uncertain social status encountering someone like herself often adopted either a roughneck insolence or an ingratiating obsequiousness. The former she found exasperating; the latter thoroughly disgusted her. And so she'd behaved badly. Deliberately slow in setting up the silver service, she'd engaged in sardonic posturing as patently false as their self-important brio. Such a waste. And that hurt more than the effrontery. For what was life but relating?

Mrs. Webber leaned her cello case against the grandfather clock and looked in the glass. Under the towel her hair was hardening in the henna pack. Her face was tightening under the egg-white masque. She watched the pendulum swing across her reflection for a moment, saddened. What would her father have said of her performance out there in the carriage house? The throaty tick of the clock reminded her that the cleaners were due at three o'clock. She and the judge were expected at the Hyatt Regency for the bon voyage arranged in their honor at eight. Mrs. Webber headed toward the Dutch doors that led to the breezeway. She swung the top half open. The packers and the new housekeeper had their backs to her as they looked out over the patio.

Under the guise of admiring her gardens, two of the female guests had escorted Mrs. Webber to the doorway of the carriage house before she had time to indicate which pot held coffee, which tea. Supplies were being unpacked, charts taped to the wall. She'd lingered, hoping the materials would clarify the nature of their business. But then one of the seated women burst forth to *épater la bourgeoisie,* so scathing the cups had rattled in the saucers. A burlesque, Mrs. Webber had thought, of all the hysterical clamoring aimed at the city administration. But far from regarding the tirade as either neurotic or satiric, the others had received it with high solemnity as apocalyptic in vision, some of them even feeling spurred to flex their vocal cords as well.

Such an exalted sense of themselves, Mrs. Webber was thinking. Egg white flaked down the front of her cotton duster. She rose on tiptoe to look over the workers' heads. By all conventional standards those people out back would be deemed as lacking in influence. And yet it could not be denied, most certainly not by her, that they'd had the power to enlist the judge as an ally, further, to place him in a compromising position, and thus to hasten the Webbers' departure from Atlanta amid the hue and cry of many acquaintances who felt sullied by association. It was something to ponder, this power, the very thing she would have wished to discuss with them had she realized who they were at the time. She would have been disposed, had they been receptive, to bring to bear on their behalf the impressive weight of her contacts, and this despite their rudeness. She was not a mean-spirited woman.

In the final analysis, Mrs. Webber admired their pluck. Watching, she felt that whatever their agenda, it would be more appropriate to the situation concerning the children than the morbid sensationalism that had rendered all discourse in the city insensible. The unappetizing sight of acquaintances who otherwise conducted their lives in a rectilinear manner huddled over the buffet tables exchanging murder theories and off-the-record remarks from officials as though trading in commodities had made Mrs. Webber demur at more than one invitation.

Mrs. Webber signaled Hazel, the new housekeeper, and tapped her watch. Without waiting to see whether the new woman moved on to complete the inventory or continued to talk with the work crew at lunch, Mrs. Webber weaved her way to the upper hallway jammed with barrels to be taken to the cellar and those to be shipped to the steamship company. A linen runner on the sideboard in the formal dining room looked so forlorn, she closed the door and moved on past the other rooms, half-empty now and desolate. Once the scene of convivial gatherings, her home of late had been the stage for ludicrous melodramas.

Cliques of officials and civilians of various persuasions had been entering and exiting, then doubling back hoping to catch the others in flagrante delicto, a sarabande that owed as much to the role the judge had been playing as to a general and rampant love of drama. Confidant, liaison, advisor, he'd taken to imposing on himself and on the others peculiar habits of circumlocution and idiosyncratic argot for the purpose of—and this made her laugh—sparing his wife any undue anxiety. As if she were the one who needed cosseting. Her husband's faithful amanuensis seemed to think she did, all but resorting to sign language when she ventured to make conversation beyond the superficial amenities. Grown more and more furtive, the judge's secretary spent less and less time preparing the judge's papers for archival storage in favor of listening at doors, holding the household staff at bay, and monitoring the schedule of their house guest, a student from Morocco working on his master's at Atlanta U.

One morning, for motives best known to the principal players, to whom Mrs. Webber gave wide berth, the research aide had staged an unseemly altercation with their housekeeper of the past six years, the stately, albeit eccentric Mrs. Walker. Mrs. Webber was given to understand that the source of the imbroglio was a violation of diet. More likely a spy-and-counterspy transgression. In any case, it was easier to concur that Mrs. Walker be replaced than to enter into the foolishness.

After the housekeeper's dismissal, the judge, the secretary, and the macrobiotic aide remained cloistered behind the study doors for long sessions, as in the days when the judge was handing down the more notable opinions of his career. Then men in dark suits began arriving at odd hours of night to caucus, often till dawn, leaving the desks layered with memoranda of a confidential nature. Mrs. Webber took to wearing her glasses dangling on the beaded chain around her neck. She was not a stupid woman. She knew her husband was not being asked to preside at the trial. Criminal court had not been his bailiwick. And too, if the suspects were to be brought before the bar, neither his most baleful visage nor his most formidable robes could hope to produce the magic required for that particular mystery play. A black Black judge or a white white judge, not her ambiguously pale husband, would be necessary if they hoped to bring the affair to a satisfactory close using one or the other suspect groups as the villains.

She had made no attempt to extract information or to verbally censure. Rather, she had selected an opportune time to propose a sabbatical. She had placed a bottle of digitalis to the left of her husband's tray in his bathroom. And to the right, she had set down their passports and the ring he'd given her on their fiftieth anniversary. He had only to choose. She'd made her choice in their forty-fourth year together, a year spent consulting round-the-clock with physicians: with his for his heart, with hers for her ulcers.

Mrs. Webber stopped by the cartons near the study door. She pressed her cotton gloves down between each finger until the seams adhered to the cream caked on her hands. She folded back the flaps of a carton marked "Family Room Memorabilia." From the various shapes of the heavily wrapped bundles, she could identify the items—plaques, statues, but mostly photographs. Trips abroad, graduations, dinner dances, friends. Educators, legislators, sportsmen, clubwomen. People who'd helped create a world whose center still held. Some, those alive, she was honored to call part of the circle. Others had passed on, leaving a legacy subsequent generations had had to stretch to merit. *Enfants terribles,* able from time to time to make reputations by challenging the Old Guard, could match the old in boldness but rarely in stature. Most certainly not the overnight orators admitting to no impediment—"by any means necessary" indeed—except the unglamorous dailiness of building a movement. Loudly they invoked "community," "the people," and other terms of sacerdotal function as they lambasted the very circles that had the "means necessary"—the money, the background, the knowledge, the courage.

"Ha!"

Ivy Webber tossed her head. Flakes of red mingled with white sprinkled her shoulders. Where would the race be were it not for the conscientious men and women who'd built the schools, the banks, produced the art, the wisdom, and saw to it that laws were passed that guaranteed continual progress? she wanted to say to the hysterical woman out back. She wanted to take that woman by the shoulders and shake her.

She tried to think more kindly of the woman, who'd apparently been in much pain. The center is holding, Mrs. Webber imagined herself saying to the poor distraught creature, whom a woman in a batik dress had drawn back to her chair.

Mrs. Webber touched the towel, felt at her face, then looked at her

watch. It had been her intention to retire to the carriage house immediately after church. A difficult passage in the Villa-Lobos piece she'd
been practicing for her swan song needed perfecting. Removing her hat
pins that morning, she'd been teeter-tottering about the piece, about
the very idea of a swan song, not to Atlanta, but to the well-wishers
who'd begun farewell preparations while the announcement of the
Webber sabbatical was still on her lips. She'd been re-experiencing too
a more troublesome tottering as she'd taken off her hat. She'd felt
gloomier than she had in years. Then the cars had arrived and parked
back of the carriage house. Her mother would have handed her the
broom to dispatch the visitors. But Mrs. Webber saw in the situation an
opportunity to resolve her conflict, not about the cello piece, but about
a troubling split that, worse than aching joints, often woke her from
sleep: duty to others versus duty to home. A woman of her capabilities
should have been able to contribute something more vital to the crisis
than a personal check, music lessons, a two-hour march with the widow
King, and a call to the telephone company at the request of the real-
estate agent. More painful than bursitis was the suspicion that in her
haste to leave Atlanta she was removing herself from an arena in which
to develop. Her mother had found her arena in the women's department
of the sanctified church. Mrs. Webber's marriage had opened up a larger
arena in which to test her capacities. What might her parents make of
her choices?

Mrs. Webber resolved to put to rest thoughts that made her uneasy.
Aboard ship, no land in sight to distract, she'd play backgammon
should she experience any sense of loose-endedness. Strolling the deck,
she could draw about her many pleasurable memories of the Atlanta
years. For one, the Sunday musicales. How spirited things became once
she'd taken on scholarship students. Those well-mannered and oblig-
ingly devoted young people had added pep to the performances at
churches, auditoriums, and the High Museum.

All of which the crisis had drastically changed. Some of the pupils
began bringing family members along to rehearsals. Then they brought
classmates no longer willing to remain after school for music. As hysteria mounted in the city, caveats issued by her pupils' parents had altered
not only the scheduling—travel canceled and the ensemble confined to
chambers—but the overall ambience as well. All through the winter,

they rehearsed in the carriage house in the presence of stony-eyed sentinels convinced that music could lure the participants, if unchaperoned, into erotic predicaments—the theory that had gained ascendancy for a while over cult killing, although Housekeeper Walker had held fast to demon possession, her all-purpose answer to any act of aggression she viewed as "senseless."

By spring, Mrs. Webber herself had begun to play hesitantly, woodenly, in the end as badly as her most nervous pupil. No longer able to unself-consciously absorb the music, prevented from taking the wood's vibrations in full through her lap, her rapture proof of a lewd disposition to which the young should not be exposed, she'd elected to bow out altogether from the Palm Sunday program and spent the day in bed fingering the pattern in her candlewick bedspread.

"May I?" The moving man's huge hands were prying apart the doors of the judge's study before she could answer. "Think we can finish up in here now?"

She stayed his arm and directed him to the memorabilia cartons. Holding her jaws as still as possible, she said, "Make sure they're secured. The cellar is dampish."

"Yes, ma'am," he said before she had finished speaking, and hopped to it, yanking tape from the roller with a disagreeable sound.

She arched her brows at what she thought was a note of sarcasm in the big man's manner, but not without a twinge of regret as she saw powdery white sift to the floor. She would have liked to converse with this gray-haired man who kept himself so fit. What was his regimen? And what did he make of the group out back? Might not the two of them take a moment out from their respective duties to explore over coffee what two mature persons such as themselves might do to offer solace and succor to the conferees? Did he have an opinion about the appropriateness of the unfortunate mothers' decision to hold a rally in the nation's capital? What did he think the city fathers might do at the prospect of a long, hot summer? What would this man, who'd obviously been around and was no stranger to the school of hard knocks, recommend a person such as herself to do, given her capacities? She truly wanted to do some one very important thing before leaving.

But his manner discouraged her. And too, his lip hair, and the Vandyke, visible once he lifted his chin. It was totally off-putting. Insufferable, in fact. For if this man had the presumption to mimic the great Dr. Du Bois in appearance, then his obsequious shuffling was a mockery of both Du Bois and herself.

She hoped the family that real-estate agent Delia DeVore had found to lease the Webber home were as responsible as their references said. In less than twenty-four hours, she and the judge would receive the last of their inoculations in the Pan American hangar of Kennedy Airport. Only a masochist would persist in teeter-tottering having already decided on a course of action. Her mother had taught her, "Dammit, Ivy, don't flounder, simpering like a ninny. Make a decision and be done with it."

Mrs. Webber made out a card to place on the arm of the divan, a reminder to the packers that the piece should be crated with a generous supply of cedar chips to ward off moths and mildew. Moreover, they should refrain from wrapping it in that infernal bubbled plastic companies seemed to love so much these days. The plush would be rubbed bald in transit to and from the cellar.

Mrs. Webber capped her pen, shoved it deep within the pocket of her duster, and glided into the study. The room was a labyrinth formed by the drums of odds and ends not yet sorted. Mrs. Webber opened a length of unbleached muslin and spread it across the velvet divan. She sat down quietly and crossed her legs at the ankles. She clasped her hands on her lap and leaned back, straining to hear what her husband and his visitor were saying across the room.

The judge was seated in front of the fieldstone fireplace in a ladder-back chair, his slippered feet on a hassock they'd brought back from their trip to Cairo. Opposite him sat his visitor, an impatient young man kneading his fist and cracking his knuckles. The judge was presenting a short treatise on the legal conundrums of wiretap evidence. Had he been speaking with other than calm equanimity, his wife would have interrupted, but the flat, measured cadence of his voice never varied, despite the young man's frequent interruptions. Content that her husband was honoring their pact, Mrs. Webber smoothed the muslin on either side of her.

"Can we get back to the issue of the wiretaps, Judge Webber?" Spence planted his foot by the fireplace screen. "Did they begin bugging after the threat to Lubie Geter, or does the tap date back to the Terrell case, when a caller said he was holding the boy in Alabama, or did they begin with the manager of the Cap'n Peg's food joint getting the call from Yusuf Bell that he was about to be killed?"

With his ring finger and thumb, Webber dragged the bags under his eyes down, a gesture Spence took as a signal to continue.

"I need specific dates in order to file an FIA. We know that the Justice Department arranged a meeting between the Task Force and a sex-exploitation consultant from Kentucky when the Terrell case was still fresh. Was that the point when the wiretaps began?" Spence waited. He thought he might have misread the earlier cue, for now Webber sighed deeply, as if it was all too tiresome.

"You are convinced that having the wiretap reports will—"

"Having them and making them public," Spence interrupted.

"May I refer you once again to the Nixon caper and remind you that the American public did not give a hoot about the Watergate tapes?"

"I don't agree that people didn't give a damn. There was outrage. There was talk of impeachment. There was a groundswell of support for Barbara Jordan's demands for the tapes."

"Talk."

"All right," Spence said, leaning toward Webber's chair. "What's your answer? Why didn't Nixon destroy the tapes and why didn't the people demand his head on a plate?"

Webber repositioned himself in his chair. The sun shone through the curly gray fringe of hair that ringed his head like a horseshoe. The freckles and skin moles on his pate looked bright red.

"Why not? Because, Mr. Spencer, of the overwhelming, all-consuming, thoroughly compelling desire of the American people not to know. They do not want to know how close we came to losing it, how close we'll always be to losing this country, because we do not wish to know." He waved Spence's objection away with a frown, then started up again, sweat glistening on his forehead.

"That close," Webber emphasized, squinching his fingers under his eyes. "Those rogues came that close to stealing the country with the co-operation of the entire intelligence community and the attorney general's office. Did I say 'cooperation'? I misspoke myself," he laughed, slapping the armrest, his chest wheezing.

"I don't laugh out of cynicism," Webber said, collecting himself.

"Fear," he whispered, popping his eyes wide. "So close . . . so close." He shuddered.

"Of course many saw in the public's lackadaisical response to the Watergate scandal evidence that the American character is inherently totalitarian, arguing that the American people are not particularly alarmed to discover that the country's become what we say the Soviet Union is. Debatable. And beside the point. The point is, the majority don't give a hoot in hell. They don't want to shoulder the burden of knowing.

"It's so dangerous," Webber croaked. "And such a terrible waste."

Spence rubbed his sweaty palms together and tried to get back on track.

"I am interested in the results of the wiretaps. The Atlanta tapes."

"Alleged tapes."

Spence took in a deep breath. "I don't mean to be quarrelsome, but it's been established that either the state or the feds or both conducted wiretaps. It's been established by too many sources, including you, to keep up the subterfuge of 'alleged.' "

When the old man did not respond, Spence reminded himself not to crowd the man. Webber might not know anything useful. But Spence had a hunch he did. If not about the GBI's secret investigation or the FBI's secret investigation, at least know of what was going on in the DA's office.

As Webber took off on a rambling explanation of how various law-enforcement agencies related to each other, Spence glanced at the one photograph that remained on the otherwise empty bookshelves.

"But have you seen the LEAA memo, Judge Webber? The one that describes the mutilations? I've reason to believe that it does exist and that the information was gotten through the taps."

"You do realize, Mr. Spencer, that the medical examiners' reports lend no credence to theories of castrations and ritual stabbings. Having taken the pains to read through the depositions of the police, I would concur with the reports. The battered condition of some of the bodies could be explained by the action of rocks and debris in the water. Those currents are strong despite the seeming calm on the surface. And both in the case of the bodies recovered from the river and those found in the woods, the wildlife . . . dogs . . . the elements . . ." He wound his hand around in the air, not bothering to finish the statement.

"Would concur" . . . "could be explained." If we both didn't know better, Spence was thinking. He was sure that Webber could verify the existence of the rumored memo. It was even likely that he had a copy of the document in his possession. Why was he suddenly so chary? He was a wealthy, powerful person on his way out of the country. What the hell was he afraid of? Spence gripped his hands together and forced himself to take it slowly.

"I get the feeling, Judge Webber, that you're sidestepping my question."

"Hmm."

Spence listened intently as Webber began talking again. Often, in otherwise innocuous answers, he inserted crucial bits of information. He was now describing favored conduits the DA's office and others used for "leaks" either to shape public opinion or to bait other agencies into trading evidence. Surely Webber was not suggesting that the authorities had started the rumor of the LEAA memo. Nor could the two most recent public statements by the FBI come under the heading of "leaks."

A few days ago, an agent addressing a Rotary club down in Macon had announced that at least four of the officially acknowledged twenty-three cases were virtually solved: parents had murdered their children. Considering the agent's timing—hard on the heels of STOP's mobilization for the D.C. rally and the peaking of on-the-street discussions about the mutilation memo—the agent's statement seemed designed to scuttle support of STOP and to deflect attention, perhaps, from the memo. The recent statement of FBI director William Webster, countering the theory of race hatred as motive—"It may be a preference for Blacks rather than a prejudice against them"—struck Spence as a panicked attempt to defuse the contents of the memo whose secrecy could no longer be secured. Spence concluded that the old judge was directing him to monitor the conduits, alert to the fact that what was being revealed was a clue to what was being obscured.

"And what of the memo itself? Does it exist?"

"I've good reason to think so, Mr. Spencer, having heard repeated references to it. . . ."

Webber seemed about to name names and cite passages. He shifted in his chair as though to get up, but only moved to adjust his jacket. Looking ill at ease, he ran his hands back and forth along the carved armrests of the chair.

"The memo exists, Judge Webber. And it does describe mutilations. And there are secret memos about the wiretaps as well. They date
back, I suspect, to the phone call the authorities refused to air—for the
public. At least as far back as that." Spence paused but was not contra-
dicted.

"I suspect too that there was something overheard through the tap
that prompted the authorities in February to put the Walker boy on the
list the minute he was reported missing from Bowen Homes. And that
that 'something' supports the evidence that the explosion at Bowen
Homes back in October was not an accident caused by a faulty boiler.
You'll excuse me, but this is not an intellectual exercise for me."

Webber stiffened.

"One final thing, if you would," Spence said. "The Dewey Baugus
case. Did the friend of the Baugus family become a suspect in the children's case because he'd vowed revenge for the Baugus boy's slaying? Or
did the DA keep him under surveillance because the beating death of
the white child in spring of '79 is related in some other way to the
deaths of the Black children which supposedly began in summer '79? In
other words, did the man murder both the Baugus boy and some of the
other children? Is that it? You said on previous occasions that he was
brought in for questioning and kept under surveillance. Is he a link to
the killers? Does the DA think that?"

Webber ran his hands along the armrests. Spence watched the spots
in the wood blur from the sweat of the judge's hands, then gleam from
the buffing of his sleeve.

"I'm hoping you realize, Judge Webber, that a number of lives depend on our ability to move. The authorities won't. Somebody has to. If
you have information and aren't willing to share it, I hold you accountable for the life of my son."

The judge wrenched away, but it was Mrs. Webber's gasp that made
Spence wheel around. He hadn't been aware of her presence in the room,
or of movers dawdling in the hall by the open door. The big moving
man with the patch of lip hair stepped into the study as Mrs. Webber
rose from her seat.

Then the four of them froze, transfixed by the sound of sirens approaching the estate. Ear-splitting, the alarm was accompanied by a
blare of lights. Blue flashed from the brass candlestick to the French

doors leading to the gardens. Red spun across the wall of bookcases and lit the photograph on the shelf: the judge in a derby, swallowtail cut-away, striped pants; his bride in veil and gown, the train swept to the front in a lake of bright satin that cascaded down the cathedral steps. Motionless, they watched each other as the vehicles sped past the Webber estate to some desperate situation elsewhere.

Mrs. Webber was the first to move. She crossed to a drum of costumes and slid the lid into place. The judge stretched in his chair. Mrs. Webber nodded to the big man, who waved the other packers in. She turned and scanned her husband's face. A dose of salts, a nap, and he'd be right as rain, she thought.

"Please clear the room swiftly," she said very pointedly, then left the room.

"Is this a documentary or a movie movie?" someone called out in the dark.

"This is the real deal," the projectionist explained. "The movie clips I mentioned are on another reel. This is a work print," he added. "As you've no doubt already guessed."

Horizontal lines passed through the grainy print, jumpy, rough footage of an underground garage.

"Deep Throat."

"Quiet."

Leaning against a silver Rolls-Royce, a woman with short auburn hair softly curled and streaked with gray was knuckling her chin as she listened to the off-camera interviewer clumsily framing his question. With her pinky, she played with the paisley scarf cowled at the neck of her hunter-green jacket and dug the point of her knuckles more deeply into her chin. Then, straightening, before the interviewer had an opportunity to paraphrase the question once again, she zipped open her briefcase and smoothed it flat on the hood of the Rolls.

"It is our task to support the growth of Freedom Focus through publications which we distribute to our various organizations. We research issues related to troublesome groups in order to provide our members with the necessary materials for helping those groups become less troubled."

She withdrew from the accordion pocket a yellow binder and slid the pages free. The camera moved in over her shoulder. "For example," she said, setting the yellow plastic aside, "in order to assist the Blacks in their plight, we are looking at statistics on teenage pregnancy."

"Your purpose is to assist the Blacks?"

In profile, the woman's face was a model of forbearance. "As it happens," she said, leafing through the pages, "actual statistics of the past six years show a marked decrease in the incidence of teenage births among the Blacks. But the Blacks are an emotional people. They do not respond to facts or care about who's conducting research and compiling statistics. They do, however, respond to charges of low morals and poor family life. On issues of social parity, they may be militant, but regarding domestic life, very conservative—that is to say, defensive. Predictably so. So we are looking at various figures related to illegitimacy and other perniciousness."

"Even though, as you say, the figures show a decline?"

The camera swung around in time to record, full-face, the expression of tight, terse strain. Then it zoomed in on the loose pages spread on the hood of the Rolls. With one hand fisted, the joint of the index finger gouging the cleft in her chin, she selected pages to be placed before the lens. Tables, graphs, bibliography, study guides with questions and an answer key, directories of media people, then photos and rough sketches for posters. Pregnant Black girls, seated, standing, kneeling, photographed from an eye-level angle perspective, underwent a stark metamorphosis in the drawings, their expressions blanked, bearings slumped, surroundings made shabby in some, ridiculous bad-taste consumption in others. Girls gazing longingly through the bars of a school gate while junkies brushed past on the street. A teen seen through the window of a tumbledown shack as she folded diapers, schoolbooks abandoned in a cobwebbed corner. Several big-bellied girls in angora sweaters and glittery skirts compared jewelry in the intake office at welfare.

"Is that correct?" the interviewer persisted. "Figures for teenage pregnancy among Blacks show a decline? It's tapering off then, not such a big problem?"

"It is perceived as a serious problem by both the American people and the Blacks themselves."

"So your organization 'assists' by publicizing it as a big headache, as a drain on the taxpayer, is that it? About how much, would you say, is your particular organization prepared to spend to—"

"The American taxpayer needs little encouragement to view Blacks as a burden. The welfare system"—the camera caught in close-up the slight curl of her lip—"has been in a shambles since its inception."

Papers reassembled, the woman slid them back onto one binder.

"Is there a contingency plan if Blacks stabilize their situation? As you say, the incidence of teen births is decreasing. So if through your organization's assistance the issue is taken up by that community and re-solved in such a way as to—"

She snapped her briefcase closed. "And how long would it take for people to perceive it so? No, we feel that the American people will see the necessity for declaring these families unfit." She jingled her car keys.

"What exactly does your organization propose, in plain speech?"

"We feel that those babies should be separated from those young people who cannot care for even themselves. We propose special board-ing schools where they can grow up to become useful citizens without resorting to crime or depending on welfare."

"Forceful removal of children?"

"Voluntary, purely voluntary. There are many among the Blacks who favor this approach. Ministers, doctors, teachers, and others as well."

"But . . . I mean, you don't really think—"

"He don't get it, does he?" whispered a viewer.

"I'm not sure I get it either. You're sure this isn't a movie?"

Horizontal lines ran across the scene. A light flashed; then, as the camera was directed on the Rolls going past the navy-deck-gray columns toward hazy daylight, the film was overexposed. After a jump shot, quivery white subtitles against a black-and-white poster of a preg-nant Black girl looking up from a tub chair, wrist upturned as she tested the temperature of milk in a baby bottle, verified that the footage was shot in Silver Springs, Maryland, September 1980.

"I need a smoke. This is spookier than the mercenary camp stuff."

"But what kind of 'assistance' is that? That's . . . that's . . ."

"Kidnapping."

"Hold up, y'all. There's a reel here somewhere that's about that—white people and their need to grab colored children."

"Just so it ain't some more of those mercenary training camps. I've had my fill. . . . Vernon, you going with Laf?"

Zala followed Mason out onto the patio, collecting last-minute pledges and statements on the way.

"Any word yet?"

Lafayette was squatting down, turning on the one radio someone had thought to bring along. He shook his head. There was no mention of the latest missing person, Larry Rogers, he reported. They moved aside as others stepped out into the sunshine.

" 'Voluntary'?"

"Ain't that a bitch! An infant's going to sign up for a boarding school."

"I'm not sure I get it," the sister from SAFE said. She looked up at the rooster weathervane swerving on its pole on the roof. One of the fathers looked up too. "I mean, are all these movie movies or what?"

The father turned his eyes from the roof.

"Don't ask me," he said.

"In your opinion, Judge Webber, since both the prosecution and the defense would be saddled with messy, incomplete records, can there be a trial? If, as you say, the wiretap evidence—"

Spence turned from the French doors when the judge began laughing. It was a long, wheezy laugh that ended with his cuffs in his eyes. As good an answer as any, Spence supposed, closing the doors behind the movers. "Virtually solved" and "impending arrests," then, were to discourage "cottage-industry sleuthing," as one City Hall rep had put it at breakfast in Paschal's. And, more to the point, to discourage defense squads or "vigilante groups," as both the mayor and the commissioner denied having said when the Techwood group's lawyers threatened to sue for slander.

"I guess there'll be no trial unless citizens bring it about."

Citizens. The word hung in the air like a life sentence.

Ever since the Patrick Baltazaar "slip-up" and the step-up of disappearances of men, women, and children in March and April, the ratio of energy invested by the authorities in the children's case was panning out as four parts PR, mostly praise for a well-behaved citizenry and appeals to frightened conventioneers and businesses; three parts empty announcements, whenever civilian tempers grew hot; two parts threats and accusations, aimed at both civilians and official agencies; and one part investigation. More than ever, Spence was persuaded that the city was playing a waiting game.

"Son of Sam" had held the city of New York in terror for over a year before the police stopped him, his Ford Galaxy sedan pulled over for a traffic violation. The Yorkshire Ripper had been on a five-year rampage of slash attacks and murders before he was stopped, arrested initially for theft. John Wayne Gacy managed to lure, through his Pogo the Clown act and his ability to hire through his contracting business, thirty-three young men and boys over a three-year period before the Illinois police followed odd tire tracks leading from the river to his yard. And now Joseph Paul Franklin of the Defenders of the White Seed—sought in six states in connection with burglaries, robberies, synagogue bombings, and murder spread over two years; wanted in connection with the shooting of Larry Flynt of *Hustler;* wanted for questioning in the sniping of Vernon Jordan of the Urban League; and implicated in the New York Subway Slasher case—was still on the run.

How long would it take for one of the Atlanta killers to run a red light or to bungle a bank heist with a missing child in the getaway car? How long would it take after the arrest and questioning for information about Sonny and the others to trickle out? The Charles Manson band had been on trial for 129 days, with information about orgies of murders inching out daily, before we heard about the Benedict Canyon rampage, which they hoped would start a race war. The People's Temple trials were still going on in California two and a half years later, the whereabouts of many who'd been at the settlement but not among the more than 900 dead to date unknown, the case building up against U.S. and Guyanese authorities still being refuted. The hunted-for suitcases of money and the posted rewards hadn't resulted in any more information than the Atlanta reward had.

"I don't envy Maynard Jackson," Webber said suddenly.

"I don't either."

"I'm surprised to hear you say so. You've had a change of heart, it would seem."

"I'd like to think that if I were in his shoes, I'd handle things more . . . well, differently," Spence said. "But I hate to think of how many Black people would have been rounded up, beaten up, railroaded, and worse if Maynard and Lee Brown were not running things. I hate to think of how this state of emergency would be used by . . . But I'm in my own shoes. Do they know about the feds' taps? Were they done with Brown and Jackson's knowledge?"

Beyond the French doors, at the far end of the walk, the big man was restacking cartons onto straps that lay crisscrossed on the ground. How many families, Spence wondered, had recently moved to new quarters and then had a member disappear? Might a mover return to a home to ask if everything was accounted for, then pick out his next victim? Bible Man had told the group that the man with the satyr-like beard had accosted him getting out of a cab. "Secret society up there?" He'd lifted his hairy chin in the direction of the reconverted stable at the top of the hill. Spence had just about brought his mind back under control from the outlandish stories of zombies, human sacrifices, blood rituals, but each time he saw the man, paranoia washed through him.

"I don't have much time," Spence said, crossing the room. "And I apologize for tiring you out and keeping you so long, but I've got to know—"

"If my doctors had their way," Webber cut in, "I'd be resting in bed from here on out."

Released from his usual self-imposed ban on personal references, Webber stretched. His socked feet snuffled against the fireplace screen. The joints of the chair groaned.

Panic gripped Spence. Webber was broadly hinting it was time for a nap.

"After a brief vacation on the Adriatic, I'll be sojourning to some of the places of my misbegotten youth. If my heart holds out," Webber added, patting his breast pocket. He whipped out his handkerchief and wiped his face and hands. He was definitely making motions to adjourn. Frantically, Spence surveyed the room. He could not leave without getting the tapes he came for.

"Judge Webber, five minutes more."

"So much has changed, I imagine," his voice drowsy and far-off, "since Brazil's development of the interior . . ."

Spence was not listening. He was feeling around the fireplace for a loose brick. He went to the bookcases and opened the glass doors underneath. He crossed back in front of the fireplace to the log box built under the window. He moved kindling aside; there was nothing but old newspapers. He looked out the open window. The heavy scent of flowers and damp loam distracted him for a moment. Mattie had taken one look at the gardens and said to Paulette, "I've never seen this much foxglove outside of a *curandera*'s botanica. It's larger than the herbarium we have at the lab. Who would cultivate this much tannia and mandrake but a witch?" And off they'd gone spinning tales of the supernatural.

The Inquiry Committee was full of characters, and he was dependent on an old codger lost in reverie about treks in the bush to study lawmaking among the "naif." As Spence drew back into the room, he remembered the framed wedding picture and went over to the bookshelves.

". . . When one is lost," Webber was saying, not hearing the crackle of glass, "it isn't the number of days that one will recall, but the immense uncertainty that eats at the heart second by second by second . . ."

Whether the judge meant to describe the vastness of the Brazilian interior, or the course of the Atlanta investigation, or the various avenues of assistance open to him, Spence used the opportunity to step in close with the glass-spattered piece of paper, kick the hassock aside, and lean down into Judge Webber's face.

"That is so. Now, let's discuss the rest of the wiretap report. Names, dates, places. Let's talk particulars, Judge. Does this report mean the Georgia Bureau compiled a case, then sealed it up? Does this paragraph mean the FBI have sealed their books too? Judge Webber, please."

"Mr. Spencer," Judge Webber began, his voice warbly. He stared into the fire, then spoke again. "You've said on numerous occasions, and I quote you, 'Nothing's in place.' Do you think for one minute that you and your associates are in position to contain the storm that would erupt if results of various investigations were disclosed to the public?"

"Spell it out."

"Sit down, Mr. Spencer, and collect yourself."

Reluctantly, Spence seated himself again. He braced his wrists against the reinforced inseams at his knees and the paper stopped shaking. He could wait. He'd learned how.

Thumbs hooked in his sash, Mason inhaled the energizing aroma of consensus. They were all in accord about the basic things. One, that the official investigation was hamstrung and that the combination hobbling the Task Force was the official list, the official victim profile, and the stubborn resistance to acknowledge the links a map made obvious. Two, that they, the Community Committee of Inquiry, had five solid things to go on: their list of victims, their map, the testimony taped at Bowen Homes, the thirty-eight reports from witnesses, and their list of seventeen suspects. Three, that whatever theory individual members favored—cult, Klan types, drugs, prostitution, porn, or "pederasty" (the term the gay community insisted upon to counter the media's use of "homosexual" interchangeably with "porn," "sex for hire," and "sexual exploitation of children")—Inquiry should conduct their investigation discreetly; further, that Inquiry's work should have top priority on everyone's agenda for five straight weeks. Mason had expected Mac and Speaker to balk at the last two items. And from the way Marzala, Lafayette, and Herman were going through the pledges again, evidently they did too.

Recent plant closings had been taking up all of Mac's time. When he wasn't conducting stress-management seminars for community workers or group raps with the laid-off workers, he was hogging Inquiry meetings to tell them about it. Conditions were ripe for wholesale despair, Mac had concluded. Were overripe for a socialist groundswell, Leah had predicted. Or for more right-wing demagoguery, Marzala had sighed. Same ole same ole, Mason had thought.

But Mac had signed the pledge. Speaker too. Below his signature, Mason noted as Herman passed it across the table, Speaker had suggested that members of Inquiry be polled as to their preparedness to go underground, a strong possibility given the wolfish tone of the intelligence memos.

Mason completed his summation, then turned to Detective Dowell, who immediately went to the board to instruct them on triangulation and to show them how to use the scanners, the radio device for foxing on a moving target's position.

"You understand that this equipment is for the purpose of visual aids only," he said solemnly. "And that I will not be accompanying you over the route."

The sister from SAFE raised her hand. She was pretty sure that Dowell was being facetious. She thought he would wink at any second and clear up her confusion. She looked at the other two cops for a clue.

"Check this out!" Vernon said breathlessly as he ran in, reloading his trusty Instamatic. Everyone in the carriage house swung around toward the door.

"We were on the Stewart-Lakewood strip making our contacts. And up by the Pickfair intersection, where a lot of kidnaps were tried—" He was pointing the camera at the map to direct their attention to the red-alert markings in that area of the route when Lafayette ran in behind him.

"They've made it a play street!"

"You got to be kidding! That's one of the most dangerous—"

"See what I mean?" the SAFE sister said. "And people in the neighborhood don't even know."

"Pickfair? Man, you can't mean Pickfair!"

"You heard me. Parks and Recreation are setting up playground equipment."

"What's the matter with those mugs?"

"No coordination of information." Dowell rolled the chalk in his hand. "Typical. But did you locate Innis?"

"Not yet, but we're on his trail. We think he's got a caravan together checking out some of the locations his witness mentioned. We think Sondra O'Neale is with them—the sister from Emory U, the one who's been riding James Baldwin around gathering info for an article. We *think*," Vernon stressed, crumpling the Kodak wrapper.

"We need to move quickly," Lafayette urged.

"What about the films? The projectionist began unbuckling the straps of a Hot Spot case.

"We'll stick to the agenda," Zala said. "The first team get ready."

Dowell chewed on his lower lip. He'd not completed the chalk talk to his satisfaction. Nor were they giving him time to turn his back while one of the scanners was being removed. For the record, he'd meant to absent himself. But things were happening too fast. Mason was giving last-minute orientation. Gaston was double-checking the tool kits made up for each team. Before the projectionist could fit on a new reel, Team One had followed the vets out the door. Dowell ducked out to go over points about the triangulator.

"Don't forget," Mason called out, "if you can't report back here, we rendezvous at the Hyatt at nine p.m."

Zala groaned and leaned against Mattie's shoulder. It was the one piece in the overall operation she'd vetoed. The Hyatt was too conspicuous a place for them to be meeting. The lobby phones were rarely free. The conversation pits were near the fountain, making it hard to talk in groups. She'd argued hard for the Marriott. Parking was easy, and the lot was visible from the wide-paned lounge area. The restaurant–coffee shop stayed open all night. More phones were accessible. But Spence had been persistent, persistent and persuasive, though he'd offered nothing particularly convincing other than "It's important." Thinking he'd arranged for Teo to meet them there, she pointed out that the Marriott was as convenient from the highway as the Hyatt was. "Trust me," he'd said again, not meeting her eyes.

"Damn," the schoolteacher said. "I can't get over that." He beckoned several people over to the map. In addition to a cluster of markings for victims and attempted abductions, there was a large asterisk and a pink dot in the Lakewood Heights section, the stomping grounds of a group of prime suspects fingered by an anonymous witness who'd walked into the STOP office in February. He continued to shake his head.

"Um-believable, as my students would say. Doesn't anybody in city government check with each other first?"

"No, that's why they can't come up with one damn thing," Alice Moore said.

The others turned in her direction. It was the first word she'd spoken since sounding off at lunchtime. She opened her bag and searched for a tissue, uncomfortable with the attention.

"Heard the one they're telling down at Simmons's barbershop?" Mattie called over to Preener and crossed her legs to draw attention away from Alice. "Seems there was this three-time divorcée who couldn't get laid. Her first husband was a dwarf—he couldn't reach it.

Her second husband was gay—he didn't want it. Her third husband was on the APD—he couldn't find it."

"Revun Mattie!" Preener said.

"Not in good taste?" Mattie fingered her earrings.

"Not in good taste," Zala said, checking off item number 4 on the flipchart. She was pleased to see that Alice was chuckling into her tissue, for one split second wasn't clutching her handbag as though ready to run out at a moment's notice. "The next item is the upcoming issue of *The Call*. Specifically, is there a conflict between pledged confidentiality and the necessity for informing the community?"

"Aren't we ready to roll?"

"That's next, brother." Speaker reached across the projectionist's arm and turned off the lamp switch. "I've left the lead page free should any of us have a sudden urge to draft some copy tomorrow morning," Speaker called out to the group.

"We get it," the sister from SAFE said. "In case we uncover anything tonight."

The members followed Speaker to the table and began reading as soon as he set down the pasted-up sheets of heavy paper.

Mason caught Zala's signal and inserted himself between the two people most likely to stretch the critique into an all-night blowout; Mac, with his psychosocial sermonizing, and Baba, the cultural nationalist. With Leah gone, her trigger-ready-Marxist-teacher reflex absent, the probability of another impromptu seminar was reduced considerably. As for Speaker, the film notes inside the suitcase lids had him occupied.

"We need hard, critical feedback, people," Speaker called out, shuffling through the stacks of video cassettes. "Whether it's principled, reasonable, or not."

"Noted," Mason answered and leaned closer to the pages.

In a glance, it was clear that the issue in progress would continue to do what other recent issues of the newsletter had done: relate all local, national, and international news to the specific situation in Atlanta.

The secret Broederbond, guardian of South Africa's White National Party, was compared to the ultra-right's growing influence on United States foreign and domestic policies, suggesting that it was mandatory, the editorial argued, for Atlantans not to be sidetracked by charges of racist paranoia or appeals to good race relations. In Chicago, the lawsuit being brought by the ACLU and the Alliance to End Repression against the City of Chicago, the FBI, the CIA, and the Defense Intelligence Agency for the illegal surveillance, harassment, infiltration, and intimidation of numerous organizations—active PTAs and local chapters of the League of Women Voters among them—occasioned *The Call*'s editors to suggest that safeguards against agents provocateurs be built into those groups pushing for a civilian review team in Atlanta. The authorities in Chicago had gone so far as to compile lists of people who borrowed public library books by and/or about Black people.

"Wake up, Africans," *The Call* warned in bold type. "If Black books are considered a threat to national security now, what will tomorrow bring? Organize! For if conditions had fundamentally changed, would things like this be going on in Chicago, would the killings be going on in Atlanta with local, state, and federal agents continually hindering the investigations?"

Mason exchanged a look with Zala. The paper was at its best when Speaker's rhetoric was subordinated to analysis, Mason felt. For example, there was a two-inch discussion of U.S. aid to El Salvador that was crisp and brief. Thousands of unionists were being murdered in El Salvador, a situation that American industrialists, greedy for union-free areas, found convenient. Mason slid that page to the side of the table where Mac stood reading. Let him read too how Mellon Bank was investing in South Korean steel while workers in Pittsburgh "despaired." Maybe that page would wake Mac up. Runaway capital had nothing to do with coffee breaks or poor job skills.

"You should send a copy of this edition to Mary Davis," Mattie called over to Speaker. She held in her hand the story devoted to clandestine prisons in Argentina and the demonstrations by the Women of the Disappeared. The same page contained the list Inquiry had compiled.

"Davis?" Alice started.

"She's the chair of the city council's Public Safety Committee. The parallel drawn with Atlanta is right up her alley. The list, I mean. She's in a position to demand from Commissioner Brown a list of all the disappeared and dead." Mattie removed that page from the table and walked over to Speaker to confer.

Mason spread out the centerfold. On one half, surrounding a photo of the SCLC's Reverend Lowry castigating Reagan for $1.5 million federal aid to Atlanta as compared to $2.5 million foreign aid to fascists in Central America, was an exposé of U.S. support to repressive regimes, to right-wing torture squads, to elite death corps, to terrorist policies of disappearance and murder. The other half centerfold, surrounding a collage of photos of white commando units and mercenary training camps, once again spelled out the implications of the country's antidemocratic alliances abroad to domestic life in the States.

"Wouldn't it be more encouraging," Mac asked, "if *The Call* focused on successful community organizing? This material tends to overwhelm."

"I appreciate that criticism, brother."

Speaker's response sounded perfunctory. From the way he was helping the mass-com intern, it was clear that he was now as anxious as the young college student to see the films.

"And the Klan still ain't on the FBI list of terrorist organizations," Dave said, passing one of the paste-ups to the youths behind him to read.

A chronicle of lawlessness by the ultra-right was interrupted by a penciled-in note about the Atlanta wiretaps. In lieu of verified particulars, the editors were going to discuss instead those cases that community investigators laid at the feet of Klan-like formations—the Bowen Homes deaths and the Lubie Geter murder. There was another two inches of space, with "RMVAB" penciled in.

"What's this?" Mason pointed.

Marzala read upside down. "You haven't seen copies of that newsletter? Two or three pages stapled together?" She went to Speaker, the person most likely to have a copy of the pseudonymous broadside that had been appearing around the city that documented acts of "Racist-Motivated Violence Against Blacks" throughout the country.

"No," Mason heard Speaker telling Zala. "I don't know who the editor is, but I'm glad whoever it is has taken on that responsibility." He pulled a batch from his backpack and Zala laid the copies in the center of the table for members to pick up. Mason reached for one, then continued looking over the paste-up of *The Call*'s next edition.

"Hey, Marzala." He looked up. "You've got part of the what-you-call-it."

"Byline," Speaker said from the front of the carriage house. "She did the interviews with the Griers."

"You never cease to surprise me." Mattie reached across the table to pat Zala's arm.

The top half of the solidarity page of *The Call* was dominated by a photo of the Day of Action demonstration in London on March 2, organized by the African and Asian women's organizations, the West Indian Federation groups, Black trade unionists, and community and youth leaders. In what was the largest manifestation of Black political power in thirty years, twenty thousand Black Britons and supporters marched in support of the New Cross Massacre Action Committee, which currently was petitioning the Court of Appeals for a new inquest into the South London bombing in January. The bottom half of the page was dominated by photos of the Atlanta march and the Harlem Mothers' March, both held the week after.

"Did you conduct the interviews with the folks in London too, Marzala?"

"Yes. And before we break up, Mattie, I may be passing the hat to pay the phone bill."

"Don't pay it, sister," the brother in the cufi said. "When it gets up into the thousands and they still don't cut it off, you'll know you're being tapped."

Several members of the group looked up to see if Baba was kidding. He was looking at the solidarity page, and his expression was anything but humorous.

In the middle of solidarity-with-Black-Britain was a boxed-in section with two columns: the officials on the right, the community on the left. Hours after the fire on New Cross Road, the police said that it was the partying youth who'd burnt down the building. The community contended that members of the British National Front had thrown a firebomb at the house. Two days later, the papers ended coverage and quoted the police as saying the crisis was over. But three hundred people showed up for a community meeting that day, and thousands turned out for the first demonstration protesting the roundup of Black youths. British authorities continued to ignore the massacre in New Cross but issued condolences to victims of a fire in Ireland. Commissioners from Africa, the Caribbean, the United States, mainland Europe, and England expressed outrage at the authorities and announced their willingness to participate in a fact-finding commission organized by the New Cross Massacre Action Committee.

The alliance, the article continued, caught the police manufacturing evidence and charged the media with complicity; parents then sought an injunction against the coroner, who'd used the police report at the inquest but would not read NCMAC's Fact Finding Commission Report. The police sought to close the case by naming the party host's boyfriend as the perpetrator, said Black man unavailable for questioning, having fled to the U.S. Whereupon the community had mobilized the demonstration on Monday, March 2. And on March 15, NCMAC began organizing an International Commission of Inquiry. Readers of *The Call* were invited to draw parallels between New Cross and Atlanta: slow acknowledgment of the crime, blame-the-victim, denial of racist motives, the Black-man-as-culprit ploy, and the discrediting of people's right to mobilize, organize, and investigate.

"This is a good place," the Academy brother said, "to say how the city won't deal with the community except through them patrols the Justice Department's Community Relations Council set up. That's how they're trying to pull the rug out from under us. Like, undermine our leadership."

"They give their patrols flashlights and walkie-talkies that don't even work," one of Dave's boys said. "Chumps."

"It might do well to include a criticism of the Techwood Squad in this issue," Mac said.

"Now, wait a minute, brother," Baba said.

"Mac's right," Speaker told Baba. "If your analysis leads you to charge some of the Techwood members with adventurism, write it up. But the presence of a few undisciplined cowboys doesn't mean we don't have the right to organize in our interest."

"That was some goofy shit," the boy in the green visor said to Dave. "First they tell the New York Guardian Angels to get lost. Then they turn around and help them. And then call people who live here outside agitators."

"Maybe Marzala here can interview you as a panel," Mattie suggested, just as Mac brushed by her, muttering. He'd been reading, she noticed, the end of the solidarity article, a report of the uprising in the Brixton district of London. The article predicted insurrections in London's Southall district and in Liverpool's Toxteth, where police repression was said to be particularly brutal in response to broad-base organizing by West Indian, Pakistani, Indian, Bangladeshi, Sri Lankan, Tasmanian, Sudanese, and Ethiopian peoples.

"I take it *The Call* is recommending street rebellions in Atlanta," Gaston said. "Is that what's implied?" He looked from Mac to Zala to Speaker, then smoothed the wrinkles out of his jacket where he kept his lug wrench.

Speaker muttered something about collective responsibility.

"There's a question on the floor," Mac persisted.

Unusually quiet, Dave wandered away from the table to look over the suspects chart. Zala followed. Mason too left off reading and joined them near the potbelly stove.

Utilizing information gleaned from the DA's office, from TF head-quarters, from Dowell's police informants, from the newsrooms, from the vets who'd maintained ties with the Bowen residents, from tenants council members who monitored the Justice Department spies who in turn were monitoring their city-controlled patrols, from a Community Watch captain who was keeping tabs on the Laundromat attendant named in summer, from three youth workers keeping tabs on the house on Gray Street, and from community workers on the case since Roy Innis's witness had sessioned with the authorities, they'd drawn up a list of suspects. Eight of the seventeen names were marked three times, meaning they had been cited by three separate sources. Several had more than three checks by their names. Five were asterisked, indicating connection to more than one victim. Color-coded dots designated seven suspects who palled around together on a regular basis.

"Teo come up with anything new, Zala?"

"If we could coordinate information from every source in the city and have one weekend set aside for a think tank . . . then put all the data into Aquarius . . ."

"Maybe," Mason said when Zala trailed off. "But so many sources didn't pan out." He lowered his voice. "The parents, for instance. They're not telling all they know. I don't mean you, I mean . . . They're not telling half of what they know, is my feeling."

"Understandable," Dave said.

"I know. Even the most innocent thing can make you look real bad when there's trouble," Alice Moore said.

"We can line up two for you to see," one of the Grady nurses offered, beckoning Alice Moore back to the table.

"What'd you have for breakfast, Dave? That's an innocent enough question. Now watch how weird you sound," Mason smiled.

Dave pushed his lower lip out trying to remember. "Swiss cheese on raisin bread and a box of frozen strawberries. . . . And a couple of pieces of chicken from last night's bucket," he added.

"Well, I had Jell-O and ice cubes and leftover pizza," Mason said.

"Ice cubes?" someone asked.

"Makes it jell faster."

"Uh-hunh."

"Is that too out?" Mason asked the boys. "We might have thought so when we were kids. Before we started hanging out in each other's households. But you figure it out after a while, don't you? You find out that the ways of your household ain't the ways of the world, just the ways of your household.

"And what'd you have for breakfast?" Mason was asking the shy boy, but the leader spoke up.

"Didn't have breakfast today. Sometimes . . . spaghetti. He likes spaghetti with nothing on it."

"Yeah," the dancer piped up. "He stands in front of the 'frigerator and eats it out the pot while he talks to his girl on the phone."

"That's all right, ain't it?"

"Guess so."

"I mean, if you'd said bacon, eggs, toast, and orange juice, I'd've tagged you for a maniac. It's them 'out' people who do them normal-type things—meals the same time every day, bed by dark, so forth and so on. Gives their lives the feel of normality.

"But they be out."

"Exactly."

"Jell-O and ice cubes, hunh?"

"Not all right?"

"Yeah, I guess so. What did you eat if not spaghetti?" the leader asked the shy boy, suspicious.

"Uhhhmm . . ."

"Whatever," Mason said. "And it's all right, right? But what would it sound like if your girlfriend was found murdered and as they're dragging you into the station house the reporter asks you, 'Say, what'd you have for breakfast this morning?'

" 'Uhh, a Moon Pie and a bottle of Yoo-Hoo.'

" 'Lock him up—lock his ass up with no phone privileges!' You see what I mean?" Mason turned to Zala, but she had sat down and was staring into the cold grate of the potbelly stove.

"We gave up trying to get anything out of the parents," Mason said, turning back to Dave. They walked out the side door, the boys trailing behind them.

"Braxton in there—" Dave indicated one of the fathers and moved around toward the front of the carriage house to get away from Mac's blue tobacco cloud—"he took three days before he reported his boy missing. Never did go to the police. His social worker did that."

"Where was the mother?"

"Visiting her folks down in Alabama. Matter of fact, they're the ones who buried Zala's stepfather. They run an undertaking business."

"Braxton was afraid to go to the police because he has a record?"

"I don't think so. He works two or three jobs and maybe didn't claim two so he could get food stamps. Braxton bent over backward to get his wife to take him back," Dave said, leaning on the words. "He had the social worker in there slugging away on his behalf. 'Kid needs a role model,' 'A broken home is a drag,' 'Life ain't shit without a man in the house.' "

"All that good stuff. Social workers never met my old man. But that's another story," Mason said, scraping grass off his shoe.

"Braxton couldn't bring himself to face it, that he blew and the boy was gone. Three days he spent looking for the kid. Would not call the police."

"Maybe when he and his ole lady separated, she slapped a peace warrant on him."

"Maybe. But it's like you said, Mason, it doesn't have to be anything big to make you clam up."

The two men wandered over toward the cliffside and watched the movers on the private road below arrange things in the van.

"The police weren't much of a source either."

"Yeah, well, I don't know who Zala was thinking about pulling together for a think tank."

"The police don't do nothing," one of Dave's boys said, coming up behind them. "We had a break-in and you know what they told us?"

"Told you to get a gun, but they told you that off the record."

"Naw, Mr. Morris. They said, 'You'll let us know if the TV turns up.' We'll let *them* know. That's where the police at." The boy turned to his buddies for five, but they were talking with Mr. Logan, whose son had run off with a cult, while others had wandered out to get some sun or to have a smoke.

"The medical examiners were a bust too," Mason continued. "We're the ones, the public, who want to think all that equipment and training adds up to something. Guesswork. Like everything else. It's real discouraging. And I won't even bring up reporters."

"*Miami Herald*," Dave said. And everyone on the patio within earshot cracked up.

"*Miami Herald*," the boy echoed to keep it going.

In response to the press conference Roy Innis had staged on the steps of City Hall on April 21, the Florida newspaper had run a story on Shirley McGill, whom relatives and co-workers were quick to say had a fondness for far-fetched, attention-getting tales. The only problem was that the paper had researched the wrong Shirley McGill. The subject of their story was not the witness Roy Innis had under wraps. She was not the woman whose testimony Commissioner Brown and FBI agent Glover had discounted. The *Herald*'s error and chagrined retraction seemed to have left egg on the face of the whole fifth estate, for no paper followed through and the silence left open as many questions as had been raised about McGill before the faulty write-up.

The Shirley McGill people wanted to know more about was the woman who'd received a phone call in winter from a former boyfriend, a cabbie still living in Atlanta. He told her that he was part of the kidnap ring that would soon be grabbing retarded adults. In spring, when the authorities began adding to the list young men they labeled "retarded" or "childlike," many readers suspected the labels had more to do with validating the TF profile, which had been used before to exclude missing and murdered adults whose cases seemed related, than with describing the young men. But McGill was prompted to return to Atlanta, where she sought the advice of a media Blood who put her in touch with the splinter group from CORE.

THOSE BONES ARE NOT MY CHILD

Community workers who'd stuck close to Innis and his group, particularly after a photo of the cabbie boyfriend was recognized by the family of one of the victims and identified as a person seen in the neighborhood on key dates, put out the word that McGill's actual story had more meat on the bones than the version the local papers told. She'd given highly incriminating testimony that placed her on the scene of a kidnap shack on the outskirts of Atlanta, according to the grapevine. She'd seen a boy threatened with a form of punishment that made "asphyxia," the term on most of the death certificates, graphic—a plastic bag would be shoved down his throat if he didn't do as he was told. McGill, the story went, had expressed a willingness to take a polygraph and to be interrogated under hypnosis.

"I don't know if the media's been asked to dummy up, but all we get in the dailies is the same ole same ole," Dave said.

"It's the rating game," Mattie said, walking past the men and the youths for a closer look at a patch of purple flowers entangled in the ivy. "They prefer to serve the mothers up like Renaissance Pietàs," she said, breaking off a sprig to carry back to her friend in white.

It was Preener who noticed Mattie squatting down and snapping her fingers at Mason and Dave, and he went over. Below, to the side of the steps, holding on to the shrubbery, was the beefy brother in the leather cap. The ends of the dingy straps dangling over his shoulder were caught in a bush.

"What's the score, partner?"

The big man looked up and the sun turned his graying goatee silver. "White boy's still in the lead," he answered, drawing his massive arms up to one side. "But then I ain't been to bat yet."

Then he swung around from the waist so convincingly, his arms sweeping across the top of the bush with such force, that those watching from the ledge above could feel the wallop. He carefully two-stepped past the shrub, yanking the straps free and sending twigs plummeting down to the sidewalk.

"Who is this old dude?" one of Dave's boys wondered.

"If him and Mr. Morris got into it, I put my money on Morris," another said. "He could take that guy."

"Yeah, he big but he old."

"I Spy has definitely got a nose problem," Mason said as he helped

Mattie up. They watched B. J. shoot past them and intercept the moving man under the trellis.

"You wanna be a man?" Dave asked, yanking the boys' ringleader up on his toes. "You jokers kill me. Is that what it's about? How much pain you can put on somebody without feeling bad?" He shoved the boy into his buddies.

"Think men go around offing each other for your amusement? You? How about you? What are you mugs going to be doing when the schools close and the kids got nowhere to go and no one to watch out for them? Hanging tough on the corner lying about how much pussy you've had and how many heads you've whipped?"

"Lighten up, partner," Preener said.

"C'mon, Mr. Morris," one of the boys said, shading his eyes from the sun. "We here."

"I know you're here." Abruptly, Dave walked back to the carriage house.

"They gave him a rough time in the can," the ringleader said, looking at Preener, Mason, and Mattie in turn. "But he's all right."

B. J. was coming across the flagstone from the trellis, giving the okay sign.

"We're going to start!" Zala called out, and those on the patio turned to go in.

"Shouldn't we wait for Spence?" Mason asked.

"No." She handed him the sheet of muslin to drape in the doorway.

"Don't worry, we're bonded," the big man said when the housekeeper handed over the last of the large silver pieces, an elaborate candelabra.

"It's not like it was my stuff, Mr. Bingham."

"Then we have your permission, Miss Lady, to return in the night and break into the basement?"

"If it suits you. All the same to me. I'm done here come seven o'clock."

"Silver don't excite you. You an undercover heiress. Is that it?"

"Ask yo' mama."

"She just like you," he laughed, "full of vim and vinegar."

"Then go see yo' daddy."

"A great lover, my daddy. Just like his son."

Ed Bingham laughed as the housekeeper sashayed out of the room. She probably had a peephole in the kitchen, he thought. He helped the men shove the barrels onto the hand truck, then taped up the cartons marked for the van.

Another crew had arrived and were doing the upstairs windows. A buffing machine, cans of denatured alcohol, and boxes of steel wool were set by the sideboard, a reminder that Bingham's crew should have been through and out of the way. He wondered how long it would be before the carriage-house group finished their business. They were the ones holding things up.

Watching his packers wrap up the silver dinner service put him in mind all the more of the household he'd grown up in, where the most-often-used phrase was "Go see Father." Whatever the problem—personal, religious, in the home, on the job, with the police, matters of the pocket or of the heart—"Go see Father."

His grandparents had joined Father Divine's Peace Mission in Sayville, Long Island, when the original Mother Divine was still alive helping folks pool resources to pull each other through the Depression. His parents had practically been raised in the Broad Street headquarters in Philadelphia. And under the tutelage of Professor Pearly Gates, Bingham had gotten his high-school studies together in the family hall of the Divine Lorraine Hotel.

He strapped the load onto his back and went out, wondering who there might be in that city for those burdened people in the carriage house to go see.

A courtly man named Fess who'd once worked for the Pullman Company had taken him to rallies, marches, and meetings, explaining their meaning and relating them to earlier moves. Protests against lynchings. Secret gatherings with A. Philip Randolph to form the Brotherhood of Sleeping Car Porters. Rallies in support of the Scottsboro Boys.

His uncle Connie used to take him everywhere else, on trips to National Negro Baseball League games, to give him something better to think about doing with his large frame and powerful arms than getting on his knees to pray. Connie had nothing against making use of the Peace Mission enterprises. He took Big Boy for haircuts at the Peace barbershops—a quarter if you had it, "Peace" and "Thank you" if you didn't, or were too stingy, which Connie was about everything but baseball. The time they went to St. Louis just to see Quincy Troupe on the diamond, they'd made use of the Peace boardinghouses, hotels, and restaurants. The Salisbury steak dinner was two bits—less than that in the restaurants where everyone ate family-style at long tables.

The banquets, on the other hand, were free, announced by messenger "whenever the spirit moves Father," as his daddy would say. Ducking under the trellis, Bingham remembered the floral arrangements on the sparkling white tablecloths, the stiff cloth napkins, the gleaming glasses and silverware. Throngs of people with heads bowed as Father Divine gave the blessing. When Big Boy had put down the bat and put on a bow tie to work on Colonel Black's plantation, Chock Full O' Nuts, he'd once been invited to the estate for a picnic, along with relatives who'd come north on the Dixie Maid "express" and wound up behind the Chock Full counters after years of standing on the corner designated by the Dixie Maid agency for white folks to look them over and maybe give them a job, for which the agency got cash and they got old clothes. The colonel's spread, for all his fanfare, couldn't hold a candle to Father's banquets.

Bingham turned sideways and went down the steps, the load balanced against the back of his neck. He stopped to kick aside a clump of ivy and purple flowers that had spilled over from the border of calcimined rocks and glimpsed a movie screen through the shutters of a side window of the carriage house. Over shots of an emblem, a circle with a cross inside and a red spot like a drop of blood, a saditty voice was saying that many seeming suicides and homicides by strangulation were actually accidents, self-induced choking while masturbating. Then another voice, an interviewer voice, asked a woman who wouldn't shut up long enough to hear the question what bizarre sex practice had made her leave.

Bingham whistled to himself. Had the woman in the neat bush given him a bum steer? If sex was what that conference in there was about, the children of Atlanta were in deep trouble.

Mac took the floor when Mason and Baba folded back the shutters so the reel could be changed. "We're so accustomed to thinking of the Klan as a paramilitary terrorist outfit, we often forget that it's a religious cult as well. I don't know if this is the time for a discussion, but I regret that the narrator didn't speak to the difficulty of trying to penetrate delusional systems to rescue its believers from psychological bondage."

Mason turned his back to watch I Spy disappear down the steps when the brother in the cufi launched into reasons why enemies of the Black man should be left in bondage and not be the subject of any sympathetic discussion. Mason heard the thuds from below as the cartons were loaded onto the van.

"I was saying that for the benefit of Mr. Logan," Mac interrupted. "Delusional systems pose the same problems in terms of deprogramming, regardless of the type of cult."

"Yeah, well . . ." Baba leaned against the shutters, and Mason fieldstripped his butt before flicking it out the window.

Logan declined to take the floor when Mac called on him. Earlier he'd informed the group about his yearlong attempt to locate his college-dropout son through the renowned group of specialists led by a brother named Patrick. He'd come to Atlanta from Athens, Georgia, when the cult theory of the killings gained currency.

"I'm anxious to hear from the Innis witness," was all he would say, pinching the crown of the hat that he twirled on his lap.

"The film also failed to point out the difference between terrorism performed for political purposes and terrorism performed for religious purposes. I bring it up because many people who think it's the Klan talk themselves out of it by saying that the Klan would boast were they involved. Political terrorists act to call public attention to an outrage. They commit acts in order to draw the media, politicians, and the public to the situation, or to provoke an uprising. Religious terrorists often act to call attention to a moral outrage, but in the classical tradition, the acts are committed purely to attract the attention of a deity."

"You're on to something," Mason said, turning around.

"In other words," Mac, encouraged, continued, "it's the victim's experience of terror that matters, not public acknowledgment of the deeds."

Mason signaled the projectionist, who turned off the lights, though the film was not yet threaded.

"Pay attention to that business about masturbation and strangulation," B. J. spoke out in the dark, "especially when you look over the chart and see how many times 'asphyxia' is listed."

"Rolling."

The second reel of "Rough Cut," footage spliced together with little attention to the finer points of cinesthetics, was, for the most part, interviews with people who had serious misgivings about their association with the Klan, or who had already left the fold ("Renegades listening to renegades," Zala piped up), followed by panels: social psychologists, historians, political scientists, newspaper types, and law-enforcement persons discussing the "New Right."

"What's of interest, good people, is the repeated reference to factionalism. That's in our favor. How many people here are members of the newly formed National Anti-Klan Network? Think you need to consider changing your name to include all right-wing terrorists?"

"Hold up," Gaston interrupted. "He just mentioned dynamite bombings."

The man on the screen—white, young, clean-cut—was sitting on a brown-and-beige plaid sofa in a knotty-pine den. A musket hung on the wall overhead. He slung one leg over the other and looked at the bottom of his shoe.

"That's where I had to draw the line," he said, jiggling his foot. "I joined because my father and my grandfather were members of the Georgia Klans. Back then 'Night Rider' meant scaring the Negroes. Whooping a few if you had to. Mostly you didn't have to. They're superstitious, so you can scare them. But now . . . And see, the biggest problem is that leaders don't want to know. Criminal types in the ranks take things too far. Criminals and snoops. The leaders take a no-see attitude and that's bad. I work for ATF, so they asked me—that's the Federal Bureau of Alcohol, Tobacco, and Firearms. That's mostly where the FBI snoops get the dynamite. So that's where we got it, from the snoops. . . . I thought it was to scare people a little, not . . . You have to draw the line somewhere." He shook his head and fingered his shoelaces. The camera stayed as he fidgeted.

"Leah was saying the other day," Speaker said, "that that's where the white Left should concentrate their work. With people like that."

"And white feminists should work on the wives," Zala added.

The man on the screen finally left his shoe alone and looked up. "If the leaders would act like leaders, I'd've stayed. Because the country's being handed over to the inferior races. . . ."

"They really do talk like that, don't they?"

". . . No-see attitude and the splits may be the downfall of the country, of all white Christian civilization. . . ."

"Burn, baby, burn."

"Look at him. Damn, he's about to cry!"

"Oh, wow!" the projectionist bellowed when the next scene came into focus.

"The Mystic Knights of the Sea meet the Knights of the Invisible Empire," Mason said, recognizing the *Amos 'n' Andy* show music.

Bingham ripped thick handfuls of ivy and flowers from the sides of the steps as he came up. He sucked his teeth in disgust when strains of a familiar radio theme from childhood reached his ears.

"*Amos 'n' Andy.* Now that's a doggone shame," he muttered, walking quickly away.

"Now, I could be wrong," Bingham argued with himself, tearing away the dripping lianas that had fallen through the top of the trellis. "The woman said 'research,' so maybe that's research. Could be I've been on the road too long."

He thought of a flyer someone had stuck under his windshield wiper his first day in Atlanta. A group of airline workers were raising a ruckus because they wanted to take up a collection for the dead children's families, but the other members of the Metropolitan Airlines Association voted it down: "None of our business." Well, what could you expect from people who spent their lives up in the air? Maybe he was in the same boat, his head in the barrels too long. He'd see what Miss Lady thought. She had her feet on the ground.

"But *Amos 'n' Andy?*" He wiped his feet briskly on the mat.

The music, familiar to most from TV rather than radio, continued over a color shot of robed figures parading by the camera. IN THIS SIGN WE CONQUER, the motto said on the satin robes, green, purple, red, white. Then the film shifted to black-and-white. Dogs were being led from trucks—Dobermans, German shepherds, bloodhounds.

Close-up of an Alsatian husky snarling at a white man in black-face, who waves good-naturedly at the camera as another man pulls the dog away on a leash. The camera follows the parade of dogs past a panel truck and lingers. White men in short sleeves unload sections of a stage.

A jerky jump cut ends in a tracking shot of a series of tables. The insignia is on shirts, tie clasps, bumper stickers, necklaces, pillow cases set out for sale. Women and children behind the tables wave at the camera. Teenagers sitting on the hoods of cars wave too, then put on their robes. Another tracking shot shows book displays under the banner of the American Nazi Party. Other tables feature *Battle Axe News,* the organ of the National Emancipation of Our White Seed. Pamphlets and posters from the Minutemen and the Christian Identity Movement share a table.

"This is grainy," the intern explained, "because it's a blow-up from Super-8."

"Shhhush."

A large field. In the foreground, members of a kleagle, the women's auxiliary, set up concession booths. Mid-ground, a stage being set up under the direction of the white man in blackface makeup. The camera follows him up a pole. He hangs a loudspeaker with a C-clamp. The *Amos 'n' Andy* tape rises in volume—Kingfish and Calhoun outconning each other in a real-estate scheme. On stage the blackfaced white minstrel cuts a caper. People straggle over from the trucks. In the back field, men wrap burlap around a cross. Others wait with cans to douse it. Five men position themselves at the ends of the ropes, waiting the cue to hoist the twelve-foot cross for burning.

The camera swings back to the stage, where the performer is shuffling, scratching, drooping his lower lip out with lots of spittle. Those around the stage who spot the camera come awake to clap and stomp in time with the song:

> Someone had to pick the cotton
> Someone had to plant the corn
> Someone had to slave and sing . . .

Several do a half-hearted hambone to the refrain "And That's Why Darkies Were Born."

The ex–carny pitchman tissues off his makeup on the front seat of his customized jeep. In a sweaty close-up he explains that his is one of the most important roles at a klavern.

". . . from all walks of life—Telephone linemen, prison guards, teachers, librarians, salesmen, hospital workers, highway patrol. Matter of fact, less than twenty paces from your sound man, we got a sheriff and a hospital superintendent. All sorts of folks. Bluegrass pickers, and ex-carny people like myself." He smiles, jerking his thumbs at his chest. "I'm the one that gets them in. I get things started. I got the best sound equipment in the state too. Why?" He leans forward to hear the question of why people join. "'Cause it's neighborly. This is like a fraternity, you see. No, no, no sir"—he wags his head—"pranks, maybe, but no rough stuff."

His image dissolves into another close-up, a young woman in a hooded robe. She turns to motion someone to her side. The camera pulls back to include a man who declines to be interviewed. The woman listens to the question and looks toward her husband again. He folds his arms across his chest and stays put, one eye on the cross preparations in the back field. He motions for her to answer the question.

"Some people can trace their roots back to the original Scottish clans," she says. "Others—some of them are here too—can claim blood roots with the original patriots like William Simmons and Nathan Bedford Forrest. My mother is an officer in the DAR. My father was with a vigilante group that started up when the niggers come into the restaurants and stores. My sister used to run a booth with her husband's outfit. Now we're all together. Yes, my husband's very proud of me. Hank?"

Hank does not want any part of it. The camera wanders away toward a group of teenagers helping youngsters into their robes. They complain that satin is hot.

A woman steps into the lens and invites the camera crew to her trailer. The camera focuses on the woman's feet as she goes up the metal steps and onto the carpet. A dark-haired woman in a black pants-and-shirt uniform looks annoyed at having been caught scrambling over the seat from the trailer's cab. She scowls at the woman who invited the camera in, then hands the woman a Dustbuster she's plugged into the cigarette lighter outlet. The woman is nonplussed for a second. The uniformed woman bends her over with a slight shove to her back. The woman kneels down and runs the vacuum over the carpet where bread crumbs have dropped.

"That's right," the woman in uniform says. "I'm with security. I worked my way up through the ranks. There's a place for women in this man's army," she says, arms akimbo, legs astride. Women making sandwiches briefly glance over their shoulders at her. The camera backs out of the doorway at the direction of the security woman.

Outside by a truck, the security woman leads a black Labrador retriever over to a man dressed in a similar dark uniform. The woman speaks into a walkie-talkie, looking toward the far end of the field, where the cross is being doused by two men with cans, who jump back, stains on their pants. The cross is hoisted twelve feet high. The dog barks.

"That could be the same black Labrador retriever that Son of Sam got his instructions to kill from."

"Hey now, Spencer." Gaston was up reaching over heads to grab Spence by the shoulder before he could stumble toward a seat. Others greeted Spence's arrival too, but were glad when the two men sat down and removed their shadows from the screen.

Zala looked over at her husband. He looked exhausted. He looked flushed. In the glare of the burning cross, he flashed her a broad smile. And she forgot what it was she'd been mad about for so long.

"Sounds complicated to me, Bingham. Mind if I call you Bingham? I can't fix my face to say 'Big Boy' without smirking." The housekeeper turned back to the loaf of date-nut bread on the cutting board.

"If that's for the researchers, Miss Hazel, I'll take it out." He could tell by the way she paused before bearing down on the knife that she'd planned most particularly to do that herself. "That tray's too heavy for you."

"You plenty nosy yourself, Big Boy." She waved her knife toward the pantry shelf where a Coca-Cola tray was filled with Styrofoam cups. "We'll divide the load. And no sense dirtying up dishes. Come seven o'clock sharp, I'm through."

"Not going with them?"

"I'm going home to New Orleans, sugar. I ain't had a decent meal since I left. You should've seen this pantry when I got here. But they don't know the difference."

"I get the feeling they're running. I got the call for this job two days ago. Big rush to get out of here, huh?"

"I don't tell tales out of school, Bingham."

"Sounds interesting."

"Shows how much you know. Some days I drop the muffin pan just for the noise. That's how interesting things get around here.

"But they're all right. He's a good egg. And she's nice, in a wiggy sort of way. Here, have another piece—then we'll go and see the movies. They've got the butcher-block cart out there."

"So you think they're on the up-and-up? They're investigating the killings?"

"Man, who ain't trying to get that reward? Maybe I'll hit on something myself watching them movies. Grab that pot holder and get the pots off the stove. Coffee's in the drip pot. Spiced tea's in the spatter ware. We'll dispense with fresh lemon. It eats right through the Styrofoam."

"I don't think it's the reward so much."

She looked him up and down for a minute, then tossed him the pot holder. "I guess anybody who'd move from Philly to Hoboken is subject to mental fits of all sorts," she said, loading the trays. "So, what did you do in real life, Bingham? Before you decided to become a pack mule?"

"This and that. Played some ball. Got a break just before the war—the forties, I'm talking about. Spent a season in Cuba and Peru. By the time I came back, the Negro leagues had about played out. So I went into the restaurant business."

"Peru? How'd you do that?"

"The scouts used to come up from South America and raid the Negro leagues. They'd lure a lot of the players away. We'd be glad to go. Barnstorming was great, but it had its low side. Like being all-stars."

"That was bad?"

"White teams wouldn't play you unless you let them advertise that your team was made up of the Negro stars. They'd only play the best. But you better not win. They got a helluva complex. You win and you'd never see your take of the gate. I was glad to leave."

"Only scouts I remember were the talent kind that never showed anywhere I was booked. And the only raids I remember were them other kind. Whole congregations would pull up stakes and go north, things were so awful."

She banged the fridge door open and removed two tall glasses from the freezer, then unplugged the box. Bingham watched silently as she bruised fresh mint in a saucer of sugar and plopped the leaves into the two frosted glasses. He had memories too of ministers bringing whole towns from South Carolina to Philly.

"When vaudeville played out," Miss Hazel said, measuring the liquor, "I missed my chance to go to Europe." She put the bottle in a tote bag, then put the finishing touches on the juleps. "Just as well. Ida Cox got caught in a roundup in Denmark. Whole lot of the entertainers did. Many a troupe had to abandon their costume trunks and everything else to get out of Europe. Nazis were all over the place—Paris, Copenhagen, Amsterdam, everywhere. Funny, we never hear about all those colored people they threw in the concentration camps."

"Yup." He waited for her to turn around so they could go. But she kept her back to him for a long while, holding on to the sides of the tray and not moving.

Suddenly she wheeled around and motioned him to hurry. "I don't know. It's complicated."

"What is?"

"What you were saying before about leaders and them people in the carriage house. Till something big comes along like in the sixties, I'm just going try to swing my way from gig to gig and be satisfied with a little get-along money. Something'll turn up by and by. Won't take long for this new generation to wake up."

"Then what are you going to do?"

"Whatever it takes. Long as things don't get too complicated."

He was starting to explain that it was the elegant simplicity of Father Divine's philosophy that had attracted so many people from so many walks of life to the co-op movement, a lot of white people too. But then he found Old Man Webber looking right down his throat.

The judge was in the chairlift on the back staircase, the lift mechanism ticking noisily as he went up. The old lady was on the midway landing in a yellow quilted housecoat, seated on a hassock, talking on the phone. She wagged a finger at Miss Hazel, then continued nodding and scribbling on a pad Bingham could see through the Lucite table.

Miss Hazel called up to them cheerily. "I'll read them the riot act out back if you want me to. In the meantime, the pause that refreshes."

"Wait, wait!" Mrs. Webber was flapping the phone message she'd written and was coming down, beaming. Hiking up her housecoat, she took the stairs with a jauntiness Bingham had not thought her capable of.

"There's a message," Mrs. Webber said, smiling breathlessly. "For them." She motioned toward the patio.

"I'll deliver it." In swift, deft moves, Miss Hazel had taken the message in hand, given Mrs. Webber the two juleps, and was heading for the patio door, jerking her head at Bingham to get the lead out.

Embarrassed for Old Lady Webber, her disappointment and bewilderment as naked as her joyful excitement had been a moment ago, he had the impulse to turn and look before stepping out. But the sight of her with maybe two perfectly good drinks spilling out onto the Oriental runner would have derailed his train of thought.

Catching up with the ex-hoofer, he said, "You could sum up Father Divine's philosophy in one word—restitution."

"Restitution, you say."

"Sure enough. Quit lying, backbiting, pay your debts, and clear the decks to get right with God. Ask each other's forgiveness for wrongdoing in the past. Balance the books."

"In my book, there're two columns, debits and credits. What about my forty acres and my mule?"

"That's what my uncle Connie used to say," he laughed. "Restitution without retribution ain't hitting on a dime."

"To tell the truth, I was thinking more of 'reparations,' but I say, right on to your uncle Connie. One lesson we could take from the Mafia—ain't no justice without some vengeance."

Bingham laughed and the kettle of spiced tea sloshed in the tray. It was all he could do to keep up with Hazel and not waste another drop.

She ducked under the trellis, though her head cleared the trumpet vines by two feet. "Come on now, Big Boy, and let's see about this research."

"Here go the spook," Gaston said with a husky laugh and got up. He and the rest of Team 2 were leaving, throwing their shadows on the screen, blotting out the Blood who was seated at a desk with neat stacks of papers and books, a plastic cup and a brown-and-black water jug on a tray. Clear again, he was folding his arms on the desk and leaned forward slightly. He spoke directly into the camera with a steady, confident gaze.

"This was shot last January, good people. Atlanta is mentioned at some point, according to the notes."

"I was recruited from Boalt Hall," the brother on screen was saying. "That's the lefty law school at Berkeley. There were twenty-three in my unit in the beginning, thirteen after the first phase of training. But four Black men didn't make it past that. The one Jewish guy, a lawyer from New York, was bumped. Two of the six white women were dismissed. And an Hispanic from Albuquerque and two Black women. After phase two, there was one other Black person besides myself, a woman from Bismarck, South Dakota. One Latino, a guy from New Hampshire. And three white women, whom I felt it was best not to be chummy with. One of them was definitely a plant, there to encourage bickering and complaints. The Black woman hipped me to her.

"We were trained to shoot on the firing range and from a sniper tower, shoot to kill. Most of phase two was learning how to handle urban disruptions. You had to be gung-ho but not overdo it to play on the varsity. We had to shine, for as you know Hoover had complained to Bobby Kennedy that the minority requirement was weakening the Bureau. But of course Hoover knew how to get around the Justice Department to deal directly with Lyndon Johnson, which he did. So there was six of us before the last loyalty forms."

He placed his palms flat on the desk as though he intended to push his swivel chair away and rise. Instead, he motioned toward the certificates on the wall behind him.

"I made the varsity, so did the Black woman, the Hispanic, and one of the white women, the plant—she was assigned, I learned later, to room with the one person, a Black woman, who'd made it past the prelims with a new unit, thirty-three out of thirty-four bumped by the gunnery instructor. I don't know what detail the others drew. As for me, I collected the plastic bags of confidential debris. In other words, this spook was a garbage man."

"I heard that."

"In my eleven years with the Bureau, I put the trash can down three times for field assignments. Once during the Chicago Days, I helped process some of the lefties I'd gone to school with." He looked off in the direction of the window. When he turned back, he unbuttoned one of his cuffs and started to roll up his sleeve, stopped, then composed his face and continued.

"The Democratic Convention in Chicago," he mused, eyes moving slightly away from the center of the lens. "They brought in a few squadrons from Fort Carson, Colorado. The local riot divisions had a lot of Blacks too, but the army troops were predominantly Black. My sister's oldest boy was there. A draft evader, he'd been given a choice—informant, the service, or jail. Eighteen months he spent on the front line in 'Nam. He thought he'd finish out his tour at a desk job in Colorado. But there he was on the streets of Chicago. He and I and a whole lot of other Black men, Black women, and youngsters were there, but the TV cameras worked around to blot us out. We saw each other. My sister and I haven't seen eye to eye since college, so it was the first time I'd seen my nephew grown. I'd been . . . offered, shall we say, an opportunity to shift from international relations to national security specialization my last year at Berkeley. That was the last decent conversation my sister and I had. It was war after that."

While he poured himself a cup of water, someone behind camera whose voice did not pick up on the track asked a few questions. But the brother gestured for silence and pulled his notepad closer.

"The second time I got to put the garbage can down was in connection with an operation that resulted in the Panther trial, particularly in relation to the government's case against Ericka Huggins. I'm not proud of the role I played. I discuss it fully in the manuscript I'm preparing. Quite frankly, by 1973 I was coming apart. There's no way to maintain civilian friendships or those from the past when you play on the varsity. And there were few colleagues in the Bureau that I cared to . . . On the one hand, it's a fraternity, a microcosm with a definite culture of its own, and many are content to let that be the whole of their life, but—I'm sure I don't have to tell you what it would cost a person like myself to fit into that world.

"As I said, my role in the Panther 11 and Panther 21 operation was beginning to tell. Or maybe it started in Chicago. But after Wounded Knee, I knew it was over. I don't mean to play the virgin. I'd be glad to discuss that later.

"I was flown to South Dakota to keep tabs on Angela Davis, me and the sister I mentioned before. We were both assigned to Davis and to keep an eye on other Black radicals who'd come in support of the American Indian movement. Our job was to make the most of any links we could observe—and if necessary, orchestrate them, if not invent them—between those we were assigned to watch and others who were on the wanted list: members of the BLA, the Symbionese Liberation Front, the Weather Underground, not to mention free-lance KGB informers. The Wounded Knee trial was the beginning of the end for me, I would say."

He played with the lid of the brown-and-black plastic water jug, glanced quickly at his notes, and resumed talking, his eyes fixed on some point below camera range, possibly at the person who was trying to feed him questions as he spoke.

"You will recall that during cross-examination by Attorney Kunstler, a lot of Bureau misdeeds surfaced, especially once they got Agent Douglas Durham on the stand. He'd not only successfully infiltrated the AIM, he'd worked himself into a position as their security chief. That success was second only to the agent who became keeper of the books at SCLC for a time, a maneuver you'll be reading about in another book in progress by an old classmate of mine, a researcher who's covering the government's campaign against Martin Luther King Jr. I doubt if SCLC to date is aware that they had an agent on staff for more than four years who was passing information to the Bureau with such regularity. I wonder how he could have done his work for the organization.

"It's amazing, isn't it? My naiveté, I mean. Thorough brainwashing. Black militants had been pulling the cover off of COINTELPRO and other intelligence operations of the FBI, the CIA, and the military for years. But I didn't come to my senses until Durham took the stand. Call it ego, call it pride, or an investment of time . . . I don't know why it took so long. And I don't know why Durham's cockiness should've been the turning point. Or maybe it was my particular assignment. The sister and I were both afraid to come clean with each other. The truth was, we very much admired Angela Davis. She's one hell of a person.

"Then I saw the movie *The Spook Who Sat by the Door.* It made me feel shitty, really shitty. It's taken me several years to try to get back . . . to my family, old friends . . . roots. My sister has washed her hands—"

He took another swallow, then leaned forward, grateful now that someone below the lens was asking questions.

"The FBI develops the cases that the federal government will prosecute, if that's what you're asking. In other words, that the U.S. attorneys will act upon. . . . Atlanta? No question about it. The Bureau was involved sporadically as early as the LaTonya Wilson kidnapping. Their involvement has been consistent since the autumn of 1980 when the nursery school was bombed."

"You'll notice he said 'bombed,' y'all."

"Noted."

"You can be sure there are reams of information on file. The STOP organization would be wise to go directly to the U.S. attorney general. It's unlikely that they'd get any cooperation from the Atlanta field office."

"He'd better talk fast, we're running out of film."

"Shush."

"As you know, the Freedom of Information Act applies to federal records only. Access to state and municipal records depends on local laws, and they vary from place to place. But since the FOIA passed in 1966, the onus is on the federal government to justify secrecy, not on the applicant to prove that the requested information is a matter of life and death. But there's a catch."

"Turn up the sound."

"Under the Privacy Act of 1974, requests for files can be rejected on the grounds that the information sought might be detrimental to other persons—that is, might invade someone else's privacy. The same holds for state and local records. Access can be restricted or denied if the information one requests mentions others. A just enough restriction— and handy too, because it justifies massive deletions if rejection on grounds of privacy is challenged. In the Atlanta case, then, the shrewd thing for the STOP organization to do is to file on behalf of everyone who could possibly be mentioned in the records."

"Got to have information to get information, sounds like to me," the former SAFE worker said.

"That's the truth."

When the lights were switched on, Bingham helped the projectionist shift things from the cart to the footstool the moving crew had left after clearing out the carriage house. On a signal neither he nor Hazel Blanchette caught, another group of people got up to leave.

"Counting the spoons, Miss Lady?"

"Laugh if you want to, Bingham, but damn if the salad tongs ain't missing." When she turned around to seek out the culprit, she saw the few left in the carriage house all seated on the floor, watching the TV screen and the movie screen at the same time.

"On the UHF monitor," the projectionist called out, "is the tape Miss B. J. said to put on, said one of you might recognize the Holmes woman."

"Holmes?" Zala and Alice Moore exchanged a look. "Nancy Dorr Holmes?"

A panel discussion was being broadcast on the smaller screen against a background of commando gunfire on the movie screen. The wife of an admiral, the sister of a mafioso, and the daughter of a Klansman were discussing domestic violence. Zala had the feeling that the three hadn't been in the same studio; that they'd been spliced together, perhaps by error or not.

"People's lives," someone moaned in the dark.

"She came all the way from Santa Cruz to Atlanta," Alice Moore said, "but Innis stole the limelight. Maybe we'll hear her story now. She claims her father and his friends are killing the children."

Miss Hazel touched Bingham's arm and whispered, "I changed my mind. Let's get out of here. Another hour of this and we'll be as crazy as forty ugly yard dogs barking at the moon."

They wheeled the cart out between Gaston and Spence, who along with the other men had turned their attention to the muzzle flashes of the mercenary training camp when one of the panelists interrupted the show host to exclaim that her efforts to have a career had been trivialized for the whole twenty-five years of her marriage.

"Did you catch that? She said James Earl Ray was driving the setup car and her father was driving the '65 white Mustang reported to the MLK commission."

"Yeah, by the very witness they locked up in a state asylum. Who is this Holmes woman?"

"She tried to see Commissioner Brown," Alice Moore said. "She writes to everyone. I can collect her letters." She reached for Zala's hand. "I'll try."

Alice Moore had wanted to be alone with Zala to compare notes, but there'd been no opportunity for privacy. Now the navy wife was talking again about life on the base, and Zala was resisting being pulled away from the screen.

Alice Moore held fast to Zala's hand. Home, she would have to go past the room. The door was half open, half closed. That, so far, was the best she'd been able to do. But she'd gotten the bed right. The sheets and the spread tucked tight at the bottom and sides, top folded back twice to a three-inch band underneath the five on top, and tucked tightly too. But he was no longer there to bounce the ball on the bed and say it wasn't right yet, ripping the whole thing apart and flinging the bedclothes to the floor.

The other wives and her in-laws had been confident that a child was the answer. A baby would straighten her out, settle her down, teach her to fit in. Years and years watching the child, contorted, making herself small to slip under the covers without wrinkling them. Night after night, the girl flattened in bed, a few hours relief when Alice came in to loosen the covers, then returned to tighten them before reveille. Till she'd found the ball in his closet, held it over the burner, tore loose both the beds, took her freedom. And lost her child.

Zala was trying to shake her hand loose. Alice Moore let go long enough to find a clean tissue. On the video screen, one of the women was nervously scratching her leg. The mafiosa woman had taken out a new identity, but as she bent down, part of her face was on camera.

"Listen," someone on the other side of Zala said, "turn off the movie and rewind to where the Holmes woman names the names. I've got 'vice-president of the United Klans of America,' 'FBI agent,' and her father. But let's get the names."

"Zala?"

"We move forward. Compare notes with each other on the route. What's coming up next on the screen?"

"Movie clips," the projectionist said. "Some footage from documentaries. Then some stuff we haven't seen—rites, ceremonies. 'The Great Monk Comes Out of the Cave.' 'The Imperial Dragon and the Black Beast.' Stuff like that."

"Well, if the Holmes woman is through, could we run something else on the TV monitor? All this navy wife wants to talk about is her career, and the Italian broad ain't said shit anyway."

"Zala?"

But Zala had gotten up with Alice Moore, who was leading her to the door talking a mile a minute.

A light drizzle sifted down through the trees and dotted the crumpled napkins on the butcher cart. The two elderly people patted each other affectionately as they hugged goodbye.

"Take care now, Big Boy."

"You too, Miss Lady."

Miss Hazel had taken her eyes off Mason in his white gym suit for no more than a minute, she was sure. But now, as she ducked under the trellis, there he was around the side of the carriage house stretching and kicking, dressed completely in black. The little woman whom everyone seemed to defer to but who didn't strike Miss Hazel as the leadership type had changed her clothes too. The others were carrying out maps, charts, and equipment to the cars around back. They were off to something risky. She could feel an electricity in the air that wasn't altogether the weather. Parlor games indeed.

In the lower hallway of the Webbers' home, Miss Hazel Blanchette's eyes traveled along the telephone wire tacked to the baseboard. There was no one expecting her in New Orleans, no one she could think of to phone. Home, she'd lock the courtyard gate, go in to her apartment, open the shutters, turn on the fan; then there'd be no other task to perform, nothing that would make any difference in the lives of Black people. And that shouldn't be.

She locked the Dutch doors to the breezeway, then headed toward the kitchen for the final washup. "I didn't come into this world to be some miscellaneous Negress," she said. "It's time for a change." From upstairs came the sound of her nibs coming down with Miss Hazel's check.

Sunday Evening, April 26, 1981

D etective Dowell dialed the Hyatt, then turned to check on the progress Spencer's wife and Preston, the narc from Florida he'd been teamed with, were making. The place was a jumping after-hours joint during the week but half-empty on Sundays. A few drowsy couples leaned on the kitchen-counter bar blinking at the colored lights, staring at the red carpet, watching the clock in a ship's wheel over the microwave oven. The barmaid Marzala was talking with pulled a bag from the rack of chips, peanuts, and pork skins and came from behind the bar with her drink. She handed the bag to a listless couple on the dance floor.

"Look, baby," she said, winding the red plastic straw from her collins around her finger, "the Marquette Club is where you should be asking those questions." She slipped the straw free with a snap and immediately wound it again. "Sure the Silver Dollar and them other bars near Greyhound get hassled. But what's it mean, and who cares? What are they going to do, walk around the corner to the blood bank to get up the scratch for a lawyer? Now, the Marquette's another deal altogether. Hassle them and it's repercussions." She sipped her drink, then set it down and resumed winding the bent-flat straw.

"See, cops don't go in the Marquette Club there on Hunter, or MLK Drive, like they say now. Cops go in the Cameo, show the pictures, roust a few drunks, throw some muscle around, and leave. Cops try questioning people in the Marquette about the children? No way. That place is strictly them men with fat wallets and some classy fags, a few of them sissies you see working the corner near Ashby too. But hear me, you don't want to go in there alone, get your feelings hurt. Lotta slipping and sliding in the Marquette—dark glasses, costumes, not using your real name, the whole bit." She waved greetings to a couple coming in past the man at the door.

"I'll tell you another thing, since you come recommended." She whipped the straw free with a snap, then leaned down.

Dowell stepped from the alcove and collided with a boy who looked too young to be there. The boy gave him a look and glanced at the barmaid, having caught Dowell eavesdropping. "Be surprised how many buffet parties going on in this city, baby. Black, white, men, women, you name it, the whole bit. That's why they gots to nail somebody quick. Too much quiet money changing hands, and tempers be rising."

Kool and the Gang drowned out the rest of the barmaid's discussion. The boy, whom Preston had followed from the bumper pool table, was at the jukebox, punching buttons. Then someone picked up at the Hyatt.

"Spencer party calling in for messages," Dowell said, feeling foolish. ". . . Then have 'Spencer' paged in the ballroom—table 23. I'll hold."

The boy feeding the juke was definitely too young to be there. He was combing his hair with both hands, watching Preston out of the side of his eye crease a five-dollar bill lengthwise.

"You don't say much for my money," Preston said, wrapping the bill around his knuckles.

The boy ignored him for a minute while he folded a blue and white bandanna, then tied it around his head and shoved his hair back. "You wanna give me a lotta shit, man, and the kid don't need your money or your shit. Five dollars a question was the deal. But you think you funky asking ten things at once." The boy passed in front of the phone alcove going back to bumper pool. Preston looked over at Dowell and shrugged, then followed the boy.

In his ear Dowell was told that someone was coming to the phone. He waited, watching the barmaid, nearly a foot taller than Marzala, slide off the stool to confide.

It had been years since Dowell had heard "buffet party" in a conversation. He knew the term from the old records his father had owned, rough country blues from the twenties. Anything goes at a buffet: the erotic, the exotic, the low-down and kinky. Deputy Eldrin Bell could fill him in on places in the present. Dowell's father could tell him about the Marquette Club's past. He hadn't thought about it in years, but

knew its story; oldest gay club in America, established around World
War I.

His parents had come to Atlanta from Tulsa around that time, their
business bombed in '21 in the so-called Tulsa Race Riot. It had been a
series of military maneuvers, the way his parents told it. The Negro vets
of Tulsa would not surrender their weapons what with riots all over the
country being the welcome-home the GIs got for fighting for democracy, but under the French flag because the presence of Negroes with
guns in the American army was deemed not in the country's best interests. Pops and the others had stationed themselves at the jail to protect
a colored man from a lynch mob. Routed and mad, whites had invaded
Greenwood, the enviable business district known as the Negro Wall
Street—burning, looting, shooting, killing.

His father would open the old trunk sometimes and remove the top
tray where he kept the old picture postcards that read, "Running the
Niggers Out of Tulsa, OK." They'd begun circulating the week after
Greenwood was bombed from the air, private planes commandeered by
the police, the 101st Airborne flown in with the dynamite.

Dowell felt a spasm in his gut and leaned away from the wall to
clear his throat. Someone was on the line. He had to identify himself
twice before he got the report that Lafayette had tracked a caravan of
cars to the Chattahoochee and that his team should spot-check the
McDaniel-Glenn and Lakewood-Stewart areas. A lot of traffic was going
over the route in these areas.

"Look," Preston said, following the boy back to the jukebox. "You
got me wrong." He'd acquired a pamphlet since last he'd passed the
phone alcove.

"You make up your mind, man. You in here to promote a deal, talk
to somebody else. The kid don't deal in product, only tips. Dope ain't
no part of this thing anyway. That either," he added, slapping at the
pamphlet in Preston's hand. "Ass is the deal. Candy-ass Asslanta, man.
You wanna know something? You need to go see *The Night of the Generals*. That'll tell you what you want to know. All kinds of crazy people
mixed up in the thing and they got titles. You sew up your asshole good
and go looking. You'll find the killers."

"That's worth five dollars, 'Go see a movie'?"

"Worth ten, but you ain't listening. I gave you the whole case right
there, but you fucking stupid anyway," the boy said, plucking the bill

from Preston's fist and running out of the place before the narc could move.

"Son of a gun," the man at the door said when the boy sped by. He looked to Preston for explanation.

Preston turned to Dowell, shrugged, and riffled the pages of one of the pamphlets he'd found.

Dowell looked at the phone and pursed his lips. He'd called the precinct at 1700 hours to make sure the duplicating machine on loan was operating in case Spencer came into possession of tapes that needed copying. The question now, as he fingered the belt buckle bearing the number of the Georgia Penal Code that governed most of his decisions, was whether to go home and catch a nap; continue patrolling with the others, which he had not originally planned to do; or check in at the station. He had a court case in the morning and needed to pick up a lab report and sign a weapon out of the property room. And too, he needed to leave a message for two fellow officers who'd asked for his help. They'd been called before Internal Affairs after writing up four senior officers they'd charged with misconduct. Dowell had not understood the importance of what they'd told him until that afternoon, when he learned that the man the senior officers had been patrolling in off-duty hours was the Reverend C. T. Vivian, founder-director of the Anti-Klan Network.

Dowell put in another dime and called home. He'd leave a message that he could be counted on. While he waited for his wife to pick up, he watched Marzala and Preston head for the door. They were going outside to compare notes. As he waited, Dowell wondered what connection there might be between the Marquette Club, the house on Gray Street, Bowen Homes, the vehicles Lafayette was tracking, his team's assignment, and the films they'd watched all afternoon.

"What was that?" Vernon whirled around and glued his eyes to the shaggy part of the bank. Roots and withered weeds hung down in mud-caked fringe where solid dirt had dropped away. The bulged-out part of the gorge looked like a buffalo head.

"Beavers, Vern. They beat the water with their tails." Lafayette led the way down into a culvert, directing Vernon to shine the light where the swamp punk had been crushed flat. "Thought so."

"Building dams this time of night? Some crazy-ass beavers."

"I don't know their business hours, Vern. Building dams was your story. Look, I think we got a make on a boat, if not a car."

Vernon leaned down and nodded. "Drag marks. Looks like some-one hauled a boat up from here." They both turned and Vernon tossed Lafayette the flashlight. "I've got three flashes left on the Instamatic." He followed behind as Lafayette moved toward the storm drain, paus-ing at intervals to inspect the ground covering, shrubs, and branches that were shoulder height.

"That wagon train we've been tracking was in this vicinity, but where?" Lafayette saw no signs. "No stakeout either," he added, looking toward the bridge. With a broken-off twig, he fished around in the storm drain and came up with one very muddied shoe. They inspected it, then moved up the slippery bank. "Watch it—soil's thin in through here."

"I see it." Vernon stopped when another faint splash sounded from somewhere around the bend. He stared into the dark until the surface of the river was smooth again. "If the Chattahoochee could talk."

"Moving to higher ground."

"Right behind you." Hand over hand, Vernon pulled himself up be-hind Lafayette until they ran out of shrubs to grab onto. He sensed his buddy go taut. A second later, fixing on a scatter of rusted beer cans caught in a tangle of roots at his feet, and concentrating, Vernon heard it too: footsteps.

"The teacher." Lafayette dug into the mud with the tips of his boots and moved up the rest of the bank sideways like a skier.

"How can you tell, Sherlock?"

"Loafers. Loose around the instep. Ground's wet. Squish."

"You're making it up," Vernon said, his voice low. He allowed him-self to be pulled up by the wrist to level ground.

"I think I got left behind." Vincent looked only partially relieved in the darkness.

"They probably heading for Plaza Drugs. The wife of one of Spencer's army buddies left a package for pickup. Any news from your end?"

Vernon hunched Lafayette in the back as Vincent gave his report, distractedly, casting his eye around the wooded area and clearly afraid.

"So they think Innis split after all?" Lafayette used his stick to point out what they'd been investigating. "A boat was down there where you see the weeds bent and broken. And up there." He waited for the teacher to swing around in the direction of the hill terraced by wind and rain. "A boat was there and it was heavily weighted."

"Pretty long boat," Vincent said, gauging the length of the lines cut into the grass and mud up above.

"Drag marks. Where the lines cut in deep is where the rowboat was sitting. At least three people were in it to make that depression."

"A rowboat?" Vincent looked from the hill, where a three-foot-wide swath cut through the greenery to the bank, and then to the river, iridescent with filth. He turned to follow the two vets up the hill to take pictures.

"Watch it," Lafayette called over his shoulder.

"I see it." Vernon waved the teacher away from a patch of leaves.

Vincent stopped, patted the leaves with his foot, and jumped back when the leaves and dirt caved in. He was still leaning over looking into the pit when a flash went off on the hill, and then the two vets returned and squatted down by the hole.

"This was dug," Lafayette said, shining a light. The hand he reached in with was swallowed up by the dark.

"Big enough to hold a body?"

Vernon looked across the ditch at the schoolteacher. "You don't look like you want an answer to that." He took the stick, measured the diameter, then held it down and reached way in to demonstrate the pit's depth again.

Vincent looked from one man to the other. "What outfit were you two in?"

It was Vernon who answered. Lafayette was rubbing his head again and swiveling around squinting at the bank area and the crushed-grass swath up above. "Twenty-fifth Infantry, Easy Company. That's a laugh. You?"

"Sat that one out. Volunteer?"

"You could say so. Thought I'd get me an athletic scholarship to college like my buddy here," he said as Lafayette stood up and began lining up the three target areas with the stick. "Ole Laf here left me behind. So I tried ROTC. Figured I'd work during my freshman and sophomore years, then buy my way out of the contract. But I didn't read the fine print. Break your contract with the army, there are two possible paybacks, service or cash. Only, the choice ain't the cadet's, it's the army's. Lay your chickenshit savings on the table, they hand you a uniform. Dar Tieng." Vernon stared off into the thickets where Lafayette had disappeared.

"Those were some films this afternoon."

Vernon nodded, listening for telltale signs. Either his buddy was taking a piss or he'd found something.

"Kind of makes you want to camp out in the woods." Vincent's laugh was forced. He couldn't make out Vernon's expression, but he seemed attentive squatting there, his back straight, his neck pulled up.

"You've probably seen these pamphlets that're all over the place calling for action," Vincent continued, dropping his voice. "Clearly a bunch of misfits, but I want some action too. I think we all do. And when you're feeling impotent, your first recourse is to want to take over."

"First a good fuck," Vernon said, turning his head when a twig snapped. Vincent could see the cords were bunched in his neck now.

"When it looks like the leaders aren't going to move, your own sense of impotence gives you crazy ideas. You find yourself thinking about—"

"Running for office."

Lafayette had returned and was squatting down, twirling the stick in the pit.

"Try to line all three areas up in one shot, Vern, so we can picture what might have happened here." He led the way up the hill, jumping over a patch of brush flowers.

"I see them." Vernon veered around the purplish flowers, pulling his Nikon out of his bag and fitting a telephoto lens on.

Vernon didn't skirt the flowers, he walked straight through, bending down to scratch his ankles. "What do you two make of that cop from Florida?" He turned his face away when the flash went off.

"Everyone's got their own angle," Lafayette said, leading them down the slippery hill again.

"And what's your angle, or the others'?" Vincent asked. "I don't know how to say this, but Logan and I were remarking that there're a lot of vets and ex-cons in this outfit. Were either of you struck by that?"

Lafayette turned Vernon around by the elbows and held him steady on the slanted bank while he took pictures. "People who've lived in hell maybe have a stake in seeing things set right. Lower, Vern—try to get the storm drain in the lineup too."

"Egos and dollars about covers everyone else. In the city, I mean," said Vincent.

"I know what you mean." Vernon swung his camera bag to the ground. "I don't know why it's so hard for politicians to say 'No comment.' They think they got to mouth off about how the killers are trying to test their philosophy or ruin their career. If the killers were all that interested in challenging them, they'd go after them and leave the children alone."

"Sells papers, I suppose. But the sad part is, many of these sheriffs believe what they're saying. It's not just an opportunity to put their record before the public. I find I agree with McClintock—people are making careers out of this crisis."

"Nobody in their right mind wants these killings to go on," Lafayette said quietly. "Not even the most cutthroat opportunist. Give the Atlanta brass some slack."

"But notice how you qualify it—'in their right mind.' That's the rub. Nobody is in his right mind in Atlanta. Nobody's thinking clearly. People keep interpreting phenomena in terms of their own careers. And the public's buying it. Soon the focus will be on Maynard and the others—they're the victims, not the children. And that's a dangerous cast of mind. It's not unlike the misguided people we saw interviewed in the films today. Do you know what I mean? I mean, by the time any of us discover who knew what and covered it up, people will be predisposed to forgive and forget. 'Poor guy, his career would have been ruined.' "

Lafayette pulled Vincent to his feet and held on to his arm while Vincent slipped the back of his loafers snugly over his heels. "None of which is the point. Is it?"

"I'm not saying that we are in a dangerous frame of mind. But have you stopped to think what frame of mind the people we're tracking are in? Who's to say how frustrated they might be feeling? Who knows what their agenda is?" He bent to scratch his ankles.

"Which is still not the point. Is it? Let's get over to the state police barracks and see what Mason's found out."

Lafayette was immediately moving up the bank, his body on a slant; then he was swallowed up in the thickets, his clothes brushing up against the leaves the only clue to his whereabouts. Vernon took one last look at the Chattahoochee and the buffalo head, then pulled himself up hand over hand to level ground before he trotted off. Vincent took a deep breath and followed, sprinting in the direction of noisy traffic. Cars bumping and rattling over the metal grids of the Jackson Bridge muffled the sound of his squishy loafers.

"What've we got?" Mattie was still buttoning her crinkly dark gray jumpsuit as she pulled out of the parking lot past the all-night drug-store. Sue Ellen's car turned for Briarcliff and beeped twice—goodbye, good luck. Mattie freed her hand and beeped thanks, then turned up Ponce de Leon.

"A hand-drawn map," Clara said from the backseat. The rest of her answer was inaudible as she pulled her dress up over her head.

"A map?" Mattie leaned back in the seat. "Does it include the building where they found the altar?" She pressed further back, then looked in the rearview. Clara was pulling a dark T-shirt down over her head. "Asterisk . . . whereabouts . . ." was all Mattie could make out.

Ever since she'd learned that the first two bodies had been dressed all in black, in clothing the families of the Hope and Evans boys did not recognize, Mattie Shaw had suspected cult involvement in the murders. And although other theories held weight, supporting, as time went on, a multiplicity of patterns, it was the combination pattern of cult-Klan/cult-porn/cult-drugs that swayed her. "There are four times as many adult porno shops as McDonald's," B. J. Greaves used to say, but she too was coming around to a Klan-cult-porn view. Even Dave Morris, the last to hold out for a single-pattern theory, was revising his position.

"I want to see that map," Mattie called out, turning up Peachtree and heading for the print shop. "I think we all will want our own copies of the material."

"Well, be quick about it," Clara said, pulling her slacks up over her hips. "I'll see if there's any indication of the building you mentioned."

At the precinct in February, Mattie Shaw had gotten only a glimpse of the Bible being held as possible evidence. Closed flat for over a month, the torn paper around the knife hole no longer folded in or out, so offering no clue as to where the knife had been driven through, Isaiah or Ezekiel. Even those who'd seen it nailed to the wall were no longer certain which part of the book had been facing out, only that it had been folded open so that the front and back covers were on the same side. Whether it was right side up or upside down was still being debated.

In either case, Isaiah or Ezekiel or both, Mattie was sure of its meaning. A cult defector had surfaced, not to bid for the reward but to build an altar in a place not far from the Mathis home and at a time when the area was being scoured for the still-missing boy. The defector had brought a Bible along, knowing the sight of it nailed to the wall would make the papers. The defector was not communicating anything to the public but was using the media to send a message to friends, members of a cult—shape up or face judgment. There'd probably been other messages left, overlooked, misinterpreted, or kept hidden from the press.

Mattie pulled past the green minibus parked in front of the motel, beeped but got no response. She saw the motel sign in her side view and remembered its importance on the big map.

"If we don't locate Innis, I hope we can connect at least with the woman who's been driving James Baldwin around. Like him, she's well versed in Scripture, Clara. She's an expert too on its use by cult groups." Mattie got no response until she backed into a space across from the Cameo Lounge and asked, "Decent?"

"I see Mr. Sanders has changed too," Clara said, closing her door.

Up ahead, walking with a determined step, was Bible Man. His long-sleeve, dark-green shirt was bunched in the center of his back where his suspenders crisscrossed. He wore his pants high, and the cuffs flapped around the tops of his shoes.

Mattie smiled at Clara. The top four buttons of her cotton jumpsuit were open. "Aren't you hot?"

Clara had changed from all white to all blue. She wore a jacket over the T-shirt and jeans. She pushed up her sleeves in response and they walked into the Greyhound bus station.

Logan was standing on line behind two men arguing loudly about the recent McIntosh case—so loudly, several passengers on line at gate 3 turned around and strolled over.

"I thought Logan was supposed to be on Memorial Drive with your good-looking friend from the barbershop."

Mattie shrugged. "We've been changing cars so fast at the checkpoints. . . . Or maybe he tracked a car here on one of Dowell's range finders."

Logan came over, looking ill. "One's arguing that the identification took so long because the young man had been castrated. The other insists there's no way to cut a man to look like a woman. They don't seem to understand the condition bodies are in fished from the river." His voice caught at the end and he hurried off toward the men's room.

Clara took Logan's place in line and kept her ears open. Mattie went in search of Bible Man. She was sure he'd gone behind the lockers, but when she reached the area near gate 1, there was only a couple sitting on upended suitcases sharing a Danish. Mattie leaned against the travel-insurance counter and surveyed the depot for Bible Man. Then something the man seated on the black alligator suitcase said caught her attention. The couple were discussing hypnosis. In the Vernon Jordan case, an employee of General Telephone was able to recall the license of a car seen just before the sniping. She didn't recognize the other cases, amnesia victims able to describe their attackers or remember causative traumas under hypnosis. But when they began discussing federal guidelines governing the use of hypnosis on witnesses, Mattie saw an opening.

"Do you think the testimony of the Innis witness will hold up under hypnosis?"

They both turned immediately, eyes wide and eyebrows raised; then the woman laughed. "Funny you should mention that," she said, rummaging in her handbag. "We were talking about that less than five minutes ago. How I'd love to audit that session."

"You're forensic psychologists?" Mattie looked from the man to the woman.

"Close," he answered, placing two fingers against his temple and staring off at the arrivals/departures sign. "I have the feeling, yes, it's coming clear as a picture. A group of pilgrims from Chicago will be parading past any minute now."

"A mentalist," the woman said. "Nightclub act. Vegas."

"Mostly kiddie parties," the man demurred.

"You in the business?" The woman was eyeing the jewelry Mattie had neglected to remove for the night's activities. "Well, I'll tell you what I think," she continued when Mattie shook her head no. She withdrew a small square of newsprint from her wallet and unfolded it. "I think the McGill woman is already in an altered state and that she volunteered to undergo hypnosis in an effort to be deprogrammed."

Mattie bent to look at the photograph. It was the right Shirley McGill, but there was nothing in her expression that spelled brainwashing. She nodded anyway. And when she looked up, Logan was leaning against the lockers listening to the woman on the suitcase.

"You're in town to investigate?" he asked.

"Heck no," the woman said. "We've been back and forth all year here trying to build the southeast regional of the National Association of Magicians." She produced a spread of aces from under the photo, then looked up and laughed, hunching the man. "Ahhh, I see what you're thinking, madam, and mindreading isn't even part of my act. We only entertain children. Neither of us have ever hypnotized a child, though they make the best subjects."

"You think that's what's been happening?" Mattie glanced over at Logan and continued. "Do you work with deprogrammers, or have you had any experience with cults?"

"None at all," the man said, turning to look at Logan, who in that split second moved away, disappearing around the side of the lockers. "But I think — *we* think," he corrected himself, bowing from the waist to his companion, "that a cult is an angle; definitely hypnosis. But it would be impossible for the police to question everyone with that ability these days, not with every magazine under the sun offering correspondence courses." He got up, set his case flat on the floor, and sprung the lock. "Health magazines, metaphysical magazines, and look, even comic books."

Mattie reached in and withdrew a magazine she'd seen quite a bit of that afternoon on screen.

"Oh, those." The woman made a face, then clamped her mouth and imitated a barf. "Those *Soldier of Fortune* magazines especially."

"What's your angle in the children's case?" The man looked up. "Are you one of the mothers?" He exchanged a worried look with his companion. "Reporter?"

Mattie concentrated on ads with local PO boxes. One mail order for a house offering a series of learning tapes had a familiar ring from Marzala's niece Gloria talking about her boyfriend, a tech whiz.

"Are you with the police?" the woman asked. "Is that your interest in the case?"

"This is my home," Mattie answered.

"Yes, it must be hard," they both murmured.

"Well," the woman said, brushing crumbs from her lap, "I think the McGill witness was programmed by the drug cult she worked with. I really do. And I also think she's key in the solution of the case. I don't believe the police dismissed her story as quickly as the press reports."

"Keep it," the man said to Mattie. "Keep the whole copy. I get the feeling . . . yes, a definite picture is coming through . . ." He gazed off in the direction of the game arcade with one finger pressed against his temple. ". . . that you are about to take a correspondence course in hypnosis."

"You're good." Mattie winked.

The boys had no heart to go walking. Dave didn't either. It was all they could do to keep to their schedule.

"This street's a dead end." Jonesy was dancing the dance of hot wires.

"Ezra Church Road," Raymond said, pulling his visor down and his shoulders in. "And it's raining."

"You see something, Mr. Morris?" Eddie stuck close.

It was only a hedge. But the damage was noticeable. Smoothly clipped in a boxy shape, the hedge was separated in the middle by a rough, bushy section where the twigs were snapped white. Leaves were scattered on the sidewalk below, and dirt had been kicked up. Had a child run through toward that house? A block captain sign was in the window. Had the pursuer crashed through, not giving a fuck, right there in plain view of the living-room window?

"Wait here a minute." Dave went up the front walk.

But they didn't wait. They recognized the area from the map. One of the two Rogers boys had lived on the block. They followed the youth worker up the front walk and hung back by the mailbox while he knocked on the burglar door. Eddie was the first to go all the way up on the stoop. He found the bell and rang it, then stepped back when Dave glared.

"Whattya think?" Raymond leapt onto the stoop next to Eddie when Dave went in. He stood on tiptoe in an attempt to see downtown over the roofs of the neighborhood. The good-looking girl he'd gotten a chance to talk to before leaving the fancy estate had said that she was going to a party downtown.

"Think what?" Jonesy danced along the walk. He held his elbows in close to his sides as he spun, his shirttails fanning out from his waist.

"Think the cops are holding the McGill lady and just cooked up the story that Innis is a stiff to sucker the cult Klan?"

No one answered right away. From inside the house the "Let's Keep Pulling Together, Atlanta" tune was playing on TV.

"I hate that song." Eddie shivered.

They were silent again, huddled together under the metal awning watching the rain speckle the gray cement walk, each picturing the scene that played over and over on TV. Black and white citizens of all ages holding fast to a rope in a tug-of-war against an invisible team, pulling hard on the rope, some smiling, some seriously straining, pulling up the hill in the sunshine. But what was being dragged up on the other end of that rope? The ten-second public announcement was supposed to be reassuring. It gave them the creeps.

"I say the Al Starkes guy will blow the thing open. The cops keep saying so-and-so was last seen at such a place, and he jumps in every time with 'Wrong.' That mug's swift. He's got the information. He catches them every time they slip up and give out stupid information. He lets Innis take the weight when they want somebody to look bad. Starkes's the brain. They ask him what he's up to, and he says, 'Our agents are in the field.' Smooth. All right, all right." Eddie and Raymond slapped fist.

"I can't relate to that," Jonesy said. "I say they got a safe house somewhere, holing up with the witness. I bet you Starkes and Innis got outstepped and don't even know where the cops and them got her."

"Hmm," Eddie said, and the three watched the walk darken.

"I bet it comes out something like Mr. Morris said, though. Say two or three Bloods were dealing smack in 'Nam and after they got out they worked their way into the Florida-Georgia drug gang. Say one of them got into that kung fu mystical stuff over there, so now over here they're dealing dope and doing some deep religious shit and stuff. So it's a mix—Mafia, spics, dope, spades, religious stuff, 'cause—everybody deals. And when it comes to money, them cult Klan jokes don't give a shit about race hate. Say they got little kids carrying the goods. And say this McGill lady don't like what's going down and books."

"Wait up. Don't forget one of her girlfriends got offed for dipping in the strongbox. That's what made her split."

"Okay. So the group gets her to do something to keep her quiet."

"Like drink blood or eat a dead——"

"Man, shut up. Like take part in some low-down sex stuff or one of them rituals like we saw."

"Like killing one of the kids, or witnessing it, holding him down or something."

"Say they made her stuff the plastic bag down the kid's throat. She won't talk after that. She's scared."

"So she goes to Florida and keeps her mouth shut and maybe dabbles a little at the drug end but stays away from the sacrifice-cult part. But then the reward starts looking good."

"Wait up. First her boyfriend phones and says something about the group's going to grab some retarded guys. She don't pay him no mind. But come March, Eddie Duncan, Larry Rogers, Mike McIntosh, Jimmy Ray Payne——"

"Them guys ain't retarded."

"Would you shut up. The papers say retarded and she's in Florida, so what does she know? Okay, so then she better get something at her back before she makes her move for the reward."

"She hears from somebody that Innis is into guns."

"I heard he was getting guns for that African guy, Idi Amin."

"Okay, so then the cops hear her story and they got to keep her alive to talk at the trial."

"Yeah. So they hole up in one of them fleabag hotels," Jonesy said out of the side of his mouth.

The three were quiet again, gazing off in the direction of downtown. Hanging over a building under construction that shot up through the dark blue haze of the city's neon was a tower crane, its rectangular bar squatting among the rust-red girders of the building like a monster mosquito driving its suckers in, draining the building white.

"Yeah," Eddie said, wriggling in his jacket, "a fleabag hotel."

They could see it. A naked light bulb dangling from the pock-marked ceiling. A bottle of cheap whiskey on the dresser. The hotel sign blinking off and on alongside the window. Shirley McGill chain-smoking in an uncomfortable chair by the closet, away from the window, away from the door. She ain't happy. She ain't talking.

One of the bodyguards tips his chair back against the wall. He's got an automatic across his lap pointed at the window. Another bodyguard, with a hip leather holster strapped across his chest, pours a drink of the cheap whiskey in one of those plastic hotel glasses. He sits half-assed on the dresser, watching the television. The sound is low.

Maynard Jackson is pacing back and forth sweating like Edmond O'Brien in that movie, D.O.A.. He asks a lot of intelligent questions. Real polite, not trying to be tough or anything. Smiling in fact, the way he always does in case any minute he might shake hands with somebody who voted for him. He wouldn't be drinking any of the cheap whiskey, at least not from one of those glasses. Maybe he'd unwrap a glass and rinse it good to drink some Tab.

"Think Maynard carries a piece?"

"Hunh? I was thinking, I hate plastic cups. They split 'fore you can get your head bad."

They couldn't picture Commissioner Brown drinking or carrying a piece either, or sweating, or pacing. They placed him in the bathroom doorway to catch the breeze. Bathrooms had to be guarded. The killers might be across the way with a telescopic sight ready to plug the witness when she got up to pee. Then, just when everybody was looking at *Hee Haw*, one of the killers would zip across on a cat-burglar wire and kick in the window. Maybe he'd get off two shots before Commissioner Brown could wheel around and plug him.

"You think Brown packs heat?"

"Naaah."

"'Posed to, ain't he? He's the top cop."

Jonesy put the smoking gun in Chief Napper's hand and placed him on the toilet tank, unseen by the killers with the binoculars. But the gun didn't seem right in Napper's hand either.

"What about that FBI dude that cooled Innis out? He must carry a piece, hunh?"

"He a jerk. Bet you he empty the trash just like the brother in the movie this afternoon. Come out when they need a nigger for shit detail."

"But wait up. None of Maynard's bodyguards look like they carry pieces to me. They too pretty in them suits. Black belts or something. Wouldn't mess up their threads with a bulge."

"I wouldn't want to be Shirley McGill," Eddie said, leaning against the burglar bar. He could hear Dave talking with the people inside. "Uhhh, where you figure we go from here?"

"Up to Lake Forrest Drive. Just before you get to 285, you run into Lake Placid by the Windmere Apartments. That's where the fat lady in the gypsy getup said to check."

"Who got offed from up that way?"

"Nobody yet. Some Klan-cult joker who deals drugs live up that way."

"What time is it?" Eddie pressed against the wrought iron and peered through the pane of the front door.

"You punkin' out?"

"Naw, I just gotta get home."

"He's punkin' out, the punk."

When Dave opened the door, Raymond and Jonesy had Eddie in a double headlock, wrassling him down the stairs. The shaft of light fell across the walk from the foyer. They heard Dave clear his throat. The two danced Eddie toward the bushes, playfully rubbing his head, jabbing him in the stomach on the sly.

"You clowns," Dave said. "Next time I'll issue little permission slips for you mugs and take you to the playground."

"Oh, wow." Jonesy curved his body around and aimed two index fingers toward the asphalt. "That's cold. That's really cold, Mr. Morris." He hugged his waist with his elbows and twisted around to mask the view, angling his thumbs and pinkies down toward the base of the hedges. "Ain't that cold, y'all?"

"Yeah, Big Dave," Raymond said, ramming Eddie's head in the bushes. "You really know how to hurt a person."

"It's like a bad marriage, isn't it?" the former SAFE worker asked the college girl. They let another bus go by, their eyes glued to the door of the State Police building. "You know he's cheating and he knows you know, but he tells you it's your imagination. Says he loves you. Says, 'Trust me.' And maybe he does love you, but it's not important to him that you doubt yourself. You see the signs but you talk yourself out of it. You go on cooking the food and washing the clothes and coming to bed like a good wife."

"I can't make love to a man I'm mad with," the young student said, walking over to drop the newspaper into the trash bin. A red-haired man came out of the gray metal door with a tripod. She signaled the Blood in dreads parked at the curb. Mason had already moved near the van where the redhead was unlocking the door.

When the student returned to the bus stop the worker continued. "What's going on in this town is really frightening to me because, getting back to the bad-marriage analogy, say your husband's girlfriend is a very violent sort of person. She's bought a gun and is hanging around your apartment building. She could call up your job and say something to make them fire you. You won't even know how to protect yourself. 'I love you.' 'Trust me.' He wants your loyalty but he don't care about your safety. And you cooperate. It's stupid and crazy. What else can you call that?"

"Feudalism," Speaker said, passing by them and crossing the street.

The student laughed. "First of all, my man come at me with some simple shit like that, I'd shoot him in the foot."

"You'd shoot him?"

"In the foot. To get his attention." She jotted down a description of the van. "He's got to know we're about to have a serious discussion and that there are consequences for lying."

"I see what you mean. Maybe when people run for office, they should be shot in the foot first."

"To remind them that they're accountable."

"That's probably a good idea. Because you can't know who they're holding hands with. I love Maynard. I think Lee Brown is a fine person. I don't know George Napper but I hear he's very nice."

"My sister took a course from him. He's real decent."

"That's what I mean. But who knows what kind of people they're holding hands with—on the force, I mean, or in the FBI, or with the state bureau. They tell us to remain calm and everything."

" 'Trust me. I love you. I'll take care of it. Don't worry about it.' "

"That's just how they do, don't they? Meanwhile, somebody's out there with guns and ropes."

"And bombs," the student added as they headed to the car. "And now with these," she said, shoving over, placing the stack of pamphlets on her lap to make room.

"That's why I had to leave SAFE. I liked my job, but you can't love the people if you lie to them."

The student drew the safety belt across her lap, glad to see the brothers coming. It was just a matter of time before the sister she was cooped up with started to cry.

"I think I know where he's headed," Mason said, climbing in. "Either back to Lakewood Heights—" he roamed his finger over the map—"or to that room in the City Hall Annex."

"I don't think so." Speaker leaned his head in the window, reached in, and spun the map around. "He'll steer clear of the feds. I think he'll make contact with an informant. Maybe here," he said, tapping a marked-up portion on the route.

"Let's go," the student said, focusing. "That light won't stay red forever. And these binoculars can't see around corners."

The near-collision of the Camaro and the two lead cars of the McDaniel-Glenn patrol left Preston shaken and with a welter of questions. Zala took the wheel before Dowell could speak up. With Preston climbing in back to straighten up the pamphlets the patrol had dumped through the window, Dowell had no choice but to ride in the bucket seat. No matter how many levers he was directed to lift, push, punch, yank, the seat wouldn't lock. Zala turned onto Georgia Avenue and Dowell pressed his feet against the hump in the floorboard in a futile effort to keep the seat from bucking.

"I don't get it," Preston said. "All the cruisers in the area and not one stopped to see what was going on. Those guys were really pissed off with you, buddy. Worse than with me. A cracked reflector's no sweat. But you, you didn't look too good back there. They expect you to be on top of things. Oh yeah, the cop on top of things."

"At the moment," Zala said, heading for Cap'n Peg's, "the police are more interested in gathering up those copies. Besides, nobody was going to jump anybody. The men are trying to get the youngsters off the street, that's all." She glanced at Dowell as she pulled up in front of the fish joint. The seat was still sliding on its track. "I want to see if there's been any word here. I'll meet you back at the Hyatt or hook up with you at the last checkpoint."

"Well, I still don't get it," Preston said, climbing in front when Dowell took the wheel and headed for I-75/85. "What's so hot about a bunch of ungrammatical rags?"

"No one knows where they came from."

"So?"

"You think you've got the neighborhood secured, then something like this happens, a mass delivery right under your nose."

"Right under *your* nose," Preston cracked. "No, you really looked pretty bad back there. And why'd they unload their copies in this car? They want you to hold them in case the police stop them? I don't get it." He leafed through the booklets, glancing from time to time at Dowell, who was keeping his eyes peeled for cars that might be traveling together. He changed lanes and tailed a Galaxy that seemed to be following a brown-and-beige Chevy.

Once before, the city had been swamped by a phantom delivery of booklets. The Weather Underground's *Prairie Fire* had turned up one morning on stoops, in mailboxes, slipped under the doors of student unions, and left by the bundle in shopping malls, at Street Academy sites, and at Jobs Corps centers. No one knew how they had done it. But their manifesto hadn't produced nearly the flurry this anonymous little booklet was causing. Dowell tried to recall what the political climate had been like five years ago when *Prairie Fire* appeared.

"Subversive literature pop up much in your neck of the woods?"

"Oh yeah. Was some leafletting back in December when the Beatle got killed, especially in Miami, but nothing out-and-out political like this. A few peaceniks. Biggest thing I can remember was down in Key West when I was in school. Big scandal about the water supply. That ring a bell, Dowell? Experiments down at the naval base? It was a big stink."

"I think I heard tell." Dowell changed lanes again, keeping the blue Ford and a two-toned station wagon in view. "Flu virus, wasn't it?"

"Germ-warfare testing was the charge. A lot of paper got thrown around the streets behind that one. I remember it because a navy recruiter came to speak in our assembly and got booed."

"That was the Korean War era, wasn't it?"

"The tail end." Preston's fingers tapped rapidly on the cover of the pamphlet as he tallied up the years. "I'll be putting in for retirement soon."

Dowell ended pursuit when the Galaxy exited and the two-tone continued on. He took the ramp and looked over at his colleague from Florida. That morning, Dowell would have said forty at most, a boozer, red veins prominent in the cocoa brown of his face, slightly flushed, thoroughly inflamed around the nose. Not particularly clean. But hardly middle-aged-looking.

"You get women out on the streets sometimes handing out flyers in front of the triple-X movies. But not like these things. There's no logo, no sponsor, not even a printer's name. What do you make of it, Dowell?"

"What you just said gives me an idea. Someone you might know. Once we find out who's going over the murder route, managing to stay a jump ahead of us."

"Something I said?" Preston folded the visor down and leaned into the mirror, searching the oily area under his lower lip for pimples. "Porno movies, you mean? I guess you guys had trouble up this way a few years back with that flick where the actress gets it in the end? I didn't see any booklets, but there sure was plenty of flyers about it."

"I don't get movies like that," Dowell said, heading for the Lake-wood-Stewart strip. "I don't see how tormenting women can be arousing. I know a little about this business they spoke of in the films too, people so-called adopting poor children from overseas and using them in sex-hate films. You hear all sorts of things in the squad room. Children. That's what I don't get."

"Sex hate." Preston laughed, lumping his cheek out with his tongue. "That's a new one. I never heard that expression before." It seemed to amuse him, or maybe it was squeezing his face that gave him so much pleasure. Dowell kept his eyes front.

"Look at that." Preston leaned out the window. A shoving match was taking place in front of a grocery store. "Going to kill each other defending a street corner. My people, my people. Bad as down my way. Miami is where you really see it, though. I was on a three-week assignment there after the riots in Liberty City. I was nowhere near northwest Fifty-fourth or Brownsville. What a mess. Lot of political leafletting then too. Yeah, they had demands, but that was something else. Talking drugs, you'd die laughing, Dowell, to see them dudes out there killing each other defending turf for 'the man.' "

"Same here," Dowell murmured. "Breaks your heart to see our young men caught up in that."

"Breaks *your* heart," Preston corrected. "Nobody forcing them into it. They see the bodies in the street every day, dealers slumped over the wheel with a bullet between the eyes. Nobody forcing them to get in the life."

"They think it can't happen to them."

"No, they know it can. They know it *will*—just a matter of time. But they don't care."

"The money's that good?"

"The money's that good. Live it up for two years—three if they're lucky and halfway smart. Then, if they got to go down, well, it was beautiful while it lasted."

The two men in Dowell's rearview wore armbands on their sleeves. "I don't think that tussle back there is drug related. Those are neighborhood patrollers. Probably having a difference of opinion about whose turn it is to go on night watch."

"If you want to believe that." With two hands, Preston squeezed the enlarged pores at the base of one nostril. Dowell turned his eyes front and kept them there.

"I've seen some of those films," Preston confided. Leaning back, he rubbed his hands along his thighs. "Let's be honest, a naked body is a turn-on whoever it is."

"A child? Maybe that's true for some people, but you check that kind of feeling, you control yourself."

"Why?" Preston braced his legs to keep the bucket seat from riding. "Don't kid me. You see these young schoolgirls flipping their asses around," he said, clutching the air with both palms, "and oh yeah, you want to get into some of that."

"I can't get to that," Dowell said with finality. The rest he left unsaid. He had an ongoing discussion with some of the junior officers about capital punishment. Despite the way the death penalty had been applied to the poor and the colored, some people needed killing, badly. Those who enjoyed murdering. And those who thought exploiting children was a turn-on and made no effort to check themselves.

"So this is the Lakewood-Stewart area," Preston said after a while. "Personally, I think we ought to shake this committee tour and follow through on what I've done so far. With the tips from Lee Gooch, we could be sitting pretty, Dowell. You and me. We pool our information and nail the perverts. What do you say?"

"Same's I've been saying."

Preston held his legs still for a moment and looked out at the houses and stores. "I understand the district we just left was once an affluent neighborhood. It's hanging on by the fingernails now same as around here."

"This piece of real estate has had more than its share of sorrows," Dowell said. "You'll notice how the highway separates the shopping plaza from the customers who might have made it a go. No accident."

"Now you sound like that character with the militant hair. The Committee of Inquiry," he said with a sneer. "Funny company you keep."

"That's true." Dowell hoped that would hold Preston for a while. He didn't like a lot of gab while on assignment, even unofficial assignments.

"I still think we could join up and maybe go see the Gooch kid together, or take another look in his neighborhood."

"There's a team covering the Cape Street section of the route," Dowell said. The young reporter with the good diction knew that area well. Just as Dowell knew the Lakewood-Stewart area from growing up there. Since the division by the highway, those neighborhoods were going down a little year by year, definitely not part of Atlanta's boomtown show.

"Damn shame," Dowell murmured, cutting through the parking lot of the shopping plaza.

"Yeah, it's pret-ty grubby," Preston said, looking around.

The sodium streetlights cast a sci-fi spell over the area. Deserted, the stores looked grim, sour. A scatter of paper bags and broken-down boxes were in the lanes for handicap parking. Poles installed to prevent the removal of shopping carts were plastered with "Keep Our Children Safe" stickers. No one was around, Dowell was pleased to see. No children vending tapes, batteries, car deodorizers, jelly apples. No youths coming up to the car with an armful of watches for sale, or sidling over with two-for-one bargains—jeans, killer weed, or "buffet" at the motel.

"Looks pretty quiet," Preston agreed as Dowell nosed the car around the back of the supermarket for a shortcut to the street. "But who are they kidding over there?"

On the sidewalk, a redheaded man setting up a tripod glanced over at the car, then kicked the legs open and screwed his eye to the viewfinder. Further down the street, his partner was pulling a measuring tape along the curb. "That guy is wired," Preston said.

Nothing about the street that Dowell could see warranted surveying, assaying, protecting, or casing. If the one in the gutter was that obviously wired there'd be trouble, a sign of a backup team somewhere.

"You ought to run them in on GP. If they're undercover, they ought
to be sent back to the academy for a brushup." Preston turned in his seat
to watch the surveyor team from the rear window. "What kind of scam
do you think that is? Speaking of scams, how do you think this Abscam
case'll turn out? A good lawyer should be able to get them off with en-
trapment."

"Which reminds me," Dowell interrupted, "I need to find a phone."

"Well, you got lots to pick from," Preston said, taking his hand
from his face long enough to make a sweep of the area. SISTER MARTHA
READS . . . JESUS SAVES . . . CORRECT CHANGE ONLY AFTER 10 P.M . . .
THE NIGHT ATTENDANT DOES NOT KNOW THE COMBINATION TO THE
SAFE. ELECTRIC PACHINKO . . . BEER BY THE KEG . . . TOPLESS A-GO-
GO . . . MOTEL ROOMS—SPECIAL RATES . . . ADULT BOOKSTORE.

Dingy pennants strung around the used-car lot hung limp in the
April night, and Dowell on the phone wished he'd kept to his original
schedule and was home with Rose. A van cruised by and the driver
slowed down as Dowell dropped another dime. The van not one of Inquiry's, he turned his back.

He left a message at the station house for the officers to call him at
home. He felt duty bound to back them up. He'd not been listening to
their troubles, had mistakenly assumed that the "preacher" who'd been
the target of the zealous senior officers was Reverend Carroll of STOP
and not Reverend Vivian of the anti-Klan group. The junior officers
would have to watch their backs. Payback could be more deadly than
anything Internal Affairs meted out. On occasion Dowell had been advised to take time off, to go to Quantico, Virginia, where the FBI offered courses, until things blew over. And then he'd be extra wary of any
new partner they assigned him on his return.

"That Abscam business," Preston was saying as they sped off. "Hard
to say no when everyone else is saying yeah. How can you know they're
in cahoots setting you up? Brainwashing is what it is more than en-
trapment. That would be my defense. Brainwashing."

Dowell ran his hand over his belt buckle, shaking his head. "I once
took a course at Quantico on brainwashing. The instructor had been
with Army Intelligence in Korea."

"Sweet deal, that place," Preston sighed. "I lay up there sometimes. I've never connected with any course that was useful. Know what I mean? But take the situation with Logan's kid. That's brainwashing. The kid drops out of school 'cause his buddies are running around in sheets with begging bowls and they talk him into it. They're already brainwashed. Pretty soon he can't think straight. They're all saying the same thing, so he goes along with it. Were you there when Logan was telling about the time he almost had him?"

"I didn't hear that part."

"His wife spotted the kid with a bunch of other kooks near a bus terminal. I forget what city they were in at the time. The kid's eighteen, so what can they do? The desk sergeant advises them to swear out a warrant and charge theft. You know, the family car, the tuition checks. A detective tells them to wait at the hotel while he makes the collar. They wait and they wait. Finally they catch the detective at the station and he gives them some song and dance. But you and I know, same as he pocketed Logan's check, he had them kooks empty their bowls in his hand and bye-bye."

"I don't know if I know that," Dowell said, pulling into the gate of the Atlanta Junior College campus. "He paid the officer to arrest his son?"

"Aw, come on, Dowell, you act like you've never heard of that before."

They bumped over the speed breaker and Preston slid into the dashboard. Dowell reached for the booklets.

"Who's he?"

A man had stepped from the campus security booth. He bent down to look through the windshield, then sauntered over, looking from Preston to Dowell to the make of the car.

"Friend of mine," Dowell said. "Used to own the newsstand in my neighborhood until they ran him out of business. You want the magazines you need, you've got to buy the ones they want you to sell. He said no."

"Muscle?"

"Porn ain't a polite business, Preston."

"Same in my neck of the woods—same all over, I guess."

The security guard stopped where the light from the booth ended and planted his hands on his hips, barring entrance to the grounds.

"Family man," Dowell said. "So what do you say to your daughters when they drop by the stand with their friends and see those magazines?"

"Some women like that kind of thing," Preston said.

Dowell got out and slammed the door.

"Am I glad to see you, Jess!" The security guard shook Dowell's hand and walked him away from the car. "Things seem to be taking a nasty turn and I'm here all alone—my partner's on the highway side of the campus. Won't do me much good if they come back. Got a make on those yet?" He steered Dowell toward Area Tech, the vocational college that shared the grounds with the junior college. A plane from a nearby base was parked there. It gave the quad a movie-set look.

"I was hoping you had something, Jake."

"What I have is the shakes. Pretty weird, this delivery business, wouldn't you say?"

"I was hoping you'd say, like, where these pamphlets came from?"

The guard unbuttoned his shirt and pulled out a copy. Same sloppy typing, hastily placed staples, a few pages upside down and slanted margins lost in the cropping.

"When I came on duty Friday night this place was a mess. They missed this one. I found it stuck under the propeller. I guess they were so busy keeping tabs on the Iranian students they didn't do a good job in collection. But I say it's the skinheads. And they could come back."

"Jake, I wonder if we could get together on some of this," Dowell said, following the guard around to the back of the plane. "They were delivered on Friday?" He watched Jake's Adam's apple ride up and down. "And was it the APD or the college administrations that scooped them up and fingered a group of students?"

The guard pulled out his cigarettes and thought back for a minute. "I came on duty and found a bunch of new officers I've never seen before. That happens sometimes. We don't like the meddling, but it happens. You never know which bureau is coming on board to keep an eye on the Iranian students. Sometimes Immigration, sometimes the APD Intelligence boys."

"Iranian students . . . But you don't think they put these booklets out. You say the skinheads. Who are they?" Dowell shook his head no when the pack was offered. Two skinny joints were in the pack. "You know I don't partake."

They leaned against the cool gray metal and examined the how-to manuals again, how to take over the city before it was too late. In the four pages that preceded the how was the what and the why. The facts of the case were mixed with some of the better-known rumors, together with high-flying charges that were new to Dowell, one being that a high-ranking APD official had had insurance policies on some of the victims, kids that he often entertained on his boat up at Lake Lanier; further, that he was the lover of one of the slain men.

"Thrown together," the guard said. "That's what I make of it. Thrown together and tossed from a speeding car is what I hear. No deliveries were made in the northeast, just our side of town. And the patrol cars rushed in so soon after to gather them up there's no way they could have missed catching them, except of course they did. Then the second bunch of cars, sneaker cars, drove in and thoroughly ruined my day. Talking about 'Pick this up,' 'Pick that up,' like I'm the janitor on their payroll. I had to set them straight. I don't care what rank you hold at your bureau, it cuts no ice with me. You know what I mean? That goes for this security job too. Fuck this job."

"Can we reason this out together, Jake?" Dowell slowly turned pages.

"Sounds like our people, don't it? Until you read it aloud and then it don't. It's the skinheads, I'm telling you. Stockpiling weapons and ready for war."

"Skinheads?"

"Those motorcycle gangs that shave their heads and paint swastikas. You know, busted up the rock concert last month. Gotta watch those guys. But who's to watch them white boys? Administration too busy watching Black folks on faculty. Bureau guys like I said jumping out of the trees every time one of these Iranians yells 'Down with the Shah.' I thought that cat was dead and buried, but once a week somebody's got a sheet strung across the quad demanding his head. I come to work, no telling who's in my chair with his feet up, taking pictures, taking names, cops stepping all on each other and trying to lord it over me. I ain't confused. And I ain't impressed with their badges."

"What's the college's stand on all of this?"

"Mum's the word is their policy. They think the Black faculty is into it. But I say no. There's no mind here." He slapped the booklet,

then took a toke, holding in the smoke and gulping. "I've been studying this thing. And it's not us. The language is too dippy. Who calls
Maynard "Jackson"? When have we ever run around talking about
stringing somebody up? And then they say near the end that Black
folks need to be rounded up for their own protection. Dead giveaway.
It's the skinheads. I've seen some of the flyers they put out trying to recruit punk rock groups. It's them all right." He buttoned the booklet
back up in his shirt.

"They hang around here?"

"Are you crazy? These students bust their humps all day and don't
want no shit when they come here. Those skinheads would be grease
smears before they could even hand out one of these. That's why they
threw them and kept on trucking. Nazis, Jess. Dead giveaway when
they start talking that roundup talk. I wish somebody would come up
to me talking about rounding up folks for our own protection."

"Any connection between this and Innis? What's the word on the
wire?"

"They ran his ass out of town is my guess, ran him out before he got
too much stardust in his eyes. He should've brought his own cameras
along. People here ain't going to let an outsider get but so big in this
case."

"What about his witness, his evidence? Heard anything about the
boyfriend?"

"If you mean the girl's cabdriver boyfriend, he's back on the street.
So I guess the evidence didn't add up to nothing. You the cop, Jess, you
tell me."

"I'm sorry to say I don't know anything."

Jake drew on the joint, eyeing the shorter man for a minute before
a slow grin bloomed into a sly smile, then erupted into signifying
laughter. "I hear you, Jess. 'Cause the one thing this little book got
right—and it's my guess it's the reason the blue boys were grabbing
these up—is that they're on to that pal of yours."

"Pal of mine?" Dowell waited for Jake to stop laughing. "Who's
that?" He held his face still, but that only sent Jake into another giggling fit. "I don't suppose you want to whisper his name in my ear?"

"You suppose right. Mean a bastard as he is, I wouldn't even give
you his initials for a pound loaf. Aww, Jess, I know I owe you one. You

bailed me out and I ain't forgotten. But you're the detective. If I know and these skinheads know, you've got to know. So get him. Run these Nazis in and get him. Then we can all get some sleep."

"You're telling me that there's a connection between the skinheads and . . . my pal? Now think, Jake," Dowell said. "Consider the source."

"Like you say, all right. But I find it real interesting that they seem to know more about him than you do."

Dowell heard the beeper sound in the booth. The guard started in that direction, then waited as if he wanted to be prodded. Smoke streamed out of his mouth and he sucked it up into his nostrils, a trick that never failed to stump Dowell. He was not thinking fast enough. What Jake had said about the pamphlet's authors trying to stir the Black community to revolt seemed right—it was in line with attempts at manipulation by groups he'd seen interviewed on screen. And more than once he'd heard talk in the squad room that members of the Charles Manson gang were in Atlanta on a helter-skelter mission. But what made Jake give credence to the "pal"'s involvement, given the source?

"You don't think you're being had?" was as far as Dowell got before Jake moved off to catch the beeper. Dowell followed him across the quad. He waited while Jake picked up, looked around at the bushes, the dim-lit buildings, the stranger in the crumpled clothes leaning against the red Camaro, then shook his head no, no deal, no more discussion. Duty was calling. Jake immediately left the booth and headed toward the highway side of the campus. Nothing in his gait suggested an emergency or a situation Dowell should wait to hear about.

So Dowell walked slowly back to the car. Maybe Rose could get more information from Jake's wife, her bowling partner. And maybe it was time for him to go down to the station house and poke around, see what the word was on these booklets and on the skinheads and on this "pal." It didn't take great intelligence to figure out who was meant—the boat up at Lake Lanier the key clue—but Dowell put no store in rumors.

Preston looked eager. "Something?"

"I need to find a phone."

"You know, Dowell, with half the reward you could buy you some AT&T shares," Preston joked, tossing the car keys to the stodgy detective. "I still say we ought to pursue the leads I've already got from the

Gooch kid. The right-wing angle's only one of the patterns. The easier angle is the one you guys keep overlooking. It'd be a cinch to collar the perverts. No one's going to let you uncover the Klan angle, so let's go for the easy money."

"The easy money," Dowell said, his voice flat, and over the sound of the motor he could hear the visitor from Florida making a noise in his throat, something between a grunt, a gargle, and a groan of exasperation. Dowell backed the car out onto Stewart Avenue and spun the wheel hard, jerking the bucket seat off its track.

"Was it something I said?" Preston laughed, playing with the levers.

"Perhaps you'd like to substitute a fruit salad," Delia said helpfully when once again Carole attempted to dip her spoon into the cream of cucumber soup only to have the surface pucker. "Looks like pond scum," she added, turning to call one of the waiters over.

The waiting had begun to frazzle nerves. Few tables were filled, and many had been totally abandoned by guests who took their place cards to other tables to be with friends.

The two women looked toward table 31, where Bryant, an ample supply of business cards tucked in his cummerbund, was glad-handing the Lederers. At one large table were four generations, from glistening pigtails to snowy white chignons and beards, a few jerri curls and forties-styled pageboys in between.

At table 17, several men reared back in their chairs, laughing loudly, ribbing the other men, who rolled from side to side fumbling for their wallets. Last year, Delia had learned, bets had been made on the outcome of the trial of Jimmy Carter's ex–budget director. The winners at the table near the dance floor were gloating, boasting political realism. The losers grumbled about nepotism and good-ole-boyism, and continued fumbling, maintaining that the bet should run until the next trial, for there had to be a next trial, the crooks.

"It'll be all right, Delia," Carole said with a bosomy sigh, and Delia smiled, grateful for the encouragement, though whether Carole was referring to the evening's festivities or to the "Spencer operation" was unclear.

The bellboy glided up, bent, and whispered into Carole's ear. She didn't take her handbag, Delia noted; she simply rose, her lavender strapless rising too but in a breathtaking three-second delay, and swept off across the dance floor.

Delia watched heads turn as her employee went out the doors. She felt tired. The heady anticipation of an evening out hobnobbing, the elegance of the gathering, the prospects of profitable encounters, had been initially spoiled when they'd been seated at table 23, close to the door to the ladies' lounge and obviously a last-minute addition. The table, much smaller than the others, and round, not square, was draped in white-on-white only, different from the peach-and-lime color scheme that marked the gala's decor. Added to that were Carole's constant comings and goings, with only the slimmest hints as to what she was up to. And only after a great deal of prodding did she share what, after all, was their business, being family. "Why you, Carole?" and the thoughtless response, thoughtlessness a rarity in their years of working together, "Who else can he depend on?" Delia had not sufficiently recovered from that, with Bryan's affectionate squeezing of her hand under the table more annoying than soothing, when Carole, leaning down to retrieve a slip of paper, said, as Delia was pointing out young people on their way up, "You mean wired up."

She'd been mistaking cocaine confidence for success. She must have been on the threshold of that knowledge for some time. Drugs certainly explained a lot of behavior, alliances she could never fathom, directives that gave her the responsibility of covering others' mistakes and making them look good. In recent years, watching people who'd been under her in seniority and know-how go off to Washington when Carter was elected, she'd told herself she'd been outclassed by youthful stamina and the confidence that came with family background, good education, and connections. But all along she'd been competing against the euphoria and enthusiasm of cocaine and didn't know it.

Delia poured herself a glass of wine. In spite of it all, and while running their real-estate business too, she'd managed to become a supervisor. There was something to be said for that. She toasted the silver-papered gift she'd brought along for her brother and resolved to have a pleasant evening, whether the Webbers showed or not. Their delay was merely impolite; the lateness of the children was worrisome.

"Such a good-looking bunch of people," Bryan said, hiking up his jacket in back to sit down. His chest high, his eyes shining, it could have been his testimonial dinner and not a bon voyage for the Webbers, who some said were leaving Atlanta at "someone"'s request. She'd thought of eavesdropping to learn about this "someone"—the DA, the mayor, the governor. She hoped their leaving had nothing to do with the favor she'd asked of Mrs. Webber. Mrs. Webber had interceded and gotten the phone company to tap Marzala's incoming calls.

"Who is that keeps calling Carole away, do you think?" Delia reached over and patted Carole's evening bag. "Not even a key or a lipstick, Bry." Paper crinkled inside the silver mesh bag. "She must know that when Nathaniel brings the children Zala will likely come along."

"They're grown people, Dee," was all he said, and was up again and gone before she could answer.

A number of people were crossing the parquet floor to the main doors. Those already there were chattering excitedly. When the doors were opened, a commotion from the lobby below attracted more people. Several musicians peeped from behind the curtain, then stepped out on stage. The piano player took up his position on the bench, looking for the emcee at table 21 to give him the high sign. Judging from the way people rushed out squealing, either Lena Horne or Prince Charles and Diana had come to the Hyatt.

Delia caught a glimpse of her niece and nephew stepping back to let people out. They turned in the direction of the corridor that led to the ladies' lounge. Delia placed her napkin by her plate and got up, carefully. She gathered up the skirt of her gown so as not to upset the ashtray where Bryan's cigar was smoldering. She resisted the urge to stub it out.

Delia swept toward the side door as the band glided into *La Mer.* Moving expertly in the narrow aisles between tables, she smiled hello to those who looked up in greeting.

A lovely young woman in green and a handsome young boy in a dark blue suit stood in the corridor. Not recognizing them, Delia moved directly to the mezzanine rail where Kofi and Kenti leaned over waving to someone below. By the fountain, seated on the nubby white sofas that encircled a glass coffee table, were her brother, an old man in suspenders, and Judge and Mrs. Webber.

"Walk on by like you don't know us, Mother!"

Delia wheeled around just as the smaller children leapt at her and almost knocked her over. She felt something pop. "Well, look at you!"

"Well, look at *you!*"

"And look at you two."

"We'll be out here all night talking silly and miss the food." Gloria took Kenti's hand and went into the ballroom.

Delia bent down and inspected her strap.

While Alice Moore passed a snapshot around to the housekeeping staff and B. J. conversed with hotel security, Zala looked out of the Hyatt Regency's glass elevator at the adjacent building. It was gray, gaunt, cold as a cliff. She was supposed to take up her post there in less than ten minutes.

As they rode down, collecting guests who gazed out on the rooftops below, Zala recalled the days in the sixties when Gerry and Maxwell would drag her from one tall height to another, directing her view through binoculars. They'd taught her to observe which roofs bore large white X's, either chalked thick or painted with a wide brush. Homes of civil rights workers, supporters, donors, churches that hosted interracial meetings were kept under constant surveillance from street level to the sky. The Student Non-Violent Coordinating Committee building on Spring Street was the one roof she could pick out from any vantage point—from the Equitable Life Building, from the bank towers, later from the rooftop restaurants of the new skyscraper hotels. It was Zala's privilege as a child to transport the can of black spray paint to the top of the building owned by SNCC. As often as three times a week she sprayed the X black so armed helicopters could not easily locate it.

"Who's the man in the picture?" B. J. nudged her arm from the rail and Zala turned. Alice Moore was huddled with the security man in his gray flannels and blue blazer. Zala shrugged and B. J. moved to that side of the car.

Everyone who boarded was in a chatty mood, the talk tinged with giddy nervousness as the glass car floated down past vine-tangled balconies toward the city streets below. A tourist just in from vacation in South America was telling his companion about the corrugated lean-tos in Lima, relieved that no unruly *cholos* threatened their family-reunion holiday in Atlanta. A woman joined their conversation to say that in Rio the geography was the reverse; bandits lived in the hills with the poor and frequently came down from the favelas to raid the estates below. The threesome, chummy by the time the car reached the thirtieth floor, agreed that travel in Third World countries was dodgy.

On the twenty-sixth floor, another couple got on talking of "Les toits de Paris"—the roofs of Paris. The woman, clinging to the man's arm, hummed the song in a jangling fashion. On Peachtree Street below were tourists in straw hats taking a buggy ride to Underground Atlanta, where the couple were going. Dante's Down the Hatch had a good jazz combo, the woman interrupted her singing to say. Zala heard B. J. mutter something. Like the Omni, the Underground was feeling the impact of the curfew. The Omni skating rink was now closing at nine. The Omni movie theater, in a last-ditch effort to balance its books, had lowered its prices, vying with the dollar movie houses. Pan bands, breaker crews, and assorted young noisemaker artists who used to set up in the Underground parking lot weren't there anymore to be chased away. Word was, someone had been hired to lure them back.

On the nineteenth floor, another tall, slender preppy type in gray flannels and blue blazer boarded, palming his walkie-talkie and saluting his colleague, who immediately drew him over and introduced him to B. J. The word was the same. Reporters, plainsclothes detectives, STOP members, and amateur sleuths were still streaming into the Hyatt looking for Roy Innis, Al Starkes, and Shirley McGill.

"I wish we could post a notice," the new security man said.

On twelve, the guards changed over. The two lookalikes held the door open for the two new men in blazers and flannels, and apologized to those aboard for the delay as they got off. Strains of "You Light Up My Life" drifted up from the mezzanine ballroom and Zala turned again to look out at the hard, buff-gray line of the building next door. Lights in the lower three stories were blinking like failing fluorescents. She pressed close to the rail to make room for two businessmen with shiny, tight, fresh-shaven faces who, though slim, seemed to need a lot of room to trade roof stories.

In Tokyo, one explained, it was best not to book quarters anywhere near the university: students in post-exam disgrace were known to fling themselves from high ledges like kamikaze pilots. The other spoke of the pigeon coops on the roofs of the San Juan hovels across the river from the Hotel Flamboyan. Eyesores, they spoiled the vista as one looked out from the casino windows to watch the sun set.

B. J. beckoned Zala over to hear what the security men had to say. It didn't vary much from the earlier reports.

Days after the CORE group had checked out of the Hyatt Regency to the Downtown Motel at fifty dollars a night, then to the Atlanta at thirty dollars, people were still questioning the housekeepers and over-tipping the bellboys. Hypnotists, private detectives, and free-lance bodyguards left their cards at the desk should the New York–Miami group need help with their witness. Narc squad detectives and members of the Organized Crime Unit were interested in more detailed information from McGill about the cult's drug operations. Members of rival CORE chapters had been in town too, holding forth in the lobbies at each of the three hotels, explaining that the Innis group were not "legitimate" CORE people, that Innis had been ousted at the South Carolina convention, that his term in office as national chairman had been vetoed because of misappropriation of funds, as a recent exposé on 60 *Minutes* documented, that he was a publicity hound, that his self-aggrandizing schemes had threatened the credibility and functioning of the organization—in short, that the man was full of hot air. No word, though, about McGill, one way or the other.

"But what I find peculiar," the older of the two guards said, lowering his voice, "is that members of Atlanta Intelligence and members of the State Organized Crime Squad are in and out of here tailing each other. It's a circus."

He turned his back to the others in the car and looked down to the lobby. B. J. hung in close by his sleeve and made room for Zala. For a long time he was quiet, looking over the people below.

"Two guys in particular have been in and out of here since the Sinatra show."

"Back in February," B. J. said, when he lapsed into silence again. "When there were threats that something would happen during the Sinatra-Davis benefit. So?"

"They were definitely together. They come in within five minutes of each other and leave within five minutes of each other. You never see them actually together, but a few of us have been able to put it together." He turned toward the balconies, looking around. He pressed his back to the rail and gazed out onto the streets, then pivoted around again, surveying the lobby.

"What's your hunch?"

"I don't know. But every time society Blacks have a banquet and the City Hall crowd shows up, we know it won't be long before one or both of them turn up too."

B. J. fingered the gold loop in one ear, then removed both earrings and pocketed them. "Keeping their eye on someone in particular, you think?"

"It's only a feeling on my part," he said, smoothing his hair from his forehead. "There," he said suddenly, his finger bent against the pane. "That's the other one. I forgot about him."

They mashed themselves against the side rail for a glimpse of a thirty-five-ish blond in a blue-and-white sports jacket swiftly walking away from the bell captain's stand. Zala felt B. J.'s elbow in her side. Tailing the man from the far side of the lobby was Mason.

"GBI or APD?"

"Neither. My partner pointed him out a few weeks ago. He was using a key on the room we'd seen the redhead come out of."

"And the redhead?"

"GBI Organized Crime. Haven't seen him all night. But he'll show. I've got five dollars riding on it."

"What about him?" B. J. said, pointing at the floor of the car.

"Just a feeling," he said again, signaling his partner. The partner handed Alice Moore back the snapshot. "But he strikes me as a professional informer. As I said, it's just a feeling. We pool information and try to come up with a story. Probably nothing more to it than that, making things up." He blushed.

"I know what you mean," B. J. said, sticking close as he moved toward the front of the car. "I guess we all do it. What do you think? I won't hold you to it, but what's your idea?" She glanced at Alice, who pushed the button to hold the car.

"Well, in my version, the guy in the sports jacket was an informer for the Organized Crime officer and got double-crossed. Maybe the Intelligence guy blew his cover. Or maybe the three were in together to break the case and were told to forget it by the higher-ups. And now they're tailing each other to be sure whoever does break the case cuts them in."

"You think they're trying to get to the mayor or the commissioner?" B. J. followed the men out of the door, gesturing behind her for Zala and Alice to go on. "Or are they blocking each other?"

Alice pressed the button and looked across at Zala. The others, who'd interrupted their conversations when their smooth descent had been interrupted, looked from one woman to the other. A woman in a black jumpsuit held up her wrist but did not look at her watch. Another one in a dark pantsuit pressed 3 and fished a dime from her pocket.

Zala turned back to the side rail. It should take no more than five minutes for Alice to phone the contact for an update and then join her out behind the U.S. Government Printing Office. Music from the ballroom filled the car when Alice stepped off, and Zala was tempted to get off at the mezzanine to see what Kofi and Kenti had dressed in, most of their things still down in Columbus. But she saw Bible Man below, quick-stepping behind the blond man in the sports jacket. Reaching the lobby, she was the first out of the car.

She shoved through the revolving doors and went down the drive toward the street, nearly colliding with a drunken couple who were reeling up the circular driveway, drinks in their hands.

"Oooops!" the woman said, protecting her coconut. The paper umbrella and two lipstick smudged straws in the shell poked her chin as she sloshed the rum drink on the front of her dress.

"Easy now," the man, a sailor, said, holding her shoulders till Zala moved past, his white jacket slipping from the woman's shoulders, a paper umbrella falling from behind his ear where it had been tucked.

Coming up the driveway was Preener, who looked at the couple, reached in his pocket, threw his keys to the ground, and bent down, signaling Zala to keep walking.

Zala kept close to the building line, wondering how the couple fit into the scheme of things. She stopped before turning the corner and looked back. The blond man in the sports jacket was handing a handkerchief to the sailor.

"Keep moving," Vernon said, coming up on her right and heading toward the Hyatt. Just then Bible Man appeared at the foot of the driveway and headed her way, his face blank.

Zala turned the corner and headed quickly toward the rear of the gray building.

She saw Speaker halfway down the street in the driver's seat of
Leah's van, dreads arranging themselves around his face as he wrote
quickly on a notepad. He reached up and switched off the overhead
light as Bible Man climbed in. Further down the street, Braxton and
Lafayette were in a car near the back entrance of the building. They
flicked the headlights, and Lafayette pointed to Dave's station wagon
parked behind a silver-tone Mercedes.

She crossed the street and climbed in. "Have we got something?"

Mattie nodded but continued to draw lines on a map. She switched
felt-tip markers and continued drawing. Several lines intersected; four
in particular overlapped at one point on the map. But before she could
begin the debriefing, "Catch this," Dave said, pointing to the back door
of the FBI office.

"Slick!"

"What is?" Clara leaned over Mattie from the backseat.

"Not what—who."

"Eyes front," Dave instructed, and the four smiled and chatted as
Slick walked to the corner, took a look at a red paper umbrella on top of
the newspaper box, then doubled back to the silver-tone Mercedes.

"That's it," Mattie said, drawing the marker back round to complete a circle. Braxton's lights flickered and then came on as the Mercedes pulled out. A minute later Braxton's car sped off after it.

"Very colorful," Zala said when Mattie handed her the sheet of
paper. "But what does it mean?"

"That's from Sue Ellen and Teo. The cast of characters include four.
In the past three hours they've been crisscrossing. One of them stopped
off at a phone booth on Memorial a block away from the state police
barracks, then showed up near the Lakewood Heights checkpoint where
the Klan family in the Geter case live. He hung around there a long
time. Number 2 was over in the Gray Street area, then Lakewood
Heights, passed Number 1 in the street, then showed up in a sailor suit
at Trader Vic's." Mattie pointed to the tourist restaurant across the
street. "Fifteen minutes ago he ducked out of the restaurant and placed
that umbrella where you see it. Wasn't the least bit drunk. Five minutes
ago he couldn't stand up."

"He's in the Hyatt," Zala said.

"I'm not surprised. Number 3 was at Lakewood Heights too earlier,
also at Cap'n Peg's."

"Baseball cap?"

"The same. After you saw him then, Larry and Paulette spotted him near the GBI office. Rice followed him into the Hyatt. He had a drink at the bar. The fourth man was with the GBI man."

"The redhead?"

"That's correct. They were together out the Lakewood area earlier. Dowell, Gaston, and Preston were told to follow him if the two split up. They did. Gaston passed Number 4 on to Mason."

"Okay. What does it mean?"

"I think it means that at least individual members of the bureaus are cooperating," Mattie said. "My guess is they're putting their heads together to find Innis, or rather McGill."

"Well, let them lead us. They're the pros."

"Move out," Mason said with only one leg in the car. "They're all leaving at once."

Overhead through the trees, the moon kept pace with the green minibus. It bumped along the hard-packed dirt road, the last of the houses and gas pumps far behind. Dipping, swerving—ruts in the road, an occasional hunk of truck tire—the bus slowed as it approached a fallen branch, and the passengers on the floor in back were thrown forward. One hand on the eight-ball cap of the gearshift, the driver curved around a narrow bend. Roots showed thick at eye level in the walls of red clay on either side as the road twisted. Those behind the front seats slid back along the metal floor to the rear when the nose of the van rose sharply. The rear doors, handles looped loosely with a coat hanger, rattled, then separated long enough for a breeze to blow in with the sting of pine resin; then the doors grated against each other and closed.

Steadying themselves against the boxes that held Sunday clothes and the sacks of tools, the passengers pulled up toward the front again, grabbing straps and levers where the rear seats had been removed. They saw it at once when the road widened a bit to an even grade, the brooding water tower in the distance, their cue to douse the lights, cut the motor, and coast downhill to the 6 Star Storage Company warehouse. But the driver only dimmed the lights and drove past the fortresslike building dark inside a circular palisade, its stout wooden stakes irregular in height, width, and thickness, but its message clear: Keep Out.

One mile beyond, no buildings, no vehicles; two miles, a large grassy field, but no signs of a stakeout; three miles, all quiet—the driver then maneuvered a skillful U-turn in a strip of scrub and drove back past the warehouse and parked under the trees a hundred-yard sprint away. She held her hand up to signal for attention, then angled it down in warning. The bus was on a tilt, the shoulder narrow, the drop swift and dangerous to rocks below. They divided up. Were they all to disembark from the passenger side, the wheels opposite would lift from the ground.

Pine resin was sharp as they got out; then it was masked by gasoline fumes as they inched around the van to survey the terrain. The doors were left slightly ajar. Sound traveled far at night in the country silence. Two members of the team, with the same thought from facsimile operations years ago, hunched each other. On their return, they would finger around in the tailpipe and check underneath. In threes and fours they scooted across the road, two dropping out to take up their posts as lookouts.

Twelve shadows came up from behind the twelve members, grew long, then marched up the stakes of the fence before they faded. Two metal signs—NO TRESPASSING, K-NINE PATROLLED—were old and rusty. The chain on the gate was old too. It gave under the wire cutters and one good tug. Work on a herringbone pattern of bricks at the very entrance had long been abandoned, the last bricks, loose, disappearing under the weeds. Midway between the gate and the front door of the warehouse, they found themselves walking on trash.

The yard was dense with bottles, stomped cans, and stacked papers. One stack had been set afire but hadn't burned. A sturdy see-through bag of flattened tin cans was slumped against a ground-story window. Electrical wires ran through the heavy mesh between the windowpane and the burglar bars. The door, though, was wooden, and the lock was a Singler. It gave after nicking two corners of a Tillie card. Pried open with the flat end of the chisel, the door swung out. But behind it was a heavy metal fire door. A red horizontal rod, waist high, ran left to right. It was coiled with electrical cable that had been stripped. It looked alive.

They split up, going around the sides of the three-story building to the rear. There were more bundles, some reduced to ash. The windows were barred, meshed, and wired. The fire escape had been removed.

Parts of the support brackets that remained were jagged and too short for a handhold or a foot up. The gutters above, though, looked promising. Fairly new, they were thick and reinforced at twelve-inch intervals by bolted bands of heavy metal. They held the most athletic member, who then pulled his partner up by the wrist. Boosted from below, two others reached the second-story ledge and hooked their arms around the metal bars of the wide industrial windows. It took the others five and a half minutes to form a climbable pyramid as one of the team instructed, making ascent easy for those who weren't wearing thick gloves and tennis shoes.

With the tools, they pried off the roofing material. They dug through the wood to the tarpaper and cut through, then tried to chip away an entrance. One of the team spotted a countersunk magnet. It looked like a claymore mine. They found the second alarm in the framing of a trapdoor that had once been a skylight. Carefully they unpacked their own magnets and inserted the horseshoes they'd liberally coated with adhesive compound. Pressed against the alarms, the Woolworth toys stuck and the warehouse circuit remained unbroken. They gouged out the frame of the trapdoor till the opening was large enough to lower the first person through, the lightest member of the group.

Squeezing through and using the tool to enlarge the opening, she was glad to find that insulation was foil-back packaged, not loose fiberglass that cut the skin no matter how well greased with Vaseline. She heard a ticking, froze, and tugged at the rope. It tightened across her breastbone and burned through her jumpsuit. Bomb? Had one of the suspects planted a bomb to destroy evidence? She kicked around to the right, twisting the rope. There was a red eye suspended, it seemed, over industrial shelving. She kicked in the opposite direction, the rope biting under her armpits. There was no matching eye on the opposite side. Not an infrared beam, then, that she was about to interrupt. Bomb? She hung loose, her arms prickly, and forced her eyes to make out the forms in the dark. A box was around the red eye. She tugged the rope and threw her head back toward her shoulderblades.

"Ticking. Sonic rodent deterrent."

She was lowered close enough to the floor to disengage herself. It was like dropping to the ground from a playground swing. She crouched, listening, then stood up and gave the rope a hard yank. She massaged herself as she waited to pull the next member down.

The second-lightest member, ropes around her hips, realized that tough skin built up over the years against the chafing of her Sam Browne belt was as tender now as a rookie's. Wordlessly, the two women pulled the others down. Then they spread out for a general reconnoiter.

The first and third floors of the warehouse were joined by huge, rough-hewn support columns. Wheelless bicycle frames and galvanized garbage cans hung on butcher nails along the crossbars. If there'd ever been a second story, all that was left was an office set kitty-corner in the rear of the building, access provided by the fire-escape steps and a foot-wide metal catwalk. Half the team went down, pausing to inspect a block-and-pulley chain that dangled from the grid of the catwalk. It might have been the chain that once operated the wide windows mid-point between the ground floor and the top, where the other half of the team searched.

Lit from the trapdoor opening above, the third floor was easy to cover. Shelving divided the space into living quarters on one side and storage on the other. A table set between booths and pushed flush against the window held ordinary things: a glass ashtray with a horse-head imprint etched in silvery white on the bottom; Hummel-like salt and pepper dwarves; plastic squeeze bottles of ketchup and mustard; a Welch's grape jelly jar half-filled with sugar and covered with a square of gauze held in place by a red rubber band. A spoon was stuck to the green painted table. The two booths, from a bar or a diner, gave the area an innocent breakfast-nook look. Then a box of candles was found under the table. The camera flash went off and two candles were put in a bag.

On the walls were no cabalist drawings, no cowled robes hanging, no rifle rack, no Bible stuck through, no Polaroid shots or rebel flag, only a calendar. Not a child pinup, or a 6 Star promotional, but a bank calendar. Two dates were circled. April 11. For the arrival of Roy Innis? Had it been the announcement of evidence, of a witness, that had sent 6 Star scurrying? Broom tracks and drag marks led the eye from the metal shelving to a trash heap by the stairs where a broom leaned. April 30 was the other circled date. The next kidnap? Walpurgisnacht? What? The thumbtack was removed, and the calendar dropped smoothly into the bag.

The pile by the washroom was not rocks, nor boots, nor children's underwear. Just rags, girlie magazines, a used can of Sterno, a few matchbooks, the torn cover of a *Reader's Digest,* and some plastic bread wrappers. With the salad tongs, the wrappers were eased into a bag. A ragged remnant of a curtain with brown teddy bears with green bowties on a yellow background was placed in a bag after a quick conference decided that a stain—shoe polish, rust, or worse—needed more careful inspection. One of the matchbooks was plucked up in the tongs; red foil bore the name of an Atlanta restaurant mentioned by a colleague on the Task Force.

The boxes on the top shelves of the metal unit in the middle of the room held reams of paper—white, blank, no logo, no address. Below were cartons marked "Cleaning Supplies"—abrasive cloths, bristle brushes, cans of lubricant, needlepoint oilers. An already open box was full of small plastic funnels, rubber tubing, and various-sized tweezers in glassine bags. On the middle shelf was a shallow box with bottles that looked like India ink, but the labels said "Gun Stock Wax." Next to it was a square box of aerosol cans, gun solvent. Dust on the bottom shelf told the rest of the tale. Several cartons had evidently been removed and dragged across the floor. The flash went off when someone on the other side of the shelving found a crate, empty, but with stenciled lettering on the side, a munitions supplier.

On the bottom shelf in the boxes that remained were CO_2 cartridges for air guns and .22 balls and pellets. Samples were taken to go with the snapshots. A shopping bag of white nylon rings gave them pause until one member, bending down to scratch his ankles, mimed breaking a rifle stock, inserting one of the rings into the breach of the barrel, then snapping the rifle closed before taking aim at the worktable against the far wall. The bag of sealing rings was replaced, and the team moved past the large wooden bins and empty metal lockers.

A pegboard hung over the worktable. All that remained were the outlines of tools that had hung there—chisels, scrapers, a mallet, a drill, a rack of bits. Near the end of the table between four screw holes was a rectangle of raw wood where a Versa Vise had once been clamped on tight. The front drawer was lined with a September 1980 program guide of the American Forces Network. In the side drawer was a tool with a cloven end, the kind used for removing tacks—the only thing in the area that did not spell a gun workshop. The overseas program guide was placed in a bag as the team moved back past the crates and lockers to the "living" side to explore the washroom.

It looked ordinary: sink with a washpan underneath, a toilet, splotchy mirror, odds and ends in the medicine cabinet; slivers of soap in a dish in the stall shower, a hose on its cement floor. The showerhead and a roll of toilet paper were on a low stool by the radiator. But behind the radiator was a length of spattered board, a large hole near one end. If one end of the board rested on the window ledge and was supported by the toilet and radiator, the stool became the exact height to hold it at the other end. Once the basin was placed under the hole in the board and the hose was nozzled to the faucet, the washroom no longer looked innocent or ordinary.

They vacated while pictures were taken, several retracing their steps to the storage side of the shelves to check again. The only thing that had escaped notice on the first go-round was a belt doubled up between two stenciled crates marked "Ammunition." Assembled at the steps to go down, they scanned the area again, hoping that whatever they missed would collect in the lens and emerge unambiguously in the developing pan.

In the office file cabinet they found no invoices, ledgers, or business flyers. No Bible, Vedas, *Battle Axe News,* or copies of *Gung Ho!,* either. Only the rest of the *Reader's Digest* in one drawer and several rippled circulars that had been used as coasters under a coffee mug in another. In the rest were husks of insects, roaches, water bugs. On the desk was no telephone, no jumper cable with pincers, no dry-cell battery with lead wires and a tube of elastoplast, only more junk mail addressed to Occupant. The address of 6 Star was not 666 or any other number of significance, though two members studied long and hard. In the drawers of the desk, a few thumbtacks and paper clips, a stubbed-out butt, and a crumpled napkin from the coffee shop of a Cobb County hotel. The napkin was bagged. A pint bottle, greasy with fingerprints, was removed from the green metal waste can and placed in a open brown bag.

Going down to the first floor, several stood on tiptoe to see what was in the galvanized cans hanging from the cross beams—spare parts of trucks and cars. Others bent down for a closer look at the block and pulley; the hook on the end had a shred of cotton cloth that took ten minutes to remove. Two others squatted to unwedge a thick book in the crook of the L bar of the catwalk grid. Not a phone directory, as they'd thought, but a mail-order catalog, with a burnt corner, torn-off cover, and the order blank removed.

The first floor was a combination garage, gym, and lounge area. It

seemed odd that the exercise rings were on ropes looped over the cross-
bar and not attached to the pulley chain; the four feet of chain would
have alleviated the need to climb on a beer crate to reach the exercise
rings. While one member stood there pondering the meaning of that,
another shimmied up for samples of rope fibers. The rest moved off to
inspect the lounge area under the metal staircase.

A beat-up couch, two folding chairs from Aaron Rental, and a
leatherlike La-Z-Boy were assembled in a semicircle around a hotellike
coffee table. Delta Airlines playing cards were spread on the table, the
two jokers leaning against a Coors beer can. Smudges of orangy-pink
lipstick covered the punctured opening in the can. What looked at first
like burn holes from a cigar in the back of the recliner proved to be, after
poking under the vinyl, gunshot holes. With the tip of the chisel blade,
three spent bullets were jacked out of the stuffing and into the coffee
can the magnets had been in. The sound was thunderous. Several
ducked, two slapping their hips for guns, three pushing others down as
they hit the floor.

The member with the can muffled a husky tee-hee and helped the
men to their feet. Together they took the chinning bar apart. The bar-
bells were taken apart too. Fibers from the exercise mats were removed
with tweezers and placed in the newly acquired glassine bags. Photos
were taken to go with the fiber and ballistic samples.

Those by the truck up on blocks had taken a vote not to remove the
license plates from the premises. The five license plates in the toolbox
were spread out, photographed, and replaced. There was one clear mud
print of a sole and heel on the floor mat in the truck. In a crevice of the
passenger seat was a square of slightly curled wood shaving. It was held
up with tweezers for inspection. From a bark canoe? The front seat
cushion was lifted out. In the compartment below were tools—ratchets,
wrenches, channel-lock pliers, an electric drill, a propane torch, a battery charger, and a blue plastic ice tray with an assortment of screws and
wing nuts.

While fiber samples were taken from the truck's interior and paint
and rust were scraped from the fenders, the drill and the propane torch
were carried over to the cellar door, where those who'd been taking
turns trying to pick the lock of the burglar bar or bust the hinges on the
side were chided for overlooking valuable resources in the unlocked
truck.

An hour later—their throats dry with the dust, eyes stinging with sweat, nostrils burning with the acrid smoke of hot metal—one of the team gave up rubbing his neck with his thumb and kicked the door in frustration. Miraculously, two bars buckled enough to insert a stout pole from the chinning bar and wrench the base of the door from its metal groove.

Flashlights held low, the three fathers led the way when the cellar door was opened. The bottom of the stairs could be the end to an old agony and the beginning of a new grief. A finish at least to the worse-than-useless comebacks to "I'm looking for a boy": "Whatsamatta, your wife on the rag?" "Ole lady got lockjaw?" "Fuck off, punk."

The first thing they saw was the wood pile. Logs, planks, two-by-fours, railroad ties, stumps, posts, and six slats from a junior-size bed. Flashlights next converged on a large mound in front of the furnace. Sacks of sand, gravel, cement mix, and river stones. Already a fortress, was 6 Star Storage preparing to strengthen its barricade for a major siege?

The youngest of the fathers squared his shoulders and led the group single-file into the darkest recess of the cellar. There behind the furnace was a large, army-green cabinet. More than the upstairs shelves, crates, and lockers, it justified "storage company." Built like a safe, it measured five feet high, four feet across. While the torch, drill, and chisel were applied, the others joined the youngest father standing by the water heater fingering his belt buckle.

Back of the water heater was a space startling in its cleanliness. Swept, scrubbed, and polished, the area was no more than three feet all around but seemed immense in the otherwise grim and filthy dungeon. One of the fathers shouldered through to add his light. He brushed at his mustache and stared at the floor, as if in staring he could reproduce the contour drawing made with fluorescent chalk as described in the confidential memorandum coaxed from an ally who finally came across over drinks.

"Bonanza!" someone said in a constrained whisper behind them. The doors of the army-green cabinet were open. Those wearing rubber gloves, courtesy of Grady Hospital, waited for photos to be taken before they moved in.

On the middle shelf, a marked-up map of Atlanta lay haphazardly folded on top of a box of dynamite. The box was seventeen sticks shy.

On a higher shelf, in a scramble of clockworks and batteries, was a key ring. If four of the keys fit the outer gate, the two front doors, and the cellar door, that left six keys unaccounted for. Had they overlooked a room, a bank of lockers? Might they be the keys to the killers' homes, or to the kidnap houses where the children were being held?

Carefully, painstakingly slowly, the keys were lowered into a plastic bag that had been blown open so fingerprints would not be blurred by the bag. The operation was too much for one of the team, who fainted, her right arm bent and close to her side, as if afraid to drop the alligator handbag she was no longer carrying.

Two flashes went off simultaneously. Those without cameras stepped back close to the wall while more photos were taken. It wouldn't do to appear on the pages of *The Call,* or in the packets that would be pitched through the transom, shoved through the mail drop, and placed in editors' desks.

VI

BEE POLLEN AND OIL

OF EVENING PRIMROSE

Thursday, June 25, 1981

Z ala held on to the refrigerator door and leaned in, oddly starving. Purple plums sweated in the china bowl Mattie had
brought in with the late-breaking bulletins from her now famous
neighborhood. Edged in fleurs-de-lis, flowers of announcements, the
bowl had been given as a good-luck gift. Who knew what information
the arrest of Mattie's neighbor might yield? In the amber Ball jar next
to the leaky milk container were the irises from Paulette's backyard.
Those flowers were also symbols of forthcoming messages. Zala roamed
her eyes over the crammed shelves. White spots were turning gray on
the egg carton. Drops of milk slid down the plastic wrap covering the
melon and dropped through the bars of the shelves to the top of the veg-
etable bins. They were so full the drawers wouldn't close properly.

Zala made no move to take the milk out. "When *The Call* comes
calling, Spence wants to be able to say he's broke from stocking up.
Then how in hell will Speaker get the money for the printer to release
the most important issue of all?"

Mattie and Paulette looked up from what they were doing, arranging headlines in chronological order. It was urgent that a fact sheet be
circulated given the recent turn of events, the arrest of a young Black
man from Verbena Street named Wayne Williams.

"Why be upset with Spencer?" Mattie said gently. "He's not to
blame for the turn things have taken. Who could know our disclosures
would force the authorities to act? And we don't know for certain that
they did arrest someone simply because of our mailings."

As Zala continued to lean into the cool of the refrigerator, Paulette
clipped headlines, swinging her foot in time with the music. From the
corner of Ashby and Thurmond the piano tuner was testing his work
with "I'm on the Battlefield for My Lord." Paulette murmured a few

lines, then sang out, "And I promised Him that I would serve Him till I die . . . Yessss, I'm on the battlefield," then hummed the rest.

She broke off to hold up a torn sheet of paper from a spiral notebook. "Where does this go? Says, 'February 13, P.B., green Chevy Impala, 20, white, brown shoulder hair, wispy mustache, eyes close set'? That refers to the Baltazaar case."

"The Coffee Papers," Mattie answered, holding open the portfolio that contained Zala's blue notebook and a collection of index cards and other notes. "I want to go through this batch in a minute," Mattie said, tapping the folio. "To my knowledge Williams doesn't match the description of any of the suspects."

"I don't feel so good," Zala said, leaning her head on the refrigerator door.

"Girl, you've been telling yourself that ever since your pastor asked you to give the Woman's Day address in church. You could have been up there with Monica Kaufman and Jacqui Maddox, Zala. You too simple. And I wish you'd sit down."

"You could have read the names on the real list—ours—and asked for a moment of silence."

"I was scared, Mattie. I'm scared now. I mean the arrest. What do we do?"

Mattie put the cellophane tape down and turned slowly. "You think we made it hot for the authorities, don't you?"

"Don't *you?* There's a connection between that gun-shop warehouse, the Klan, and the murders."

Mattie looked at Paulette. Paulette blotted her face and neck with a napkin and blew down into her blouse. Mattie fanned herself with the morning edition. Neither of them answered.

"Why don't we move this operation over to my place," Paulette said after a long silence. "I'm about to dissolve. If you're going to let the groceries melt, at least step aside so we can get a little of the breeze."

It was a record scorcher. In the entertainment section, movie theaters bordered their ads with cartoon icicles. Old Man Winter blew frost across June sales of fans and air conditioners. On the front page, the heat wave stole the secondary headline, warning of an energy crisis and directing families with babies and senior citizens to the emergency relief shelters. A small photo near the bottom of the page showed a man leaning his arm out of a car. The caption identified him as an investigator of strange phenomena, who claimed to have gotten on film two cases of spontaneous combustion of Georgians.

The lion's share of page one was devoted to the capture of a local man papers across the country were referring to as "the Atlanta Fiend," "the Monster Killer," "the Crazed Beast." Since the arrest on Monday of Wayne Williams, charged with the murder of twenty-seven-year-old Nathaniel Cater and implicated in the murder of the other adults and children on the official list, it was no longer necessary to wade through columns and columns of local color—the Shriners convention, the Piedmont Art Festival schedule, the Dogwood Golf Tourney, the Atlanta 500 stock car races, tulips in Hurt Park, the Druid Hills Arts Festival—to find the continuation of page-one taglines: SUSPECT ON BRIDGE QUESTIONED . . . WILLIAMS'S ATTORNEY DEMANDS END TO STAKEOUT . . . SUSPECT'S HOME SEARCHED . . . FBI CALLS FOR ARREST . . . VICE PRESIDENT BUSH ASKS GOVERNOR BUSBEE TO ARREST . . . WILLIAMS ELUDES POLICE . . . SUSPECT HOLDS PRESS CONFERENCE . . . WILLIAMS ARRESTED AND CHARGED.

In the middle section of the paper, international news was squeezed into skinny columns and stories on Williams were run in four fat sections side by side, page after page. One purported to give biographical information, though the data was frequently contradictory and tended to change from day to day. Twenty-three years old, only child of Homer and Faye Williams of Verbena Street, Wayne was described as an electronics prodigy, having built his own radio station, WRAZ, as a youth. An entertainment promoter, he'd been known also as an ambulance chaser and allegedly had a record for having impersonated a police officer. That he'd been a free-lance newsman for radio and TV was scantily mentioned; that he had access to police calls was mentioned frequently.

More damaging was the development of the lead sentence in the second column, which said Williams had frequently distributed leaflets at schools and parks advertising his nonexistent music company called Gemini. With lengthy quotes from psychologists and law-enforcement officials, "Gemini" opened the door to wide speculation on the Jekyll-Hyde character of the "mass murdering child killer"—who thus far was charged with the murder of one adult.

The third column beefed up the case against Williams by quoting people in the target neighborhoods who claimed to have seen him talking to Patrick Rogers, or walking with Aaron Jackson, or having a drink in a bar near the Greyhound terminal, hangout of the victim Nathaniel Cater. Helen Pue, mother of Timothy Pue, listed in the papers as victim number 18, was said to have identified a photo of Wayne Williams as a man she'd seen talking to her son.

The fourth story described the evidence, choosing not to belabor the point that the colors of the incriminating fibers and the species of the dog hairs had changed drastically since Williams had become a suspect some time in May. Violet-colored fibers from a bedspread removed from Williams's home were said to match those found in the hair of Nathaniel Cater, whose decomposed body was fished from the Chattahoochee several days after Williams had been stopped on the Jackson Parkway Bridge. A stakeout officer posted beneath the bridge, a rookie, thought he heard something thrown in the water, and a stakeout officer posted closer to the top thought he heard Williams's station wagon stop before continuing across the bridge. Hairs from Williams's German shepherd were said to match hairs found on Nathaniel Cater's body, on the decomposed body of Yusuf Bell, found in '79 under the flooring of an abandoned schoolhouse; on Aaron Jackson, found partially nude in the Chattahoochee in the fall, and on Charles Stephens, found near a trailer park in the fall. Fibers from the Williams carpet the investigators had cut up and hauled away were said to match those found on Stephens, Jackson, and several others. Blood samples taken from Williams's car were said to be the same type as that of William Barrett, seventeen, found in May near I-20, and of John Porter, twenty-eight, who had not been on the Task Force list and whose "official status" was still uncertain.

Two photos accompanied the copy. The caption of one described Williams "cocky." Taken sometime between June 4 and June 11, when Williams, questioned, released, then kept under surveillance, his home a camp-out area for media, police, and the nosy, broke through the police cordon and disappeared for hours, it showed a pudgy young man in glasses. Some said he'd eluded the police to dispose of damaging evidence overlooked in the June 3 search of his home. Others said he'd gone to warn his cohorts. Still others felt he might have headed for Mayor Jackson or Commissioner Brown as he'd once done to make fools of the stakeout. Others said he'd gone to DA Slaton to make a deal, names in exchange for immunity.

The families of still-missing women, men, and children badgered the authorities at their offices and at their homes, demanding to know if a bargain had been struck and if the authorities were guarding wherever it was kidnapped relatives were being held. But the only *officially* missing person was Darron Glass, *officially* unaccounted for since September 1980, though his foster grandmother said she'd received calls from him, and reports had come in from Alabama to the effect that he'd been spotted at a baseball stadium selling peanuts. On the other hand, a worker in the Fulton County coroner's office was convinced the Glass boy had been found, misidentified, and buried under another name during a hectic period in the spring when medical records got mixed up.

The other photo of Williams showed him handcuffed and climbing into a police car on June 22. In neither of the photos, nor in any other that appeared, did Williams resemble the suspect drawings on the corkboard down in task force headquarters or the descriptions given by eyewitnesses to abductions, or murders, or dumpings. He did, however, fit the description offered by psychic Lillian Cosby on a Tony Brown TV special aired back in April. For most media, the Tony Brown show was not a reference point, and so was not mentioned. *The Call,* however, and a few out-of-town Black newspapers, did pick it up. And it was the source of many conjectures in the barbershops and other neighborhood news forums in the Atlanta Black community.

In the April telecast, psychic Cosby described an individual who would be arrested as a light-skinned Black man, young, chubby, wearing glasses, receding hairline, sharp-witted. No two people seemed to agree as to whether she named the individual as *the* killer, *a* killer, or simply someone closely involved. A skeptical radio DJ threw out a challenge at every station break for someone to produce either the psychic or a videotape of the show.

Three other things had been part of the psychic's description. The suspect had an identity kink—that is, he dressed in women's clothes and wigs from time to time. The officers who stopped Williams on the Jackson Parkway Bridge in the early hours of May 22 saw both men's and women's clothing in the white station wagon. And though his story was fishy—he was checking out an address of a potential client at three in the morning—they did not detain him for more than a few minutes. Given the official victim profile, the police were programmed for boys' clothing. The psychic also reported that the individual was well connected with the authorities. Those who remembered the spring telecast as they followed the unfolding of the case in summer made much of the fact that Williams had once had an office in the same building as Zone 4 of the APD, had use of a police scanner, and had once, it was said, impersonated an officer. It was common knowledge on the day of his arrest that he'd been photographed with several Atlanta personages who'd written him letters of recommendation—or so he boasted: a plentiful supply of salt was necessary in weighing his statements. Hadn't the resumé he'd brazenly handed out at the press conference he called in early June, together with the audacious challenge that made June 14 headlines—EITHER CHARGE ME OR EXONERATE ME: WILLIAMS FILES LAWSUIT AGAINST MAYOR, COMMISSIONER, GA. CRIME LAB DIRECTOR—proved to be only profiling. But "well connected" encouraged speculation about where Williams had gone the night the police gave chase only to have one police car rear-end another and earn the tag "Keystone Kops" in Williams's later statements. Scuttlebutt at political potlucks had it that DA Lewis Slaton had resisted pressure to arrest exerted by the FBI and the governor until the White House arranged a meeting at the governor's mansion. And though the DA's office had charged Williams with one count of murder, word was Slaton still felt the case against the man was very flimsy.

The psychic had concluded the April telecast with a prediction that the man would be captured in ninety days. Local newscasters ignored her. They preferred to quote the GBI and FBI agents and FBI director William Webster, everyone except the Black woman on the PBS channel, as they gleefully announced, teeth glistening, eyes shining, that it was a Black man after all and not a racist conspiracy. So militants should shut up, *Pravda* could go to hell, BBC should go home, STOP should disband, and Maynard Jackson should calm down. The beast had been captured.

The radio newscasters echoed the "lone wolf" theme, but several of the disc jockeys didn't go along, which gave music programs' reports tone and texture.

"Turn it up," Paulette said. "Let's hear the latest word on his motive." When neither Mattie nor Zala moved, she got up and went to the counter. Three tea bags were lying on top of the pot holder. Water had nearly boiled away in the saucepan. She turned up the radio and refilled the pot. "I believe you said something about iced tea a while ago."

Zala opened the freezer. "You know them, Mattie, try to think. Is

Williams a black belt, a marine? Does he dabble in the occult? Show dirty movies in the basement? Hold satanic meetings in the backyard? We keep waiting and waiting to hear some connection, but all they say is that he did it and he did it alone. Nothing about the evidence we turned in."

"That might be a good thing," Paulette said, flopping down on the step stool. "Trespassing, breaking and entering, vandalism, theft. Jeepers," she said, tugging at her hair, "I feel like Goldilocks. All we missed was the porridge." She wrapped her long legs around the stool's and sighed. "Where's that Shirley McGill is what I'd like to know. Maybe she can identify Williams as part of the drug cult." Paulette looked up. "Someone at the door?"

"Why didn't I put the curtain back up, dammit!" Zala peeped over the top of the refrigerator door and looked toward the front of the house. "I can't take Alice right now. She spooks me."

"Alice Moore?" Mattie glanced toward the living room, then continued clipping the newspapers. "She's been showing her husband's picture to everyone. Do you think she suspected him all along of killing their daughter, or was that triggered, do you suppose, by the domestic-violence panel we saw at Judge Webber's? She reacted so strongly to that Holmes woman."

"She'll go away in a minute," Zala whispered, staring at the blue plastic ice trays. "We made it hot for the authorities all right, and forced them to move. Williams may not be connected at all. Could be he was just . . . handy."

Paulette turned toward the fan and pulled her blouse away from her skin. "That's dirty, Zala, leaving poor Alice out there baking in the heat."

"She tells me things I don't want to hear. Intimate things. I feel helpless to stop her. Her husband used to clean his revolver at the table while she washed the dinner dishes. Then he'd run his hand up her dress."

"She really think he did it? Sounds to me like Nancy Holmes all over trying to pin everything from the King assassination to the Atlanta murders on her father. Revenge, in other words. I'm surprised the authorities haven't picked him up, then gone after all the STOP men."

"They're satisfied they've got their man," Mattie was saying when there was another knock on the door.

"Why don't we let her in?" Paulette whispered.

But no one moved one way or the other, and the whirring fan blades began to drag.

Jessica Grier wheeled the Herby Curby in from the street as far as her side window. Silas could take it from there; it was too hot to push it. She hadn't intended leaving the house at all, but she'd found a letter for the Spencers slipped inside the Spiegel catalog the mailman left. Eventually they'd come to the front door and see it. She glanced toward the church on the corner where the piano was being tuned. The tuner was cranking one note, higher, higher, the sound tightening her temples.

Her garden was dying. The greens were crispy. Vines on the A-frame Silas had built in the spring were withered. Clusters of blue-gray grapes, dusty underneath and shriveled on top, were trying to hide from the sun under seared leaves. In the next yard a young woman in shorts got up from a deck chair and went inside. Across the fence the woman Mrs. Grier usually saw only during planting time was seated on her back porch, a bowl of ice under the fan on the wringer-type washer beside her, her feet in a basin. Mrs. Grier waved, not really expecting the parboiled woman to respond.

Mrs. Grier walked slowly to her own back porch. Prickly heat had already popped under her brassiere band. She looked at the back door of the unit next to hers, wondering if she shouldn't knock. The letter might be important. It was from New York, handwritten; might be a friend in trouble. There was so much trouble. She and Silas had been to a memorial program for Walter Rodney, killed by a bomb planted in a walkie-talkie by, many said, one of Guyanese President Forbes Burnham's henchmen. The loss of Dr. Rodney, scholar, organizer, freedom fighter, was a great tragedy, a terrible loss, not only for the people of Guyana but for thousands outside the Caribbean community as well. Rodney had planned to journey to London in an act of solidarity with the embattled West Indian community there. There was another memorial scheduled by some of the university people. The Griers planned to go to that one too.

Mrs. Grier stepped over the raised brick that divided the back steps of the duplex. Perhaps the letter from New York was cheering news that she should deliver. Perhaps the Spencers had news to share too, now that the child killer was in jail, where he could be questioned about their boy and the others. She couldn't be sure with so many radios and televisions going all day and at once, but it seemed that the radio was on in the Spencer kitchen, though no one answered the door. On the back porch by the sack of barbecue charcoal was a stack of papers. On it was a program from a recent Soweto Memorial Rally. Forty-seven children, it said, had been found in mass graves in South Africa. She bowed her head and fingered the rickrack on her apron.

"So much hatred," she said, and knocked one last time.

She curled her toes to hold her slippers on and stepped back over the brick to her own rear door. There was no danger of the letter blowing away; she'd stuck it behind the front door knob, and there was no breeze at all. She went in slowly, looking over her shoulder at the houses beyond. What would neighbors say of the Griers if television cameras set up in the front by the jade trees? It was hard to believe that the people she saw on the news offering all sorts of comments about the Williams family were real people, not actors in a very bad drama show. All the Williams boy had done that they could prove was drive over a bridge. And who could say if the fibers they were talking about in the papers hadn't come from the police blankets or the carpet in the coroner's van or from the clothes the people who handled the remains wore?

Slowly she moved into the shade-drawn cool of her living room and sat down on the sofa, which she'd covered with sheets. She could hear water running next door. She'd ring them up in a minute. She couldn't blame them for not coming to the door. It was too hot to stir.

Mattie held her glass up and Paulette squeezed the lemon in it, reading the catalog over Mattie's shoulders. "In the market for a nine-millimeter Luger, are you? Or is the bipod you're after for your automatic? Feeder belt comes equipped with a ball of beeswax, I see. That's nice." She dropped the lemon in her own glass and sat down. "I say we order something from this outfit and see what happens."

Mattie wet her fingers and turned the page. Zala shook out the extension cord and moved the radio to the table. Paulette searched the out-of-town papers for a scrap of evidence that the packets they'd gone broke assembling had sparked someone's courage. The news reports on the radio all resembled each other. They each repeated the "lone wolf" theme, condensed events from May 22 to June 22 into one minute, then used the update since the arrest for a special touch. One commentator, preferring gossip, shrewdly inflected quotation marks around statements potentially libelous and built on what neighbors in the Verbena–Anderson Park district had said; he concluded that the Williams household was pathological, son and father reportedly seen fighting in a downtown parking lot years ago, father and son said to have kept the missus locked in the attic without food or water, alleged affection extended to the family dog of an allegedly unnatural order.

Another station took a scientific turn, interviewing a serologist who said that though sexual activity had long been denied in all of the cases, one should not rule out the possibility that semen might still be detected in the anal cavities of the victims and through analysis be linked to Williams's blood type. A guest on another news show was a forensic specialist who stated that the scanning electron microscope, or SEM, could magnify specimens such as hairs from an Alaskan malamute or German shepherd to a powerful degree. A more dramatic specialist on another station described the ability of the gas chromatograph and the mass spectrometer to analyze and make matches between material samples such as paint.

The three women propped their elbows on the table, drank iced tea, glanced at the weapons catalog, and brooded about equipment they did not have in order to examine their samples thoroughly.

Paulette recommended once again that they make use of what they did have, the catalog from the 6 Star warehouse. "For twenty-four ninety-five we could order a canister of mustard gas. That includes postage and handling." She smiled wryly. "Should I get the phone? Might be Stuff-'n'-such."

"That's Alice, I can feel it." Zala set her glass down, hungry for a soda cracker.

"Could be Dave calling to say goodbye. He's packed up and ready to move out. I need to pack myself and see my mama. If that's your pastor, I'll tell him you can't stir. You need all your strength for suffering."

"Go to hell," Zala said. "It's Alice. She'll give up after a while."

"So what do we do, wait for the printer to release the issue of *The Call*?"

"We could hold a press conference. Everybody else does."

"It's more than a notion."

Mattie turned pages. Paulette read over her shoulder. And Zala changed the station once again. One station wrapped up its news report with stab-in-the-dark theorizing about Williams's reasons for killing. He was jealous of children, having once been a celebrated child prodigy and now an unemployed adult. He hated the little street hoodlums; they offended his sense of race pride. He despised the ability of unremarkable children to hustle money while he, with his superior IQ, had yet to make a killing.

"Please, *please* change that, Marzala."

The wrap-up on the next station called attention to White House interference in the case. The meeting between Vice President Bush, Governor George Busbee, the FBI, and Fulton County District Attorney Lewis Slaton had "the aroma of politics about it," the newscaster said, dropping his voice low.

The three women moved the news clippings to the side and placed the radio in the center of the table. One DJ was rapping the rap, saying that those who'd boarded the buses for the STOP rally in D.C. on May 21 came home all fired up and had Atlanta turning on the spit for a month. That's why the brother had been bagged: things were getting too hot. Police in the various counties weren't getting any of the federal money for overtime. A lot of other sectors were threatening insurrection and mutiny. But especially fired up were the people back from the rally. For openers, they were determined to get answers to their questions about the rumored LEAA memo and the redneck phone call. The first thing they learned was that STOP was being hassled by the consumer affairs office for illegal solicitation of funds. The next thing they knew a Blood was in cuffs and white commentators were grinning all over themselves.

Many Atlantans were returning from D.C. in the early morning hours of Friday, May 22, when an FBI-conducted stakeout squad of local, state, and federal officers focused on a 1970 white Chevy wagon driven by a young Black man. He was questioned as to why he was driving across the Jackson Parkway Bridge at that hour, then let go. Newspaper readers would not hear of the incident at the bridge until June 4, after the man was called in for questioning by the FBI. Commissioner Brown continued to echo the refrain "no connection," "no suspects," "no arrest expected," up to the moment Williams was taken into custody.

One DJ was saying, as Marzala fiddled with the tuning knob, that the FBI was conducting the murder investigation because the White House wanted to see something for the money it was pumping into Atlanta. On another station, the word was: "The White House was pissed about all the demonstrations in the capital and were calling for blood, Bloods!"

On the college station, a student read from notes she'd taken at the STOP rally in D.C. Thousands had been there to protest the erosion of affirmative action, of the Voters Rights Act, of legal aid to the poor programs. There to protest the efforts of the Senate Judiciary Committee, headed up by Strom Thurmond, to set up a Senate Subcommittee on Terrorism and Security and usher in a new McCarthy witch hunt / HUAC era. There to protest Senator Jeremiah Denton of Alabama's charge that Mobilization for Survival was a mob ruled by the KGB. There to protest the expulsion of the Libyan embassy from the United States and Mobil and Exxon's pressure to escalate the government's terrorist moves against Qaddafi. There to protest the role of USAID in the infant formula controversy in the Third World. And thousands representing the National Anti-Klan Network and similar organizations had been there to demand that fascist terrorists groups be outlawed and their training camps prohibited. The student had been there with a green ribbon and STOP button to protest the obvious coverup going on in Atlanta. "Now we find out," she said, "that they'd picked out a scapegoat before most of us got back to the city."

A community worker was being interviewed on a call-in show, offering his version of the events that had turned Atlanta into a tinderbox and Williams into a scapegoat. In May, while Mayor Jackson was in Washington getting the pledged federal dollars released, the FBI had once again announced that they'd solved the case, and Maynard had hit the ceiling. Within hours, seventeen-year-old William Barrett had disappeared from the McDaniel-Glenn area, where John Porter and Nathaniel Cater and several younger victims on the TF list had lived. Barrett was found the next day, strangled and stabbed on Glenwood Road near I-20, where six others on the TF list had been either last seen or finally found. He was called the twenty-seventh victim in twenty-three months.

"If the FBI was on the case and ready to wrap things up, why weren't they staking out those two obvious areas?" the community worker asked. "Now all the bureaus agree that the case is solved. But all they mean is that they've turned their attention to Williams and are no longer investigating cases of disappearances and murders. If people have information about missing children or adults from the area, I invite you to call in," he said.

Then he turned his attention to another case, the police murder of Fenton Talley.

"I don't argue that Talley should be on the official list. But the fact that we've heard so little about what occurred the day before the announcement came over the air that the Missing and Murdered case was solved should make responsible people wonder."

In pursuit of Fenton Talley, twenty-six, who allegedly had hit the back of a school bus with a stick, SWAT and a corps of one hundred APD regulars and an armed helicopter had occupied a four-block area in the Black community. After a two-and-a-half-hour, one-way barrage of bullets and tear gas, Talley was dead. And his friend, cowering in the wreckage of his home, was charged with resisting arrest.

"Before Maynard Jackson took over," the community worker said, "Atlanta was the leading city in per-capita deaths by the police. In 1973, the APD gunned down twenty-nine people; all but two were Black males. Fourteen of those twenty-seven were under twelve years of age. I'd like to know a few things. How many of those cops last month who shot up the neighborhood and killed Talley had been among those demoted by Reggie Eaves for having brutal records? My second question is, Are we on the threshold of a new reign of police terror now that the state and federal authorities *think* they've pushed Maynard Jackson aside?"

"I recognize his voice," Mattie said. "He was on the air when the Techwood bat squad was arrested. He called Deputy Eldrin Bell and City Attorney Mays on the carpet for misleading the squad about their right to carry weapons, then turning around and arresting them."

"When did the Fenton Talley thing go down?" Paulette sucked on the lemon. "We must've been busy developing the photos and getting the 6 Star packets ready for distribution. What he said makes you think. Who is keeping track of disappearances now that the Task Force is busy building its case against Williams?"

"I don't wish my next comments to be misconstrued," the worker said on the air, "but of course they will be, because we've all been indoctrinated against communism. No, let me correct that: indoctrinated with the phantasm of communism, and that's not the same thing."

On May Day, he explained, the Revolutionary Communist Party had burned flags at Techwood and were roughed up by the police who made little distinction between demonstrators, the Techwood Squad, tenants, and onlookers. Many of the same officers who'd jumped the RCP when they doused the TF office with red paint and later raised a red flag over Bowen Homes had asked for the Techwood assignment on May 1. Since the media failed to go out and cover the event in a responsible manner, residents had had no opportunity to say whether they regarded the RCP as a nuisance, the police as brutal, or whether they felt police action and red-baiting were being used to discourage and discredit every attempt at community organizing.

"It's been clear for some time," the worker said, "that the authorities were bound to arrest a Black man, and soon, preferably a militant or a radical or a Rasta. Failing that, a sexual deviant or a weirdo, someone no one would wish to be associated with by coming to his defense or by challenging the so-called evidence against him. Someone they could isolate."

He then took a call and stated again that Williams was a scapegoat. "Guilty or innocent, he is a scapegoat being used to protect a number of people's careers. People say that DA Slaton bowed to pressure and agreed to charge Williams when he didn't want to. I say Slaton was glad to get off the hook."

"What are you doing?" Mattie reached for Zala as she got up. "You look terrible, girl."

"I want to call in. He's gotten on everybody else. Maybe he doesn't know that Commissioner Brown was scheduled to turn over the list to the city council of all unsolved killings, deadline June 30. Now he's off the hook too."

But she didn't go to the phone. She went to the refrigerator and looked inside. The shelves seemed a mirage. Reaching for the bowl of Jell-O, her hand seemed to fall through space.

"Don't keep the flowers in the refridge, Marzala. Let's have them on the table."

"I feel a little peculiar." Zala stretched out her hand toward the jar of flowers. The jar seemed to recede.

"You mustn't keep giving yourself that message or you will get sick."

"Think you're pregnant?" Paulette said, fanning her skirt.

"That would be lovely, wouldn't it?" Mattie smiled.

Zala looked at Mattie. An ordinary smile, an ordinary face. The face of a person she'd once attributed extraordinary powers to at a time when she was hoping that Mattie possessed the ability to bring off a miracle. Sitting there with her mascara about to run, Mattie Shaw in her yellow-and-white smocked dress looked like nothing more or less than a good person, a friend, a middle-aged woman with a fondness for makeup, stories, and clanky jewelry.

"If you ask me, I'd say three children at your age is already one too many." Paulette was glad when the phone rang, sparing her whatever criticism went with the pained expression on Mattie's face. Mattie's eyes were rolling and her lashes were fluttering like a person who'd used the wrong eye drops.

"Take that call."

The ferocious whisper made Zala move obediently toward the living room. Mattie's face had gone vacant and her eyes were suddenly still.

"You all right?" Paulette reached for Mattie's wrist, then shot to the freezer for ice. Zala was in the living room, wound in the cord, trying to keep track of what was going on in the kitchen, when someone on the phone asked first for a Miss Foreman and then a Marsha Spence. Another woman came on the line and corrected the operator.

"I think it's for you, Paulette. Central intake, a hospital. Miami, I think."

Paulette slapped a dish towel of ice against the back of Mattie's head and pressed her head down. "Take a message."

"This is Marzala Spencer speaking. May I take the message for Nurse Foreman?"

The woman began again when the operator clicked off, explaining that she was a clerk at central intake and calling about a patient.

"At first we thought he might be one of the boat children," the caller said. "He was suffering from severe exposure. He wouldn't speak.

We thought he might be Haitian or Cuban. After the first IV, he detached the tube and hid in the bathroom, curling up in the tub as many of the boat children do. But something in the workup sheet reminded me of the missing children flyers Nurse Foreman distributed when she was here doing volunteer work with the refugee committee."

Coming in the door on the heels of the children—literally stepping on the back of Kenti's sandal—Spence wasn't sure if Zala was pleading with someone on the phone or begging the children to be quiet. Kenti wanted no part of the SAFE summer camp programs. And Bobby reported that camp counselors like himself weren't about to spend the summer indoors with no air-conditioning, either.

Kofi dropped his load of library books, missing the arm of the sofa by four inches, when he saw his mother's face.

"That's my foot, you know." But Kenti cut it short when she turned and saw Zala.

"Don't worry," Gloria was telling Spence as she latched the screen door. "Bruce can tap into six county systems and trace those license plates for you." Turning, she snapped her fingers. Her uncle was bending down, listening in on the phone. Her aunt was staring at the mirror mounted on the back of the door and not even seeing her standing there.

"What's the matter?"

Zala saw her mouth in the mirror trying to form the words "front tooth" and handed Spence the phone. His free hand was scattering things on the table and then the contents of the folder, the photo, the medical report, the dental card, the flyer.

"Does he have a chipped tooth in front? The uppers," Spence said, his hand in his mouth until Kenti reached up and pulled it free. "The tooth to the right of the two big ones in front, is it chipped?"

Walking backward, Zala watched his face contort. She didn't have to hear it. The John Doe Jr. in observation in Pediatrics, found wandering in a daze on the highway, barefoot, in khaki shorts and a ragged child's undershirt four sizes too small, was so badly battered, it was difficult to isolate one area of damage from another. One chipped tooth in a jaw they'd had to wire shut when the X rays came back could not be readily remembered.

Zala raised her arms in front of the window to be sure she was there. She was hung out in space, pale in the glassy blue, no more solid than gelatin turned out of a mold and trying to cling fast. She knew she was not dreaming this time.

"Mama gonna fly."

Kenti's words stayed in their ears and moved in their blood for the next three cruel hours it took to empty pockets and bags on the table, Paulette across the street borrowing from the boarders, Peeper screaming from the window as they unloaded Dave's station wagon that a rearview didn't matter so long as the tires weren't bald and the tank was full, the dresser refusing to come unstuck, one leg loose and jammed in a corner back of the seat, and Silas Grier pulling up, listening to Kenti and Mattie, and handing over his Gulf Oil card and thirty dollars and going in to dinner without a word.

"Only maybe," Spence said as they flew down the highway, the half-ironed clothes folded on the backseat.

"Don't." For she was already at the hospital running up the three side steps as Paulette had described them, racing past reception, where Spence would stop and ask that the intake clerk be called and the doctor paged. A left past the water fountain and on past two doors, first the social worker's with a green plate, then the volunteer office, where a trolley of books would be parked. Take those stairs, elevator's slow and you need a pass, to the third floor, then left past the first ward and straight through the playroom with the rocking horse. Then right at the fire extinguisher, the red In Case of Emergency Smash Glass box, to a narrow corridor where the tile ends. First door in front of the locked ward knock and ask for Patti with an *i*, never mind the last name, she's Ghanaian and keeps her surname off her plate, a serious sister with no time for gab and no tolerance for silly conversations about names' meanings. She will take you to the boy. Trust her. She's had good rapport and is the only one he allows to find him.

"Let me drive, Spence."

"No."

She didn't insist. It would be dangerous to change seats doing 85 mph, and stopping was out of the question. So was too much talk. They must do nothing to rob the car of its energy. When he said "God?" she didn't ask what he was praying for.

Spence changed lanes again and zipped past a Spitfire, keeping his eyes on the clouds of vapor billowing up over the shrubs where the road curved in front of them. The vapor settled into the green like angel hair. He knew it was a sign, a paradox, and kept on flying. Where the road straightened again, the mist from the dusted crops far beyond the highway rolled onto the shoulders, wisps curling across the road and under his wheels. He deliberately slowed to 65 to show God he was paying attention. He had faith and was placing the backseat clothes in God's hands.

Spence felt her turn toward him with a question which she must have quickly answered for herself because she turned back, reading off the signs, keeping watch in the traffic ahead for openings and not checking the speedometer or urging him to speed up.

He'd proved he had faith. Now he proved he had wisdom, for he recognized that he'd become what he'd always ridiculed, a superstitious fool and a lane jumper. He wasn't above calling himself names. For the next thirty miles he thought up names to whip himself with, wondering if God was so stupid not to know he was really whipping the needle back up on the gauge. Then he thought of other names to call himself, in the way folks in the back country did it, renaming themselves Short Rations or Misery Love, naming their children Li'l Bit or Dolores, to let God know they were humble but knew what was what. To remind God too that they'd had their share of sorrows and to lighten up if you please. And, merciful, God would take pity.

Saturday, July 18, 1981

K enti wriggled her shorts up and followed the girls around the
side of the house toward the garden.

"Anna fanna ba-nana, fee fie fa-canner, Nannnna!"

"It don't go like that," Kenti said.

"Yeah it do. Down here in Alabama it do."

"Goes different ways in different places," the other girl said, doing
a walkover. "And she does can things," she said, talking upside down.

"Well," Kenti said, turning around in the driveway and looking
past the rows of snap beans, "her name ain't Nana. My other grandmama named Nana."

"But Miss Loretta do put up tomatoes and things, now, don't she?"

"Jam too."

"So?"

"So yourself."

"Well, so your own self."

Grandma Lovey kicked the basket into the row of cukes and looked
up. The three little girls were pushing on each other, but they were
being real careful not to trample anything in her kitchen patch. She
bent again to her work. Legs wide, elbows resting lightly on the inside
of her knees, she snatched up carrots, beets, and a few tough, spiky
okras, shook the dirt loose, and tossed the vegetables into the basket.
When she heard the tinkle of china, she straightened up and looked toward the house. Her broad cheeks crinkled as she squinted.

The girls heard the tinkle and then a bump and looked up at the
screened window midway between the downstairs parlor curtains and
the upstairs bathroom shutters.

"Stuffy, scruffy, ba-buffy, fee fie fa-toughy, Cuffffeeeee!"

"Kofi ain't even up there," Kenti said, her hands on her hips. "That's my mother."

Zala got a good grip on the tray and continued up the stairs. She could hear her daughter below telling the girls from the Girard Stables that her brother wasn't named nobody's Cuffy. And then she spelled Kofi's name, slowly, loudly, leaning on each letter the way she'd seen Grandmama Lovey do trying to get a number from the information operator.

Zala inspected the tray before she bumped the bedroom door open with her hip. Gerry had set it up all wrong, with a white napkin, plastic dishes, and the vial of medicine. Everything that smacked of the hospital was now down in the kitchen drawer. Zala didn't trust the medication. Didn't trust their approach. Hadn't liked any of them on sight, except Patti.

They had wheeled the boy out from the solarium. A shadow of a boy, the sun behind the nurse, the doctor walking beside one huge wheel of the chair. She saw the boy's feet first: one barefoot, curled on top of the other in a short white sock, his pajama cuffs flapping loosely around his bruised-blue ankles. She'd expected him to be in khaki shorts and a cotton undershirt, but he wore sea-green pajamas, the tops unbuttoned. His hands were in his lap coming into the light. Too weak to sit erect, he was strapped in the chair, his head bobbing like an old man's. One strap was loose across his lap, the other strung across the wide white bandage around his chest.

Patti had been standing by her talking rapidly about the way they had to strap him down in bed or he'd wander around the ward, cowering in a corner. Zala had left her to run to him, to free him from the bindings he fell against when the wheels came to a halt.

His face stopped her.

She'd had to refuse the tea they brought her there in Miami, refused three times before they took it away. Had to slap away the nurses' hands trying to feel her forehead. She'd submitted to the gray mat they wrapped around her arm, though, and didn't grumble too much when they squeezed the bulb. They were smiling that starchy smile. She told them she was angry. "I know you are," one of them said in that way they had. It brought her up off the couch to swing. She meant it to hurt. But the blow landed soft and comic in the doctor's shoulder pad, and she fell back on the couch.

They kept looking past her, asking if she recognized the boy. Spence handed over all of Sonny's charts, so she had to get them straight. They were not in the adoption business, no matter what her husband said. Perhaps some other nice couple could provide a home for the poor boy. They kept looking past her, and Spence bent down to tell her to look at the boy again.

Zala backed into the bedroom and went immediately to the dresser. With a corner of the tray she shoved the clock all the way back to the mirror. In it she could see the foot of the bed. Kenti's plush elephant in the folds of the coverlet, Kofi's Darth Vader laser sword on top of the checkerboard. She saw his feet, yellowish, and his shins like dark iron. There was a sticker burr on his pj's, which were wrinkled at the knees.

"That is not my boy," she had told them. She'd rehearsed the line months ago in the Quonset hut in Atlanta. "Those bones are not my child." Brushing Spence's words away from her ear, she told them it was fruitless to try and palm the damaged boy off as their son. But Spence kept saying things to bring her around, to take a good look, to concentrate.

"I hope you're hungry." She talked to him in the mirror. "Hot broth with fresh vegetables from the garden." She felt like she was saying lines in a play. She laughed, to show that she could, to show him she was not put off by his wounds. She left the glass of ice and the container of orange juice on the dresser.

His face was turned her way, his head against the wall, the pillows bunched behind his neck. His eyes stayed on the juice as she approached. His hands crossed over his stomach.

Holding the saucer lid down and gripping the spoon tightly, she carried the bowl to the bed. It wouldn't do to drop anything. He was skittish. She sat down gently and felt him tighten up. She eased the bowl onto the night table, taking her time so that he would learn to take his. There was a father in Winston-Salem who'd written that his son didn't speak at all the first eight weeks. When he finally did, he spoke not as the seven-year-old that he was but as the four-year-old he'd been when he disappeared from a Founders' Day parade at the college.

She eased around, lifting her leg and placing her knee carefully on the bed. She was learning how to do things in slow motion. She would have to learn other things too. How to open her lungs again, retrain them after a year of shallow breathing. How to unclench her thighs, teach her back to relax. And she would have to learn to call him Sonny again.

"You don't look comfortable," she said when he squirmed against the pillows. She placed her hands carefully on the corners of the pillow behind his neck and tugged, expecting him to help, to raise himself a little. "I guess you're too sore to move?" She fluffed the pillow and slid her hands down onto his shoulders. She could feel his boniness through the blue-and-white cotton. She could feel his heat, clammy and sudden.

"I couldn't . . ."

It was a croak. And the sound seemed to scare him as much as it did her. He fell back against the pillows and clamped his mouth shut, though she hadn't shushed him this time. This time she looked at him squarely, to show that she could, to show that whatever he'd been through he was seeable.

"No matter what," she said, then lost what she'd planned to say next because his face was moving, rubbery and stiff at the same time. She couldn't make out what he was trying to tell her. When he pried his jaws apart, she turned away from the smell of him, a rusty, unfamiliar smell, and picked up the soup bowl. She leaned closer so she could feel his breath on her hands. It shivered the hairs near the base of her fingers. She hadn't known she had hair on the base of her fingers. And she'd never been so aware of the size and shape of his head. His neck seemed too fragile to carry it.

The bad smell came out of him again and she almost pulled away. She concentrated on not spilling the soup. He leaned forward from the neck. She watched his mouth close over the spoon. And he watched her, his eyes inching forward from deep, purplish sockets to the puffy blue swells of his cheeks. She felt a tiny wind ruffling in her uterus and wanted to say something, wanted to use his name. But then his grip loosened and she hesitated, for if she pulled the spoon out, words would follow. And she was no more prepared now to hear it, the rush of it, tumbled and confused, than she'd been on the Fourth of July when he'd limped into the bathroom to hide from Dave, come for the car.

"Eat," she said, letting go of the spoon. She pressed the bowl to his chest until he took it. He turned his face away sharply. The sun on that side of the room caught him full in the face and he had to close his eyes and turn his head again.

She slid toward the foot of the bed, moving Kofi's toy out of the way. He sat there a long time holding the bowl, the spoon stuck in his mouth. He hadn't forgotten how to feed himself. She'd seen him doing it spying from the adjoining bedroom through the keyhole; she'd seen Kenti sitting cross-legged on the windowseat, asking him how come he hadn't used his kung fu to get away from the kidnappers. He was wolfing down the remains of her cheese toast, leaving the breakfast tray Gerry had set on the table untouched.

Zala waited. She'd learned how. And now he would have to learn a few things too. He would have to learn to understand food again. She too. Meanwhile, she would learn how to hem up the dragging flesh of her life with careful, tiny stitches. She watched him. And he watched her. Staring for so long without blinking, she saw specks of black and green clouding her vision, but she could be as stubborn as he was.

He blinked when the children called out to the mailman. His glance flickered away from her face for a split second to look at the juice on the dresser. When his gaze returned, she smiled. Angrily, he pulled the spoon out and ate, greedily, rapidly. He was fuming and would not look at her.

When he threw the bowl down on the bed and flung the spoon after, hoping to break the bowl, she said, "I've done that. I've gotten into a car because I thought somebody called my name." She watched the smeared trail the spoon made across the checkerboard dry before she spoke again. She measured her words to teach him how it was done.

"Yes, I got in. And yes, I knew better, but I got in anyway." He obviously thought she was making it up. His mouth was sneery, but the rest of his face didn't join in, so she continued, slowly teaching him how he should tell his story. "I didn't recognize the car either," she added. A little at a time so he'd know how to do it. Small bites, tiny sips. "Or the driver. Didn't recognize her either. Didn't even look. Just got in."

He was moving his head like a swimmer with water in his ears. Then he stopped and formed a word with his lips, his mouth still closed in doubt. He thought she was making it up.

"Yes, me. And I was cursing God at the time." She could see that that shocked him. "That's right. I was cursing God when the car—it was a van, a green van—it pulled up and I was ordered to get in."

She tensed when he leaned forward, pressing his knuckles into the bed. He was suppressing a cough. She thought he was going to laugh. She was afraid. She'd left no room in her plans for panic.

On the fourth day in Miami, she'd been flipping through a medical journal waiting to see him when she heard him coughing. Hammer blows against the walls of his lungs, crashing tissue, blood, and water together in a crackling tidal wave. He'd recovered, his face twisted in pain; but she hadn't.

"Careful," she said, touching his foot. He stretched out a little and blew the bad smell down the front of himself. She took his feet onto her lap and rubbed them until he pulled them away. Watching his face gray, she began to doubt the wisdom of what she was doing. Mouth grim, balling his fists, his eyes darting over her face, he was clearly worried. Maybe he thought she'd meant as a girl.

"Juice?"

His nod came in stages. He dipped his head, and his eyes moved right, left, then came to a rest and closed. She thought he might be drifting off, but he was clenching his fists more tightly. He raised his head to complete the nod, then opened his eyes, swiveled them toward the dresser, and sighed. One day soon, she thought, rising slowly from the bed, they would speak of this moment, and she would imitate his gesture, and call it regal. They would laugh with no fear of bruising his lungs.

She poured the orange juice over the ice. He watched her in the mirror. "It was a Monday morning in autumn," she said, turning away from the dresser to address him directly. "October 13 of last year." She walked back to the bed. He was concentrating hard on what she had said. What had he been experiencing that day as she was on her way downtown to be lied to once again? He eased back against the pillows and slid his arms out to the side. His palms were sweaty. The date relieved him: she'd not been a girl getting into a van but his mother.

He reached for the glass with both hands. She helped him hold it, trying to prevent him from gulping it down. "That was the day a nursery blew up." His frown didn't seem to mean he'd heard of it but that the glass was empty. He shook it and looked at the ice cubes, then allowed her to take the glass from him. "When they brought the bodies out . . . me and Daddy were praying that . . . We feared you might be . . . We . . ."

She hadn't meant to go that far. His eyes grew dull when she set the glass on the night table and gathered the bowl and the spoon from the bed. It was a long time after she'd sat down again that he seemed to come back from a great distance away. He was trying to say something, not necessarily to her, but something important that pained him. When he opened his mouth, there was a bubble in front, a thin spit bubble. It had colors in it like a rainbow.

"It's hard, isn't it?" she said and left it at that, wondering when he would seem real to her.

Her back turned, Gerry unwrapped her bubba, shook the wrinkles free, then secured the cloth around her hips again, tucking the ends in tightly around her waist. She glanced over her shoulder at Spence, then continued slitting the mail open with the steak knife.

Spence was leaning against the little water heater and looking up at the ceiling. It was the first day Gerry had been able to ease them apart. Reluctant to let each other out of sight, obsessively attentive to what each was doing, the Spencers communicated what it meant to have lived in Atlanta in a state of siege. The murmuring from above had stopped, but he continued to stare at the grate until satisfied that no more conversation would be traveling down the duct from upstairs.

"There's a letter from New York," Gerry said, "with a June postmark." She read it through quickly and offered as compact a synopsis as she could, for his attention span was worse than the week before. "From a Charles Logan. He's in touch with a firm called G. Kelly Associates. They're specialists in destructive cults. Says Innis and McGill are in attendance. More to follow." She waited to see if the message registered. She looked at the pile of mail to go, anxious to get to the unopened mail addressed to Sonny to see what Spence would instruct her to do.

"Save the Logan letter," he said, running his hands over the tank. The only portion of the water heater still white was the rectangle where the trademark plate had fallen away, leaving two small, brownish holes.

He tightened the screw in the porcelain knob and swung the gate open and shook his head.

"A little faith, my brother." Gerry brought him the box of matches. "It's really quite reliable despite its years."

"Faith," he said and turned on the gas. "The faith of the bather." He struck the match and stared in at the rusty entrails.

She had to nudge his arm before he moved the match. He held it against the orangish iron, and the flames sprang up around the ring. "Surprise, surprise," she said, since that was the expression he wore.

He tilted his head and looked at the ceiling again, and she waited. She'd been in the company of parents often enough to know they could hear sounds that other people couldn't and would leave the room before anyone else registered a thing. She'd been for a long time in the company of people who lived in a state of siege, people who could hear a jeep twenty kilometers off, could distinguish the sound of a government motor from one of a raiding party from across the border, could cock their head to the side and tell whether the vehicle was slowly carrying the wounded or was triumphantly transporting Israeli weapons confiscated from the invading South African troops.

When his attention returned to the water heater, she went back to the table. "The STOP organization has made an appeal to accountants to help them get their books in order." She was not sure she understood that. "Does that mean they're preparing to apply for part of the reward?"

"No. They're being hassled. Upsets people to see poor folks with money. Now that the cops have got Williams to take the fall, it's open season on STOP."

Gerry shook her head. The logic of the case continually escaped her. "I don't understand this," she said, flipping through clipped-together newsprint. "The papers talk about Williams's motives for killing the children, although he's not been charged with murdering children. For example, 'Williams, charged with the murder of two ex-cons, Nathaniel Cater, twenty-seven, and Jimmy Ray Payne, twenty-one . . .' And what's more curious—" She interrupted herself to locate an article from earlier in the week in which the death certificates had been cited. She was certain that one of the deaths had been attributed to drowning and had been called a probable suicide. She could have sworn the other document mentioned a history of suicide attempts by strangling, a description her stepsister Marzala's husband had said might be a misinterpretation of or a euphemistic term for "enhanced masturbation gone too far." She was sure that the death certificate of one of the men had listed a history of heart disease, and was sure that neither death had been termed a homicide until after Wayne Williams's arrest.

"Of course, I wouldn't put it past the coroners to change official documents. In my part of the world it's the rule rather than the exception. The Pretoria regime originally listed suicide as the cause of Biko's death, for example. Then it was changed to heart trouble. Of course, any who knew Steven Biko knew that his health was excellent and knew a lie for a lie. Once the counselors for the family were able to get the body released and people saw—ah, my brother, what they saw—then the state termed it 'a necessary death for the preservation of the nation.' " Gerry looked over at Spence. She was not so surprised to discover that he'd not been listening. From the first, they'd all been so totally absorbed with the feeding and comfort of Sundiata, a whole day might go by without a word or a kiss between them.

"What is it?"

"Ex-cons." He wagged his head. His smile was ugly. "That's what they're calling them now? Having a good time—street hoodlums, retards, ex-cons, and the Fiend. Trash it, Gerry."

Reluctantly, she dropped the envelope and its contents into the box by her feet, then hurried on while she had his attention. "Con helping police establish links between Williams and other kidnappers disappears the day Williams is formally charged."

"Trash."

"One moment." She read through the now familiar story of a brother who'd managed to talk his way out of prison even though "Extreme Escape Risk" had been stamped all over his record. His police escort had hung back to allow him to locate supposed companions of Williams who allegedly frequented the bars near the Greyhound terminal. Gerry wondered if the escaped prisoner, Watson, had information that was related in any way to the story her nephew had been narrating piecemeal in the past few days. "You're sure you don't want to save it? Looks important."

"The authorities are committed to a solo murderer. Watson's lucky he wasn't iced by the cops his first night out on the street."

Gerry continued reading. "They'd feared he'd made contact with

Williams's fellow kidnappers and met with foul play. But his mother reports he contacted her. So the fugitive is still at large."

It was a long while before Spence answered. She watched his jaws tighten; he was grinding his teeth. "Trash. Get on with it."

"Governor Busbee says the Georgia Bureau completed their investigation of the KKK and their slate is clean. Julian Bond challenged their findings."

"No mention, I suppose, of who headed that GBI whitewash? Save that," he growled. And when he moved, she expected him to take the letter with the taped-down clipping from her. But he walked right by and into Mama Lovey's dining room.

"Is this one of the cover-ups you were talking about?" Gerry grabbed up the mail, lowered the flame under the pots, and followed Spence, who was trailing his hands across the lowboy as he strolled toward the master bedroom.

"Well, my brother, what are you going to do, and how can I help?" She stood by the china cabinet as he hooked his fingers around the exercise bar jammed high in the bedroom doorway. From where she stood on the raked floor, the cabinet tinkling its contents, she could see the big iron bed with the two dents in the mattress. In time, one dent would plump up again. Spence was swinging his body a little the way her father had tried to do to convince himself he had not shrunk, was still the hale head of the house.

"What did you say?" He turned to her. "Do? You mean about notifying the FBI and the police? I assume the Florida police relayed the news about Sonny."

"The medication, Spence. The medication is in the drawer again today."

He blew air through his nostrils and walked into the living room. He looked at the fireplace he'd help to build. He looked at her projector and the carousel of slides, but expressed no interest in what she'd been doing in Africa. He moved around the sofa, fingering the mudcloths she'd sewn together and draped across the back cushions. One side still needed fringing. Gerry still hoped to get Zala and Lovey to sit down together to do it before she left to join Maxwell in Maseru.

"Shall I go on?" If Spence was not prepared to stop dodging the issue of the medicine, they could at least get through the mail that had piled up. He was looking at the paintings above the stereo. There was a picture of Jesus kneeling at the rock with a valentine heart. He gazed up at a sunbeam breaking through the clouds. Next to it was Martin Luther King Jr. on black velvet, resting his cheek against two fingers; he gazed up at an oil painting of her stepmother a local artist had done from a color photo.

"Like she knows how to get to heaven without first dying," Spence said, smiling up at his mother-in-law. "This is a good family," he said unexpectedly. "And you're such a good person," he said, which threw Gerry off balance. She was out of her slippers now, for he was moving fast, heading for the foyer, and she did not intend to lose him this time. For when he went up the stairs brooding, gray seemed to gather in the house and dim the light. She did not wish to cook food in the somber house or serve the women from the co-op somber stew. The women were due in a few minutes, and there was more mail to handle.

"Please," she said, "let us accomplish a little more before supper. Then perhaps tonight we might feel like Talent House. Yes?" But he was facing the front porch and she couldn't see if he remembered. There was nothing particularly stimulating to look at on the sleeping porch. One of her wraps was slung over the top of the shutters. There were books in the hammock she slept in. It swung slightly, the breeze sweeping the fragrance of wisteria and jasmine into the foyer.

"Go on," he said.

"Authorities say the decision to apprehend Williams grew out of the suspicion that he might flee." She saw his shoulders move. "After leading the police on a merry chase, Williams and his father reportedly attempted to hire a pilot. There was no pressure politics involved in the decision to arrest."

She heard his derisive laugh, and he turned. "First the GBI grabbed the ball and made the feds look bad. But then they'd been looking bad, their own agents kept fucking things up. They had to send agent-in-charge Glover up to Washington to convince the JD that their case was airtight before the big chiefs would lean a little on the locals. We heard what they were basing their case against Williams on—what a laugh. But those jerks up in D.C. went for it. Trash that shit."

She tore it up and looked about for somewhere to throw it. And when she tried to back into her slippers, the backless red leather slippers slightly curled at the toe eluded her across the buffed floor. He was laughing at her attempts. He was laughing from the staircase, three steps up.

"My brother, do you know that I love you?" That stopped him on the fourth step, and he waited for her to come to the banister and reach up. "We must all make an effort . . ." She patted his hand, but the words would not come, so she settled for "I'll be in the kitchen if you need me. The women from the co-op are coming over. Try and get Zala to join us in the sauna. She's in knots, and that can't help Sundiata, can it?"

Gerry lingered in the foyer as Spence slowly moved up the stairs. She wasn't sure if anyone but the boy had gotten more than two or three hours' rest in a given day. She turned toward the old piano, several yellowed keys missing. She refrained from striking the notes; it would sound mournful. One of the piano legs had broken and her father had fixed it. Shorter than the other, it was propped on a wad of cardboard that pulverized at the corner when her slipper brushed against it. She went back through the living room thirsting for music. Kofi had been playing the Wailers all morning, the volume on low. She put on Fela and turned it up high. Then she went back to the kitchen, glancing quickly at her things on the coffee table.

From all over the region, she'd received invitations to give slide-show presentations about apartheid and the South African regime's attempts to reannex neighboring countries and extend its pernicious influence into Lesotho, Botswana, Namibia, Zambia, Mozambique, and Angola. But within her own family, the slides, the photo album, the large looseleaf of letters and notes remained undisturbed, unnoticed, all of them totally absorbed in convalescence.

Gerry brushed her cheek against her shoulder and stirred in a little peanut butter to thicken the ground nut stew. She glanced at the grate in the ceiling, then moved to the mail on the table. All of Sonny's mail looked the same—square white envelopes. One felt especially thick, like the greeting card contained cash. She slipped it down inside her cobalt-blue patterened wrap, then tucked the fabric in more tightly around her waist.

Spence paused at the landing window when he heard Kofi telling the two big boys who'd come to ask after "Sunday" that he was not interested in going to see the bees. The boys were on the path that took a fork down by the chicken coops, the skinny dirt path going past the toolshed to the hives, the wider grassy path leading to the cedar sweat cabin the co-op women had built for his mother-in-law. Spence pressed his face against the window screen. He could see her below. Her behavior confused him. As long as daylight held, she avoided coming into the house. And at night—he couldn't be sure, he was so whipped by the time he bedded Kofi and Kenti down on the cots in the big bedroom upstairs, but she seemed to prowl around like an insomniac. So soon after the death of Widow Man, she was mourning, restless.

"And here we come," he muttered, moving away from the window. Maybe Lovey would insist that Zala join the women for the ritual sauna. And perhaps then there'd be time to take Sonny for a drive and be back before Zala could accuse him of kidnap and coercion. Pressure, she'd said, was damaging. Pressure and probing had been the doctor's careless game. And he was a stupid son of a bitch for adopting their methods on the traumatized boy.

She'd been adamant on the subject of psychological testing. "Interrogation," she'd called it. By the third day in Miami it was "violation" of the boy's privacy, a "rape" of his mind. He had a right to himself, and had a right to legal counsel as well. Who the hell did they think they were, breaking and entering, ransacking his dream life, interpreting his drawings, plastering labels on him, and for what? To fill up their folders, fill up professional journals with psychobabble. Not once in all their jargonized bullshit had they acknowledged that a crime had been committed against the boy, a monstrous crime. They talked about psychosomatic disorders and coping mechanisms and so forth. Nothing about the torment that had shattered the boy's identity.

And then she had turned on him so fiercely—wasn't he going to protect the boy, wasn't he the father, was he going to just stand there and cooperate in the rape—that he hadn't realized she had stepped over the line and had called the boy Sonny, had said "your son," "our child."

"You ain't scared?" Kofi's voice was high-pitched, the way it had been on first sight of Sonny. He and Kenti had backed away, as though battered bruises might be catching.

"They Georgia bees."

"Well, Georgia bees sting. That's where I'm from, Atlanta."

"You from Atlanta? Ain't that where they been killing children?"

"Aww, man, quit. Let's see the bees."

Spence continued up the stairs. Zala was right. Pressure, before Sonny had made up his mind what he would tell and how he would tell it, only forced him to lie. Spence was sure that a lot in the story was lies. Maybe not the first part, going with the woman he'd thought he'd seen at school. Maybe not the part about the risqué tapes the couple played, then accused him of being a nasty boy for listening to. But the parts in answer to who they were, the first set of captors and the second, and then the last . . . those parts he always fudged. "He owes no one the truth," Zala had argued, as if he, Sonny's own father, were the enemy.

"Let me tell it." One of the boys with Kofi was outshouting the other. "Your grandmama was out here one day putting flour on the crops. And all these bees came. A bunch of them, a whole gang of them. Your granddaddy hobbled out here with the fly swatter to give her a hand. But she didn't call the exterminator man like some people do. She called the bee man. Now y'all got a lot of hives. Make a lot of money when you got a lot of hives."

"Y'all used to have four. Now y'all rich."

Spence yanked the water on hard and the handle fell into the tub. He left it there and plugged the stopper in. Then he went to the wall and leaned his ear against it. But the water was running full force and the girls were playing around that side of the house.

"Funny money ba-bunny, fee fie fa-runny, Sonnnyyyyy!"

Spence tiptoed into the hall and stood by the door listening. In the version he heard Sonny tell Kofi one early morning when Spence noticed the cot in their bedroom empty and bent to the keyhole, Sonny had been sold to a slave gang of boys and forced to work on a plantation that outsiders thought was a state-run reform school. This last part seemed a tacked-on improvisation in answer to Kofi's question how come the mailman or the meter readers or the neighbors didn't think it was weird that two white men had a bunch of Black boys living with them and didn't call the police.

There was no keyhole on the hall door of the bedroom. Spence held his breath and concentrated. He could hear a slight wheeze on the intake of breath, a slight whistle on the out. He tapped softly on the door and turned the knob slowly. He had to wipe his hands on his jeans and try again. For a moment, he was homicidal with the thought that Zala had locked him out.

.   .   .

Zala opened her eyes and turned her head toward the sunny corner of the room. Voices were coming up through the grate.

"Can you believe it? For nearly two years they'd been questioning people who used to work for the co-op and poking in our files, and couldn't find one irregularity. So they said they'd have to impound our records."

"So we said, all right, but we want a receipt."

The women below in the kitchen whooped and hooted.

"Little man sits himself down and writes out a receipt. 'Ohhhhh nooooo, man, we want a separate receipt for each piece you remove, and we want the piece and the receipt numbered so they tally, and we want a full description of the piece written on the receipt. We know our rights, dammit!' Think that stopped them? Don't you know they called in some other IRS agents to help them do it. How long they park their hocks in that office, Ruby?"

"Did nearly two hundred pieces worth 'fore they threw in the towel."

"Go on."

"I'm telling you, Miss Loveyetta. That's how they spend the tax-payers' dollars."

"Couldn't stick it."

"No, they really couldn't. They really slung some lowdown dirt on the project. But they couldn't stick it. Threw in the towel like she said."

"We lost some troops though. Lost support money too. They scared off a lot of people. I tell you, I just don't know about some people some-time, Miss Lovey. Run for cover in a minute."

"It's the way people bring up the children nowadays. Raising their children to be mindless workers. Half the people around here would turn in their own mama just to be considered cooperative by some damn authority type. They just roll over. Give up information you'd have to torture and beat out of me."

"You know it. The Federation of Southern Cooperatives going strong."

"And going to be be-bone badder than ever soon's we catch our breath."

Zala sat up when the cheering rose up through the grate. Something stuck her. There was a burr on the bedspread where Sonny's feet should have been. She jumped up and was partway down the stairs before the sound of sloshing brought her back up and to the bathroom door. Someone was drawing the shower curtain, the plastic rings clicking across the metal rod. When she leaned her ear to hear, her hair brushed against the door.

"Zala?"

"Yes."

"We're okay. Sonny's taking a bath. I'm about through shaving. We're going to go for a drive."

She chewed over the two "we"s. Neither included her. He seemed about to say something further, in fact did, but mumbled it. Something about her going to the sauna. She tried the knob, making as much noise as she could, uncertain whether the shower curtain had been drawn closed or open. Since the evening Gerry had walked in on Sonny while he was changing into fresh pajamas, he'd made it clear he didn't like Gerry around, pulling the coverlet up over his head when she came up the stairs with breakfast.

"Why is this door locked?"

"The door is not locked, Zala."

It was the voice he'd used at the hospital, the long-suffering voice he'd used to tell her to look again. Her throat swelled so she couldn't swallow. She knew the anger she felt was unfair, but she was helpless against it.

Spence shook his razor briskly and set it on the sill by the plants. "Unplug the stopper?" It was a while before he heard him do it, longer still before he heard the shower curtain being pulled back again. He turned, and when a foot emerged, hesitantly, then a leg, Spence stepped on the end of the bathmat so it wouldn't slip. But Sonny would not step out with him standing so near.

Spence filled the toothpaste cup and turned his back to water the plants. "Don't worry about the tub," he said as casually as he could. "I'll wash it out." One day soon, they would joke about the crud Sonny left each time he took a bath. Where the hell did it come from? All he did was lay around in bed, play checkers, once and a while sit in the window.

Spence took his time watering the plants, watching the water bubble up around the base of the begonias before the thirsty roots sucked it down through the soil and he could pour a little more without fear of overflowing the pots. He listened to the buff of terry cloth against Sonny's wet skin. The slow, careful dabbing when he came to a sore spot. The hard rubbing to get the adhesive residue off. If only he'd talk. "Ahhunh," "uhn-uhhhn," and "pamb-uhhh-uhn" didn't say very much. No one mentioned going to Lovey's minister anymore, or to "somebody" who might be good to talk to—most definitely not to the police. Sonny talked with his sister and brother a little. That was progress. And he seemed to manage a few words with Zala.

When Spence turned, Sonny jumped, clutching the towel in front of him. Rage swelled Spence's neck. Who'd done this? Who'd wrecked this moment, father and son, a shave and a bath? When Spence knelt down and took the sponge and the can of cleanser, his foot knocked against the hamper and the lid banged down. Sonny looked at him and smiled, but there was no fun in it. A smile to ingratiate, to disarm. He was shivering.

"Your robe's on the door, Sonny."

It was the faded plaid cotton flannel one hanging on the back of the door. They'd chosen it over the new one still wrapped in Christmas paper in the hall closet at home. Sonny was backing away and not taking his eyes off of Spence. "You'll catch cold," was as much as Spence could say before anger welled up again. He scrubbed at the ring in the tub. And when he turned the tap on to slosh the suds away, he looked up at his son. For a minute he looked almost like himself, taller, thinner, slowly tying the sash around the robe and watching him, tense, alert.

"It's all right, Sonny." He stared at the boy's neck. Scrawny, but not as emaciated as before; the flesh was not sagging in folds. The doctors had told them that they'd had to clear a passage in his esophagus. He couldn't eat without choking. He'd still been on intravenous feedings at night their fifth day in Miami, his daytime meals graduating from gruel to bland soup with a few solids by the end of the week.

Spence took his time getting up when he heard the children. He tipped his head in the direction of the window. Sonny would not take his eyes from him until he turned to look out. One of the boys was chasing the girls with a stick. When they screamed, Spence started, but the shrieks got no reaction from Sonny at all.

"Bet that stick is supposed to have touched a rat or something." For his efforts Spence received a wan smile. And then Sonny was watching him again, wary, backing toward the door, his hand behind him searching for the knob.

When he noticed Sonny's gaze move up from his face to his head, Spence smiled. "My hair, you noticed?" He ran his hands over his bush and tried not to be too eager. "Yeah, had to get rid of that curl. Like it better this way?"

It was an obedient nod, quick, unengaged. Spence would have given both arms to see him cock his chin, push his lips out and size him up, then issue some outrageous remark about his hair. It was enough that he was standing there, the bruise on his upper lip faded to a smudge. Or maybe it was the beginning of a mustache. He was nearly thirteen now.

It was in fact a miracle. Members of the American refugee committee, which Paulette had worked with, had come to inquire about the boy. Handbills Paulette had brought down from Atlanta were examined, one in particular placed apart from the others on the bulletin board. A worker from a child-find agency had inquired too and left behind a stack of handbills, one of them from the mass mailing Zala had done. The intake clerk thought she saw a resemblance and went daily to see the boy, checking his chart against the description—height, weight, dental work, blood type, chicken pox scar, smallpox vaccination. It was the vaccination scar that said he'd been born before 1970, the year inoculation methods changed.

"Sonny?" When they'd asked if he was Sonny Spencer, he'd tried to slip away. Now he was trying to make himself small to back out of the door. He hadn't exactly denied who he was, but he'd not been eager for the hospital clerk to place the call to Atlanta.

"I love you, boy." Zala was waiting in the hall with her arms open wide. But by the time Spence stepped out of the bathroom, Sonny had wriggled free from his mother's embrace and darted into the bedroom. The door clicked shut on a corner of the bathrobe. Together Zala and Spence watched the small piece of flannel disappear. Then they searched each other's faces for a progress report, listening to the movements behind the door.

"I'll get the truck," Spence sighed. He touched her face. She looked as worn out as he was. "Whatever happened to happily ever after, Zala?"

. . .

"Don't trample in my yellow root tea, girls." Mama Lovey tossed the eggplant back and forth and watched the truck churn up dust along the road. The two little girls waved goodbye to Kenti. Then they turned to the kitchen patch on the lookout for a china cup or a teakettle.

"What yellow root tea look like, Miss Gerry?"

Gerry didn't hear them. Slippers in her hand, she was hurrying through the rows of snap beans in the direction of her stepmother. The girls studied the different kinds of greens, searching for the particular ones the women in the sauna had asked for. There were thin blades that smelled like furniture polish and tasted like lemon when they crammed in a mouthful. There was curly stuff they recognized from lunch, swimming in butter on the Irish potatoes. There were tall fragrant stems for putting in iced tea to make it taste like green gumdrops. There were needles that Miss Lovey boiled up in the yard with ladled-up rainwater, to rinse her hair with. The plant with the round blue-gray leaves that smelled like cough drops they broke off in bunches to take to the cabin and put in the steamy basin on the stove down there.

"They bare all over, all the way up to their titties," one of the little girls whispered, taking off down the wide path. The other giggled and ran behind her, hands over her mouth, her shoulders hunched to her ears.

Gerry tucked the loose slip strap up under her stepmother's cap sleeve, then pinched her. "Talk to me. You haven't said a word to me all day. I've missed you."

Lovey extended her cheek and Gerry kissed her. Then the two turned toward the road, their arms around each other's waists, and watched the truck get smaller. When it turned off, Lovey pulled the handkerchief from her head and wiped her hands with it.

"Like having a sneak thief in the house," she sighed.

"He is exactly the topic I wanted to raise with you, Lovey."

"What makes you think I ain't talking about you, Geralanna?" Chuckling, Lovey squatted down and lifted the basket. "Could be talking 'bout most any of us, and I probably should."

"What I want to know is, where does he go when he climbs out at night?" From her blouse pocket Gerry produced a tattered piece of blue-and-white cotton. "I found this hooked on the chicken wire this morning. I almost missed it. Looks like one of the black-and-white striped feathers, doesn't it?" She held it up. "Another two nights and his pajamas will be ripped to shreds."

Mama Lovey tucked the basket under her arm and moved Gerry aside when she attempted to take it from her. "Sundiata come round once they back off and give him some room. He'll quit the shimsham if they give him time."

Gerry bent down and brushed soil from between her stepmother's toes. "Has he come round to you? I saw you out here last night in your nightgown. Over there," Gerry said, looking toward the white field of Regale lilies, artemisia, cotton-lavender, and Queen Anne's lace. "You were standing by the white roses. Later I heard the thump on the porch roof, and when I looked, I saw him over there." She pointed to the part of the field where the daisies mingled in with hydrangea, delphinium, foamflower, candytuft, foxglove, and silver mound. "Do you two meet at night to talk? What does he say?"

"It'll all come out in the wash," Lovey said, tramping off toward the back porch. "Everything in good time."

Gerry followed her up the steps, where they wiped their feet on the rug. "Think it would help to have talent night?"

Mama Lovey laughed a good hearty laugh and pushed the screen door open. She reached up and swung one of the smoked hams aside, then ducked under the sprigs of drying herbs. But she didn't go through to the kitchen.

"Here," she said, turning around in the cramped space, inviting her stepdaughter to take in the shelves of jars, funnels, pectin, the zinc tub they washed their feet in, the stool used to get light bulbs down from the storage bin. "Here's where he comes to do his talking, but only to himself. I expect this little squeeze place is like the room they kept him in." She left Gerry there staring at the stool.

In years past, when the family gathered for holidays, Talent Hour could usually draw the boy out no matter how aloof he was trying to be, how much he thought himself too grown for silly games. Lovey would put the old Decca records on. Sometimes she could get Gerry's father up to join her. Maybe he'd tell an anecdote. Zala would recite poetry. Kenti would do ballet and sing a song. Spence would read part of a speech from Douglass, Malcolm, or King. Maxwell would get them on their feet for the Guinea-Bissau marching song. Kofi would say he'd act out an episode from *Space Raiders* but Sonny had to go first. So Gerry would do one of her magic acts and Sonny would watch, then call it stupid. Then they had him. He would have to do something for the show. Once he brought the house down after gesturing in dumb show, then lying down on the floor. "That was 'Silent Night,' y'all." They'd thrown the sofa pillows at him, and the general free-for-all had almost toppled the Christmas tree.

Gerry found Mama Lovey in the bedroom on her knees, the dusty handkerchief on the bed by the Bible, her braid hanging down her back. She always prayed before the ritual bath at the sweat house. Gerry went into the living room and started arranging things for Family Talent Hour. Reluctantly, she put the projector and her slides aside for another time.

"Mama, where'd you get this from?" Kenti reached to the floor of the truck and took the wax tablet from Zala's handbag.

"It used to be mine. It was in the attic. You can write on it with your fingernail or a bobby pin. See? When you lift the top page, it disappears." But there was a collection of messages that remained, faintly visible to the eye but definitely there to her fingers. Zala moved her fingertips over the impressions, reading her past.

Kenti knelt on the seat, facing the back of the truck, and started writing. She lifted the top sheet and the writing disappeared. She passed it through the cab window to her brothers.

Sonny was sitting in a tire with his arms around his knees. He wouldn't look up. Kofi took the tablet from her then leaned back against the stacks of straw and started writing with his nail. He handed the tablet to Sonny and tapped his arm until he took it.

"Remember?" Kofi moved close to the tire and waited for Sonny to read what he wrote out loud. "Member that earth science project you did?" When his brother didn't answer, Kofi read a few billboards as they drove on. Sometimes Sonny took a long time to answer, and when he did, the answer was short. It took time to make up short answers, so Kofi waited. He didn't have anything better to do. He wasn't even hungry. They passed a McDonald's and he saw his father watching them in the rearview mirror, expecting them to say something. Sonny wasn't even looking.

"What's that say?"

Kenti was pointing to writing on the wall of a brick building: MIS-CARRIAGE OF JUSTICE! FREE MAGGIE BOZEMAN AND JULIA WILDER! Kofi touched Sonny's arm. "What's that first word mean?" Sonny didn't move his head. But when the truck stopped, he moved his eyes to watch the train coming.

Kenti leaned her cheek on her hands and looked at her brother in the tire. "Awwww . . . you don't know how to read anymore? You for-got?" Then she lifted her head up. A bug was crawling over the mound of her thumb.

"Don't move," Kofi said, crawling toward her. "A ladybug's good luck." He put his wrist next to hers and the red-and-gold speckled bug crawled onto his hand. "You're supposed to make a wish." He closed his eyes and made one, peeking at Kenti. Her mouth was moving, her fore-head was wrinkled, and her eyes were squeezed shut. She was making the same wish he was. He turned around to show Sonny, holding his wrist right under his nose.

"Ladybug, ladybug, fly away home, Babylon is on fire 'cause Sundi-ata's back home."

He knew that would get him. Sonny kept his mouth closed over his teeth, but he was smiling, then he was laughing, then he wasn't. He was shivering like he was scared the train was going to jump the track and crash into the truck.

Kenti was standing on the seat reading the cars. " 'Ral-ston Pur-rina Co period.' 'North-thern Rail-way Line.' 'South-thern Cent-tral Su-per-shock Con-trol.' 'San-ta Fe Piggy Back Ser-vice.' That's funny. Look, there's the Cheshire cat!"

Kenti turned around.

"Where you going?" Kofi pulled Sonny back down.

"What's the matter?" 'cause Kofi was yelling.

"Sonny crying, Daddy." But Spence had already jumped out of the truck.

Kofi put his arm out stiff and Sonny fell against it, but he didn't fall over. He was trembling. And he was working his fists back and forth like they were tied together. Kofi got an arm around his brother's back and held on.

"I got you. It's all right. Ain't nobody gonna mess with you." Kofi flexed his muscles hard so his brother could feel the strength of the arms around him.

"Nobody gonna bother you," Kenti said, climbing through the window. "Daddy blow they head off anybody try to mess with us." She worked her face in between Kofi's arms to kiss Sonny. "Don't cry. Awww, don't cry, Sonny."

Spence was leaping over the side of the truck when Zala gave up trying to reach Sonny through the window. Sonny lunged toward her, his wrists locked together. It took all she had to pull his hands apart. She kissed his knuckles. "No matter what, no matter what!" When he opened his hands, she kissed his palms. "We love you. Ohh, Sonny." She prayed he would not start coughing.

"It's okay," Kofi said, ordering everybody away. "I got him, Dad. Let go, y'all. I got him."

When the train thundered by and the truck stopped rattling, Sonny slowly lifted his head. He tried to sit up straight but fell down into the tire. He laughed a little. Kofi laughed a lot but didn't let go. Kenti giggled and leaned over to poke her father who smiled. Zala was still holding her breath, making vows, taking notes, and praying he would not start coughing.

Sunday, August 30, 1981

Z ala draped Sonny's sheets across the rack she'd improvised out
of old tomato stakes and chicken wire. Every bush but the butterfly bush held towels and underwear to bleach in the sun. She watched
the white-suited bee men through the close weave of leaves at the vanishing point of the two laundry lines.

"They're gathering propolis today," Zala heard her mother telling
someone around the other side of the house. She left Sonny's coverlet in
the basket and went to see who Lovey was talking to. "Got to leave
some, though. Can't take it all." The girls were going "Ahh-hunh" but
kept picking blackberries along the fence. "Keeps the hives germ-free,
you see," looking toward the house, as though the house had no natural
immunity of its own against its monthlong guests who'd tracked in a
disease.

Zala watched her mother bend and lift a bedspread from the basket,
her dress hiked up in back, veins bulging in her legs. Zala did not move
to help her. Only a few minutes ago she'd told Gerry that she was not
angry with Mama Lovey, denied she'd set her heart against her mother
for not coming to her in Atlanta, for choosing Widow Man over her
own child, and Gerry had said, "Uhn-hunh." They all went around imitating Sonny. There was nothing funny about it that Zala could see.

Zala moved back around to the yard and slapped at her neck. She
wasn't quick enough. The mosquito drew blood and flew off. That
morning, what Mattie had dubbed the Coffee Papers spread out all over
the bed, the worn portfolio she'd mailed them in on the floor, Sonny had
told her that he didn't know any of the people, did not recognize the descriptions of the suspects, though he did hesitate when it came to the
white man with the zigzag scar down the side of his neck, the man from

the Lubie Geter case. Said he didn't know any of the children, any of the women, the men. She'd said nothing; gathered the papers up and did not point out that he'd gone to school with Jo-Jo Bell. That he'd once competed against Patrick Rogers's music group. That he'd met Wayne Williams at least once. That one of the murdered women had worked in the candy store on Northside Drive before they'd moved to Thurmond. She'd just slipped everything back into Mattie's portfolio.

She had not pressed him. He didn't owe anyone anything; not even his family did he owe the truth. But he had to understand that people had a right, the stricken families had a right, to ask him questions. She was trying to prepare him for home.

He had put his shoes on and left the room without a further word about the year he'd spent away from them. That was all right for the moment. It might have to be all right forever. If not all right, just so. Hugging the Coffee Papers, she'd felt nothing but a deep throbbing as after a hot bath.

Zala looked around for someplace to hang the rest of the wash. There was a squabble down in the chicken pen, Lovey's prize rooster laying the law down to the hens.

Sheena sat back on her heels and held the pail for Kenti to stand on. Even on tiptoe and stretching up, up to the sky like they did in school in the mornings, she could only see the helmets of the bee men over the roof of the henhouse. They looked like camping tents on their heads. Then a breeze came. Kenti jumped down and grabbed her end of the wicker tray. Sheena poured her pail of berries in it and lifted up her end. They shook gently so the berries wouldn't bounce out or mush each other. What the wind didn't blow off fell through the holes—bits of twigs, leaves, and dirt.

"You could stay here and go to school with us, Kenti. You already missed a week, you know."

"We going home soon," Kenti said, hoping that was so. Every morning at breakfast now they had to go over how to act when they got back to Atlanta. She guessed they couldn't leave till they got it right. But a limo was coming to take them to the Rawls cousins first. They could go swimming in the ocean.

"Well, you better hurry up or you'll get left back. People make fun of you when you get left back."

"I know," Kenti said, thinking about Sonny. She was glad Sheena stopped talking. She hoped the horns would blow soon, so they could go to the stables. She looked toward the fields to see if Kofi was coming.

"Spacemen." Kofi stabbed the loose hay with the pitchfork. He couldn't talk and keep up with the rest of them, so he stopped looking at the bee men. Everybody, including Cookie, was way ahead of him. The men were bundling faster than he could collect hay in a pile. But it felt good to be working. He liked how he smelled. And not only was he going to get paid, he was going to ride down to the stables to get it.

Someone clear over on the other side of the field was asking who was it that could spin straw into gold. It was too far to yell over. But he knew the answer: Rumpelstilskin. It was better to keep working. His father was on the truck and coming, pulling his gloves on tightly and getting ready to grab up the bundles. Kofi really put his back to it, waiting to see what his father would say about how strong he was getting.

Spence packed the haystacks in tightly and looked toward the field where the young medical students were moving along with their sketch pads, drawing the plants. The smoker the bee men were carrying left a dark, smeary trail. They disappeared behind thick tree trunks, then materialized suddenly in the field back of the bone-white boxes of the colony's brood chamber. He let his mind roam freely over the far field, picturing himself and his children running, looking up at a kite. He would hold the spindle, feeling the tug of the string, something live at the end of the line. They might go fishing too. His in-laws in Brunswick had a boat.

Spence reached for his shirt and mopped his face, neck, and chest, then rapped on the roof of the cab. The truck pulled up toward the last batch of haystacks. What wouldn't he give for nine straight days and a boat in the middle of the water.

"We going to the stables now?" Kofi trotted alongside the truck. When it stopped, he pulled up his T-shirt and wiped his face with it.

"Where's Sonny?"

"Someplace," Kofi said, glad to be away from the others so he could know that the smell was his own and not theirs. He was standing there squinting, sniffing himself, before he realized he was being sent to find his brother.

Without disturbing the look of the ripped-open envelopes, Gerry pushed the mail onto a tray and placed it between the sandwiches and the thermos. Since Lovey was determined not to set foot in the house till dusk, she took a plate out to her and then waited for Spence. Shading her eyes, Gerry watched Kofi trotting toward the mangle Mama Lovey had one of the med students set up in the yard. She intended to iron the sheets outdoors when they were dry enough. Lovey was pointing Kofi in the direction of the toolshed.

Sonny kicked the front wheel. It was completely flat. And the gash in the back wheel was longer than his finger. He didn't remember it being that bad, but it had been dark last time he'd searched the shed. The round cardboard box of bicycle patches wasn't on the shelf where he'd put it back, either. He searched around, trying not to get nervous.

There was a jar of ground-up Japanese beetles. Probably the same beetles he and the old man had crushed for the ground crops. There were two large, squarish glass jars with green screw tops. Self-rising flour with extra baking powder was in them. It used to be his chore to sprinkle the green things, especially the collards and cabbage. The bugs would eat it, swell up, and fall off the leaves and hit the ground splat. There were flat plastic jars of soil, some with specimens, as the old man called them. He'd mail them to the agricultural people and they'd write back and tell him what to add to the soil. But there was no sign of the box that looked so much like Kenti's can of pickup sticks he'd almost overlooked it before.

On the wall of hooks hung the old man's cap, a red plaid corduroy cap with a long bill. The old fishing bag was covered with dust. So was his box of lures and weights. In the bait bucket in the corner was the fish knife. Sonny slipped it into his pocket when he heard Kofi call his name.

Sonny stepped out into the blazing sun and couldn't see. He fumbled, but he got the shed door latched before Kofi came walking up.

"We almost ready," Kofi said, winded.

"Got any money?"

Kofi didn't answer right away. He was looking at the spaces in between Sonny's teeth. "Gap?" he'd heard Granny Lovey say on the phone. "Like a pasture gate, sugar," laughing with the cousins in Brunswick, Georgia, where Kofi didn't want to go.

"I want to go home, don't you?"

"What's home?"

"School," Kofi said.

Sonny skeeted through his teeth. Spit landed close to Kofi's shoe. "Hey, little brother, I said do you have any money?"

"To do what?"

Kofi stepped back when Sonny took the knife out. He started flipping it overhand and underhand in the dirt. Kofi watched, then bent down with him to watch better. The knife pinned a leaf to the ground.

"Money for what?"

"I want to go see Nana Cora."

"Why you want to go there? It's better here, 'cept for the bees." Kofi was going to say it was better 'cause there was work and pay, but something told him not to. "You could call them. They call here lots of times asking about you."

"Where was I?"

Kofi looked toward the house, then turned in the direction of the chicken pen. "You were incommunicado."

Sonny started laughing. He rubbed his chest and the laugh trailed off with a hissing sound, like he was fixing to say that was stupid. But he didn't. He kind of winked. His skin, shiny and tight from the sun, crinkled up under his eye. Some of the bruising had let up. He didn't look so much like a raccoon anymore. "You all right, little brother."

"You don't want to go to Brunswick either, hunh? Or Jekyll Island, or Sapelo?" Kofi couldn't remember the other islands where their mother's father's relatives were. Sonny kept on pitching the knife in the dirt. Kofi didn't blame him. Them Rawls people liked to laugh and joke too much. And even though Sonny had been to the dentist and the barbershop, he didn't look so good. He just didn't have two black eyes was all.

Kofi had thought Granny Lovey was being mean on the phone laughing at his brother, but maybe she was cracking so the cousins would run out of things to say by the time they saw Sonny. "What's the matter with the boy's face—furnace fall on it?" "Hey, boy, been eating rock sammiches?" Granny Lovey had been slapping herself all over, kind of pushing her nightgown up so she could rub her legs, talking on the phone. Kofi took a good look at his brother. For all the cocoa butter his Mama smeared on him every night, Sonny still looked like one of them tough boys always getting in a fight.

"Whereabouts Granny Lovey sell honey around here?"

"Don't ask me."

"Go find out."

Kofi pulled the lacings of his moccasins tighter and made new knots. He stood up and brushed straw from his shorts. It would take all day to pick the straw off his legs.

"What about the mailman?" Sonny stood up and slipped the knife in his back pocket. "Think he'd give us some money? Bet he would if you said Gerry wanted it. They kind of like each other. We could do something if we had us some money."

Kofi's heart tripped over a beat. He'd thought about this for a long time. But this didn't feel right. This felt sticky and wrong. He picked at the straw glued to his legs.

"That was you calling them times, wasn't it?" This time Sonny bunched his eyebrows so they met. He kind of nodded. Before, he used to act like he hadn't heard. "I thought so," Kofi said. "I was waiting for you to tell me to come where you were."

"You wouldnawantedyou to be there," Sonny said, quickly, turning away from him.

Kofi stumbled over the pushed-up roots of the tree when Sonny kept turning away. Kofi had to grab the back of his jeans to get him to stop.

"I wouldnawantedyou there," Sonny said, crossing his arms. "Go find us some money," he said and walked off.

Zala was spreading the coverlet over the butterfly bush when she saw Kofi heading around toward the back of the house, his hands dug down in his pockets, head low, muttering and unhappy. He reached out suddenly and whacked a milkweed but didn't wait to watch the pod release its feathery seeds into the air.

"Kofi?" She was afraid to let go of the coverlet, afraid the bush could not hold the weight. She crooked her finger when he looked her way and he came slowly, stubbing his toes every third or fourth step. "What's a ruby cue, Kofi?"

"You late, Ma," he said, climbing up and swinging his legs over the back-porch rail.

"Well, what is it? Kenti said I should get Sonny one."

He threw his arms out. A small boy with the world's troubles to handle and she was weighing him down with trivia. She eased the coverlet down over the bush. She wanted to talk with him about going home. They might not have the chance to talk family during the trip. Once everyone heard that Mercer was sending a stretch deluxe limo down, the passenger list to Brunswick had grown.

Spence offered Kofi a bite of his sandwich, and he stepped back. "Something the matter?"

The men were getting up and going out. The trucks had come and were tooting their horns. Kofi followed his dad out.

Sonny was hanging his arms out the truck window, beating his elbows on the door.

"You staying?" The skin under one eye crinkled. "You got things to do, Li'l Brother?"

When Kofi hesitated, Kenti stood up in the back of the first truck and waved her arms to shush everybody. "We gotta wait for my brother Kofi." She turned to him all serious. "You got to go to the bathroom first?"

Before Sonny could laugh, Kofi climbed up beside Kenti. It wouldn't have been a good laugh; his face was screwed all up like he was disgusted with him.

There were no horses. And the moo cow turned out to be a big ugly bull. Long after the others went off to swing on the ropes and Sonny, really mad 'cause there weren't any horses, went off by himself somewhere, Kenti kept watching, hoping the bull would do some interesting thing she could tell the class about when she got back to Atlanta.

She pulled her halter up and hooked her arms over the next-to-the-top log that went across, and watched the bull through the space. It was eating something with its mouth open and the spit was coming down like a washing machine with too much soap. It made a low rumbly noise when it chewed. She could hardly hear the tractor, the bull was so loud. Seemed like her daddy, riding along with Sheena's granddaddy, could hear it.

Kofi was way over by the pig house with Cookie, fooling with the pump. She was holding the bucket and he was working the handle. Rattle rattle, lift, squeeze, and the water thudded out. They were too far to call to. But maybe Kofi would think to come on and see something about the bull that she could tell the class. Sheena and Junior and them were standing on the knots at the bottom of the ropes. The ropes were hanging down from a big log somebody strong had set in the elbows of three pecan trees near the stable where there weren't any horses on account of Junior's daddy had sent them out to work. She wasn't sure where Sonny had went to, but he said he'd be back.

She bent down and loosened the buckles on her new white sandals, watching the bull Sonny called the Beast. She could make up something about the bull, even something about the horses, act like she'd fed them carrots and apples, patted their necks, taken a ride. But that would be lying. She'd heard Aunt Gerry telling Granny Lovey that Sonny was prone to lying.

"Prone." She did her mouth to say it again and liked the way it felt. The Beast looked her way and started pawing the ground with its big foot. "Prone," she told him. The bull swished his tail. Sonny had said to be careful, not to get close or do nothing stupid like give the Beast clover to eat. It made her laugh, the way he kept saying "the Beast." But then he teased her for calling it a moo cow, teased her for acting like a silly little child, kept saying she better grow up 'cause look like she hadn't grown any since he'd been gone.

Kenti looked down at herself. Her halter and shorts were the same ones from last year. Maybe Sonny was right. She'd have to see what she weighed on the school scale and see where the ruler pressed at the top of her head hit the wall. But the way he said it was like she was a baby because he wasn't around, like he was big stuff. He wasn't nothing but just a ball nobody could find. That's what Granny Lovey had said to Aunt Gerry—he was a lost ball in the high grass.

Spit was coming down the bull's chest where his muscles bulged like black ropes. He was pawing the ground again like he was saying to come in and play.

"I look like a fool to you, Beast?"

From where she squatted, looking between the two bottom logs, she could see his feet good. He took a step coming and then another one. And his paw landed right on top of an anthill. Ants starting running away. Some of the ants were carrying yellow specks from the bluebonnets there in the pasture. Some were carrying their dead ant friends.

Sonny had told them a scary story about a slave boy they gave a whipping to and made him die. Sonny and another boy snuck down to the basement and got him. They were carrying him to the garage to get away, that's when he died. But they put him in the car anyway and didn't cut on the lights when they drove off. Then the police stopped them and took them to jail on account of the white men told the police they stole the car. And the police wouldn't believe Sonny and the other boy. The police said they were the ones who killed the boy in the back.

She wasn't sure she believed the story, because one time the other boy was named Buck but later when the police said they killed the boy in the back of the car, Sonny said "Roger" like her goldfish Roger, the poor little goldfish Mama let dry up.

Kenti wiped her face on her shorts and looked up. She wrinkled her nose. The bull was taking a crap. Right in front of her, the bull let go with another big plop to the ground and swished his tail like he'd done something to talk about. Kenti walked backward without even standing up first it smelled so bad. Then a bird came and sat on the top log. It had a blade of grass in its mouth. But when it lifted its head and smelled the stink, the bird dropped that grass and flew up. But it didn't fly away like she would've. It flew down to the bull crap and started pecking in it.

"You nasty, bird."

She ran off toward the ropes to tell what happened. But then she slowed down. Sheena and them probably saw that every day. But she had to tell somebody there. She sure couldn't tell that in class.

No horse, no horses, six stalls and no horses, eight saddles, hay, harnesses, but there weren't any horses. In the old shed back of the barn, though, was a bike and it was in great shape, an air pump on the bar, a tool bag behind the seat, and in the bag a Prince Albert can with four patches and a full book of matches. The bike was leaning against the wall boards. But when he pulled, the whole shed shook. The kickstand was caught in the space between the boards. It took a while to work it free. When pulled from the bar, the strongest part of the bicycle's frame, the front wheel turned and the handlebar got wedged between the boards. He lifted the bike as much as it would go and rammed it against the wall, twisting the wheel and freeing the handlebar. It made a lot of noise. He was sure someone would hear it. When the dust settled and no more pebbles fell on his head, he pulled again. And the boards shook again. He hadn't watched the pedals. The inside one had knocked a knot hole clean out of the wood and was jammed tight.

Close to crying in frustration, he jumped when Kenti peeked through the boards and said, "I see you. You hiding?"

He moved quickly to the door but she'd run around and beat him. "Who's playing?" She tiptoed in and pulled the door closed behind her. He stepped to the right to block her view of the bike. But, running around for places to hide, she saw it.

"Whose bike?" she whispered, going to it. "Can we ride it?" She straddled the front wheel and hooked the inside of her elbows up under the handlebars. "It's stuck, Sonny."

"We can free it, though," he said, coming over.

"Better ask Junior. It's his bike, I bet."

He didn't like the way she was eyeing him as he unfastened the tool bag and took out the tobacco tin. If someone stopped them, at least he'd have the patches. He slipped them in his pocket, then reached in for the matches.

"That's not yours."

"Lean against the wall and stick your foot against the pedal," he told her. "And when I lift it up, push hard on the pedal."

"You smoke now?"

"It's to fix a flat. Stand over there and push hard. It's the pedal that's stuck."

"You stealing stuff to smoke, hunh?"

"Would you push the damn pedal. I'm doing this for you. You want a ride, don't you?"

Kenti backed away from the bike and walked around behind him, heading for the door.

"Where you going?" He meant to catch her by the arm, but he caught hold of the rubbery red-and-white halter, and when she pulled away the elastic snapped against her back.

"That hurts, you know!"

He could tell she wasn't mad, so he had a chance. She was ready to play if he wanted to. So he snapped her top again and rushed at her to tickle her. She was too fast for him and ran. When they reached the door his father was standing there and his expression made Sonny cringe.

"I've been holding these, Zala."

Gerry tossed the envelopes on the table. They landed on the letter from Mason. Zala realized she hadn't been reading but staring. More children murdered. The murders officially disconnected from the case. All news of the murders suppressed. Pressure to call off the rally organized weeks before the arrest.

"And you opened my mail?" Zala looked at the mess, the torn-open envelopes, a clipping someone had sent from a New Orleans newspaper nearly torn in half, a letter from Paulette with the second page missing, an empty envelope curled in the roll of the map. Zala looked up at Gerry. A cloth tied around her and knotted under her armpit, two towels slung over one shoulder, Gerry was braiding her hair and looking at Zala with one side of her mouth hiked up.

"Not I. You know that." She pulled the chair out next to Zala.

Zala let out a long breath and removed the ironed sheets from the seat. "Yes, I know that," she said.

Mama Lovey was outside beating two bath mats together. She turned away from the clothesline as the tufts of lint blew through the yard. She looked toward the kitchen and Gerry blew her a kiss.

"Anything new from your friend Logan about the hypnosis sessions?"

Zala watched her mother moving between the clotheslines feeling the towels for dryness. "They're on their way to Atlanta now—Innis, McGill, Logan, and a few others."

"Think they'll wind up at the same field you all located near the warehouse?"

Zala shrugged, but she had no doubt that the field not five miles from 6 Star was the cult's ceremonial grounds McGill had described under hypnosis, even though Inquiry had seen no shack, the shack in which McGill said she'd seen victims tied up, one victim murdered, a plastic bag shoved down his throat.

"And the Committee of Inquiry?" Gerry was rummaging in the mail.

Zala sighed again and said nothing. At the community meetings Mason spoke of, little credence was given the findings of the committee, though many felt there had to have been wiretapping by the state bureau and the feds, and were convinced too that the network of professional informants must have produced things that had since been suppressed. The mortician's assistant had left town. The Bowen witnesses had either absented themselves from meetings or come and kept quiet. Only two of the community workers were still monitoring the house on Gray Street. Mason and Lafayette kept watch on Slick; Speaker stuck to Red. And the word on Dettlinger, the leading STOP investigator, was that he would work with the prosecuting team. An equally strong rumor was that he would work with the defense. Zala wondered what was preventing Mason from asking Dettlinger to declare himself at one of the meetings. Camille Bell would assist the defense. Other members of STOP said they'd wait and see. A major rally was scheduled for the next week. Buses were going up from Alabama.

"And Sonny?" Gerry asked quietly, breaking into Zala's thoughts. She was fitting the torn news photo together. Zala looked at the picture of Hazel Blanchette. The Webbers' former housekeeper, writing from the Algiers district of New Orleans, had drawn a parallel between the bogus official version of the Atlanta case and the bogus version the New Orleans authorities offered to explain away the murders in the housing project by the New Orleans police. It had been too much to read.

"I don't know," Zala said, leaning against Gerry's arm. "I got a letter from a neighbor this morning." She smoothed out the fancy stationery from Old Man Murray's landlady. "Such a nice note. But she says we should go on TV." Zala laughed; it came out short and breathy. "I can barely piece two bits of Sonny's story together and she wants a neighborhood celebrity on prime time."

Gerry took the letter. "I never have understood the desire to appear on those talk shows. But in your case, it might help. You seem to know more than the Task Force."

"It would be helpful if they allowed the families to tell their stories and let people call in with any news they have. It would be helpful if we could play the phone call the Task Force recorded. I know someone would call in. But that's not what they do. They want you to cry so the cameras can zoom in on your personal tragedy. They ask questions that have nothing to do with the real case. It takes the whole time to straighten that out before you can get to the case as it really is. And so personal. They get right under your clothes."

"I can never fathom why guests submit to it as though they're not free to say, 'I'd rather we focus on the whys and wherefores of the situation,' " Gerry said. You'd think we'd've learned something since the sixties—how to keep your eye on the ball, the issue."

"It's so childish," Zala said. "This need to go public to be understood—as if you can be understood by people who don't even know you."

Mama Lovey came toward the back porch, a bunch of flowers in her hands. She was stripping away leaves from the stems.

"So," Gerry said, going to the stove for the kettle. "The witness was cross-examined under deep hypnosis by the cult specialists. Did any of the descriptions McGill offered of her partners-in-crime fit Williams?"

"Possibly one. Hard to tell."

Zala left the map on the table, but piled the rest of the mail on the tray with Sonny's envelopes on the bottom. She shoved the tray in the cupboard as Mama Lovey came up the back steps. Gerry beckoned Zala to the pantry, where she poured warm water into the foot tub.

"Mama's trying to make peace with you, Marzala." Gerry draped the towels over Zala's shoulder and hugged her.

"We're not at war."

"Yes, well . . ."

Gerry held the door and Mama Lovey came in and stepped immediately into the tub.

"My girls," she said, pressing the flowers to Zala's breast. When they leaned to kiss her, she complained, "I'm sweaty," extending her face all the same. She turned and held on to the shelf of jarred gooseberries.

"Then get out of these clothes." Gerry lifted Mama Lovey's dress, ordering her to raise one arm, then the other, pulling the dress off, the black slip clinging to it.

Zala set the bouquet on the shelf between the crock of spearmint soap and the box of Gloria Brand Unlimited labels Kofi had not put back properly. With the back of her wrist, she shoved the cardboard lid down on the honey labels and continued lathering the sponge as Gerry stepped back into the kitchen, leaving the two of them alone.

"Like my beads?"

She sounded like a little girl. Even as a younger woman when she'd asked "How do I look?"—really meaning it, her generation taught that to spend much time in the mirror would bring you to a bad end, and so her mama and other women really needed Zala's eyes, because they didn't know what they looked like—she'd sounded more grown than now, turning around with little steps in the zinc tub, lifting one hip, then the other, to show Zala. On a narrow, soft strip of leather around her hips were small, oval brown beads strung at intervals between knots. Zala examined the knots, disc-shaped open rosettes, a knot Zala did not know, and smiled in answer.

"You'll stay?" Mama Lovey held her arm out as Zala soaped it, moving close to the tub to do her armpit, then run the sponge down her side, turning her mother around, casually lifting her breasts to soap her stomach, then patting her thighs for her to squat and open her legs.

"With the bees, the chickens, and the garden and fields, we could eke out a living. Haying alone can carry us into the autumn. You think about it," she said, patting Zala's shoulder when she knelt to tip the kettle into the dipping gourd. "And you talk to Geralanna little bit, hear?"

"You want me to talk Gerry into staying?"

"You talk to her a little bit," Mama Lovey repeated, and turned and caught hold of the shelf. She bent her head as Zala sluiced the suds from her neck down her back, guiding the water over her buttocks and patting Mama's behind to again squat, the way Mama had done to her years ago.

"Stay at least till Kofi's ready for that Benjamin Mayes School," Lovey added. "The boy's got his heart set on going for science up there in Atlanta." She smiled over her shoulder at Zala.

How could they go back to Atlanta? And how could they not?—it was home. Zala moved her head like a swimmer with water in her ears. When she thought of Atlanta, it was the media mob that she pictured. Sonny strapped in a chair, the wire from the clip-on mike snaking around his throat and down his back. Her son a memorial object, a hope symbol, a boy come back from the dead, with the malignancy still plaguing the city and the authorities still hoaxing them all. And the killers, would they know the connection between the couple that had picked Sonny up near Ashby and held him somewhere outside of the perimeter? Was there a connection between themselves and the old man who'd stropped the boys about the legs till they dropped to their knees and called him Master? Would they come to silence him? Kerosene sloshed against the side of the house? Or Kofi's worse fears, a bomb thrown through the window?

Her mama took the damp towel from her and washed her face. Zala dried one foot and one leg and Mama Lovey threw down the face towel and stepped out, leaning on her daughter's shoulder. Zala dried her other leg and foot, massaging the bottom with her knuckles.

Lovey held her arms out and Zala wrapped the big towel around her, then hugged her. How small her mother had become. Friends of the Twins used to say "adorable," and Zala had never been able to see it before.

Zala squirmed to make her mother let go. But her mother did not let go.

"Don't be cross with your poor ole mama, she doing the best she know how."

"I know it." Zala kicked the kitchen door open with her heel and steered her mama through.

Zala went around the house twice, smiling to herself and only once remembering to feel the clothes on the bushes. The sun was on the rim, so they had at least three hours before the trip to the fields. When Zala looked toward the kitchen window, Gerry was leaning over the table unrolling the map. Mama Lovey must have called her, and when Gerry turned, the map snapped to. Zala thought she heard it, but it was the banner pinned to the side of the Girard truck flapping in the breeze.

Sonny and Spence were standing up in back, Junior leaning over to talk to the medical students. Spence seemed to be supporting Sonny, one arm behind the boy's back, the other crossed in front of Spence and holding the boy's arm, as if he were in the middle of telling about the beatings and might drop to his knees. She was only imagining it, for Spence let go of his arm and they were looking at each other, talking, smiling, Spence's hand moving up the boy's back to massage his neck. But from where she stood by the fence, she could see Sonny stiffen.

Zala turned away and went into the house through the sleeping porch. A neat pile of books was on the table with a transistor radio. Lengths of fabric were piled neatly on top of Gerry's suitcase. A half-painted, carved calabash was on the floor. Gerry's diary, covered in a cloth made from baobab and still smelling of cream of tartar, was in the hammock. Exhausted, Zala looked at the small pillow and almost climbed in. She knew Gerry and Mama Lovey had left a place for her in the middle of the big bed so they could have one ear apiece: "Come to Africa," "Stay in Epps." Zala continued through to the foyer, smiling at the snaggle-tooth piano no one played anymore. She trailed her fingers through the fringe of the mud cloth, then made her way into the bedroom and took off her clothes.

There was a bright yellow-and-orange bubba for her to put on. And at the foot of the bed where she climbed in was the Bible opened to the Book of Daniel. She crawled into her place on her hands and knees as she used to when she was pregnant and took naps in the afternoon. She eased down on the freshly laundered sheet and fell asleep dreaming of her children running across a wide savannah, a baobob silhouetted against the red sun, the legs of the gazelles a blur.

They followed Lovey into the green, the fields that would become in Indian summer acres of tall golden grass. The children, spread out, were doing swim strokes in the dusk-shaded field, Sonny joining in at the last. Spence squeezed Zala's hand and they rushed to keep track of Kenti, who turned her head expertly each time she brought her arm around past her ear, marveling at the bone-and-socket action of her shoulder. The elder Girard brought his knees up high, his elbows held out level over the grass. Like Lovey, he let each step twist his body at the waist, his knees cutting a path, her hips leading the way. The student workers closed in on either side. Those who'd lingered in the aloe garden brought along a sprig for study and became Lovey's right flank. The others, who'd stayed awhile in the going-to-seed garden of phlox, forget-me-nots, foxglove and flaming hearts, became her left flank.

Lovey came to a halt seven feet from the big bushes at the end of the field and turned the sprig over in her hands. The high grass that had swayed freely and parted for them was now tangled and snarled by renegade vines that had weaved their way from the honeysuckle-covered shapes ahead.

"Parboiled in potash," she said, "it dissolves like starch to a transparent glaze. Good for inflamed joints." She handed it back. "Draws out the fever and the ache."

Zala squeezed Spence's hand. Lovey had applied glutinous poultices to Sonny's wounds, and Sonny was nodding in recognition. The two looked up at the moon, turned to the fields behind them, the cabin's chimney gleaming in the night, and exchanged sly smiles, increasing their pressure on each other's hands. Lightning bugs lifted, flashed, then sank down low again in the grass, faint telegraph signals all around them.

"Or you take ordinary salt," Girard was saying, "and heat it up in a black iron skillet, stir in apple cider vinegar, and you got you something almost as good."

"You soak the rags in it," one of the students spoke as she wrote, "then you wrap the rags around the inflamed joints."

"Thank you."

Girard brushed the brim of his hat with four fingers, his outdoor version of removing his hat when addressing a female. "Good for horses and people too."

Lovey, with meticulous care, was parting the grass as though combing the hair of a tender-headed child. When she put her hands together like a diver, the children followed suit. They shoved off through the green, Lovey directing attention to the base of a bush up ahead.

"SNAKE!"

Junior threw out his arm to halt Sonny and Kofi. Lovey threw up her arms to stop the shouts and the sprints. In the murmured conversation were two votes for killing the snake, wrapped round a tangle of saplings.

"Why kill it, unless you plan to eat it?"

"*Eat* it?" Kofi backed away from Junior, looked at Bernard, then looked back at the thick, moist coils of brown wrapped round the stalks. There were bright orange diamonds on the snake's back. Sonny moved up close and hunkered down the way Aunt Gerry did sometimes when she wanted to think hard. Kofi kept his distance.

"That snake there," Bernard was saying, "he'll kill himself if he thinks we fixin' to."

"Bite hisself," Sheena added, "bite that bush, spit on everything he see, try to kill the whole world."

Sonny wrapped his arms around his legs and watched. The snake hadn't moved. The orange lozenges were now as brown as the rest of him, the brown looking more and more like the stalks. The rough scales seemed to smooth out too. Sonny rested his chin on his knees and studied it the way Grandaddy Wesley had taught him on outings to the zoo. If he blinked, the snake would have him convinced he was seeing things. If he looked away and then back, the snake would have vanished, only thick stalks in its place and doubt in his mind.

"No good for eating or for medicine either if he poisons himself," Girard said. "But there are ways to kill a snake. Ways and ways. You got the right idea, son," he called over to Sonny. "Got to be his match 'fore you can beat him at his game."

"The oil's good for lumbago," Lovey said, leading the group away to a gap in the bushes. "Careful here, the way gets rugged."

The students conferred amongst themselves, wondering aloud if they might not apprentice themselves next to a snake-oil huckster. Maybe there was something to the elixirs and tonics peddlers stumped the rural section beyond the Tombigbee.

Kofi followed his grandmother through the hedges and over the stones, on the lookout for snakes and other dangerous things in the overgrown brush that led to the woods. The girls were behind him, turning their ankles, Old Man Girard telling them to stay on the path. Kofi then realized there was order to the wild woods. The stones were arranged in footpaths. So long as he stayed on the stones, the briars and thorns couldn't scratch him.

"Good for worms." Lovey pointed to a plant with freckled leaves but kept moving toward the line of trees. "Good for dogs and people too." Over her shoulder she raised her voice in Girard's direction. "Miss Erma would've passed those gallstones if she'd've put herself on a tea regimen, Titus."

"Told her so," he answered.

"Not everybody can be told something," she answered, pointing out something else to the students. "This here's good for bad nerves," she told them when they trotted to catch up with her. "Not like it is now. Too much slick on top."

Kenti examined the bush. The leaves were thick, shiny tongues going "ahh." The berries were dishwater gray. The twigs were sticky white with cobwebs in the crooks.

"In a few days," Lovey said, "when the stems are softish and everything goes pale, it's good. Time, see? Just one more instance of that law of life, time. Right now, it's poison. In a few days, good medicine."

"Like fish," Junior said, calling over to Sonny, who was wandering toward the path to the creek. "Some kind of fish can be good to eat most of the year. But don't try it when they pregnant."

"A pregnant fish." Kenti came to a stop to picture it, and Cookie plowed into her.

"Take a look here." Girard motioned them around a low, sprawled-out bush, but Lovey did not come back to lecture. She had her elbows close to her sides and was moving flat-footed and fast through the trees. Girard snapped out his handkerchief and broke off a switch. When one of the students, drawn by the musk, reached for it, he snatched it away.

"This stuff will hurt you. You'll itch and stay itchy, lose your sense of smell, and that's only the half. I don't know the scientific name for it. Could be related to dumb cane, but I call it the family plant—won't see some without you see a lot congregating around."

"Its use?" Pencils poised, the students studied the held twig.

"If you're ever in a fix with tracking dogs on your tail, do yourself a favor and stomp around in this bush before you run on. I don't care how high your odor is, the dogs come this way will forget all about you. They stick their muzzles in the family plant and they'll be walking backward barking at the moon." He chuckled and moved on, an anecdote about a man on the chain gang lost as the children outdid each other being wild dogs, coyotes, and wolves.

Lovey had cleared the trees and had broken into a run. Zala took one strap of the gathering basket. "And to think that I worry whether I can possibly leave this poor old woman to manage by herself," Gerry said with a laugh. Elbows tight against her sides, fists pumping like pistons, Lovey was running flat-footed through the fields toward the wildflowers, the children racing along. Titus Girard, huffing and chuckling, brushed his brim as he went past the two women.

"I think it's time to count the cattle and gather the cowries, my sister," Gerry said.

"Girard and Mama?"

"Crazy about each other. You hadn't noticed?"

"Too busy watching you and the mailman, Gerry."

Gerry threw her head back and laughed, and Zala joined in, more for the memory the arched, supple neck recalled than anything else: Gerry the teenager laughing at little Zala, fresh back from summer Bible school and worried about the state of her soul.

"I'm laughing, Zala, because that crazy brother of mine has been trying to marry me off for the past year. First to a teacher in Botswana who's not in the least interested in a woman who owns no land. Then to a Zambian medic who works with the Flying Doctor Service. A very fine man, he has two wives—a city wife and a bush wife." I don't know what Maxwell can be dreaming of."

She tugged on the basket to hurry Zala along. "One bull, six horses."

"Sixty hives, eight hens, one rooster."

"Forty-six meters of cloth."

"Six macramé planters."

"Harnesses and saddles."

"Beeswax."

"The collected writings of Nkrumah and Cabral."

"Back issues of *Klanwatch* and *The African Call* and one dog-eared copy of *How Europe Underdeveloped Africa* by Walter Rodney."

"Ahhh, my sister. We've got treasures to match the Girards' treasures for certain."

"BEHOLD!"

There was a hush. Everyone came to a halt. Lovey was standing in the middle of a spread of evening primrose, her arms flung wide.

"Evening primrose blooming in September?" one of the students whispered.

"They weren't even here last year," Bernard said to Kofi.

"Just one or two," Titus Girard corrected, smiling. "She's been out here talking to them a little bit. While the others sported their colors, these little tricksters were laying in the cut."

Gerry moved into the spread, searching for flowers that had

dropped their petals. She and Zala plucked the pods that contained the seeds that had the oil that, pressed and refined, kept their mother going financially.

"Very costly," Gerry explained.

"You were saying, Mrs. Loveyetta, that this is better than aloe for burns?"

"Fire burns, X-ray burns, eczema, ulcers, arthritis, thrombosis, dandruff, baldness, cholesterol, blood pressure, hyperactive little chirren, fat, alcoholism, childbirth, cramps, a heap of female complaints, various allergies, migraines, glaucoma, toxemia, hepatitis." Lovey dropped to her knees and scooped up the pale yellow buds in her hands, then let them go. They danced on their stems. She was radiant. Titus Girard patted himself down for a clean handkerchief to give her.

"Good for razor bumps too," Junior said, scratching his chin.

"Watermelon rind just as good," Bernard said, "or the sloppy side of a papaya skin. This stuff's too expensive when watermelon just as good." He elbowed Junior when Kofi started feeling his "mustache" and "beard."

"Waaaaatermelon, red to the rind," Sheena sang out. Cookie joined in to sing the fruit wagon's chants; then they all went back to being wolves again when a cloud passed from in front of the moon.

Titus Girard lifted Miss Lovey from the ground, and the two grown-up ladies picked primrose in earnest.

"I like that man," Gerry said. "One spring-open umbrella for the broker."

"A radio that plays in the shower."

"An audience for my slide show."

"Fresh flowers for my hair." And when Zala turned, she saw Sonny approaching with a bouquet of tiger lilies and swamp punk.

"If, as you say, it's a case of wishful thinking or of mass brainwashing, then the sponsoring organizations will want to call off the rally, won't they? Obviously Atlanta is not going to turn out in numbers. On the other hand, I can't see how they can stop the momentum in other cities. Buses are leaving from Birmingham—are you listening to me?"

Gerry reached across the basket and pinched Zala's arm. They rounded the bend, and Spence glanced up at the tin chimney gleaming in the green-purple foliage.

"I'm listening," Zala said. She would wait for him in the cabin. The glow from the logs would be all she could see by until he opened the door and the moon spilled in.

"If there's a rally, I guess we'll be there," Spence said, listening to the crunch of needles underfoot. He pictured the trail of clothes he would leave from the house to the cabin, how his pants would look on the bed of needles when he turned up at the door. "I'm not sure the rally is the time and place for Sonny—" He cut himself off when the boys dashed by, zinging pinecone torpedoes over their shoulders. "Not that he's told us anything concrete as yet." The girls pursued with vines and twigs that their shouts turned into snakes.

"It's an odd thing about the tortured," Gerry said, then waited until the chickens quieted down and the children's noise, far ahead now, grew faint. "When political prisoners slip through Pretoria's grip and reach us, torture is the last thing they tell us about. The beatings, the electroshock, the burns—that is not what's on their minds. To read, Spence, that's what they wish to speak of. Think of it, sentenced to 10 years on Robbens Island, and on top of everything else forbidden to read. "Mostly they speak of the hungers. Five unrushed minutes on a clean toilet. A cake of milled soap. A real toothbrush. To read. Which do you think you could endure the least, Zala, twenty lashes or twenty weeks without writing materials and something to read? And music. It's quite an adjustment out in the world again,—car horns, transistors, laughter. Laughter after the screams of the tortured, the screams of the broken gone mad in their cells. Or the silence, the absolute silence of solitary confinement. Clandestine whispers for months and months, and then free, across the border, to see people walking two and three abreast in the streets, lambasting the government or discussing the news or just talking nonsense. People at the cinema club, in the coffee bars, people freely assembling in a free country. Well, not so free. Not so long as the mad dog across the border is given free rein by the 'free world.'"

"In Africa they have a saying," Gerry continued after a few steps in silence. "'A borrowed fiddle cannot complete the tune.' I think of it sometimes watching the two of you practically giving Sonny mouth-to-mouth every five seconds. Are you listening to me?"

"We're listening," they both said.

"What strikes me is, if it's difficult for adults—adults armed with an analysis, men and women who, no matter how cut off from the world or from the rest of the prison population, know at least why they are there and know too that they are not alone in the brutalization or the struggle, for the struggle goes on all around them behind the walls—then how impossible it must be for Sonny. He's a boy."

"You think he's protecting them, is that what you're saying, Gerry? You think he's protecting . . . his tormentors, through silence?," Spence asked.

"Do they denounce their torturers?" asked Zala.

"Not with the passion you'd expect. And not because they've accepted it or gotten used to it. Not because their minds recoil from the memory. Though certainly some of that applies. And not because they identify with their tormentors. That's what your friend McClintock suggested, isn't it—confused loyalties? I've thought a lot about this," Gerry said. "Long before I met banned people and torture victims. The Stockholm syndrome, as they call it, rarely applies with freedom fighters with a passionate ideology.

"But a child. It's good that you have a friend who's skilled to assist."

"Mac. Yes," Spence said.

"I hope I'm making sense. It's the only context I know," Gerry apologized.

In the soak tub the surface of the water was silvery. The branches where Zala would hang her clothes were silvery too. The moon would wash the floorboards white and she'd ask if he'd come like that from the house, what would her mother think? That hers was one lucky daughter, he would say, striking poses in the doorway. She'd kick her feet against the ceiling, egging him on. And when he came inside the cabin, she'd roll onto her hip and extend her foot to catch on to so he'd know how to move in the dark.

"It's the same with us and the sixties. Neither Maxwell nor I dwelt on the beatings. I'm sure we spoke of the fear. We didn't want to shield you from that."

"Mostly I remember the singing," Zala said.

"Yes, the singing. Perhaps there is no way to talk about torture and hatred, because they aren't images, they're un-images. I don't mean I can't picture the clubs and the guns and the electric prods. But it's all an un-image. Half the people I work with have been political prisoners in one liberation struggle or another—and even with ANC members in numbers transforming prison conditions . . . torture is an un-image. That's as far as I can get. It's similar to your situation, isn't it? You've not spoken of the yearlong torment nearly as much as . . ." Gerry could not find the words.

"The longings," Spence said, but his mind and body were elsewhere. He would find his way to the lower bench, groping, then put his knee on the slats and climb up to her.

"The hungers, as you say."

She'd roll onto her hip and grip his in her thighs and with her heels in his buttocks guide him to where he wanted to be.

"You don't want me to speak of these things."

"It helps, Gerry," said Zala.

Gerry took the whole of the basket to carry, scooping up the seeds and letting them sift through her fingers. Zala and Spence crowded closer to hold her.

They heard Girard's truck backing out the side gate. Lights went on in the house as they approached. In the driveway between the rows of snap beans and the kitchen garden was the limo, long and sleek. It gleamed like a dream car. It lured them away from Gerry's voice and even their thoughts of a late rendezvous. This time tomorrow, they'd be on the Georgia coast, grinning slyly about their night in the sauna.

"I've been trying to pin down what it is that always makes me hold back a little," Gerry went on. "It's not lack of sympathy, or lack of knowledge. I know the degree to which propaganda can contaminate. And yet, a part of me is always thinking that they must have called it down on themselves somehow.

"Had it coming," said Spence.

"Yes."

"Not like you and me, pure and safe."

"Yes. Even though we know better. I certainly know better. We listen and say all the right things. But inside we hold back a little and don't empathize as we should."

"Yes," Zala said. "We study the persecuted to see some difference between us that will make us feel safe."

"I've been doing that with Sonny all along, I think. From the beginning." Gerry's voice was small and cramped. "Please forgive me."

And when they did not recoil, she flung herself at them to kiss and be kissed.

"You think we don't understand blame-the-victim? It's—attractive, especially if you can't get your hands on the . . . the . . ." Zala could find no word loathsome enough.

"I love you both," Gerry said, and moved around quickly to the front of the house.

They clung tightly as they listened to the porch door knock closed, then the squeeze of the hammock as Gerry threw herself into it for a night of armed dreaming.

Spence looked up at the windows. "I'll tuck them in," but he did not move.

"I'll be waiting," she started to say, but his tongue was in her mouth.

"Mushy, mushy," Kenti called down from the landing, her face pressed against the window screen. They looked up as the light from Sonny's bedroom went on behind Kenti's head.

"What the hell are we going to do, Zala, if he won't talk?"

She buried her head in the crook of his neck, then tugged him toward the path to the cabin.

Mama Lovey broke out switch after switch, searching for one special one, supple but stout. Switches sap-sticky or split she didn't bother to test but dropped, lifting the hem of her nightgown to kick them with the side of her foot under the delphiniums. By the time the bush gave way at the heart and splayed out, she'd found the best of the bunch. And best had always been good enough for Lovey. She'd had her fill of the worst—grandson vanished, Mr. Williams ailing, her daughter on the telephone broken, her voice flat and unwilling to forgive. Lovey would hang up and resume her vigil. Chair tipped back to the wall in the bedroom, she'd fall asleep with the Good Book open on her face and sliding.

When Death came to the house, it caught her dreaming about peaches and cream. She awoke still cranking the handle, but it was the arm of the chair: She could have sworn she'd been shearing off a corner of ice a second before and packing in rock salt, then hurrying the churn because Mr. Williams was fond of ice cream. She'd been shearing the ice and dreaming the meadow was crowded with children on snowshoes of cardboard. So many children, children on TV, in the papers, in Sister Myrtle's talk from New York, not one of them Sonny.

Mama Lovey pulled the switch through her fist and stripped the leaves off. The child had come back, had come back from hell, tracking into her house a strange contagion that had them all fetching and scurrying, spying and whispering, but not paying attention to his get-away plans when their questions and their love became too much. She brushed bits of leaf from her pleated bodice and took up her post. Never ever had she whipped a child in her life. But if it came to that, they'd have to forgive her that too, just as she'd forgiven them without anyone knowing that Mr. Williams had quit breathing in order to free her to the claims of blood kin.

She waited under the tree, her feet cool in the pool of pollen that gleamed lightning-bug green even in the darkness. She kept watch on the house, her eyes tacked to the window above the roof of the porch. But that's not how he came. He didn't so much come as be there, giving flesh and form to a shadow she'd thought was thrown by the fancy car parked by the pole beans.

Then there he was, the boy, the baby named for the great bowman of ancestor epics. There he was, crouched low, hobbling toward the fence like a burglar, shaming the blood. And she had to stop him now or she'd be guilty of the unforgivable.

"You know one thing?" She pitched her voice in his direction and pinned his shadow to the ground. "Them people sleeping up there are at the end of their tether as it is, Sundiata. And one of them people is my girl. Do you know what I mean?"

He didn't move, playing her for a blind woman or an imagining old-soul one. So she walked toward him, wriggling the switch through the grass like a snake so he could see what it would cost if he vaulted over the rail. She brought her arm up and around and slapped the top post hard, slicing the better part of the bark away. The whistling hung in the air a long time. Then he stood up and gave her his attention like he hadn't done all summer long.

"Hey, Gran, I was just—"

"Did I ask you what you were just?" She brushed past the dry blooms while she took his measure. So grown, thirteen and grownish, casually out for a stroll at three a.m.

"I'm caught between two stools, Sundiata. I know there's all kinds of people waiting for you up there in Atlanta, and could be some of them don't wish you well. So maybe, like the saying goes, the better part of valor would be to run. You're my grandson," she said, watching his face in the darkness. "And I care about you.

"But then again . . ." She swung her arm and the switch came whistling with it. He jumped. She moved the switch right past his cheek to point at the house. "She was my own baby girl long before you came. So. What do you make of the situation I find myself in, Sundiata? Must I let you go and make my own child lay down in ashes?"

She placed the tip of the switch in the well of his left collarbone so he should know she didn't require her sewing glasses to thread this needle.

"I know what you thinking, Gran, but I was only—"

"Wait now," she stopped him. She could see by the way he held his hands out like a baby boy that there was shimsham coming. "I know you're going to tell me something intelligent."

He rolled his eyes, folded his arms across his chest, and stood hip-shot like no child had ever done to her except this boy. She wriggled the switch a little bit and could tell the minute he shunted his cargo to another track by the way his arms slid down and his chin softened. But when he opened his mouth, she saw a boxcar of ballyhoo riding the rails.

"Think first." Her voice like a shot, he cringed. She trailed the green bulbous tip across his throat to snuggle it in the well of his right collarbone.

"Oh, child. They taught you good, them people. They taught you fear, them people that took you. Seem like the people that brung you into this world would matter more. Them people up there that raised you and loved you all the while—you were no easy baby, you know. A colicky baby can try your last nerve." She invited him to grin with her. "But I guess them up there don't matter no more now that you've decided to go off somewhere, being grown and all, hunh?"

"Granny Lovey, would you get off me?! I don't know about them children. I keep telling y'all I don't know. Ask the cops, why ask me? It ain't my fault they got some joker locked up in jail."

"Did I ask you that? I didn't ask you that. Maybe you think you grown enough to take that tone with them," she said, tilting her chin toward the upstairs bedroom. "But this is me you talking to. Don't be confused."

"Gran . . ." He hooked his thumbs in his back pockets and kind of swung himself like a boy fixing to tell a joke in Sunday school, flirting with the idea, flirting with his audience. It wasn't much of a chuckle, just enough to alert her. She got a good grip on the thick part of the switch. She could hear sass coming down the pike.

"What is it you want to say to your grandmother?"

"Quit saying 'up there.' They ain't up there. They're down in the cabin." And then he did laugh, swinging himself just enough to turn his head so it couldn't be said he was laughing in her face.

"Think you cute laughing at your grandma. Grin on," she said, moving up on him while his head was turned. "Think I don't know what you smiling at? Don't you know I know you spy on the women when they come to use the sweat cabin? Think I been here in the country this long and don't know a boy in the bush from a bird? Think it don't make me shame to know what you've become in this lost year? You need to see about yourself, little Spencer. Just so much other people can do for a person. You know what I mean?"

He was listing to the side. She thought he might be falling. But he was only leaning to spit through the gap in his teeth. She wanted to hurt him. When he straightened up, he looked right in her face while he did something rubbery with his to give himself a hangdog expression like he was properly chastised. But all the while he was trying to frown a hole through the fence and be gone.

"You never were a false child," she said. "But you getting smaller every day. You need to look at that, Sundiata, 'cause could be you'll be called upon real soon to do something big that requires the kind of straight-up courage you've let strangers trash somewhere."

He hiked his shoulders up and left them there. "I don't know what you all want from me," he said, his voice wavering between the decision to whine or to tough it out. He crossed his legs at the ankles and teeter-tottered for a while. Then he looked like he'd heard the meeting had been adjourned and he had permission to go to bed.

"Sundiata."

"Yes ma'am."

"Beg pardon?"

"I said—"

"I heard what you said. And 'yes ma'am' been rarely in your mouth that I recall, and I've been knowing you since before you had a name. Don't be a stupid child, what with me standing here with this switch in my hand. No telling what a poor old crazy senile widow woman liable to do at this hour of morning, 'cause grief can make a person do crazy things. Do you know that?" She pleaded with him with her eyes to understand that he was in mourning too, mourning himself, the loss of himself. But she could tell by the way he was staring back that he was on another track.

"I'm sorry, Gran. I didn't get a chance to say nothing to you before. I'm sorry you lost Grandaddy."

"I didn't lose him, sweetheart. Doctors lost him. That's what they told me. 'We lost him on the table.' Ain't that something to tell somebody about somebody? Like a matchbook they'd scribbled a telephone number on, then tossed among the coffee cups in the doctors' lounge. 'Lost him on the table.' Isn't that something for me to hear on top of everything else, Grandson?"

He shifted his weight and stared at his shoes. Then he looked at her bare feet and stole a glance at the pebbles in the road. She kept her feet where they were but slid her upper body closer along the rail.

"I'm sorry Grandaddy Williams died. I miss him too."

"Sounds like hokum to me, son. You didn't like him very much."

"Yeah I did. Sometimes. But he was kind of strict."

"Strict."

"Kind of mean. I mean, he was always doing stuff. I remember one time he made you get out of bed to get him a glass of water. He was right there in the kitchen, I could hear him, 'cause I was asleep on the couch. He kept yelling for you to come get him some water. And the house was cold. I had both quilts over me. But he nagged until you got up. He was always pulling stunts like that."

"Well, now. I'm glad to know you were concerned about my welfare, Grandson. What did you make of it, my life with a mean man and all?"

His hands talked to each other for a while as he bobbed his head up and down. "I don't know. Why we got to be standing out here in the yard? It's getting chilly. Ain't you cold without your bathrobe?"

"You thought I was a fool?"

"Naw, Gran."

"Sure you did. Whatcha call a pushover. He used to think so too, you know. But who fell over, me or him?"

His eyes went wide for a minute and then he chuckled, sounding like his daddy for the world. But when she didn't join in, he stopped, studying her for a sign of how he should act. She thrust her face toward him and, ornery, he didn't back up.

Then the green taper arced over his ear and the thick part of the switch was against his chest, her fist a ball of heat in his solar plexus. She felt him come to attention.

"You know what, sweetheart?" She was close enough to smell him. Vanilla from the vanilla bean she'd slipped in his underwear drawer mingled with adolescent musk. "I loved him," she said quietly. "He was mean, but I loved him anyway. Why set conditions? Most people know they ain't worth a damn. That don't mean they undeserving. Deserving ain't even the question—question is, can you take it? Can you take it, a heap of loving? Takes courage."

He gave her a toothy grin. "This is some weird stuff you talking." And on the pretense of scratching his neck and shaking his head at her ideas, he moved the switch aside. "I don't even know what we're out here talking about."

"Sure you do. Sundiata."

He moved closer when the crickets stopped abruptly. His breath was fluttering the pleats of her bodice. He was close enough for her to grab him, lick him, bite him. He stepped back and looked at her.

"You smell like him," he said.

"I'll be smelling like Grandaddy Williams a long time," she said, then stopped to caution herself. Maybe he was recalling the smell of somebody else. His nostrils were flaring, his head tilted back. She sniffed the air too. It smelled of rain. She waited to see if he would speak of some other "him."

He took another step away from her. "I know when people live together a long time, they start to look like each other."

"Get to smell like each other too, 'cause they swapping their juices. When you get down to Brunswick, you ask Cousin Sonia to tell you about it." She followed his gaze to the limousine. He was nodding his head, a conscientious student ready to do the assignment right away.

The sky was making its slide from indigo to blue-bottle blue. The birds were still faint. She could hear the throaty laughter of her daughter travel up from the cabin on the breeze that smelled of moist spruce and burnt wood. She heard the rumbly low laughter of her son-in-law. The sound of them put her in a soothing mood until she caught her grandson watching her eyelids droop.

"I'm sapped, Sundiata. So tell me now, are we going to make this run up the road together, you and me?"

"Get off me, Gran. I don't understand nothing about none of it."

"Whole lot of things you've yet to understand. But instead of measuring the distance between your little-boy understanding and big-boy wisdom, you standing there plotting how to get past me. Yes, you are, too. You so scarce in understanding, you think you can get past your own flesh and blood. Well, you can't, Sundiata. It's a law of life. But you too small to take that in, so take this in." She stepped to the side and flopped the switch over the rail.

"There'll be hell to pay should you move. That spot you standing on, scheming with little-boy understanding, stay put. 'Cause if you run, I will lash you all up and down this road to wherever you planning to go to throw yourself away like this family had nothing better to do with its love than raise garbage and grief. Hear me now, 'cause if you don't care, I don't care."

"Yeah, you do," he said. His grin was as crooked as the embrace he offered, his arms more and more lopsided as he edged away from her.

She held the switch up in front of him so he could study it and could see that her arm was ready for the task.

"It'll be one helluva skin-peeling time on Randall Road, I'm telling you. 'Cause this time, I choose her, not you. You been through it, I know. But I can't think about that right now. You can mend. But my girl, you see, I don't think she could take your going off, and she's my child. You do see my point?"

She took a good look at the road and could feel him gathering himself up for the jump. She knew just how he'd try it. One hand on the post, young knees springing him up and over. She'd seen him try it many a time.

"It'd be a punishing trip, I ain't fooling. I ain't all that tired and I really ain't that old."

She felt ready when he made his move. But she wasn't prepared for how he moved. The sudden solidness of him against her made her drop the switch. He heaved the whole of himself at her in a torrent of words that rushed the wind from her lungs. He called himself names, ugly names he'd stored up from the devil knew where burning through the pleats of her bodice. And all she could do was breathe and hold on and declare the love of the blood. As painful as the dirty words were cleaving through her breastbone, his hiccups shuddering clear through to her spine, part of her called it shimsham. A part of her wanted to beat him down to the ground with her fists, then drag him to the road by the nape of his neck and say go on then, go on, go on. But the best part of her locked him in tight while she prayed for a long, hard driving, relentless rain.

VII

BONES ON THE ROOF

Thursday, October 29, 1981

Gummy orange and sticky black waxy wrappers from molasses candy fluttered out of the school bus window. Alongside the bus a girl in ruffled pantaloons and cat whiskers pedaled a bike decked out in crepe-paper hubcaps and handlebar streamers. Children on the school bus, late returning from the planetarium, pelted her with peppermint candies, searched the sky for the Greater Dog, then sat down again in their seats to connect the dots in Orion's belt or draw on breath-fogged windows with their fingers the instruments that measure the winds, tides, and stars.

Kofi's buddies, sullen, stared out the window wishing themselves to Orlando's Sea World like they'd voted for back in September, half the class eager to go see the dolphins zip around on roller skates. Kofi, silent in his own wish, adjusted his helmet as he climbed into the cockpit at the Huntsville Space Center in Alabama, a suggestion that had received twelve votes in the class election. But every year the same phony election was followed up by the tried-and-true trip to the planetarium he used to love. Disappointed, he looked out the bus window at aliens.

For it was that time again when doors were opened to vampires, buccaneers, and moon men come for the loot. Grown-ups also dressed up and gasped in mock terror. A rubber knife, a water gun, hands up, your house, your life. The very masquerade a sign of harmlessness, this time. Officialdom had erased the terror of months before by planting the "no more listed" equals "no more killed" equation in the public mind, the official silence about fresh kills as fraught with danger as the babbled din before when all houses in Atlanta were haunted and everyone was suspect. Memory was being rubbed out by the official erasure as gray settled in all over the city.

Gray dead moths swept up in the dustpan in the room over the bookstore where Inquiry planned to meet. Gray clumps of hair on the floor of the barbershop, where Preener and Bible Man prepared to go meet the others. Gray dust and fibers matted in the bag of the vacuum cleaner down at headquarters, where Dowell read over the reports on the police search of Williams's family home: closets ransacked, attic tumbled, drapes and carpets butchered, lawn trampled and trashed, life totally disrupted for one more family while the rest of Atlanta's citizens were urged to return to forgetfulness, to the tranquil gray, as after a hellish war.

It was that time again too when sound trucks blared through the neighborhoods. Andy Young running for mayor. State rep Mildred Glover also a candidate, and becoming more and more drawn to the case and the upcoming trial. Former Public Safety Commissioner Reggie Eaves the only candidate speaking out on public safety; the people turning a deaf ear. Maynard Jackson was chided for calling Black backers of Sidney Marcus "handkerchief heads" and for introducing race, a dead horse, into the campaign. The Missing and Murdered case pulled through the gray, but only to point out that the suspect was Black. Except that in the paper Spence read at the red light, it said "killer," "mad killer," "child killer," "mass murderer," "fiend," "serial murderer," "beast," not "suspect."

Spence folded down the page where Leah and Speaker appeared in a crowd protesting an expeditionary force flexing its muscles to encourage enemies of freedom in Central America and the Caribbean. Operation Amber, launched from a base in Puerto Rico, was being protested by Nicaragua, Cuba, Grenada, and the independence fighters in Puerto Rico, in demonstrations from Atlanta to Orlando. He didn't know why he felt a connection between Operation Amber, 6 Star, the explosion at Bowen Homes, the Missing and Murdered. He turned down another page where the support gun-control acquaintance of Teo and Sue Ellen appeared in a Police Appreciation Day photo. He then turned to the continuation from page one on the upcoming trial that he would tear out now that Zala had abandoned her news-clipping file and no longer cared to discuss the case.

The trial, to have begun before Halloween, was rescheduled for late December. No two quoted sources agreed on the number of charges: the murder of twenty-eight or twenty-nine; or two of twenty-eight; or two adults with ten, maybe twelve, maybe fourteen other cases attached.

But the accused was a Black man. Not the Klan but a Black man, not a crazed white or a rotten apple in the police barrel but a Black man. At the next light Spence read on, the papers linking the names Wayne Bertram Williams and Marcus Wayne Chenault to further insinuate that Black men were the dangerous menace to the Black community. The mention of Chenault, killer of Martin Luther King Jr.'s mother three years before, was justified several lines later by the reminder that DA Slaton's last homicide prosecution was the Chenault case.

The car behind Spence beeped. He was trying to remember the cult rumor at the time of Chenault's arrest. Might it be the same one that figured in the Innis-McGill testimony the authorities had dismissed and the media had since ignored?

The coupling of the two Black men who shared more than the name Wayne caught Sonny's eye as he scanned the papers. Not interested in tricorner hats or papier-mâché masks or the costume his cousin Gloria wore going out the door, he was looking for the events-of-the-week section. There was to be a Halloween dance at the community center following the Careers Day Fair. He paused for only a minute when he recognized two of his parents' friends in the paper. She wouldn't care about that. All she did was watch him and booby-trap the house when she thought he wasn't looking. He'd seen her slip bits of paper in the door or leave a match stem on the floor. She continually grilled him without actually asking him anything.

Kenti set the damp eraser on the windowsill and walked back to the blackboards. Marva lingered at the window to watch three children from the middle school near Gordon that was going to close down before she even got out of elementary school. The three were pulling the stuffing out of the porch glider cushions and slinging the cushions all over the yard. When they ran out of the yard, she joined her friend at the blackboard.

Kenti liked washing blackboards. What she liked even better than washing away the numbers and letters was watching the slate dry. It dried like sky, the wet disappearing like clouds drifting away. The whole board turned pale and even again. With Marva standing beside her, she didn't feel lonely like at home. They measured themselves against each other, hiking the inside shoulder up, cheating and laughing about it. Then they rushed forward and threw their arms up all over the blackboard, so clean they wanted to hug it.

Across the lane at the community center, people were screaming hello to each other. Adults carried folios like the one gathering dust on the TV table in Kenti's house. There were busloads of little children. High-school children and college students came on foot. Neither Kenti nor Marva wanted to go over there to be chucked under the chin by a grown-up and told how cute, I want to gobble you up, I want to snatch you and take you home. Each was waiting for her daddy to come bring her costume to wear to the program. They held hands and looked toward the window, one side of the flagpole going dark, the side facing the light looking greased. They looked at each other waiting to see who'd say it first. Let's wash the blackboards again, 'cause gray slate wasn't as pretty as shiny black.

"Think them killers are after you all?" The velvety beads around the brim of Andrew's gaucho hat swung when he turned from Kofi to make a face at the driver. Andrew pushed Kwame up the aisle and both boys did their best to fall all over their classmates bouncing on the seats as the school bus rumbled over the train tracks. They cracked on the driver, a creep. No stops in between, even though he had told them they'd be going right past Kofi's house.

Kofi's ship headed into a nose dive and he gripped the controls. His spacecraft was rattling and coming apart. Once wrecked and moving through alien territory in his bubble suit, could he read enough of the sky to guide himself safely to Grady? What if, shook up and stumbling along the highway, he couldn't find his way to a hospital, the way Sonny had? The train was passing, the smooth metal skin of a storage tank marked 'Propellant' like an enemy craft.

"Aaaaarghrghhh."

Kwame and Andrew piled on top of him, and Bestor Brooks's little brother led the raid from the back of the bus. Kofi was trapped in the mangled mind center, with more trouble in the engine room.

The broken white arrow in the newspaper picture his mama tucked in her diary had showed how far the train had dragged the car along when they crashed. An iron fist had smashed the nose of the car in. The roof came down over the windshield. The sides crumpled, and the whole front seat was torn out and thrown on the ground. Two wheels had come off the car. One on its side in the middle of tiny white dots for the broken glass. The other wheel was on the far side of the track, hunks of rubber all over the place. Next to a white outline of somebody taken away already dead was a shoe. It wasn't Sonny's. He'd been down on the floor in the back and had gotten away.

"Shove over, Kofi." Andrew opened the window and the wind gusted up homework and picked at the papery Woolworth costumes.

The children were yelling, the bus driver too, and Kofi was trying to remember how many names. Seven. Two from the car, five from the train. That's what the newspaper his mama had sneaked from the library said. Just like Sonny had told them, except he had the day wrong and the place wrong, and he said there were three men in the car, one driving and two in back holding him down on the floor. "I'd never seen dead bodies before," he'd said, pouring syrup, and before Kofi could recover from the way Sonny said it, Kenti had stabbed the last piece of French toast for herself.

Sonny pulled the blanket across his right shoulder and Zala tacked it, smelling Noxzema on his neck when she leaned down to bite off the thread. He backed up till the table stopped him. The TV shook and the Coffee Papers fell over. She moved so he could see himself in the mirror. He stood up straight and held the staff away from his body.

"I should shave my head," he said. "Like Lafayette. That would really be kicking, hunh?" He couldn't remember what he'd originally been designing when Aunt Paulette gave him the blanket, but when he'd draped it around himself and she started calling him the Prophet, that did it.

He looked down at his sandaled feet. "How would socks look?" It was blowy outdoors already. And after the fair and the Halloween dance, it might really be cold. "Ma, would socks look stupid?"

Zala piled the bolsters on the back of the sofa to cut off the view from the window. Powerful spotlights had shone on their house their first week back in Atlanta, out-of-town journalists covering the September 9 rally mostly, and the curious, to see how near the fire the Spencers had come.

"Let's go, Sonny."

"Ma, my feet."

"Look at me—look at me—*lookatme!* Socks. Yes, wear socks."

The same two-toned Seville was going past the house. The landlord, it looked like. No place to park. The Robinsons were hosting a Halloween party for their grandchild's Girl Scout troop. Mean Dog, chained in the yard, was barking; the Seville moved on. Zala had wanted to argue for a new stove. But so far the repairs were holding. It was best to find a new place anyway. Paulette hadn't decided whether to sell or to rent her house after she married. But her boarders had given notice. Zala thought about the spacious second floor with its own sunporch.

"Let's go, I said."

Sonny sat down in the chair, shoved the Coffee Papers folio out of the way, and smoothed out his socks with his fist. "Somebody needs to kill that dog."

A skeleton, a cowgirl, and a boy with padding under his green sweats under ripped jeans and wearing a dusty wig were going up the walk, Mean Dog panting but quiet as they rang the bell. Their shopping bags were heavy. Mrs. Robinson dropped in boxes of animal crackers and they skipped off, jumping to the side when the dog yanked on his chain. They ran off with their booty—to the neighborhood inspection center to X ray the goods, Zala supposed. But what could the machine detect besides razor blades? Poison wasn't part of the pattern. But then, since the pretrial hearing, "pattern" referred only to fibers. Not that anyone discussed the case anymore. The city had voluntarily taken as law Judge Cooper's gag order, and she couldn't care less.

"Let's go, Sonny." She threw his jacket across the room.

He took his time turning his jacket inside out. He planned to wear it on the shiny side. He'd warned Kofi about his school sweatshirt and warned Kenti about her birthday barrette from Nana Cora with her name on it. He'd argued so loudly with the coach about the sports jackets, she'd gotten a call from school recommending a psychologist. But he'd been right. Wearing your name in plain view of strangers was stupid.

He bent down and buckled his shoe. She wondered if he knew and was stalling. She'd not put much store in his descriptions at first. But when she spoke to his former principal, a woman who'd volunteered back in May and a friend she'd recommended for an assembly program had both fit the descriptions.

"You can go 'head, Ma. The party's not gonna start till you grown-ups clear out anyway."

"We go together. Wouldn't hurt you to find out something about college scholarships, Sonny."

"But I'm going in the army, Ma." He looked up at her with a crooked grin.

"Don't start," she said.

He straightened, still grinning. "You can go on. I'm not gonna run away."

"I'm tired. It's late. Come on."

"I tried to come home, you know. I really did."

"I know. Get your keys."

"You mad 'cause you think I didn't want to."

"I'm not mad with you, Sonny."

"Yeah you are. I can tell."

She sat down on the arm of the sofa, feeling his need to go over it again. Five minutes, no more. The boots, so long by the doorway she'd stopped noticing, fell over when she swung her leg. Those stupid boots he'd inherited from the previous owner of his locker had loomed so large in phony importance.

"I wasn't going off nowhere. I was just mad."

"I know," she said.

The car had pulled alongside, a white Toyota Tercel. The driver, a woman, called out "Sonny" or "sonny" or "honey." He'd walked a little faster to catch up and say hello. The car had pulled up six feet ahead of him at the service station at Mayson Turner. She got out. Brown knit dress, flashy glasses, olive complexion, dark wavy hair held back by a tortoiseshell headband. She rapped her knuckles on the top of the car and said something to him, talking softly. He had to lean forward and concentrate to hear. He thought he recognized the car from the school lot, parked next to the principal's blue BMW. But then she said something about going by the club, so he moved the car to that lot and parked it near the snub-nosed bus. Then he attached her first to the director, then to one of the counselors at the Boys' Club.

"She seemed to know me. I really thought she did."

"I know what that's like," Zala said, glancing at the clock. "You were being polite. You thought any minute her name would come to you."

"Then the door, you know, the other door, on my side, it like . . ."

"It opened."

"Yeah. I should have known. I didn't see nobody but her, and her hand was on top of the car. She kept knocking her knuckles on the top of the car and talking to me."

"To keep your attention on her, Sonny, so you wouldn't wonder too much about who was in the car with her, who opened the door."

"But I should've known. You always told us to pay attention and not take rides."

"Of course, Sonny. But they tricked you. You got in because you didn't want to be rude, not because you were stupid."

"And I was mad, don't forget."

"Yes, you were mad with me."

"So I got in."

"That's not why you got in. You got in because those two were clever and tricky."

"Yeah, but . . ."

"They tricked you. That's why you got in. You weren't looking for trouble. Being mad at your mama don't make you bad. They tricked you."

"Yeah. They tricked me. They tricked me."

She stood up. He didn't. He stared straight ahead. She'd hung the African poster on the wall. The zebra in the extreme foreground had his head turned toward the herd of gazelles. The eye on the side of the zebra's head was bright. Animals with eyes on the sides had a broad range of vision. The bird in the baobab had eyes in front. Creatures with eyes in front had to keep them open or be eaten.

"It's time," she said. He wasn't looking at the poster. He was tipping the chair forward, riding in the car. She sat back down.

When he started up again, he would probably concentrate on the man in back who told him not to move, not to yell, and to keep his eyes on the floor or he'd blow his head off. The woman scolding the man, laughing and talking, pleasant and friendly, shifting gears while Sonny watched her feet, memorizing the jewelry and the shoes, the luggage brown leather, the black scrollwork around the sides and the toe, the light tan saddle stitching, the reddish brown stockings that wrinkled when she worked the pedals. She smelled of expensive perfume. She told Sonny her friend was a bit of a character, to pay him no attention. She would be dropping him off in a minute and would then take Sonny wherever he wished. He was able to keep his head down but lift his eyes enough to recognize the streets they shot through, speeding over the dips and mounds he used to take his bike throwing papers.

Sometimes, if he was tired, he skipped over that part of the ride and picked up the story on I-20 west heading past Hightower, then jumping lanes to the left to swing off onto 285 north into Cobb County. When he started seeing signs for Smyrna, he really got scared. He didn't know anybody north of Bankhead, and it was clear by then anyway that the woman in the designer glasses and the man who spit when he talked were not his friends and he was in trouble.

"They played these tapes," Sonny said, reaching through the rungs of the chair to show her where the tape deck had been. He drew his hand back and closed his eyes.

"Of course," Zala said. "And they laughed at the nasty parts and tried to get you to laugh too."

"I did laugh."

"Because you were scared. You were hoping to disarm them, to keep them friendly."

"I laughed and then he called me . . . he kept calling me names."

"That was the plan. They tricked you into laughing so they could make you feel dirty. Make you feel like whatever happened, you deserved it 'cause you're dirty."

"He kept it up. But she said not to pay him no mind. She was trying to get him to shut up."

"No, she wasn't. They're partners. Two against one. Two grown-ups against one child. He scared you and she acted friendly. That's how they planned it. To keep you off balance. A trick, Sonny."

"Yeah, but she was—"

"An evil bitch, Sonny. Don't be stupid. She got you into the car in the first place."

"Yeah."

"They tricked you, him and her. Both of them. They're friends to each other, not to you. You were the victim."

He tilted his head away as though to look at the woman who was not an ally. She'd said she would drop the man off at a friend's house, and they might stop in for a minute, just for a minute. There was a party and they would be showing movies, the adult kind. And seeing as how he'd enjoyed the tapes and was a mature boy, not silly and giggly like some kids his age but grown-up and sensible, maybe he'd like to watch for a minute, just for a minute. And then she'd take him right back home if that's what he wanted.

"I said okay, like a jerk."

"You were playing along. There was nothing you could have done that would have been any better than what you did. You played for time, watching for a chance to get away."

"I was hoping she'd keep her promise."

"That's only natural. You are not a crazy person. You don't know crazy, evil, tricky people, so you can't think the way they can."

"But I was kinda . . ." He plucked at the skin on his neck, and his Adam's apple disappeared for a minute. "I sort of wanted to see . . . you know, the movies."

"Of course. They planned it that way. That says nothing about you. That's about them, about Maisie and . . . what was his name?"

He kept pulling at the skin on his neck. She made herself look. He'd been so malnourished when brought to the hospital in Miami that the loose skin had sunk into the cartilage of his throat, blocking his esophagus. They'd had to surgically open it to feed him broth.

"Stop it," she said.

He wheeled around and hit his elbow on the table. When she moved to comfort him, he turned away and hugged his arm.

"I kept thinking you'd come, you and Dad. I kept waiting for you to come get me. But it wasn't you. It wasn't you."

A knocking at her heart, the police at the door. Always when she got close to the names, he'd accuse her and Spence. Concealment and distraction, twin ploys of deception. What had they threatened him with? And how could he be cured of deception in a place where his heroes, his leaders did it too? Concealment. Distraction. Atlanta heading for the open drain. Inquiry and STOP keeping the faith, theirs the solidarity of the shipwrecked.

"You didn't come," he said again.

She would not bite. He'd told Spence how he'd been sent to the door of the three-room prefab the following night when neighbors complained about the noise and the likelihood of a lewd party. He'd told the police a story—no carousing, just a birthday party. The woman came up behind him to confirm it, to promise to bring the noisy children under control.

"They didn't even come in to look, Ma."

"Maisie was pretty convincing, I guess."

"They didn't even take a look around," he said.

The nonchecking police, the nonarriving parents. But nothing about why he'd been trusted to go to the door. Why he'd put the police off with a story. Why he hadn't run out. He'd known at that point that the children were being moved in the morning, but he did not tell the police.

"What happened to the other children, Sonny?"

"I told you, Ma. They weren't the ones you showed me. I don't know nothing about the ones that got killed."

"Sonny. There's a man in jail."

He popped his fingers against the folio. He snapped the tie string till it came off. He poked his finger through a frayed corner and a paper clip slid out from her papers.

"Maybe it's better to talk these things over with Mac on Saturday."

"I knew you were mad. I can tell. You keep saying you're not, but you are."

"I'm mad. And I'm worried."

"You worried about me?"

He could have been four years old, coming to the bed to tap her. "You glad about me, Ma?" She'd been glad about him. No matter what stories he'd heard about an unwanted pregnancy and his mama not finishing school on time, she'd been glad about him.

"I love you, and I've always been glad about you, Sonny."

He smoothed out the creases in his prophet outfit and looked down at his socks and sandals, then shrugged.

"I don't know anything about this stuff," he said, smacking the folio with the back of his hand.

She didn't, either. Not anymore. The ceremonial grounds the Innis caravan had found in September should have strengthened her belief, but didn't. She had as many doubts now as she'd had the autumn before. Uncertain because once she looked at it with a cold eye, she no longer cared about the children's case. It was this child's case she had to crack.

"Sonny, it's time we left."

"I kept thinking Dad was going to kick the door down any minute, and you . . . you. But you didn't come."

"I am sorry that we didn't know where you were. We did the best we could. And it worked. You're here."

"It didn't. They beat me up and you didn't come."

"We came. You're here. Stop telling us we didn't come. I'm not going to spend my life apologizing because we didn't know where the hell you were. When we found you, we came right away and got you, Sonny."

"You didn't find me. I got away. I got away on my own."

"We're going now." She got up and opened the door.

"I knew you were mad."

"Move."

He got up slowly, adjusted the blanket, took up his jacket and the staff, and strode to the door like he meant to go out. But he pushed the door slightly into her for a last look at himself in the mirror.

The community center was a beehive gone mad. Small children changed into costumes in the lobby. Parents rushed about snatching up brochures and booklets. Guidance counselors herded students into the booths of IBM, Dow, Polaroid, and Union Carbide to hear how good marks, good attendance, and good conduct led to good prospects in science and industry. GE bulbs in the hands-on booth were buzzing. In halls PTA members were haranguing fathers for lackluster involvement. One of the cornered fathers was loudly protesting the decision to raise money for the children to hear Handel's *Messiah* when no program for Black Month had been planned.

Zala left Sonny behind with Bestor Brooks and his sister and pushed through the halls in a bulldog frame of mind. From the tables under the banner COMMUNITY SERVICE CAREERS, she picked up an announcement for free legal-aid workshops and a brochure put out by Women for Economic Justice. She heard a few parents, members of the recently formed New Justice League, comparing strategies to organize for an independent party.

Up and down the halls, everywhere Spence turned was talk of ROTC, National Merit Scholarships, vocational schools, the seminary, and performing-arts curricula. He broke through a group discussing a recent TV program about latchkey children—what a shame, working mothers; thank God for grandparents—and sidestepped a dietician explaining the importance of eating a good breakfast. He caught up with Zala, who let the coach—holding aloft a tape measure like a prized trophy—run interference. Twenty teenagers followed the coach to the penny-waist dance, sucking in and counting change as they ran.

"Did you get to the bank?" She could barely hear herself above the noise.

"Next time I'll wear a ski mask," Spence said. "They don't pay worth a damn, Zala. But I got two applications."

They followed a man carrying a window pole into the auditorium. The band was setting up on stage and that was all. She headed out into the hall again and he followed, waving to Kofi and Kenti, who were racing toward the cafeteria with their friends.

"Where are we going?"

"Careers in Science." Zala pointed out to the upper corridor, where reps from the five magnet schools passed out literature.

"I'll pick up the Benjamin Mayes School material for Kofi," Spence started to say when he spotted one of Judge Webber's friends. In the Law Careers booth was the attorney who worked for the Victims Aid Program out of the DA's office.

"Remember the gunman who took over the FBI office in summer, took hostages? He lived across the street from Middlebrooks's half-brother, a cop? I'm going to ask her about that. There's been nothing in the news for months. And of course no connection."

"Ask about Curtis Walker's uncle too, murdered out there in Bowen Homes. That wasn't in the papers, either."

Zala cut through a stream of people going into Careers in the chemistry room. The demonstration she was after would be in the booth up ahead near the water fountain. The sign hung on the side of the panel said GLASS. She walked in. Six folding chairs were set up, two by two by two. Another chair was up front by the table. An asbestos cloth was thrown over the table; a footlocker rested on the floor underneath. She sat down to wait for Maisie and the man who'd threatened to blow her son's head off.

A woman walked in, bumping Zala's knees with a square metal box.

"I'm sorry."

"Glass Design?"

"We start in five minutes." The voice was small, pinched, and shy.

Zala could not see the woman driving a stick shift in a slim knitted dress saying, "I have to choke it when it threatens to stall." This woman was shapeless inside a capelike brown coat with flecks of white and green. Her hair was hidden under a dark green tam with a stem. She sat down in the chair by the table and set the box on the arm. When Zala looked at her oxfords, the woman drew her feet in under the chair. She then set the box on the floor and got out of her coat. Brown-skinned and ashy, she drew her hands into the shapeless sleeves of her sweater. The blue-and-green plaid skirt, like the tam, smacked more of Catholic school than a three-room prefab and dirty movies. The woman was a disappointment. She got up to unpack the box and the locker and line things up on the table and began to assemble the parts of a torch.

"Haven't I seen you at Herdon Elementary?"

"Me?" She turned slightly toward Zala with a timid smile. "No, I went to S. Agnes Scott."

"May I help you off with your sweater? They've turned the heat on."

"Oh no," she said, clutching it to her. "I don't have on anything but my slip."

No trace of the perfume Sonny had mentioned. Zala watched as the woman lined up lengths of glass tubing, then hooked up what looked like a vacuum pump for inflating wading pools. Zala was making the woman nervous.

"I've seen you somewhere," Zala persisted. "I keep thinking it was a school. Do you know Maisie, or maybe it's Mazeen? I never can get her name straight. She's a friend of . . . ahh . . ." She motioned toward the equipment.

"Mr. Haynes?" The woman shrugged. "I don't know, I'm new. I found this job through the placement office. It's just for two weeks."

"The placement office?"

"At Atlanta Junior College. Maybe that's where you've seen me? I work in the bookstore there."

"Is Mr. Haynes's wife named Maisie?"

"You can ask him." She looked at her watch. Kmart. Maybe Sears.

"You don't hear that name much anymore, do you? I once knew a nurse named Maisie when I was in kindergarten."

If she's Maisie, she gets first prize, Zala was thinking when she heard familiar footfalls behind her in the hall.

"For some people," the Victims Aid attorney was saying to Spence, "no lamp shades, no anti-Semitism. Either show them the lynched body or shut up about mistreatment of Blacks." She scraped one of the folding chairs out of formation and sat down.

"But the evidence—"

"Evidence? Unless you can put the killers on the stand to confess in open court, forget it. They've got their man."

"They're going to go with Williams, then?"

"That's right. The defense team's efforts to introduce another . . ." She held up two fingers, forming a zero. "Zilch. What goes on here?"

The assistant was about to answer but instead stood up. Zala turned but missed the entrance of the glass man, Haynes, who came in talking and handing out his cards. More importantly, she missed any look of recognition that might have passed between him and Sonny, who was standing in the hall pointing her out to Jonesy. She glanced down at the card Spence passed across the aisle—CHARLES A. HAYNES, LIGHT DESIGNS, INC., a PO box in Decatur—while Jonesy told her something about a call he'd gotten from Dave.

"If you'll form a semicircle," Haynes instructed, motioning the youngsters jammed behind Zala to sit on the floor up front, "I'll begin."

Tall, slender, dancerlike in a sky-blue jumpsuit with many zippered pockets, Haynes didn't look like a man who crouched behind seats and made threats. A charmer, he held a gold-tipped cigarette in one hand and an industrial igniter in the other, and he didn't spit as he talked. She turned to look at Sonny as the man lit the torch and gave the frowzy assistant instructions.

Sonny was standing in the hall next to Bestor, who was dressed as a pirate. They leaned against each other looking in. Their arms folded across their chests, they wore expressions of mild interest. Older students stood behind them. From somewhere Sonny had found a strip of leather with a cowrie shell. He wore it tied around his head, the shell centered on his forehead. Zala studied Haynes. Spanish or Seminole in the ancestry maybe, or Luzana Creole, he was closer to the description of Maisie. She listened carefully to his voice.

"Next to being a movie star," he smiled, "being a neon glass artist is the quickest way to get your name up in lights."

His audience laughed appreciatively as he pulled on a pair of shiny white gloves.

"The job requirements are minimal," he continued. "An ability to work with your hands, and a desire to manipulate and to mold."

His aide held up two halves of a mold, boardlike pieces with a hole at the end for inserting the glass. Zala and Spence exchanged looks.

Addressing those at his feet, Haynes went on in a light baritone. "A glass designer can earn anywhere from ten to twenty dollars an hour, depending on the kind of firm you work for. Advertising agencies, for example, that furnish stores and other businesses with signs, frequently contract designers such as myself. I consider myself more of an artist than anything else," he said. He picked up one of the blue tubes and slid his hand over it caressingly.

"I prefer working in homes with an interior decorator. I design special things to hang over people's bars. People's names usually." He held up a sample. "Sometimes in this line of work, you have to be outdoors, though, to make sure your piece is hung correctly on a motel or a restaurant."

The Victims Aid attorney, bored, got up and squeezed past those crowding into the booth.

"I should mention that a fun part of the work is playing with fire." He leered as he twirled the tube in the flames, and the children laughed. "Ahh, you like to play with fire?" he asked one of Kofi's classmates. "You apply heat to soften it up so it can be shaped as you desire." He held the tube to his mouth and blew, continually turning the glass in the flame. "A little hot air to keep the game going. We don't want the thing collapsing before we've had our fun, do we?"

"Noooo," the children up front said.

"This can be done orally, with your mouth," he explained, "or with a pump." He fitted a length of rubber hose around the end of the glass tube while his aide squeezed the accordion bellows.

"With experience," he said, selecting more tubes, "you can handle several at once. You develop a sense . . . how much heat . . . to soften things up . . . when to blow . . . and when it's time to bend them to your will. I'll need a volunteer."

Hands shot up. But Haynes continued blowing and rolling, closing his eyes each time he placed his mouth on the tube's opening. His lashes seemed long and thick for a man. Zala outfitted Haynes in a silk knit, expensive pumps, and a tortoiseshell headband. His hair was dark and wavy, his skin smooth, his shoulders narrow. When he'd fitted the glass rods to the pump he looked toward the back in Sonny's direction.

"We'll need a name. And we'll need a few volunteers to bend the tubes." He held up pairs of gloves and swung them, still looking toward the rear of the booth.

"Valerie!"

It was Bestor Brooks supplying the name, Sonny beating him on his back and trying to muzzle him with his hand. But three of the younger children up front jumped up and grabbed the gloves.

" 'Val' will be fine for our demonstration," Haynes said, helping a robot volunteer push the silver-sprayed boards off his arms so he could bend the pink tube into a V. Cinderella twisted the blue tube into a cursive L. A gangster in white suspenders twisted the green tube into a cursive A.

Several children supplied grunts. The older students hummed the *Superman* theme as the boy in the robot suit played to the audience. There was a scatter of applause when he bowed and sat down, wolf whistles when Cinderella curtsied, and stamping of feet when the gangster gave up his tube and shook his own hand over his head.

"And now we'll fuse them together," Haynes said, twisting the nozzle of the torch and directing the thin flame to the bent tubes. His aide stood by with a sticky jar with its brush cap lifted. "Manipulating is a matter of knowing when to apply heat and when to let things cool off. That's how you stay in control of what you're doing. Hands on, hands off. It's an art."

He picked up a pink tube and a tool and with one crack lopped three inches off one end. "Just to cut it down to size," he explained. From the jar he brushed on a substance that looked like mud and directed the flame at the bottom of the letters that now lay on the table.

"How'd you learn this? Did you have to go to school?"

"The best way to learn this art is from a master. There are books you can read and courses you can take. But I recommend finding someone to study under. And this is one skill you don't have to worry about the robots taking over," he smiled. "It needs the human touch. A special touch." He inserted the sticky piece against the bottom of the letters, played the flame over it for a second, then turned off the torch.

"Do you have to know how to draw?"

"All you have to know how to draw is people—draw people to you. If you can attract customers," Haynes said, peeling off his gloves, "you'll do all right. Neon is the sign of the times. People like to see their names in lights." He held the piece up. It spelled "Val" in script with a slash running underneath ending in a finlike tail. The applause was hearty.

"And this is a skill you can travel with. As you can see, it's portable." He kicked the locker, then strode toward the hallway with the finished piece.

"Where have you traveled? Go to Smyrna much, or Florida?"

Haynes stopped by Zala's chair and gave her a quizzical look, then moved on, answering one of the questions a parent asked about colors. "I work in a range of forty to fifty different colors. Most people limit themselves to twenty. But I have lots of helpers to prepare my own tints."

"Might Maisie be one of your helpers? Or do you tend to use children?"

Spence stood up when Zala did. No one else seemed to find her questions odd or her tone peculiar. Most people were oohing and ahhing and getting up to see where Haynes was going. Bestor Brooks was holding his arms out to receive the piece, but it was to Sonny that Haynes presented it. Spence moved quickly and grabbed Zala by the belt of her dress.

"Where do you get your helpers from, Mr. Haynes?" She fairly growled it.

"Volunteers. As you can see," Haynes smiled amiably. Already children were rushing him, waving their Careers Day flyers under his nose for his autograph.

Kofi joined the others crowding around the glass bender. He didn't know whether to ask for the name of a book to learn from or for the man's phone number, but he couldn't take his eyes off the glass bender's hands. He was like a magician. One minute he had a gold-tipped cigarette in his hand, and then it vanished and he was unscrewing the cap off his pen. The pen had a glass nib just like the one in Grandaddy Wesley's dresser drawer.

"That's neat," Kofi turned to tell Sonny, but Sonny was hunching over the piece named after his girlfriend and his father was arguing with his mother about something. Kofi moved around to the other side where the bigger kids were asking the glass bender about classes.

"Don't start that again, Zala."

Kofi heard it. It made him shrink up inside. They would come in the house together and she would stop them and make them listen. Maybe there'd be scratchy noises in the ceiling, but that wouldn't be it. She'd say she'd left the TV on and now it was off. Or she'd say the circus poster or the African picture was slanted like somebody bumped into it. Or she'd say her book was on the wrong page, pointing to her notes that said page 40 and then to the book opened to pages 32 and 33. Then she'd make Daddy check the windows and doors and say the locks had to be changed and she'd pick up bits of paper and say somebody had stepped on them while they were out. Then he'd say, "Don't start that again."

Kofi went to the fountain and let water splash on his face. It scared him the way his father said it. He would say it to him too. But Kofi kept on hearing a prowler around the side of the house at night. The wheels of the Herby Curby would squeak. Buster the cat wasn't big enough to do that. And if it was a dog, a dog would make noise. Then he'd hear footsteps on the roof. But he'd be too scared to move or call out. And then it would get light. But when Sonny climbed down from the upper bunk and shook him awake, there was nobody out there sloshing gasoline up against the house or trying to dig a hole through the roof to drop a bomb through. He stopped telling his father about it 'cause he would say, "Don't start that again, Kofi."

Kofi saw his mother tear away and rush up the hall with one of Uncle Dave's boys. It looked like she was after Sonny, 'cause he was running ahead. And now his father was leaving without him, like he'd forgotten all about him and Kenti. Kofi weaved through the students talking to the glass bender and ran after his father.

"Stick close, Kofi. Where's your sister?"

"Eating. She's always eating. Trying to grow."

Kofi adjusted his helmet and checked the buckles holding his oxygen tank in place while his father stood there raking in his mustache and sweating.

"What's going on?" Kofi followed his father's eyes and found himself looking at the glass bender who was looking up the hall at them for a moment before he turned his back and talked with the big kids and some of the parents.

"Kofi, this may sound a little peculiar, but could you picture that guy passing himself off as a woman?"

"The glass bender? Oh yeah?"

"I'm asking, do you think he could convince you that he was a woman?"

"Guess so. I mean, he's not very muscular or nothing."

"You were standing in back. Did you get the impression he and Sonny knew each other?"

Kofi concentrated. The more he pressed himself for details, the heavier the oxygen tank seemed on his back. "I don't think I was paying attention." And he was sweating too. His father threw back his head and put his hands on his chest like he was having a heart attack, so Kofi thought some more. "Why don't we just ask Sonny?" But when he headed for the gym, his father clapped his hand on Kofi's helmet and stopped him.

No streetlights, no bus-stop posts, no mailboxes. The neighborhood was devoid of color too. Mouse-brown bushes, gunmetal strips of sidewalk.

"How far, Jonesy?"

"We're almost there."

A gust of wind stung the cab windows with grit. Crickets were loud. Moths beat against tufts of spiky grass in the scraggly yards. In the headlights, white was sprinkled around a cinder-block doorstep. Too generous to be soap powder, too early for snow, but then the area seemed to exist outside of the seasons. Borax for ants and roaches, she supposed.

Jonesy leaned forward and tapped the driver. "Right up there." He pointed to where houses slanted uphill fifteen yards to their right.

"The street ends here," the driver said.

"You can go up. It's not much of a hill."

"You talking circus talk, T. J."

She looked around wishing she'd been in when Dave called. "What sort of people are they?" What kind of lives were lived around here?

What sort of work did people do—sell poor whiskey, hot clothes, mean dogs?

"They're cool."

"I can wait here," the driver said, leaning back and plopping his cap on his face. "Or I can go find me some coffee and be back in twenty minutes. Which?"

"Whatever." Jonesy put his hand on her pocketbook when she tried to pay the driver. The locks were sprung, and the boy reached across her and pushed the door open with his fingertips.

Clumps of trash stopped up the sewer, and the backed-up water stank. She swung her legs over to a bank of dirt she took to be the curb and dug her heels in.

"Wait, I'll come around." Jonesy got out on his side.

Though they walked uphill, it felt like going down dark basement steps. She followed the boy into a narrow lane, front doors where she expected backyards to be. A door close to her elbow snapped open suddenly, rattling a chain, then slammed shut with a grunt.

"They're all right," Jonesy assured her when she jumped. "Mr. Morris knows them. Watch it."

On the ground on top of neatly arranged brown wrappers were two fishheads and a tuna can of curdled milk. There was no cat in sight, but a dog barked somewhere to her right and was answered by a dog to her left far in the distance. Up ahead, in defiance of all known geometry—and of the fire codes as well, she was thinking—were two houses jammed together that dead-ended the lane. One house had a light in a round window shaped like a ship's porthole. She hoped that one was it. There was a laundry pole out front, the kind that worked like an umbrella. A peely oilskin bag hung on one of the spokes, its side seam torn; a clothespin and the leg of a doll poked through. Under the porthole a piece of Masonite covered with shiny butcher paper leaned. The childlike drawings were the kind Kenti used to make—stick people with birdnest hairdos, lollipop flowers, and a green dog with an enormous, pointy tail.

"No bell," Jonesy said, feeling around the door frame. He rapped with both fists. The house shook. Approaching footsteps felt like an earthquake.

A door was opened. Zala then realized she was looking through fine mesh at a curtain. Draped in front of them was a vegetable-dyed length of unbleached muslin. Light shone through the splotchy saffrons and purples. A hand pulled back the curtain and a greeting rumbled up out of a woman who turned out to be not heavy at all.

"T. J., whatchu say! Get on in here. Big Dave said you'd be around." The woman pulled Jonesy in by the neck and kissed him, then opened the door wider and inspected Zala from head to foot as she stepped over the threshold into the pungent smell of kerosene.

"I'm Em," she said, as a group of men spilled out of a side room and roughed up Jonesy and asked after Big Dave, then returned to a card game inside.

Em handled Zala familiarly, taking her down the hall. Toward the rear of the house people stirred. A boy of sixteen or so stepped into the hall, holding a piece of bread and a knife. He too looked Zala up and down. He was evidently the boy she'd come to see. He stepped back into the room and she could hear the knife clinking against the inside of a jar as she passed and was suddenly yanked forward into a room of smothery heat by a man who shook her arm and swung her around and out of her coat before she could catch her breath.

"Welcome," he said. "I'm Jersey, Em's ole man. Any friend of Big Dave's should make herself right at home. That's the Lady Bee," he said, indicating a woman who came sailing out of the kitchen with two tall glasses of water.

Em dropped down on the sofa and pulled Zala down beside her. The Lady Bee put one glass in Zala's hand and handed the other to Jonesy. "Butter beans on the stove. Cornbread and light bread both," she announced.

"I've eaten," Zala said, looking at the glass, "but thank you kindly." She hoped it was water, not vodka or white lightning. Both Em's and Jersey's voices sounded whiskey thick, though neither of them looked or otherwise sounded tipsy.

"It's boiled," the woman said, and sailed around the room in her peach peignoir. The sleeves were two yards apiece and trimmed in maribou. Smells of supper trailed her as she shut off the TV, rearranged the trophies on top of it, then waved people coming out of the kitchen eating something hot and dripping that they held over napkins to go up the hall. "I always boil it," she said. "I don't trust nothing that comes out a city tap."

Zala sipped and smiled at the trophies and the graduation and wedding pictures on the wall, and the Lady Bee went back to the kitchen. Zala hoped there was a fire extinguisher to go with the sleeves.

Em shook off her slippers and waved Jersey out of the room to get the boy. "Maybe I should tell you about Lorraine, since that's how it started." She paused when the boy appeared, brushing crumbs from his shirt. He hung in the doorway. Jonesy unfolded Sonny's missing flyer and handed it to him. He looked at it, then looked at the floor. Zala hoped Em would not be too long. It was the boy she wanted to talk to.

"Lorraine was no kin to us," Em said, "but her mother and me used to sing in the choir. You know how that is like, when an old chum is on her ass. So I took the girl in. She'd run off before, arrested too. Wasn't but thirteen. I don't know what story she gave them, but when it suits them they put the girls in with the women."

"Did Lorraine know Angela Bacon and Cynthia Armstrong?" Zala was hoping to push the story along before the boy hanging in the doorway fell asleep. The fumes from the kerosene heater were already making her eyelids droop.

"That girl knew too many people for her own good. Call themselves ministers. Call themselves getting these youngsters out of the life and on the straight and narrow. Bunch of Jesus Joes on the hustle. You know the type. Those girls would come out of that Salvation Army shelter and the pimps and dopers would be lined up from the front steps to the bus stops, them so-called ministers right along with them. Yeah, Lorraine knew about five or six of them young women that got murdered. Met them at a camp where they pay the kids to stick around to make it look legit." She turned to the boy. "Get me my bag, Michael.

"I'll show you the pay stubs. I saved them. No two in the same amount. Lorraine was getting checks long after she moved in with us. That camp was summer before the last one, and she came to stay with us about this time last year—November maybe. You'll see," she said, taking the bag the boy brought her. "Seemed like an awful lot of money for camp kids."

"Stipends," Michael said.

"Stipends my behind. That girl would walk in here sometimes with a roll that could choke a horse. I tried to school her. She was just a kid. You the first person to take an interest other than Big Dave. The police didn't even ask to look at her things. But I'll show you if you want so you'll see what I mean. Now, here. This is Lorraine. This one too."

Zala handed back the check stubs in amounts ranging from $150 to $285 and took the snapshots. In one, Lorraine, a dark-skinned girl with large eyes and long dimples, was dressed in a shiny blue low-cut dress that was hiked up to one side with a fabric rose. She wore arm-length lace gloves with the fingers bare. In the other photo she had on a blue skirt and a simple white blouse, the sort of outfit Zala used to wear for Wednesday assembly.

"And this, one of them four-for-a-dollar."

The brownish pictures in the photo-booth strip showed a sweaty Lorraine with her hair standing on end hugging a man with a heavy ridge over his brows, bushy sideburns, and a dark five o'clock shadow. "Who's he?"

"One of them jokers she met at that camp. Football camp, I think it was. You'll notice it doesn't say a thing on the stubs. That Cynthia child you mentioned was at that camp too. This guy used to come for Lorraine. Wouldn't never come in. Jersey went out to the car and spoke to him about blowing the horn like she was a ho. You know, come on up and knock on the door with some respect. But he'd blow, and she'd tear out of here and we wouldn't see her for days. No sense asking for nothing. She'd tell me same as she tell her mother, nothing. One of them fast-talking girls, a whole lotta talk but no information. She tried to get Michael to go along with her."

Michael sat on the arm of the sofa, still holding the flyer. He had grabbed his arm and twisted it to examine the scabs on his elbows. Zala wondered if he also had scabs on his knees.

"Tell'm, Michael."

He cleared his throat and picked at a scab. "Meetings," he said, and looked toward the blank TV screen.

"They'd have prayer meetings, only the real meetings were in the back. These minister types would get the kids to go out on the street with collection cans. But that's not what they wanted Michael for. Tell'm, Michael."

"They wanted me to pull some kid's pants down."

"How you like that? In a church."

"Warehouse."

"Warehouse? Either you were lying to me or you lying to Big Dave's cousin here. They don't want to hear no stuff. This lady came all the way over here to find out about her boy. You got to do better than that, Michael," Em scolded.

"One time, there was a meeting at a warehouse over there near Whitehall."

"Near McDaniel-Glenn? Did you know Yusuf Bell?" Jonesy asked.

"Only from the papers. Another time, we were over at the Krystal hamburgers on Memorial and this guy—" he leaned over to tap the photo-booth picture—"he came in and walked us around to a church in a store. I didn't hang around. But something happened that night. Lorraine was scared after that."

"She was plenty scared," Em said. "Kept saying things were coming apart and she was going to stay with her father, which was news to me 'cause I've been knowing her mama for more than twenty-five years and the man I thought was her father died in Vietnam. Next thing I know, the police are knocking on the door to tell me they found her body. Didn't even ask to look at her things. Come on, take a look. You'll see. A couple of hundred dollars' worth of makeup, underwear that would make your teeth fall out. I'm talking about bras with no cups and drawers with no crotch. You come too, T. J.—be a real education for you."

Em pushed Michael ahead of her up the hall, talking all the while about drugs, orgies, and blue movies. It wasn't until they came to a door that had to be shoved open, so many clothes hanging on the back of it, that Michael spoke up again.

"After that, they started following me. They'd come to the house asking for Lorraine but really trying to see if I was in. When I'd go out, they'd follow me."

"That's when you should've called Big Dave. But oh no," Em said, flinging a crinoline lamp shade onto the bed covered with rough dry clothes. She changed the bulb in the lamp but the room remained dim. "Come on, sit down," she urged, clearing a few spaces. She pulled a red leather model's hatbox from under the bed and zipped it open. The makeup and the underwear she mentioned were on top. Photographs, an angora sweater, a leopard-skin boa, and jewelry were crammed inside.

Zala sat down and went through the photos, realizing that the faces of the murdered men, women, and children had faded from her mind since the summer. The girls in the pictures were mostly teenagers and the boys seemed Kofi's age. The grown-ups were all men. The man with the thick ridge over his eyes who looked like a boxer turned up in several snapshots, usually standing over one of the girls and gesturing with his finger. She worked through layers of photos, flipped through an address book, found two torn movie stubs from the Coronet in a white clutch bag, and worked down to a pack of looseleaf whose cellophane had been slit at the top. Between the sheets were two folded pieces of paper. When she shook them out, Michael came around and sat on the night table near her. She tried to handle the papers with care. It was clear the girl had meant something to him and that he thought these papers important.

"She wrote poems," Michael said just as one of the creases tore.

Feeling the pain of causing pain, Zala took more time reading over the tried-lied, love-God above, reality-eternity verse than she wanted to. On the other piece of paper, which looked as if it had once been in the rain and dried on the heater, crisp brown lines indicating the coils were several names followed by numbers: "A. Wiley 246," "P. Putnam 336," "S. Burr 516." In different ink and block-printed was Dave's name and phone number, and at the bottom the single word "Bell."

Michael was leaning over her, but she couldn't remember the names of the men in the Bacon and Armstrong cases. And if "Bell" referred to deputy Chief Eldrin Bell, she wasn't sure what that meant. Perhaps it referred to Camille Bell. Maybe the girl had meant to visit STOP and tell them something.

"What do you think about them numbers?" Michael asked her.

Jonesy crawled across the bed and looked over Zala's shoulder. "Hotel rooms, could be." Michael's face went flat. "Might be taxi ID numbers," Zala offered, "or swimming pool lockers."

Em began gathering the things together, her face wet, and Michael looked far away.

"Is that why you left Atlanta?" Zala asked him. "You were afraid they would try to silence you because you could identify them?"

"You need to speak up, Michael. They wouldn't be here if Big Dave hadn't sent them. And he's done more for you than anybody. But instead of sticking close to Jersey and Fred," she said to Zala as she zipped the case closed, "he thought he saw a chance to make some change, so he started calling up the papers and the television people saying he knew something and could get the reward. Like he hadn't noticed how kids around here who talked to the police or reporters wound up in Juvenile for beating up an old lady they never saw before. You know how things go. Soon's you talk to somebody, your ass is grass. Didn't I tell him, try to school him, but he fronted me off. Kids."

"What happened, Michael?"

"This guy called, told me to meet him at the train station out there by Channel 11. I thought it was one of the reporters calling me back, so I went."

"White guy?"

Michael looked over toward Jonesy and nodded. "He gave me thirty dollars and a ticket. Said to keep my mouth shut and he'd check out my story. Said it would take a few days, then I should call him, and if they hadn't arrested anybody, then he'd tell me where I could get a job till they made the arrest and I could come back for the reward."

"Blow over in a few days," Em snorted. "Four months later they grabbed Williams, and now they've tied ten or twelve of them children to his tail. Half them cases could have been solved last year if they'd wanted to. So you know the trial's going to be one hell of a joke. And my son here, he don't even call home. A white man tells him to get on the train, he gets on the train. I'm telling you."

"I think I would care for some butter beans if it's not too much trouble, Em. And Jonesy, could you get my glass and a piece of ice maybe?"

"Why, sure," Em said, slapping her son on the knee. When he winced, Zala moved closer to the night table. "You tell this woman what she wants to know, Michael," Em said. "She's like blood."

Zala handed him a picture of Sonny that Lovey had snapped. "That's my son. It was taken this summer."

"He's home?" When she nodded, he asked, "And he's all right and everything."

"Yeah," Jonesy said at the door. "And it wouldn't be stooling, 'cause he's been trying to tell us what happened. But they messed him around so bad, they broke his jaw. And they got him wired." Jonesy reached his arms around to clamp his face in a vise. "They got to feed him through a glass straw, Mike. He can't talk, but he wants to."

When Em and Jonesy were heard down the hall talking to Jersey,

Michael looked at Zala and they smiled. "Leave it to Jonesy to take it out," he said. Then he looked at the photo. Sonny was by the fence near the chicken coops. Blackberries and grapes were thick behind his head, the leaves painted red and blue from the juice; armies of wasps covered the scuppernongs that had burst their skins. Michael gripped the photo by the edges and ran his thumb over the berries as if to bruise them, to make them spurt.

"He was on a farm like the one they took you to, Michael. Did you know him?"

He kept rubbing. And each time his thumb moved, the skin wrinkled on his elbow. Under the scab, infection still threatened, the skin around it puffy and blistered. Under the city's rug, sweepings were festering too. Only part of it was of interest to her now.

"I remember in April when ten boys who'd been reported missing came home. The papers said they'd been working crops, but I wondered," she said.

"They forced me into a car," Michael said. "I had this drink, a Dr Pepper I got on the train. I was going to the phone to see if I could stay at the YMCA. And these two guys, white guys, jumped out of a car and knocked the can out of my hand." He tucked his lips in and pressed and his whole face looked tight. He stared at Sonny's photo again.

"Were you beaten, Michael?"

"Some."

"Were you forced to work?"

"They started me digging potatoes the minute I got there. There was a lot of jane growing on the place. That's how they paid the older guys. They'd be sitting against the wall smoking. We slept in a shed. They would lock us up. It had these concrete bunks coming out of the walls like shelves. That's what we had to sleep on."

"Could you leave?"

"You'd hear about people thrown in a ditch or dropped along the highway 'cause they tried to leave or got sick. Sometimes they threw them in the river. Sometimes they just let them rot in the fields."

In spring, when the papers said "not related," she'd asked around, and so had Spence. From Florida to Texas, then back up the coast to North Carolina, thousands of migrant workers were transported from April to November to harvest sweet potatoes, cucumbers, grapes, oranges, lettuce, tobacco. Bodies were always being dredged up from the Tar River. It crossed Interstate 95 in Nash County. She thought of Nancy Holmes, who'd been back in the city since the arrest still telling her story, naming names, and making a connection between murders in Memphis, North Carolina, and Atlanta.

"Were there children there from Atlanta, Michael?"

"From all over. Was some people there spoke only Spanish. And some that spoke only island French. They stuck to themselves. Everybody stuck to themselves. They didn't want you buddying up together. I started vomiting one day, vomiting blood. Everybody was scared and got away from around me. When I fell out, these two guys, they were overseers—they were the ones that carried blackjacks and rubber pipes but not the guns, only the white guys handled the rifles—they threw me on the back of a flatbed. I didn't know where they were taking me to. I rolled off and hid in the woods. Took me two days to find a phone that was working. I called my aunt in Gainesville and she came and got me. Took her two days too 'cause I didn't know where I was. I know I crossed the Georgia line walking, but that's about it."

"I'm glad you got away." She was about to ask again about Sonny when he spoke up, looking at her squarely for the first time.

"You got a counselor? One of them lawyers that takes migrant workers' part? They call it an advocate."

"Sonny's seeing a therapist kind of counselor. We can't fit enough of the story together yet to—" She didn't have to finish; he was nodding and rubbing the photo.

"I know he was raped," she said.

He made a sound. A high-pitched, irritating, metallic sound, it rolled out into the room like a siren. Neither of them moved.

"If he says he knows me, maybe so." Michael's voice was wiry thin. "But I don't remember him." He held the picture toward the light and studied it. "I got a court date," he said in another voice. "My advocate counselor is getting the FBI in because it was kidnap and slavery. It'll be out of town. Big Dave said not to talk to anybody in Atlanta."

"Michael," she said, moving closer. "I'm going to describe several people to you. I'd like you to tell me if these people seem familiar. Would you do that for me? It could be that the people who grabbed my son are connected to the people who grabbed you."

He wiped his nose and nodded.

"And it could be they're connected to the people who killed Lorraine."

"Think so?"

"I think so."

"I'll tell you one thing. There was a white guy at that farm who looked like one of the men who was slapping around this preacher at the storefront church near Memorial. They could have been brothers."

"Why don't you describe all the people you can and I'll take notes. Then I'll describe who I can and let's see if any match. Would you do that?"

"I guess when Big Dave said not to talk to anybody in Atlanta, he didn't mean you."

"No, he didn't mean me," Zala said, holding up two fingers. "Me and Dave are like that."

"Cousins like?"

"Like blood," she said.

Kofi waited until Sonny rolled all the way to the wall on the top bunk before he could get in without the upper mattress banging him in the head.

"I'll be glad when we move," Kofi muttered, facedown in his pillow.

"Me too," said Kenti from her cot. "'Cause I want a cat and a room to myself. You make this room small, Sonny. You going be a giant any day now. Mrs. Grier said it, I didn't. You should sleep on the back porch. That way Kofi can have his place back and I can sleep where I was."

"It's cold on the back porch."

"Aunty Paulette giving away stuff. She got an electric blanket. You could get a hammock like Auntie Gerry sleep in and move out of here. You make the whole house small."

"Goodnight, Li'l Bit."

"Goodnight yourself. I'm not finish talking to you, Sonny Spencer."

"You mad with me?"

"Yeah, 'cause you hurt my feelings. You told me to get out the gym. Nobody else minded me coming to the dance. You all the time think you so big. You ain't nothing but a lost ball in the weeds. And I don't see how Valerie Brooks could think you cute, 'cause you ugly."

"You finished?"

"Maybe." She pulled the covers up and thought some more. "If you would move out of here I'd like you better."

"Goodnight, Kenti."

Spence thought he heard Sonny in the kitchen. Later he thought he heard the backdoor click. Zala kneed him in the back. It was a while before he could rouse himself, though he was only dozing and very much wanted to give her room. At the community center, he'd thought she was going to jump the glass designer. She'd been even worse when she got back from the trip with Jonesy. The counselor Mac had referred the whole family to wasn't available till mid-November. But they needed relief now.

There was no sign that Sonny had been in the kitchen. Spence headed for the bedroom. Kenti had kicked her covers off again. She had a new sleeping posture: one hand under her cheek, the other under her pillow, left leg flexed, the other out straight. He adjusted the covers and looked in on Kofi. He was facing the wall, his knees drawn up tightly, his head under his pillow. His grip on the covers was tight. Spence massaged his back until he stretched out a little.

In the upper bunk, Sonny was on his back, but not in the old position, legs apart, arms over his head, centered, in full command of the mattress. He was facing outward, one leg crossed over his body like he'd planned to step out into the air. One arm was over his stomach, protecting his viscera, the other forearm across his forehead, his hand balled. But he was on his back and in the middle of the mattress, not scrunched up in the upper corner of the bed with fists. Progress.

Spence re-inserted the nails in the window frame and wedged a comic book in to keep the pane from rattling. He was about to tiptoe out for the third time that night when he spotted the beeswax on the bookcase Paulette had given them.

The coach said Sonny was using the balls of wax to build up his wrists and fingers. Soon he'd be able to span a basketball like a pro. Mac had told him Sonny pressed the balls of wax to relieve tension. He had a lot of rage. Zala said he sometimes molded the wax into figures, then set them down near the pot to melt down again into balls. He'd inherited her artistic genes. Everybody had something to say about them damn balls of beeswax.

When Spence had seen the first one back in August, the only thing the wax brought to mind was keys, making an impression to duplicate keys. But there was nothing locked up at Lovey's place. There was nothing worth locking up at any of the Rawlses'. He'd kept watch, wondering what locks Sonny had in mind to open. Then the balls became two and grew as fat as tennis balls. He had a whole can full of wax. Spence hadn't seen him handling any lately. They would harden, collect dust, and by the time someone ran across them packing to move, they'd be unidentifiable.

Spence walked back into the living room. "Wayne who?" he'd heard someone say at the community center. He wasn't sure which side was holding up the trial, the defense lawyers, who kept changing, or the prosecutors, who kept trying to attach the whole list to Williams.

First light was coming through the pane of the door, giving shape to things he'd previously stumbled over: Sonny's jacket, fallen from the back of the chair; Zala's sweater coat, off the knob; material she'd taken about the law workshops, no longer a neat pile under the table. He moved toward the window and looked out. Spencer could make out the glint of Peeper's binoculars. He reminded himself to ask Paulette's boarder about the car that parked two doors down from the Robinsons' every now and then, the driver in it. On good nights, Spence figured it was a late-shift husband doubling back to check on his wife. Or a family man on the night shift who'd lost his job and couldn't talk about it yet. On bad nights, he imagined the driver was watching the house, their house, waiting for a chance to grab Sonny.

Spence turned. One of the children, bundled in the quilt, was stumbling toward the kitchen. Sometimes Kofi coming out of the bathroom half-asleep took a wrong turn. Spence headed for the kitchen, hoping it was Sonny. He'd suggest they raid the fridge, though he wasn't hungry, only longing for company.

"What's up?"

Sonny turned, his hand on the doorknob. "I want to see how cold it is out here."

Spence followed him onto the back porch. Sonny stomped around,

nosed a stack of newspapers over his toe, sized up the room, and looked
out the barred window.

"This could be my room."

"You'd freeze your ass off out here."

"It's a drag sharing a tiny room with two children, Dad, especially
with you checking every five minutes."

"Who you calling a child? You a child yourself," Kenti said, snug-
gling up against Spence for warmth. "You ain't grown till you eighteen
or twenty-one, that's what Mrs. Grier says."

"You oughta move in with them, Li'l Bit. Then you two can gossip
all the time."

"We don't gossip. I keep her company 'cause she feels bad 'cause
Buster won't come home. He took one look at you and ran away. You
took my quilt."

"Ssshhh, you two will wake everybody up."

"I'm glad you changing rooms. I can't do nothing in there with him
in there, Daddy."

"Summit conference?" Zala trailed the bedcovers behind her.

"Sonny thinks maybe we can fix this up to be his room."

Zala looked from Spence to Kenti to Sonny to the backdoor leading
to the yard.

"Is that car out there one of your friends?"

"Aw, hell," Sonny said, brushing by them.

"See," Kenti said, trying to follow him and bumping into a groggy
Kofi. "You make Daddy nervous and Mama don't trust you neither, and
me, you just make me mad."

"Somebody light the oven," Zala said. "Wake me when it's warm."

"I don't feel so good," Kofi said, following her.

"Me neither. Can I sleep with you, Mama?"

Spence locked the backdoor and stood alone in the kitchen wondering where matches might be. The students who'd rented the place in
the summer had strange ideas where to keep things, and everything was
still topsy-turvy. Especially his feelings. He found a book of matches on
the table by a paperback and lit the oven.

They were making progress, though. The question of new sleeping
arrangements, which Mac had raised, seemed to be working out without Spence having to do anything. He stuck a pan of water in the oven
and looked into the living room, feeling he'd been a coward. He'd been

putting it off. But how would he have put it: "Son, I don't want you sleeping in the same room with your sister and your brother"? It was time to think about separate quarters for Kenti and Kofi as well. There was the minor problem of finding a job. Delia had certainly been generous, but each time he'd gone to borrow he had to hear about white-collar pill parties and discrimination against nonjunkies. Spence sat down in the chair and opened the paperback his eldest had checked out of the library, *The Exorcist*.

"Great," he said, and put his head down on the table.

Tuesday, January 12, 1982

"Ready?"

Her lunch hour almost up, Zala adjusted the sonic earmuffs and nodded. Schumake could do the shouting. That part of her preparation she had no need to perfect.

"Any damn fool body down range?" Her instructor's voice ricocheted off the basements walls. No one stirred. Below zero for the second day, the booths on either side of her were empty. "Ready on the right. Ready on the left. Ready on the firing line. Commence firing!"

She emptied a round into the stationary target. It was a pleasurable feel, the weight in her hand, the ping and thud of collision solid in her gut. She snapped open the cylinder of Schumake's practice pistol, spun it for his amusement, jacked out the spent shells, and reloaded quickly.

"Ready on the firing line," she said matter-of-factly and immediately began firing again.

Schumake reached around her and set a brand-new revolver on the counter. He pressed the buttons that brought the target rattling toward them. "You're getting damn good, I'd say—damn good." He secured his scarf more tightly around his neck, no heat issuing from the pipes along the wall behind them. "Better leave your weapon in the locker if you're planning to go to court from work." He tapped her on the shoulder and she secured the sonic earmuffs in place again.

Zala shoved in the clip of the new pistol. Then she loaded her Walther, the .22 caliber, sound-suppressed automatic she'd ordered in a fit of recklessness. In the catalog of 6 Star, which was supposedly closed down and out of business, the gun had been advertised by a comic-book drawing of a man with three right arms: One arm snatched the weapon free from a holster strapped to his right leg; the second arm whipped it upward to aim; the third fired it, not from the shoulder but from the hip, gung-ho style. "Order Your Merchandise Early," the cardboard blank in the middle of the catalog said, its drawings appealing to those who reveled in broken teeth, bloody fingernails, and gore. The brass knuckles, bolo knives, and ammunition cases on the order blank brought to mind the man with the same name as a Klan founder. Teodescu and Sue Ellen said he'd been in court on the first day of jury selection. The Walther had arrived on the day of trial when the prosecution and the defense made their opening statements. Not out of business, 6 Star had merely changed its name and address. The return sticker she'd handed over to Lafayette; the PO box was in Glyco, Georgia. Once a week, Lafayette followed Slick from the FBI office on Peachtree to the agent training center in Glyco, Georgia.

Her co-workers in the bank tower went to considerable lengths to obscure certain aspects of reality from themselves. "Which trial?" they would have asked, blank-faced, when she left her post, a footstool in front of the file cabinets, to go to the courthouse. A good Black woman, model mother and model citizen: No one questioned her comings and goings; her crazy-quilt schedule was attributed to familial and civic duties. She could describe to co-workers going down to the lobby exactly how her children would be dressed and whether they'd be standing by the guard waiting for their father to come down from the third floor, or by elevator number 5 waiting for her to come down from the bank tower. Certain set habits, such as meditating by the window rather than gossiping by the coffeemaker, the older accountants advanced as a virtue to the younger typists. They held keyboards and adding machines quiet when she was on the phone checking on her children's progress at school, occasionally calling a network of friends—from church, it would seem—who looked after shut-ins who lived on Gray Street and kept in touch with former church members who'd moved from Atlanta.

Daily Zala's sense of isolation deepened. The Inquiry meetings in her home meant little to her now. The comings and goings of Lafayette and the other trackers simply meant more out-of-pocket expenses for Inquiry. Like an automaton she went to work and mindlessly relayed information from Spence to the others and back.

One day she would look out on Peachtree and see the white Toyota pull up across the street, front wheel wobbly. The driver would get out, tucking a wave of hair behind her ear, to look at the tire. Her friend would come around to see, the two careless of oncoming traffic. Struck down, they'd lie in a pool of blood until Zala, sprinting from the bank lobby, could climb into the ambulance with them. Friend of the family, she'd say—would say whatever it took to get in and get to the tanks, the knobs on the tanks and the masks.

WAYNE WILLIAMS FOR PRESIDENT was scratched on the side of each newspaper box at the bus stop at Five Points, Zala noticed as she headed back to work. The day before, she'd seen the handbills flying around Center City Park and the meaning hadn't registered until later, when from the tower window she'd seen two white youths putting them up around the fountain and she'd gone down to dispose of them.

"We signed you out," someone called to Zala. Three co-workers from the tower took turns shouting that a blizzard was predicted and she could go home. Zala waved thanks and headed in the direction of the courthouse.

At Alabama and Peachtree, AVFW vets were collecting for the Vietnam War Memorial, fifty-five thousand names engraved on a slab of polished black stone to be set in a mound of earth in the country's capital. At the last Inquiry meeting, Spence and the others had talked about organizing buses from Atlanta for the Veterans Day dedication. The announcement of the upcoming memorial ceremonies had triggered off protests by Vietnamese Americans against the United States for Operation Baby Lift at war's end. On public radio, a Vietnamese woman compared the situation in Saigon in 1975 to a burning building from which frantic parents had dropped their children to those below for safety. "Who could know," the woman was saying as Mason attempted to get the Inquiry meeting underway, "that those who caught the children felt they had the right to keep them, fly them away, sell them, or give them away? Like puppies."

Lafayette had given his report. Slick had been followed to the Bureau Training Center in Glyco, where he seemed to be a consultant or liaison officer between the Immigration agent training school and Arms, Tobacco, and Firearms school. Vernon showed a photo of Slick passing Red of the GBI in front of the Federal Annex post office in downtown Atlanta. Speculation turned to whether Slick and Red were investigating or covering up the links that seemed to exist between Immigration and the Stoner convention the weekend of the Bowen Homes explosion; between the ATF, the Innis-McGill cult, and the "Klan justice" threat against victim Lubie Geter; between the "clean bill of health" the governor had given the Klan and White House pressure for the governor and the DA to arrest Williams. Speaker voiced a possibility that Spence found too plausible to ignore: Maybe the arms deal that the GBI informant alluded to in the memorandum that had been in Judge Webber's possession—the one who'd infiltrated a particular Atlanta Klan family to find out about the arms deal and then heard members boast of their involvement in the Missing and Murdered case—maybe the arms deal was bigger than just the Klan. Given the number of mercenaries being signed up all over the southeast region to go down south of the border, maybe it was a government-conducted operation.

Horses tethered to the fence diagonally across from City Hall were stomping the sidewalk and snorting in the cold. Visitors coming out of City Hall, the capitol building, and the courthouse paused before boarding their tour buses, their eyes drawn to the horses. They were Tennessee walking horses, Morgans, and quarter horses—not particularly effective in riding down criminals or controlling unruly crowds, but nonetheless crowd pleasers. With the recent purchase of more horses there was increased opportunity for mounted duty, and according to Dowell morale in the squad room had lifted somewhat. There was still a lot of grousing because of overtime hours amassed because of the case. But the horses were beauties. When six mounties approached, smelling of coffee and cigarette smoke from the City Hall cafeteria, one of the horses pricked its ears forward in recognition, twisted its neck, and clomped noisily on the pavement.

City Hall looked like a postcard. Its landscaping stiff with frost, its window ledges glazed, it was a study in stasis. Crossing over, Zala wondered where Maynard Jackson had moved on to. People said that Benjamin Hooks had a clearer shot at the post Maynard was after as national head of the NAACP. She supposed ex-mayors returned to private practice. In recent days she'd been learning what former state legislators did. In a group she'd come to call the shuttle group, because they

moved triangularly from the courthouse to City Hall to the Capitol Police Office in the basement of the domed building, were several former
members of the Georgia legislature, junior and veteran lawyers, and reporters who covered the court beat, the city hall beat, and the capitol
beat. Ex-state legislators kept abreast of what was going on in the "triangle," the three buildings right next to each other. The usual next
stepping stone was becoming a local DA.

At the corner, Zala looked down the street toward the capitol. She
often found the casual conversation of the shuttle group more informa-
tive than the trial itself or the media commentary on it. According to
them, Williams had made a big mistake in hiring an out-of-town attorney to head the defense team, someone not sensitive to local customs
and biases, not attuned to local speech patterns and style, not privy to
hunches and tips on the various grapevines. Sure, there were foot soldiers to run down tips; there were aides who assisted in the mysteries of
glance and gesture; and of course there were Mary Welcome, who'd
stayed on as assistant attorney, and Chet Dettlinger, who sat at the defense table to second-guess the prosecution's moves, and Camille Bell of
STOP, who'd made herself available. But Alvin Binder, a white man
from Jackson, Mississippi, was further handicapped by having had only
a few days to prepare for the trial; and, most serious of all, he'd inherited a defense that was running on an empty kitty.

She'd heard them refer to Williams as a dupe, a setup, a dummy.
The shuttle group's speculation about the kidnap-murder ring echoed
Miss Em's description of the church group Lorraine had fallen in with:
The real operators connived behind closed doors. And so—like Oswald,
Ray, and Sirhan, they argued, moving from point to point on the
triangle—the defendant would sit tight and reveal little simply because
he'd been set up.

Zala crossed again and headed for the courthouse. No one in the side
street and no one on the roofs, either. During the first two days of the
trial, sharpshooters in goggles and high leather boots had lined up
along the roofs' edge, weapons pointing down at the crowds milling
around the courthouse. Officers in flak jackets and riot helmets had
been on the front steps and against the walls of the inside staircase looking shoot-to-kill grim. Police dogs were led through the corridors, up
the stairs, taken to the elevators to sniff for bombs. In bulletproof vests,

sheriffs and platoons of deputies kept the traffic moving through the halls and through the surveillance. The tocsin sounded every few minutes at the airport-style setup, people forgetting to remove jewelry, key rings, and coin from their pockets, electric razors and cans of toiletries from their travel bags.

On the second day of the trial, a marshal had pulled Speaker out of the line bunched up in front of the surveillance archway. He gave Speaker the once-over with a hand-held metal detector. "Expecting an invasion?" Speaker had been the soul of cooperation, removing his knit cap, shaking out his locks, turning around good-naturedly as the marshal searched him. "His cohorts might try to spring him," the marshal then said. Bible Man had been holding the larger tape recorder and Leah the miniature one. "No comment," the marshal had said, spotting the mike. "We're not with the media," Leah coaxed. "No comment anyway." But when he'd done with Speaker and moved down the line, Bible Man followed him, just as Preener and some neighbors from his former safety patrol followed the shuttle lawyers around. Inquiry was determined to find some channel through which they could get the 6 Star packets impounded by the court.

The amount of security those first days had everyone wondering: Was there a surprise witness waiting in the wings? No defense witness would cause such heavy guard, people were certain. The name "McGill" was on the lips of some who reminded others of developments last spring. While transcripts of the trial were being peddled at a dollar a page, people compared hunches. Logan had written Inquiry from New York that McGill, McGill's son, and a former "personal friend" of McGill's had identified Williams. Under hypnosis and subjected to both the psychological stress evaluation and the polygraph, the three had placed Williams on the periphery of the drug-running, child-murdering cult. That he knew not a great deal but far more than he'd revealed thus far, had been Logan's summation in the fall when the Innis caravan, led by McGill, found a huge, partially burned cross and animal corpses on a burial ground just outside the city. Logan's summation jibed with the shuttle group's theory and much of the hunching in the fourth-floor corridor. But those who snooped around the offices of the defense team said there was little material on this angle in the Brady file, the volumes of reports gathered by the prosecution that was then, by law, made available to the defense.

Inquiry members were pretty sure who the witness would not be, but should be. For Spence it was the youngblood who'd testified at the St. Louis–Hardy–Wilcoxin sodomy trial. The three white men convicted of sexually molesting minors were said to have been involved with two or three victims on the Task Force list. The media, however, did not pick up the link, nor had the authorities. And according to B. J., the snoopers had found less than a line of it in the Brady file. Since the child porn angle had been Dettlinger's theory all along, and he and *L.A. Times* reporter Jeff Prugh had amassed a great deal of material through independent sleuthing, B. J. was hopeful that a young teenager known to the two would be called by the defense to give the jury another suspect to consider. A boy from Miss Em and Michael's neighborhood had been out one night filling a prescription for an ailing relative and had witnessed the murder of a youngster. He'd shared this information with a neighborhood worker and was, shortly after, picked up and charged with beating and raping a schoolmate he swore he barely spoke to; he swore he'd been framed.

Mason was all for calling J. B. Stoner to the stand. "Whereabouts unknown," the paper said. "Jumped bail," Vernon reported. "On vacation," a crony maintained. "I'm confident that my client will not forfeit his bail," Stoner's attorney was quoted as saying. The bail bondsman merely grinned for the reporters. Lafayette continued to hope that the GBI agent who'd infiltrated a Klan family in Atlanta would be subpoenaed. A Kluxer had told the wired informant that he and his friends had killed nigger boys before and would do so again. That was in the April-dated memorandum Spence had secured from Judge Webber. There was no word from the snoopers on this angle. That the prosecution had tagged to Williams ten additional cases, one being Lubie Geter, mentioned in the wiretap, the other Clifford Jones, about whose murder several witnesses had given testimony to the police over a year ago, forced Inquiry to conclude that either the Brady file had been doctored or there'd been a hell of a lot of tampering with investigative reports before the DA's office began assembling its case.

While Inquiry members continued to update the packets and look for an opening, others in the corridors those first few days converged on one name as the prize witness: "Cheryll Jenkins," the name Williams had offered on May 22 when asked by the stakeout detail why he was on the bridge. To make sure he'd know where to meet her, a prospective client he'd made an appointment with, Williams was checking out her address.

By the second day of the actual trial, security had been relaxed. The thousands of out-of-town and overseas reporters who'd been expected to create havoc with the courtroom seating never showed. Surprise witnesses and anticipated media throngs crowding into the sixty-seat press box were forgotten about. A space in the press box was made available for former mayoral candidate Mildred Glover. Seat passes were made available to the defendant's parents, to attorneys' relatives and errand runners, and for various friends of the court. Relatives of "official" and "unofficial" Missing and Murdered victims had to scramble for seats like any other miscellaneous persons.

Near the first checkpoint in the courthouse lobby, Zala noticed a law professor and her students, a class who'd been in attendance from December 28 to January 5 for jury selection, discussing the Miranda law and flipping through their notebooks to answer the professor's question, how many times Williams had been questioned but not read his rights. Either they'd arrived too late to be seated upstairs in courtroom 404, or the trial had recessed early because of the expected blizzard. But people were still noisy overhead. Zala went through the surveillance, glad she'd taken Schumake's advice, and headed for the stairs. Perhaps she would spot someone who fit the descriptions Sonny and Michael had given.

She'd been shocked by the eagerness people displayed to be picked as jurors. Some, of course, asked to be excused because of young dependents or ailing relatives at home; none on the grounds that the trial was a hoax. After a few rounds of elimination, the judge asked those remaining if they could live within the limits of sequestration and the prospect of a lengthy trial. A very few had asked to be excused, citing medical conditions or claustrophobia, or other reasons murmured so low only the hired lip readers who worked for either team understood and passed ahead to the tables on squares of yellow paper.

Asked if he or she had formed any opinion concerning the guilt or innocence of the defendant, each prospective juror had said no. Despite the round-the-clock repetition of "beast," "fiend," "mad-dog killer," and "child snatcher finally jailed" from June to December. Despite the "no more murders since Williams's arrest" official bulletins. Despite the well-publicized behavior of the authorities; state patrol roadblocks discontinued; FBI agents withdrawn; undercover police on park duty reassigned; Task Force personnel drastically reduced; Task Force posters removed from phone booths, corner waste bins, public walls. Safety education programs in the schools were no more, civilian search teams had disbanded, Community Watch had wound down, people had stopped wearing green ribbons; but no prospective juror had formed an opinion concerning the defendant's guilt, and Sunday sermons urged people to give thanks and return to normal.

Nor, they had said, were they related to or acquainted in any way with the defendant. The man whose picture, whose parents, whose bio, habits, home, dog, car, resumé, and psychological profile had filled the news for six months running. Not acquainted in any way with the man whose photo had been flashed at community centers, parks, skating rinks, music stores, funeral parlors, recording studios, schools, gas stations, movie houses, bus stops, and MARTA stations, the Neighborhood Art Center, Cap'n Peg's fast-food joint, and apartment complexes from Dixie Hills to the Jackson Parkway Bridge as the attorneys' foot soldiers scoured the city, frequently crossing the path of Inquiry scouts, looking for potential witnesses. Two prospective jurors who'd survived the first few rounds of peremptory challenges used to live in the Verbena–Anderson Park neighborhood, an erstwhile neighbor had notified the defense table.

"You didn't miss anything this morning," a woman on the landing was saying to her companion, whom she recognized as one of Mattie's neighbors. "A bunch of landlords and apartment-house managers testified that no Cheryll Jenkins lives anywhere near the bridge. Like those guys know who the hell's in them apartments."

"So big deal. Since when do you need an alibi for driving over a bridge?"

Zala made way on the stairs for people coming from the Techwood trial. Judging from their dress and conversation, they were supporters of the "outside agitators" and "jungle joes," the members of the Techwood Homes Defense Squad who had been charged in the spring with displaying weapons in public, and a few for possessing weapons without proper permit. Additional charges against three dated back to 1979 and 1980. For demonstrating on the Atlanta University campus when Lester Maddox was giving the commencement address and later when then First Lady Rosalynn Carter came to speak, they'd been charged with disturbing the peace. Though those charges had long since been docketed, they were used again at the trial that had been going on since December 4. Things were apparently going well for the defendants, though they faced four-year sentences and fines of four thousand dollars.

Zala recognized the woman ahead of her at the corridor checkpoint as an aide who used to help pick jurors, help read the judge's expressions, the opposing teams', witnesses', and jurors'. A host of lip readers, body-language experts, linguists, behaviorists, sociologists, criminologists, and psychologists were in court each day as guests of the prosecution, the defense, or the judge. It was their job to study postures, gestures, facial expressions, tics, eye movements, breathing rhythms, all the numerous variables that might help them determine the outcome of the trial. Along with the defendant's family, the attorneys' relatives, friends, and errand runners, a few members of STOP, court artists, and media people from newspapers not prestigious enough to secure them a seat in the press box, these experts had seat passes and filled up the first five rows on either side of the center aisle. Male relatives of victims on the Task Force list, unfamiliar to the bailiff, had frequently been locked out.

The Williams family seemed to be totally friendless in court. There was no cheering section for Wayne Williams other than his parents, who sat behind him slightly to one side or the other each day.

Past the checkpoint, Zala continued on to courtroom 404. Opportunity, means, and motive thus far had not been established as promised in the prosecution's opening statement on January 5, day 1. Nor, as far as Zala could tell, had the prosecution even established that the two dead men fished from the Chattahoochee were in fact Cater and Payne and had been in fact murdered. Payne's and Cater's relatives disputed several key features of identification, just as several relatives of victims attached to the charges by "fiber pattern" disputed the clothing identified as their child's. Binder, in cross-examining the coroners about Cater and Payne, had succeeded in having heart trouble, suicide, and accident not ruled out as cause of death. According to the law students who spent the recesses below by the vending machine, the whole trial was illegal anyway because of venue. The splash the stakeout team said they heard on May 22 would have occurred in the Cobb County sector of the river, not in Fulton County. On day 2, when the prosecution introduced a twelve-foot model of the bridge, the place where their expert witnesses said the bodies had entered the water was also in Cobb County.

What did the prosecution have? A splash, some fibers, some hairs. On day 3, the stakeout officer who said he'd been a lifeguard and could distinguish the splash of a human body from that of a beaver was forced to answer no when Binder asked if he made any attempt to jump in and save the person he thought he'd heard hit the water. Watching the police on the Jackson Parkway Bridge attempt to simulate the May splash had become an October spectator sport. People watched the authorities heave rocks, cinder blocks, and other objects into the river, watched them try to attempt to muffle the sound of car tires going over the expansion plates in the bridge to justify "Williams sneaked across," and pointed out to one another how high the rail had been before it had been lowered, asking whether the short, pudgy Williams could have heaved Cater over the rail unassisted. As for the prosecution's witnesses, so far they were on the order of the apartment managers Mattie's neighbor had said the courtroom laughed at.

But then, what did the defense have? They had no money, that was for sure. It was as out-of-pocket an enterprise as Inquiry. From STOP members, Zala had heard in the corridors that there hadn't been a case quarter to retain Dettlinger's services. This had been said over and over and early on to squelch the rumor that the reason he'd turned down the prosecution team's offer was that they hadn't met his price. The defense didn't have much by way of appeal, either. Binder was abrasive, and Welcome fumbled badly with names and dates. On the other hand, Jack Mallard, the assistant district attorney handling the questioning, won jurors over each time he made an incisive point, then smiled slyly their way. It looked bad for Williams.

Squares of a manila folder were taped over the door panes of courtroom 404. When Zala pushed at the door, she felt resistance on the other side. She could hear Attorney Binder shouting at a witness. There was no way that the body fished out of the river on May 24 and ID'd as Cater could have been the splash heard on May 22; bodies don't decompose that badly in water, and he'd been seen on May 21. Actually, Zala had heard, Cater had been reported seen on the twenty-third as well. She leaned her ear to the crack. Stivers, the Fulton County medical examiner, argued that bodies can decompose swiftly. Binder came at him again. Stivers was firm: No, he wasn't trying to make the autopsy fit the splash theory, the facts were facts.

Zala draped her coat over her arm and headed for the water fountain, then sat on the stairs and eavesdropped on the two officers at the checkpoint.

They were discussing how they would conduct the trial. She sat up straight when she heard them name two witnesses they would call to take the stand: Hosea Williams, state rep and community worker, who'd had many a run-in with the police over, presumably, traffic violations; and state rep and civil rights leader Tyrone Brooks, who apparently was not a favorite either with the two white policemen. Hosea Williams and Tyrone Brooks were the subjects Zala had heard being discussed whenever she dropped by Paschal's to pick up chicken dinners to take home. The cigar smokers who held court in the entranceway and the toothpick chewers who lounged against the window of the pool hall two doors down often traded versions of what must have transpired the day Williams and Brooks went to Wayne Williams's house before his arrest. The stories differed widely but converged on two points: The politicos had urged him to tell all, to name names, to come clean. And he'd said, no way.

The Kibitzers downtown were certain that Hosea had promised to get a huge portion of the reward awarded to Wayne Williams's family if he would talk. Wayne was in cahoots with a bunch of religious kooks who molested children, then disposed of them so they wouldn't squeal. Zala had heard them theorizing as to what would come out at the trial and how it might impact on Andy Young's administration if it looked like Black people couldn't run the city. "If Maynard had just walked out of his house and gone around the corner to express condolences to Mrs. Mathis, none of this would've happened," one of the cigar smokers had said the other night. This version of the case Zala had had her fill of: the notion that it never was a real case, but that the media had exploited the grief-stricken parents of the kind of kids that often got into deadly trouble; then, the thing blown up to create a phantom whodunit, those predisposed to exploit the situation got into the act; and next thing you knew, the administration was saddled with a nationally known embarrassment.

The officers at the corridor checkpoint seemed to have not even a chewed toothpick's worth of evidence for feeling that Hosea Williams and Tyrone Brooks knew what Wayne Williams had been up to for two years.

No matter how Zala strained to hear around the corner, no sound came from the courtroom. There'd been times when the only activity going on at all was the sketching. Often, for as long as five minutes, Judge Cooper would stare into space as the two attorneys waited for him to render an opinion as to whether the jury would be escorted out to the jury room while the attorney played out the scenario he thought relevant and legally appropriate, or could remain to hear it. The jurors would doze, waiting. The bailiff, having admonished spectators to put newspapers away and cease talking, would lean against the wall, waiting. The sketch artists alone remained busy, one fist full of drawing pencils, pens, and colored chalks, steadying the sketch pads, the other hand working swiftly.

Zala sat on the steps hugging her coat and bag and stared at the shadows thrown on the floor by the banister rails. For a minute she was back in the Georgia Sea Islands, squinting at the blue-green-mauve gray of the Spanish moss that hung from the live oaks in the cemetery five walking miles from Cousin Sonia's house. Sonny kneeling at her father's grave, examining the decorations. Sonny turning to ask her if she knew for sure that she was her father's daughter. Spence had gotten around finally to telling the family that he'd been adopted. The issue of blood ties and obligations was very much Sonny's theme for two straight weeks.

"Looks like they're eating well, though," the first person out the door was saying over his shoulder.

Zala got up and slid along the wall, hoping to see someone trying to hail her—a member of Inquiry, the stalwarts of STOP, Teo and Sue Ellen, the mortician's assistant who'd sworn last fall he'd demand to take the stand and testify about the state of some of the bodies: hypodermic needle marks in the genital area, ritually carved, castrated.

"The trucker, you mean," the man's companion said, brushing by Zala, her heels on the baseboard.

"Guess dinner is the highlight of the evening for them," someone sighed sympathetically.

Nine men, three women; eight Black, four white; two Black

women, six Black men, one white woman, three white men. The jury
was indexed, cross-indexed, described, and analyzed, but mostly felt
sorry for. When they weren't penned up in the box, they were being escorted out under armed guard to be locked in the jury room. Back at the
hotel out by the airport, they were locked up in a common room for a
game of cards and some small talk about anything but the case. Escorted to the bathroom or to the hall for a smoke. After dinner, locked
alone in a hotel room with no radio, TV, newspaper, magazine, or
phone, until the knock on the door in the morning to be escorted back
to the courthouse.

Several more people went by discussing which jurors had gained
weight and guessing how much weight the defendant had lost. Weight
wasn't all Wayne Williams had lost, Zala was thinking, craning her
neck to see whom she might talk to. After months of playing musical
chairs with his attorneys, Williams hiring and firing Mary Welcome
and Tony Axum, the two in turn dismissing each other, Williams had
lost his seat, leaving Binder and Welcome to battle the state's five attorneys and their well-oiled, moneyed machinery. No more press con-
ferences, no more showboat statements for his lawyer to feed to the
public: Wayne Williams was no longer even a consultant in the thrust-
and-parry that determined his life. He was captive in what Leah called
the Slaton-Binder-Cooper troika. By the time he took the stand in his
own defense, the parameters for disclosure would be as hard as cement.

Of the three men of the troika, Judge Clarence Cooper was the least
discussed in the press and the least mentioned in the corridor. A specter,
an icon; the facts about him were few. Zala knew that he'd been responsible for the use of the airport-type detectors. That he'd worked for
District Attorney Lewis Slaton his first eight years out of law school.
First Black assistant prosecutor in Atlanta, thanks to the urging of the
Urban League's Vernon Jordan. For five years a judge in municipal
court, thanks to Maynard Jackson's appointment. Then he ran for and
won a superior court seat as prosecutor in 1980. Word was, he maintained close ties with his first boss, DA Slaton.

No, things didn't look good for Williams, Zala heard over and over
going down to the lobby. And she thought, spotting two young attorneys from the shuttle group, annoyed that court had recessed for snow,
that whatever information Williams might have could be easily kept

under wraps. People might never know the means and motives and identities of the killers who'd wiped out over a hundred Black children, women, and men. Killers free to strike again while attention was fixed on one man being used to close the books on the officially Missing and Murdered twenty-nine.

"They're bound to carry the recess over a few days," one of the law students was saying on the courthouse steps. "It's supposed to be a big snow."

"Big snow *job* you mean," the professor said, following Zala down to the sidewalk.

Zala looked at the clock up front in the West End Mall A&P. She'd lost twenty minutes somewhere. At 3:07 the snow had begun to come down hard. By the time she'd gotten off the bus, it was sticking. Traveling up and down the aisles, she'd heard someone remark the time and predict that by 4:00 it would really be blowing. She'd looked at the clock then. She stared at it now as people grabbing up whole fryers on sale jostled her. The old men were leaving, she heard, the old men who carried shoppers to and from the mall for a dollar or so. The line in front of the telephone outside by the shopping cart depot was long, running all the way past the front windows and doors to the new soda machine that talked back when a coin was dropped in. Zala loaded three whole fryers and two hamburger packs in her cart and shoved on.

In produce a young worker was hosing down the greens while another mopped. People were losing their footing reaching over each other to snatch up mustards, collards, and turnip greens without the usual finicky inspection of leaves. Her cart skidded and she rammed into a stack of grapefruits, toppling the fruit. A little girl playing open-sesame with the front door was yanked off the mat by an older brother. The door continued to whoosh open, wheeze closed, then spring open again, snow swirling in on the black rubber mat. Near the door, women with babies on their hips were asking each other how they planned to get home. Zala put three grapefruit into her cart and replaced the rest on the stack, then started up another aisle, to the frozen section.

People were leaning way over into the cold box stacking TV dinners up to their chins. Boxes of frozen chitterlings were traded for frozen pizzas as carts jammed with white parcels from seafood-deli on top and dog-food sacks below stalled, the bent lower racks blocking the wheels.

"Take it easy." The security guard was trotting, with one hand holding his holster steady. He urged people up and down the aisle to calm down. Every few feet he was stopped by an elder who required something from a high shelf—coconut cream, bottled guava, Jamaican hot pepper sauce. The guard was called back to the front, the store manager on the mike. Arguments had broken out on both express lines. Someone was holding things up clipping coupons at the register; another was trying to buy space heaters with food stamps. "Take it easy . . . take it easy," the guard kept saying as he trotted along.

The man in front of Zala on line turned around and Zala jumped. "Bet they get the snowplow out this time," he chuckled. "And if we're lucky, somebody actually knows how to operate the damn thing."

"Assuming it ain't rusted out altogether," the woman in front of the man said.

"Leastways they'll take a pause in evictions," said a woman in the line next to them. "I never heard of throwing people outdoors in a storm such as this. But then you never know."

The man in front of Zala stepped out of line to empty a box of Baby Ruths into his basket, and she saw Murray up front by the window shelf that in summer held sacks of charcoal briquets, in winter held manufactured fireplace logs. He was biting off his gloves and looking at her.

"Let a little air out of your tires, that'll help," he said to two men loading their arms with the logs. "And if you're heading Northside way, get you some sawdust from the lumberyard. Strew that around in your driveway. As good as cinders and better than salt," he told them, still looking at Zala.

"Guess so," one of the men said, grunting loudly when his friend piled on two logs at once. "Salt will eat up a car."

"Attention!" The store manager leaned up over the partition of his booth, then kicked something back there into place to stand on. "Please remain calm!" he said, his voice tinged with hysteria. "Let's be neighborly! There are plenty of cars and trucks outside, enough to get everyone home in time for supper. If we're neighborly—" he was adding when whatever he was standing on caved in and he disappeared with a crash. People laughed more heartily than they might have had it only been raining.

"I can get you home, Miz Spencer." Murray had materialized by her side and startled her. He pointed to his truck blinking in the parking lot beyond the telephone queue. A sliver of ice slid from his hat brim into her basket. "A bus skidded onto the median out there by I-20. No telling when they'll get that straightened out."

"Thank you," was all she could think of to say.

"All right. All right then."

When she walked into the house and dropped the bags, they didn't give her time to get her coat off.

"Look at this, Mama!" Kenti was pulling her toward the TV, where she turned from one snowstorm to another.

Kofi swung her around to get her attention. "Guess what all that noise was on the roof? Guess what the landlord and them found up there?"

"The landlord? The landlord was here?" Zala looked around for Spence. Sonny was stretched out on the couch with a book, his feet on the cushions, his shoes on. "Who let him in? Where's your daddy?"

"The big bald-headed guy came and got Dad. They went somewhere and Gloria had to go home. But Dad called back and said it was all right for Glo to leave. But come look. Lemme show you. They were raccoons on the roof them times making all that noise. The leak was on account of them. They roofers are gonna fix it." He was pulling her toward the hall closet.

"Wait a minute. Hold it. What was the landlord doing here?"

"Look at this, Mama. Guess which snow is Atlanta, Channel 11 or—8?"

"Hold it a second."

"He brought the roofers by to see the leak."

"How'd he know? Who talked to Gittens about the leak? I only noticed it this morning looking for my boots." She turned to Sonny. He plopped the open book down on his face. "Who let them in? I told you not to let anybody in this house."

"He's the landlord, Ma."

"I don't care if Jesus comes—we've told you! Did he use a key or did he ring the bell?"

Kofi looked toward the sofa, then down at the puddles around Zala's boots. "Sonny let him in." Kofi moved to the groceries, but Sonny got up and got between.

"One minute," she said, but Sonny went past her and into the bathroom.

"You better take your boots off, Mama. You messing up the rug."

"I beg your pardon, miss." Zala sat down in the chair and looked from the bathroom to the TV.

Kenti swung herself around and went back to the knob. People were slipping and sliding out of view between snowbanks. On another channel, a bus was up to its eyes in the snow. The weatherman in New York, calm and friendly, pointed to the weather map. Then New Yorkers climbing over dirty white mountains waved at the cameras.

"Now watch this," Kenti said, turning channels. In Chicago, people holding their coats and hats ducked down past the camera; the screen went opaque. The weatherman, neatly groomed and chatty, pointed to the weather map with a schoolteacher pointer.

"Now this is Atlanta!" Kofi chimed in.

The weatherman in Atlanta was out of his jacket, sleeves rolled up, tie loose, hair wild. "He's going to pop a vessel!" Kofi laughed, throwing his body around the living room as the weatherman gestured crazily. Kenti was lowering, then turning up, the volume.

"Please turn that thing down, I can't think."

Motorists along Peachtree got out of their cars; cars were skidding around them and stopping at odd angles in the street. Drivers walked off looking helpless and left their cars where they were. Elderly people with rugs and blankets across their shoulders waved to the camera from the warmth of an emergency shelter. People wrapped in newspapers huddled under the highway ramp. Buses, patrol cars, and tow trucks blinked red, amber, white, blue, their lights in sync with the yellow blinkers of the highway barriers. In a hotel lobby people crowded around a grinning man standing on an end table. He waved a room key, auctioning it off.

"I asked you to turn it off. I want to hear how the landlord got here."

"He just came, Ma. Him and the roofers. They said they wanted to see the problem. But guess what? All them noises? It was a family of raccoons raiding all the garbage cans and taking it up on our roof to eat.

There were chicken bones and potatoes and steak bones and orange peels. The stuff up there was rotting right through the roof. That's how come we got that leak in the closet. They patched it after they saw what it was."

"Who was inside doing what and who was outside and where were you all? And where was your father?"

Kofi plopped down on the floor and crossed his legs in his lap and took it slowly. "We were washing the dishes, me and Kenti."

"Like you told us to," Kenti added, then turned to Florida. Huge stakes had been stuck in the ground of the groves and lit. They glared an ugly, smoky orange.

"And Sonny went to the door."

"You heard the bell or the knock or he just went?"

"Whatcha mean?" Kofi shrugged and looked up at Kenti. "I guess he heard the knock. I was washing the dishes."

"Me also. I don't like how the landlord told us to stay out of the way. But he got the closet fixed." She talked over her shoulder and began raising and lowering the volume again.

"So then what?"

"The landlord came in and said he wanted the roof men to see the problem."

"I'm trying to get the sequence straight. Your father and Gloria got you from school. Your father left with Lafayette. Gloria went home. It's snowing hard, and Gittens shows up with some men who say they want to check out the house. You three are here alone and let them in. But who called them?"

Kofi rolled over on the floor and pulled two of the bags toward him by their plastic handles. "Don't look at me."

"Well," Kenti said, twisting a braid around her finger. "I told you yesterday there was a hole in the closet. But you didn't listen. I told Mrs. Grier this morning when I saw her. She probably called the land-lord."

"I see."

"Sonny brung them the stool."

"Did what, Kenti?"

"The step stool from the kitchen. Sonny got it so the landlord could climb up into the spooky space in the hall ceiling.

"Where were the roofers?"

"First they were standing around in here, then he sent them outside."

"Did they have a ladder?"

Kofi rolled up onto his knees and looked at her. "I see what you mean, Ma. No, they didn't have a ladder. They just climbed up. But they did clear out all that garbage. And when they came back in, they asked for some water to mix the plaster and stuff. Then they fixed it in the closet. At least I think they did."

"Go see, Kofi. Go and see."

"You don't believe they were real roof men?" Kenti turned the TV off.

Zala pressed her lips together and listened. There was silence from the bathroom. From the closet, Kofi came and held out his hand. Globs of white were on the tips of his fingers.

"Go back to the part where the roofers were outside and Gittens was inside. Where were you?"

Kofi worked his mouth. His bottom lip disappeared under his top teeth while he thought. He wiped his hands on the back of his pants. "Me and Kenti were in the kitchen mostly, and Sonny was helping the landlord. You know, holding the stool steady."

Kenti came and stood by the arm of Zala's chair. "We were in the kitchen, Mama, 'cause he said we should stay out from underfoot on account of the roofers charge by the minute."

"Uh-huh. Sonny and Gittens were in the hallway. Were they talking, laughing, or what?"

"I didn't hear anything. Except the landlord poking around in the crawl space. You know, Ma, like the time we were up in there. That's all I heard."

"They were whispering then?"

"Mama, you scaring me."

"I'm sorry. Then what happened?"

"Nothing much. The roof guys mixed up the plaster and fooled around in the closet."

"Fooled around."

Kofi laughed. "You're making me say things I don't mean, Ma. I mean they fixed it. One of the guys had a trowel. Then the roofers told the landlord what the problem was and that they could come back and do a good job after the snowstorm. Then they all left."

"They all left together? The landlord didn't hang around for a few minutes?"

"We were in the kitchen, Ma."

"How long were Sonny and he in the hall without you two or the roofers?"

"You mean alone?" Kenti whispered.

Kofi grabbed up three bags of groceries and lugged them to the kitchen. "Ask Sonny. He let'm in, he was in the hall with'm. I'm hungry."

"Kenti, how long was it after Daddy left that the landlord came?"

"Mm . . . um . . . uhn . . . But I know you better get out that coat. You wetting up the chair."

"Beg pardon?"

Kenti lifted two bags but set them down quickly and looked in instead, taking out what she wanted. "You gonna fix dinner now?" She pulled out two boxes. "I see you got macaroni and cheese. I can fix it, I think."

"Just put the groceries up."

"If you come and watch, I can do it."

"Put 'em up, Kenti."

"Put 'em up? Put 'em up on the ceiling?"

"Put the groceries away, please." Zala got up and looked at the bathroom door. She went instead to the front window.

"I'm going to cook, Ma."

Zala waved her on into the kitchen, then looked out to the street trying to piece it together. The landlord had been hanging around, circling the block perhaps. And when he saw Spence leave, the coast was clear, he made contact. Lafayette had come, no doubt, for whatever reason had kept Inquiry from court. Zala then thought of a more likely scenario. Lafayette, at Spence's request, had been tracking Gittens. When he spotted Gittens's car in the area, he and Spence, as previously planned, cleared the way. Gittens then made his move and confirmed their suspicions. Zala looked across the street. Surely they would not have gone far, and they'd see she was home. There was no sign of anyone hiding behind the low hedges in Paulette's yard. There was no bush big enough to speak of in the Robinsons' yard. Perhaps the two had gone after Gittens. They would call now.

When Zala turned toward the phone, she found Kenti still standing by the chair, a box of cereal under one arm, a box of Kraft macaroni dinner under the other.

"You could've brought the groceries home in dry boxes, Mama. Then we coulda used'm to start packing."

"You better shut up and get in here!" Kofi hollered. "If you know what I know!"

Zala took a good look at her daughter. How grown she seemed, standing by the chair, her legs astride, the boxes under her arms, her gaze unwavering. She didn't budge when Kofi called again. She didn't hunch her shoulders up and lean against the chair under her mother's stare.

"I'm sorry, Kenti, I didn't mean to snap at you before."

"You did mean it, 'cause you did it and you didn't have to, you grown."

Zala bent down and unbuckled her boots. "Please help Kofi put the groceries away, and I'm really sorry."

"You coming?"

"In a minute."

"I'm going to put the big pot on to boil the water, then I'll need watching to see how to do this. I want to do this."

"All right."

"If you waiting for him to come out of that bathroom, the food'll be all burned up."

"Be there in a minute."

Zala thought she would need more than a minute to think it through. But she couldn't get past the part where Spence had used the children as decoys. So it had to be the other way around.

"I want you out of that bathroom, Sonny. Right now."

He opened the door as Kofi let out a groan in the kitchen. "I wish you would calm down," Sonny said, going to the kitchen, turning his head only slightly in her direction. "Things are all quiet and peaceful, then here you come." He pulled a chair out from the table and whirled it behind him on one leg, barring her way. "I'll do the hamburgers, Kofi. You don't half cook'm through," he said, done with her.

"Sonny, I want to hear what you know about all this roof business," she said from the hall.

Sonny walked back from the stove to the table so she could see him fully. It wasn't the same as he'd done months before: lookatme, lookatme, the haircut, the capped tooth, the hat his father had bought him. He had his hands on his hips, and his mouth was hiked up to one side.

"Would you leave it. You want to make a big thing out of nothing, save it for Dr. Perry. She'll go for it. Me, I just want to eat and finish my homework."

"Who the hell are you talking to?"

He sucked his teeth and went back to the stove. "Get the rest of the groceries," he said, tapping Kofi on the shoulder.

"Who you think you talking to now? I ain't your slave."

"Everybody be quiet." Kenti banged the box of cereal down on the table. "Everybody in this house is talking all the time and don't even hug or say hello. So why don't everybody just be quiet."

Kenti looked around at her mother, whose eyes were still blazing. Then she turned her back and tore the top off the blue-and-white box.

Wednesday, March 10, 1982

"We got grits. We got hot skillet biscuits. We got Southern fried chicken, quiche, nachos, lox, sushi, pizza, egg rolls, and paella. We got Six Flags Over Georgia, Stone Mountain, the zoo, and the lovely Chattahoochee. Got the Falcons, the Braves, and *E.T. the Extra-Terrestial* on a first-run basis. Got carpeted subways, decorated tile in the stations, a stadium, a symphony, the ballet, and an art museum. Got the Merchandise Mart, the World Trade Congress Center, the world's tallest hotel, and an airport so big it's liable to run its own candidate for Congress. . . ."

Spence followed the tour bus weaving leisurely up the newly widened street respecting none of the freshly painted lines and dashes in the blacktop. Placards on the back and sides of the bus promoted Broadway shows on the Southern circuit. On the Saturday night of February 20, a festive *King and I* crowd had been caught in the glare of TV lights there to catch the jurors' return to civilian life: after nine weeks of listening and twelve and a half hours of deliberation, they had brought in two verdicts of guilty.

"Aunty Paulette's plane gets in at 10:10, Dad."

Spence looked in the rearview at his sons, confused for a minute. They should have been in school. The soccer ball to his chest, elbows stuck out, Sonny was swiveling the globe against his shirt front, looking at nothing. Kofi was waving to passengers on the tour bus, those who weren't looking over the roof of their car, Aunty Delia's car, to an apartment building going up on the next street. The formal facade stopped abruptly at the third floor.

"Always building," Spence murmured. "But it's always a thing."

"We got steel-and-glass towers. Got Georgia red-clay straw bricks, and the famed Georgia pine. We got long, long-burning fuses, short memories, and coolant systems that are state of the art. Got false fronts in place and flax at our backs. Got covens and klaverns and twitchy commandos. Got funeral wreaths fading on doors in our neighborhoods. Black armbands and green ribbons discoloring in the back of dresser drawers. Got Twinkies set on saucers and chocolate milk for curfew-free children bounding in from play at 3:30 or 9:00 or even 10:45. We got names, dates, events boxed, locked, and buried. Got walls well erected against question and challenge. And roofs bolted fast against all types of storms. . . ."

"Crowbar," Spence muttered, passing the bus and entering onto the highway for the last clip of the trip to pick up the wedding party.

"Crowbar?" Sonny leaned forward for a minute, then felt he knew what his father was grinding his teeth about. He never let up. There was a case in the paper lately about murdered women. Lafayette and them were trying to get the police to see that the women were part of the whole Missing and Murdered thing. They'd been running around doing that since the big snow. They hardly came to the house anymore, for meetings. Only a few now; mostly they hung out at the garage on Memorial or stood around talking in the side lot junky with car parts. They kept saying they had to move fast 'cause the Task Force kept getting smaller and Williams's new attorney was getting nowhere arguing for a new trial.

"Hope yet," Spence said, talking to himself, both sons with their faces turned to side windows ignoring him now.

There was hope. Like Lux the Leather Illuminator down at Simmons's had said, "All closed eyes ain't sleep and all goodbyes ain't gone." There were still pockets of interest and people who wouldn't let the case go. James Baldwin had been coming to town off and on; a book was rumored. Sondra O'Neale, the Emory University professor, hadn't abandoned her research, either. From time to time, TV and movie types were in the city poking around for an angle. Camille Bell was moving to Tallahassee to write up the case from the point of view of the STOP committee. The vets had taken over *The Call* now that Speaker was working full-time with the Central American Committee. The Revolutionary Communist Party kept running pieces on the case in the *Revolutionary Worker*. Whenever Abby Mann sent down a point man for his proposed TV docudrama, the Atlanta officials and civil rights leaders would go off the deep end. Dettlinger and Prugh were putting their heads together on a book. So long as there were people who kept the thing going, Spence could stay on the case without feeling he was alone, or hallucinating.

Spence stole a glance in the rearview at Sonny. If he let out the rope and gave Sonny some slack, the boy would eventually lead him to where he wanted to go. Zala kept harping on the landlord, browbeating the boy. But there was more than one way to skin a cat.

"We're going to make it," Kofi said, looking at the clock on the airport tower.

Mother and daughter sat on the floor by the TV, the younger unbraiding the older one's hair. The house around them stood back, separate and chilled, aloof from the cartons and barrels, apart from the furniture pushed together and numbered with squares of red stickers. When the news came on, the three females gathered as round a campfire. Through naked windows the sky showed gray like lead.

Brass handles of a casket gleamed. Schoolmate pallbearers in white gloves carried their chum down the steps. Grieving mothers seen through the gauze of black veils. School pictures, the long-ago smiles fading as the image dissolved and the courthouse appeared. The flag, the paneling, the gavel in its wooden saucer. Then "clearance," the leitmotif of officials. Ten, then twelve, then fourteen, cases "cleared by arrest"—why try him again, trials being costly?

Homer Williams: "I don't see how anybody anywhere could find my son guilty." Camille Bell in her trademark glasses: "The jury was given no one else to look at; the real killers have not been found." An unidentified Blood in a leather-trimmed beret: "He's a political prisoner." Then Andy Young, confident that the jury knew what it was doing, rubber-stamped the entire enterprise.

An expert from the FBI Behavioral Science Unit came on the screen to say that Williams's behavior jibed with three of the nine classic features of the serial murderer's profile. One, serial murderers were invariably police buffs. Williams was a scanner freak and owned a car purchased at a state patrol auction. Zala blinked. It had been said so many times, on the block at least, that the white Chevy wagon had been bought from an uncle in Columbus, Georgia, she wondered what car the expert was talking about. And would he mention that ambulance and fire engine chasing was Williams's work as a free-lance news pho-tographer? She dropped her head to the left as Kenti brushed her hair. Delia reached over and massaged her shoulder. Zala closed her eyes.

Two, serial murderers usually went out of their way to make post-mortem contact. According to the authorities, Williams had attended one of the funerals and before that had applied for a job as a morgue photographer. Zala opened her eyes again and tilted her head to the right as Kenti brushed. How many features did Leah fit, or Vernon, or Dowell? She was sure Williams had applied for the job in 1979, not postmortem.

Three, serial murderers invariably collected souvenirs. The stakeout officers who'd stopped Williams on the bridge had reported seeing clothing in the car that could not have been Williams's, and the family had boxed up numerous items between the bridge incident and the first lengthy questioning on June 3. But, Zala frowned, Dettlinger main-tained that the bag of clothes from the Chevy was still on the back porch of the Williams home, and no one had had any interest in it.

The review continued. Zala tried to stay awake to see if they would interview or even mention Mildred Glover and Annie Rogers, mother of Patrick Rogers. They'd begun to organize a second committee, Par-ents for Justice, during the period when agency after agency had been going after STOP. But there was only the now-famous shot of the con-victed man in an isolated cell, the camera looking down on him through the bars, the shadow of the bars slanting across the no-longer-pudgy Wayne Williams. Then a series of on-the-street remarks from children playing in the parks, women hanging clothes on the line, men hosing down cars. In one crowd scene, Zala recognized some of the men and women who'd come down from Harlem for the September 9 rally. They'd questioned her closely about the zoning method. "What, no precincts!" They couldn't get over it. "You mean it's all centralized in one or two buildings per county? That's insane!" they had screamed, collaring others who'd come from Detroit, Chicago, Cleveland, Dayton, and Philly to compare notes. "Police work is all about squealing. Who the hell is going to hop on a bus and travel ten miles to go up into some big-ass building to talk to a cop they've never laid eyes on?"

Zala waited in vain for the appearance of the new group that had been formed to badger the Task Force into beefing up its personnel and getting down to a real investigation. There were still at least six cases open on the books. And too, the story of the murdered women was being forced back into the news by adamant community workers—this was the work Inquiry had concentrated on when they realized the trial would disclose nothing. The review did not include Parents for Justice; there was not even a word from the Williams's attorney Lynn Whatley.

"You should try to take a nap," Delia urged, holding on to the hall-closet doorknob to get up from the floor. "I can help you set up the reception buffet and help you get the children dressed, but the Webbers are due and I've got to get the house reopened and spruced up. They ask about you all the time—did I say that?"

"You're a good soul, Delia."

"I'm going to be the flower girl and the pillow girl," Kenti said, getting up. She tried not to stand between them just in case they quit being so grown and just went on and hugged. Aunty Dee was smoothing the wrinkles out of her skirt and looking at Mama. Mama was looking down at the TV.

"Pillow girl?"

"I'm carrying Aunty Paulette's ring on a pillow."

"That's nice, honey."

Aunty Dee looked over at the table where Mama's pocketbook was, then she looked at Mama. "Zee, give it up," she said, and pulled her into her arms and hugged her. "Try to give it up. It's crazy."

Zala looked at the screen. The wrap-up was winding down.

"Case closed," the TV announcer said in front of the board full of school pictures. The children's faces hung on long after the news went off.

Between the suntanned legs of kids in college T-shirts and army youths dragging duffel bags, Spence saw the boys halfway down the concourse, scrambling after the ball, zigzagging past briefcases and flight bags, kicking and elbowing each other out of position, then broken-field-running down the carpeted gray expanse. Their sports play didn't draw the attention of any security guard. "Got yourself a couple of Peles there, brother," a skycap congratulated Spence and moved on.

With the tip of one sneaker, Kofi was edging the ball up over the top of the other the way Sonny had been teaching him all morning in the one corner of the yard where the jonquils had pushed through. The ball bumped up to the top of his shoelace and Kofi snapped his foot up and bunted the ball with his knee. He kicked a ground ball past a gift shop where a demonstrator was sending a model airplane out. It flew around in an arc to come back again to his hand.

Sonny, hearing his father's name being paged, brought the ball to a stop and kept it tight under his foot so Kofi couldn't move it. He motioned to Kofi, who stopped trying to wrestle the ball and turned. Dad was sprinting to the Delta information desk. He was bent over like he was trying to get a pencil and pad out of his pocket.

That's how Gaston would run dribbling an inner tube around the garage trying to get Sonny to play. Kofi would drop what he was doing, which was usually fooling around in the trays of metal parts, to go guard the "basket," the machine the tire was set on its side in. Sonny kind of liked Gaston, or at least he liked hanging out in the garage. There was a lot of long-handled junk and heavy steel tools for giving rubber and metal a good wallop, as Gaston liked to demonstrate, sweat flying and him laughing that weird laugh of his that sounded like someone up to no good in the night around the back of somebody's house and about to get caught. A goofy laugh of someone who was born to get caught. But that was the interesting thing. Gaston would scratch his head and scuff his boots and play country dumb, but he wasn't. He knew things.

While the others would talk war talk, Gaston would be watching him. So Sonny was extra careful around Gaston. He knew a lot about things that didn't go with his act. He knew all about explosives. And he sure had known how not to become a morphine junkie even though he'd been hit bad twice. He didn't even smoke or drink. And he knew how not to get caught up in war talk. Dad would be cracking his knuckles and pacing back and forth in there sweating from the talk and forgetting himself and next thing Sonny knew, Dad would pop his fingers upside Kofi's head and yell at him to stay away from the crossbow contraption Gaston had in there. It would take Dad a long time to get himself back together and apologize to Kofi. He wasn't a hitting father..

Gaston knew things like that Sonny wanted that bow. And when Lafayette asked him if he'd sell it to him, Gaston laughed his laugh and looked Sonny's way. Or like when Mason asked him about the white guys who'd come around asking if Gaston had souped up any cars lately

for "colored boys" who might be thinking about springing Wayne
Williams, Gaston had looked his way when he said they were Legionnaires. It was impossible for Ole Tee-Hee to know, but it was almost
like he did know that the word meant something to Sonny.

Grandaddy Wesley used to tell stories about Legionnaires, not so
much to Sonny and the others, but there'd be company, old people who
sat around drinking out of mayonnaise jars and talking over old race
stuff. Legionnaires with bats and clubs used to storm the railroad yards
where Grandaddy worked in the old days. They'd beat up on the
hoboes, then they'd go down to the river and bust up the bums who
lived there cooking food in tin cans over fires. Black people, cripples,
carnival people, drunks, and anybody else they could call scum and get
away with it, they'd bash them and fuck up their living places, whatever they were. And the sheriff would stand around chewing tobacco
and looking up at the sky the way Kofi did sometimes making up shit
like he knew all about constellations and the space program. But ole
Gaston, he didn't sidle up and ask Sonny things outright like the others did trying to get him to talk. Gaston laughed his laugh and did his
little two-step and watched.

And Sonny found out, standing there watching his father run from
the white phone at the information desk to the little alley where the
regular pay phones were, that he didn't mind that Gaston ran the country number on him. He kind of liked the guy. Mostly, he decided as Kofi
started pulling on the ball, because of the explosives. He wouldn't mind
getting his hands on a couple of sticks of dynamite. And he kind of had
the feeling Gaston knew this and might actually help him without
telling Dad.

"I bet I know what's up." Kofi waited for the two stewardesses
to understand that he wasn't moving and they'd have to split and go
around. "It's Ma. Betchu Michael remembered something and Ma
wants you home right away."

Kofi trotted after his brother, in no hurry to catch up. He wanted to
see if Sonny would walk into the phone area and ask, or if he'd hang on
the edge and spy.

Whenever Miss Em brought Michael by, the two big boys would
walk around each other like gangsters or cowboys, sizing each other up.
It was stupid. But then Miss Em was a little stupid too. She said mothers with growing sons needed to show boys the places white people

liked to put Black boys before they got to be men and couldn't be con-
trolled. Sonny was by the hall closet eavesdropping. Michael was in the
kitchen helping himself to the last of the baloney. And Mama was saying that that wasn't her idea of an educational outing. She'd been taking a first-aid law course at the Office of Equal Opportunity center,
where she and maybe Dad were going to be working soon. Sons and
daughters needed to be taught about their rights, was her comeback.
And then Miss Em said, "Well, they need to learn something, 'cause
boys think the whole purpose of having knees is to use up a can of Band-
Aids." Kofi didn't see the point of that joke.

"Who is it?" Kofi stood near the ice-cream machine.

"Paulette."

But before he could ask any more, his Dad took off with Sonny right
after him, and Kofi had to run like hell to hear what Sonny was saying.

"They're already at the house?"

"They haven't left Houston airport," Sonny said over his shoulder.
"There's a big crowd in the airport, she said, waiting for the new Houston police commissioner to touch down."

"So what? I thought they were getting married up here."

"You see who I see?"

Winded, Kofi came to a halt in front of the gate for the flight to
Houston. "We're not going to Houston, are we?"

"Use your eyes," Sonny said.

Passengers were ready to board. A couple was helping an old man
out of a wheelchair. An attendant was holding the line back until a
woman carrying a baby and tugging on the straps of a little kid carrying a panda went through the door. The line was long. On line were
Commissioner Lee Brown and his wife, Yvonne. He looked at Dad a
long time with his eyebrows up and then he nodded. Before Dad could
jump over a garment bag a man had unzipped on the floor to put something in, Brown and his wife had gone through the door.

"What's the deal?" But once again they were running, back to the
phones again, Dad looking like O. J. Simpson, hopping over tall ashtrays and stuff.

"The mayor of Houston was going to announce her choice for the
Houston police chief job this afternoon," Sonny explained, running
sideways. "The reporters got wind that the new guy was coming in on
flight 1154, so they're waiting for him."

"Brown?"

"Brown. Ole No-Rap Brown has slipped out of town without any-body knowing. And all this time, people were all over Napper because he got a job offer from California and if they let him go, that's the end of any chance to make the Task Force get down to business. But Brown split."

"Why is that so funny?"

Sonny never did say. He threw the ball from hand to hand double-daring Kofi to try for it. After a while the laugh was one of his sarcastic laughs like everybody was a stupid jerk but him.

The wedding guests were on the first floor. In the hall at the foot of the stairs, people took turns making calls on the phone and answering the door. Those in the living room made polite talk with the Foremans and the groom's relatives, one eye on the TV and one ear cocked toward the radio. What the hell could Andy Young say at this late date? The news broke in Houston at 10:54 a.m. when Brown's plane landed. By the time he and Yvonne left the airport at 11:15, the shit had hit the fan. Rank-and-file HPD were up in arms—not because Brown was Black, they said, but because Mayor Kathy Whitmore should have selected a local candidate for the post. The Houston City Council balked—not because Brown was Black, they explained, but because the executive search had been conducted in secrecy. They'd never heard of the guy till reporters called in from the airport. Who the hell was he anyway? The roving reporter queried Houston citizens, who echoed the beef. Who was this colored guy with a Ph.D.? Not that race was any problem, but the mayor had overlooked a lot of local talent to import this colored fellow, and that wasn't right.

The wedding guests buzzed through the first-floor rooms checking dates with each other. Brown and Whitmore had held a secret meeting in an undisclosed town outside of Houston about three and a half weeks ago, it had been learned. Damned if that wasn't when Brown had re-duced the Task Force personnel to a skeleton staff.

The musicians came in and their entrance broke up the talk. For a while people questioned each other about the groom, the honeymoon plans, and said lovely things to the Foremans about their daughter.

Ten minutes before Mayor Young's press conference was due, Brown was the subject again. He was the focus too of special news reports from Houston. The first Black Ph.D. in criminology from the University of California at Berkeley, he was also the first nominee for the post from outside of the Houston PD since 1941. The newsmen said, sounding more personal than professional, that many citizens were busy enough trying to get used to a woman mayor when out of the blue an out-of-town Black was slipped in under the very noses of the city's movers and shakers.

The wedding guests brought finger sandwiches by the plateload to the sofa and finally moved a small table with stuffed celery and fruit salad closer to the television. The Atlanta murders were offered as the most current episode in Brown's past. Since he'd been on the West Coast before he'd come to Atlanta, California's Zodiac Killer of women and girls was trotted out, followed by the case of Juan Corona, who'd killed twenty or more migrants. To cover Brown's Seattle years, the story picked up the torture-rape-bludgeon murders of Ted Bundy, who'd been on a killing spree through Oregon, Utah, and elsewhere in the late seventies. Local Houston cases were introduced, going back to the mid-seventies with the case of Dean Corll himself murdered by an accomplice after being accused of the murders of twenty-seven young boys.

Mr. Robinson snuffed out a cigarette in a paper plate. "What the hell are they trying to do, pin all those murders on Brown or something?"

Wiping their fingers free of cream cheese and chasing slippery melon balls across the buffed floors, various wedding guests made bets that in the next set of man-in-the-street interviews someone was going to say that while race probably had nothing to do with it, it did seem that serious murder cases followed Carpetbagger Brown around and even preceded him.

"Here we go." One of Paulette's boarders, who'd stayed an extra day to assist in the reception, sailed through the rooms to the foyer to notify everyone that Andy Young was about to appear.

By the time Mayor Young came on the screen, everyone in the room had heard via the phone that his staff had to locate the resignation letter and pull a statement together. There were no side bets on whether Andy would say he'd been shocked by the exit, not to mention pissed off to be jumped by the media when he was unprepared. Spence, leaning forward in his chair, had called both STOP and Parents for Justice so that if one of any reporters still on the case planned to catch them on camera with their mouths open and their eyes rolling up like morons, they'd be forewarned. He assumed Mason had called someone on the City Hall staff. Spence wondered if Brown's exit was related to the latest mailings of updated 6 Star packets.

"Aww, whattaya expect him to say? Of course he was in consultation with Lee Brown." Mr. Robinson was more interested in the ham, turkey, and roast beef that were scenting up the living room each time the woman who used to live there, dressed to the nines but wearing men's shoes broke down in the back, sailed through the door from the kitchen, teasing them with dishes of meatballs with toothpicks stuck through them.

In the upstairs room that Peeper had occupied, Zala stood unwrapping a bunch of baby's breath. She could look right down into her living room, could almost read the sticker on the back of the Sony still sitting on the hallway floor midway between the living room and the kitchen. How awful, no privacy; what was somebody doing about people like Peeper? She chuckled.

The corps of bridesmaids, women who looked totally unfamiliar, though Zala knew she'd met a few of them before at the Webbers' estate, were lined up in front of the bathroom. Paulette was blotting her lips and smiled on the tissue when Zala came into her room. Six yards of champagne bridal satin, the bodice cut on the bias for graceful cowling across the breasts. Two yards of ecru lace for the peplum that flounced over Paulette's hips and dipped down in back. Thirty-six dollars' worth of seeded pearls hand-sewn on the lace. Zala felt bad that her only contribution was the headgear.

"You gorgeous long drink of water, you!"

"Don't make me laugh, Zala, I'm trying to hold it all together. And whatever you do, girrrrlllll, don't look my way while I'm taking the vows or you'll crack me up."

"I'll behave if you behave. Sit."

Paulette held on to the edge of the dresser as Zala fitted an the satin halo she'd made from a length of welting. She pulled it forward and tugged part of the halo down toward Paulette's left eyebrow. Satisfied that it would stay put, she arranged sprigs of baby's breath inside the halo at the crown, then, parting Paulette's hair gently with her fingertips, pinned the stems down. With the extra bobby pin she fluffed the hair back in place.

Zala backed up, shoving the sewing basket out of the way, and looked at her friend.

"You may not know it, girl, but you're going to miss the hell out of me!" Paulette held on to the dresser to stand up.

"I know it, Paulette. I've been missing you for months."

"It's going to get worse. It's going to come to you that we've been more than across-the-way neighbors, Marzala Rawls Spencer. And you're going to cry your eyes out. So I want to tell you now, while we have this moment together . . ."

"Yeah?"

"Just suffer, bitch."

"Laugh if you want, but you won't be laughing when I trip your ass down them stairs."

"Oh, God. I have to walk down the stairs in these shoes, don't I?" Paulette hiked the hem up and lifted one shoe and groaned. "My father's going to have to carry me down on his back."

"Don't you want to climb out the window first or go through any of them numbers brides go through at the last minute?"

"I think I'd better go pee is what I think. But before I figure out how to do that with this gown on, let me say I'm glad y'all are going to be living here. It'll give the joint some class."

Zala stood by the window. Mr. Robinson had built an arched trellis in Paulette's yard that was grander than their own. All morning, neighbors had been bringing over whatever flowers had come up early to decorate it. Mrs. Grier had forced paperwhite narcissus bulbs in the basement. They were on the altar in the brass pot Gerry had given Zala on their last day in the Georgia Sea Islands. There was to be a two-lined procession from the foyer to the side door, then out to the yard. Zala was glad there was no wind blowing. The dress she'd made for herself was a quickie wrap—no buttons, no zippers, no Velcro or fasteners. She looked up. On the western rim, the sun was glinting around the edges of a cloud bank. No longer like lead, the sky was rinsed blue.

The film convinced them they were driving through Aspen. In church basement chairs, the senior and junior choirs overhead in call-and-response singing, eight members of Inquiry were driving through the town of Aspen, Colorado, at 35 mph. They stopped at a light and children in shorts crossed, names stitched on the sides of their swimming-pool satchels. Driving again, they passed a troop in ski clothes reading a menu in a restaurant window. Turning down a leaf-strewn lane on a crisp autumn morning, they paused to watch a man reshingle the scalloped eaves of a Swiss chalet. On the main street again, in heavy night traffic this time, icicles reflecting the light from a movie marquee, their headlights strobed the green door of a tavern. Then down a rain-swept driveway, they followed a collie carrying a sack by its handles. Going into a garage, the dog dropped the bag and a jug of cranberry juice spattered as the garage door slid down.

Lafayette scraped the bottom of his shoe on the rung of Zala's chair and they sped up a mountain bluff, plowing through flowers of ice like a kayak. Snow was banked to their elbows on both sides. They shivered and huddled together. McClintock turned the wheel of his notebook and they climbed a peak to the left and felt suddenly airborne. From their new vantage point, they looked down on the movie house, the restaurant, the Swiss chalet, the tavern door, and the collie's garage. Buffeting her stomach in the updraft, Zala held on to the back of Dowell's chair. Water bubbling practically under his feet, he kept his eyes on the ski lodge whose rear deck held the huge hot tub. The ski lodge was built like a ship.

Preston, the Florida narc, had called from a shipyard in Norfolk, Virginia, where the ornate fittings of the S.S. *United States* were scheduled to be auctioned off. He'd driven over from Quantico, where he'd been taking in an FBI seminar and, snout ever to the ground sniffing out money, picked up on a few things. He'd confirmed from that end that agents for the U.S. Customs Service had infiltrated a group involved in an illegal arms deal and had traced the dealers to the same Klan family in Atlanta that a GBI informant had. Preston had proposed on the phone that Dowell throw in with him and try for the reward. Not the reward from the children's case; the feds would obviously separate the child murders–international arms deal tie-in. Local murders complicated things. By now they would have suppressed or destroyed any evidence that linked the two. The reward Preston was talking about had to do with the weapons. It was customary to award a percentage of seized property—in this case maybe as much as would fill the whole of the 6 Star warehouse—to agents responsible for making the collar.

Dowell had seen through it. "Hush money, you mean." What else did a Florida narc and an APD homicide detective have to offer those assigned to the armament case but their silence? Preston had laughed and called him chicken shit. And when Dowell laid out the possibility—a possibility that grew more and more probable each time Lafayette came back from Glyco—that the arms deal might be a government caper, Preston had laughed even louder, dropping more coins in the phone. "The bigger the better," he'd said. Judging by the speed with which the regular agents were squeezing out free-lance and contract part-timers, the arms deal might well be a CIA covert operation the other bureaus had happened across. In which case, Preston argued, there'd be beaucoup hush money to pass around. Wasn't it time some colored guys broke into that private country club anyway? Preston was playing with fire. Dowell no longer accepted his phone calls.

"Too bad we're not driving through Atlanta," Lafayette murmured as they observed the highway patrol in Aspen. The sensation of being in a car in Colorado was so strong, Lafayette felt around to his left for the armrest of the car door.

A videodisc, Dolph Newcomb, a.k.a. Claude Russell, had informed them, can store as many as 54,000 stills, which can then be called up on the screen in one-twentieth of a second. Single images, footage, graphics, any visual can be segued to allow the viewer to reconceptualize or recontextualize a particular site, detail, or relationship. Any feature of the targeted terrain can be seen from multiple perspectives, they'd discovered driving through Aspen, with Dolph working the dials so they could experience what the area felt like at any time of day, night, or season and under varying weather conditions. They were now going over the same terrain, the children in their shorts with snow on the ground, the collie dropping the juice at twilight.

With the aid of a videodisc, an entire city could be learned. A particular district or neighborhood could be mastered without leaving one's chair. Half the stills could be gathered from guidebooks. A team with cameras could leisurely walk through a district taking snapshots.

"Such as the killer's route," Dolph said, "or the segments of the route where murders occurred after Williams's arrest."

"Or the Gray Street area," the young reporter said next. "Where the house we had under surveillance mysteriously burned down."

"Or the neighborhood where we keep losing the boy," Vernon said, looking across Zala to Spence.

"You can be there in ways you wouldn't dare be there for real," the visitor from Hot Spot continued. He pressed the fast-forward button to show them something else. "Believe me," he said to hold them, "it's a matter of time before our neighborhoods become the target of this new branch of surveillance research."

They were walking through a campus now, clusters of windburned faces reading the notices on a columnular bulletin board ten yards from the student union. Lafayette put his feet flat on the cement floor. McClintock sat up straight as they went up the steps. Vernon's hands left the camera in his lap as they pushed through the revolving doors.

"If we had more equipment, I could turn this room into Aspen. With holograms, you'd be so convinced, you'd step right up to that counter and order." Dolph turned in Spence's direction. "Remember the raid at Entebbe, Nat? That's when the Defense Department got into this research. They're funding a group up at MIT. Need I say more."

"Talk money." Spence leaned forward to catch Zala's eye. On an anniversary card from the Webbers, the judge's wife had pledged financial assistance toward Sonny's rehabilitation. "What would it take to make a videodisc of a six-block area, for example?"

While Dolph was scribbling on the lid of the suitcase holding the tapes, Mason leaned in toward the rest of them.

"Speaking of money, I'd sure like to know where Atlanta's federal dollars went."

"The long hot summer was the threat," Lafayette said for the benefit of the Blood from California. "That's how the local authorities got the money. There were more community groups organizing than the authorities could contain. Word was spreading and it was spreading fast. It wasn't enough to call people outside agitators and vigilantes anymore. The official fiction was unraveling. People were waking up."

"Can't prove it by me," Dolph said, shaking his head.

"Mellow?" Spence chortled.

"Brain dead, jim, brain dead. I think they've mickeyed the city's drinking water."

Mac sighed and set his notebook on the floor, as much to prove to himself that it was the church basement floor and not the cedar planks of the college dorm hallway as to get up and fix a cup of coffee.

"I wish the rest of us were here," he said as the young reporter jumped up from his chair.

The Inquiry group had dwindled to ten. Leah and Gaston, still hanging in, were out scouting a neighborhood for the Spencers. On the table by the coffeemaker were three dog-eared copies of *The Turner Diaries* that Speaker had sent. The 1978 novel, which blueprinted the ultra-right takeover of America, was his way of saying not to count him out. But he'd not been part of the group for months. He'd gone to New York when it was thought that Maurice Bishop, prime minister of Grenada and leader of the New Jewel Movement, would take the case of the independently developing Caribbean nation to the UN. The one viable economy in the Caribbean that wasn't a client state, socialist Grenada had been the target of destabilization schemes since the New Jewel Party had come to power. When last heard from, Speaker was in D.C. President Reagan had rebuffed Prime Minister Bishop, refusing to meet with him and sending a marine officer from the National Security Council in his stead.

Mac turned to ask if anyone else wanted coffee. Mattie, whom he hadn't seen since the break-in at the warehouse, had driven him through a snowstorm to see Alice Moore at the state asylum. Despondent, Alice had called a suicide hot line. At the volunteer's recommendation, she'd called the police, who had arrived and handcuffed her, informing her that threatening to take her own life was a crime. She'd spent thirty-six hours in an isolation cell, without food, water, or clothes, then been shipped to Milledgeville, where it took her three days to walk off the near-overdose of medication. Drugged or not, she was daily propped up in front of a chart in the hall, "The Aid to Daily Living," until she agreed to abide by the 5:30 a.m.–to–8:30 p.m. outline. Fortunately, a nurse's aide one day walked her two feet down the hall to another chart, fly-specked, that read "Patient's Rights."

By the time they got to Milledgeville, Alice Moore had her hospital insurance papers in her seersucker robe pocket. She'd decided to stick it out for the money. Mac was never clear as to whether Alice was suing her husband for divorce and alimony or was planning to charge him with the murder of their child. She'd not been particularly coherent.

Mac brought over a cup of black coffee for Dowell, who remarked how he missed a good cigar. Mac missed B. J. Greaves; flinty though she'd always been, she was straight-arrow and worked hard. B. J. was in Wisconsin with Dave Morris, training staff for a runaway shelter. She called from time to time, mainly to remind them, as she put it, that Klan-arms-drugs was but one of the patterns, while the one playing the largest role in the murders was child porn.

"One last thing I want to show you," Dolph said, looking at his watch. "This will give you an idea of how to scout an area and collect material." Vernon watched closely. Overhead, the choirs were singing in eight-part harmony "Take It to the Lord in Prayer." Zala pulled back from the streets of Aspen and bowed her head over the straw pocketbook in her lap.

Spence glanced at the door of the basement room, usually used for Wednesday-night fellowship. Someone was outside the door. Was it Sonny eavesdropping? Spence turned back to the monitor. Streets and yards were emerging on the screen as more familiar ones had in the developing pan that morning, Vernon swishing the heavy paper back and forth with the tongs, four pairs of eyes glued to a figure emerging as in a seance: Sonny ducking under a tree and disappearing into a black hole that looked like a doorway in 'Nam about to receive a fragged lob.

Miss Butler had stuck a bookmark in at Luke, chapter 4, verse 18. But that was about Christ coming to the world to bring good news to the poor, Bernie's lesson for Sunday school. Kenti had asked to do a play for the young people while the grown people did their program upstairs. She flipped to Luke, chapter 15. The bookmark told her that what she wanted was in red print from verse 11 to verse 31. Kenti had already cast the Prodigal Son play. All she had to do now was write out the speaking parts for the father, the two sons, and the people the Prodigal met when he was away "wasting his substance with riotous living." There didn't have to be anybody onstage to send him to feed the swine when the famine came. As the storyteller, she could just say it, and Jimmy Crow would act it out. The best part was what the jealous son had to say when he saw the fatted calf being roasted. She would have to write a good last scene, though, so the two brothers, the foolish one and the jealous one, could make up at the end. She put her pencil down and scanned the story again. There was no mother in the Bible story. But there had to be a mother in the play, because Kenti had good lines for the mother to say.

A daddy longlegs was crawling over the piece of paper Kofi had used to hide the firecrackers he'd found in the basement closet. It was a big insect. Its head was like a crinkly leather drum. On the end of each bent leg was an orange shoe. They were supposed to bring good luck. She knew a family that needed some. There hadn't been many good times since they left their Rawls relatives. They could make anything fun, even going to a graveyard. One of her girl cousins pulled moss down from the tree and wore it for a boa to prance around with. Kenti had been taken with the decorated graves. Kofi and Sonny too thought they were interesting. Their dead grandfather's grave was covered in seashells. Pliers and a beat-up coffee kettle were stuck in the dirt of his grave. Other graves had favorite things the dead people liked. There were baskets made out of marsh grass half-buried in some. She didn't go and look in because lids were on the baskets. She had the feeling, though, that Sonny had snuck a look. One grave had a saw stuck in it. But the dead man hadn't been a fix-it man like Mama's daddy; he'd played the saw for music.

Sometimes at breakfast, somebody would say something and they'd talk friendly awhile. One time Mama put aside her books and helped her stick almonds and raisins in the gingerbread boys she was making for Marva's birthday. Daddy was balling up socks from the wash and Kofi was pulling strips of bacon apart, licking the salt from his fingers while he told about the latest danger Captain Singh was in. That was the first Sunday they'd spent in the new house, Aunt Paulette's house, Mama getting up to stretch and say how good it felt to have space. The second floor even had its own sunporch. Then Kofi asked who'd go if a spaceship landed and let down the ramp. Right away Mama said she would, which made Kenti feel bad. But she didn't even know she felt bad, because they were all talking at once about *E.T.* and the adventure of being out beyond the moon seeing things they never saw. Then Sonny said to Mama, "You sure didn't have to think long about running away from home, did you?" Things went back to like before then.

From the other side of the sliding doors, Sonny could be heard explaining to Kofi's group what the grown-ups' sermon had been about. Jacob at Jabbok. Miss Butler had a bookmark for that too. Genesis, chapter 32, verses 22 through 32. Kenti followed, liking Sonny's version better. Jacob was getting ready to cross the river Jabbok one night when somebody jumped him. According to Miss Butler's bookmark, the man in the dark was an angel from God, but Sonny said "mugger." They rassled all over the riverbank, and Jacob was winning. But he wouldn't turn the man loose until the man blessed him. And that didn't mean "bless him out," Sonny had to say to one of the boys who interrupted. Jacob was crippled because the man wrenched his thigh out of joint, but Jacob wouldn't turn him loose till he got that blessing. Then they took it to a verbal level, Sonny was saying, and got into the naming business. Jacob, who used to be a cheat and a hustler, got the new name "Israel," meaning "God-ruled." When Jacob got his blessing and limped away, he named the Jabbok neighborhood "Peniel." Kofi and them had to haul the dictionary open to find out that the word had something to do with "penance," or doing good deeds to show you're sorry for doing dirty before.

When Sonny left the room, Kofi's group had to figure out on their own the so-what of the story. On the back of the bookmark Miss Butler had scribbled the answer, more for herself than for the children. As far as Kenti could make out, the lesson was that people who struggled in the dark and got scared should keep on with the struggling and then they'll be blessed and can change. She wanted to tell Kofi's group that, 'cause they were in there talking about Jacob Israel's broken leg instead of talking about how people can change things if they keep fighting. But she had her own work to do.

She heard Sonny on the first flight up, going out the side door, it sounded like. He was supposed to stay around for the program after church because he was a tuning fork. That's what she heard Mrs. Grier and Miss Em saying on the steps the day they moved and Miss Em had gone to the old door. Put Michael, Sonny, and all the other boys together in a room, strike one and the others would sound. Miss Em might bring the boys to the program. So Kenti carefully wrote out the speaking parts for the play she'd put on at the end. Once again, she ran her finger up and down the red print looking for the mother. If the father wanted to make merry, and the jealous son had an attitude, surely the mother wanted to ask the foolish son for the name of the harlot so she could go and slap her face for making him "waste his substance in riotous living."

From the side door, Sonny watched the tables get set up in the vestibule. Two times DEFEND THE RIGHT TO ORGANIZE was taped to the wall and fell down. Then he saw his mother come out of the minister's office. She went out the front door without stopping to shake Reverend Thomas's hand. He was holding on to each hand an extra long time, telling people to be sure to come right back for the special program. Sonny went up the four steps to see what was being put on the tables. Nothing much—some newspapers, a few pamphlets, and the petition people were being asked to sign. He stepped out onto the portico and hid behind one of the pillars.

His mother was helping a woman out of a car. It wasn't the woman he'd been on the watch for. This was just an old lady his mother was helping. She had on heavy brown stockings, the veins lumping through. Over her homemade dress she wore a vest that looked like a man's. He'd seen Granny Lovey do that sometimes: take the husband to church, dead or not. He moved around the pillars when his mother went up the street. He was half hoping she'd turn and see him. He had the feeling lately that she could read his thoughts. He'd be fixing a sandwich and thinking about places on his body to hide a few sticks of dynamite, and she'd come into the room quickly as if he had called, or she'd close her book and look up at him like she knew his mind.

"Let's go watch Kenti's play," Kofi said from the far end of the portico. He was pulling leaves off the high hedges. "She wants us to be there."

When Sonny made a face and turned back to what he was doing, spying on Mama, Kofi made up his mind not to talk to his brother anymore. He'd tried, he'd really tried, but Dr. Perry didn't know what she was talking about. And he wasn't going there anymore with them either. If Sonny could stay later for therapy, he could stay too. He went back into the shady, cool vestibule, sorry he'd bothered to leave the cool basement in the first place.

One of the men who sometimes came to the house was clicking a counter down till it read zeros straight across in the little windows. Some of the people who'd been in church for the service weren't leaving. They were standing around the information table talking about Wayne Williams's parents. They were suing the police and the city for wrecking their house and tapping their phone. Kofi went down the steps thinking of the time his mama had pleaded and hollered to have their phone tapped. But these people were talking about an illegal tap and other kinds of violations of privacy. He continued down to the basement without stopping to look through the side door to see if Sonny was following Mama. It would have been great if Sonny had stayed on with Uncle Thaddeus and them on the island, he was thinking. Tiptoeing into the room where he'd stashed the firecrackers, Kofi was muttering that it would have been even better if Sonny had never come home at all. But that wasn't true, 'cause he'd loved him and missed him when he was away. Down at the shore with the cousins, he could just be missed.

Spence glanced into the room where Kofi was muttering and kicking the table leg. He went down the corridor and looked in on Kenti. She was ordering boys and girls about dressed in odds and ends from holiday pageants from the past. She warned them that this was their last chance to get it right before the curtain went up. Spence went up the stairs. Cars were pulling up in the side lot. He went out to shake hands with the brothers from the mosque. They'd not met since the winter of '80/'81, when they'd opened self-defense classes. The media had referred to the First of the Nation as "gestapo squad." Spence salaamed and kept moving.

Like at other meetings that had been going on since the fall, there were groups between parked cars in the lot holding caucuses beforehand. There was usually a group reliving the sixties, whether they'd been in it or not, the nostalgia ridiculous, the glorifications ludicrous. Legend making was the impulse to exempt the ordinary self from responsible action. And always at the pre-meetings and at the meetings themselves there was someone who stood apart, usually Spence himself, while Mason charged through the circles, saying to one group what he never failed to say to McClintock, that it was naive, stupid, and dangerous to seek psychiatric solutions to political problems, then charging through to the next. The elite and would-be-elite types taking up as armor against him and others like him the argument that what Black leadership said was good, was good for the grass roots who'd put them in office. And reps from the gay quarter against any analysis that included child porn as a pattern because it was too much like the official version that claimed homosexuality as a motive.

What had been striking Spence lately about the meetings was that even the radicals, white and Black alike, did little more than react to the authorities' agenda, as if there were no alternative way to organize or to think. They appealed to the same fear and hatred the "enemy" did to promote a version of reality that didn't match any other in the room, including each other's, though their main tactic was the same—to provoke the authorities and keep the leadership in a bad light, and then appoint themselves as saviors of the people. Spence had stood apart. So had an actor-model friend of Sue Ellen's, who kept turning the television down when the Falklands or the World's Fair in Knoxville appeared, then turning it up for the commercials, as though a new and improved detergent could clean up the ideological and intellectual confusion that reigned at the meetings.

It was Dowell this time who stood apart and alone. Grinding on a cigar in his back teeth, he glowered at the ground. The dusty patina was so even on both his black shoes that they looked brown. He stood apart because the parents planned to sue local, state, and federal authorities for obstructing justice, while at the same time they were going to petition the feds to re-examine the case, plans that seemed contradictory to him. He stood alone because nobody wanted to hear that, and especially not from a cop. Spence walked around Mason and Vernon discussing the possibility of escorting the parents to D.C. Some top brass were trying to prevent the Vietnam War Memorial dedication ceremony on Veterans Day. Groups of volunteers were guarding the site where the memorial stone, engraved with 57,939 names of the dead and missing, would be set.

Up the street, approaching, were the usual shark-nosed snoops who always turned up for the meetings. Usually quiet, they occasionally broke discipline to praise actions taken by various law-enforcement agencies committed to the protection of the community. Spence hoped there were groups forming that were committed to the liberation of the community. He scanned the streets for signs of his wife.

Zala headed toward Gordon Road looking for a pay phone. Reverend Thomas's office had been jammed with helpers calling the shut-ins and others running off extra copies of the program. Several cars were double-parked on the street. She cut through a yard for the quick route to the Jiffy Mart. Dowell had given Leah and Gaston a beeper, but no one had called them to see if it worked. She hurried past a school that would not be opening in the fall. Not three months before, school-children closer to home had been at the community center selling cooking-class fudge from the middle school that was also being closed down. The children hadn't raised funds to save it, but to buy new pom-poms for the pep squad. She hadn't heard of any PTA activities to save the schools in either neighborhood. She went past a driveway where a couple were taking in pole lamps, a clothes rack, and other remnants of a Saturday yard sale. Two houses up, a real-estate sign was stuck in the lawn. Soon there'd be a stampede, and those left behind would have to fight harder than ever to make sure garbage collection was kept up and the block didn't go down. But how the hell did people think they could let their schools close and still maintain viable neighborhoods?"

People were parking their cars as far away as Gordon and taking the long way to the church. Among familiar STOP members were two unfamiliar couples, one dressed up as though they were heading for a dinner dance, the other down as though for a picnic outing. Just in case they were spotted by parishioners from their own church, they wanted it clear that they didn't usually worship at Seven Hills Congregational and hadn't defected, like all those people from every denomination attending services at Reverend Barbara King's church of late.

Zala crossed over to the Jiffy Mart. Two undercover cops in a sneaker car were watching Parents for Justice cross Gordon Road. They got out of the car. The Black man had a square of toilet paper on his freshly shaven jaw. The white guy's shirt buttons were about to pop off his belly. He slung his jacket over his shoulder with two fingers. Crossing, the Black cop, in a shiny gray suit that matched his glasses, yanked on the short-sleeve shirt of the fat guy, telling him to put on his jacket.

Zala tried twice from the outer-door phone to get Leah or Gaston on the beeper. She watched the two plainclothesmen take the long way to Seven Hills Congregational.

"Sonny coming?" When Kofi turned up his nose, she handed him the narrator's part and went upstairs to get her brother herself.

Coming into the vestibule were people she'd never seen before. The program was going to start soon, because everybody was men and men liked to stand around and be last. There was a reddish-brown man with a white turban on his head; his beard was bound in a hairnet. There were some very dark men in short-sleeve brown suits with no collars. Some African men came in too. Their shirts were very pale and very crisp and the creases in their pants were very sharp. They wore sandals. A tall redheaded white man wore sandals too. He had on a long shirt that looked like a girl's. Flowery and sheer, it went down to his knees; his white pants were crinkly and not very clean.

A nice-looking man who used to come to the house was standing next to Baldy Bean and Mason clicking a metal thing every time somebody went through the inner doors and sat down in church. She was just about to go outside and tell Sonny all about himself when a lady stuck her head out of the office and called Baldy Bean to the phone. He winked at Kenti before he went in, or maybe he was winking at Mason, 'cause right away Mason pulled the man clicking the thing and pointed his finger at the man with red hair like the clicker had forgotten to count him.

"You coming to my play or not, Sonny Spencer? We're doing the last rehearsal and I want you to come. I come when you play ball," she said, appealing to fair-is-fair. "Whatchu doing? It's hot out here."

He was looking at the people on the sidewalk, on the steps, and in the doorway.

"You did good with Jacob at Jabbok—I listened. I want you to come and listen to me. This is your last chance."

He tried to brush her out of his line of vision like she was Raggedy Ann. Kenti refused to move, so he had to walk around one of the big white posts to keep spying on people behind their backs.

Sonny had been overhearing juicy bits about hair standing there on the top step. Stuff about Negro pubic hairs and head hairs from Caucasians. Witnesses had lied about hairs. Cops had been sent to the dog pound to collect hairs. Scrubbing the bottoms of their shoes on the mat, not eager to go in and cut their conversations short, people had been talking about money too. Money that SCLC and other groups had doled out to the families. An older woman had ducked to the side by the high hedges she was so angry, she was telling her friend what Venus Taylor had done with her share of the money: she'd had a tummy tuck. The woman was fuming and spitting so bad, her friend had to take out a handkerchief. Right there on the church steps on a Sunday, the woman had said Venus Taylor, mother of the murdered girl, should be flogged for what she'd done with her money. Sonny had wanted to laugh in her face. "Yeah, let's stone her, stone her at the altar." People were a trip.

It was like his mother had written in her diary: gossip was some people's idea of citizens in action. Calling the emergency hot line was what they thought participatory democracy was about. Polls were taken and that was supposed to be as good as intelligent debate. People coming up the stairs sounded like they'd handed their heads over to the pollsters. Did Williams do it? Did he get a fair trial? Do you still think it's the Klan? Circle yes or no, check a box, call this toll-free number.

"People are dumb," he said, his lip curled. "Dumber than shit."

"So. Everybody's stupid and rotten but you, hunh?"

Kenti expected him to lift his chin in the air and say "That's right," but he didn't. His mouth drooped and then pulled his whole head down to watch an ant who'd come out of the cracks. The ant was as fat as a blackberry and would be a big spot if he squashed it, but he didn't. He just kept stepping and stepping to hurt it and keep hurting it with the edge of his big, heavy shoe.

A Boys' Club van came up the street and went past Zala, boys back from an overnight trip, sleeping bags stuffed in the rear window. Something caught her in the back of the knees. She didn't look around for a cause. It had been happening often enough for her to know a few of the old demons were still hiding out. She concentrated on getting from one telephone pole to another. A posted sign where she'd expected to see LOST DOG REWARD turned out to be someone offering free kittens. On the next pole was a poster advertising a local production of *Deathtrap*. She almost laughed. Paulette, on her honeymoon in New York, had urged Zala and Spence to fly up and join them, maybe take in a Broadway play. The long-running thriller about a burnt-out playwright who schemed to murder his wife for her money had been Paulette's choice, especially after learning that one of the backers of the nasty drama was Claus Von Bülow, on trial again for attempted murder of his wealthy wife. Zala laughed—like they had flying money.

Often, out walking in the morning, her lungs clear, joints oiled, no guck in her eyes, she'd be overtaken by a vitality and would feel like a character in a musical about to burst into song, a hundred violins sawing away, a French horn in an achingly lyrical solo. But just as sudden it could be the blow at the back of the knees.

She was sure she could keep moving and walk the strange charley horse out of her legs. She stepped on a candy wrapper that crinkled like the blue tissue airmail from Gerry. Gerry had applied for a position with UNESCO. A major conference; the issue, who would inform the world about Africa, colonialist Africanists or Africans? Partway down the side of the letter was wet-on-wet brushstroke, an ink blot.

She could see Sonny on the portico and people moving quickly up the steps to go in. When he saw her coming, he played Samson between the pillars. Zala laughed as loudly as she could, to show him she could and to invite health into her lungs.

"How's it looking?"

Instead of answering her, he was searching her face. She was sure she had a mustache of sweat and looked wilted, but he seemed to be aware of something else. She studied him for a clue.

To get away from her eyes, which seemed to be frisking him, Sonny took three steps backward and bumped into his father's friend from California.

Dolph backed over the threshold. "People sure are whistling a lot for a city that's supposed to have everything under control."

From where Spence stood, passing out programs, it looked as though Zala were backing Dolph and Sonny into the vestibule. If they'd had their hands up, the picture would have been complete, the picture provoked, he supposed, by the sight of so many undercover types.

"Keep the focus on the petition," one of the Parents for Justice members was saying to Mason, who always looked strange to Zala without his right hand, Lafayette.

"Let's try to get a civilian task force formed before we adjourn,"

Reverend Thomas said from the corner. He was pulling on a roll of tape, preparing to rehang the DEFEND THE RIGHT TO ORGANIZE sign.

Sonny was behind her now. His hands on her shoulders like clothespins, he turned her toward the sign. "Somebody's added 'Without Spying or Harassment,' " he told her. From the way he said it, she had a pretty good idea who it had been. She tucked her pocketbook under her elbow firmly. His eyes seemed to bore through the straw even after he moved off and worked his way toward the stairs.

People crowded around those listed to speak and offered handshakes of solidarity. They didn't miss the opportunity to pass out brochures, but did miss the eyeball messages that telegraphed between members of STOP, Parents for Justice, and Inquiry and shut the congratulators out of the circle. The shared past of the families, vets, and community workers had led to a consciousness that overrode expedient alliances with those who also worked hard to encourage people to battle against forgetfulness, but only for the opportunity to market glow-in-the-dark merchandise.

More people were moving into church as the choirs trooped up the stairs. Spence had seen the look on their faces before at other memorial programs and meetings: slack from so many revisions, new theories, changing stakes, sifted facts. Their step was wary as they entered the church.

Reverend Thomas squeezed Zala's shoulder as he went past to enter in front of the choirs lining up two by two to march in. Support of the program was voiced loudly. Confident predictions were made. Backs were slapped and Zala's hand was pumped. Spence flashed a broad smile as he went in. But Zala felt that Sonny alone knew her heart's desire.

When the junior and senior choirs split at the center aisle, Zala followed behind the seniors, quick-stepping down the left aisle. She scanned the faces in church on the lookout for a particular pair as she advanced toward a pew in the front.

> You may run on for a long time
> Run on for a mighty long time.
> Run on for a long time
> But Great God Almighty's gonna cut you down.

Go tell that midnight rider
Go tell that long-time liar
Tell that ram-ba-lah gam-ba-lah backbiter
That Great God Almighty's gonna cut'm down.

The floorboards thundered. Gladioli in the vases along the pulpit
shook. Saints glowed at the windows. Panels of the Twenty-third Psalm
turned amber in the sunlight. Tape on one cracked pane had covered
portions of THOU PREPAREST A TABLE BEFORE ME IN THE PRESENCE OF
MINE ENEMIES for so long, even old-timers referred to the scene as the
Last Supper, ignoring the inimical faces closing in on the diner.

Zala pulled a T-shirt from her bag and drew an index card from her
pocket. She looked up. The pulpit had never seemed more elevated, the
padded wine velvet chairs more thronelike. "Great God Almighty" slid
without pause into "No Hiding Place Down There"; then they sat. She
was glad they would remain in the choir stall. She didn't want to be
alone in that high place. If only Mama Lovey were present, or Paulette.
Zala slipped the T-shirt over her head and used the hardwood back of
the bench to brace her shoulders. Can't live with your heart in your
mouth always, she counseled herself.

Reverend Thomas got right to the point. "If people are to win vic-
tories over their worst terrors, the noblest traits in them must be appealed to." This he directed to those scheduled to speak, taking his time
to roam his eyes over the gathering to pick them out before he continued, speaking of the children and the community, the love and concern
for their care being the noblest and oldest sentiment in the Black community.

"We've all been favored before with articles and talks that point
up the inaccuracies and untruths concerning the Atlanta Missing and
Murdered Children's Case. One would think further education would
be unnecessary. But many of us are still unwilling to dismantle the
authorities' myth. While we may despise the treachery of lies, we seem
to fear the squalor of the truth even more. Let us bow our heads and pray
for the strength to overcome our own fearfulness. Let us pray for the
strength to become more accountable to the generations to come. And
for the strength to make this city responsible to people's need for the
truth, so that our children will not grow up cynical and warped by our
failure of courage."

He looked the assembled over and gripped the sides of the lectern. His shiny, black, fulsome sleeves draped down over the sides of the wood. He bowed his head finally and began, "Father, Mother, God, Spirit," pausing a long time for this departure from his usual invocation to sink in before he asked that the gathering be blessed and the tongues of the speakers be touched with the light. And as the people said Amen, he nodded to Zala. She mounted the steps as Reverend Thomas pointed the crowd's attention to her name on the Cradle Roll. Then he praised this longstanding member of Seven Hills for the courage to come before the 204 in attendance.

Zala braced her knees against the shelf that held a water glass and a carafe. Looking up from her note card, she gazed out. She knew now how ministers could be so perceptive about individual members of a congregation. From where she stood, everyone was distinctly visible. A whole row of men, their shirts opened at the throat. A woman powdering her nose. A patch of tissue on a shaving cut, a pair of hands folding a crocheted-edged handkerchief, a couple who sat close together rubbing shoulders. She spotted a pair of old patent-leather dress shoes in the aisle: the undercover cop, legs crossed at the ankle, had tried to mask a hole in the bottom of one with shoe polish. She was strengthened by the encouraging nods and smiles. Someone in the choir behind her said, "Hmm-hunh." The woman in the center pew closed her compact with a click and lifted her powdered face, expectant. Zala began.

" 'We are all each other's harvest, we are each other's business.' From a poem by Gwendolyn Brooks. 'We've always been at the center of the theft.' From a poem by Andrew Salkey. 'Of all the virtues,' says Maya Angelou, 'the most important is courage, for without courage none of the other virtues can be practiced with consistency and passion.' " Zala held on to the lectern and stepped carefully to the right and then to the left, still holding on, she turned to her chair so that her T-shirt was visible to all. She stepped back and repeated the two-word inscription. "From a poem of the same title by Alexis DeVeaux—'Question Authority.'

"From the start, there was silence. Not only in City Hall and in the squad rooms and newsrooms, but there was silence in our neighborhoods too. Even now there is a taboo against speaking out. Those who do speak out are put down with a look or a sarcastic remark that says, 'You're making too big a fuss and are trying to make our leadership look bad by washing dirty linen in public.' " She was bolstered by the murmuring of the elderly woman she'd helped out of a cab, a woman who probably still did her washing outdoors in big pots and knew no better way to get linen fresh than to let the sun at it with a breeze blowing through.

"We are too quiet. We fail our neighbors and we fail ourselves and our children too by going along without a mumbling word. For our silence we are patted on the head for not turning somebody with a bat or a gun into the Messiah. I don't know how it was for you in the beginning, but I kept telling myself it wasn't happening, not here. In Alabama or Mississippi maybe, but not here in Atlanta. Our own son was taken and we were being told to be quiet. We all were told that. I didn't want to believe the worst, and so I was easily silenced. I was easy anyway," she added, with a shy smile. "A lot of us, I imagine, were raised to be quiet, obedient, and dependent."

"Tell it!" someone remarked, and a wave of heavy sighs worked its way up to the pulpit. The heaviest sigher was a pregnant woman who sat on one end of a pew, her feet in the aisle, her ankles swollen.

"We raise our children to have respect for the truth. We stress the importance of being honest, and honesty is right. In the law courts, that's how they distinguish the sane from the insane—the ability to know right from wrong. But we're lied to every day, from advertising to the government. And we know it. The government invented the term 'credibility gap' to cover the distance between what officials know and what they tell us. In other words, a lie. We say deceit is wrong. And we all think we believe it."

A woman sitting behind some of the parents settled her scarf around her white eyelet dress. She wore an implacable expression that softened as Zala related the agony of days from "Went" to the Bowen Homes disaster to the ride to Miami.

"When we got our son back, there were no parades for him. Friends sent good wishes and gifts, but there was no hero's welcome for our boy, who was a hostage for nearly a year. On the one hand, I was grateful that the police and the FBI didn't come around. But on the other hand, think of it—'No stone unturned'? They should have been lining up to question our son."

Spence was thumbing his finger over his shoulder. Sonny had come in. He was standing behind Kofi and Kenti, his hands resting lightly on their shoulders. When people began turning around to see what had caught Zala's attention, she continued quickly.

"There's something else I have to say about when our son came back to us: I didn't care after that. The case, I mean—the children, the others. I didn't care about anything but my family. All I wanted to do was close the door, because I did not care. That's not how I put it for a long time, but that's the truth of it. I had been privy to a great deal of information about the case that never made the papers. But I was no longer interested in getting to the roots of the murders. Maybe . . ." She searched the faces for Leah's, but Leah, she remembered, was out on a mission. She hurried her eyes past Spence and buried her gaze in the empty air of the center aisle.

"Our son was stolen from us and from you and from the streets of our neighborhoods. And he was made to feel that he deserved it. That he deserved what happened to him. And the things that happened to him."

"Take your time, sister."

She saw Sonny back out of the doorway, saw Kenti go and bring him back. Her pink index card was useless to her now. Like Reverend Thomas that morning, she'd strayed far afield of the text. Several of the parents had their heads lowered. People behind them leaned forward to pat their shoulders.

"Worse happened to others. Death happened to others. Because we allow it. We allow ourselves to be manipulated by name calling—'paranoids,' 'agitators.' Our understanding of where we are and what is what led many of us to say 'Klan' and 'cover-up' under our breath. But we silence ourselves because we're afraid of being called names like 'traitor to the race.' We swallow the line that security means secrecy and silence. How do we balance that?" she asked, holding her arms out to the side, her palms up. "Our children in danger on one hand, and our fear of being called names on the other? In a just order, crimes against children would be dealt with more seriously than crimes against the state. Because it is more serious. What could be more serious?"

"Tell the people."

"It wouldn't be right and it wouldn't be fair if I left the impression that everybody sat back and left it up to the leaders, the police, and the media to define things for everybody. People from the community, not least the children's parents, joined forces and voices to demand answers that didn't insult their intelligence or the memory of the children lost. We all know the official answer the authorities came up with is no answer at all. The children who escaped could have told us that much and a lot more. But maybe—" She looked to the rear of the church. "Maybe they feel why should they tell everything when nobody else does. And what right do we have to badger them when we don't demand answers from the people we pay to run this city? What they're hiding has tremendous importance for the well-being of hundreds of thousands. Doesn't it?"

Sonny nodded from the rear. Mason held up his arm and tapped his watch.

"So. You won't get what you came for, if you came looking for the enchanted box. We're here today to put some facts together. To get some commitments to work. And yes, to pass the plate. The immediate purpose is to get signatures for a petition so that the parents can take it to Washington, D.C., and demand that United States Attorney General William French Smith reopen the case. I know that many of us here are split on the issue and call it a case of the fox and henhouse. But what we're after is a congressional investigation spearheaded, perhaps, by the Black Caucus, with the parents calling the witnesses and asking the questions."

Already Mason and Vernon were hefting the box containing the map and a sheaf of papers. Members of Preener's neighborhood safety patrol were signaling those from Techwood to move up front to assist. Two of the brothers from the mosque leaned forward, their hands on the back of the pew in front, to see when Spence would move and signal them to join him.

"Before turning the program over to a number of people we've been taught to regard as troublemakers, I'd like to close with this reminder: coerced silence is terrorism."

"Say it again, sister. Got some sleepers in here, God bless'm."

Kenti leaned forward, her cheek on the back of Zala's hand. "Were you scared?"

"When I actually heard myself talking, yeah. But the old folks in the choir would hum me along." Zala leaned her legs against the hump of the gear box and turned to look at her children. "But wasn't Miss

Kenti the hit of the day." She kissed Kenti's cheek just as Spence swerved around Griffin and pulled up short at the stop sign.

"We going to Paschal's?" Kofi scooted forward to see how many men had gathered in the open shed at the side of the Pool Checkers Tournament Association building.

"You guys are," Spence said, watching Sonny in the rearview. "Aunt Dee and Gloria and Uncle Bry are waiting for you in the dining room. We've got a run to make. Got to get this car back to Gaston's."

"You going to Gaston's?"

"Yeah, Sonny. Want to tag along?" Spence's hand slid from the wheel, but he refrained from reaching across the gear box to squeeze Zala's.

"Where we going, Pop?"

"Ya know, Sonny," Spence began, "if you were only a neighbor's boy, I'd still find you special enough to want to get to know you." He found he could not go on to say all he felt. A white Toyota was parked at the curb. Sonny's eyes were straight ahead, Spence noted, stealing a glance in the rearview. Spence had been stealing glances at his son since the day he'd come home, and even more so since the day, unpacking pots, pans, and everyday dishes, books, balls, and a gadget that belonged to the sewing machine, Sonny had lashed out at Kofi for packing something Sonny had thrown away. By nightfall, Spence had in his possession the wax that bore a sweeter fragrance than the bees had ever intended. Sliced open like grapefruits, the molds had only to be turned over to Dowell for five sets.

"Recognize these?" Spence passed the keys over his shoulder to Sonny.

Her knees against the hump, Zala turned to read his expression. His face was muted. But his brain was revolving like a prayer wheel, nut and bolt on tight. Through his window she saw the green minibus half-parked on the sidewalk. A cluster of sunflowers hung over the windshield. Between two beds of sunflowers was a path that led to Cower Road. Birds plucked at the seeds and kept the flowers bobbing and swaying. The seeds were large enough to press for salad oil. She moved her eyes back to Sonny.

"Which house is it?"

"Whaddayamean?" He looked around the street from both side windows but not straight ahead or behind, she noticed. "I don't even know where we are."

Spence parked the car. He put his back against his door and slid his arm across the top of the seat.

"When I was growing up, your nana Cora and gram Wesley used to make big speeches about lying. Lies were sin and crime. There was nothing worse than a blue-gummed, bald-faced, bandy-legged liar. Though that didn't prevent your nana Cora from painting a prettier picture of our status than the facts allowed. I guess the problem of lies stayed on their minds because they'd been lying to me. They wouldn't tell me I was adopted. They fed me plenty of clues, though. They wanted me to know what they couldn't bring themselves to simply tell me. Lies are like that. Or rather, the truth is like that. It leaks out, because, I think, we by nature want to be up front."

Spence turned off the motor and turned his body more in Sonny's direction. "Your mother has told you that you don't owe anybody the truth, including us. I sort of agree with that. I like counting on your basic nature to help you spill whatever you really wanted us to know. So I don't have to ask you where you've been going when you tell us you're off to see Valerie Brooks. You've led us here."

"Here? Where? I don't even know where this is."

"We're here, Sonny, because you want us to be here. In various ways, you led us here."

Sonny slammed his weight against the back of the seat and one of the speakers Gaston had installed in the back rattled. Zala got out and slammed her door. As she bent to open his, she caught a movement on the roof of a house they had passed. A one-and-a-half-story building, it had a louvered attic. There were plants in the large lower window and shiny blue drapes. The stoop was to the side of the window, a rain spout running down the bricks. Three big dogs were flopped on top of each other on the top step in front of the door. One looked like a grizzly bear. The yard was bushy. There was a gate.

"Come on," she told him, prepared to lean in and pull Sonny out if he balked. Spence got out and came around to the sidewalk. He looked up and down the street, then caught her glance and began walking.

"Is that the house, Sonny?" She walked close on his heels, steering him toward the gate.

"Which house?" He stopped to look at the houses across the street so that she had to crowd him. "I've never been around here before. Where are we anyway?"

Zala walked him up to the gate. The grizzly dog lifted its head and bared its teeth. Its teeth were yellow, its eyes were milky. The other two scrambled up. When the grizzly started barking, head jutted forward, claws scratching the brick step, the other two joined in.

"Open it," she said, "and go ring the bell."

"Use the key," Spence added, quietly unlatching the gate.

When the gate creaked open, the leanest dog, bowed like a starving greyhound, shot from the steps directly to the dirt. The grizzly came down the steps barking, strong jaws lined with thick white spit. The barrel-headed dog stayed on the steps, barking and snapping and backing his rump into the door.

"Go in? Are you crazy?! You seen them wild dogs!"

At the sound of Sonny's voice, the bony dog flattened himself on the ground and inched toward Sonny, tossing his head like he had the catch of the day, a chewable slipper. Barrel Head nosed the grizzly out of the way and came through the yard. Dog tags clinked in excitement, rumps wagged. Spence pushed Sonny into the yard ahead of him, and the three dogs moved in to nuzzle Sonny's hands, which he quickly withdrew and held up past his head. Barrel Head reached up on his hind legs, trying to bury his muzzle in Sonny's hands, Grizzly aimed for the elbows, the greyhound mutt dove for Sonny's pants leg.

The dogs shouldered each other out of the way to escort Sonny up the walk. They doubled back to sniff at Spence as he inched toward the steps. They eyed Zala, growling low in their throats, one sheepish eye on Sonny in case he swatted them for threatening company. They did not bark again until Lafayette slid down the drain in front of them and the gate creaked open behind Zala. The dogs were turning every which way as the front door opened.

She could hear Gittens telling the dogs to be quiet as he reached a hand out to greet Sonny, who recoiled—the greyhound mutt shot past Gittens and into the house over the tile as Spence pushed Sonny aside and rushed the door with Lafayette. Another voice from deep inside the house made Zala take the steps two at a time. It took both dogs to slow her down.

EPILOGUE

Wednesday, July 8, 1987

Y ou're at the keyboard trying to answer a letter. The TV is on, a
summer rerun of baby-remember-my-name *Fame*. Your child,
on her way out, flips the channel to your brand of drama, the news; then
the porch light goes on. And you, on red alert now, swing your head up.
The years swing up too, the room does at least, it's three years older than
the time on the page you've been typing. Moon or no, you become Larry
Talbot each time your child no longer child goes through that door.
Hair everywhere on your skin at attention, mouth muzzling out to
match the menace beyond the house. Kneecaps and spine rearranging
your line, you lope to the porch with a no. "No! Why?" Because of the
washer worn in the bathroom faucet that drips all night wrecking your
sleep and this that and the other, there are claws in your voice. She's
groaning but patient. Her friend on the porch asks how the project is
going. With so many fangs in your mouth, a normal-toned answer is
not easy. They're only going next door to a VCR party, *Under the Cherry
Moon*. Your daughter, by way of pulling your coat to the time, the hour
and year, mostly the year, says, "Hey." You still not caught up, or rather
too much so, won't relent. You escort them to check out the adults, your
convoy sailing under the flag of what again did "Pass the Dutchie on the
left-hand side" mean? It's still '83 on your hit parade, if not '79. Your
daughter, the soul of tried patience, warns you to get done with the project, eight years, enough is enough.

You go back to the desk to finish the letter. It's got to be long in lieu
of a visit. Your friend is in a hospital bed in St. Thomas up to her chin
in plaster of Paris. She wants news of Atlanta.

Your attention is on the letter. You hit on an idea. By packing up
things and mailing them to Flavia, you can answer the letter, and at the

same time clear off the dinner table, and put an end to your daughter's cracks about 'stove buffet.'

First, there's *The List,* the book written by Chet Dettlinger with Jeff Prugh. Originally serialized not in an Atlanta paper but in the *Chicago Sun* in April 1984, the book arrived in Atlanta bookstores in May. An important book, it dismantles the myth of the official version. It (1) offers what should have been the pattern noted by the authorities—the geographical and personal links between the victims; (2) makes more than a strong suggestion that the child-porn ring behind many of the murders was known to the authorities; (3) points out the blunders made by the police, the media, city hall, and the trial judge and attorneys; (4) names a lot of names—suspects under surveillance but never questioned, suspects questioned but then released, witnesses who at their own risk fingered neighbors who'd been seen with victims, who'd been seen molesting victims, who'd been seen going off with victims, who'd been seen carrying child-size bundles, who'd been seen on the phone tipping the authorities to where a body could be found. On local TV and radio, those who interviewed the writing pair together or singly kept the focus on the book's formal imperfections—the book has no index, the book has no coherent structure, the book the book the book, its tone is bitter, its criticism of police and media methods harsh in general and in particular—and didn't get into the findings of the detective and the investigative journalist.

You slip the *Sentinel* piece into the cover of *The List* and pack it. You wish you could also pack the Glover book, the long-awaited book by Camille Bell, and the book overdue from Sondra O'Neale, but they've not appeared. Baldwin's *Evidence of Things Seen,* however, did. Had it been a voice in the chorus and not out there alone, *Evidence* would have helped round out the story. Alone, it didn't fill the expectations of those expecting a hard-hitting look at White House–FBI–CIA machinations in Atlanta as both the Baldwin and Glover books had been rumored to do. You jot a note that the proposed film Nancy Holmes was to do with CBS News and Amnesty International fell through. You clip it together with tearsheets from out-of-town periodicals that covered a petition drive in Atlanta, Tallahassee, Santa Cruz, and other parts of the country calling for stricter child-protection laws based on the Atlanta case. Several of the articles triggered by the broadcast and rebroadcasts of *Alex,* a teleplay about a missing child case. The program used the same postplay format as other social-problem dramas—*The Burning Bed,* about battered wives; *Consenting Adults,* about gay offspring; *Something About Amelia,* about victims of father rape; and *Surviving Teenage Suicide*—namely, panel discussions or interviews with experts and a hot line furnished by helping organizations.

The sheaf of local and out-of-town articles dated 1985 is fat. In late January '85, when Abby Mann's five-hour teleplay of the Atlanta Missing and Murdered Case was previewed, city and state officials went off. How dare Mann say that we were more concerned about image than about the investigation? That really makes us look bad, puts the entire city in a bad light! Those who paid any attention to the teleplay's promotion, designed and paid for as well as designed and unpaid for, took note of how many verbs of "seeing" and how many synonyms for "image" were crammed into statements by Bush, Young, and others without one mention of children's well-being. Earlier, when Mann's point man had been in Atlanta and drawn fire from then Mayor Maynard Jackson, the point man, self-righteous, claimed that Mann's only concern was the protection of Black boys. Where the hell was that concern, Maynard fired back, during the Inman reign of terror?

In a word, the two-part CBS telecast on February 10 and 12 was vicious. A wholesale attack on the very concept of Black leadership. Dopey lines jammed into actors' mouths like, "We've lost that good white cop, now what do we do," ad nauseam. On the other hand, the broadcast did reopen the discussion and gave numerous people the opportunity to try to pry the lid off. Because the script was supposedly based on *The List,* both Dettlinger and Prugh got an opportunity to put some information out to the public.

Sometime in the summer or autumn of 1985, the Williams family's attorney Lynn Whatley must have pulled together the team of William Kunstler from New York, Alan Dershowitz from Cambridge, and maybe Bobby Lee Cook of Georgia to plot strategy based on the GBI files that linked the Ku Klux Klan to the killings. In autumn, the team would file for a writ of habeas corpus for Whatley's client, Wayne Williams, and demand that Williams's conviction be overturned. A

new trial was demanded on the grounds that the authorities had with-
held crucial evidence about a secret investigation conducted by the
Georgia Bureau of Investigation. The team would also demand eight
additional volumes of material that cover events from 1980 to 1981 and
that seems to implicate local, state, and federal authorities in a cover-up
that grew out of a relationship between a police informant and a Klan
family. In spring, attorney Bobby Lee Cook would take depositions
from the GBI and Atlanta Police Special Services. In the fall of 1986
Spin magazine would publish a three-part series that reviewed the
whole case in light of the new evidence. News specials appeared on TV
too in this period, focusing most especially on witnesses who'd lied and
witnesses who'd died since the trial.

In 1980, a police informant had infiltrated an Atlanta Klan family
with ties to J. B. Stoner and to the National States Rights Party and
other extremist organizations. Originally, the informant was tracking
down weapons stolen from National Guard armories.

In February 1981, while FBI director Webster was saying "Not
racially motivated" and local Atlantans were pressing to have a "redneck" phone call aired on the radio, the informant tipped his contact
that a Klan family he'd infiltrated had bragged of their involvement in
the child killings—death squad practice.

A month later, in March, while Mayor Maynard Jackson was asking
for outside help, in particular for fed dollars to underwrite the no-stone-
unturned investigation, the informant, wired now and escalating his activities, was having his info relayed to a GBI official higher up than his
contact. The official decided to question the Klan family members on
his own.

In April, while the killings continued, the GBI official gave the
implicated Sanders family a clean bill of health. Days later, the informant complained to his contact that his cover had been blown.

In May, with Webster still running the same line, and an FBI agent
announcing at a public gathering, "The parents did it," buses left for
the STOP-sponsored rally in D.C. and Maynard Jackson was finally getting the fed dollars released to Atlanta. Williams was stopped on the
bridge the next day, questioned, released, but kept under quiet surveillance.

By December 1985, network news people and free-lance writers were filing for access to the new material and conducting investigations of their own, researching old news stories, interviewing people, and trying to make contact in particular with witnesses and jurors, neo-Nazi types and free-lance informants. In 1986, writer Robert Keating and others published articles and produced video documentaries and news specials that cracked the case wide open coast to coast. At least one docu in the making focuses on the weapons—the automatics, the bazookas, machetes, explosives that, according to evidence from the GBI secret investigation, the Sanders family were ordered to obtain and stockpile by Edward Fields, head of the notorious National States Rights Party. Other articles focus on the drugs, again based on evidence in the GBI records, attempting to highlight the link between the paramilitary nature, the ritual cult nature, and the underground-mob criminal nature of the Ku Klux Klan and other extremists on the Right. More locally, writers began to speculate on how the costly Williams trial from December 1981 to February 1982 might have proceeded had the defendant's attorneys had access to the suppressed files. Others raised the question, would Williams have been picked up at all?

Storage box packed, letter finished, you look around at the TV in time to get a final glimpse of the man being turned into a matinee idol. In addition to arming the thug Savimbi to topple Angola, Oliver North also organized the invasion of Grenada.

You lick the envelope closed and dump your bag on the floor for your keys. It's 1981 all over again until you two reach the sidewalk heading for the post office. People are shooting off guns still and flinging firecrackers all over the street. They must have foreseen that you two would need an extension of the Independence Day celebrations.

ACKNOWLEDGMENTS

Books begin and end in huge debts. To begin with, Miss Adelaide's mother used to flag me down on Cascade to inform me that someone had a nephew overseas and also had arthritis. She'd lean in the car window and say, "Well? You're the writing lady, aren't you?" After witnessing letters I'd write and contracts I'd draw up for people, she'd tell me that it was unfortunate that I had such a bad hand because there was a lot of writing to be done in the neighborhood. In 1979, we had a bit of an argument about it while folding clothes in the washerette there on Cascade near Oglethorpe. The talk of the day was the rash of abductions and murders, and it was her notion that I march myself over, shy or no shy, and write down the mothers' stories. It was my notion that that might wind up to be a hustle or an appropriation of their tongues, in that my forte was fiction and my fictional impulse tended to override my documentary one. "Chicken shit." Miss Adelaide's mother said.

In 1979 and 1980, while I was still in the throes of *The Salt Eaters,* a number of friends nudged me into the realization that the sketches, narrative essays, and stories I'd been drafting about events which would later be called the Atlanta Missing and Murdered Children's Case were really portions of a book. Special thanks to the Pomoja Writers Group for their pitch-perfect ears and their generous shoulders, which kept my chin, let us say, from dragging during several drafts from '79 to '85; especially to Joyce Winters and Malaika Adero, who did some leg work, and to Nikky Finney, whose discipline was such a model; to Alice Lovelace of the Southern Collective of African-American Writers for those talks on the wall at the bus stop near Ebon's; to Charles Riley and a number of Brothers who covered my back during public readings in various years and who hipped me to tighten my security, and not a moment too soon; to Ida Lewis, Tony Batten, and other media friends whose calls and questions kept me moving and also prepared me to recruit those who'd call later for "an angle" as research aides.

I was particularly blessed from beginning to end with a sense of familiar care, thanks to my ever-supportive mother, Helen Brehon; my consistently understanding daughter, Karma Bene, and my best friends, Jane and Sarah Poindexter, all of whom kept things rolling even though I frequently failed to hold up my end in the household or my end of the conversations. Thanks too to Jane for continuing to keep an ear out and clip the papers and for bearing up with people's "Ain't she done yet?" long after I'd cloistered myself. Special thanks to Karma, who ran the house and didn't allow me to walk out of doors in my bathrobe. And to Sarah, who makes me think I wasn't too bad an example, as she writes a mean story among other things wonderful. And me mum, who never doubted that I knew what I was doing, which must have taken a great deal of imagination and grit.

On my visits to New Orleans, my ole high-school pal Pat Carter would jump right in and ask how I was tackling the dodgy business of writing a novel about real events—a question a lot of people ask, but when Pat asks, you answer. I devised a few simple dos, don'ts, and maybes early on.

DO: Assemble a cast in line with the actual events. Whether the book was fictional or nonfictional, the obligatory cast members would be the Missing Child, the Family, the Police, the Media, the Psychologist, the Suspect, the Judge, the Attorneys, the Community Spokepersons, the Independent Investigators, the Real Fiends.

Hence, Sonny, the missing child; his family, the Spencers; Dowell and B. J. Greaves as well as real police persons; the network guy as well as the real Jeff Prugh; Mac; there should be no fictitious suspects, so all suspects alluded to were actual suspects to the actual police and/or actual community investigators; real Judge Cooper; real trial attorneys; Inquiry as well as real people such as Hosea Williams; Inquiry as well as the real Dettlinger.

DON'T: Treat real people as though they were fictional; it's rude, it's confusing, and it ought to be illegal. Of all the real people—Brown, Williams, Napper, Jan Douglass, Julian Bond, Dettlinger, Prugh,

Camille Bell, et al.,—only Maynard Jackson is ever an on-the-scene talking presence. His words, however, are the words several million people heard and are a matter of public record.

MAYBE: The best way to bring onstage those people who played an important role in the actual events is to invent a "shadow" colleague or acquaintance. B. J. Greaves, purely fictitious, was originally devised solely to enable me to tell the reader about actual police officers. Just as Mason, Vernon, and Lafayette, purely fictitious, enabled me to tip my hat to the numerous vets and community workers who were on the case since the Bowen Homes disaster, if not before; many of them have not skipped a beat to this morning despite the "bad press" they've received from relatives, employers, and friends.

In 1981 and 1982, I set the project aside several times, once when Lawrence Schiller and Penny Bloch, of Lawrence Schiller Associates and ABC, respectively, offered me a crack at a script that didn't pan out. Each time Pomoja got me back on the track, as did Billy Jean Young and Monica Walker while they were in Atlanta; and while I was in London, Siva, Gail, the Huntleys, and most especially Menelik Shabazz (in both London and Atlanta); while I was in St. Croix, Gloria I. Joseph, who offered a gig and sanctuary and who times her support cards and calls over the years in an uncanny manner, Roseann Bell, Audre Lorde, and Winnie Oyoka; in New York, the late Gerri Wilson, the best person I ever knew to talk with about children; in Ibaden, Nigeria, Esi Kinni-Olasunyin, who lost a lot of sleep during my talking jags; and in my neighborhood at the time, Ernie "Tech" Pilot, who clued me in to the fact that if he could tap in on "redneck" transmissions, maybe the APD, GBI, and FBI were doing it too.

A special thanks to all the elders who ever told me to learn to be still. Research need not be running around in an effort to apprehend information. It can sometimes be accomplished by being still and comprehending. By climbing into my chair and working, a lot of things came my way via the phone, the mail, drop-ins, and what some people would call intuition and others would call history.

In 1983–84 I was into the third draft thanks to Camille Bell, whom I've never met, and Sondra O'Neale and James Baldwin, whom I've known for years; all three were working on books, a fact which made me

feel a lot less alone in my obsession. The work was going well, thanks
to Susan Ross and Andrea Young, whose growing-up-in-Atlanta stories, which they'd shared with me two years prior, filled out Marzala's
past; Kwame Penn, an old pal from my daughter's Pan African preschool days, who steered me to the latest in comic books so I'd know
what Kofi might be reading; Sue Houchins and Lynda Sexton at the
Djerassi Ranch and Cheryl Gilkes of Boston, who gave me a way to read
the Bible that was more to my liking; and especially Madame Chin for
a lot of good talks and support; the late great Anna Grant and Edie
Ross, who discussed the trial from a particular angle in a conversation
at Joanne Rhone's house in the winter of '81, I think it was; my good
sister friend Cheryll Chisholm, the best person for talking about the detective genre and cinematic structures; and while on the road, Gwendolyn Brooks and Nikky Giovanni and Guadaloupan writer Maryse
Conde.

In 1985–86 I was continually bolstered by Gloria Joseph, Hailie
Gerima, Tom Dent, Sonia Sanchez, my family, the Poindexters and Sandra Swans, Terri Doke, Ishmael Reed, and my hearts of hearts Eleanor
Traylor and Toni Morrison. And Kristin Hunter, who saved me once,
and my mom several times when funds were zero.

I bow forehead to the floor to the typists for their patient eye-
detecting and speed: Tracy D. Bonds, Medina Holloway, and Eileen
Ahearn.

Thanks to numerous people who forgave me the broken appoint-
ments, missed deadlines, and unanswered communications. Especially
Gloria Hull and Maryse Conde.

Warm thanks to my agent Joan Daves and my Vintage editor Anne
Freedgood for their quiet notes. I cannot thank enough my former Random House editor and ever sisterfriend Toni Morrison for the git-up
phone calls and the git-down cards and the genius strokes in the
margins.

Many people from all over the place sent or gave me tapes, documents, photos, posters, drawings, tips, maps, flyers, banners, newspapers, records, books, poems, stories, questions, and contact people's
numbers. Many packets bore no names; other names were in quotes or
were struck through. Many names I've lost; please pardon. Some of the
anonymous senders identified themselves as hotel chambermaids, office
workers, garbage collectors, prisoners, waiters, barmaids, librarians,

former and active police persons, media persons, and Klan defectors. Also while I'm at it, I'd like to thank several crank callers, threat-makers, hecklers, and writers of poison-pen letters, et al., without whose fierce opposition I might not have been so damn dogged. Special thanks to Grace Paley for handling one heckler at our reading at the museum in Houston on March 12, 1982, and to the Brother in rimless glasses who took the other heckler out and introduced his head to the fire extinguisher.

Of the namable suppliers:

IN THE SOUTH:

In Atlanta: Malaika Adero; Helen Brehon; Alelia Bundles; Cheryll Chisholm; Imani Claiborne, the Committee on Research into Racial Violence; Jan Douglass; Faraha; Miller Francis, WRFG; June Jordan, for the Atlanta poem while at Spelman, and the model she offers; Joy, Carl, Randy, Zeke, Terry, *Revolutionary Worker;* Ernie Pilot; Jeff Prugh, then *L.A. Times;* Jane Poindexter; Tony Riddle; Susan Ross; Elizabeth "Purple" Siceloff, SRC; Lowell Ware, *Atlanta Voice;* Monica Walker; Saundra Williams; Andrea Young; National Anti-Klan Network; *The Monitor;* the Committee for Democratic Renewal.

In Alabama: Billy Jean Young; Stella Shade; and Janet of the then Mothers Against Madness.

In Mississippi: "Fran," an invaluable source for ultra-right white publi-cations and tips.

In New Orleans: Pat Carter; Kalamu Ya Salaam; Tom Dent.

In North Carolina: Bob Hall and the folks at *Southern Exposure.*

IN THE NORTH:

In Washington, D.C.: "Fran," for materials on Western Goals, a D.C.-based right-wing intelligence group.

In New York state: David Gandino, for invaluable material on hypnosis in general and in particular; Howard Nelson, Lois Drapin of Cayuga Community College; Gerri Wilson for children's toy catalogs; Car-men Ashurst, for her Grenada film screened at the Atlanta Third World Film Festival in '84.

In Philly: Clark White; Terry, *Revolutionary Worker.*

IN THE WEST AND MIDWEST:

In California: Carole Brown Lewis; Sue Houchins: the National Children's Day Committee of Santa Cruz; Ishmael Reed; Saundra Sharpe; Lawrence Schiller; Penny Bloch.

In Minnesota: Therese Stanton, Pornography Resource Center.

In Montana: Lynda Sexton.

In the United Kingdom: Jessica and Eric Huntley, Walter Rodney Bookstore; Gail, Pat, and Pava, Black Women's Center in Brixton; John La Rose, New Cross Massacre Action Committee; A. Sivananden, *Race & Class;* Manny, *Spare Rib.*

And to my former Rutgers student. I hope that session in front of Wicker Store was as valuable to you as it was to me. Many, many thanks.

And to my orisha, who has many names and forms, imagination her dominant disguise, mother of Mnemosyne born in *Meno,* who is memory, midwife to all muses, and who offers anecdotes, antidotes and anodynes against agnosia, the loss of pictured memory; aphasia, the inability to recall verbal usage; and amnesia, the inability or unwillingness to recall due to trauma or enforced taboo; and she speaks sometimes in the voice of the grandma with auburn hair piled on her head who visits with the aroma of sassafras, witch hazel, and linseed oil to say, "Don't forget."

For financial support:

A National Endowment for the Arts Individual Literature Grant in 1983 funded most of the third draft.

A Djerassi Foundation Artist-in-Residence Grant in August 1984 enabled me to complete the third draft.

A Kristin Hunter Hey-Girl-I-Know-How-It-Is Check in the miserable winter of 1986–87 put food on the table.

And Helen Brehon shared hard-earned wages in her seventy-fifth year.